From the Royal Palaces of Britain to the Temples of High Fashion, from the Mansions of Bel Air to the Gutters of Fleet Street and the Villages of the Third World, Prince Richard's Destiny Was Linked with Three Extraordinary Women.

JO. A wayward beauty with emerald eyes and a wide streak of ambition, she grew from Hollywood brat to celebrated actress. This fascinating woman is accustomed to getting everything she wants—but can she win the offstage role she longs for as Richard's princess?

HARLEY. Her unique brand of exotic sensuality made her a top model. But when she learned how deep prejudices run in her royal lover's country, she turned her back on fame. Now, after three years in Jamaica, she's returning to London—and His Royal Highness is the reason.

VICTORIA. A British beauty with classic looks and aristocratic lineage, she's the favorite with the oddsmakers. This gently bred woman was Prince Richard's first love, but will she be his bride?

D0358327

Also by Celia Brayfield
PEARLS

THE
PRINCESS

Celia Brayfield

BANTAM BOOKS

NEW YORK • TORONTO • LONDON • SYDNEY • AUCKLAND

THE PRINCESS

A Bantam Fanfare Book

PUBLISHING HISTORY
Bantam trade paperback edition published May 1991
Bantam paperback edition / July 1992

FANFARE and the portrayal of a boxed "ff" are trademarks of Bantam Books, a division of Bantam Doubleday Dell Publishing Group, Inc.

ISBN 0-553-29836-4

Bantam Books are published by Bantam Books, a division of Bantam Doubleday Dell Publishing Group, Inc. Its trademark, consisting of the words "Bantam Books" and the portrayal of a rooster, is Registered in U.S. Patent and Trademark Office and in other countries. Marca Registrada. Bantam Books, 666 Fifth Avenue, New York, New York 10103.

PRINTED IN THE UNITED STATES OF AMERICA

RAD   0 9 8 7 6 5 4 3 2 1

ACKNOWLEDGMENTS

This book began after years of listening. In offering my thanks to all the people who have helped me with it, I am aware that my deepest gratitude is due to the many friends and acquaintances whose lives I have drawn upon for my story. Most cannot be named for reasons of discretion; before this book was conceived, neither I nor they could have appreciated how their experience would become part of my resources. I thank them for their confidence and admire their courage, hoping that they will not consider themselves to have suffered too much in translation.

For her friendship and her invaluable assistance in Jamaica, I am indebted to Barbara Blake Hannah, who with her friends and family took me more deeply into that beautiful country than I could possibly have travelled alone. My thanks are also due to Senator Olivia Grange, Sonia E. Jones, Polly Perry of the Jamaican Tourist Board and Elomar M. Radwanski.

Christopher Wilson, Tim Hodlin, Veronyka Bodnarec, Judith O'Connell, Jack Gordon and Denise Kingsmill have also given me the benefit of their expertise, judgement and encouragement, which was of enormous value. My particular thanks are also due to Michael Sparrow, for his warm interest as well as practical help, and to Annie Hutchinson, for whom no challenge was too daunting in the field of research.

For their patience and support, I am grateful to my publisher, Carmen Callil, and editor, Alison Samuel, at Chatto & Windus, and as ever my gratitude to Andrew and Margaret Hewson is beyond words.

PROLOGUE

MEN WERE SURE that they knew why women adored Prince Richard. He possessed a dominating grace which could make any adversary subject to his will. He had a soft manner, a hard mind and a lean body; his extraordinary combination of merits and ambition would have ensured that, had Richard been born into any other family in Britain, he would have risen to an equally exalted position in the world. His Royal Highness, The Prince Richard Alexander William Nicholas, was one of nature's princes, as well as a prince of the most successful royal house in the modern world.

The tops of the tall trees in the garden of Buckingham Palace thrashed as the heavy Wessex helicopter passed over them to set down. Prince Richard's Private Secretary, Clive Fairbrother, watched his master sprint away from the aircraft towards him, resenting the way his glossy brown hair fell back smoothly after the wind ruffled it. The man had every possible unfair advantage.

Prince Richard was not a big man but his physical presence was overwhelming. From his own height of well above six feet, Clive Fairbrother was always surprised to find himself looking down on Richard's imperiously poised head.

It fell to the Prince, as it always did, to give his Secretary's most urgent preoccupation pause.

"Busy morning?" he threw back over his shoulder, a tightening of his full lower lip indicating irony.

"Pandemonium. Every newspaper in the world seems to think you're getting married now. The Press Office is really under pressure."

The bigger man lengthened his stride to keep up with

Richard's dynamic pace down the red-carpeted Palace corridor. The Prince either stormed through life like a tornado or idled with a lack of haste that was almost feline.

"They'll cope. They've always coped before. Amanda never loses her cool. After all, the press have been trying to marry me off for years."

"It seems different this time, they're very positive."

His Royal Highness raised an eyebrow and puckered one side of his mouth in a very characteristic grimace of amusement.

"Positive? They're taking bets, aren't they?"

His private sitting room on the second floor, a substantial, high-ceilinged chamber, immediately shrank to the proportions of a toy theatre when he entered it. As he approached his thirtieth birthday Richard reminded people more and more of his great-grandmother Queen Mary. His shoulders were carried with her regal bearing and his mouth, otherwise loose and sensual, had her decisively chiselled upper lip.

"I'm sure that's just a rumour, Sir, the bookies wouldn't . . ." Why am I lying, Fairbrother asked himself angrily. He was new to this game. He saw himself as a courtier only by profession and hated to find himself succumbing already to the sycophantic atmosphere of the Palace offices.

The Prince took his customary place before the plain white marble fireplace. The logs in the basket were rarely burned; he was suspicious of comfort, and was never in the Palace long enough to make lighting a fire worthwhile.

"Oh yes, they would. I called Ladbrokes myself. They're giving two to one on Tory Hamilton and six to four on my darling Harley. Princess Stephanie of Monaco, Princess Louise of Meinenbourg, Jo Forbes and that go-go dancer they snapped me with in São Paulo are all at 100-7, which will no doubt annoy them all severely." His loud, clear laugh resounded to the corniced height of the room. "Can you beat it, Clive? They're actually running a book on who I'm going to marry. Isn't life rich?"

The room was considerably less cluttered than the apartments of other members of the Royal Family. Richard did not accumulate objects for sentimental reasons. His cousin David Hicks had decorated the room in dove grey and gold. His cousin David Linley had designed the only modern piece in the room, a small marquetry desk of English fruit woods which held Richard's private correspondence.

All the surfaces were bare apart from a seventeenth-century bronze statue of Theseus abducting Antiope, the queen of the Amazons. The walls were similarly unadorned, apart from a large looking glass above the mantelpiece and, on the opposite wall, a double portrait by Van Dyck of two melancholy black-clad gentlemen of King Charles II's court.

Men were wrong about Prince Richard; women loved him not for his strength, but for his weakness, which was well hidden. Only women's eyes detected the signs. His deep-set eyes were normally narrowed against intrusion. There was frustration in the tightness of his jaw, anger in his energy. Everything about him betrayed a man of enormous emotional strength who had never been able to commit himself. There were many women who thought they knew him intimately, and each believed that she alone could unravel the knot of his heart.

As they went through the business of the week together, Fairbrother noted a new lightness in the Prince's manner. Vulgar speculation about his love life usually enraged Richard; there was still a mark on the pearl damask wall where he had hurled a glass of whisky on receiving the news that *People* magazine had voted him the World's Sexiest Man of 1984. Fairbrother knew, but was far too discreet ever to say, that the Prince was oversensitive on the subject of his empty heart. Now he was joking about the rumours of his marriage. If he could find this sordid media circus amusing, he was a changed man.

"You're obviously thriving on the excitement," he ventured.

The Prince caught his meaning instantly, and chose to ignore it. "Well, you have to laugh about things like this, don't you, otherwise you'd go out of your mind. There's only one woman in my life, and that is Sister Bernadette of the Nansen Trust, and when we're through I'd like you to ask the office to get her on the phone for me."

Fairbrother knew his man and kept silent a few seconds longer than was polite.

Then he said, "Seriously, Sir . . ."

"Seriously, Clive," the Prince mimicked his secretary's persistent Australian vowels. "*Seriously* you know I can't say anything until I've spoken to my mother." He had a casual way of saying "my mother" which somehow emphasised invincibly the fact that his mother was the Queen. The Queen was not due to return from a tour of the Far East until two days later. Fairbrother refused to be intimidated.

"Will you be speaking to her, Sir?" he inquired, stone faced. Speaking in this sense did not mean a pleasant filial initiative on the telephone. If Prince Richard were to marry, he would need his mother's formal consent, and the tradition in the family was that matters of gravity were always discussed face-to-face and in private.

The Prince paused, shook his head like an animal bothered by gnats then turned with a resolute air. "*Finita la commedia*, then. Yes, you can tell them I'll be speaking to my mother as soon as she gets back, tonight. They can have a statement in the morning. Although by then," he moved towards the door, his step noticeably more buoyant than of late, "our friends in the media may have something else to think about."

"Thank you, Sir." Fairbrother had not picked up the emphasis in that suggestion, and Richard decided to let it go. There was a luxurious pleasure in being able to share a secret with one of the very few people he could call a friend, but this time he could resist. Nevertheless he needed to test the bond now, to reassure himself that it was there. As he walked to the door he demanded, "What's your fancy, Clive? After all, you know the form better than anyone. Who's your hot tip for the Royal Wedding Stakes?"

The reluctant courtier gave his master a look which would have extinguished any man with a less armour-plated ego. "Fuck off, Richie," he growled.

The Prince's laugh echoed from the corridor after the door closed behind him.

•   •   •

A TWO-MILE tail-back of stretch limos crawled towards the Shrine Auditorium. The temperature in Los Angeles was 90 degrees. The air on the street was so thick and enervating that the gawpers who tried to glimpse the famous faces behind the tinted windows and security grilles moved in slow motion.

In the great Scandinavian tradition of Greta Garbo and Ingrid Bergman, Lorna Lewis and her daughter Jo Forbes were actresses who could never give of their best when their shoes pinched. Even now, with a Best Actress nomination each and three more for *The Dawn of Dreams*, their first picture together, they saw no need to torture their toes until it was absolutely necessary. On the floor of their limousine two pairs of handmade sandals lay abandoned; two pairs of practical but impeccably pedicured feet wriggled in the cool pile of the carpet.

"Who paid for our page in *Variety*?" inquired Jo.

"Our producer, of course." *The Dawn of Dreams* had been a family affair; the producer's credit was for Robert Forbes, Jo's father and Lorna's husband, who sat beside his wife, his long, elegant legs half-hidden in the ultramarine satin folds of her skirt. Even in his eighties he was a fine-looking man, the more so in any kind of formal dress. The truth was that the two women between them had raised the nine million dollars needed to make *The Dawn of Dreams*, and they had done it with such consummate feminine grace that the handsome, silver-haired head of the family did not quite understand that his title of producer was merely honorary.

"That stingy bastard—what did you have to do, sleep with him?" Affection gleamed in Jo's large sea-green eyes.

"I just told him I hadn't won an Oscar for almost forty years and it was about time, that's all. He was quite reasonable about it." Lorna patted her husband's hand.

"But I thought we didn't have a lot of cash left over for publicity?"

"We didn't, but when I heard the whisper about the picture I decided to beef up the budget," her father explained. "Didn't make any sense to hold back. I've lived in this town long enough to know that when people are talking about a picture in a certain way you don't need to spend a lot of money on hype, just a little in the right media and the nominations start piling up. Then your picture's just about made." He enjoyed his new role of producer. Producers, successful ones at least, were the lords of Los Angeles.

Jo caught her mother's eye and saw that she, too, was amused by her father's instant expertise in their business. A few years ago Jo would have been unable to resist a put-down, but the Hollywood brat had grown up and knew how and when to be gracious.

"People will want to see this picture because it's damn good," she said, checking her make-up in the vanity mirror.

"Five nominations won't do any harm," her mother added reasonably. "And it wouldn't surprise me if you won Best Actress, Jo. You know you more than deserve it."

Jo refused to discuss the Oscars; the whole idea was too exciting to bear serious thought, and besides she knew something about the events of the next three and a half hours that her mother did not, and would not until her name was called.

"And people will come just to see Lorna Lewis at the top again," she said.

"People will come to this picture to see *you*, sweetheart. Especially, let's face it, when your wedding is announced."

"And boy are they going to be disappointed!" She threw back her head and laughed, dislodging a portion of her dark brown hair. *The Dawn of Dreams* had not been her most glamorous role—to play the central role of a disturbed adolescent Jo had gained 20 lbs and spent hours creating the greyish, pasty complexion of a kid raised in institutions. It was dedication of that order which had won her the reputation of one of the finest young actresses around.

Expertly, her mother reached forward and repinned the falling curl. "They won't be disappointed," she reassured Jo. "Hold still now, let me just fix this . . . there now." She settled back in her seat. "I'm so happy for you, darling. I know you both are going to have a wonderful life together."

"Do you? I wish I did. I love him, but he's so difficult sometimes . . ."

"All men are difficult sometimes, even our wonderful producer. And you're not always a dream to live with, you know. Besides, he's not difficult, it's just his position."

Her mother was the original cockeyed optimist, Jo thought fondly, as her eyes strayed to the window. "Oh my God, look where we are now." The cortège had been routed through one of Los Angeles's poorest neighbourhoods. A group of derelicts seated in the trash-strewn gutter amiably waved their bottles at the passing parade. "This town is just incredible. Sometimes I think the people should get out and leave the place to the automobiles."

Even after a lifetime in Hollywood, Lorna could not look comfortably on squalor. "You look absolutely fabulous," she told Jo to distract her.

"Uh-huh." Jo pulled nervously at the top of her dress; it was also of satin, a pink so pale that it appeared white at first glance, swathed tightly around her long-waisted body and embroidered all over with pearls, brilliants and crumbs of coral. Jo thought the dress was gorgeous, and cunningly kind to her voluptuous shape, but she was always uncomfortable in formal clothes. Leggings and sweatshirts were more her style. And all that was going to have to change.

"Who do you think I should ask to make my wedding dress? Let's face it, no one can make me look like Princess Diana."

Lorna shook her head, her famous blond hair stirring like a cornfield in the wind. "I think the British people would appreciate it if you chose one of their designers."

"But they all make those frou-frou little-girl party frocks . . ."

"Not all of them. What about . . ." she reeled off half a dozen names.

Of course. Trust her mother to know everything. Jo momentarily relaxed. She felt tired and detached. So much had happened so fast, and the man she loved was so far away. She had the echo of his morning telephone call in her memory, and even that seemed faint and distant.

The limousine was finally slowing to a halt and they scrambled for their shoes. There was a pause while they waited for Michael Douglas to go in ahead of them, and then the door opened wide; beyond was an incessant glare of flashlights, the roar of the crowd. They were screaming for Lorna, and Robert handed her out first, then steadied Jo on her unaccustomed high heels. The three of them walked slowly forward in the dense heat, deafened by the crowd and blinded by the lights.

A man struggled towards her, calling her name and waving a piece of paper. She thought she knew his narrow, deranged face. From the corner of her eye she saw the security guards wrestle him to the ground.

Jo raised her hand to wave, feeling the unaccustomed heaviness of the pearl and diamond bracelet which her mother had lent her. The weight of the matching necklace was already giving her a headache. She hated being on display like this, hated crowds and hated people snatching photographs, and trying to touch her. Her mother had a genuine affection for humanity in the mass, which she knew she lacked. She liked people one at a time. Feeling severe misgiving, she gave the crowd her best smile.

• • •

"YOU CAN JUST leave the bags here," Harley waved the porter with his load to the centre of her apartment's immaculate sitting room, then pressed a few pounds into the man's furtively extended hand and hustled him out.

Impatiently she struggled out of her blue gaberdine suit and began to rip open the thick, shiny bags and the gleaming boxes. She tore away the tissue paper and threw the dresses over the sofa. Oh, it was great to have clothes to wear again, *real* clothes, beautiful clothes, clothes that had been created with genius and handled with adoration, shy, deceiving little artefacts that seemed just lengths of cloth but once you possessed them would flow over your body like enchanted water and transform you into something magical.

She crushed the last dress to her face and inhaled the scent, the faint, delicious musk of fashion lingering in the fibres, the incense of the temples of elegance mingled with the stink of sweat, debts and cruelty. The smell excited her like a pheromone, even now, three years after she had walked out on all that madness.

As if remembering the steps of a dance she walked to the long cheval mirror in the bedroom and tried on the dress, a dark grey beaded silk gown by Bruce Oldfield. It was magnificent; the neutral tone accentuated the rich tints of her skin, which, after three years under the Jamaican sun, was the colour of medium roast Blue Mountain coffee. But tonight's objective was to please Richard and be photographed by every goddam paparazzo in London, and that meant colour, the brighter the better.

She tried a red-and-pink Chanel shift, a Lacroix confection splattered with turquoise roses and a long green tube by Azzedine Alaia which made her six foot, 128 lb body look like some exotic serpent. It was stunning. She turned sideways and admired the long sweep of her neck, mentally accessorising the garment. Long hair would be good, but hers was cropped short now, too short even to pin on a fall. Life as a lawyer in Kingston did not allow much leisure for hairdressing. And she needed ear-rings, big ear-rings . . .

The telephone rang, and as soon as she picked it up and heard the echo on the line from the Prince's lofty Palace rooms, she knew who was calling.

"All set for tonight?" he asked her.

"I can't find a thing to wear, you know," she complained. "You've got to help me choose now, darling—would you like me in red, green or blue and white flowers?"

"Anything—you always look fabulous. Why are you asking my advice, you know you never take it. You're the top model. What do I know about frocks, for heaven's sake?"

"What do *I* know about frocks, I'm asking myself. I used always to look fabulous, but that was then and this is now. I've had other things to think about just recently. Now I'm standing here in this thing and I don't even know if I've got it on back to front or not."

"Well, what does it look like?"

"Like I fell out of a tree in the Garden of Eden." Harley's laugh bubbled down the line. Hearing it made him feel human again.

"Just shut up and pass me that apple."

"Not bad, not bad—who's writing your material nowadays?"

His voice suddenly dropped to a more intimate key. "God, I've missed you. We had such fun, didn't we?"

"Just because I'm the only woman in the world who shares your crazy sense of humour . . ."

"No, don't put it down, I won't let you do that. I love you, Harley, I'll always love you, and you'll always love me, and that's settled, we both know that."

"Tonight will be just fine, you know," she reassured him, sensing the anxiety that consumed him.

"You can always tell, can't you? Thirty years they've trained me to give nothing away and you can still read me like a book."

"Can you get hold of some ear-rings for me?"

"Don't change the subject."

"Rich, the dress needs ear-rings, long long *long* ear-rings, maybe diamonds or diamonds and emeralds . . ."

She was nervous, too, he realised. It was always Harley's

way to get more frivolous the more serious things were. "I'll find you some ear-rings," he promised, "and the car will come for you at six, ready or not."

"I'll be ready," she told him.

• • •

IN SILENCE, VICTORIA HAMILTON gazed across her children's heads, thinking about their future. The early summer sun streamed through the yellow Provençal-print curtains of the kitchen and illuminated a room in which the only sound was the faint crunch of toast in their mouths. Unformed as their faces were, Sarah and Alex had the look of all her family, generous and strong-boned, with thick, fair hair above a wide forehead. Agincourt faces, Jo had called them; the bony, resolute features of a dynasty which led the people of England for centuries.

"Look, Mummy, I've got another wobbly tooth," Sarah pulled her rosy lower lip down and demonstrated the tooth's instability with her finger.

Victoria switched her attention to the present, flinching at the sight. "Don't do that, darling, it makes you look ugly."

The child's face, shiny with butter and dotted with toast-crumbs, folded up in a huge smile. She was delighted at having achieved her aim and made her mother notice her. "Were you being sad again, Mummy?"

Animation returned to Victoria's features; it was so touching when your children tried to make you cheerful with no conception of what was on your mind.

"No, darling, I was just thinking." Perhaps this was a good time to prepare the ground. If they were all to get on as a family, she would have to be careful about introducing Richard to the children. "I was thinking," she began with caution, clearing her throat, "that in time you might like to have a new daddy."

The suggestion was received with complete lack of interest. Alex had spilled some juice on the table top and was drawing his finger through the orange puddle with enjoyment; Sarah seemed completely preoccupied by the last mouthful of toast. Their father, Patrick Hamilton, had died dramatically a year ago, blown up by an IRA car-bomb a few yards from what was then their home in Dublin. Patrick had not been a demonstrative man. His nature had been over-mature and he had been focused so much on his career that he had never had a great deal of time for his family. Having herself lost her mother when she was three years old, the same age as Alex now, Victoria had watched the children carefully to see how they reacted to their loss. She had concluded, with relief, that apart from a few episodes of moodiness from Sarah, they had taken it very well.

In many ways, the tragedy had brought the three of them closer together. Victoria had discovered that the traditional upper-class way of raising children took all the fun out of it. On her own as a mother, she had relaxed all the rules and found all the unexpected joys of being a parent. She loved sitting up with the children until long past bedtime, playing silly games or just holding them in her arms and carrying on a conversation at their absurd level.

"What sort of new daddy would you like, do you think?" she persisted.

"One who is fun," Sarah said with decision.

"With a big car. Daddy had a big car." Her brother also saw some advantage in the proposal.

"Only sometimes, darling. It was the embassy's car really. And do you think he should have dark hair or blond hair?"

"Doesn't matter but he must be nice," Sarah pulled thoughtfully at her pink hair ribbon. She had been seriously into pink for a year; Victoria indulged her with delight and stifled the protests of her own aesthetic sense.

"And what sort of job do you think he should have?" She smiled to herself, reflecting that this was the question that had been torturing Richard all his life. Perhaps the answer out of the mouths of her babes . . . he had this mad idea of working with refugees; politically, of course, it would be an absolute nightmare, but she was sure she had talked him out of it. "Blond hair and a farmer," Alex said slowly, his grey eyes wide with thought. "With a lot of pigs."

Victoria laughed. "Oh dear, are you sure, Alex? Pigs are awfully smelly. Couldn't he just have a tractor?"

"Oh yes, a tractor."

"Well, that's settled then. I'll go out today and see if I can find a new daddy then, shall I? A nice farmer with blond hair and a tractor. But suppose they haven't got one at the shop?"

Sarah gave her mother a look of absolute disdain. "Don't be stupid, Mummy. You don't get families at the shops."

"Oh dear, where shall I find him then?"

"In the dustbin," growled her son with a naughty chuckle.

The new nanny, a reassuring figure in her brown Norland uniform, came in with the children's coats and Victoria automatically dropped the conversation. She was longing to tell them everything, but even five-year-olds gossip and it was vital, at this stage, that no one should know.

"Do you like my new dress?" Sarah asked the nanny, standing on tip-toe to see herself in the gilt-framed mirror in the hall. "I like it because I look pretty like Princess Di. Mummy knows Princess Di, don't you, Mummy?"

"Only a little. Off you go to school, darlings, and have a wonderful morning." The nanny hustled the infants emphatically towards the door. She had already gathered that her new employer was extremely well connected and, as might be expected from a woman of her standing, required absolute discretion of her staff and the encouragement of her children in a properly modest attitude to the family's privileged position.

"Here she is!"

"Can we have a photograph, Mrs Hamilton?"

"Vicky! Come on out!"

As she opened the door Victoria saw the small group of photographers outside, waiting patiently under the small horse-chestnut tree opposite her house. Heads turned all along the quiet Kensington street. She quickly smoothed her hair, then kissed the children and said goodbye to them. They looked at her in surprise as the lenses clicked.

"Why are they taking our photographs now?" Sarah asked with anxiety. "Has somebody else died?"

Four grey eyes were demanding an explanation. "No, nothing like that. It's a nice reason but I can't tell you now. It'll be a surprise."

"Can you just come forward a few steps? You're in the shadow of the porch." Obligingly, Victoria took her children's hands in hers and posed on the steps while the nanny stood aside and looked on with pride. Standing between the two stone urns which Victoria had thoughtfully filled with pink geraniums and ivy the previous day, they made a pretty picture.

"Off you go now, darlings. Mustn't be late for school." Looking anxiously behind them, the children set off down the street with the nanny. The reporters were fumbling for notebooks.

"I'm sorry, you know I can't possibly say anything." With a polite smile, Victoria went back into the house and shut the door.

It all seemed so much easier this time round. She was more mature, more experienced. The sight of the photographers no longer made her startle with something close to guilt. She was calmer. Of course, she was still taking tranquilisers to quieten her nerves, but that was to be expected so soon after her loss. She would be able to do without them in due course. There had always been a feeling of pre-destination with Richard and now that they had both suffered so much it seemed stronger than ever. She hoped the photographers had not upset the children. Of course, they associated being photographed with their father's death, she ought to have foreseen that.

Victoria's whole life had been lived within the aura of the Royal Family, and she reacted by instinct to nurture that relationship. It did not occur to her that she valued her relationship with Prince Richard more than the love of her children, and had anyone suggested this to her, she would have been mystified; such a comparison was impossible. Loyalty and morality were the same thing to her.

Her friends, who were many but not close, agreed that Victoria had about her the rich glow of a woman who excelled at everything which constituted a woman's work. She was a good mother. She had been a good wife, too. The perfect ambassador's wife, according to one of the senior diplomats who had been delighted to promote her husband. Now she was a young widow, dignified but vulnerable, busy but not tastelessly careerist; she believed that she always put her family first.

She was also beautiful, in a very English way, uncontrived and romantic, her large and imperfect features artlessly combined in her own unique grace. Her eyes were big and dreamy. Her hair fell thick and straight to her square shoulders; it was a shade too dark to be fairly termed blond, but Victoria's canon of style rejected tinting

—or at least, tinting which could be recognised as such. A few highlights were enough.

She was tall and generously made, and her clothes were self-effacing—this morning a faintly nautical look, a square-necked navy cotton sweater and a white skirt. The skirt did not reach her calves at the ideal point for flattery. Victoria had very long legs and skirts seldom finished where they should on her.

She considered her reflection between the gilded curlicues of the eighteenth-century looking glass in the hallway and decided to begin a diet. And perhaps she should take up jogging or something. White always made her look heavier, and she wanted to look perfect on her wedding day.

•   •   •

"LOVELY." A WOODEN coat-of-arms dangled from the heating duct above Sean Murray's head. At 10.30 am, first thing in the Fleet Street morning, his desk at the *Daily Post* was still stacked with the detritus of the night before. On top of the pile were the pictures of Victoria and her children, which he leafed through with satisfaction. "Old Keithie would have made more of it, but this'll do. Excellent."

"But what's he playing at, Sean? We've got these as well from last night. The old dusky beauty. Pretty hot stuff." The picture editor spread out a selection of shots of Richard and Harley entwined on the dance floor at various nightclubs. "They started at L'Escargot, went on to Annabel's, then Crazy Larry's, then L'Equipe Anglaise and finished up at the Chelsea Arts Club. I mean, that was a heavy night out."

"It's the heavy nights *in* that count, old boy. He's just a randy little shit, up to his old tricks, putting it about all over town, Victoria Hamilton's the one, mark my words. We'll keep the mystery going today and then I'll splash it tomorrow." The picture editor was relieved. Murray was becoming increasingly flamboyant in style, which meant that his rages were fearful when the rest of the team did not get him what he wanted. His attitude was that he was the greatest gossip writer on Fleet Street and only the best was good enough for his column. It was not a position which enhanced his personal popularity, but while he was still coming up with the stories Murray's position was unassailable.

"Are you putting your money on her, then?" Sandy, his assistant, returned from the library with a pile of cuttings.

"Absolutely. The horse's mouth, old girl. Jane Brompton called me from the Betty Ford clinic last night and it's absolutely 100 percent sure. Pop down and put a bet on for me while I'm in conference, there's a love." He handed the prints back to the picture editor and looked at his reflection in the dirty window to check the alignment of his snaffle-printed Hermes tie.

"But how can you trust anything Jane Brompton says? She's been on the sauce for years. I saw Colin Lambert last night," her New Zealand accent sounded excessively plaintive when she argued. "And he said it was all over Los Angeles that it was Jo Forbes."

"Colin Lambert hasn't got two grey cells to rub together and will say anything to get his name in this column. For Christ's sake wise up, Sandy. The first rule in this business is never believe anything any actor tells you, especially about another actor, *especially* if he's fucking you at the time." When she blushed Sandy's normally lacklustre face looked almost pretty. "Use your head, girl—the throne of England's been rocked by an American once, they won't let it happen again."

With a sulky expression, Sandy watched the two men prepare to leave. "You can start getting the page drawn," Murray ordered her, handing over a sketch. "There's the headline—At Last! Rich The Bitch Gets Hitched! As big as it'll go. We've got the bastard this time—that'll wipe the smile off his face."

CHAPTER I

THE GARDENS of Balmoral in the middle of August displayed as much glory as the devoted skill of the gardeners could achieve in the short-lived Scottish summer. On the west lawn a large motor mower progressed slowly across the sward shaving off the last half-millimetre of grass before perfection. The turf, dense and springy after the summer's rain, was rolled into even stripes which led the eye away to the pine woods in the middle distance; the forest obscured what had once been an inspiring view of the valley of the Dee, but shielded the castle from curious passers-by on the road that followed the river banks.

In the sunken garden, orange snapdragons and pink asters, raised in the sheltered nursery beds, had been set out in lurid masses. The borders blazed with purple loosestrife, golden rod and ox-eye daisies. A waterfall of begonias, of every colour known to the plant breeders of the 1960s, filled the conservatory. The men who tended the garden were well aware that to modern eyes this planting scheme was gaudy and banal. It followed the taste of Queen Victoria and Prince Albert, for whom highly coloured bedding plants had been newly fashionable; successive generations at Balmoral, monarchs and men alike, had valued continuity above innovation.

In the vegetable garden rows of watery English lettuces had been sown in succession to provide sufficient salad for the Royal Family and their guests throughout their summer holiday. The gladioli were staked in gaudy ranks and the sweet peas had been assiduously kept in bloom for a month to provide the maximum quantity of flowers for the house. By the bed of alpine strawberries at the bottom of the slope two small children stood hand in hand watching one of the young gardeners at work covering the plants with black netting.

"Why are you doing that?" the boy inquired, his curly dark head on one side like a curious robin.

"To stop the birds eating your father's pudding, Richard."

"Do birds like those strawberries very much?"

"They're nae fools, they always know the best."

"Do *you* like them?" By the age of six, Richard was well aware of the beguiling property of personal concern.

"I do not. They may be all right to eat but they're the devil to pick because they're so small you can hardly see them."

"They are *very* delicious, these little strawberries, aren't they?"

"Aye, if that's your fancy. I dinnae care for them myself." Expertly, the gardener pinned down the last of the net with a wire stake.

"I've never eaten them," Richard gazed up at the man, his clear chestnut eyes, starry with their thick lashes, open wide as he judged the amount of pathos necessary to achieve his aim.

"Have ye not," the young man's voice was noncommittal as he straightened his back and wound up the spare netting on a wooden stake.

"Nor has Tory, have you Tory?" he presented the girl, a golden-haired child with the high colouring of a Joshua Reynolds portrait. Overcome with shyness, she looked down at her feet, twisted the hem of her much-washed pale blue smock and said nothing. The two children were of equal height and made a pair pretty enough for a Victorian painting, the boy dark and vivid, the girl fair and withdrawn. The sight alone would have won a more sentimental soul, but the Balmoral workers shared their countrymen's pride in hard headedness. Besides, the Queen did not like her children to be indulged.

"And who is Tory, now? I've nae met her before. Is she another of your cousins?" With practised twists of his fork the gardener spread a small pile of stable manure around the strawberry plants.

"Well, sort of." Richard knew he was related to Tory

somehow, but was not sure if cousin was quite the right word. "We were cousins in olden times, I think."

Suddenly the girl raised her immense grey eyes to look at the gardener. "My mummy's in hospital," she whispered, twisting a lock of hair around her finger. "She isn't very well."

"I'm sorry to hear that," the young man could not be sure, but it seemed that the child's eyes were glittering with unshed tears. "But she'll be home soon, eh?"

"Yes," broke in Richard eagerly. "And when she does come back we're going to ask her if we can get married." A smile at once curled the girl's red lips. The two tiny hands clasped together swung back and forth with excitement.

"Well, now . . ." Charmed in spite of his suspicion that all this was nothing more than an elaborate strategy to get the best strawberries, the young man leaned on his fork. "Do you not think you're a little young for all this? You're nobbut six years old, if I'm right. When you grow up you could change your mind, you know."

At once the tiny girl was crushed in a one-armed embrace from Richard that almost unbalanced them both. His small face crinkled in resolution. "I couldn't change my mind. I love Tory."

"I can see that." The gardener's heart was melted. "I suppose you're after picking your girlfriend some strawberries now?"

"Oh yes, *please!*" Squeaking with excitement, the two children jumped up and down.

The young man bent down once more and carefully undid half his morning's work, lifting the netting off one row of plants. Very soon every ripe strawberry on the row had been picked and tipped carefully into Tory's cupped hands. The gardener, an honest youth of little imagination who was by now enchanted by the whole affair, remembered that the taste of strawberries was improved by setting them on a cabbage leaf, and strode down to the brassica beds to cut a broad green plate for the feast. The two children retired to a nearby bench where Richard ceremoniously selected the largest and reddest strawberries for his companion.

When the illicit treat was over Richard insisted that they find their benefactor, now at work in the hot, wasp-infested interior of the raspberry cage, and thank him.

"I don't know what I've to tell the chief when they want strawberries for the house," he protested in embarrassment. "Get away with you now, and mind you tell no one."

Their strawberry-stained hands still clasped together, the two children strayed in search of further excitement. Tory adored Richard. For the past few days he had brought security into her child's world of distorted perspectives and half comprehended fears. Until she saw him each day her small face was blank with anxiety.

Although everyone had tried to persuade Victoria that spending the summer with her cousins in their untidy house at the edge of the moor would be a wonderful adventure, she was not convinced. She was not yet fully converted to the philosophy held by her family and their circle that fresh air and the country were the ultimate enjoyment.

With her infant's intuition, Victoria knew that major shifts were taking place in the adult world above her head. She was accustomed to her parents' absences and proud to endure them as a member of a sailor's family should, without complaint, but now the absence of her mother and father disturbed her. Lately there had been too many hushed conversations and long telephone calls behind the doors of their London apartment.

Her brother Alex, two years older and much more robust in temperament, was her bulwark against the world. Marie, their high-spirited young nanny, had endless patience with the timid child who was always the first to dissolve into tears. Although both these comforters were with her, Victoria could not settle in the strange environment.

Aberknowe was one of several substantial granite houses on the Balmoral land which were occupied by the estate managers. Victoria knew her Uncle Donald was something to do with the Queen's castle, and that Aunt Rose was her father's sister. Her four cousins were all older than her and their dogs were boisterous enough to knock her over. The house was always cold, full of stale animal smells and decorated with grotesque knick-knacks made from deer's hooves or ram's horns which gave her nightmares.

All the adults pronounced the name of Balmoral with a unique excitement; the cousins were soberly proud of their duty to play with the royal children. Alex, who in London shared lessons in the Buckingham Palace schoolroom with the little Prince and two others, was regarded almost with awe by the other children, but to Victoria these privileges seemed merely frightening.

She had drifted unhappily around the estate, dragging her feet and shrinking back from the noisy pack of children which romped around the gardens. Alex, her brother, was big enough to be included in the older children's activities and without him she had felt unprotected. Several times Marie had found her alone and in tears.

One afternoon a nurserymaid from the castle had appeared with Richard, and her distress had melted as quickly as it had grown. The girls in charge of the flock of children assembled from this extension of the royal Household watched in giggling amazement as the two children fell in love.

To the relief of the nursemaids, Victoria's mood of weepy apathy subsided. She knew that Richard came from the castle and understood that his family was the family to which all the others deferred, but now instead of intimidating her Richard's status seemed to impart a sense of protection. He more than filled the gap left by Alex; his presence animated her with a mysterious excitement.

The sweet precocity of this infant romance delighted every adult who observed it, which in turn encouraged Richard in his chivalry and Victoria in coy connivance.

"I should like to marry Tory when I grow up," he told Marie decisively during a rainy afternoon which drove the children in to the chilly shelter of the Aberknowe kitchen. "Will you mind very much? You can come and live with us afterwards if you like."

"I shall know what to do because I'm going to be a bridesmaid next year," Tory confided in a diminishing whisper. "Do you think Mummy will say I have to wear the same dress? I know she doesn't like me having too many dresses because we can't afford it, and I don't mind—only it might be the wrong colour."

Suddenly anxious to direct the conversation away from Mummy and her preferences, Marie proposed a formal engagement and began a hunt through the button boxes and trinket chests of the house for a ring. A tiny circle of bright brass was found at last in the fishing tackle cupboard, slipped over Victoria's finger and proudly displayed to the rest of the party.

They wandered out of the kitchen garden. When she

worried that they might not know when it was lunch time, he explained that when they saw his sister come back from her ride, then they would know.

"We can find a bird's nest in the woods, I bet. Would you like to go and look?"

Anything Richard could suggest was irresistible and Tory nodded. They ran across the lawn and found a rabbit path through the light undergrowth between the red-barked pines.

When she suggested that they might be lost he was comfortingly scornful. "I know all the trees in the wood," he told her. "My father knows all their names. This one is a Chinese Pruce." He patted the trunk with a hesitant gesture. "Or maybe it's a fir, a Noble Fir, I think."

Richard now admitted to himself that they might be lost after all but knew instinctively that saying so to Victoria would destroy the flattering confidence she placed in him. He wandered crossly around the tree, kicking up dead needles.

"Maybe Alex will come and find us," Victoria suggested.

"Alex doesn't know where the path is," Richard was annoyed to find his beloved's allegiance wavering. "He'd have got lost ages before we did. He's really stupid."

The grey eyes instantly overflowed with tears and the girl's features, unformed miniature suggestions of the wide-browed Fairley face, distorted in misery. Dismayed at the pain he had inflicted and at the pain he himself felt in consequence, Richard rushed forward, then stopped a few feet from Victoria twisting from side to side in frustration, wondering how he could stop her crying.

A jay flew out of a nearby tree, startling them with its clattering wings, and then they heard the unmistakable sound of distant adult voices calling. Hesitantly, Victoria stood up, wiping the tears off her cheeks with the back of her hands.

A few moments later Marie and Richard's nursemaid appeared, panting as much with distress as exertion, with Aunt Rose, her old-fashioned roll of black hair half unpinned, behind them. A few yards behind them came two of the gardeners and the young detective on duty at the nursery that morning.

"Richard! You little monkey!" Relief and anger were mingled in the nursemaid's voice. "You know you're not to go wandering off like that! We've been so worried about you—whatever possessed you?"

Marie knelt down beside Victoria. "Are you all right, Tory?"

Victoria nodded, her lower lip quivering, puzzled by the sudden drama around them. "I was frightened. But I'm always all right with Richard, aren't I, Marie?"

"Yes, love, of course you are." She stroked the child's hair and Tory, suddenly babyish, held up her arms to be carried.

They walked back towards the lawn in a procession at the pace of Richard's small strides until he stumbled over a tussock of grass, admitted that he was tired and accepted a ride on the detective's shoulders.

"Have the children not been told?" the nursemaid enquired of Aunt Rose once Victoria and Richard were ahead and out of ear-shot.

"Not yet. My brother is coming up at the end of the week to take them back with him, and he'll tell them something then."

"Poor wee mite. It's a terrible thing to happen." Victoria's head lolled on Marie's shoulder; she was almost asleep.

"She's a very sensitive child, though she's had to put up with a lot already, her mother being ill so much." Aunt Rose pinched her thin lips together, uncertain how much to confide. She regarded gossip as a mortal sin, and encouraging it almost as bad. The estate girls, for all their loyalty, could be as foolish as any other group of young women with dull lives and minimal education, and on this occasion most of Britain was also speculating about the death of her brother's wife.

Caroline Fairley, wife of Lt-Commander The Honourable Charles Fairley, RN, had apparently lost control of a car that was not hers on a small country road in Oxfordshire and crashed into a tree. The car had burned out and the body had been difficult to identify. There had been an inquest and the coroner had dwelt with what the family considered unnecessary emphasis on the theft of the car and the woman's motives for driving recklessly about the countryside at the dead of night.

With all this in the headlines daily there was no hope of preventing gossip; Aunt Rose would not normally have considered imparting any personal information to a servant, but she was concerned to protect the children from the truth until they were judged ready. Furthermore, the Fairley family considered themselves to be people of consequence and were careful of how the world perceived them. They had three centuries of expertise in oral disinformation on which to draw in these situations.

"My poor brother," Aunt Rose said softly as they trailed across the drive to the side door of the castle. Victoria was asleep and the detective paused a few yards away to swing Richard down to the ground. "He's being very brave but he did adore her, you know." The servants said nothing. Richard's mother appeared in the doorway holding out her arms.

"They hadn't gone far—where did you find them?" She ruffled his hair, pulling out a leaf that was still caught in his curls.

"Just away beyond the gardens, Ma'am."

"I was looking for a bird's nest to show Tory, Mummy."

"You mustn't run off like that, Richard. Look at all the trouble you've caused. Poor Tory must have been terrified. Weren't you frightened?"

"What's 'frightened'?" His attention skipped the strange word. "Can we find a bird's nest for Tory after lunch, Mummy?" Energy revived, Richard was now intent on keeping Victoria's company as much to himself as he could for the rest of the day.

His mother shook her head, smiling. "Tory looks as if she's had enough of birds' nests for one day. Besides, it's too late in the year, all the chicks will have grown up and flown away by now."

"But the nests will still be there—can we? Oh, please . . ."

"Wouldn't you rather go for a ride this afternoon?"

"No! I want to play with Tory."

"Oh dear, you and your girlfriends . . . well, perhaps Tory could come too?"

There were uneasy smiles. Richard's enchantment with girls sometimes raised echoes of anxiety in his parents. He was also showing a distaste for outdoor pursuits that ran against the grain of their family life. His mother and father told themselves that he was only six and was bound to change, but the incident that had made his grandfather King already coloured his life.

After lunch, it was decided to harness two Shetland ponies to a dog cart and give all the children who were too small to manage their own mounts a ride around the park. They proceeded slowly in the afternoon sun, Victoria content to gaze up at the massed conifers as they passed and listen to the rhythmic grating of the eight small horse-shoes on the roadway. She had Richard beside her and Alex, her brother, who was a much larger boy, sprawled on the opposite seat. A groom led the ponies and the two nursemaids formed a chattering rearguard.

The road Richard chose sloped gently down towards the river, levelling out where the Balmoral bank sloped steeply down to the waterside.

"Why are the flowers in the water?" Tory asked suddenly, pointing down to a strand of granite pebbles by which a group of bright blooms apparently sprouted out of the shallow water.

"Flowers in the water—oh, I see. How funny! How did they get there? No one planted them, surely?" Marie turned enquiringly to the groom who gently halted the ponies.

"The lupins, you mean? They used to be in the garden here, but Her Majesty doesnae care for them so they were thrown out on the rubbish heap, but the rubbish heap was by the river so the seeds were carried down by the water and sprouted by themselves on the bank. You can see them away down the river for miles now. And the water's high at the moment because we've had so much rain, so it's come up around their roots."

"But why doesn't the Queen care for them?" Tory asked at once.

"She just doesnae," the youth replied, loquacity exhausted.

"I think they're pretty." Tory turned back for a last look at the rejected blooms as the ponies moved off.

"That's just because you're stupid," Alex, her brother, announced, immediately receiving a punch in the ribs from Richard.

Afterwards the flowers growing in the river were all that Victoria remembered of that summer. The Fairley family considered that they dealt with their tragedy very well, because both children afterwards showed no signs of trauma. They were told a carefully graduated series of lies: first that their mother was staying in hospital for a while, then that she might not come home for a long time, and finally that she might never come back. As their mother seemed already to have been in hospital for most of their lives, Alexander and Victoria saw no change and since the family followed the form of their class and delegated the day-to-day care of their children entirely to the nanny, the absence of their mother hardly affected their routine.

When they returned to London, Victoria settled peacefully to walks and naps, nursery lessons each morning and Madame Vacani's dancing class on Tuesdays. Their father, occasionally grand in his uniform with gold stripes on his sleeve, went out in the morning and seldom returned before the children's bedtime.

One day Victoria and Alexander were called to the drawing room after tea and saw a strange woman in a dress printed with yellow lemons sitting on the fender beside their father.

"Pamela is going to be your new Mummy," he told them.

"But I don't know her," Alex protested.

"You will grow to know her and love her as I do," their father took the woman's hand and she smiled up at him.

Alex threw himself on to the floor and rolled over and over shouting, "I don't want her! I want my Mummy!"

"Get up and behave yourself or Marie will have to take you back to the nursery," their father ordered. He was not a harsh man by nature, only by training. He himself had been brought up first to obey orders and then to give them in the expectation of instant compliance, and was unacquainted with more complex patterns of relationship.

Alex worked himself into a crimson-faced rage and bit the curled corner of the carpet, whereupon Marie picked him up bodily and carried him out of the room. His angry yells sounded from the corridor as their father closed the door. Then he took Victoria's hand and led her towards the strange woman.

"Tory's a sensible girl, aren't you, Tory? Would you like to give your new Mummy a kiss?"

Obediently Victoria stepped into the warmth of the fire and delicious aura of scent which the woman emanated.

She bent down her face, which was covered in pink make-up, and Victoria pressed her small wet lips to it.

"Well done, Tory, that's my girl," her father approved at once.

"We're going to get along famously, aren't we?" The new Mummy patted her shoulder. "Would you like to show me your dolls before bath time? I expect you've got lots of dolls, haven't you? I had when I was a little girl."

Alexander, who resolutely persisted in being rude to his new parent, was judged old enough for boarding school six months later. There was a quiet wedding, which the children did not attend, and Pamela became part of their household. She seemed over-conscious of her position as a step-mother and pitifully anxious to integrate well into her husband's family.

Victoria, always pretty and amenable, was taken on a round of the treats considered traditional for an upper-class London child: the zoo, the Changing of the Guard at Buckingham Palace, ice-cream at Fortnum & Mason's soda fountain, a visit to the enclosure reserved for some over-weight rabbits near the statue of Peter Pan in Kensington Gardens and a Christmas pantomime called *Where the Rainbow Ends* in which four intrepid children fed their pet British lion a medicine called the Commonwealth mixture.

Marie sulked and complained that Victoria was always worn out and was being spoiled. What she really meant was that the child's affections were being alienated; this was not wholly a fair charge. Victoria seemed to be growing shyer than ever, now less prone to tears but also less ready to smile. The nursemaid felt a withdrawal of affection and was hurt, not noticing that the child was shrinking back from all emotional expression; the hugs and kisses once lavished on Marie had not been transferred to Pamela. A crescendo of resentment built up between the two women, which reached its finale when Pamela lost Victoria's precious blue rabbit, whereupon Marie gave notice.

"Daddy has been posted to Hong Kong, darling; it's a very, very long way away. We shall have to go in an aeroplane for a whole day, can you imagine? And it's very hot and not nice for children, so you can stay in England and go to a boarding school like Alex—won't that be fun?"

With a new rabbit and a short-haired piebald guinea pig in a box, Victoria arrived at a once-grand Queen Anne house in Wiltshire that was now a school devoted to raising the daughters of the gentry. Most of the new girls cried a great deal; Victoria did not and the teachers were pleased.

Thirty girls between the ages of six and ten slept, ate and did their lessons in rooms with noble proportions, blistered stucco and peeling paint; they were each permitted the character-building company of one small pet and one pony, and slept on iron beds left behind from the mansion's use as a hospital for the wounded of World War I.

The school belonged, her father explained in reassurance, to some cousins. Great Stourford had been built as the ostentatiously fashionable home of a sugar millionaire whose wealth was so substantial and political skill so keen that his grandson was elevated to the title of Lord Chamfer by Queen Victoria. One daughter was triumphantly married into the Scottish aristocracy and the family thus connected through succeeding generations to the net of blood ties which included both the Fairleys and the house of Mountbatten-Windsor.

Three generations later, fortunes founded on sugar alone were lost and the current Lord Chamfer retired with his wife to the dower house. The family home, dilapidated as it had become, was the last tangible talisman of their pride and, rather than relinquish it, the Chamfers leased the building and what remained of its land to an educational trust, retaining shooting rights, fishing rights and the right to have their female descendants educated gratis. Suzie Chamfer, a sturdy, high-spirited child with thick brown hair which no ribbon could effectively restrain, became Victoria's best friend.

The school was but one institution in a network created to educate, employ and entertain those members of the British nobility who had the inclination to live as courtiers. Birth was the least of the requirements for co-option to this introverted community. Many hundreds of cousins, the majority of the proliferation that linked the Fairleys to the other great families of England, the Pagets, the Cavendishes, the Churchills, the Devonshires, and the Spencers, did not choose lives predicated totally on loyalty to the ruling house; those who did entered a circle in which loyalty was the supreme virtue—to family, to the extended clan of the courtier caste, to the Royal Family and to the British ideal which they embodied. Victoria and Alex learned first never to call this loyalty by its name, never to identify or analyse it, but to live it. The morality they absorbed, the way of life which they assumed, were beyond question.

It became clear to them that their trust was to maintain the essence of their country in themselves. Their class were the guardians of the mysterious quality of Britishness; it was their duty to be fair, honest, and clean in a partial, deceptive and dirty world.

For the next ten years their father was posted from one naval establishment to another, around most of the strategically retained vestiges of the British Empire, from Hong Kong to Aden, to Gibraltar, to Singapore and finally to Malta, and Alex and Victoria, rejoining the family during holidays, became seasoned travellers.

They learned also that they had privilege to complement their responsibilities, and they learned to deny that privilege absolutely. Wealth was not to be flaunted, although as the children grew older they became aware that their father's circumstances were not the same as those of brother officers who lived only on their Navy pay. Victoria continued to wear handed-down Liberty dresses from Aunt Rose's daughters, and wasting money by the excessive use of electric light, hot water or heating appliances was a vice which Pamela rigorously discouraged in children and servants.

Possessions were to be valued for their family associations, rather than their artistic or commercial value; the Fairley household gods—three glorious red Beloush rugs, another huge Persian carpet woven with a deer-hunting scene, two handsome gilt-framed mirrors, portraits both human and animal, and an assortment of silver—were carried from one featureless Navy married quarters to the next, becoming chipped, torn and battered in the process, but no mention was ever made of their material worth or aesthetic quality. Like most officers' children, Alex and Victoria were educated in Britain and had very little contact with children of any other class but their own. They were nevertheless encouraged to play with the children of other service families, instructed to be polite to these less fortunate beings and discouraged from arrogance. Snobbery might be innate in their parents' way of life, but it could never be admitted.

Their father called himself "just a sailor" in the same deprecating way as King George V, King George VI, Lord Mountbatten and many other naval officers of royal or noble lineage had done. It was their claim to simple humanity. Aboard a ship naval ranking was the status system which over-rode all others. The Royal Navy relieved these men of the burden of privileged birth, gave them a peer-group of brother officers and an isolated, artificial microcosm of society in which they were free to be themselves. In return, the Royal Navy gloried in the title of the Senior Service and looked down on the Army and the Royal Air Force.

Outside the immaculately maintained and smartly guarded naval enclaves, where minds were drilled as thoroughly as bodies in uniformity and obedience, the privilege of royal society was granted on condition that it would be denied to all outsiders. The children learned from the example of adults that it was their supreme duty to protect the Royal Family from the degradation of other people's curiosity.

Victoria and Alex occasionally returned to Aunt Rose at Aberknowe for summer holidays. Pamela presented their father with three more children, two boys and a girl; this second family were collectively called the "littles." She preferred the hazards of local naval hospitals to leaving her husband and returning to England for each birth, but the strain of pregnancy in hot climates and the diversion of her own children made her willing to billet the older two on their aunt whenever it was convenient.

At Balmoral they internalised the lesson of loyalty completely. At fourteen and sixteen years old, tall, well-built and strikingly similar in their strong bones and tawny colouring, Victoria and Alex naturally became temporary additions to the royal circle. They resembled each other so markedly many people thought they were twins. Since the brother and sister were always invited together, they were dubbed "V and A," and the appellation headed many a hostess's guest list for the boisterous informal balls organised during the summer.

Victoria was a graceful partner for Prince Richard, now a small, slender and self-conscious boy, but he forgot the sequence of steps to the eightsome reel and did not impress her. Very few boys impressed Victoria; they all seemed inadequate beside her brother. While a fervid interest in sex overpowered other girls, she listened to their confidences unmoved. The perverse laws of sexual attraction ensured that this lack of interest only added to the appeal of her generously-made, rosy beauty.

Victoria was also popular with adults. She was said to mix well, a social attribute particularly esteemed in one of such high birth and breeding since it implied the correct unconsciousness of her status.

"You mean you really danced with Richard?" Suzie Chamfer demanded during the animated dormitory chatter that characterised the first night of the new term at the larger boarding school to which at least half their class at Great Stourford had progressed *en bloc*.

"Yes. Everybody did."

"Wow! Gosh! You lucky, lucky pug! What was he like? I bet he was really dreamy! Come on—tell us all!"

"He was rather shy, I think."

"But he's gorgeous! You mean you let him get away?"

"Mmmn . . . there were loads of boys there."

"Didn't you even go outside? Did he kiss you?"

"It wasn't that sort of ball. You know what those Scottish things are like."

"Yeah, draggy." Suzie sensed that Victoria was withholding information and knew why. "Well, I got kissed lots these hols, how about that? Do you want to hear about it?"

"Oh, yes, of course."

"Good, 'cause I'm going to tell you anyway." She chattered on, unaware that in the next bed Victoria silently registered her curiosity about a member of the Royal Family as a threat.

Suzie's interest was not easily quenched. "Is he taller than you?" she demanded the next morning as they awkwardly shared the small mirror intended to discourage the girls from vanity.

"Who do you mean?" Victoria brushed back her thick, honey-brown hair. The question seemed to her to be doubly hostile, implying both that the Prince was too short and that she was too tall.

"Richard, of course."

Victoria settled a broad black velvet band on her hair with a single efficient movement. School rules required all girls to tie back their hair, and Victoria seemed to have a knack of observing the most oppressive and trivial regulations with grace.

"I really didn't notice." She turned away from the mirror.

"Well, when you looked into his eyes were you looking up or down?" Suzie persisted.

"I can't possibly remember," Victoria gave a patient smile.

"You danced with the original Prince Charming and you *can't remember*?"

Victoria remembered perfectly well that Richard's eyes were brown, a rich, glowing brown rayed from the pupils in shades of chestnut, bay and bronze. She was rather surprised that she remembered them so clearly. She did not intend to disclose such information to Suzie; defence by denial was a strategy she already operated well.

"I can't remember the colour of the eyes of every boy I've ever danced with, for heaven's sake. It was only a few minutes. Alex talked to him more than I did. Come on, Suzie, we're going to be late for breakfast and the tea will be cold."

Suzie dragged her unruly locks to the nape of her neck and snapped a clip across the tangles, scowling at the dishevelled effect her best efforts always created. Everything that was easy for Victoria seemed hard for her and she never understood why.

As the two girls whirled downstairs towards the clattering dining room, Victoria realised that a wedge had been tapped into their ten-year friendship. Sometimes Suzie and Victoria had added Prince Charles or Prince Richard to their oft-revised list of the men they would most like to marry when grown up, along with Robert Redford, Steve McQueen and Mick Taylor of the Rolling Stones. That had been harmless fun. Now Prince Richard was no longer an imaginary distant idol and Victoria felt offended by Suzie's sudden fawning fascination. At that instant she chose the path of her own life, and understood that in time she would have to part company with her friend.

Victoria was happy at school. Alex attended a similar establishment for boys ten miles away and visited her at every weekend *exeat*. The rules and routines of the institution made her feel secure and offered her plentiful opportunities to do what gave her the most satisfaction, to comply.

"Victoria, you're a sensible girl, you go first," was an order she heard often and with pleasure, for whatever ordeal into which she had to lead the rest, from construing straight-faced a suggestive passage of Ovid to pushing her pony through a muddy ford, was always rewarded by authority's approval.

She accepted responsibilities gladly and discharged them well. When the headmistress, with some guilt, asked her to take over the school's unpopular Commonwealth Society she rolled up her sleeves and cleaned out the dusty room that had been hung with torn posters depicting "Tea-picking in Ceylon," "Coffee Growing in Kenya," and "Sheep Farming in Australia." In their place she pinned up a poster of a starving black child and a chart which eventually recorded a handsome donation to the Biafran famine relief fund, amassed by the girls from a summer fair, Christmas carol-singing and a sponsored fast during which Suzie Chamfer histrionically fainted in the lavatories.

The next year, to the dismay of all who knew her, Victoria altered. Alex decided to follow his father as a naval lawyer, and was accepted at Trinity College, Cambridge, to read law as a student sponsored by the service. Expressing a desire to see the world first, he set off to spend a year teaching elementary mathematics in Kenya. Victoria pined and cherished his infrequent postcards. Severed from the only person with whom she had ever shared a meaningful degree of closeness, she lapsed into a state of almost trance-like disconnection, all energy gone. Distress replaced serenity in her wide grey eyes and every task suddenly seemed impossibly difficult. A test paper which she should have found easy was turned in uncompleted, with "I can't do this, sorry," scrawled at the foot of the page.

Her English teacher found her crying by herself over the job of rearranging the drama cupboard.

"I'll never see my brother again," she moaned, hating herself for sounding so foolish when her grief was so vast.

"Don't be silly, of course you will. He's coming back next year, isn't he?"

"Yes but he's g-g-going to C-c-cambridge and he's the only person who really c-c-c-ares about me."

"Now come along, Victoria. You know that isn't true. We

all care about you. I shouldn't be surprised if you're head girl next year."

"Oh no, I couldn't possibly . . ."

"And anyway, Cambridge isn't the end of the world. Why don't you apply to go there, too?"

The bubble of agony quietly burst. Victoria sniffed and pulled a tissue from the pocket of her dress to wipe her nose. "I couldn't possibly, they'd never take me—would they?"

Victoria was intelligent but typical of her class in that she had conscientiously allowed herself to be educated without imagining any particular use for her good and well-trained mind. A dozen girls from the school went to universities each year, very few of them to Oxford or Cambridge. Those who did achieve such distinction, however, reflected glory on both school and teachers, and the English mistress at once saw how to gain advantages all round from Victoria's unhappiness.

"You've most certainly got the ability," she told her earnestly, "and you're a good worker—if you like, I'll write to your father. I'm absolutely sure you could make it if you put your best foot forward next year. Why not talk it over with your family and think about it for a week or two?"

Victoria made up her mind at once. For two years she applied herself to her studies with an energy no one had suspected she possessed. Commander Fairley saw at once the wisdom of keeping the two children of his first marriage together for the last years of their progress to maturity. He was promoted to the rank of Captain and a desk at the Admiralty offices in Whitehall, which meant an end to the family's wanderings and a large apartment in a turreted neo-gothic building overlooking the Thames in London's legal district. It had a circular room with a compass inlaid in mahogany in the parquet floor, and here father and daughter sat side-by-side on the window seat while he coached her each evening in the school holidays.

He also wrote letters to bring the full weight of the family's influence to bear on Cambridge University. The examination papers written in Victoria's large, even script were considered adequate; her interview was unexceptional, although the examiners at Girton College recognised her at once as she had been universally described by all who knew her: an extremely pleasant girl of excellent character.

When the letter arrived telling her that she had been accepted to read History of Art, she shouted "Hooray!" and flung her arms around her brother, then burst into uncontrollable tears of relief.

"Don't cry, Tory, you'll look like a boiled owl," he advised, mopping her eyes with his handkerchief. "You big silly, you should be happy. You've done it. We're going to be together for three whole years."

"I know," she sniffed, taking the wet square of frayed cotton from him and blowing her nose. "That's what I'm crying for. Why shouldn't I have a good old weep? I've worked for it, I deserve it and I'm jolly well going to do it." Her long, strong legs folded under her and she sat down on the rug in the hallway and sobbed to her heart's content, while Alex patted her shoulder and wondered if he really understood his sister at all.

CHAPTER II

MARTHA HARLEY sat down on the mossy stone parapet of the old bridge to put on her shoes. She paused and peered down the rocky road to make sure that none of the children who lived in the lower houses had followed her. They tormented her enough on the grounds of her pale skin, her thin body and her grandmother's pretensions to gentility and the shoes only gave them another cause to tease.

She buttoned the tight bars over her insteps, feeling the patent leather cool against her skin; lying close to the river's cold water all day had chilled the shoes.

The river was called Rush River, because of the speed with which it roared down from the Blue Mountains, scoring a twisted gorge through the forest. The water came down so fast from the cold heights that it remained icy even in the thick heat of the valley. The children played a game, jumping into the deep green pools in the torrent from the big rocks under the star apple tree; the cold of the water was so intense that Martha felt her body flush to its core with a spasm of heat; even after she had scrambled out of the water her flesh still tingled from the shock.

As she trudged awkwardly up the valley road her feet began to sweat and the toes rubbed painfully against each other. The leather chafed her heels and the straps felt as if they were going to crush her bones. Martha hated her shoes. They were ugly, they hurt her, they drew attention to the ever-increasing size of her feet. None of the other children had to wear shoes, and to Martha's contrary seven-year-old mind the reasons Nana advanced for insisting on shoes were not satisfactory.

The journey home each afternoon seemed endless. The

children emerged from the elaborate wrought-iron school gates, which were red with rust-preventer but had never got around to being painted. They scattered across the dirt plaza that gave the low-lying village its air of consequence; those whose homes lay uphill began their journey with scuffling games of last-lick which ceased as the road became steep and the heat too strong.

A few at a time Martha's companions would turn into their own yards, until at last she continued alone to the highest village in the valley, her uniform a civilised patch of blue and white against the wild green tracery of the jungle. Martha was not the only child who lived in the highest settlement, but she was the only one who was ordered to school each day.

She was usually alone, which she preferred to be; the roar of the river water seemed louder when she climbed the road by herself. Martha thought that the river was angry. Its depths were treacherous and swift. The shallows lashed themselves to white foam over the limestone boulders of the valley floor. In spate it was a terrifying torrent which uprooted whole trees and smashed them to driftwood; in drought it was an evil-tempered stream which grudged them water and tugged the pots from her hands if she did not hold them with all her strength. The stones at its margins were bleached like bones and nothing grew at the water's edge except rank thickets of bamboo.

At last the track grew level and the valley floor widened into a clearing lined with small board houses. Martha could feel now that her toes were not only wet with sweat but also sticky with blood. She greeted their neighbours absentmindedly as she passed them in their yards, her mind occupied with the new argument against the shoes.

Nana's house was the only painted dwelling in the row. Its yellow distemper had faded to the palest sulphur over the years. At the rear, Nana's yard was grassy like a sparse lawn, not worn to dirt by chickens and children as most of the others were. A high hedge of hibiscus screened all of the front from passers-by, except the window at the end which Nana used as a shop counter, letting down the shutter when she was open for business. This was another futile pretension of formality, since anyone wanting to buy from Nana's small, dusty stock of essentials when the window was shuttered simply wandered into the yard and called for attention.

Having her argument prepared, Martha took a deep breath and opened negotiations.

"Nana, you know, I can't cross the fording in my shoes any more," she began as she came through the gap in the severely-clipped hedge. "The water wet them up, I got to put them off."

"Say *take* them off, child," her grandmother corrected from the dim interior. She tried to make Martha speak high English at home as if she were still in school, but the old woman often lapsed into patois herself. "And you can't go without shoes, I've told you before. You got to wear your shoes all the time and thank God Almighty you got shoes to put on your feet at all. You can step across the fording on the rocks."

"But I *can't* Nana, the river too high just now."

"What for the Lord give you fine long legs, child? Don't tell me you can't jump above the water." The old woman glared down her straight black nose.

"I *can't* Nana. Don't make me wear them, Nana, the other . . ."

"What the other children do is nothing to do with you, Martha. Don't judge by other children, they got no ambition."

"Anyway, the shoes pinch me, see they mash up my toes, Nana. Look, my toes are ready to bleed right now." Martha sat down on a rough wood bench in the yard and pulled off one shoe to show her grandmother her sore toes.

"You always argue, Martha, you make me tired." Reluctantly the old woman prodded the unyielding toecaps of the other shoe, feeling Martha's long bones crammed painfully together beneath the worn leather. She screwed up her face as if Martha were growing on purpose to prove her wrong. The child was soon going to be taller than she was. Nana was small and scrawny, and the sinews in her neck stood out like guy-ropes above the demure white collar of her dark blue dress. "What a way you growing now."

"So can I take the shoes off, Nana?"

"No, you may not. We got to buy you new shoes again and God Almighty knows where we can find the money."

"But why, Nana, why must I have shoes?" Martha felt ready to weep at the unfairness of it.

"Child, I tell you a hundred times and you don't hear me yet. You never learn. You got your mother's hard ears, and hard ears people never learn. You're fair like your mother and you can't run around without shoes like them ignorant dark pickney. Now go on and coop up the fowls and don't bother me any more with your obstinacy."

Angrily, Martha flounced into the yard and flushed the chickens out of the bushes and into the pen where they passed the night, fiercely calling "shi-shi!" to the birds with the resentment she felt towards her unreasonable grandmother. Once the birds were enclosed she leaned against the low cocoanut tree behind the house and examined her arms in the gentle afternoon light, wondering what colour they were.

Her grandmother never used the words white and black to describe skin colour. She termed people fair or dark, and there was scarcely one of the valley's many-hued inhabitants whom she did not classify by colour. Fair did not seem to Martha to be a colour at all, merely an excuse for a hard old woman to persecute a child. The children at school, with whom Martha's struggle to be accepted was lost before it began because of her colour, called her Red Ibo. Certainly she had the lightest skin among them, but she was not red-coloured, like the red of an egg.

Nana could make a chocolate drink with cocoa beans and goat's milk, and that was the only thing Martha could think of that was coloured like her. Not that her grandmother wasted much time preparing treats for her troublesome charge.

Martha Harley never felt she belonged in the valley. It was just a place where she had been left, and as she grew out of infancy she knew that it was her mother who had left her there. The horizons of her life seemed unnaturally close; she could see no further uphill than the lofty breadfruit tree that overhung the road at the edge of the clearing. It was their tree; although distant from Nana's house, it was one of several passed down as part of the family's inheritance. It leaned over the track which disappeared in the deep shade below its deeply cut dark green leaves.

At the front of the house the space cleared by the road and the river enlarged her perspective. She could see rising tiers of treetops, the endless green punctuated in its season by the brilliant orange flowers of the tree called the flame-of-the-forest. Often there was a lonely John Crow wheeling over the hilltops in an unhurried search for carrion, and Martha thought that the big black bird must enjoy a superior view on the world.

There were mountains beyond the hills. Most days they were invisible behind low clouds, but if Martha could not see them she could always feel them in the cold fury of the river and the eddying downdraughts of chill air which occasionally penetrated the valley. The sudden cool of evening made it advisable to keep the cooking fire alive and in the morning a cold, heavy dew dripped from the leaves.

Knowing the mountains were there, Martha passed hours gazing upwards, waiting for a break in the curtain of vapour that would give her a view to the summit, her attention fixed at that mysterious level where the mist descended on the tree-tops and blotted out the perspective entirely. She was full of a formless curiosity about the distance, but had no mental vision of the world outside the valley. Her mother visited rarely, and Martha had no clear picture of her either. All she had was a yearning for everything that was out there beyond her knowledge.

Martha soon heard a new opinion on her colour. Beyond the hedge of red-leaved crotons that marked the uphill boundary of Nana's yard stood a dilapidated shack that was unoccupied, the property of a woman in one of the lower villages who owned several plots in the valley. One day on the weary way up from school a truck stacked with furniture ground past Martha; when she reached Nana's house she found the truck stopped in the overgrown yard next door, and a fat woman in a pink dress buying soda pop for a brood of children who stood around her looking fearfully at their new home.

"Mrs. Joyce has come to live here," Nana presented her customer with formality.

"Is this your gran-pickney now?" the woman demanded cordially, skinning a gold tooth as she smiled at Martha. "She so white! I like that, pretty and white. And she got good hair. But she thin!" The woman's square-palmed hand almost encircled Martha's upper arm. "You don't eat enough, me love, you got to put more flesh on you. How old she?"

Nana remained seated on her stool in the dark front room, below the curling photograph of Queen Elizabeth that was pinned to the shelf that carried packets of Albion sugar, brown on one side, white on the other. Martha could see from the humourless stretch of her grandmother's mouth that she judged Mrs. Joyce and her offspring an unwelcome addition to the neighbourhood.

"Martha is seven years old," the old woman announced in an aloof tone, anticipating the vulgar interest this information would arouse.

"Seven? Just seven?" Mrs. Joyce whistled in amazement and stepped back to look at Martha, her fists now buried in her wobbling hips. "She already tall like my Hyacinth and she twelve, jus' left. Hyacinth! You see this gal! Come stand together so we can see you both."

The biggest of the children, a girl with a sweet, oval face and a stout stomach that strained the buttons of her green print dress, handed the baby she was carrying to a smaller sister and stepped eagerly forward to stand beside Martha. Mrs. Joyce turned them back-to-back and the smaller children chuckled and somersaulted in their amusement to see the two girls were the same height. Embarrassed, Martha stepped aside.

The moral gulf between the households was soon judged by Nana to be impassable. Mada Joyce did some higglering in the neighbourhood, taking produce from the smallholdings down to the market in the coastal town of Annotto to sell and buying any goods the villagers might require while she was there. In Nana's opinion this was not only a common occupation which gave a woman vulgar, loud manners but it was also bad for trade.

Mada Joyce expected Nana to trust her for goods from the store, but never expected to pay. Mada Joyce had, it seemed, no husband but seven children from three different fathers, each apparently blacker than the one before and the latest, who occasionally visited and made half-hearted repairs to the shack, Nana dismissed as "nothing but pure Negro."

Martha, however, was ready to question her grandmother's notions of colour since, whatever colour she was considered to be, it only seemed to bring her trouble. She found Hyacinth, placid and biddable, an agreeable playmate and Mada Joyce a fine source of entertainment. She knew stories about Anancy the spider and the Maroon people who fought the British in the mountains. She scolded incessantly but never beat her children.

Mada Joyce also told the truth, which Martha considered the best virtue an adult could possess. While Nana denied that there were such things as duppies and forbade Martha to look under her old iron cot for them before she went to bed, Mada Joyce was expert on ghouls, ghosts, spirits and apparitions of all kinds, and had known a woman in another village who had actually seen the skinless old hag who sucked babies' blood reach into the cradle of her new-born child and disappear with a shriek when she touched the Bible on the infant's pillow. Mada Joyce also told stories of Jamaican people coming to the island as slaves from Africa.

Martha pondered this thrilling information for a day. After school she went to do her chores, but soon fell into her customary trance of curiosity. Eventually her grandmother came to rouse her, infuriated as always to see the lanky child leaning against the cornerpost of the verandah, craning her long neck to look between the palms at nothing.

"You tidy the house yet?" she demanded.

"Yes, Nana." Martha turned and shook off her idleness, realising that the old woman would continue enumerating chores if she were not distracted. "Nana—how we come in this valley here?"

"All the people in this valley is descended from four brothers from Scotland called Leekie," Nana sat heavily down on the upright rush-seated chair which was the most she would permit herself in the way of comfort, and began the tale as Martha had always heard her tell it. "My husband's name was Leekie, so my name is Leekie and so was your mother's before she marry. And at the bottom end there was also a family of Portuguese Jews named Da Silva. Everybody living in this valley descend from those two families and their people."

Although everyone in Rush River told the story the same way, most of them said "and their slaves" instead of "and their people," but Martha knew that Nana did not like the word "slave." She had never mentioned the people Mada Joyce had called Maroons, either. Nana's form was to skip the next two hundred years of Jamaican history and tell Martha how her husband had gone away to work in Panama and never come back, and how Martha's own father was in America now.

Knowing the route Nana's history took, Martha tried to subvert it. "Are we Scots then, Nana?"

The old woman laughed, baring all her yellow teeth. "No, child, we not Scots. What a question you ask me now."

"Well then are we African, Nana?"

Perceiving the child's intentions, Nana got up and walked stiffly to the front room, returning in an instant with the curling photograph of Queen Elizabeth from the sugar shelf. "We are citizens of the British Empire and subjects of Her Majesty Queen Elizabeth the Second," she announced, as if to pre-empt any further questions, pushing the photograph into her grandchild's hand.

Obediently, Martha studied the image of a glassy-eyed young white woman in a long white dress and tiara. The picture had been before her eyes every day of her life, and consequently had no meaning. "But your *grandfather*, Nana," she persisted, "what was he, was he an African?"

"What kind of a question is that?"

"Well, was he a slave?"

"Slave days were long ago." Nana's small, knobbled hands were picking at her skirt, a sure sign of agitation.

"But was your grandfather a slave?" Martha continued, her head on one side in an attitude of persuasion.

"No, he was not."

Nana's evasions infuriated Martha. The old woman was always threatening her with a stick-licking if she told lies, but told them herself. She was a hypocrite.

"This family has always been poor, but they were not slaves," the old woman almost shouted, snatching back the photograph as if Martha's impious fingers would stain it. "You too idle and too curious, child. God Almighty must look out for you now—Satan putting ideas in your head."

"But the children of Israel were slaves in the land of Egypt, Nana . . ."

"You dare to argue the Holy Bible with me? You think you're too big to get a beating? Where is my stick?" The old woman hobbled around the verandah, consumed with frustration, peering uselessly into dark corners in the pretence of looking for a switch.

The next day, a Sunday, Martha dawdled silently home

from church behind her grandmother, watching without sympathy her painful, crablike progress on bowed legs and misshapen feet. Hyacinth came with them, more for company and the irrefutable excuse to avoid work than from any religious inclination.

She lagged behind them, pausing more and more often and holding her belly.

"I can't breathe," she complained, gasping like a fish. "Me breast tough up."

Martha paused with her, noticing that Hyacinth was sweating heavily and her skin, normally plump and smooth, looked oddly withered and sunken around her eyes.

Hyacinth shook her head, her heavy braid swinging between her shoulder blades.

"I can't go on, I got to sit down," she gasped, collapsing heavily on the grass. "Oh God! Lord Jesus! Oh God! It hot! Me belly hot!" She clutched again and again at her stomach with her crossed arms, then rolled on to her side and lay moaning, her face contorted with pain.

"Nana!" Frightened, Martha called after her grandmother, but the old woman kept walking uphill with stiff, arthritic strides.

"Nana—we got to help Hyacinth!" Martha ran after the old woman, but she did not look round.

"Hyacinth can get up and walk," she said, her nose in the air in a familiar pose of disdain.

Fury filled the child and picked up her feet. She leaped up the track and ran until she felt as if her lungs would burst. The forest became a blur of green around her until at last she tore into Mada Joyce's yard, her long limbs flailing, sending the fowls squawking under the house in panic.

"Hyacinth can't walk, she fall down on the road, Mada Joyce, come quick!" Mada Joyce's round face appeared in the doorway, frowning in anxiety.

"She just fall down in the road screaming. She say her belly hot." Mada Joyce suddenly nodded and gave a smile of understanding.

"I expect I know what happen."

Hyacinth was lying where Martha had left her, curled in a foetal ball at the roadside, her eyes shut. She was moaning and dribbling and her Sunday dress of aquamarine nylon which Martha admired greatly was streaked with mud, a sure sign of extreme distress.

"Now, me love, what the matter with you?" Mada Joyce bent ponderously to feel Hyacinth's brow and the child's eyes fluttered open. The curious children stood around like statues, stilled by the drama.

"It hot so much," Hyacinth whispered.

"Yes, child, I know. Hot all the time or it come and it go?" Mada Joyce picked a wisp of grass from her daughter's hair and stroked her round cheek.

"It come and it go."

"Try if you can get up now."

Her eyes wide with apprehension, Hyacinth rested her arm on her mother's well-padded shoulder and stood up. She paused, frightened but feeling no pain, then gasped and looked down with embarrassment. Silent drops of scarlet were falling on the grass around her feet.

Mada Joyce nodded again, a mixture of satisfaction and irritation in her manner. "See there now. I think so, I think it your period. You know I ask you, Hyacinth, if you see your period yet?"

The child nodded, glancing fearfully around the small circle of onlookers.

"So long you been growing out of childhood, now you step into womanhood. You turn big woman, now. This is your period," Mada Joyce's concern began to turn to sternness. "Now you got to take care, child, stay away from the boys. If you have anything for do with a boy now, you will get pregnant." Hyacinth shook with a new thrill of fear, and her mother's tone softened. "Don't mind the pain, child. Woman's life full of pain always. Come up now, I make you some bush tea and you will feel better."

Martha was burning with curiosity but the solemnity of the affair checked her questions. They proceeded slowly back uphill, with Hyacinth walking taller at each step as she appreciated the glamour of her new condition. Two of her brothers, boys of Martha's age but half her height, fell into an exchange of sniggers and whispers, and Mada Joyce paused to smack them around the ears.

"You Granny keep Safex in her little store?" Mada Joyce enquired of Martha, who had no idea what Safex might be. "Ask her," she was commanded. "Ask if she got Safex and maybe some gin."

Eager to take a role in Hyacinth's drama, Martha sped ahead and found Nana resting on her porch, her church books still in her hands.

"Hyacinth is turn big woman now," she announced, radiant with sympathetic pride. "Mada Joyce ask if we got some Safex and some gin."

A flash of black fury shone in the old woman's eyes. "*On Sunday?* That woman have the impertinence to send you to ask for unmentionable things on Sunday?" Nana's rage struck like lightning; now she shot from her chair and grabbed Martha by the arm, dragging her into the stuffy gloom of the bedroom. "Stay out of that house! I told you to have nothing to do with that woman! Why you always want to go with those ignorant worthless people!"

"They not ignorant nor worthless either!" Martha felt her stomach churn with emotion and her tongue loosened with anger. "You're the one who's ignorant! You tell me lies all the time! You go to church so fine and holy and when your neighbour fall down sick you pass by on the other side! You are like the Pharisees and the hypocrites!"

The old woman gave a scream of outrage and began raining slaps on Martha's head. Feeling her strength almost equal to Nana's, Martha thrashed her arm to break her grasp. She lost her balance and fell back on the iron bedstead, pulling the old woman off her feet. For a few seconds she felt the bony weight of her grandmother on top of her and smelt the sickly powder she used; then Nana struggled upright, her breath rasping painfully in her throat, and pulled a thick length of bamboo from its hiding place behind her dressing table.

"Those who cannot hear must feel the rod of correction," she declaimed, raising the stick as she advanced. Martha let out a shriek, leaped to her feet and, barely aware of her action, hit the old woman as hard as she could on the side of the head, knocking her against the wall. Her spectacles clattered on the board floor.

Martha bolted out of the door and crashed through the hedge into Mada Joyce's yard, expecting to hear her grandmother's shout of rage behind her and all the more fearful when only silence pursued her.

At once her own drama was engulfed in the tumult of Hyacinth's entry into a woman's estate. The boys were screaming around the yard outside with companions attracted by the commotion. Mada Joyce and a neighbour bent over the cooking fire arguing over the best decoction of herbs for the girl's condition. In the bedroom the females of the clan gathered in awed silence. Hyacinth, now well advanced in hysteria, lay in state on the old striped pallet on which she slept, moaning through clenched teeth and clutching her belly. Around her hovered two younger sisters with a washing towel and an enamel basin.

Martha watched in silence, unconsciously rubbing her palm on her dress because she could still feel the crisp impact of Nana's hair against her hand. Mada Joyce at last brought in the bush tea, hauled her daughter into a sitting position and persuaded her to drink.

"This will ease the pain, my love," she promised. "Drink it all up."

Unconvinced, Hyacinth sipped cautiously, then gagged, seized the enamel bowl from her sister and spat into it. Mada Joyce retrieved the mug and clicked her tongue in annoyance. "It can't do you no good if you spit it out. Drink it all up and all this painful agony finish."

"It too nasty—me can't drink that stuff," Hyacinth implored, close to tears, but her mother resolutely grabbed her head, held her nose with one hand and poured the potion down her throat with the other. Retching and weeping, Hyacinth subsided on the mattress and the bitter herbal odour of the brew filled the stifling interior of the hut.

Having anticipated that Nana would be unable to supply gin and Safex, even in an emergency, Mada Joyce had sent her oldest boy loping down to the Chinese store in the lowest village for these essentials. When he returned more water was boiled with leaves brought by a second neighbour summoned from her home in the upper forest.

Martha, mesmerised by her friend's ordeal and grateful to feel the guilt of her attack on Nana ebb away in this greater crisis, watched silently from the corner of the tiny room. In the distance she heard a car engine, normally a sound which compelled curiosity but now of no interest.

After more anxious discussion, the woman who had come down with the leaves, bony and greyish of skin with her hair wrapped in a yellow turban, poured half, then all the small bottle of gin into the steaming mixture and ceremoniously put it in the centre of the floor.

"She must sit on the pot until it cool so the vapour can come up her inside," the thin woman commanded. Hyacinth, quieter now, glanced around the room in embarrassment and her mother at once shooed out the smaller children.

With an expression of furtive apprehension, Hyacinth allowed herself to be helped to her feet and settled, squatting, on the pot.

"Too hot! It burn me up!" she squeaked, leaping away at once.

"It must be hot as you can bear or it can't do no good," the thin woman insisted, motioning Hyacinth back with her knobby hand. Voices called outside in the yard, and the girl glanced nervously towards the doorway; with difficulty Mada Joyce pulled the door approximately shut on its rusted hinges.

Hyacinth nervously straddled the pot again and, supported by her mother, was lowering herself over the steaming brew when the door crashed open.

"Martha! Ain't no use to hide yourself in here! You got to come out directly. Here's your mother come to see you now." Nana's voice, distorted with tension, sounded so unnatural that at first no one recognised it. Hyacinth leaped to her feet with a yell and knocked over the pot, screaming again as its scalding contents splashed her legs.

Into the intense atmosphere of the hut, now additionally aromatic with herbs, juniper and alcohol, walked the most beautifully dressed woman Martha had ever seen. Her tall, slender body was tightly swathed in a pink dress and she stepped warily across the uneven boards on white sandals with heels so high and narrow it seemed barely possible that they could support a human being.

Behind this graceful form Martha could see her grandmother in a state of strange tension, arms folded and brows contracted in the effort of masking her feelings. The elegant one turned the neatly-coiffed head on her long neck and looked apprehensively around the room, careful to suppress her alarm at the primitive scene into which she had intruded. With almond-shaped eyes thickly outlined in black she looked from one face to another. Mada Joyce, appreciating the situation immediately, pulled Martha forward.

"Martha she here," she smiled hopefully.

"Martha, my daughter, my darling child." Two slender arms extended towards her and Martha realised that this must be her mother. "My what a big girl you are. When I last saw you you were just a tiny little pickney." Martha scented a fresh aroma of cleanliness and toiletries as her mother kissed her. "But you're so thin! Just skin and bone!" Her mother held her at arm's length and examined her like a piece of merchandise, turning her this way and that, searching for concealed flaws. Then the almond eyes gazed fiercely over the child's head towards Nana. "Let's go back to Nana's house, shall we?"

In a silence vibrating with silent accusation the three of them filed through the gap in the croton hedge. An enormous powder blue car, gleaming and new, its plentiful chromium winking in the sunlight, was drawn up in front of the house and against it leaned a man in a white suit.

"This is my husband, Martha, his name is Denzil." The man shook her hand and smiled. He was slight and a light yellow colour, with round shoulders, and Martha felt he was friendly.

"We came here today to see how you were doing, up here in the bushes with Nana," her mother explained, leaning against the hot side of the car and avoiding the child's eyes. "I thought to myself, Martha must be growing up now, it's time she left the country and came to live with me and go to a good school."

"Leave Nana's house?" Martha was not sure she understood the suggestion. Much as she disliked living with her grandmother, she had never thought of any other arrangement in concrete terms.

"Yes, and come to live with us in Kingston. In our house. We have a lovely house up on a little hill." Martha was speechless. The simplicity of the rescue her mother proposed astonished her. She was dazzled by the vista of liberty.

She gave Nana a quick, guilty glance and saw the old woman, arms still folded, standing a few paces apart, maintaining her vacant expression. "Can we go now?" Martha asked at last, testing her good fortune.

The man and her mother laughed. "As soon as we can gather up your things, darling," her mother promised. "Go on and find your clothes, I have something to clear with Nana first."

Martha's school dress and books, her one skirt, two blouses and handful of frayed underwear were swiftly parcelled up in the coarse paper Nana used in the shop. The old woman scarcely said a word and betrayed no emotion, although Martha felt an obscure sense of triumph and her mother was plainly anxious to leave as fast as possible. A parcel of mangoes was also assembled and loaded into the car. Martha and her grandmother said goodbye without looking at each other and then the newly constituted family climbed into the shining blue vehicle and bumped slowly down the track.

"She is so thin," the man observed in a soft, concerned voice. He leaned forward over the steering wheel to see his way through a deep pot-hole in the road. "What kind of food were you getting, child? Nothing but callaloo and green banana porridge, I'm certain. Did you get hungry, Martha?"

"Nana said I was always hungry."

"Maybe she's been ill—have you darling?" On the wide bench seat her mother held her close. Martha shook her head, feeling tiredness descend on her like the low cloud on the mountains, muffling all her emotions.

"I never sick," she whispered with pride.

"I should have come before, I meant to come before," her mother's smooth voice was tight with anger. "Nana is too strict and too hard for a little child all alone like you. It was different for me, I had my brothers, she was so busy beating them she never noticed me." The car wallowed around the last bend in the descent and cruised across in front of the school gates leaving two trails of dust behind. Martha wanted to look back but was too tired to turn her head. By the time the car reached the coast road she was asleep.

• • •

THE HOUSE WAS pink like her mother's dress, and sat high on Beverly Hills with a view out over the whole sprawl of Kingston to the hazy bay beyond. It was made of concrete and had a beautiful garden with a white hibiscus bush and one small, resinously scented tree.

Inside everything was modern. Martha delighted in turning on the taps in the bathroom and watching water pour out at her command, and when that attraction palled she took to rushing into the kitchen to watch the maid turn on the fire.

Her mother proudly showed her a room which was all for herself, with a pretty bed made up with white sheets and two pillows. For the first two nights Martha peered under the bed for duppies and enjoyed having no one to forbid her; by the third evening she forgot.

The sudden materialisation of a mother who fulfilled all her formless dreams, seemed to Martha confirmation that her discontent with life in the valley with Nana had been justified. Now, she felt, she was cherished and valued, the centre of attention, and her real life could begin. As if to confirm these notions of her importance, an enormous party was held in the villa a few weeks after her arrival. From the balcony, she was pushed forwards to see an immense display of fireworks above the town below.

"What's it for, Mama?" she asked, watching open-mouthed a huge waterfall of silver sparks hanging in the smoky night sky.

"This is the Independence celebration," her stepfather told her solemnly, handing her a pair of heavy ex-Army field glasses so she could see better. "The Queen has given Jamaica independence from Great Britain now, so we can be our own country by ourselves."

"Is the Queen down there?" Through the glasses it seemed as if the whole sky was showering brilliance on the town below.

One of their guests gave a sarcastic laugh. "The Queen's thousands of miles away and she's not stirring herself on account of Jamaica, of that you can be sure."

"Norman Campbell, why must you always be so cynical and spoil things for the child?" Her mother put her arm around Martha's shoulders, enveloping her in a cloud of scent. "The Queen sent her own sister, a real princess, instead."

"Is it the princess who's down there then? Can we go and see her?"

"Well, darling . . ." her mother was never anxious to mingle on the streets.

"Why not?" Denzil broke across her refusal. "You can come to my office with me in the morning and we can see her as she leaves King's House."

And so in the blazing heat of the next day Martha was

supplied with a small replica of the new green, black and gold Jamaican flag and hoisted on to her stepfather's shoulders at the gates of what had just ceased to be the colonial governor's mansion, to see a small erect figure in the back of a Rolls-Royce drive slowly away.

"Independence," Martha repeated the word solemnly to herself. In her child's understanding it seemed that it was her own liberation that was the cause of the celebration.

"You're going to have a little baby brother, Martha," her mother told her one day. "Or maybe it will be a little sister."

"Can I have a sister, please, Mama?" Martha assumed with delight that this was another special recognition of her preciousness. Nana and her earlier life faded from her consciousness, the emotional charge of her parting not neutralised but stored deep within her. The next few weeks were the happiest of her life, but then she sensed that her mother was losing interest in her.

She knew that her mother wanted her to be fatter; at each meal she willingly cleaned her plate, eating ice cream and fried chicken until she felt bloated. She willed herself to grow solid flesh like Hyacinth, but nothing changed. Every rib and every vertebra could be counted.

Her mother was better satisfied with their trip to a beauty parlour, where Martha's hair was released from its braids, anointed with a number of glutinous white creams, cut to the level of her shoulders and wound upon enormous wire rollers. When her coiffure was dry, Martha saw her small oval face framed by curtains of hair that was stiff and immobile but appeared at least to be straight.

The face was another disappointment. "I don't know why you should be so dark," her mother said with irritation, accidentally scraping Martha's cheek with her long, scarlet thumbnail. "Your father was lighter than I am."

"Nana's very dark," Martha suggested helpfully.

"Yes, well . . ." her mother's pencilled arcs of eyebrows contracted in anxiety. "You know, the only ambition she ever had for me was to marry well and bring up the colour of the family." Unconsciously she patted the slight swelling of her stomach under her smart new navy-blue smock. "Never mind, darling, just remember that the colour of your skin is not the colour of your mind."

This maxim Martha repeated fervently to herself during

her first week at school. Her mother and the driver escorted her to a complex of low concrete buildings in a parched garden high on a nearby hill. Martha thought it was a beautiful school; all the pupils were girls, most of them were white, and some of them arrived in cars even larger than her own. Her teacher was white—indeed, all the teachers were white—and told them with great pride that she came from England.

Martha longed to show off her advancement in reading and writing, for which she had been noted in the valley, and was bewildered and humiliated when she could make no sense of the books she was given. She ended the first day with a headache so severe she could hardly see.

She could not find any satisfactory playmates. From being the palest child in her school, Martha found that she had become one of the darkest. She was unwilling to ally herself entirely with the three truly black girls in her class, who were scholarship students from poor families.

Martha saved herself from relegation to a junior class by reciting the whole of Psalm 103, one of Nana's favourites, in morning assembly; after this feat her teacher had a long conversation above her head with her mother, and began to come to their house on Saturdays to give her extra lessons. Martha found these even more difficult; she screwed up her entire face in the effort of deciphering print.

"What are we going to do with you, Martha?" the exhausted woman exclaimed, attempting jollity because she saw that the child was distressed by her failure. "You've got the memory of an elephant, you're probably the cleverest girl in class and you can't read."

"This book's so difficult," Martha rubbed her eyes. "The pages just mist up."

"Is it easier if you hold the book closer to you?" The teacher had noticed that Martha held her books almost at arm's length.

The child shook her head. "It's easier if it's further away."

"Can you read the names on those packets over there?" They were seated at the breakfast bar in the kitchen, and she pointed to a row of cereal boxes at the far side of the room. Martha instantly rattled off the names and descriptions, hardly stumbling over strange words like niacin and riboflavin.

"Can you tell me what's on the table in the living room?"

It was a copy of *The Daily Gleaner*; from a distance of twenty feet Martha could read all the headlines and some of the smaller print.

"You know, I believe the problem is with your eyes not with your brain at all." She took Martha's hand and together they went to the terrace where her mother was resting on a new cushioned lounger. "I wonder if you would consider having Martha's eyes tested," the teacher suggested, her commanding tone precluding any disagreement.

Shortly afterwards Martha's world came sharply into focus. She was supplied with a hideous pair of spectacles with yellow frames and thick lenses.

"You'll only need them for your school work," her mother reassured her, also trying to talk herself out of her own dismay. "You can take them off the instant you don't need them for reading." Martha, eager to reassume the status of the cleverest child in class, could not appreciate her mother's concern. "Don't you see," her mother explained, drawing her close with an arm around her bony shoulders, "you'll be looking after boys soon and things are just like they say, boys don't make passes at girls who wear glasses."

Martha sniffed, unimpressed equally by her mother, by boys, and by any benefit likely to be acquired through beauty.

CHAPTER III

JOCASTA FORBES WATCHED the headlights of her mother's car as it drove carefully up the twisting canyon drive, and began to die inside. It was gross to be collected from a party at midnight by your mother when you were fourteen years old. When your mother was Lorna Lewis, and still got called the last great blond in Hollywood even if she hadn't made a picture for ages, it was worse than gross, it was a total bummer. At least, she could have sent the driver, instead of always bringing her daughter home herself.

Someone passed her a fresh joint and she took a deep drag, feeling the smoke burn her throat. Her mother drove like a cripple. She had a few more minutes.

"Is that your fairy coachman?" Ryan was pretty sensitive, he could always tell when she was upset.

"Yeah, watch me turn into a pumpkin any minute now." Forcefully, she blew two thick streams of smoke down her nose and passed on the joint.

They were lying contentedly together against a stack of white floor cushions, the whole of Beverly Hills twinkling in the distance outside the semi-circular window. Ryan's father's house was small, really not much bigger than Lorna Lewis's guest cottage, but it was in a great situation right at the top of the canyon. In the daytime the view from the huge windows on the south side was smog, but when darkness hid the mass misdemeanours of the city, Los Angeles glittered like a fairy kingdom.

"It's ridiculous; she treats you like a child. Me too, you know—I could drive you home, couldn't I?" Ryan had just turned sixteen and the object which he counted his proudest possession after Jo was his new red Porsche.

"Oh God, that's just what she's afraid of—she's afraid if I got in your car we might go somewhere and *park*, for God's sake." They giggled heartily. Jo and Ryan had been dating for six months and had progressed some way beyond parking now. Because of Jo's curfew their first priority at every party was to find somewhere quiet and get the screwing accomplished in comfort.

She tossed her hair and preened, imitating her mother. "Trust me, Jocasta, I know what's best for you. You can't stay out all hours at your age. There'll be plenty of time for all night parties when you're grown up. You'll thank me then, sweetheart. You're just like me, you need your sleep. I have to have the full eight hours or I can't do a thing the next morning, not a single thing. And I look like death warmed over." Ryan rolled over on the floor, shaking with laughter. Jo could imitate anybody and always made him crease up, even without the dope. The way she did her mother was the best, though, catching that tiny lisp she had and the way her English was just a little bit awkward. According to the publicity department of the studio which had trained her, Lorna Lewis was a luscious Swedish beauty whose parents were leading actors at the famous Stockholm National Theatre. In fact she was born Gunilla Horrigan, the illegitimate daughter of a waitress in Cottonwood, Minnesota, and raised on her grandparents' farm, speaking Swedish at home until the day she ran away. Either way, the soft Scandinavian sibilants lingered.

"As if I've got such important things to do tomorrow morning," Jo grumbled through her giggles in her own voice. "As if I needed to look my best to watch the Archies, for Heaven's sake."

Affectionately, Ryan twisted the drawstring of her new embroidered blouse around his fingers. It was a Thirties classic, made of fine white crinkled cotton with multicoloured smocking and red poppies worked around the puff sleeves and low neckline, the perfect complement to her Minnehaha skirt of pale chamois leather. Jo had bought it that very morning at Aardvarks on Melrose. The fabric was so delicate that if she wore it without a brassiere you could just see the outline of her nipples.

Jo loathed her blobby nose, her receding chin, her long body, her short legs, her droopy ass, her fat thighs, her white skin that absolutely refused to tan and her brown hair which frizzed and which her mother wouldn't even let her frost; she accepted that she would never look like Faye Dunaway, never be a Prom Queen and that most of her body was a total disaster area, but she knew with absolute certainty that she had great tits. The upper slopes rose softly almost from her collar bone, the lower curves were rich and full and the nipples pointed invitingly upwards.

Most days Jo left the house with her breasts strapped into a brassiere that had been tailored for her by her mother's corsetière, two thick white cotton cones attached to a four-inch band, meagrely edged with broderie anglaise. Ryan called it the Iron Maiden. Her mother insisted the device was essential to stop her skin from stretching, but Jo merely saw it as another strategy to make her ugly. She played those games—anything to keep the girls children as long as possible and not face up to the fact that she was over the hill.

Most days Jo headed straight for the nearest john and took the hideous contraption off as soon as she was alone, muttering, "If you got it, flaunt it!" as she threw back her shoulders and felt the liberated flesh bounce free. Now, however, it was time to tie the tits down again before her mother threw a blue fit.

"Oh shit—my brassiere! Did we leave it in the bedroom?" They scrambled to their feet, feeling distinctly stoned, and picked their way over the outstretched legs of their friends to the door. In the next room half of Beverly Hills High was freaking out to The Doors. On the stairs some man with a twelve-string guitar was improvising for the benefit of three skinny girls with long blond hair.

They got to Ryan's bedroom just in time to stop a bunch of kids they didn't even know putting his treasured copy of the Beatles White LP on the turntable. Ryan's father was in the music business and he could get all the hot albums before they were released.

They found the brassiere under the bed and Jo let him hook it up at the back for her. There was no way to put that garment on alluringly—she knew that with certainty, having spent hours struggling in front of her bedroom mirror.

Thanks to the operation of Murphy's Law relating to parents, they were coming downstairs hand-in-hand just as Jo's mother walked in the door; nobody in the whole room could have missed the flash of alarm in Lorna Lewis's huge, upswept, blue eyes when she saw her elder daughter coming *downstairs* with a boy. *She's so fucking naïve*, Jo told herself angrily. *If only she knew*.

Then it began, the stuff she hated, the stuff she had been forced to stand by and watch all her life. Lorna Lewis might not have made a picture since a flopperoo called *It Happened in Monte Carlo* three years ago, but she was still Hollywood royalty. As she advanced into this room full of teenagers, pretending not to smell the rich aroma of Acapulco Gold, gracefully rippling the caftan of pink flowered silk which she considered appropriately hip casual wear, the kids all stopped what they were doing and collected admiringly around her.

Somebody put on Herb Alpert instead of The Doors. The guitar player strummed along respectfully. Ryan's father appeared from the den, seated the star in the centre of the white sofa and ordered Ryan's sister to fetch orange juice from the fridge. He always had their maid squeeze some fresh juice when Lorna Lewis was scheduled to put in an appearance. Everyone in her orbit knew she never touched alcohol.

Then her mother would graciously conduct half an hour of polite conversation with all these people, who Jo knew were otherwise pretty cool and mostly also pretty sane, and they would all pretend to be interested in whatever dumb thing she said, and laugh if she made any of her awful little jokes and store away any personal information she disclosed so that they could tell it to their friends the next day and make it absolutely clear that they were on intimate terms with a really big star.

By the time her mother rose in an elegant flourish of Pucci and swept her towards the door in that ostentatiously motherly way she had, Jo was in a sulk as deep as the Pacific Trench. She slumped in the far corner of the white Corniche and watched her mother nervously hugging the steering wheel and peering at the road ahead. The throb of Marvin Gaye's Grapevine followed them down the twisting road. Her mother had a cute, sharp, upturned, little nose. Her sister Tina had the same nose. Why, Jo wondered, did she have to have a nose like a cross between a doughnut and a ski-jump? She felt her brassiere tighten uncomfortably as she heaved a vicious sigh.

"Do you want some air, honey?" An uncertain but immaculately manicured forefinger hovered over the dashboard. The car lurched towards the far side of the road and her mother anxiously wrenched it back on course, then turned her attention back to the dash and at last flipped the switch which folded the roof down. Suffocating warmth enveloped them.

"This car is air-conditioned, Mom. You don't put the roof down for air, you turn the air-conditioning on."

"Sorry, sweetheart, you know I don't understand mechanical things . . ." the car swung wide around a bend as her mother searched again for the switch.

"It's fine, Mom, just leave it." Jo's voice was sarcastic with patience.

"I thought you wanted some air, sweetheart, that's all . . ."

"No Mom, wrong again. I wanted to stay at the party, have a good time, be with my friends, dance with Ryan . . ."

"You need your sleep, sweetheart, or you'll be no good in the morning."

"What do I need to be good in the morning for, Mom? It's only Sunday."

"Yes, and you haven't done your school work. You went shopping this morning when you should have done it, so now you have to do it tomorrow."

"It's not important, Mom."

"Of course it's important—you want to get good grades, and you won't get them if you don't study." They turned left on to Sunset and her mother put the roof of the car up again without any argument. Neither of them wanted every driver on the street gawking at Lorna Lewis having a fight with her daughter in her white Rolls-Royce.

Jo sighed again. Her grades were always the best in her class; she didn't need to study. There was no point telling Mom that, because whenever she did so her mother just told her that everyone needed to study and her grades would drop if she stopped.

"Some of the other kids were going down to the Ash Grove later," she complained.

"For Heaven's sake, what kind of a name is that?"

"I said the Ash Grove, Mom, not the Hash Grove, for God's sake. It's just a place people go to listen to a little music, you know? No big deal, nothing heavy, nothing depraved . . ."

"Don't talk to me like that, Jocasta. There were people taking drugs at that party, I could smell it."

"That was patchouli oil, Mom, can't you tell the difference? God, you're so *naïve*, I can't believe it. Anyway, so what if there were people smoking a little—everybody does it, the teachers in school do it . . ."

"I don't believe it, not at your school." Jo and Tina were chauffeured every day to a small exclusive private school for the cosseted daughters of those Bel Air families who valued high moral standards and hard work more than the pretence of being regular folks.

"There are plenty of other schools in town. Ryan says a teacher tried to score off him. And the soldiers in Vietnam do it . . ."

"I suppose Ryan does it?"

Jo paused. If she admitted that Ryan smoked her parents would probably break them up and she didn't want that. She wasn't in love with Ryan, but he was cute and they had a good relationship. They didn't expect it to last forever especially since he was planning to go to college back East.

Ryan had come along just a few weeks after they took the braces off her teeth and the tits started to look like something; in those few weeks Jo had had more attention from boys than she could handle. It scared and disgusted her the way every male she met suddenly started ogling the blancmange under her blouse. She tried going around in overalls to disguise things, but Mom didn't think they were ladylike. Once she was dating Ryan things were easier. He was muscular, athletic, good-looking and his folks were rich enough; he scared off the other guys. With Ryan's ring, made of a silver spoon bent into a spiral, on her finger, Jo felt safe.

"Ryan's dad smokes, Mom," Jo answered at length. "Everybody does it."

"Your father and I don't do it, Jocasta, and neither do you."

"Only because you're always fussing around me like a fucking *jailer* . . ."

"Don't say that word, Jocasta! Just don't say it, that's all!" Her hands flew up in horror then slammed down on the steering wheel. The Corniche shot across two lanes of Sunset with a squeal of tyres.

"Why the fucking hell shouldn't I say it, I fucking mean it!"

They yelled at each other until the car passed erratically between the electric gates of the elegant, much photographed Lewis home and came to a halt on the gravel before the porch. It was beyond her mother's skill to put the car in the garage while distressed.

Jo ran straight up to her room and fell on the bed. She pulled off her clothes and left them in a heap, then lay on top of the covers looking up at the ceiling. She was too wound up to sleep. She didn't want to fight with her mother all the time, but there didn't seem to be any alternative.

After a while she soothed herself with her favourite fantasy; by a succession of miracles she grew divinely tall, with long, sinewy, racehorse kind of legs and a small straight nose of classic proportions. Her breasts deflated to a simple 34B—no, 34A, even better. Her freckles joined up into an even tan—nothing excessive, the colour of lightly browned toast would do. Then one day, when she came out of school there was a car waiting to take her for a screen test, and something magical happened as soon as she stood in front of a camera, and she became an actress, a real actress not a washed-up joke like her mother, and everyone admired her. She imagined her face in close-up on the screen of their cinema downstairs, looming radiantly over the small audience of her family, and fell asleep.

She sulked through the morning reading *Anna Karenina*. She had chosen the book because it was the kind of volume she liked being seen around with, thick, classic and Russian. Because the story took her into an exotic, adult world, she enjoyed it. The mood of heavy tragedy seemed congenial; it was good to know that other people, far away and long ago, had felt as miserable as she did. Maybe they would remake *Anna Karenina* when she was an actress, and everyone would be amazed that such a young girl could project such depths of emotion and hail her as the new Garbo.

Ryan came over late in the morning and stood uncertainly on the terrace jangling his car keys, intimidated by the thunderous look in her eyes.

"I—uh—thought we could go to the beach or something," he offered.

"You mean you thought you'd like to drive around in your *car* all afternoon just in case there's anyone in the entire state who hasn't drooled all over it yet—that's OK, Ryan, that's cool, I can handle that, I'm sure you and your Porsche will be very happy and I wouldn't dream of fucking up your beautiful relationship."

"OK, no beach," he said lightly, "I'll call you tomorrow."

She did not want to go to the beach because the beach meant the bikini, and spending all afternoon sucking in her gut and wondering why her skin went straight from fishbelly white to lobster red while all the other kids had golden tans. She did not want to be evil with Ryan either, but fortunately, Ryan understood all that.

"C'mon, Jo, play me at tennis," her sister Tina cajoled.

"Why? Can't you find anyone else to play with?" Tina never normally wanted to play with Jo because her sister always won. Her favourite partner was her father; neither of them could serve to save their lives and most of the balls ended up scattered on the lawn, but they made a handsome couple on the court. Tina, at twelve, was already taller than Jo, and slender, and a natural blonde like her mother, with that cute nose and deep blue eyes edged with dark lashes; Tina looked fantastic in whatever she wore, particularly jeans or a tennis skirt. Jo looked like a Munchkin in anything that showed her legs.

"Dad's asleep and Mom's getting a manicure. C'mon, Jo."

"I'm busy."

"No you aren't, you're only reading."

"Call up a friend or something. If you've got any friends. Just fuck off and leave me alone."

Tina immediately burst into noisy tears and ran off wailing "Mom—she said that word to me again!" Their mother appeared in a blue face pack, waving her spread fingers, and another row started.

Sundays were the worst. Sunday was always the same in the Lewis home—now that it really was the Lewis home; for the first ten years of Jo's life her mother had been away making films and her father had been away on business so much that the main house had been a ghost dwelling; the Chippendale and Sheraton furniture was draped in dust sheets. The children had lived with the housekeeper in the guest cottage and learned early that it was futile to ask when Mummy would be home.

Because Jo's father was English and Lorna Lewis gave many interviews explaining that the secret of keeping a marriage together in Hollywood was to make sure your husband was the king of his own home, they had chosen a house built in English baronial style, with walls mantled with ivy, black exposed timbers, fireplaces big enough to hold a conference in and small diamond-paned windows through which the sun streamed defiantly in brilliant narrow shafts. First-time guests peered up the dark oak staircase to the gallery murmuring, "Mrs Danvers," under their breath.

While most of the neighbours favoured Spanish-style architecture, and their gardens rioted with purple bougainvillea and pink oleanders, the sombre, towering hedges of yew around the Lewis house looked distinctly foreign. The sweeping lawns were sprinkled daily at dusk when the shadows cast by the magnificent specimens of chestnut, oak, pine and sycamore stretched out to touch the house itself.

The manorial style was what Robert Forbes had been accustomed to portray in his early days in Hollywood, when Paramount had tagged him "the young Ronald Colman" and cast him in half a dozen minor heroic roles with reasonable success. It bore no relation to his origins. Robert Forbes was born Terence Lewthwaite in Salford, part of the industrial heartland of England, a sprawl of sour streets of back-to-back houses, cross-hatched with scummy canals and punctuated by decaying factories which fouled the atmosphere with their effluents. At fifteen he ran away to sea, pursuing the myth of his absent father.

At eighteen he was tending bar in San Francisco when an actress, taken with his clean-cut good looks, said she thought she could get him a scene shifter's job at the theatre. The director, even more impressed with the tall, meaty young man with a flashing smile and an indefinable and absolutely spurious air of distinction, gave him walk-on parts. "That was when the acting bug really bit me," he habitually recounted. "After that, all roads led to Hollywood."

He was the kind of man who looked magnificent in any

uniform; Hollywood's British Colony gave him the airs to match his looks. In a clipped, reconstituted Oxford accent he called his colleagues "old chap," and "my dear fellow." C. Aubrey Smith, the imposing king of the dress extras, liked him and he became a regular guest at his croquet tournaments. He also taught Forbes to play cricket.

As a screen Englishman, he felt it his duty to volunteer for the Royal Navy when war broke out and was amused to find that his newly-developed persona automatically promoted him to officer class. When he returned in 1945 with a wide-eyed English wife, something in his spirit had matured. Acting was unsatisfying; he was clear-headed enough to recognise that he was not particularly talented, and he was permanently detached from the narcissism of the self-styled Glamour Capital of the World.

"I didn't feel like spending the rest of my life waiting around for the parts David Niven turned down," was how he expressed it.

Then Selwyn, Lorna's agent, always added, "Since when did Niv turn anything down, huh?"

Whereupon Robert Forbes would shoot an immaculate cuff, finger the crested gold links, crinkle his eyes and rejoin, "Precisely, old boy."

His honest, square-jawed and faintly familiar face served him well in the real estate business. His wife, severely disappointed to find that her husband was happy to sink to the status of a businessman with only a distant connection with the movies, ran off with a more committed actor. By the time Robert Forbes was introduced to Lorna Lewis he was free, rich and forty-one; his hair had turned almost completely white and he was the perfect partner for a beautiful actress, eighteen years old, who was so full of ambition she almost trembled with it.

Their courtship, marriage and family life became useful promotional tools. At MGM Lorna Lewis had been given the keyword "kittenish" to help focus her identity—cute, blond and comic, more down-to-earth than Grace Kelly, less neurotic than Monroe but sexier than Doris Day. Louis B. Mayer announced that she was America's new sweetheart, exactly the kind of actress to make the kind of pictures decent, wholesome citizens needed. For a while he appeared to be correct. She made a brilliant debut in *This Girl's Army* and followed up with two light romances; the publicity department declared that she was grown up when she charmed Alfred Hitchcock and won an Oscar nomination for *Reasonable Doubt*, a sophisticated courtroom melodrama.

Pictures of Lorna Lewis picnicking in pedal pushers, marrying in white and christening her baby daughters counterpointed these triumphs, and the couple, who lived their lives from the outside in, saw themselves looking happy in magazines and believed they were happy, although the combination of Hitchcock and post-natal depression persuaded Lorna to announce that she would take a year off to devote herself to her family. It was the year in which Mayer died.

When she returned, decent, wholesome Americans were inclined to prefer television. Film scripts specified free-spirited nymphets in mini-skirts, and there were younger actresses with more malleable identities queuing up for the parts. Lorna made a comedy western, a beach musical and a spy spoof in slow succession. Hitchcock wanted her for *The Birds* but she turned him down. Then came *It Happened in Capri*, and after that, nothing. The adorable kitten had grown into an uninteresting cat; Lorna Lewis found herself approaching forty, battling against spreading hips, deepening wrinkles, an unlovable daughter and changing times.

Her film titles were recited like a catechism over Sunday lunch. The routine was always the same. Selwyn, Lorna's agent, would arrive early, with his wife and sometimes a new script. Jo's godfather, Harry, the director of *This Girl's Army*, would come late, sometimes drunk and alone, sometimes a little less drunk and with a girl. Usually one of Robert's business prospects would be invited for a lethal dose of glamour. Lorna's publicist, physician, astrologer or other senior members of her entourage might also be present. On this occasion Andy, the landscape architect, whom her father nicknamed Adam the gardener, was invited. In the beginning Lorna's illustrious co-stars frequently appeared; Paul Newman came once, Jo remembered, but three years is a long time in Hollywood and now lunches were becoming more intimate.

The event commenced with Lorna entertaining the ladies on the terrace, currently with her plans for a flower border around the pool, while the men retired to the library with Robert for Scotch and business talk. Jo heard Selwyn enunciating the words "deep, deep shit," from behind the double doors as she came downstairs and hurried towards the dining room to avoid her father, who was bound to complain about the embroidered blouse and her overalls.

"Before I forget," Selwyn announced as a plate of the roast beef of Old Idaho was placed in front of him. "Somebody called from the London office to know if you'd be interested in a revival of *South Pacific* they're planning over there."

"I've done Nellie Forbush in summer stock." Lorna never said no outright, Jo noticed. She would twitter on for a few sentences to get everyone else to give their opinions, then make a decision. "Who called, do we know them?"

"No, nobody knows 'em from Adam," he nodded jovially at the gardener who flashed back with a wall of white teeth.

"London would be nice . . ." Another cornerstone of the externally absorbed philosophy of the Lewis home was that anything British was good and Britain itself the most alluring destination. Neither of Jo's parents had been to Europe since her father returned from the war.

"Not in November," Robert growled from the side table where he liked to carve the meat himself.

"What are they offering?"

"Peanuts. I'd have turned it down without asking except I thought you might be interested—ah—because . . ." he shrugged, unable to find a tactful way of saying that this was the best offer she would get all year.

"Well, I'll think about it."

"Didya read the script I brought last week?"

"Oh well . . ." Lorna daintily unfolded her damask napkin. "It was interesting, I suppose, but I didn't really feel it was right . . ."

"It stank." Her husband sat down. "What's the matter with you, Sel—you know Lorna can't play that kind of part. A nympho barfly shacked up with a prizefighter—that's not her scene."

"Jewison wants to direct it." Selwyn mopped gravy from his chin. He ate fast and heartily, but his skinny frame never gained a pound.

"I heard he was making some kind of detective story with McQueen." To mitigate this shrewdness, Lorna lowered her eyes and chased a fragment of meat around her plate with her fork.

"Well, the next picture after that . . ." Selwyn shrugged, "I thought it could be another *Doubt*, maybe I'm wrong."

"Steve McQueen's really groovy, Mom—can't you make a picture with him?" Tina put down her fork with prim care and reached for her Irish crystal water glass. Jo flinched at the insensitivity of her sister's request. Mom would probably give her back teeth to make a picture with McQueen but nobody would cast her if they could get Faye Dunaway. She caught Adam's eye and saw that he too was embarrassed.

"Your mother doesn't operate her career for your amusement, Princess," her father admonished, pinching Tina's cheek.

There was a commotion from the distant hallway and the rangy silhouette of Harry Foster appeared against the afternoon sun.

"Apologies, apologies." He scooped back a lank blond forelock as he sat down. "New York called just as I was leaving. Ah, hair of the dog!" He seized the Scotch that was set before him and drained it. "Thank you, thank you —a little more water next time. Ah! What news, eh?" He bared well-shaped lips over handsome teeth and smiled around the table.

"What's your news, Harry? You're in fine shape this morning." Lorna gave him the intense, twinkling smile that had once agitated the hormones of millions in *This Girl's Army*.

"Fine shape! Yes, Ma'am!" Harry had not been in good shape in Jo's memory. Once a good director, now a cheerful but notorious lush, he seldom worked nowadays and when he did it was only television. However, this morning he was certainly smiling, and much less liquored-up than usual.

"What's the scam, Harry?" Selwyn folded his bony fingers.

"The scam! Ah yes! Is that horseradish?" He gestured down the table with his knife and Jo, smiling broadly, passed the relish. She liked her godfather. He was a man who was quite unable to relate to children and therefore always treated them as adults, an approach which she appreciated.

"Come on, Uncle Harry, spit it out. What's happening?"

"Happening? Happening? Johnson's going to stop bombing Vietnam. The polls say the people don't trust Nixon. We won another gold in Mexico City . . ."

"You gotta picture," Selwyn announced.

"I got a picture," Harry confirmed, reaching for the potatoes. "This is good meat, Lorna. You do the best roasts, you know that?"

"What kinda picture?" Selwyn demanded.

"Ah—the producer's calling it *Mondo Desire.*" Harry's voice evaporated to a whisper and he glanced nervously at Lorna.

"*Mondo Desire!*" Selwyn repeated with satisfaction. "You're gonna gang bang them in the drive-ins, Harry. *Mondo Desire!*"

"But you won't go with that, will you, Harry?" Lorna smiled encouragingly.

"Oh no, no, no, no way. Like I say, it's just a working title. It's kind of an emotional drama, two middle-aged guys driving through Texas, reliving their lives on the way to a college reunion . . ."

"No women in it?" It was many years since Selwyn's wife had persuaded him that it was not good manners to pick his teeth in company, but his lips still made the motions of mouthing a toothpick.

"A girl, a hitchhiker, kind of a hippy . . ." He glanced uncomfortably at Andy, who had blond ringlets down to the shoulders of his fringed buckskin jacket.

"So they pick her up and rape her . . ."

"You read it." The agent was doing an efficient demolition job on Harry's ebullience.

"Nah. I get a dozen scripts a week like that. Seems like the only parts they got for a young actress nowadays she gets six lines, they cut three and she gets raped in the first ten minutes. No wonder kids don't go to the movies any more. You—Adam, Andy, that's your name isn't it? Does *Mondo Desire* sound like the kinda movie you'd want to see with your Saturday night date?"

"I guess not," the gardener answered, awkward at suddenly being made a spokesman for his generation.

"You see? They're killing the business. Jeez! This town."

There was a chorus of agreement as the maid cleared the table. Hollywood's death wish was the traditional subject for this stage of the meal. Then they would move on to acquaintances who were ruining their careers doing television. Jo tuned out. She had an idea, a hot one. Uncle Harry was going to cast her as the hitchhiker in *Mondo Desire*. She could make him. She knew how. He may have known her all her life, but when the tits appeared he'd had his tongue hanging out just like all the rest.

When the meal was finished Harry excused himself, as he always did, and went to take a nap down by the pool. It was the perfect place for what she had in mind, several hundred yards downhill from the house and screened by tall shrubs.

She saw Harry stretch out on a lounger in the fragrant shade at the far end of the terrace and toss the last four inches of his Romeo y Julieta into the hedge. Out of sight behind the orange trees she loosened the string at the neck of her blouse and readjusted the straps of the overalls. A quick dab of Youth Dew and then she sauntered over to join him.

"Hiya, kid," he greeted her sleepily. "How's tricks?"

She didn't want to get into that kind of conversation, the kind of conversation adults had with schoolkids. Somehow she had to get into grown-up territory. She considered taking off all her clothes and diving into the pool, but rejected the option instantly; he'd never want to fuck her once he'd seen her naked in full sunlight.

"What happened to your girlfriend?" she asked, perching on the edge of the white wrought-iron table beside him.

"Uh? You mean the one with the headband and the brown-cow eyes?"

"Yeah, who came with you last Sunday."

"Oh well—she's not around any more, I guess. Got too possessive, kept wanting to play house. Broads are all the same." He unbuttoned his shirt and the sun gleamed on the astrological medallion around his neck. An Aries, she noticed, hot blooded and impulsive—great.

"You mean they put out they're into free fucking but really they just want to get hitched?"

"Does your mother know you use that word?"

Jo giggled, seductively, she hoped. "My mother thinks I'm still a virgin."

"Oh, I see . . . ." One of his rawboned hands descended on her shoulder and she felt a flash of excitement. It was going to work. "My little girl's growing up, eh? That—er—what's his name, red-haired kid . . ."

"Ryan. Uh-huh."

"Well, good." He swallowed, scanning her face with tawny eyes whose whites were becoming dull with excess alcohol. How old was she? Sixteen? Seventeen? Things like this made him feel his age. "He seems like a nice kid. You've been going together quite a while. That's the best way, in a good steady relationship."

"Oh, we're not in love or anything." She shifted her free shoulder and let the blouse slip off it, then squeezed in her elbows to make the cleavage look really inviting. This was a great pose, she'd practised it a lot with the mirror. "Ryan's cute but he's kinda young."

"So are you, don't forget."

"Yeah, but like you said—fourteen going on thirty-five." Shit, she shouldn't have mentioned her age.

"I said that?"

"On my fourteenth birthday—you've always been around at the most important moments in my life, Harry." Complete lie but what the hell, he was usually too juiced to know where he was. He was looking at her affectionately and he hadn't taken his hand off her shoulder.

"Well—hey—what's a godfather for?"

"And now I'm older, you know, you're very special to me." She spoke slowly, partly so she could drop her voice to the right sort of sexy drawl and partly because she was desperately wondering what to say next. "I can't get interested in kids like Ryan, Harry—not with you in my life. You're my ideal of how a man should be . . ." He was looking confused. Jo leaned towards him and began to slide her hand up his long, lean thigh.

"Holy shit! You're coming on to me! I don't believe it!" He jumped off the lounger roaring with laughter. "Lorna's little girl's trying to vamp her old Uncle Harry!" He cackled on, nervous with shock, glancing guiltily around the pool terrace to make sure no one was watching. "And there I was wondering why you were smelling like a—like a . . ."

"Oh shut up!" yelled Jo. Getting angry was better than dying of embarrassment. "All you so-called adults ever think about is sex. You make me want to throw up! You don't understand anything . . ."

Harry rubbed his eyes. "Don't yell like that, your mother will hear. Now listen, Jo. Don't get mad. We both know what went on just now—don't we?" He tipped up her chin so she had to look him in the eyes but she pulled her face away. "It was just foolishness, the kind of thing people do at your age. You made a mistake and you won't do it again. You're a nice kid, nice looking kid—you could lose a little weight maybe—but you're no great beauty, are you?"

Mutinously she stared at the ground. "Look, kid, I've been around, I know what happens with kids like you. You want some attention from the boys, but they don't want to know. They're all chasing the good looking girls. So you figure if you come across with what the good looking girls are holding out on . . ."

"It isn't like that. You don't understand . . ."

"What I'm saying is don't make yourself easy, Jo . . ."

God, what a moron. Her chest was tight and her throat hurt. She refused to cry. "How dare you talk to me like that! How *dare* you! You come around here every week with whatever chick you fell into the sack with the night before and you're giving *me* a morality lecture! You don't know anything about my life. You don't know anything! All you know is shit . . ."

"I'm just trying to stop you breaking your poor mother's heart, Jocasta . . ."

"Her heart! What heart! What about *my* fucking heart!" It was no good, she was going to cry. She ran off up to the house, and managed to get to her room before anyone saw her. Damn motherfuckin' Uncle Harry. He was just scared, scared of her mother. Still, he'd be sorry one day that he'd turned her down.

A blend of emotions fermented inside her. She was angry, humiliated, ashamed and most of all frustrated. Uncle Harry did not understand, but there was a trace of truth in what he had said. And why couldn't she make things come out the way she wanted?

When the driver brought her back from school the next day she was still agitated. Andy the gardener was standing around on the lower terrace looking at some white geraniums he had set out in an urn by the pool house, and although she shrank from returning to the scene of yesterday's shame, she decided to go and rap with him. Andy was cool. He understood things.

"I feel like I'm in prison and I don't understand the crime," she told him once the preliminaries were over.

"Wow! That sounds really heavy."

"Yeah. It feels really heavy as a matter of fact. Do you think I'm beautiful, Andy?"

"Ah—yeah, sure . . . you've got beautiful eyes and nice hair and . . ." She knew what that meant—that meant no, not really beautiful. Well, that was nothing she hadn't already handled.

"What would you do if you were going with someone and you liked them but you didn't love them or anything but you were only really going with them because if you didn't you'd get so much heat . . ."

"I guess it must be tough being Lorna Lewis's daughter."

"Every girl in Bel Air is somebody's daughter." Jo looked at Andy carefully. Deep tan, good body, jeans that were tight and bleached over the thighs but not looking like they were sprayed on. Yeah, she could go for Andy.

"Like Somebody with a big S, huh?"

"Yeah. It's normal around here to have famous parents."

"But your mother's really special, isn't she? I mean she doesn't act the big star and all, she's really warm and caring and—ah—a special kind of a person . . ."

Jo felt a little flash of old familiar rage. Another starfucker. "Do you know what the problem is really, Andy?" she asked, making her voice as sweet and low as she could. "Let me show you, OK?"

"OK, but . . ."

"Just turn around and don't turn back until I tell you." She was wearing the dumb preppie blouse her mother liked her to put on for school and, of course, the Iron Maiden. Impatiently she pulled off the blouse and unhooked the brassiere, throwing them out of sight into the pool house. Then she cradled the tits the way she'd seen the girls do in Ryan's father's porno movies. "OK, Andy, you can turn around now . . ."

"*Jocasta!*" Jo nearly fainted with shock as her mother stepped out of the pool house, her face pale under its tan and her freshly painted mouth twisted with fury. "Go inside and get dressed this minute! What in the world possessed you to act like that?"

In all the yelling and argument that followed Jo concluded that Andy the gardener was a starfucker in the literal sense of the term, for what else could her mother have been doing in the pool house at that time of day and why else would she have over-reacted the way she did? Jo figured that her mother was probably a nympho—after all, it took one to know one and Jo thought she was probably a nympho herself. Hadn't she just come on to two guys in two days? And she and Ryan screwed all the time and she didn't even love him.

She advanced this theory to the child psychoanalyst to whom she was delivered the next day. He was a practitioner of the old school who was intrigued to be asked to treat a child named after the mother of Oedipus, but unimpressed with anything she had to say. Jocasta struck him as a typical Hollywood brat, neglected, indulged, selfish and forced to grow up too fast. He discovered that she had an IQ of genius level and announced that she needed firm discipline and intellectual stimulation.

The Lewis home became the scene of several anguished conferences, not all of them, as Jo imagined, about her. The deep, deep shit to which Selwyn had referred concerned the collapse of a marina development in which her father had invested heavily. Robert Forbes pulled out before his partners were indicted, a manoeuvre which cost all the accumulated wealth of Lorna Lewis's golden days. Lorna and Robert did not tell the children.

Lorna decided to do the tour of *South Pacific*. The Lewis home was rented for enough to cover its mortgage, and Jocasta and Tina were enrolled in an English boarding school famous for its high fees, flexible academic requirements and tolerant attitude towards the screwed-up children of wealthy foreigners.

"It's cool here," Jo wrote to Ryan after a month. "Cool like refrigeration, the climate sucks. I can do the work OK, they're giving me really good grades, which is more than my dear dumb sister. They do Shakespeare every year. Everybody laughs at my accent. The boys are nerds. I'm not saving myself for you, or anything, but there's nothing fuckable for miles. Mom's talking about staying a few years because someone's offered her another show. They keep saying how cheap everything is. None of the kids know who the hell she is, which pisses her off no end, but she doesn't visit much."

That year rolled into the next, and then the next. Lorna

did another show in London, then went to Broadway with a revival of *Kiss Me Kate*. Jo acquired a British accent that was almost flawless, and considerably more genuine than her father's; she dated the son of a famous playwright, and discovered that the dramatic societies of the great British universities were an excellent entrée into the acting profession. When she disingenuously called her mother and asked if she might stay in England to take a degree, her parents congratulated themselves on having saved their daughter.

CHAPTER IV

THE ICY WATER streamed down Richard's face. From where he lay on his side inside the laundry basket, he could hear the noise of the showers echoing around the stone walls of the House. Big drops hammered the side of his head and his face ached from being clenched to keep the water out of his eyes. The tender rim of his exposed ear burned with cold.

There was a filthy taste in his mouth and his lips felt as if they had been stung. Across his scalp and down to his brows spread a searing pain. He could not feel his fingers; whatever his hands were bound with was stopping the circulation.

This immense physical distress was nothing to his internal agony. "You're an arrogant little shit, and this is the way we treat arrogant little shits round here, and we don't give a flying fuck who your fucking parents are!" He could hear the words as if they were still resonating in the dank air of the shower room.

It was all his own fault. Four boys had beaten him up, forced him into a laundry basket and left him helpless under a cold shower, and all for a few ill-judged words and a bar of soap. He had got into an argument in the wash room with Clive Fairbrother, an Australian exchange student a year older than him whose sense of humour was only a few degrees away from sheer malice.

"The divine right of kings doesn't mean you can pinch my soap," Fairbrother had snarled, and the three other boys in the wash room had been electrified by such dazzling insolence.

He was not using Fairbrother's soap, Richard was sure of

that, even though his mother had made sure that he had been supplied with the exact brand most popular at the school.

To argue would be prissy, he decided. Better to make a joke of it.

"I thought you colonials didn't know what soap was for . . ." He regretted the words as soon as he spoke. Clive's fist hit the side of his head before he could blink, and in an instant he was crushed under all four boys and someone rammed the soap into his mouth.

Why is it always like this, he cried silently to himself in the darkness. Nothing I say ever comes out like I want it to. Nobody likes me. Most of the people I like actually hate me. Why can't I ever behave like the person I want to be?

He kicked out as if kicking himself and yelped as his bare feet hit the end of the basket and a sharp end of wicker stabbed into his sole. The self-inflicted pain goaded him into a furious spasm, but as he strained and thrashed against the wicker walls in the darkness all he achieved was the sense that the basket had not yielded a millimetre.

He had been at school almost six months, the most miserable time of his entire life. He had a picture of himself being friendly and relaxed—normal, like the others; he wanted to be popular, or at least to have one friend, but the ideal withered as soon as he tried to achieve it. If he behaved normally the other boys stepped back and did not respond. He would try harder, hobbled by self-consciousness, and then he would say something precious, or stupid, or insulting. No wonder they all hated him.

His father had warned him of what might happen, but not about how he would feel. "Some of them will probably think you need cutting down to size; they might be quite right, of course. You'll find there's a certain kind of boy will have a go at you now because he knows he won't be able to touch you once you've left school. You'll have to stand up for yourself."

Quite how he was supposed to stand up for himself when he was tied up in a wicker laundry basket which had been left under a running shower was another matter. Anger at last took hold of him. The sods—Fairbrother and the rest, filthy, stinking, little creeps. He'd kill them for this.

His jaw ached and he realised that he was grinding his teeth, so he released the muscles and tried to relax. Instantly an uncontrollable tremor shook his mouth and his legs began to shiver in sympathy. The part of his mind that remained a detached observer wondered if his teeth were actually going to chatter.

The same faculty considered his options. His hands were tightly bound together with what felt like bootlaces. His tormentors had snapped off the lights as they wished him goodnight, and it was completely dark. It was probably about ten o'clock at night, and if he yelled it was unlikely that anyone would hear him. His detective was in all probability preparing for bed in the sanatorium, a quarter of a mile distant at the extremity of the estate.

If he lay there until the morning, assuming he did not pass out, or drown, or spew up and choke to death in the meantime, he would be found when the boys came in to wash; the humiliation would be unbearable and the whole story would be all over the school by breakfast. Then Amanda Pennington might hear about it; her cousin was in another House and they wrote to each other. The thought made him flush hot with embarrassment even though chilled to the marrow. Amanda Pennington, with her long, black maenad's hair and round blue eyes, was the girl he adored. She was two years older than him, and a thousand miles away at a girls' school in Gloucestershire, and on the rare occasions when they met he hardly dared even speak to her; but Richard was always in love with someone and his passions were all the more intense for being largely fantasy. If Amanda Pennington ever heard about this he would die of shame.

Like a caged rat, his mind ran around all the possibilities of his situation. Although still some months short of his fifteenth birthday, Richard had already discovered from experience that there is a critical relationship between the piquancy of a secret and the number of people who can keep it. Even in the largely loyal community of the school a hot little item like this one could probably only be shared by about five people before the newspapers got hold of the story. Shame on shame, and the sight of the awful mixture of distress and reproof in his parents' faces.

Killing Fairbrother was out, too, for the same reason. Also drowning himself or any other method of snuffing it. Why, if he died the embarrassment would kill him! In the darkness the Prince gave a short, barking laugh, ingested a large mouthful of water, choked and expelled it in panic through nose and mouth at once.

Don't panic, think, he ordered himself. How strong was the basket? He wriggled and heard its creaks amid the incessant pounding and splashing of the shower. The thin cotton of his pyjamas did nothing to cushion the discomfort of the wicker scraping his bony body. Richard was small and skinny for his age, part of the reason he was in this mess. Clive Fairbrother was six feet tall and heavy.

With his bare feet he strained against the side of the container, and heard a few cracks. It was an old basket, maybe he could make a hole in it. Although slight, he was well made and capable of explosive strength when he had to be.

He rocked to and fro, feeling the basket creak and trying to get a sense of its condition. There seemed to be a weakness in the wicker wall at his feet. Perhaps not, perhaps he was wishfully imagining it—but what else did he have to go on? He kicked repeatedly with all his strength and heard splintering.

Encouraged now he kicked again with greater force and application, ignoring the cuts from the sharp ends of broken wicker which clawed at his feet and legs. Soon the whole side of the basket was smashed and he was able to wriggle out and away to the side of the shower room, out of the icy water, gasping with relief through streams of mucus.

By the faint, clouded moonlight from the small window in the adjoining washroom he was able to orient himself; he struggled upright, leaning awkwardly against the wall, hampered by his bound hands and lacerated feet, and began to walk.

A yellow line of electric light shone below the door just as he reached it, and his heart jumped; he stepped back quickly as the handle turned.

"Oops—sorry!" The silhouette, instantly recognisable by its wide hips and shaggy curls, was David Murray, an older boy in the House who had so far taken little notice of the latest royal presence in the school. His rounded hand reached for the light switch. "Oh Christ! It's you. Are you OK?"

Blinking in the glare, Richard followed the other boy's gaze and looked down. He was standing in a pool of blood and water and behind him a line of bloody footprints marked his painful progress from the showers. Below his knees, his blue pyjama trousers were blotched with crimson.

"Yes, I'm—er—no, I'm not, I'm . . ." Murray's face wore an expression of dismay and Richard realised that an explanation was needed immediately. "They trussed me up in a skip and left me under the showers. Had to break out so I kicked a hole in it, you see, but I've cut my feet . . ."

The older boy's face relaxed. "I—my God, I don't know what to say. That's awful, awful . . ." He shook his head as if trying to deny what he had heard. "Bloody hell, I can't believe it. What a filthy thing to do. Are you sure you're OK? I'm busting for a pee, back in a sec . . ."

Richard leaned against the wall while Murray lumbered past to the lavatory. Flashes of warmth darted uncomfortably through his chilled limbs and he felt nauseous. He closed his eyes.

"Who was it? Don't tell me, I bet I know . . . Fairbrother was one of them, wasn't he?" His voice, hushed but full of nervous urgency, echoed over the metal partition. "He's been on your case all this term. Primitive little git. Australopithecus is alive and well and hanging round Pete's Cafe." Murray emerged from the toilet and gestured towards Richard's hands. "Let's look." He picked at the assembly of hitches uselessly with fingers on which the nails were bitten, then pulled the last knot loose with his teeth. "Ah! That's got it! No prize for seamanship, whoever tied that." He patiently unravelled the bootlaces and Richard winced with pain as the circulation returned to his fingers. His hands were marked in red and white stripes where the laces had cut into his flesh.

"Thanks," he muttered, still wary of his rescuer's reaction.

Murray looked into the shower room. "God, you must be strong—have you seen this? Or what's left of it?"

Gathering strength, Richard retraced his bloody steps and together they inspected the basket, now sagging under the running water. Fragments of wicker were scattered all around the room; a small pile of them marked the drain.

Murray splashed round the perimeter of the enclosure and turned off the shower. "Christ, I'm sorry. Here, take my jacket, get yours off, you're soaking. They shouldn't have done it to you—to you or to anyone. Anything could have happened."

"Well, they did." Richard accepted sympathy badly. "Look, let's leave the basket, we can't do anything with it. Can you go up and get me a vest or a towel or something from my locker? I don't want to bleed all over the stairs."

"Yes, yes, of course—you're *sure* you're OK?"

"You thought I was in here slitting my wrists, didn't you?"

Even in the yellow glare of the lights Murray's blush was unmistakable. Richard's round brown eyes, normally bright and birdlike, drilled into him without a trace of humour. "Well, not exactly, I mean, I didn't think that carefully . . . but you have had a rough time, you must admit."

"Yes, well, I suppose I have. Some people might say I asked for it." This, Murray acknowledged to himself, was also true. Those of the school staff who remembered Prince Charles had immediately noticed that Richard was a much more outgoing and confident boy than his brother had been. They predicted that he would make friends more easily, reckoning without natural adolescent malice and the excessive value their pupils had been taught to place on modesty, however false. In his first term, Richard's bounce had hardened to defensive, brittle pride. There was no pity for his evident loneliness and many stories circulating about his arrogance and the superior manner in which he parked the cheaply-framed photograph of his parents on his night table.

Richard found the cleaner's mop and bucket and was amateurishly wiping the floor when Murray returned with a dressing gown and some towels. He wanted very much to deliver some insouciant quip about royal blood—his sense of humour was seldom disabled for long—but since wit of this stamp had been the cause of his persecution he kept silent.

"Don't bother with that." Murray reached for the mop but Richard pulled it away and squeezed it out in the bucket as he had seen the maids do.

"No, let me—if I don't clean the place up there'll be a hue and cry."

"Look—what are you going to do? You're going to report it, aren't you?"

"Absolutely not." The floor was clean. He sat down in the doorway and inspected his lacerated feet.

"But you must. The headmaster has to know what's going on . . ."

"There'll be the most almighty fuss and I'll look like a prize prick. Look, David, thank you for helping me. I've got to trust you, since you came down and found me, but *please* just keep this quiet, OK?"

"But you must do something, you can't just take it."

"I've got to take it, don't you see? It'll be ten times worse if I don't." He wiped his nose on the sleeve of his dressing gown and sniffed. He was on the edge of weeping, but did not want Murray to realise it.

"You're not going to do anything—er—silly, are you?"

Richard was so exhausted with cold and emotion that his laugh came out as a foolish titter. "Duff them in, you mean? Clive's twice my size, for a start. Even if I could make an impression it'd be the worst thing I could do. Think about it. They'll just kick up a stink and then it'll all come out anyway. The head will chew them over, their parents will go mad, then when it's all finished we'll be back here next term and they'll hate me worse than ever."

"If they really want your guts they won't let up, you know."

Richard wrapped one vest around each foot and tied the corners tightly. "Well, I'll get Mum to send them to the Tower then, how about that? Look, it's my barney, OK?"

"Stout fella," Murray approved, helping him stand again.

"Plucky little tyke," Richard took his arm and limped into the corridor.

"Good man, Carruthers."

"Salt of the earth." He began to shake with suppressed laughter. It was almost worth all that agony to have these few moments of companionship.

"Heart of oak."

"Damn good soldier." Murray grabbed him under the ribs and they reached the bottom of the stairs. They were both snorting back their giggles.

"Sssh—for Chrissake, someone'll hear us." Making as little noise as possible, Richard struggled up the stairs.

"Don't worry, God's on our side. At least no one came and found us half naked in the showers with our arms around each other. That would have been a tough one to keep quiet."

Richard gave his rescuer an amiable punch on the arm and hopped into his dormitory. Five minutes later a plastic bag containing his wet, bloodstained pyjamas and a bottle of antiseptic fell on his bed and he heard Murray's heavy footsteps retreat down the bare boards of the corridor.

With his cuts bandaged tightly with handkerchiefs and two pairs of socks inside his running shoes he managed the morning dash around the garden, but realised as each step became stickier and more painful that there was no real hope of the gashes healing while he continued to fulfil the personal fitness goals in his Training Plan. He was considered a promising runner and there was a cross-country race at the end of the week.

Fairbrother was shuffling reluctantly out of the stone doorway as he returned, and Richard greeted him with sarcastic cheerfulness. He managed to avoid the morning shower by lingering over the cleaning of his shoes, and decided on a strategy to get him to the matron without attracting comment. Fortunately a younger boy had a dramatic nosebleed which distracted his house-mates' attention and covered any remaining smears of blood.

Mid-morning, he had a training break on the school's assault course. He unwrapped the handkerchiefs, contrived to get a good amount of mud down his boots and pretended to make a bad landing from the monkey rope and was dispatched to the sanatorium with a suspected sprain.

"Whatever have you been doing?" the matron demanded as she examined his feet.

"Larking about," he mumbled.

"But your feet are cut to ribbons—and look at your leg!" She pushed up the caked edge of his fatigues, revealing a long, shallow scrape on his shin.

"Oh, that—I, er—got cut up on the rocks canoeing, Matron. Shoes came off in the water. Broken bottle or something, I didn't see it."

"Hmn. Well, it doesn't look too bad, but I'll have to ground you till you heal up a bit. We'll have to take care they don't get infected. Come and see me tomorrow and I'll change these dressings." The matron was a sceptical young woman who had seen many different injuries in her short time at the school and heard many bizarre explanations for them. Intuitively, she knew that the little Prince was lying and the dejected lag in his steps as he left her room told her that there was a weight on his spirit.

That afternoon she sought out his housemaster, a fresh-faced biology PhD who habitually passed his free-time assembling, examining and cataloguing slides of plankton species from the Moray Firth.

"I can't imagine what he could have been doing to get cut about like that, but it wasn't falling out of a canoe, that I am sure of," she finished, leaning against the low white-painted bookcase in his study.

"I've got a good idea what's been going on." All day the riddle of the wrecked laundry basket in the showers had been exercising the teacher's faculty of deduction. It was a torture which was part of the school's underground mythology, but something he assumed had died out at the same time as the belief that bullying was inevitable, harmless and good for the victim's character. "I've seen it coming—or something like it. He's run into a spot of trouble with a couple of the older boys, if you ask me."

"No! You don't mean it! They wouldn't dare . . . the poor lad, he can't help being who he is."

"He can help the way he behaves; he's too cocky. Don't feel too sorry for him. He's not asked for our sympathy, has he? He's got to work this one out for himself sooner or later, and it looks like it's going to be sooner." As he spoke, the teacher saw Prince Richard in his mind's eye and recalled the authority in the imperious carriage of the boy's small head on his narrow but habitually braced shoulders. "I think he's decided to handle things his own way. Good for him, if you ask me. We shouldn't intervene."

"We should tell the Palace, surely?" At the back of her mind, the matron envisaged gangrene, amputation of the royal limb, a national scandal, a public inquiry and the ignominious end of her own career.

"I'll mention it to Detective Furness. I don't think it should go any further. We can't stand up and lecture them on self-reliance and personal responsibility and then wade in and take over as soon as they show signs of doing what we want. His parents didn't send him here to have the teachers live his life for him."

"All the same, I do feel sorry for him. He's a nice, ordinary lad . . ."

"He's got charm, Matron, but he is not and never will be ordinary. That's what he's got to live with. I'd save your sympathy—he's lucky, in a way. They never did anything like this to his brother, you know, because they didn't dare."

Three days later the matron had to take care of Clive Fairbrother, who lost half of one of his front teeth in what he claimed was a game of dormitory rugby after lights-out with Murray. No one believed this explanation. Murray's manner was habitually dignified to the verge of pomposity; nocturnal rugby was a juvenile predilection for which both protagonists were too old. Murray, a boy who was well-liked but who shone at nothing, was also proud of his status as a Colour Bearer and a member of the school council, and took seriously his obligations of exemplary citizenship. Obviously it had been a fight, but since Fairbrother was a newcomer to the school, aggressive and ever ready to defend himself with insults, no particular motive was assigned to either party.

As he watched his enemy climb into a teacher's car to be driven to the dentist, Richard felt agitated by a mixture of anger, fear and pleasure. Murray did not make himself available for conversation through the rest of the week.

On Saturday the pupils could enjoy the austere pleasures of going into the small granite town of Elgin, something Richard did not enjoy but decided to do because his injured feet ruled out most alternatives. In silence, with Detective Furness at his side, he dawdled aimlessly around the streets looking in shop windows. There was a particular café which the others frequented, but he knew if he went in he would be greeted dutifully, the buzz of talk would die down and one by one his schoolmates would leave.

He bought a pen, which he did not need, in a small general store, and as he was leaving stepped aside to let Murray pass.

"Oh!"

"It's me again."

"Yes. Ah—do they have geometry kits here? I've broken my compass." Murray's awkwardness was again betrayed by a blush that spread upwards from his weather-reddened neck.

"You didn't stick it into somebody, by any chance?" That

sounded OK, Richard noted, hoping with passion that the older boy would take the bait.

Murray laughed and he felt triumphant. "Can't think *what* you mean. Violence? Fisticuffs? Horseplay? Why would I indulge?"

"Just an idea I had." Now they were once more a conspiracy of two. Murray bought his compass and they walked on together, beginning the skein of meaningless jokes and catchwords which was to bind them together in the next few weeks.

By tacit, mutual understanding they returned to the school separately. In the same way, they took care to spend no more time together than the daily round of school life made appropriate, but the simple knowledge that there was now one person in the small, enclosed community who cared for him healed Richard's wounded spirit. It seemed to him that he at last had a friend. They laughed at the same things.

His transactions with his fellows began to lose their artificiality and it was generally admitted that the Prince was losing his rough edges. Murray was flattered to the depths of his heart by the affection of this special creature; he was an uncomplicated youth of shallow emotions who did not appreciate that Richard was investing their relationship with far more significance than he was.

The season mellowed. The last of the daffodils along the walk to the chapel died back and were hidden in new grass. The larches drooped gracefully, dappled with their fresh green growth; the hedges grew shaggy and a deep fringe of rushes, sprinkled with a few yellow flags, bordered the lake.

An osprey's nest was discovered above an inlet to which the junior yachtsmen sometimes sailed. A project to photograph the birds as they raised their young was launched, and at once became a passion with the younger boys. Richard had joined the birdwatching society hoping to make friends and been disappointed when the membership dwindled in consequence; now he found himself surrounded by eager acolytes. More field trips were demanded; in the new climate in which life was at last prepared to be amenable to Richard's desires, it seemed natural that Murray should supervise these expeditions. For two perfect Sundays they scrambled side-by-side over the lichen-dappled rocks of the valley wall, the aquamarine sky above reflected in the ribbon of sea below them.

In such a small group the special sympathy between the two boys was obvious to all their companions. It was all the incitement which some of them required.

"Wake up, Toady!" yelled Fairbrother, matched against Murray in the summer tennis tournament. His confident, curving serve whistled over the net into the far corner of the court, leaving Murray to lunge futilely in its direction. "Get off your knees, Toady! What are you waiting for, your knighthood?"

The name stuck and by the end of the day it seemed to Murray that every child in the school covertly sniggered "Toady" as he passed. His own closest friends looked embarrassed and avoided him. No trouble was taken to keep the name from Richard's ears, but in his new flush of confidence he paid no attention.

Murray turned back his bedcover one evening to find a dead toad spatchcocked across his pillow. The sight and smell revolted him; the creature had been a female bloated with spawn. In fury he scooped up the gelatinous mess and hurled it at Fairbrother, who kicked him in the balls. The fight was broken up by the housemaster, whose ears had been open in anticipation for some days. Murray was removed from the school council, demoted and warned sternly by the headmaster that such a betrayal of the community's trust was also a betrayal of one's best self, a suggestion whose subtlety he could not penetrate.

"It's so unfair," Richard complained miserably, having sought Murray out in his study to offer his guilty sympathy. "I can't understand how people can behave like that."

The older boy was finishing a letter to his father in which the news of his downfall was carefully translated into a voluntary withdrawal from activities which were interfering with his studies. He looked at Richard with discomfort. "Fairbrother's just a slimeball. Forget it. That's what I intend to do." He stuffed the scrawled pages into an envelope and sealed it. "I've got to get this stamped." He stood up, feeling bad about his dismissive manner. "Have you got anything to post?"

Instantly Richard brightened. "Yes, I've just finished a letter. I'll get it." He ran down the corridor to fetch his own letter home and gave it to Murray, taking this small offer of service as a token that their friendship would continue.

Murray bought stamps at the school shop and fixed the two portraits of Richard's mother to the letters, curiously reading the address on the envelope inscribed Buckingham Palace, London SW I, with the special code for personal letters to the Royal Family almost unreadable in Richard's energetic script. Two younger boys came in and, after an awkward silence, one of them ventured to mumble, "I'm awfully sorry about what happened and everything, David."

"I just want to forget it all," Murray reiterated, and in his agitation stuffed both letters together into his trouser pocket, where they remained, forgotten, until a month later when he returned to the London apartment, cramped but in a smart street in Chelsea, which his mother's divorce settlement had provided. He at once set off to stay with his father in Spain, abandoning his school clothes to his mother.

She thoughtfully left the two letters on his desk, where his older brother discovered them. Guessing that they had been overlooked, Murray senior tore up the one addressed to his father; Richard's he opened and read. It was insignificant prattle about birds, sailing and school gossip, but the last paragraph mentioned plans for a demonstration against the Education Secretary's newly-announced plans to end the distribution of free milk to schoolchildren. "It seems like a good idea to me, but then I hate drinking milk anyway. I think they really want to have a demonstration because it's a trendy thing to do." Richard had concluded with a large exclamation mark.

Murray's brother sold the letter to the ambitious editor of his university newspaper for £20. By the end of September it had reached a news agency reporter in Manchester, who offered it to the *Daily Post*, an ailing middle-market Fleet Street tabloid, for £15,000.

The editor, a nervous man always conscious that none of his immediate predecessors had lasted more than two years in the job, held his readers' adoration of royalty as an article of faith. He decided to use the letter; the editor of his gossip column astutely elected to buy himself into the good graces of Buckingham Palace by informing their Press Secretary. The police retrieved the letter in a dawn raid on the Manchester reporter's hotel room and traced its progress back to Murray. By the end of the month a summary of their findings had reached Richard's parents at Balmoral.

"Is that the boy he wanted to bring home in the holidays?" his father demanded. Behind him the tartan curtains of the drawing room framed a view of ten yards of sodden lawn and a curtain of heavy rain.

"Well, it's the same name. Oh dear. I think it'll be a blow for him; he does get so attached to people." His mother passed the two sheets of paper, typed in the smudged style characteristic of the Metropolitan Police, to her husband with a frown.

"But what kind of people? He'll have to learn to judge better than that in life." Restless with irritation, he crossed the room to stand in front of the white marble fireplace.

"He's desperately lonely, Philip. Can't you see how miserable he is, how difficult all this is for him? Only the wrong kind of boy comes forward to be his friend; the right kind are just the ones who hang back."

"That's the natural consequence of his position." Prince Philip crossed the room and paused in front of the white marble fireplace. "It'll be the same for the rest of his life, he's got to learn to get on with it."

"I can't understand what's happened to him. He was such an easy child, everyone adored him. Now he's gone wrong, somehow. He's not stupid . . ."

"No point in having brains if you can't use them." He folded his arms and leaned against the mantelpiece. "The trouble is, the boy's not interested in anything. If he could find one thing to put his heart into, it would solve everything."

His wife nodded, smoothing the collar of her pink tweed dress with an abstracted gesture. "I think everything has been too easy for him up to now, that's Richard's trouble. As soon as he's more or less mastered something, he's bored with it." It was a course of discussion they had followed several times before, each time with greater perplexity as their bright, affectionate little boy metamorphosed into a silent, awkward adolescent.

"Is the headmaster talking about expulsion?"

"He hasn't seen the boys yet."

"However you look at it, it's a despicable thing to have done."

"Well, we mustn't judge too soon. It may not have been

this boy's fault." She pursed her lips and reached for the next letter on the pile of personal correspondence brought in by her secretary.

There was a silence broken only by the faint snuffles of the dogs at her feet. Queen Elizabeth considered her son's maturing character.

There had been no doubt of Charles's sensitivity or Andrew's boisterous good nature; Edward was still too young to be a cause of anxiety. Richard was more complex. He was clever, but disinclined to distinguish himself in study, athletic but lazy, honest but argumentative. His bubbling forwardness could collapse in an excess of emotionality. He showed passionate intensity without any focus. His mother was puzzled but disinclined to judge him; Prince Philip interpreted these contradictions as wanton perversity.

"Of course it was his fault. He couldn't possibly have come by the letter honestly or even accidentally."

"Well, at least the newspapers can't get it now."

She spoke too soon. The German magazine *Die Stern* had also bought rights to the letter, and published it the next day, with a lengthy translation and a headline proclaiming, "Drink, Birds and Politics—Prince Confesses." Under the guise of outrage, the *Daily Post* self-righteously took up the story, forcing the other Fleet Street newspapers to follow suit. By the time Richard and Murray were called to the headmaster's study a sheaf of publications headlining the incident were laid out on the large drum table.

"Sir, I swear I don't know how it happened." Murray's round blue eyes glistened with the effort of projecting honesty.

Richard wondered what to say. He remembered clearly that Murray had asked if he had any mail, and his instinct was to tell the truth. If he did so, Murray's guilt would be confirmed. If he claimed to remember nothing, Murray might be suspected of stealing the letter—unless he also claimed that it was a forgery; there had, indeed, been several of those.

While he deliberated, Murray continued: "I had the letter because Richard gave it to me to post, sir. It was when I was voted off the school council and I was really broken up about that and I suppose I forgot to post it . . . I don't even get on with my brother, we've always been at different schools and I've hardly spoken to him since he went to university."

"Does that agree with your recollection, Richard?"

Richard muttered an affirmation, his gaze firmly fixed on the spotless grey carpet, and then, feeling obliged to speak up in Murray's cause, added, "I'm sure it's all a dreadful chapter of accidents, sir. David's been a really good friend to me, and he's had a tough time because of it. I trust him absolutely."

"And you haven't had too many friends, is that right?"

"Yes, I suppose it is, sir."

The headmaster paused, reminding himself of his conclusion that the privilege of educating the sons of the royal house had been conferred on this school because it was uniquely endowed with a philosophy which informed all its actions and made it equal to the task. He wondered how Plato would have advised him. Murray seemed to him to have a laziness of spirit and a lack of character; Richard, on the other hand, gave the impression of a great potential traduced by charm.

"The education you receive here," he said at length, "should equip you to realise your own powers and thus to serve your community to your utmost. This experience should be something from which you will both learn. I am sure you are as appalled as I am at the use that has been made of the private letter of a schoolboy to his parents, but it is certainly a lesson for you in the ways of the world."

Outside the study door Murray strode forward without a word and Richard, bewildered, had to trot to keep up with him.

"Thanks for sticking up for me," he snapped at last, an unmistakable sneer in his tone.

"I thought it would help. I only meant . . . you are my friend, David."

"If I'm a friend, I'd hate to see how you treat your enemies. God, I wish I'd never come to this bloody school. Why don't you just piss off and leave me alone. Go on, get lost."

They were following the perimeter of the cricket ground in full view of at least twenty-two other boys, and Richard was damned if he was going to trail in Murray's wake before this audience. In furious silence he matched the older boy's stride until the trees of the Home Wood shielded them. A few minutes later Murray turned into the Sports Centre and Richard continued towards the House in merciful solitude.

The headmaster issued a brief and dignified press statement which avoided confirming that the letter was genuine and regretted the entire incident. The Queen's Press Secretary called a meeting of Fleet Street editors and implored them to let Richard grow up in reasonable privacy. Murray's father, feeling that neither communiqué sufficiently absolved his son, left tax exile in Marbella bellowing recriminations and removed the boy from the school. A few months later Murray began a miserable round of university interviews at which he felt his prospects had been unjustly and completely blighted.

All this Richard observed with dismay which deepened to despair. His mother permitted herself to use one weekend visit from the strictly observed quota to see him. The relief of an interlude with one of the handful of people who could understand his feelings made him weep, which embarrassed them both.

He went about his work mechanically, withdrawing from contact with other children as much as he could but aware of a subtle shift in the groundswell of opinion around him. Out of his hearing there was much discussion of the rights and wrongs of the affair; the general conclusion, held in typically absolute adolescent terms was that Murray and Richard were innocent victims, while Murray's father and brother were villains.

Fairbrother yelled, "Goodbye, Toady!" after the Murrays' car, and crowed loudly with his diminishing circle of admirers over his enemies' downfall, thereby reducing his popularity still further. A brief mood of shapeless hysteria took hold of the claustrophobic young community, which ended abruptly with a short holiday.

Richard chose to stay with his grandmother at Birkhall, her house on the Balmoral estate nestling between sloping woods of birch and pine and its own concave garden hedged with yew. He was not an easy guest; he arrived in an obvious abstraction of wretchedness and his grandmother, being aware of his growing tendency to argue with the family's general insistence that outdoor exercise was good for whatever ailed one, at first decided to leave him alone to recover. He moped from one room to another to everyone's frustration, declining amusements and leaving a half-read book open beside every chair in which he sat.

"Come down to the river and do some fishing with me," she suggested after his third afternoon of idle silence.

"No thanks, I don't want to go out."

"Darling, you can't help these awful things. I know you're unhappy, but you can't sit indoors and brood about it all day." She tucked her dark blue silk scarf more securely into the neck of the beige jumper she wore under her thick tweed jacket. Her hand trembled slightly, a measure of her anxiety for this unpleasable child.

"I don't want to do anything," he mumbled. "Stop worrying about me. I hate you all fussing over me all the time."

"And I hate to see you unhappy, and you won't feel better if you stay in and frowst by the fire all day. Promise me you'll do something tomorrow? You've got to take your mind off this horrible business somehow and it's a sin to waste this glorious weather." Deeside was enjoying an Indian summer of mild, windless days and skies piled with white cumulus. Behind the trees the late afternoon sky was growing pale towards the horizon and taking on a pellucid apricot tint.

"There's nothing I feel like doing," he persisted. She sighed. When Richard's top lip set in an obstinate bow and his lower lip protruded in a sullen pout he had the unmistakable look of his aunt Margaret. Any minute now his eyes would darken until they seemed almost black with the sheer emanation of his will. It exasperated his grandmother to see this forceful spirit drifting like a rudderless boat, directed neither to work nor to leisure. Richard was already a good shot, a patient fisherman and a brave, if occasionally reckless, rider, but competence in all these sports had come to him so easily that he had no interest in practising them.

"Then do something whether you feel like it or not," she advised crisply.

"I'll go for a walk, then," he conceded in a sulky voice. "Can I go up Lochnagar? Old Fiery can come with me." Detective Furness had earned this nickname for his hair which, cropped unfashionably short, still glowed a vibrant rusty red.

"I don't see why not," she replied, in a bright tone which belied the words. This was an obvious choice made to evade her concern. It was a hard walk to the mountain top, and she was relieved he had selected a pastime which did not require her participation. "Which way do you want to go—from our side or Loch Muick?"

"Can't I go along the burn?"

"It's a very long way, dear, and bound to be boggy at this time of year. If you want a nice long walk you can go by the iron bridge and through Ballochbuie forest . . ."

"I don't like that way," he announced, decisive at last. "I'll go up Glen Gelder. Now that's settled can I carry on moping for a few hours more?"

The next morning, he laced up his walking boots while Detective Furness, squinting doubtfully up at the cloudy sky, telephoned the mountain rescue post on the other side of the peak to advise the guide of their intentions. The Loch Muick approach to Lochnagar, generally held to be both the easiest and prettiest, was the one favoured by most climbers. There were no regulations to prevent people from walking up the Balmoral side of the mountain when the Queen was not staying at the castle, and Richard had chosen a long ascent from the Balmoral side for the sake of privacy.

The mysterious mass of Lochnagar dominated the landscape. The mountain, eleven granite peaks rising between the gentle flow of the Dee in the north and the foaming River Muick in the south, was a presence which pulled everlastingly at the primitive senses of the people below it. Lochnagar seemed to hold the ancient spirit of the land. Young couples took their children to it as soon as their legs were long enough; old people accepted it as the first of their last climbs and many beery pledges were made to the mountain in the Deeside pubs.

The lower slopes, smoky purple with heather, incised by green-banked burns, and in this season splashed with the intense russet of dead bracken, rose from the woods surrounding Balmoral. On clear days grazing deer or wheeling birds added life to the stillness of the mountain. Most days were not clear, and the higher rocks were invisible behind curtains of mist and rain. The summit reached almost 4000 feet, above a mass of crags which were blotched with snow even in the height of summer.

The hold which the mountain had on Richard's imagination, and indeed on the attention of all who lived in its shadow, was not related to its height or its beauty, but to the succession of mysteries which Lochnagar revealed only to those who climbed it. Lord Byron had imagined the souls of dead Highland heroes riding the gales around the mountain's rocky heights. Local folktales made it the home of mythical monsters. Richard's brother Charles told stories about the creatures that lived around the black loch which lay hidden at the mountain's crest.

When Charles had first taken his brother to the summit Richard had been so young he still half-believed that a haggis was a little animal with one leg longer than the other, the better to run around mountainsides. He remembered a long climb between grey-white boulders to gain a flat ground scattered with lumps of quartz, which glittered like giant uncut gems in the sunlight. He had filled his pockets with stones, but the drama of the landscape had been beyond his understanding. What he had retained was the sense of an elusive mystery waiting in the heights for his return.

He declined the offer of a Land-Rover ride for the dullest part of the journey. After an hour of easy walking through heather and scrub they reached the lower slopes, and Richard strode rapidly upwards with no compassion for "Fiery" Furness's middle-age.

Their route became a steep scramble between white boulders speckled with green and grey lichen. When Richard at last paused at a twist in the track he looked back to see the detective, red-faced and sweating, a hundred yards below him. At once, he turned and sprang up the rocky path even faster, suddenly excited by the idea of being alone.

The air was thin and pure, and the sun shone on his back without warming it. To his right was the undulating panorama of the Cairngorm foothills, already capped with snow. Closer, on the other side, he could see the Grampians, a tapestry of a thousand shades of green. Thick white clouds raced across the blue sky, casting a perpetual kaleidoscope of light and shade over the earth.

At last the steep slope flattened and he reached the saddle scattered with quartz. A darker cloud bowled over the sun, bringing a sudden icy wind, and he paused to untie his Fair Isle sweater from his waist and put it on.

The detective was nowhere to be seen. Richard felt a

pang of guilt, knowing that he was selfishly, and perhaps dangerously, preventing the man from doing his job; he liked old Fiery, but at that moment the only company he wanted was his own. His life so far had been crowded with people, familiar but not friends, guardians like Fiery or the nurserymaids, boys at school or companions chosen for him. He had never questioned their presence, but now he realised that it had oppressed him.

Those whose company he would have liked, his mother, father, sister or brothers, the friends from his old school, the girl he adored, were all distanced from him. There were, he calculated, seldom fewer than a hundred miles between himself and the people he loved. Loneliness was his inevitable condition, and now at the mountain top the intoxication of solitude took hold of him. He began to run and jump across the white rocks, exhilarated by the emptiness all round.

A huge curtain of grey cliff rose up in front of him, the lay of the ground making its appearance seem instant and magical, like scenery in a theatre. As he rushed onwards it lengthened and curved, until he stood at the edge of a cold volcanic cauldron, looking down at the mountain's secret, a still, dark lake which gleamed green at the foot of the crags.

Three small pools below the lip of the crater shone turquoise in the sunlight. There was snow in the folds of the rock face, and a new sprinkling of white along the ridge. The highest point on the mountain was, he remembered, to be gained that way, but he would need to go back along the path and so would meet Detective Furness and prick the bubble of aloneness in which he was so happy.

Almost as if he had willed himself there, he found himself standing on the scree at the foot of the rock wall, staring upwards, searching with the little experience he had gained on school climbing expeditions for footholds. There seemed to be enough of them. He was good at climbing; it was a sport in which his small, sinewy build was on his side.

The vast mountaintop panorama was forgotten as the focus of the world shrank to six inches away from his nose. The dark rock comforted him with its hardness. Boldly he kicked loose stones off the ledges and heard them clatter into the silence below. The footholds grew narrower as he climbed higher, but a deep groove in the rock face opened out into a chimney in which he could brace his boots against the sides. The effort began to sap his strength and his muscles quivered as at last he pulled himself over the icy edge.

From the clifftop he watched the small figure of Detective Furness in his red anorak on the saddle below, twisting from one side to another as he strained his eyes against the bright sunlight to search for his charge. Exultantly Richard stood above the rocks and looked down once more on the lower mountains around. A large bird was riding the air currents below him, and he decided it must be an eagle. He felt triumphant and at peace, standing alone with the world spread out at his feet, hearing only the faint howl of the wind and the thunder of his own blood. People were insignificant. He looked at his hands, white with cold, the fingertips rasped to bleeding, and felt that he could hold his destiny securely in them.

Another dark cloud covered the sun, and he saw another, much lower with rain like a grey curtain below it, approaching rapidly from the north. There was suddenly an intense chill in the air. It was time to go back.

"Fiery" Furness was very angry. He was also tired and cold, and in between worrying that Prince Richard was lying at the bottom of the lake with a broken neck had been forced to entertain the idea that he himself might be less fit than he should be. All these emotions vanished when Richard came bounding towards him with scarlet cheeks and shining eyes, looking happier than the detective had ever seen him.

"*There* you are, Fiery! I thought I'd lost you! Isn't it a wonderful climb? Did you see me on the rocks? I got to the top—it was easy!"

"All the same, anything could have happened . . ."

"Nobody is going to kidnap me up here," Richard told him, jumping off a boulder for joy. "And if I broke a leg I'd have done it whether you were with me or not. Ow!" He landed awkwardly and twisted his ankle.

"Take it easy, there's still time for that." Furness extended a hand to help him up and they walked down the track together.

"That's better," his grandmother approved when Richard returned, still pink-cheeked and with the afterglow of joy in his eyes. He realised that for the first time in weeks he had not thought of school, Murray, Fairbrother or the wretched affair of the letter.

Climbing became his passion when he returned to school. His self-conscious gaucheness vanished as if it had evaporated in the thin cold air of the mountains and he found friends. The small groups who tramped across the Cairngorms with him enjoyed his wit, admired his ability and trusted his leadership. To his childish charm was added experience of people under pressure and his intuitive sensitivity developed into adept diplomacy.

His peers liked him, even, in the end, Fairbrother, who enjoyed climbing himself and appreciated Richard's gifts. His teachers were suspicious of his popularity, annoyed by his lack of interest in academic work and infuriated that he could still achieve high marks in examinations.

In his final year he took the part of Hotspur in the school production of *Henry IV* Part I and had the audience cheering at his rabble-rousing speeches. "It is fortunate," wrote the critic in the school's magazine, "that Richard was born into our Royal Family, because if he led a revolution it would probably be very successful."

CHAPTER V

"ARE YOU GOING to let him kiss you?" In the mirror of her white dressing table Sheldon saw his sister Martha's eyelids dip with embarrassment and he rolled across her white crochet counterpane with delight.

"Maybe he won't want to kiss you!" Spencer pulled his twin off the bed and tried to pin him to the floor.

"He'll have to stand on a chair to reach you! Look, this is how it'll be, this is Claude trying to kiss you!" Sheldon jumped on to a chest of drawers and struck a ludicrous pose of disdain while Spencer jumped ineffectually about below him, puckering his lips and pleading with his eyes. By the age of eight, Martha's brothers thought alike but did not look alike. Spencer was growing taller, thinner and darker than his brother.

"Will you two just shut up and mind your own business!" Martha reached out for her precious porcelain statue of a ballerina just as Sheldon knocked it over. Then she unwound the first of the rollers on which she had set her hair. After years of persistent chemical assault it hung straight and tamed to her shoulders; only a few fine tendrils at her temples obstinately crimped themselves as nature intended.

Checking with the photograph in a copy of *Seventeen* magazine which was propped against her mirror, she let the free strand of hair fall forwards to rest precariously on the bridge of her spectacles and pulled the pin from the next roller.

The girl in the picture in *Seventeen* had a glossy black bob with thick, straight bangs that hung almost to her neat freckled nose. Martha wished desperately to wear her hair the same way but her forehead was as high and domed as that of a Renaissance portrait and anyway her mother and the hairdresser both insisted that bangs never turned out right with straightened hair.

"Oh Martha, Martha, you're so pretty, you're so sweet, I love you, kiss me, kiss me *please* oh please oh please . . ." Sheldon and Spencer were snorting with mirth as they acted their malicious scenario for their sister's first date.

"Shut up and get out of here!" Martha was losing her temper. Claude was not really shorter than she was, at least not if she wore low shoes. Whether or not he was going to kiss her had been her main anxiety ever since he had asked her to the dance. If he did, it would be the kind of triumph the other girls savoured breathlessly each Monday when they exchanged their weekend news. The girls with no brains did that. Martha despised them and envied them in equal measure. Their feelings about her were exactly similar; they sniggered and called her "Sticks" because of her thinness, but watched her sidelong with jealous eyes when the exam results were read out.

"Oh Claude, you're so fine and handsome, you're so big and strong . . ." Sheldon squeaked falsetto, hand on hip and lashes fluttering over his big round eyes. Spencer jumped on the bed and began trampolining with vigour.

"Cinderella had ugly sisters and I've got ugly brothers! Go away and leave me alone!"

"Carmen says Claude's a coolie man and coolie man got lice!" Spencer taunted her as he bounced.

"Who cares what Carmen says? Mamma would go mad if she heard you repeat such ignorance." She took out the last roller and tossed back her hair. Coolie was the colloquial epithet for a Jamaican of Indian ancestry, whose forebears would have been imported as indentured workers by the British sugar planters a century earlier. Claude's family all had the refined bone structure and soft, *café-au-lait* skin typical of this descent.

"Hey-ey. Look, Spence, she's putting on new underwear!" Sheldon jumped down and squealed with triumph, snatching up the empty packet which had contained her new Maidenform bra. "Look at this brassiere! What do you want to wear a new brassiere for, Martha, you've got no . . ." He spluttered in a paroxysm of prurient giggles at the idea of referring to his sister's breasts.

"Get out of here right now!" Martha jumped to her feet and grabbed Spencer by the hair. Sheldon jumped to his brother's aid but she seized him the same way, cracked their heads together with a very satisfactory impact, threw the boys through the door and slammed it.

Their teasing had touched a raw nerve. She was so anxious about this date that her hands trembled as she sprayed her coiffure into position. If Claude didn't kiss her it would, of course, be a humiliation, but to those she was well accustomed. But if he did kiss her . . . her imagination balked at the scene and she cringed with alarm.

The role of the best student at St James's High School was one to which Martha aspired, realistically and with increasing success; frocks and boys and dates, *Seventeen* and soap operas on the radio, giggling and primping and fussing with hair and make-up, were all things at which she could not excel; she rejected them and the girls who cared about such things. Louisa Paley was the worst, a frizzy-haired blond of intense stupidity who owed her continued presence in the school to her father's position as chairman of the Rex Bauxite Corporation, or, as the *Daily Gleaner* liked to call him, the King of Hanover County.

Martha studied obsessively, played netball without great athleticism but with the immense advantage of being six feet tall, and acted in school plays in which she had enjoyed surprising success as Professor Higgins and Petruchio.

She was also president of the debating society, and so had encountered Claude, son of her father's friend, a slim, handsome boy whom her mother had pushed at her as a suitor before Martha had rudely rebelled against the incessant matchmaking. She had run rings around him in a debating competition, opposing his motion that "The future of Jamaica will be governed by geography not history," lost the vote but gained an invitation to the dance.

"Martha! Martha!" She heard her mother tripping indignantly upstairs. "What have you done now? You little witch! Are you trying to kill my sons? Look!" Her mother flung open the door and dragged Spencer forward, showing the bump the size of a bantam's egg on his forehead. "You are the eldest child in this household—you're not even a child any more, you're a grown woman almost—and you should be setting an example to the little ones not scrapping and squabbling like a pack of street kids!" Sheldon's face appeared; he was clinging to his mother's skirts, eyes rolling, pretending to be afraid. "You think you're so superior, Miss, you give yourself such airs and graces like you're too good to live in this house with us and you can't wait to leave! Well you hear this, Martha, you injure my children again this way you'll get your wish sooner than you imagine because I will not have you under this roof one instant more . . ."

Martha knew exactly which argument to use with her mother. She stood up, slowly unfolding her majestic height which was sheathed quite appealingly in a green dress splashed with white daisies. She widened her immense up-tilted eyes and looked down at the angry woman without expression. "Mamma, they were messing up my dress and getting in the way when I was fixing my hair. Can't Carmen mind the boys for just a few minutes while I get ready for Claude?"

"But they're only children, children are delicate. You could have broken his nose." Her mother, rage subsiding, caressed Spencer's face tenderly. "You could have fractured his skull."

"I doubt it, Mamma." Martha sat down again with disdain and picked up her comb. "And if I had fractured his skull there's nothing inside it could come to much harm."

Her mother hissed in frustration and turned away. "If you don't learn to mind that evil tongue of yours you'll die an old maid, Martha. No man likes a woman who runs on and criticises the way you do. It makes them feel small. Take my advice and learn some sweet-talking. Come along, darlings. Carmen will give you some ice-cream. Leave your sister alone; she can just pickle in her own vinegar."

Martha scowled into the mirror and smoothed her hair again. She opened her lipstick, Max Factor's Apricot Glow, the shade *Seventeen* suggested was ideal to complement a green outfit. The lips of the model in the magazine were long, slim and slightly bowed. Hers were so thick her mouth was almost round. The lipstick looked chalky against her skin colour; she wasn't sure it was meant to do that. Doubtfully, she wiped some of it off with a fingertip then dropped her hand in her lap and smudged her dress. Tears trickled down her cheeks and she reached for the Kleenex.

Her mother should be helping her. This was the day she

had worked towards for years, fighting her recalcitrant daughter year after year. Her mother was so adept at feminine things; she could always fix Martha's hair and make her look nice, if not exactly pretty; but now there were years of anger between them and Martha too proud to ask for help.

Through the elaborate iron grille at her window she saw Claude drive up to their garage in his father's big white Ford. All the houses in Beverly Hills now had grilles at their windows, and many had large dogs roaming their yards. The house next door had been burgled by masked gunmen. One of the girls at school had been mugged just a few streets away, so now everyone in the Beverly Hills district of Kingston travelled by car with the doors locked. The only people who walked were the maids.

"You look very nice, darling. Enjoy yourself." Her mother put her head around the kitchen door as Martha came downstairs. There was doubt in her words. She no longer fretted over her daughter's colour, since the twins had turned out darker; but in her mother's eyes Martha was every other kind of ugly—tall, skinny, charmless, clever, sarcastic and with emphatically negroid features.

"Hi."

"Hi."

"I like your dress."

"Oh, it's just an old one I got for my cousin's wedding last year."

"Well—it looks nice anyway."

Claude smoothed his bright silk tie against his white shirtfront and opened the car door for her. He had always had a precocious urbanity which Martha admired, though it made her feel doubly gauche in his company.

He drove downhill with élan and inexperience. They crossed a gully at the bottom, a green space when Martha had first arrived in Kingston but now crowded with shacks of cardboard and matchwood with an ugly yellow stream winding between them.

They conversed awkwardly as he navigated the crowded highway at the edge of the town, then took the winding road up the next hill to the house where the dance was to be held. Except for visits on school business to the state buildings of Kingston, Martha and her friends never went into the hot heart of the city. That was where there were shootings and robberies, where ghetto gangs burned down each other's neighbourhoods and women were raped in front of their children.

The dance was in a house designed by Martha's stepfather for Henry Chang, a banking millionaire, with a lofty pillared portico and spacious rooms. He had always called it the house that made his name, because its airy gracefulness had brought him the commission for a hotel complex at Montego Bay, one of the most exclusive on the island.

The dance was to celebrate the graduation of Chang's eldest daughter, who had studied medicine in Dallas. Her sister Jennifer was in Martha's class, a quiet clever girl who would have been her friend had the large Chang family not kept themselves so much to themselves.

More than half the girls at the dance were Martha's schoolmates, and she did not miss the wave of comment and speculation that drew heads together all around the room as they entered. Louisa Paley seemed particularly electrified.

Claude and Martha danced, rather stiffly since each was wary of stepping on the other's feet, and drank the fruit punch dispensed in silver cups with caution, since both were concerned not to get drunk and act foolishly. Seeking something else to do, they came out to the terrace and perched on the white balustrade, enjoying the distant glitter of Kingston by night. A big ship was leaving the harbour, a pyramid of lights proceeding slowly over the darkness of the bay.

"Do you believe what you were saying in the debate?" she asked Claude, aware that this would not be her mother's idea of amusing small talk.

"I believe it but I don't like it," he answered at once, settling more comfortably on the balustrade. "This island's like a child that's grown but can't walk. Our economy could be strong but we've got no infrastructure . . ."

"Yes we do," she contradicted him eagerly, "but there's so much corruption nothing functions . . ."

"Right! So the question is as broad as it is long . . ." Martha's face split in a grin. Claude loved tossing around such pompous legal phrases. "And a small poor country close to a big rich one . . . right through the history of the world it's always the same story. In twenty years' time Jamaica will just be a suburb of Miami."

"If the Cubans don't get here first, you hope?"

He paused. "I think communism can't take hold here because we've got an equitable system of land ownership . . ." Martha gave a pout. "Well, OK, a *reasonably* equitable system, and we've got a strong bourgeoisie, as Karl Marx would say . . ."

"And the CIA . . . Nixon won't allow no domino playing round here!"

"No, ma'am!" He casually dropped an arm around her shoulders in delight and Martha, who had been dreading the first touch, barely noticed.

An hour later they had settled the destiny of the entire Caribbean basin, planned Jamaica's industrial development for the next ten years and agreed that the Prime Minister was the biggest national disaster since the last hurricane.

"What are you going to do when you leave school?" Claude demanded, turning over her hand and stroking it.

"Are you going to read my palm?"

"You don't believe all that. Haven't you got any plans?"

"I've got plans but I don't see why I have to tell them to you," she teased. "Anyway, what are you going to do?"

"Going to UWI, take a law degree."

"The family business, huh?" Martha felt unwilling to disclose that her own ambition was also to study law, but she had set her sights above the University of the West Indies.

"Sure, why not. OK, now you tell me . . ."

"Oh, I'll wait and see how I do in my exams," she murmured vaguely. "I'd like to go abroad, get off the rock, you know."

"Oh." He seemed a little disappointed and Martha decided under no circumstances to admit that the school had entered her for all three of the island's scholarships for study in Britain.

As they walked back into the ballroom Martha, now feeling excited and happy on Claude's arm, missed the step down into the room and fell flat on her face. He at once helped her up, enquiring solicitously if she was hurt, which she was although she assured him she was not.

"Five, six, pick up Sticks!" tittered Louisa Paley loudly from the edge of the dance floor.

The intimacy, the fairy-tale happiness, vanished at once and they became again the awkward couple with nothing to say to each other. As early as she could without offending her hostess, Martha asked Claude to take her home. He gave her a decorous peck on the cheek at her porch and said he would call and take her to the beach some time.

"Well, I suppose Claude Campbell just wants a woman he can look up to," jibed Louisa as Martha curled her long legs uncomfortably under her desk in school on Monday morning.

Days went by and Claude did not call. A month later Martha saw him across the lawn at a brunch gathering of Beverly Hills' first families but by then she was so hurt that she rudely ignored him.

Her wounded heart healed in an instant when she was called to the headmistress's study and told that she had won the Commonwealth scholarship to study in England. "You have been awarded an exhibition at Girton College, Cambridge," the woman's watery blue eyes gleamed with pleasure. "You've hitched your wagon to a star, Martha, and I'm very, very pleased for you." Her tiny white hand reached out and clasped Martha's fingers hard.

When the news was announced at assembly Martha felt as if she had conquered the world, although the only girl who congratulated her was Jennifer Chang, who planned to follow her sister to Dallas.

At home, Denzil, her stepfather, to her surprise, positively swelled with pride. Her mother was delighted to be able to send her incompatible offspring thousands of miles away for at least three years. Her brothers became temporarily docile. Telegrams of congratulation were delivered every hour for almost a week. Relatives she was hardly aware she had sent money and presents. There were letters too, one in Nana's tremulous script referring to the parable of the talents, and a stiffly worded note from Claude. She threw away both of them at once.

*   *   *

DUSK IN THE Western Isles of Scotland falls with a radiance that in warmer waters would suggest dawn. Richard leaned on the yacht rail and watched the sea, the sky and the distant outlines of the islands dissolve into mist. The sun, invisible in the overcast sky, was sinking with brilliant reluctance, casting up a light that flushed each fold of cloud with pale boreal colours.

The moment was calm and optimistic, and Richard breathed deeply as if he could quieten his thoughts with the air. His hair was wet and his body, inside a heavy Aran sweater, glowed with exhaustion. He had been scuba-diving with his brother Charles for as long as they had air in their tanks, two nameless wanderers in the silent country under-water, where shoals of mackerel wavered in silver-sided indecision at their approach and scallops sped across the seabed in front of them, puffing sand into the clear water at each clap of their shells.

He heard light footsteps on the deck; Charles was com-ing to join him. "I give up," he announced, leaning back against the mahogany rail and folding his arms. "The boys are fighting over the map. Andrew wants to put in some-where calm to windsurf, Edward wants to anchor here and Papa wants to push on up North. I keep telling them the forecast's Force 6 everywhere tomorrow and nobody takes any notice."

"It's the Canute coming out in them," Richard sug-gested.

"They'll hoist it in soon enough when the wind gets up, I suppose." Charles stood beside his brother and watched the sea and sky in silence for a few moments.

"I wish we could do this every year. I like us all being together. Just the boys, you know. I seem to get on with Dad better when we're away from it all." Their mother and sister, for whom sea voyages and sports held no great at-traction, were not aboard.

"It's not every year I get four months off between post-ings. I think we need this kind of time together just to get to know each other. You're away at school, I'm away at sea, Mama and Papa seem to go round the world every year. I hardly recognised Andrew and Edward when I got back." Charles still had a deep tan from his nine-month tour of duty as a Lieutenant aboard the naval frigate *Minerva* in the Caribbean. He was not due to join his next ship until January, but still wore the dark blue sweater with canvas patches, a standard naval-issue garment, every day when neither royal nor Navy duties required more formal cos-tume.

"It's not every year our sister gets married."

"Well, let's hope not, anyway."

"At least she's not marrying a horse." They laughed then lapsed into companionable silence.

"Do you like the Navy?" Churning at the back of Richard's mind was the knowledge that this was his last year at school; he had to make the first decisions about his future soon.

"Love it. Great life." Now that the peace of the evening had settled on him, Charles was not inclined to talk, but Richard determined not to lose the chance of getting advice from the only person in the world truly qualified to give it.

"What do you like about it?"

"Well—when I'm officer of the watch and I've got three million pounds' worth of ship underneath me and I'm in charge of it all . . . it's an incredible feeling, Richard, there's nothing like it. Or being gunnery officer and knowing you're responsible for the missiles and you could start a war if you had to . . ."

"And knowing that you wouldn't have to, because they wouldn't let you. What else?"

"Well, the flying, especially the jets, the Hunter's marvellous . . ." he was aware that he was not giving his brother the quality of information he wanted. "I suppose what I really like about it is that you learn to live with people. It's probably the only chance—well, the last chance—I'll ever get to be one of the boys. Two days out to sea and they all forget who you are and you all just muck in. But you're better than I am at all that, anyway."

"Do you really think so?" Richard knew now that he had charm, but it still seemed a wayward attribute which deserted him as soon as he really needed it.

"Oh yes. You're much better at chatting people up than I am. I think you've got Grannie's twinkle. People warm to you."

"So you think I'd get on all right?"

"Yes." He hesitated, considering the temperamental differences between them. Each time he saw Richard his brother seemed more restless and more argumentative. "You'd have to toe the line, of course. Discipline might not suit you. You can't argue with your senior officers the way you do with Papa. And you'd have to stop falling in love all over the place, because you move around all the time and it'd be hopeless. Unless you had a girl in every port, of course. And you're not that type either, are you?"

"Aren't I?" Richard shrugged non-committally, resenting his brother's tone and hoping to deflect questions about love. By now the whole family teased him about his passions for one girl after another, each more intense than the last, and he was learning to hide his feelings. "I don't know what type I am."

He was sensitive because now his love affairs were no longer fantasies. In the carefully planned and restricted orbit of his social life he had contrived to lose his virginity six months ago, to the daughter of an American racehorse owner. She had sensitive hands and supple thighs, a mane of silky black hair that fell around their faces like a perfumed tent, and she was proud to give her nervous novice an excellent erotic schooling in the ecstatic week they were together. She was also ten years older than Richard and without a sentimental bone in her lovely body; her father hoped that Richard's mother might send mares from the Royal Stud to be covered by his stallions, and these prestigious unions were far more important to her than her own with the sweet little Prince. His letters had been answered with affection but briefly, and her parents had just announced her engagement to a scion of the first family in the state, a shock which had hurt Richard so much that his feelings were temporarily cauterised and the last thing he wanted to discuss was his emotional life.

"You're not thinking of joining the Navy yet, are you?" His brother had sensed Richard recoil.

"There's not much else I can do, is there?"

"Don't you want to go to university? You're supposed to be the brains of the family."

"You know I'm sick of being bloody educated."

"Well . . ." Every letter Richard had written his brother from school had been signed "yours in interminable boredom," but Charles had not taken these expressions seriously. "University's not the same, you know. It's the last chance you'll get of any peace and quiet."

"I don't want peace and quiet."

"Well, what do you want?"

"*I don't know.*"

"That's one thing you'll have in common with ninety-five

per cent of the other undergraduates. What do you like doing best in all the world?"

A vision of his American seductress, her dark hair fanned across the pillow and her warm white throat pulsing as she whispered tender instructions, flashed into Richard's mind and he wiped it out with anger. "I suppose the only thing I really like doing is climbing mountains. And I'm good, you know."

"And modest with it."

"No, but I am. Everyone says so, everyone I've ever climbed with. In America they couldn't understand why I did anything else. I'm at least as good at climbing as Anne is with horses. I really want to put an expedition together and take a crack at one of the big hills. And I will, one day." He turned to face his brother in the fading brilliance of the evening, suddenly tense and animated. "There's dozens of mountains no one's ever climbed before, do you know that? Can you imagine standing on a rock and looking down on the world and knowing you're the first human being ever to stand there and see it all?"

"Not a lot of opportunity for mountaineering in the Navy."

"No." Richard chewed his bottom lip, trying to give a form to the nameless dissatisfaction which now seemed to invade his mind at every unguarded moment. "Anne's so lucky, there's nothing to stop her doing what she's good at. I suppose what I really want to do is *something*, anything, just something I can be proud of, make a mark with. I don't just want to go down in history as a name on a family tree and that's all."

"You're sure you don't mean a name on *my* family tree?" It had never before occurred to Charles that Richard might be jealous. They were seven years apart in age, and had had no opportunity to feel rivalry over anything. With his parents Richard got away with much that Charles would never have dared attempt, but although he felt occasionally aggrieved Charles told himself that all older siblings suffered the same kind of injustice.

Richard turned swiftly and seized his brother by the arms, his eyes narrowed and intense. "No, no. You must understand, that isn't what I meant. It's the same for you, don't you see? The family is more than all of us. I just want to be something of my own. I don't want *who* I am to be more important than what I am."

"Sounds like you ought to read philosophy."

"Oh shut up, I'm being serious."

"So am I. You've got a good brain and you ought to use it."

"Yes, that's what Father says."

"He always told me that he never went to university and it didn't do him any harm."

"I know, it's bloody unfair. I don't want to go because it wouldn't mean anything. They'd take me at Cambridge even if I was as thick as a jockey's bollocks."

"They wouldn't and you're not. Why don't you just sit the exams under a false name?"

Richard's impassioned expression altered. "I suppose I could . . . do you think they'd let me?"

"You could persuade them. I'll speak up for you. And look," now it was the older brother who demanded understanding. "This is something that never meant a lot to me until now. Our grandfather never expected to be King, did he? But his brother abdicated, so he had to take over."

"And he hated it and it killed him, but you're not . . ."

"Belt up and listen. Their father never expected to be King either, did he? But his brother died of pneumonia the minute he got engaged, and so he had to take over . . ."

"Fiancée and everything, Queen and country," Richard smiled. Queen Mary had died a few years before he was born; but because people claimed to see in him a resemblance to the great-grandmother loaded with pearls and diamonds whose imperious stare pursued her dynasty from her portraits, he had been particularly curious about her and sometimes leafed through the letters in her firm, flowing hand that were kept in the library at Windsor. "But that's history, nobody dies of pneumonia now."

"Those who do not remember the past are compelled to relive it, Neddy." Charles used the quavering tones of Major Bloodnok, a voice from the past which Richard could not remember at all but nevertheless found amusing. "I'd have said the same thing until the funeral last year."

The death of the Duke of Windsor, and his lying-in-state and interment beside the graves of his immediate ancestors at Frogmore, with its attendant nightmares of precedence and protocol, had consumed the court for months. The loss of the man who had refused his duty to the nation for the sake of his personal happiness had seemed to Richard like a rite of passage for his entire family.

Charles released his grip on Richard's arm, and turned to look out over the darkening sea once more. "And William, too. Aeroplane falls out of the sky and so his brother's got to take over." Their close cousin, Prince William of Gloucester, had died in a plane crash a month after his younger brother's wedding. "It could have been me. It could still be me. I fly Jet Provosts, too. But do you know what really brought it home to me? Bermuda. The Prince of Wales, who happens to be passing Bermuda on HMS *Minerva*, goes to dinner with the Governor and has a useful chat with him about Caribbean politics while strolling round the gardens. A few days later someone assassinates the Governor and one of his staff in exactly the same place. Was that supposed to be me? Or did I make it happen just by being there? That's when you really know the danger, when it happens to someone else, someone totally innocent, someone who hasn't inherited our great ancestral right to be shot at. And let's face it, they can double up security all they like, but if anyone seriously wanted to wipe me out it would be only too easy."

"And I ought to be prepared."

"Yes. The fact is you're next in line." Richard's face now wore an expression of morbid distress and Charles realised he had frightened him. "At least," he added lightly, "until I get married and start giving myself heirs."

Richard gazed at the waves with an uncertain expression as if he expected an assassin with a speargun to break the surface at any moment. It disturbed him to hear his brother talk of death. Richard had avoided the idea that he might one day be compelled to lead the same life as his mother, which seemed an eternal burden of responsibility without power, all suffocating limitations and petty, uncongenial demands suffered cheerfully in the name of duty. It was a scenario for his future he rejected with horror. He wanted to be free. He did not want to conform to the family's fixed traditions, of which Cambridge University had become a part. Now he had to acknowledge that duty, even if he chose to evade it, would also shape his own destiny.

"I get it," he said at last with a sigh. "England expects every man to do his duty and especially us. Do you really think they'll let me sit the exams under a false name?" This concession was the only claim to self-respect he could attempt in the circumstances.

"Why not? You can persuade them, anyway." Charles had already heard their father suggest this course, but judged it wise not to say so. If Richard felt that the family were conspiring to influence him he would rebel at once.

His choice of college did not please, since Magdalene, as his father put it, was famous for educating aristocratic clots. Richard refused to be swayed. He had first consulted his Gloucester cousin who had, thoughtfully and with no fuss, taken him to dine there. They drove through a raw spring night from London at high speed, ignoring the 50 mph speed limit recently imposed by the government to force fuel economies during the long miners' strike. Power cuts and an enforced three-day working week for industry earned the season the title of Winter of Discontent, and Richard, newly in possession of a driving licence and a white pre-production model of the Aston Martin, now felt as discontented as any ordinary citizen suddenly plunged into cold and darkness by a power cut.

He was further annoyed by the silent disapproval of his new detective, Inspector Henshaw, from the back of the car and arrived at Cambridge in a mean temper. Once inside Magdalene, however, the sheer theatricality of the scene mellowed him. He at once saw himself against the backdrop of the galleried and candlelit Jacobean hall, posed with dignity below the massive painted armorial of Queen Anne over the high table, at that time half-obscured by gloom and cigarette smoke.

Surrounded at home by portraits of royalty and their retainers, he did not miss the fact that Magdalene's icons were of the college's masters, benefactors and celebrated fellows, an alternative order of merit which suddenly appealed very much. He felt liberated. "I see you're not worried about the power cuts here," he announced, indicating the massive silver candlestick in front of him with admiration.

Over port before the Combination Room fire after dinner he managed, deferentially but deliberately, to commit himself to Magdalene College in such positive terms that his decision could not afterwards be altered without giving offence.

CHAPTER VI

"YOU BLOODY LITTLE idiot! What on earth possessed you to jump the gun like that without a word to anyone?" His father angrily closed the door behind him. Richard had been formally summoned to his mother's office at Buckingham Palace. "For half the informed opinion in this country Magdalene is exactly the sort of college a member of our family ought *not* to attend."

"It was fine for our cousins and for Alex Fairley." Richard could not hide his satisfaction.

"But that's another thing—don't you see? We can't have half the family going to the same college. The others will complain and they'll be quite right. It's showing favouritism." His mother, dressed for a morning of deskwork in a coral pink twinset, closed the last of the scuffed red leather dispatch boxes in front of her and moved them to one side. She rubbed her eyes, which were already strained—the need for spectacles was undeniable—and reached for the small card on which one of her Private Secretaries had summarised the salient facts about the college her son had impetuously selected. The two dogs who lay at her feet sensed the hostility in the air, opened their eyes and pricked their ears anxiously to follow the mood of the conversation.

"I didn't think it was reactionary, Father. They were very concerned about public education and things . . ."

"Oh, yes—what kind of things?" There was a trace of a smile hovering around his mother's mouth now, but Richard mistrusted it.

"Well, they were talking about the government cutting back on building new schools . . ."

His father halted beside his wife and rested a protective hand on the back of her chair. "And what else?"

"Well," his memory of the dinner was blurred by the claret. "The recession and . . . well, political topics. You know the sort of thing."

"All very elevated stuff—I'm sure you were a very sympathetic listener. You realise that Magdalene's one of the poorest colleges in Cambridge, don't you?"

His father's anger had subsided to a weary earnestness. "As you grow up, Richard, you'll find that most people want to get you on their side for one reason or another. You can see them coming if you learn to think about things from their side. And you can always ask someone here for a briefing if it's something you don't know about." He leaned over and picked up the summary card to show his son. "Don't make quick decisions. Think how this might turn out. Now, if there's any funding that might reasonably be withdrawn from a college that's poor by the privileged standards of Oxbridge, but still much better off than any little provincial university, it will, in all probability, be left alone on our account. When they come to cut budgets, they'll take the money away from some nice inconspicuous little place that needs it desperately to keep an entire department running."

"Philip, you're exaggerating. It could quite well work the other way, especially if we get a Labour government in at the next election." His mother's smile was warmer now, telling her son she was on his side. "What's been done can't be undone now, we must simply make the best of it."

"I'm sorry, Father, I just didn't think."

"You've *got* to think, Richard." His father fixed him with a firm stare. "You're not a boy any more, and you really must learn to consider the implications of what you do. All the implications. Of everything. The Crown must be above politics; your mother is its symbol and all of us, her family, reflect upon her in everything we do."

"He can't learn without making mistakes, Philip," his mother's voice was gentle.

"Yes, but we have no option but to make our mistakes in public."

"I can't be perfect, Father, I'm only human," Richard protested.

"No you're not—not in the eyes of the world, at least." Abrupt severity at once stiffened his mother's features.

"For whatever that's worth," Richard growled under his breath.

"When you are in a public position, public opinion is worth a great deal—however wrong it may be." He was bewildered and did not understand. His mother delivered an unwavering glare of disapproval. There was an uncomfortable pause. Richard rallied defiance but found he did not need to display it. She reached for her telephone to call her Private Secretary. "But you've done it now and we shall all have to live with it. I suppose we'd better arrange a visit as soon as possible, though Heaven knows when. As soon as Christmas is over we have to go to New Zealand for the Commonwealth Games and if there's an election in the spring we'll have quite enough to cope with. I should think we'll have to manage it at Easter from Sandringham."

The fact that Cambridge was less than forty miles away from their home in Norfolk had been a major factor in making it the university favoured by the family.

The visit was arranged during the spring on a day his mother had previously set aside for a meeting with her trainers at the Sandringham stud, and if she resented giving up this cherished pleasure she took care not to show it. They drove across the flat fen country in high spirits, with a secretary and Susan, his mother's lady-in-waiting, trying to think of names for the new foals which would soon be born. To anyone else on the road the two green Range-Rovers might have contained a party of race-goers on their way to the meeting at Newmarket, not the Queen, her son, two courtiers, four detectives and a police security advisor.

At Cambridge two dozen policemen waited in Magdalene Street; since a mentally disturbed gunman had shot at Princess Anne and her new husband in the Mall in London a few weeks earlier, the local constabulary had posted extra men in cars strategically around the town. Their presence, obstructing the narrow mediaeval streets, when no distinguished visitor had been announced, naturally intrigued every passing citizen and student, so that by the time the two royal vehicles arrived at the gates of Magdalene's Master's Lodge a large crowd had collected.

When the Queen's unmistakable profile was recognised, the crowd began to shout and cheer, spilling off the pavements almost under the Range-Rover's wheels. They waved and Richard waved in response, which produced a frenzy of agitation. People crushed forward, half of them trying to touch the vehicles and the rest resisting the push of the others. The policemen were lost in the stampede.

"Oh, do take care!" Susan gasped as a small girl jumped joyfully into the road in front of the Queen's car. The driver stamped on his brakes at the instant half a dozen hands pulled the infant back to safety.

The next moment a dirty-looking blond youth jumped forward with a camera held above his head. A policeman struggled out of the crowd to drag him back, two infuriated students attacked him and the four men fell fighting to the ground.

Police sirens sounded at once and the two Range-Rovers crawled forwards towards the entrance to the Master's Lodge. Richard's mother was visibly vexed. He looked back and saw two of the college porters struggling to close the iron gates on a noisy mob which suddenly no longer smiled. The sight made him think of the French Revolution. He had accompanied his parents on public occasions before, pre-planned to the last detail of security and crowd control, but never seen how a free mass of people could react to his mother's presence.

Inside Magdalene, ancient calm prevailed. "We shall enjoy having your son here very much, Ma'am," Richard's tutor told his mother over tea three hours later, after they had inspected his suite of rooms and met the college staff selected to serve him. "We were all very taken with his *espièglerie* when he visited us before . . ." He paused, realizing that he had committed a multiple gaffe; he had recalled Prince Richard's contentious method of selecting the college and used an archaic foreign word which the monarch might not understand. He saw a startled expression flash through her eyes and froze with embarrassment.

"Espièglerie is all very well, but I hope you make him work hard into the bargain." His mother reassured the man with a small nod; she was quite accustomed to the kind of tactlessness inspired by anxiety. The tutor could not have known that *espièglerie* was a word she had not heard used for almost twenty years, the word her grandmother Queen Mary had selected to describe her sister Margaret's dangerous sparkle.

"Richard's brother," she went on, "had to spend far too much time on state occasions to apply himself as he would have liked, but Richard will have no such excuses. Especially since I understand you have no immediate plans to admit girls . . ."

"Oh, Mother," Richard protested, embarrassed. The don smiled with deference.

"The opinion of the members has always been very much in favour of preserving the genius of Magdalene," he announced slowly, now choosing every word with care. "We are aware that we have a special, perhaps a unique identity which the admission of women would change irrevocably."

"Of course." His mother twinkled at Richard over the rim of her tea cup; he said nothing and looked uncomfortably out of the window at the budding herbaceous border of the Master's garden.

They rejoined the security team and began to take their leave.

"Which way are we going?" his mother briskly asked of Susan, who had been conferring apart with the Master.

"The best plan seems to be for us all to walk to the end of the Fellows' Garden and for the cars to drive out and pick us up by a little gate down there."

"Very well. As long as the cars don't attract attention themselves . . ."

"I took the precaution, Ma'am, of sending them off a few minutes ago," Inspector Henshaw prided himself on foreseeing practical difficulties. "They can take a long route round the back of the town where they won't be followed. There is a police car behind, just in case. There are still quite a few people waiting at the front gate."

"Well done." His mother pulled on her black kid gloves and the Master led the royal party to the small gate in his own garden wall which led to the larger enclosure of muddy spring grass and stickily budding horse chestnut trees beyond.

"I don't understand, Mother." Richard walked beside her, turning awkwardly sideways to talk in a low voice. "Why are we going out the back way when they're all waiting for us at the front? Won't they all be disappointed? You're always saying we shouldn't let people down."

"Later," was all she said, indicating that no explanation could be given with strangers present.

Later meant a few moments snatched in the evening before dinner, when she was able to leave her husband to entertain their guests and take Richard aside on the pretext of seeing the dogs in from their evening walk. He had so few moments alone with either of his parents that the intimacy itself added significance to the moment.

In the hallway, cluttered with boots and coats like the hallway of any country house in England, she dismissed the footman. "Richard, you're very young . . ." she began, touching his arm with a protective gesture.

"I wish you'd stop saying that." In the dim light of the hall his smile flashed warm and white.

"The point is, I want to tell you something you may be too young to understand, but I think the time is right for you to try to understand it, at least. It was something my grandmother taught me, probably the most important lesson I ever learned. A crowd is not an audience, Richard; I know that when people gather around you the way they did today you feel you want to make them happy, just as if you were on a stage—but that's when you must hold fast to what you are, not what people want you to be. You *are* a prince, but you must live as a prince, not try to act like one. Pleasing a crowd is what an actor does; you may be called upon to do it, too, but it's just a small part of the job, not everything. Can you understand that?"

He shifted his feet, uncertain. "Not really, Mother."

The dogs, still excited from their run, were pattering around their feet demanding affection and she knelt to pet them and gently stop them pawing her green silk dress. Charles had been almost too easy to teach, Anne had the natural instinct for both her status and vocation, but this one always resisted. It troubled her because she loved him, and nothing but pain would come of it. "Oh, Richard, I'm beginning to think you're born to learn everything the hard way."

"But I do learn in the end, don't I?"

She stood up and linked her arm through his with a small sigh. "Yes, you do, I admit that. I just wish it wasn't so hard for you."

"Cheer up, Mother. When it gets too much I can always walk up another hill. Mother, can I ask you something?"

While they were alone he wanted to ask the question that had weighed most heavily on his mind for the past few months.

"Of course, what is it?"

"Do you think I'll grow any more?"

She threw back her head and laughed, her long diamond ear-rings swinging violently. "You're not really worrying about that, are you? You're as tall as Charles already!"

"Yes, but . . ." Going through life two inches short of the magic six feet did not appeal to him. "I'm still not as tall as Dad, and Andrew's nearly as tall as I am already."

They were passing a looking-glass, and he paused to check his appearance and brush a few dog hairs from the cuffs of his jacket. His new evening shirt, fine white lawn pintucked and starched to perfection, was his own design and, he thought, well worth the unction he had been obliged to pour on the shirtmaker to get it made exactly as he wanted it.

Richard was a handsome man now; the softness of youth had left his face early. Constant exposure to fierce weather had given him a permanent tan and a lean, weathered look. His mouth had a decisive firmness despite the humour given away by the twitch of his upper lip. His eyes narrowed habitually to slivers of bronze below straight, thick brows; in their depths was a piercing intensity of feeling that could turn any woman's heart upside down, including his mother's. She was about to tell him so, until she saw that he also admired his own reflection.

"You've always been a nice looking boy," she said firmly, releasing his arm. "But looks aren't everything and if I were you I'd find something more important to worry about. Now do come on, we can't keep everyone waiting."

A few days later a letter came from Charles, now serving as communications officer aboard HMS *Juniper* in the South Atlantic. "I think everyone gets lonely at Cambridge," he wrote, crystallising his own thoughts. "And Richard seems to be terribly vulnerable where people are concerned. I wish I could be around to help him. But there must be some people who'll be up there at the same time . . ."

"Some people," of course, signified candidates from among the trustworthy cadre of cousins and courtiers. Her Majesty asked Susan to make enquiries. A few months later, under a Constable sky on an uncertain June Sunday, the Gloucesters, the Fairleys and a handful of other young people with university connections were invited to lunch at Windsor.

Afterwards they watched some polo on Smith's Lawn, their conversation occasionally drowned by the overheard roar of jets leaving Heathrow Airport a few miles away. Victoria lounged gracefully in her Lloyd Loom chair, absentmindedly sipping Pimms and innocent of the effect created by her rose-printed dress, her milky complexion and her brother's plain panama hat shading her eyes.

Richard was surprised to find that Alex's sister, Tory, was now so tall; he felt almost as if she had betrayed him. And she was beautiful. Or was she really beautiful? There was something untouchable about her. He watched her whenever he could be sure she would not notice and his opposing emotions tied themselves in small, stubborn knots.

Victoria noticed that Prince Richard seemed to have grown up at last. He was, she grudgingly admitted, quite good-looking but he obviously knew it and what Suzie Chamfer and her ilk found so devastating about him she still did not understand. But her brother liked him, so she smiled her faraway smile and was pleased for his sake and, in the undeclared depths of her heart, jubilant that their royal connection was to be continued at Cambridge.

Richard politely walked with them to their car at the end of the afternoon and spoke to Victoria directly for the first time as he shook her hand. "I am sorry to hear about your uncle," he told her, having already covered the subject in depth with Alex.

"Thank you," she drew her white cotton cardigan around her as if chilled by a sudden wind. "Of course, we saw very little of him because we were abroad so much. But it is certainly going to change things."

* * *

THE RIGHT HONOURABLE the fifth Earl of Selwood, Viscount Fairley, Baron Eyre, died on the longest night of the year 1974, bringing about the promotion of his brother and heir from the status of "just a sailor."

Alex thrust his hands into the pockets of his old cavalry twill trousers and contemplated the ancestral home from the gravelled terrace in front of it.

"You're thinking one day it will be your turn." Victoria could always read her brother's mind.

"Quite a thought. Never really hit me before."

Aston Langley, a beautiful Queen Anne house of red brick and white limestone, had been the home of their family for generations. As children they had understood that the grand building depicted in one of the paintings which accompanied them on their travels would one day be theirs to live in. Its square mass crowned with thirteen tall chimneys had represented their destiny, but now that they stood on the terrace in the building's shadow both brother and sister felt a new sense of connection to their ancestry.

The house was set on the southern escarpment of the Malvern Hills, commanding a view over a landscape which was considered to be the spiritual, if not the geographical, heart of England. The rich farmland, speckled with sheep and cattle and chequered with orchards and wheatfields on that day as it had been for centuries past, had been the foundation of the family's wealth, and consequently of its titles; the first Baron Eyre had happily been in a position to lend King Charles I twenty thousand pounds to pay his royalist army to fight Oliver Cromwell and the Roundheads.

Their stepmother came out of the front door to join them, knotting her green-bordered headscarf more firmly under her chin. Her youthful beauty, although neglected, could still be guessed from her bright, dark eyes under very arched brows and the small, pretty mouth which quivered mischievously when she was amused. At this moment she was not amused at all.

"I've had to put you two at the back; they're very small rooms but quite sweet really." Alex and Victoria, unconcerned, nodded acceptance. They had never occupied a home long enough to feel any sense of possession about their rooms. "The roof's been leaking and all the pipes burst in the winter and I don't know what else. The place is hopelessly neglected. They've tried to air the rooms but you can smell the damp everywhere. I've had to put Tom and Perry in together." She paused, hands on her flat, boyish hips, and surveyed the terrace. "You can see how he loved his garden, can't you?" Pamela was not green-fingered. She gestured doubtfully at the pair of stone urns overflowing with delicate pink geraniums, the ancient lead troughs frothing with silver leaves and yellow rock roses, and the avenue of eight yews, clipped into perfect cones, which invited them to admire the valley below.

"Look at us rolling down the hill!" At the end of the yew avenue the land fell away in a steep bank down to the ornamental pool that stretched the width of the terrace. Peregrine and Rose, Pamela's two youngest children, were scrambling up and down it, covered in lawn clippings. Thomas, their elder brother, stood aloof, aimlessly throwing stones into the water.

Since the family had accumulated few possessions in their nomadic life, and Rear Admiral Fairley, the sixth Earl of Selwood, needed to keep his London flat, moving into their new home took less than a day. Evans, the butler, a small man with bowed legs and a brisk, rolling walk, served their first meal in the dining room that evening.

"Well," Pamela shook out her napkin with an air of achievement. "Isn't it marvellous to have a home at last? If I never see any of those trunks again I shall be delighted."

"I like it here, it's spooky," Peregrine announced, looking around the room. The blue brocade wallpaper gleamed in the harsh light of the chandelier. Above the fireplace Lady Caroline Fairley, her famous wit and beauty captured by Gainsborough, gazed down on them with a virginal complexion and knowing eyes. The picture was in need of cleaning; her muslin fichu pinned with a rosebud seemed grimy and the details of the landscape behind her primrose silk skirts were obscured.

"Is it true there's a ghost here?" Thomas's eyes were wide with excitement.

Their father seemed abstracted and paused before replying. "There is supposed to be one, yes."

"Wow! What sort of ghost? Does it drag chains and moan?" Thomas's conception of the supernatural was coloured by Dickens's *Christmas Carol*, which he had unwillingly read at school.

"Does it carry its chopped-off head underneath its arm?" Perry's inspiration came from a performance of Gilbert and Sullivan's *Yeoman of the Guard* by the Portsmouth Players.

"Stop it, Perry, you're frightening Rose. And no elbows please—all joints on the table will be carved." Pamela glanced anxiously at her husband, who was cutting a potato slowly and with precision.

"I've heard of the ghost, someone told me years ago. It's the Grey Lady, isn't it?" Alex, who always bolted his food, put down his knife and fork. "Didn't our mother say she saw her once?"

There was a small, tense silence. Their father's first wife was very seldom spoken of, especially in front of Pamela, who stiffened now and twitched her mouth as if affronted.

"Your mother had a lot of imagination." There was a gentle warning in his father's voice, which Alex ignored.

"She saw the ghost upstairs somewhere, didn't she? Something to do with footsteps . . ."

"The gallery is where the ghost is supposed to appear, if there is a ghost. One of the maids said she saw her when I was your age," their father now spoke in the beautifully-modulated even tone in which he had made his most difficult court martial judgements. "She claimed she was so frightened that she dropped a bucket of hot ashes on the floor. You can still see the burn on the floorboards. I rather think she made the whole thing up because she dropped the bucket by accident and was afraid she'd get into trouble."

"The whole story's in the library, I remember now," Alex sensed that his father was struggling to make light of the subject of the ghost, which made him determined to pursue it. "She has a long grey dress, and . . . ah, yes, got it now . . . she drowned herself, didn't she, and she's all wet and she leaves wet footmarks on the floor . . ."

"What absolute nonsense! You'll give the children nightmares, Alex. Do have some sense." Although both Thomas and Victoria were still eating, Pamela pressed the bell push under the table for Evans to clear the plates.

"Hey, I haven't finished!" the boy protested, applying himself vigorously to his remaining food.

"No need to gobble," Pamela told him.

"You eat too much anyway, Porky-Bunter," Perry thumbed his nose at his brother. Alex, Victoria, Rose and Thomas all shared the same fair colouring, wide-browed open face and large build as their father, in Thomas's case currently accentuated by puppyfat; Peregrine, small, dark and elfin was the only member of the family to take after his mother. Victoria relinquished a plate which she had hardly touched. The younger children normally ate in the kitchen, apart from their elders. Pamela's conception of motherhood did not involve day-to-day physical care, and on rare gatherings such as this it was Victoria who instinctively looked after the little ones. She had been fully occupied in cutting Rose's food for her and wiping gravy off her chin, and so had entirely missed the tension of the conversation.

The next day Alex went to the library and spent several hours searching for the small dog-eared volume bound in plain brown leather and dated 1825, which contained the legend of the Grey Lady of Aston Langley.

On the last day of the meagre allocation of leave which their father had secured from the Admiralty he asked Victoria and Alex to join him for a walk. They set off down the valley under a cloudless sky with a strong wind blowing Victoria's hair across her face, following a path which was almost obliterated by meadow grass. The stiles were rotten and overgrown with brambles which their father hacked back with his walking stick.

At the bottom of the hill their route followed the grey stone wall which bordered the estate; the road, heard but not seen, lay on the other side of it. They were sheltered from the wind here and creamy plumes of meadowsweet scented the still, warm air.

After twenty minutes the height of the wall dropped and they saw a squat grey stone church in a churchyard around which the wall continued unbroken. Two yews trimmed together into an arch stood over the gateway which gave on to the road, but their father led them through a small wicket gate at the side.

"This used to be our chapel," he told them, opening the oak door. "In the days when they kept a lot of staff. Then the village expanded and the old church there burned down, so your grandfather decided that the village could take it over." Obediently, Victoria and her brother looked around the dim interior. Each of the six stained glass windows in the short nave was inscribed to the memory of one of their forefathers. A marble tablet carved with a border of laurel leaves commemorated the death of the twelfth Baron at Gallipoli. Beside a pyramid of salmon-pink gladioli wilting on a wrought iron stand the names of the men of Aston Langley who had given their lives in the Great War were inscribed in gold on an oak scroll, and beside it a longer scroll recorded the dead of World War II. Three of their great-uncles and their father's younger brother were mentioned on this memorial, on which the names were divided into those of officers, non-commissioned officers and men of each service.

Feeling awkward, they followed their father back into the sunshine. The graves at the front of the building were large and elaborate and dated from the previous century. They walked around the side of the church, past older headstones which had sunk at crazy angles into the ground. At the far end of the enclosure the oldest tablets, whose inscriptions had been worn away completely, were arranged against the wall and a new line of graves had been started with a simple white marble slab inscribed "Petronella. 1929–1954. 'I sleep but my heart waketh.' "

Their father stood silent for a few moments, trying to command his emotions. He straightened his shoulders against the weight of old grief, and clasped his hands behind his back lest they should make any involuntary gesture. "This is where we buried your mother," he said in a gentle voice, a few moments after that realisation had come to his children.

"I never . . . we never . . . I didn't know that was her name," Alex felt a stab of unreasonable anger and tried not to betray it. "You always just called her Nella."

"That was what we all called her. And I used to call her Pet, sometimes. Always one thing or another. She didn't like the whole name, I don't know why really, she said it didn't suit her. But it seemed right to have the whole thing on the stone." He gave in and bowed his head.

Victoria had never seen her calm, cerebral father moved by feelings before; her heart swelled with sympathy and she wanted very much to hug him and comfort him as if he were a child, but she was afraid that if she touched him he might betray himself and give way to weeping. She folded her arms across her chest as if to hold in her impulses.

"I can hardly remember her." Alex walked slowly around the grave, as if looking at it from the other side would restore his memory. "I can remember her telling me bedtime stories, and running across a field somewhere because it had started raining and . . . a cat scratched me. Did she have a cat?"

"Burmese. Foreign breeds are always neurotic but she liked it."

"I can't even remember what she looked like. I can remember her getting dressed to go out somewhere to a ball or something and asking me to button her gloves for her and I couldn't manage it."

"She wouldn't wear anything but white kid gloves. They cost a fortune." As he spoke, the sensation of dancing with his wife overwhelmed him. He felt the warmth of her palm through its second skin of fine leather in his right hand and the soft suppleness of her waist under a boned satin gown with his left; he smelt the unique and almost forgotten perfumes of her scent, face powder and perspiration; he sensed the brush of her hair against his face and heard the intimate murmur of her voice, and all these sensations seemed more real and palpable than the bright sunlit place where he stood.

Alarmed at the chaos threatening within him, he looked around as if seeking an escape. Victoria took her cue.

"They keep the churchyard beautifully," she offered.

"Yes. I don't know who's responsible, the parish council probably but they do a very good job. Some of these country churchyards get terribly overgrown . . ." Victoria took his arm and they turned to leave.

Alex refused to be deflected. The sense that his mother had somehow been stolen from him was never far below the surface of his consciousness and now that his father had opened the door on the forbidden subject he was determined to reclaim everything of her that he could. "What did she look like, Pa?" He was talking to his father's resolutely straightened back.

"We don't look like her, do we?" Alex persisted. Father and daughter were walking slowly back to the wicket gate together but had to pause and go through it one at a time. Their father, as a gentleman, was obliged to let Victoria go first. Alex had a last try. "Do we take after her at all, Pa?"

"You've got the Fairley looks, both of you. But sometimes I think . . ." his father spoke slowly as he passed through the gateway. "Sometimes I can see a little bit of her in Victoria. You've got your mother's legs, I think. Especially round the ankles. She had very pretty ankles. Although it's hard to tell because you're always wearing those jeans nowadays."

"But Daddy *everyone* wears jeans . . ." Victoria wished Alex would be more sensitive. It was obvious that talking about their mother upset her father dreadfully.

The evening was fine and warm, and Pamela decided they should sit out on the terrace for drinks before dinner. Victoria changed into a cream crepe dress spotted with small blue flowers, with generous puffed sleeves and a pleated skirt. She looked carefully at her ankles, which seemed completely in harmony with the rest of her and not particularly pretty, and decided that her father had been carried away by sentiment.

As if by coincidence Alex and Victoria entered the small drawing room whose doors opened on to the terrace at the same time as their father.

"Come with me a moment," he took Victoria's arm and led them both back into the depths of the building, to the trunk room where a few Navy-issue wooden boxes, newly stencilled Rr. Ad. Lord Selwood, were stacked beside their grandfather's vast and battered leather suitcases.

One box was open, and from it their father lifted a picture, a sketch on pink paper of a bright eyed, beautiful woman with a wide smile and short, vigorously waved, black hair. An elaborate diamond necklace lay over her prominent collar bones, above the low, lavishly ruffled bodice of a white gown. "There she is," her father propped the picture against the lid of the box. "It's very like her, he got her expression absolutely right. She wore that dress to the Coronation Ball. There are some more pictures in these albums here, if you want to take a look later. Mustn't keep Pamela waiting now." He laid the picture down again and closed the box.

Victoria accompanied her brother with little interest the next day when he went straight back to open the four books of old snapshots. The small black and white pictures showed them both as infants, her father as a young man and her mother, always vivid and smiling, balanced on high peep-toed shoes and clinging to his arm. Nothing she saw seemed to have any relevance and in the end she grew bored.

A few weeks later the two of them took a series of trains across the centre of England to Cambridge, with Alex consulting timetables, buying the tickets, calling porters and taxis and tossing their bags into the luggage racks as he had done thrice-yearly at the beginning of each term for as long as Victoria could remember. He directed the driver to take the road to Girton first, although it was four miles from the centre of town, and kissed his sister goodbye under the red-brick Gothic arch of the entrance.

The porter directed her through the long, dark and shabby corridors to the office of her Director of Studies, who presented her with a little black book of instructions for freshwomen and explained that her room-mate was a Commonwealth student who had arrived in England for the first time that morning.

Two floors up, at the end of another long, dark corridor which was quietly murmurous with girls unpacking, Victoria found her room. It had a sloping ceiling and a narrow pointed window, and two beds. On the right-hand bed sat a black girl with the biggest eyes and the longest legs Victoria had ever seen. The girl stood up nervously.

"Hello," Victoria said with practised cordiality. "How do you do? I'm Victoria and I think we're sharing this room."

"My name . . ." Martha was so nervous that her voice was a whisper. She cleared her throat and began again. "I'm Martha Harley, how do you do?" The two girls looked each other resolutely in the eye and realised with pleasure that they were almost the same height.

"If that's your bed, I'll have this one . . ." Victoria moved towards the left-hand bed. This was much the less desirable of the two, since it was under the low ceiling and could not be comfortably sat upon by any woman of their dimensions.

"No, no, really, I just sat down on this bed, I didn't intend it to be mine." Martha was desperately anxious not to offend this gracious and beautiful English stranger.

"Well—um—oh, goodness, what shall we do . . ." Victoria was equally concerned not to offend this sensitive and well-mannered foreigner. Not being Anglo-Saxon was a misfortune which she had been trained to treat with the most delicate sympathy.

"We could toss for it," Martha suggested. Both girls simultaneously reached into their handbags to search for a coin. Victoria found one first, a silvery ten pence piece.

"I'll toss, you call," she said. "I'm not very good at this, watch out . . ."

She flipped the coin inexpertly and Martha called, "Heads."

Victoria failed to catch the coin and it rolled out into the doorway. They both leaped out into the corridor in time to see a short girl with tousled brown hair and denim dungarees trap the coin delicately under one of her platform-soled red sandals.

"We were tossing up," Victoria explained at once, lest this girl should pick up the coin and invalidate the whole exercise.

Jo Forbes raised her foot and looked down at the now familiar profile of Queen Elizabeth II. "It's heads," she announced. "What were you tossing for?"

"Which bed to have," Victoria picked up the coin. "You win, Martha, take your pick."

"Oh, I'll have this one," Martha indicated the inferior bed under the low ceiling.

Jo looked up at the two tall women and down at the two beds. "Why don't you move both beds around like this . . ." she gestured with wide arms, "so that the feet ends are over there and the head ends over here . . ."

"Of course! Why didn't we think of that?" Victoria was delighted to have this impossible dilemma of etiquette instantly resolved.

"Are we allowed to move the furniture?" Martha was extremely anxious to keep all possible rules.

"Who cares? Why not just do it?" Jo seized the end of the nearest bed and in a few moments the room was rearranged. Since she had arrived the day before and explored the college building thoroughly, she also showed them the distant, chilly bathrooms and the small gyp room containing an array of very old gas rings for the preparation of the students' own food and drink.

"It's worse than our school," Victoria announced, unsurprised since she saw nothing strange in the British notion that the deprivation of comfort was good for the character. "It's like a nunnery."

"A nunnery for pigmy nuns," Martha agreed.

"For anorexic pigmy nuns," added Jo. "I guess that lets all of us out."

CHAPTER VII

"AND I'M SENDING you another $20,000 because you'll need a car." Not even the effort of shouting down a particularly bad transatlantic telephone line could rob Lorna Lewis's voice of its soft huskiness.

"I won't need a car at Cambridge," Jo shouted back. "It's against the university rules. Students have to have special permission." She was pacing to and fro in front of the payphone at the end of the dim college corridor like an angry dog on a chain.

"But promise me, sweetheart, you'll buy something sensible, not one of those tiny little Mini things, I know you think they're adorable but just think if anything happened you'd have no protection and you know the way they drive in England . . ."

Her mother was not listening, as usual. Jo decided not to argue. Twenty thousand dollars was twenty thousand dollars and sooner or later she would certainly find a use for it —the nose job, for a start. It was a year since her parents had gone to New York, and Jo was joyfully riding the cosmic high of a young American alone in Europe. She sensed freedom of every dimension within her grasp, as long as the folks kept sending the money.

"And promise me you'll eat sensibly? Lots of fruit and salads? Do they have a restaurant in the college?" Gazing over the parched expanse of Central Park from her twentieth-floor apartment, Lorna had never felt further away from her daughter. Nothing seemed to appease the guilt that had gnawed her heart for years on Jo's account. From the moment of her birth an oceanic love for her first child had swept her away; she tried to tell her, but Jo never seemed to hear her. Now all Lorna could do was call anxious trivialities across the miles between them, knowing that they were messages which Jo could not decode.

"Yes, and it's awful. I promise I'll eat sensibly, Mother. I've lost a little weight already. How's the show doing?" Tell Mom what she wanted to hear, make her talk about herself, after all, that was her favourite subject. Jo knew how to handle her mother now.

"Well, a little down right now but that's natural for the end of summer, you know everyone leaves New York and the bookings just plunge but they say it's sure to pick up again in a few weeks . . ."

"I'm sure it will, nobody goes to the theatre in New York in the summer. The place is as hot as an oven and they just head for the beach."

Showbiz talk was Jo's native dialect. Shows did not pick up, they folded. Everyone knew it, nobody said it. Failure was forbidden within a two mile radius of the Beverly Hills Hotel, and even if her mother was not living in Los Angeles she was still subject to its merciless philosophy. "The word of mouth's really good, Mom, even over here everyone's raving about it. And about you. They love you in London, you know."

"Do they really, sweetheart?"

"Oh yes, everyone's really hoping you can come back here soon. I think they care about the theatre much more here, they really appreciate good acting . . ." Somebody had called her mother a *grande dame* of the American stage, but Jo decided not to repeat that verbatim. She doubted her mother was ready to accept institutional status. Accentuate the positive, that was the rule. Keep telling the lies, keep the system running. Anyway, if this show bombed her mother might very well come back to London, which was the last thing Jo wanted. She felt an inch taller for every thousand miles Lorna Lewis was away from her. "I'm sure the bookings will pick up in New York soon, Mom. You had such great notices. Just don't worry."

"I'm not worrying about me, sweetheart, only about you. I wish I could come over and be with you. We're so proud of you, I really want you to know that. You've worked so hard and done so well . . ."

"Cambridge is really pretty, you'd like it."

"There's no way I can get over there in the middle of a run, you do understand, don't you?"

"Mother, of course I understand. You're a great professional, people love you for that, but it costs, you can't always be where you want to be. I've been an actress's daughter all my life, for heaven's sake. Don't worry about me, I'm fine, I'm OK, everything's just great, honestly."

"You'd tell me if you had a problem, wouldn't you? You're like me, you keep things in too much . . ."

Why did she always say that? Jo could not see that she was like her mother in the least. "Mother, honestly, everything is just great. I am not sick, I am not pregnant, I am not doing any drugs, I am not hanging out with anybody who is doing any drugs. The sun is shining, and I'm sitting in my room wearing a proper brassiere and reading *Beowulf.*"

"You're reading what? This line's terrible."

"*Beowulf.* It's a poem about some Norse legends written in the tenth century."

"But aren't you studying English?"

"It *is* English, Mother. We have to begin at the beginning." Jo leaned against the wall, congratulating herself on her patience. After all, neither of her parents had stayed in school beyond the eighth grade.

"And have you made any friends?"

"Well, the place is still quite empty, a lot of the students haven't come up yet, term doesn't start for a few days. But there's a really nice girl in the room next door to me; she's some sort of cousin of the Queen."

Her mother's squeak of excitement echoed clearly across the Atlantic. Jo gave a wry grin. Now she had definitely done something right. "In the room next door, sweetheart? And she's really nice?"

"Yeah, just like you'd imagine. Tall and cool, very reserved and very polite all the time, absolutely ladylike but then I think she *is* a Lady actually . . ."

"That's wonderful, Jo, listen honey, I have to go now or I'll be late, here's your father to speak to you. Bye, sweetheart, and take care, bye now . . ."

Jo detected the whispered exchange between her parents and then her father's voice resonated amiably in her ear; a few more minutes of meaningless chat, some routine words with her sister and she hung up the receiver with relief and took the bus into town. She was going to buy a bicycle. All the other students had bicycles. Already clattering flocks of them were chained outside every college, café and bookshop. To do Cambridge properly, you had to have a bicycle, and Jo was determined to do Cambridge properly.

Initially the university had been nothing but an ingenious scheme to outwit her parents and become an actress, but as soon as she arrived the beauty of the place captured her. She had spent an entire morning walking in rapture from the court of one college to another along the bank of the slow, green river, marvelling at the casual assembly of sublime buildings.

English history, which until then had seemed nothing but a meaningless jumble of kings' names, stood palpably around her in sandstone, brick and stucco. In her mind she made a pilgrimage through six centuries of scholarship, through the mediaeval enclosure of Corpus Christi, the Tudor solidity of Jesus, the unadorned modesty of Clare and Wren's palatial opulence at Trinity until she reached King's College Chapel and sat down in the choir stalls, overwhelmed and exhausted.

For an hour she watched the glow of the sunlight in the vast interior. The ancient tints of the stained glass dissolved in the air and the light which reached the vaults of the roof was pure and colourless. With the dragons of *Beowulf* fresh in her memory the soaring white columns above her head seemed like the ribs of some monstrous but exquisite fossil. She felt her spirit cease its fretful chafing and float into the ancient space.

Rested and refreshed she wandered outside and found the gate of Christ's College, where she stood in final wonder examining the huge heraldic carving above it. Two fantastic spotted beasts, horns, hooves and tails blazing with gold-leaf, supported a coat of arms with a crown above it, surrounded by a mass of gilded, painted and carved decoration.

Below this bizarre escutcheon stood the massive black oak doors of the college. Jo approached, ran her fingers slowly over the panels, carved in the linenfold design familiar since her childhood from the walls of the Lewis home. That had been an imitation; this was the real thing. Between the two she believed there was something more than time and space.

She felt now that everything around her was true and genuine. Los Angeles, and the person she had been when she lived there, was unreal. In herself, Jo was beginning to recognise a void, and she wanted to fill it up somehow with the living integrity of this place.

The cloistered grandeur through which she had passed had humbled her rebellion. She was treading the same ground as Erasmus, Newton and Darwin, breathing the same air as Milton, Wordsworth and Tennyson, crossing the streets where Wilberforce had condemned slavery and Keynes had argued economics. To do this with the major motive of outwitting her foolish mother suddenly seemed absurdly trivial and unworthy. She released the idea as she crossed Magdalene Bridge and imagined it floating away on the glassy green river like a scrap of trash.

Did she still want to be an actress? Had she ever seriously wanted to be an actress? She sat alone on the upper deck of the Girton bus and considered. At the bottom of her heart, the ambition remained, purified now and stronger than before.

Girton College, she realised on her return, with acute aesthetic instinct and well developed feminist consciousness, was also an imitation. It was an ugly replica in harsh red brick of the hallowed institutions built centuries earlier to educate men. In place of their gold leaf and worldly arrogance, Girton was undecorated and had a convent air. It was also a long way out of the town, as if the mere presence of women might contaminate the essentially masculine atmosphere of scholarship.

She bought her bicycle with care, calling at three small, dirty shops until she found exactly the upright, black boneshaker design she wanted, complete with a wicker basket. It was the sort of bicycle people rode around country lanes in old, black-and-white, British films. The shop owner kindly lowered the saddle and adjusted the handlebars, warning her to keep the chain oiled.

Jo rode away on her new purchase, wheeling triumphantly through the sparse flock of early undergraduates in the narrow streets until she found the Girton road and discovered a flaw in her vision. From the top of the bus the road had seemed perfectly level. Experienced at close quarters it was a hill, and the gradient was against her. She arrived back at the college late and sweaty, with just enough time for a chilly bath before the uneatable dinner. She decided to henna her hair instead.

Within a few days the town filled up and work began. The days grew shorter and less golden. An occasional chill wind blew yellow leaves from the trees. Victoria and Jo frequently found themselves speeding side by side down the hill on their way to lectures, while Martha, who found something uncomfortably unladylike about the idea of a bicycle, took the bus. They met afterwards at a café called The Whim, to eat small, misshapen cakes and drink watery coffee.

"This is my brother, Alex," Victoria jumped up and hugged him as his healthy bulk loomed over their table, his cheeks flushed with cold. She introduced her new friends.

"Didn't I see you at our lecture this morning?" Alex asked Martha, mumbling as he unwound his scarf. His thick hair fell sleekly across his wide forehead.

"Well, I'm pretty hard to miss." She grinned cheerfully. Cambridge had already solved a major part of her identity problem. Here she was not dark, light, coloured, yellow or red; she was simply black. This made her conspicuous, and, she had already discovered, exotic and rather fashionable.

"You were taking an awful lot of notes." Alex pulled up his chair.

"My God, I'm going to need them. Roman law! I never dreamed I'd have to study Roman law. I couldn't understand half of what he said."

"I couldn't understand it either. But my father recommended this great book, you can borrow it for a couple of weeks if you like . . ." He could not have defined why, but Alex found Martha powerfully attractive. He had spent most of the lecture simply gazing at the long brown sweep of her neck revealed below her pinned-up hair as she leaned forward to follow the lecture. An introduction, and grounds for getting to know this exciting creature, were opportunities to be seized.

"Alex, have you telephoned Daddy today?"

"Uh-huh. Look, Martha, this chapter's got everything you need, all the Latin tags in a glossary here . . ." They drew together over the book and Victoria was alarmed. She felt her brother's sudden sexual interest, and it frightened her. She knew that one day another woman would take her brother away, but she wasn't ready for it yet; especially not a woman she introduced him to; especially not one of her own friends; especially not a black woman.

"And have you heard from *our old acquaintance* at all?" She meant Prince Richard, whom they would not identify before strangers. This was a trump card. Alex had to pay attention to her now.

"Oh, yeah, we're doing the freshers' cross-country on Sunday." He gulped his coffee, never taking his grey eyes off Martha. "It'll be a pretty good mud-bath, especially if it rains. Why don't you watch us stagger in at the finish?"

Martha at once shook her head. "I couldn't, I have to study. There's so much I haven't covered, I couldn't get the right books in Jamaica."

"Well, listen, don't go and buy everything without asking me first because there's bound to be stuff I can lend you and law books are so expensive."

"Could you really?" Sincere gratitude shone from Martha's spectacles. "That would be so kind. I was really worried about how much the books were going to cost—I thought I'd have to take out a mortgage to get them all." Her laugh filled the crowded room.

Jo watched the three of them and forgot her coffee. She could watch people for hours. There was Martha, in her sweet cerebral innocence, quite unaware that her mind was being courted only as a preliminary to her body; there was Alex, one of those puppyish English boys always helpless when lust took control; there was Victoria, so serene but now suddenly crazy with jealousy. Her body was tense, her face was clouded and her hands were almost twitching.

Victoria picked up her cup and it slipped from her fingers, crashing to the floor and splashing all of them with coffee. Alex at once came to his sister's rescue, fussing around her and cleaning up the mess, and the gathering broke up in a way that seemed quite natural.

•   •   •

"CHICKIE, I'M GOING shopping, I'll meet you in the car park," Richard announced to his detective on the private telephone which was the sole privilege granted by the college on account of his status. It was an ancient black device with a plaited cord, which connected him with the world outside and with the suite of rooms on the floor above him which housed his detectives. He also had a car, but the Aston was not strictly his privilege, since it was officially owned by Inspector Henshaw.

He had been in Cambridge a month, and the curtain was at last going up on his life. He had the sense of liberation which Charles had predicted; he was able to forget that he was his parents' son, and relieved of the duty of acting in public a role which he himself did not yet know. He was also safe from the bizarre *alter ego* of Richard the Rebel Prince which the world's press had constructed from the few facts and many fictions about him which they had collected.

He felt he stood alone surrounded by infinite possibilities, and he was greedily intent on seizing everything which would make him his own man.

What this came down to was a woman, a black leather jacket and a purpose for his existence. Most of the other 3,000 freshmen had the same broad aims, and all of them, including Richard, believed they were unique in doing so, and gazed across the willow-fringed vista of the Backs feeling lost, lonely and full of melancholy self-importance.

Richard was one of the few who knew precisely what he wanted. He wanted one of the clear-eyed girls with flowing hair who occasionally swooped across his path on their bicycles like rare birds of paradise. He wanted the sense of purpose that the men who scored those girls had, the intense focus and preternatural maturity with which they cut through the herd of dreamers to pursue their ambitions. And he wanted the kind of leather jacket those men wore, the kind that signalled arrogant street-wise virility and made the most of broad shoulders and narrow hips. You needed a leather jacket to do Cambridge properly, and Richard was determined to do Cambridge properly.

He had seen the ideal garment in a shop named Jean Jeanius near the market square. He left the detective in the car and tried to walk through the fingermarked glass door as if he always bought clothes in shops and paid with money. Until now, Richard had acquired clothes from outfitters who proudly displayed the Royal Warrant in their Mayfair shops, dispatched deferential tailors to measure the royal limbs at Buckingham Palace, had dressed his father and grandfather before him, and sent accounts which were settled by their equerries.

The interior was dim. The shop assistant, a David Bowie

clone in snakeskin boots, ignored him. Pasted on the till was a sign which read "Shoplifting *really* fucks up your karma."

Richard found a rack of leather jackets chained together at the back of the shop and began to look through them. The assistant, alerted by his purposeful manner, slipped Eric Clapton into the tape deck and nudged up the volume. Old Clapper always got the punters in the right frame of mind.

"Can I try one of these?" Richard had to raise his voice to be heard above the music. The assistant lounged off his stool with a key and released the padlock at the end of the rail, disdainfully eyeing Richard's attire, one of the finest achievements of Savile Row tailoring in the season's new muted lightweight worsted.

Richard tossed his jacket over a chair, revealing red braces and a full, striped shirt. The assistant blinked in horror; this man definitely needed help. Richard tried on the first of the leathers, and in the murky mirror on the wall he was gratified to see that it was too small.

"Here, try this one." There was hope for him—the punter definitely looked keen. The assistant noticed a cream Aston Martin outside, checked his customer's residual suntan and heavy gold signet ring, and decided it was his moral duty to make a sale. "Studs are gonna be really big this winter."

"I don't want studs," Richard was sure about that.

"No studs . . . fringes?" Richard shook his head. "No fringes. Your classic James Dean number, we had one somewhere if it hasn't been nicked . . ."

"What about the one in the window?"

"Yeah, it's the business, that one. But I gotta tell you the price—hundred and ten pounds. Italian, you see." That was always the clincher—telling the punter he couldn't afford it.

"Can I try it?"

"Sure." Without undue haste, the jacket was removed from the window. "It's a lovely garment, this one. Only came in yesterday. Beautiful leather. Glacé kid. Look at the finish on it, it'll last you a lifetime . . ."

The jacket settled contentedly on Richard's shoulders. He thrust his hands into the pockets and admired it. He loved every meanly tailored and carelessly sewn seam of it.

It was perfect. He zipped the front. He looked taller, older, a different person.

"Could have been made for you," murmured the assistant, folding his arms with confidence.

"I'll take it." Richard fastened the steel buckle at the waist and realised the silhouette he wanted was spoiled by the cut of his trousers.

"We might have the trousers to go with it . . ."

Leather trousers! This man couldn't have any idea who he was. He was getting away with it, passing for normal. Richard felt a surge of triumph. "I don't fancy that idea—I could do with a new pair of jeans, though." As if he'd ever owned a pair of jeans in his life.

"Certainly—we've got some new distressed look, flares, patchwork . . . what size do you take?" Richard had no idea how to respond but the salesman appraised his proportions shrewdly and burrowed into the heaps of blue denim on the shelves. "You look like a Levis man to me. Nothing too outrageous, am I right?"

Richard nodded. Two pairs of jeans were draped across his arms and he was propelled behind a limp curtain to change. The first pair was too long in the leg. The second fitted perfectly. He returned to the mirror, tense with excitement, and checked the effect from front and back.

Great body, now you could see it. All muscle with an ass like two prime sirloins fighting in a bag. The assistant's reptilian eyes flickered as he gave his customer the significant once-over that turned into a twice-over around the crotch then skimmed up for eye contact. No response. Pity. Still, you couldn't win 'em all.

"Great fit. Like a second skin. I could give you a size smaller but it wouldn't be fair on the chicks." He winked with a shade of regret and reached for a black leather belt with a silver Western-style buckle, shook his head then picked out another, more expensive, one. Richard eagerly threaded it through the belt loops.

"Do you want to wear the gear out? I can pack up your suit for you." The salesman felt he was doing a good morning's work, transforming this Hooray Henry into a half-way decent human being.

"Yes, terrific, please do." Richard could not take his eyes off the mirror. A few more details of his appearance needed to be changed. The brown lace-up brogues considered perfect gentleman's casual wear by his bootmakers, looked ridiculous. The linked cuffs of his yellow striped Turnbull & Asser shirt were crushed in the jacket's sleeves and felt uncomfortable. In another ten minutes he had replaced these discordant accessories with black boots and a plain white shirt with button cuffs.

"Cheque or cash?" The assistant returned to his perch behind the till and rang up the handsome total, mentally calculating the commission with satisfaction.

"Cash." Where the hell was his wallet? He had ordered one specially from Gucci for this new phase of his life, but, being unaccustomed to carrying money at all, let alone having it stolen, Richard had lost track of it.

"You'll be needing this then. I think it was burning a hole in your pocket." With a grin, the salesman passed him the wallet from the inner pocket of his old jacket and continued stuffing the discarded garments into two large boxes.

Richard counted out the notes with a little too much flourish. The assistant counted them again and casually held one of the ten-pound notes to the light to check its authenticity. A germ of suspicion sprouted in his mind. Something wasn't quite right, but he couldn't put his finger on it. Richard felt intense satisfaction as he saw the portraits of his mother stuffed into the till.

"You look kind of familiar—have you been in here before?" the assistant asked, handing Richard his receipt and noting that he hesitated, uncertain what to do with it.

"I don't think so."

"I'm sure I have seen you somewhere before?"

"Around the town, perhaps?" Richard was determined to keep up the pretence: if he was recognised the whole adventure would lose its thrill.

"You're not an actor, or anything? We get a lot of actors in here, being near the theatre . . . maybe I've seen you on TV?"

"Yeah, maybe," he agreed lightly, making for the door. "Goodbye—thanks for your help."

"Cheers, mate—come again."

The man followed him to the door, wanting to see the Aston drive off. He was not disappointed. Richard, intoxicated by his adventure, hit the gas hard and half a ton of superb British motor engineering shot down the market square like a hunting cheetah.

Richard was oblivious of the shoppers who jumped nervously on to the pavements, the two students selling the *International Socialist* newspaper who scowled and yelled abuse, and the small group of bicycles emerging from a side street. *Cheers, mate* rang in his ears. He was high on the smell of the leather, the grip of the jeans and the power in his hands.

He cornered with a squeal of tyres and suddenly a girl on a bicycle appeared dead ahead. He hit the brakes, heard a scream and the metallic clatter of the bicycle hitting the ground, and leaped out of the car.

"You fucking asshole! Why don't you fucking learn to drive before you buy a fucking Aston Martin!" The girl who jumped out of the gutter in front of him had a cloud of pre-Raphaelite red hair, eyes like emeralds and mobile lips. Richard had never heard the expression "fucking asshole" except in the cinema at Buckingham Palace.

She also had a magnificent voice; the entire market square heard every word. Heads turned. Richard took her arm. "Are you all right?"

"What the fuck do you care if I'm all right?"

"Please, I'm sorry, I was driving like a maniac, I had no right to drive like that. I'm desperately sorry. Please believe me. Are you hurt?" He was holding her gently with both hands now; she was trembling. "You must come and sit down—you've had a terrible shock."

Jo saw remorse in the stranger's eyes and heard concern in his voice. She allowed him to lead her to a bench provided by the municipality for footsore shoppers, and to brush the grit from her grazed hands. His touch was firm and delicate and his hands were warm. She felt comforted.

"I guess I'm OK. I can walk, anyway."

"You ought to clean these scrapes up." His exquisitely clean handkerchief would have done the job, but it was in his old jacket in the back of the car. He quickly raised her right hand to his mouth and licked the cuts clean. "Best way—animals do it." He took the other hand and she gave it willingly. His tongue was hot and quick on her raw flesh; it was sensual, and a presumption and they both knew it, but he had not calculated the gesture.

"You're sure you're not a vampire or anything?" She pulled her hands away at last.

"Just a lousy driver. I'm really sorry. I can't believe I did such an awful thing to you." Now there was an aura separating them from the world, from the handful of curious onlookers and the large, older man with blond hair and an ill-fitting suit who had got out of the stranger's car and picked up the twisted wreck of the bicycle.

"What you did to me was nothing—look what you did to my bike."

"I'll get it repaired, I promise. That's the least I can do." And an absolutely genuine and foolproof way of making sure he saw her again. The woman who matched his ideal had fallen immediately into his hands, as if shot down by the force of his longing. Richard felt that nothing was impossible.

"I really loved that bike."

"It'll be as good as new tomorrow."

"I liked it because it was old." He had eyes like lasers; every time she looked into them she felt a jolt in her guts.

"Well, as good as old then. The wheel's bent, that's all. There must be thousands of old bicycle wheels in Cambridge. Listen, you're in shock, you must have something to drink, a cup of tea . . ." He wanted to possess every vital piece of information about her immediately, but there were still half a dozen people loitering curiously around the car and it was only a matter of time before one of them recognised him.

"I hate tea and I've got a tutorial in twenty minutes."

"Well, let me take you there. What college are you at?"

"Girton."

Great. These would be the slowest four miles he ever drove. "Can you bear to let me drive you? You must, I insist. I promise I'll be careful."

He helped her into the car and drove away, leaving Inspector Henshaw irritated in charge of the bicycle. The detective had no sympathy for his master in this matter at all. Of all the girls who threw themselves at Prince Richard, it was sheer madness for him to take after a perfect stranger just because of the way she used foul language. She even looked Irish.

The onlookers dispersed. The sales assistant in Jean Jeanius was still lounging in the doorway when the junior from the camera shop which adjoined it trotted back from the scene of the accident with the painful expression he always assumed when deep in thought.

"He came out of your shop, didn't he?"

"Who did?" The assistant flicked back his precisely coiffed forelock. Keith from Photofix had acne and Hush Puppies, which classified him as a very low form of life.

"Prince Richard, that was Prince Richard, in the Aston, who knocked that girl off her bike, didn't you see?"

"I saw him run the chick down, yeah. You reckon that was the Royal Rich, eh?"

"Swear it. I didn't rumble him until I saw the detective. You can tell a plod a mile off even if he thinks he is in plain clothes."

"I take it he won't be running His Majesty in for dangerous driving, then."

"Nah, but His Majesty'll be running that girl in for a bit of the other, if you ask me. He was all over her. Now he's driven off with her, 'n' all. Didn't hang about. He'll be up there like a rat up a drain pipe, trust me. Now look—he did come out of your shop, didn't he?"

"Oh yeah, yeah. He was in here all right. He had the most god-awful suit on." The assistant felt personally offended that Prince Richard had not identified himself, even though he regarded the Royal Family as ludicrously ill-clad and a species only slightly higher than that which wore Hush Puppies.

"He never bought all that gear in here?" Keith was so excited he was virtually spitting.

The assistant stepped back out of range. "Jacket, jeans, the lot. Paid cash, too."

"Fantastic. Far out. Tell me exactly . . ." Keith was carrying a dog-eared copy of the *Daily Post* with the crossword half completed; from the pocket of his cheap suede jacket he produced a pen and wrote down the details of the royal purchases, half-printing with severe difficulty. "How much did he spend?"

"Oh, God, a couple of hundred—I can't remember."

"Never mind. Go on, then, what was he like?"

"What do you mean, what was he like? He was only in here half an hour. Just like any other upper class twit, if you ask me."

"Look, I got some snaps of him picking that girl up. I

can send 'em to the papers, they'll pay plenty, believe me. I'll cut you in, of course. Can you remember anything he said?"

"He might have said good morning or something. He was here to buy clothes not make conversation."

Keith saw he was getting nowhere. Still, there was one thing this posing poof always noticed. "What about the royal wedding tackle? What's he got to put in the old Y-fronts, eh?"

The assistant delivered a withering look. "I suppose you think he was wearing a string vest, too. With the royal monogram on each tit."

"So he wasn't wearing Y-fronts. What about the old crown jewels, then? Come on, don't tell me you didn't notice. You reckon that tart'll get what's coming to her or what?"

The assistant prepared to withdraw from this distasteful conversation. "Well since you ask, Keith, I reckon that when that chick gets his flies open she'll be down on her knees feeding it buns, all right? And you can quote me on that, dear."

Keith glowered as the shop door shut in his face. He didn't get it.

•   •   •

"VICTORIA, HAVE YOU ever been in love?" It was almost midnight and Jo had gone down to the gyp room to make cocoa.

Victoria was already there doing the same thing. "No, never." She smiled softly and stirred boiling water into the two mugs on the grimy bench in front of her. "Have you?"

"I don't know." Jo did not feel sleepy at all. The man who had knocked her off her bicycle, who said his name was Richard, was going to call her as soon as the machine was repaired. She was disturbed by her impatience. She wanted to see him again. A subtle uncertainty was running through her veins, exciting emotions she had never recognised before. "Don't you worry that you've never been in love? We're nearly twenty, time's running out. I mean, Juliet was only fourteen."

Victoria considered. Love was something else she avoided thinking about but after half a term of companionship with this uncompromisingly direct American her British habit of self-denial was in question. "I've been at school all my life, and if we weren't at school Alex and I were being posted round the world to so many different places. I suppose I took it for granted that nobody would come along until we settled down."

"It must be wonderful to have a brother like Alex." Jo sniffed her carton of milk cautiously. It was sour.

"Yes, he's wonderful. No matter what happened, I always felt safe when Alex was there. He just takes charge and takes care of everything. He really brought me up, I suppose."

Jo smiled, fascinated. She loved making someone talk, peeling back the layers of their personality like turning back the petals of a rose to reveal the hidden centre. She knew she had given Victoria a new taste for self-awareness, but would she ever understand how hung up she was on her brother? "And he's so good looking, too. I bet the girls were always after him."

"I suppose he is handsome, but I can't think of him that way. He's just my brother Alex to me. Look, do have some of our milk. We bought some fresh today, I'm sure we've got enough for three."

Amused, Jo followed Victoria down the corridor to her room, where Martha was still toiling through a textbook as thick as a doorstep.

"Have we got enough milk for Jo?"

"I'll just check with God's little refrigerator." Martha uncoiled behind the desk and opened one of the tiny pointed windows. They put the milk on the sill outside, where the dank chill of autumn kept it fresh. "Yes, there's plenty. My, you two look serious. What's coming down around here?" She threw aside her spectacles and massaged her tired eyes.

"True confessions time. We're talking about love."

"Oh *that* old thing." Martha's chuckle bubbled around the room.

"Yes that old thing. The stuff you try when . . ." Jo turned the book around and checked the title, ". . . when the fascination of *Torts and Malfeasances* by H.G.W. Pollitzer-Holmes begins to fade."

"Well, don't ask me. I'm a case of arrested development, still turned on by torts and malfeasances." She pulled down a pillow from her bed and sat on the floor beside Victoria, feeling deliciously lighthearted. This was the kind of conversation she could never have had in Jamaica. Nobody in Beverly Hills, Kingston, would have included that skinny bookworm Martha Harley in a conversation about love. "Do you think there's any hope for me?"

Jo sat in the room's single shabby armchair, twisted her legs together, screwed up her face and did her psychiatrist routine. "Vell, if you enter a course of psycho-analysis coming to see me three times a veek for tventy years at a very reasonable fee of only five hundred dollars each session I sink zat maybe perhaps ve can make a leetle progress, *ja*. Now if you will just take off all your clothes, lie down on the couch and open your legs ve can begin with a leetle free association."

"I think I'll stick to torts and malfeasances, thank you, doctor."

"Nein, nein, zis is all wrong, you don't understand, you are acting out with me ze hostility you feel for your father. I haff put my hands on your breasts now exactly as your father would have done to bring back to you all zose emotions you haff repressed for so long."

"But doctor . . ."

"Now you must simply relax *und* release your inhibitions. If you sincerely want to give up zis infantile fixation *mit* torts and malfeasances you must do exactly as I say wizout quvestion, *ja*?" She picked up Martha's spectacles, perched them on the tip of her nose and peered over the rims with furrowed brow.

"I mean ze torts perhaps fall wizin the parameters of vat ve in my profession call normal, alzough you understand zere is no exact clinical definition of normal *und* vun man's bratwurst can be anozzer man's cocktail weenie, if you can understand me. But ze malfeasances . . ." she sucked in her cheeks and made a tent out of her fingers.

"Ze malfeasances—vell, here we are in the borders of psychotic territory, vat ve in my profession would call definitely weird. Now vill you please take out my penis zo, *ja*, *und* now under hypnosis you vill go back to ven you vere three years of age *und* your father gave you your first lollipop." Jo suddenly catapulted herself on to the floor in a convulsion of simulated agony.

"Aaaaargh! *Mein Gott! Gott in Himmel!* Sigmund Freud! Vat do you mean, you liked to crunch your lollipops! Zere it is again, hostility! hostility!" She scrambled to her feet, every movement somehow conjuring up a small, fat, pompous person with teeth marks in his vital organ.

"Ve haff to work through zis hostility or ve can nothing do. Next time ve shall go back to ze first time you were raped by your father. You vere never raped by your father? In my long clinical experience, my dear, I have discovered zat every woman is raped by her father. *Natürlich* zis vas a great trauma *und* you haff repressed ze memory. Zis is common also. Ze hour is up now, Miss Harley, goodbye and zink about everyzink I haff said."

Her audience of two was roaring with laughter. Jo was hilarious when she did one of her acts. She amused herself as well, but once she ran out of words a kernel of uncertainty remained. It was an uncomfortable thing to encounter, and now she feared it from the moment she began to perform, and so found the inspiration to continue. Tonight had been particularly bad; she was very tense.

She jumped off the bed and joined Martha and Victoria on the floor.

"Was your psychiatrist like that?" Victoria wiped the tears of mirth from her reddened cheeks.

"No, not really. He was pretty good, he saved me from my mother anyway."

"What did he think about love?"

"I never asked him, I wish I had. There was somebody I was fond of, then, back home. But I didn't think I loved him." Jo recalled that distant period in her life and wondered what she had truly felt for Ryan. She had been certain it was not love, but now, after a long time among strangers in a strange land, she was unsure.

"There was somebody I was fond of back home, too." Martha thought of Claude for the first time since she had thrown away his note of congratulations, and discovered a degree of lingering affection. "Maybe they all look better from a few thousand miles away."

"Yes, and that was then and this is now—anybody now?"

Martha laughed again. The status of a minor celebrity which her colour gave her among the other students had been an agreeable surprise since she had expected to feel utterly inferior at Cambridge. The sexual element in the men's admiration was something of which she was unaware, never having felt herself to be in the least feminine or attractive. "Well, there's a man from Tanzania who sends me notes in the library addressed Sister of My Soul, Daughter of Africa, who says he wants to give me the perfect love of black so I can heal the wound of four hundred years of castration by the white oppressors, but I think he's probably full of shit, don't you?"

"Right *on*! And gimme five!" Jo and Martha slapped hands.

Victoria was reassured that Martha had not mentioned her brother. Since Martha was the product of an education system closely copied from the British model, the two women had much territory in common. Jo was the real alien of the three. Victoria and Martha had sung the same hymns in assembly, swallowed the same bromides selected from Shakespeare and Jane Austen and been led in blinkers through the narrow path of British history from William the Conqueror to George IV. They stood on the same high hill of British superiority to look down on the rest of the world. Most of the time they forgot that they belonged to a different race, until the question of Martha's sexual fascination for Alex slithered into the picture. Fortunately, Victoria reassured herself, Martha remained oblivious to the fact she aroused the libido of most of the male students.

"I wonder who is out there waiting for us?" Victoria tucked her legs elegantly sideways and leaned on one arm with a wistful expression. "You realise there are four men to every woman at this university? We ought to be able to take our pick."

The others agreed. The chief business of Girton's girls, whether they admitted it or not, was choosing their partners from the mass of masculinity around them. The women students at Cambridge were the status mates pursued by the alpha males among this élite; a man who failed to score one would have to choose between a foreign girl from one of the language colleges, a scrubber from the town, celibacy or homosexuality. Only the last of these might be interpreted as a good career move.

As Jo, Martha and Victoria explored Cambridge, every freshers' event, every lecture they attended and every club they considered joining had a feverish, meat-market undertone. It was not unwelcome; many Girton girls were, like Martha, unaccustomed to male attention and they blossomed in their newly desirable identities. There were also dangers. Bookwise but foolish in the ways of the world, girls made decisions about men which they would repent at leisure. Jo's room-mate, a timid but brilliant mathematician, had fallen for the first man she met, a spotty Scottish physicist who had already reduced their relationship to premature ejaculation once a week and long harangues about her inability to toast crumpets to his satisfaction.

"Can either of you tell fortunes?" Jo was prepared to try anything to salve the apprehension stirring her blood. The others shook their heads. "Read Tarot cards? Tea leaves?" There was a girl down the corridor who had the I Ching, but Jo was not in the mood for oriental mystery either. "What about a ouija board?"

"What's that?" asked Victoria.

"Oh, you must know, you have the alphabet all set out and you see if you can call a spirit of a dead person and ask it questions."

"Table-turning, that's what we call it—we used to do that at school until one girl had hysterics and they banned it. But it was great fun . . ." Victoria jumped up with enthusiasm and reached for a notepad. "We don't do it with a board, just a piece of paper, like this . . ."

Martha sat still and watched wide-eyed as the others assembled the approved apparatus for communicating with the spirit world. The one thing both her mother and grandmother had agreed upon was that supernatural beliefs of any kind were strictly for the ignorant. Voodoo rituals were cabaret for tourists, not something the modern, educated Jamaican should take seriously. She was shocked to see these two white women, both from the highest possible social echelons, preparing to indulge in country superstition.

Martha said nothing and acquiescently took her place at the table and put her finger beside theirs on the upturned glass in the centre of the circle of alphabet letters. It was well into the night now and the college was silent.

"OK. Now everybody close their eyes," ordered Jo. The glass agitated itself under their fingers almost immediately.

"Is there anybody there?" Victoria asked, her voice lowered with awe.

The glass shot towards the slip of paper labelled "Yes."

"No doubt about that—so quickly." Jo asked herself how

she could be doing something so childish, but dismissed the question with excitement. "Can you tell us your name?"

The glass whisked from letter to letter so fast that Victoria had to write them down awkwardly with her left hand. "Lady—that's clear—Lady Em—did it do M twice?"

The glass dashed for "Yes" again with impatience.

"Lady Emma."

"Lady Emma, we greet you and offer you our thanks for speaking to us," Jo projected so much solemnity in her voice that even Martha felt conjured by its spell, until an owl hooted from the trees outside with such perfect theatrical timing that she had to stifle a giggle. "Do you have a message for anyone here?" The glass hesitated, then headed positively for J. "For me, for Jo?" It hit the "Yes" again then set off around the letters once more.

"Sussex," read out Victoria, puzzled. "Does that mean anything to you?"

"Sussex? That's on the South Coast isn't it? Doesn't mean anything to me. I am not now and have never been in Sussex." Jo was disappointed.

"Can you tell me more, Lady Emma?" With rude impulsion the glass sped to "No." Then it retreated to the letter H.

"H?" The glass nudged the letter repeatedly, pushing it out of the circle.

"Do you mean H for Harley, do you mean me?" Martha now allowed herself to be as intrigued as the others. The glass rushed to "Yes" again.

"It is you, Martha," Victoria had more time to write as the glass moved more slowly but quite deliberately. " 'The queen of Paris.' My goodness, what on earth can that mean? Oh, it's off again." She snatched up the pencil again. " 'Go home.' Go home?"

"Not me, I only just got here," Martha laughed. This was all too silly. She could not believe that the others were taking it all so seriously.

There was a brief, embarrassed pause of which Martha did not understand the significance. Supporters of the underground British fascist movement had for some years chosen "Blacks Go Home" as their favourite graffiti slogan, but there were no graffiti in Cambridge and Jo and Victoria hoped Martha had not noticed any on her brief journey through London.

"We can't understand you," Jo told Lady Emma in a tone of deep respect. "Can you explain?"

The glass stirred uncertainly, then moved towards the letter V.

"Is it my turn, do you want to tell me something?" Victoria had been feeling neglected. The glass set off busily around the alphabet once more.

Martha took over the writing pad. " 'Death, jealousy and mad . . . madness.' Hey, this is a long one, '. . . my . . . destiny . . . will . . . be . . . you . . . yours'—Lady Emma, you've been reading cheap novels from the circulating library again!" She rocked back and forth with laughter. "Are we really doing this? I don't believe it! Are we three educated intelligent grown-up women sitting here in the middle of the night seriously doing this?" She swept the papers into the wastepaper basket, shaking her head. "Look at you two! This is the twentieth century, ladies. Men have been to the moon, electricity does not trickle out of the sockets if you take the plug away and reality is anything you can hit with a hammer, all right?"

Jo and Victoria felt both disappointed and grateful that Martha had decided to break up the game when it showed signs of getting serious. "It's really just sympathetic magic, sort of like mass hysteria," Jo explained, recalling the last time she had heard a ouija board explained away. "Unconsciously we all move the glass where we think it ought to go."

"Obviously we were all in the mood for melodrama," Victoria brushed a few stray letters off her skirt and picked them up carefully from the floor. Of course it was all just superstitious rubbish. She tore the top sheet off the notepad and crumpled it without looking at the message.

"Well, we started out in the mood for love. It was Martha who sent us off the rails with her torts and malfeasances." Jo yawned. "I'm for bed or I'll never have the motivation to catch that bus tomorrow."

Back in the narrow bed in her own room, with the mousey mathematician whispering to herself in her sleep on the other side of the room, Jo gazed into the darkness, still feeling the subtle agitation aroused by the man named Richard. She could not think of him as anything other than a man, even though he was probably not significantly older than she was.

CHAPTER VIII

KEITH COWLEY BUSIED himself in the dark-room at the rear of Photofix Camera Services, waiting for the boss to go to the pub for lunch. Room was a generous description; it was a malodorous shed at the back of the yard, containing a lavatory, an ancient porcelain sink and a wooden bench where grimy baths of chemicals awaited the films to be developed. The tin roof was no defence against the seeping Fenland cold and the only sources of heat were the two naked light bulbs, red for developing, white for everything else.

Since the boss seldom ventured into this squalid enclosure, Cowley could get on with his own affairs there in peace. He idled away hours fantasising about his glorious future as a world-famous fashion photographer; he flicked through magazines allegedly devoted to photography which carried large pictures of bare-breasted women and small captions mentioning the camera, film and exposure used to take them.

He could have a crafty cigarette by the rotting window, and, since the door had no lock and the yard could be entered over the rear wall, he could have a crafty shag on Saturday night. When his luck was in; Cowley needed a lot of luck to get laid, what with his acne, his distaste for personal hygiene and his undershot jaw. With a couple of beers inside him he could deliver a reasonably persuasive line about how the target chick had great eyes and ought to be a model. If she was extremely stupid, ugly, drunk or any combination of these she might be persuaded to climb the wall in the back alley and give him the use of her body on the darkroom floor. He reckoned sex was a numbers game. If he gave the old modelling chat to every scrubber he encountered in an evening, sooner or later he'd land a live one.

In this dark little kingdom Cowley also developed and printed his own photographs, taken with his ancient Nikon and films he filched from the shop's stock. Six prints were floating now in the sink and he pushed them around impatiently in their final bath. He had to admit it, they weren't the best work he'd ever done. Not exactly sharp. He had had no time to change the film already in the camera, and it was too slow. And he had been too slow. He had not composed the picture properly like they said you should at his evening classes. Prince Richard had his back to the camera most of the time. Still, it wasn't too bad of the girl. She'd come out well, which was strange, considering she was the kind of slag you could walk past a dozen of without noticing.

With great care he picked the prints out of the water and clipped them up on the drying line. Half an hour later the boss announced his lunch hour and Cowley made straight for the telephone.

"Incorporated Newspapers," growled a male telephonist.

"Picture Editor," demanded Cowley with equal surliness.

"Which newspaper, son?"

"*Daily Post*," Cowley snarled. The bastards would be calling him Sir when he'd made it.

"Pictures!" A girl's voice.

"Hullo, darlin'. I want to talk to the Picture Editor, tell him it's urgent."

"He's out of the office at present. Can I take a message?"

Out to lunch, in every sense. "My name's Keith Cowley, I'm a freelance photographer in Cambridge and I've got some shit hot shots of Prince Richard running down some chick in his Aston Martin."

"Just a minute." Keith grinned as he heard a muffled exchange at the end of the line. Then a man's voice said, "Phil Addams, deputy picture editor—what's this you got, laddie?"

Keith told him.

"Great. Great. You're a freelance, right—have we used your stuff before?"

"Yeah, you've taken quite a few of my snaps, actually. I usually deal with the Picture Editor direct." Absolute lie, but what the hell, this wally was probably new to his job anyway.

"Would that be Harry?"

"Yeah, Harry, that's right."

"Ah well, Harry got the push yesterday. We've got a new editor, new broom sweeps clean and all that, Harry's was the first head to roll. I'm keeping his chair warm while they make up their tiny minds who they want. Now what are they like, these shots—any good are they?"

"I wouldn't be offering you rubbish, would I?"

"I dunno. Send 'em in and I'll tell you. Hang about while we check the train times . . . *Sharon, thank you* . . . right, get 'em on the 2.35 and we'll get 'em picked up this end. Call me around six."

The proprietor of Photofix Camera Services returned half an hour later to find the shop door locked with a note taped to it advising him: "Sory—toothake—gone to densit." He shook his balding head over the idleness of kids today and bawled Keith out when he returned, breathless and plainly feeling no pain.

"Next time you take off like that you needn't bother to come back, you lazy little monkey. There's a dozen lads I could take on tomorrow and they'd all do this job better than you." The lunchtime beer intake was slowing the old boy down; Keith ignored him and went to make tea. He passed the afternoon in the darkroom developing a set of passport photographs, mounting some of the boss's typically hackneyed wedding pictures, combing his lank blond hair every quarter of an hour and wondering how much the *Daily Post* would pay him.

At six he commandeered the payphone in his landlady's linoleum hallway.

"Keith Cowley in Cambridge—you got the prints all right?" he demanded when the deputy picture editor came to the telephone. There was now a clatter and shouting in the background.

"Yeah, we got 'em. They're out of focus."

"Well, they're not exactly out of focus, Phil, they're just a bit soft . . ."

"We're not into soft here, laddie. The only thing that's soft in this office is the editor's cock when I tell him I've got a great royal exclusive and show him pictures like that. Christ, the only thing you can see clearly is the back of our royal Romeo's head. Doesn't even look like him."

"You can see the bird OK," Keith argued. When he made the big time he'd make this jerk beg to lick his boots.

"Granted, but who the fuck is she, laddie? You've given us the low down on his wardrobe but not the girl's bloody name. This is the *Daily Post*, not the *Tailor And Cutter.*"

"So you can't use them? 'Cause I can offer them elsewhere, you know."

"I didn't say I couldn't use them, laddie." At once Phil's voice dropped half an octave and turned mellow. The *Daily Post* had sent one of their own photographers to Cambridge at the beginning of term, but he had produced nothing except pictures of Prince Richard walking decorously into lectures. "We'll have to crop the best one down and see what the process department can do with it. Fashion editor says this is the first time a member of the Royal Family has been photographed in jeans, and the leather jacket's unbelievable—Richard—Rebel Without a Cause—it'll make a good page. You done all right, laddie."

"How much . . ."

"Hang on there and get a name for that skirt, all right? And keep in touch. Here's Sharon to take your address for accounts." There was the sound of a receiver being dropped and a crescendo of yelling, then the secretary's voice struggling to be heard over the din.

Cowley bought the *Daily Post* the next day, and opened it with eager anticipation. He passed over his picture the first time; it had been cut down to show the Prince only, retouched with a heavy hand. There was no credit line naming the photographer.

"Fucking bastards!" He crumpled the paper and threw it into the gutter. They'd print his name two inches high by the time he'd finished. He would be a fucking celebrity. He'd be the one, the figure in the photograph, and that Phil Addams would be still sitting at his desk ordering another hungry young hound to get a shot at him.

Disappointment sharpened his wits. He'd had a chance and he'd blown it, and his royal fucking highness was not going to give him another like it. His mistake had been waiting for the plum to drop off the tree. Shake the branches, that was what he ought to do. Get off his backside, get out, get hustling. Stake the bastard out. Christ, he didn't even know where to find Prince Richard. Although he lived in Cambridge, Cowley had only the haziest conception of how the university was organised. All he saw were kids from good schools with rich daddies, braying boys who elbowed him off the pavements and disdainful girls who swept past him as if he did not exist. From Cowley's perspective, students spent three years drinking, doping, partying and fucking each other's brains out, then left the town with a lifelong illusion of superiority and an unjust claim to wealth and privilege.

Prince Richard, of course, was the richest, most superior and probably the most disgusting of the lot; and on the taxpayers' money, too. To his litany of hatred Cowley added the resentment he felt every time he looked at his payslip. Driving like a maniac, knocking people over, putting it about with every slag in sight—someone should expose him, show him up for what he was, randy little sod.

By the end of the morning Cowley was clear as to where his duty lay, and determined to learn the habits of his prey. The first job was to run him to earth. Ask a few questions. And then he recalled a goldmine of royal information which had been under his nose for years.

On his half-day he drove out to see his parents, feeling ambition blaze hotter inside him with every muddy mile of the road. On each side of the road a grid of flat fields stretched to the grey horizon.

For uncounted and inbred generations the Cowleys had farmed an expanse of land south of the Wash, the twenty-mile wide inlet in England's east coast silted over the centuries by four sluggish rivers which drained the marshes of Lincolnshire, Norfolk and Cambridgeshire.

Ouseport had never been much of a village; the name itself was a description imposed by William the Conqueror's census-takers on the dozen isolated fishermen's hovels they recorded in the Domesday Book.

Whatever features the surrounding landscape might once have had had been levelled over the centuries. In a profession noted for its parsimonious practices Fenland farmers were a byword for their greed; no pocket of marsh was too small to drain, no spinney too tangled and no hillock too low to flatten for the convenience of the plough. The only trees that grew here were willows pollarded to yield osiers for baskets. No land was squandered on hedgebanks; in some places ditches were an inevitable necessity; elsewhere single strands of wire separated the fields. In Ouseport, Cowley senior proudly maintained his ancestral right to grow vegetables in the unoccupied area of the graveyard.

As he parked his Suzuki next to the decaying chicken coop in the expanse of slime beside their farmhouse Keith congratulated himself on being the first of his line to knock the mud of the Fens off his boots and escape. He had been sent out to pick potatoes almost as soon as he learned to walk, like his father and grandfather before him, and decided that he wanted out almost as soon as he learned to think for himself. At which point meaningful communication with his parents had ceased.

"I'm doing your father's papers," announced his mother, a faded woman with a grimy floral wrapper over her dress. She sat on a stool at the far side of the scarred Formica table in the centre of the kitchen. "We've had tea but I can warm the pot if you like."

Keith grunted, signifying acceptance. His father's habit was to spend the daylight hours in the fields, while in the murky afternoons his mother struggled with the farm's paperwork, decoding leaflets from the Ministry of Agriculture and completing forms recording their crop sales and claiming their subsidies.

She put his cup in front of him, a large blue receptacle with a crack in it, filled with acrid lukewarm tea. "You didn't let us know you were coming."

"Can't phone from the shop, old man doesn't like it."

"Half-day closing, is it?"

He grunted again, ignoring her suspicion that he had bunked off work.

"New regulations—can't make any sense of them. It seems to me we're getting nothing out of this Common Market business except more work." She jabbed her pencil in the direction of the untidy piles of paper spread over the table and across the tops of the two large freezers which occupied one side of the room. An electric cooking range, the latest labour-saving innovation when his grandfather bought it in 1938, occupied the other wall, its steel rails crusted with grime.

"Have some light on the subject." Keith rose from his

stool and reached for the switch. The cobwebbed fluorescent tube on the ceiling flickered into glare.

"You think we're made of money." His mother snapped the switch and turned off the light.

"It costs a penny to have the light on for twenty-four hours."

"You think you know everything since you've been to that technical college, don't you? What do you call a penny nowadays, eh? You tell me that first, since you're so clever." His mother regarded the recent innovations of decimal coinage and Britain's membership of the European Economic Community as elaborate schemes to disguise rising prices and falling incomes.

Keith got up and went into the next room. The farm house, newly built shortly before the kitchen range had been bought, had two downstairs rooms, two bedrooms above and a scullery built at right-angles to the kitchen which his father had grudgingly converted to a bathroom ten years earlier. The lounge was strewn almost to waist height with dusty piles of what his mother called her "books," publications which Keith had learned to refer to as magazines.

Ladies' Realm was her preferred title, because it contained the best knitting patterns, cake recipes and features about the Royal Family. The magazines were the only reading matter in the house and Keith's mother never threw a single edition away. Keith had leafed through them all his life. From *Ladies' Realm* and the greasy sheets of newspaper used to insulate Friday night's fish and chips, he had formed his ideas of wealth, power and fame, and turned his discontent into ambition.

After a couple of hours' application to the most recent issues he gleaned the information he needed. Prince Richard had chosen to study at Cambridge's historic Magdalene College; like his brothers and sisters he was a normal, healthy young man. The Queen had taken care to see that he had been brought up as much as possible out of the public eye like any other boy. He was an action man who liked sailing, windsurfing, climbing and running. He was good looking and charming and his brother Charles had described him as the heartbreaker in the family. He had already had many girlfriends, including an American heiress who shared his love of horses. Six particular English beauties, pictured almost identically in jeans, Puffa jackets and pearls, plus two European princesses in satin and diamonds, were suggested as ideal future brides. This last page Keith tore from the magazine and folded into his pocket, quietly lest his mother should hear and protest.

From the distance he heard the occasional thudding noise of his father's shotgun. The old man was finishing his day's work by shooting a few crows. Anxious to avoid him, Keith prepared to leave. "I had a picture in the *Daily Post* this week," he told his mother as he picked up his crash helmet from the kitchen table.

"Stupid paper. Your father always said he wouldn't waste his money on it." She did not look up as he closed the door. It was now an awkward step down to the sawn-off length of railway sleeper his father had placed below the doorstep as a makeshift extra tread. When the overworked soil dried out, it blew away like dust. Most of the doorsteps in Ouseport were more than a foot higher than their builders had intended.

Cowley remounted his Suzuki and roared out on to the road in a splatter of mud as his father's tractor approached from the opposite direction. At dusk the landscape was at its most surreal, the sky a vast dark canopy beneath which the smallest feature cast a giant shadow to the treacherous horizon.

On Sunday Cowley successfully tracked Prince Richard to the freshers' cross-country race. He waited for three hours in icy rain at the finish line and scored his first real triumph with a shot of the royal runner-up splashed with mud from head to toe as he staggered across the line in third place. Some great gorgeous blond bird kissed him; when Cowley printed the shot her face had been caught at all the wrong angles and she looked like a gargoyle. He did, however, manage to identify her name from the *Ladies' Realm* page as Lady Victoria Fairley, daughter of the Earl of Selwood. And this time the picture was in focus.

Phil Addams was ecstatic. "You done great, son, fuckin' great. Stick with this one and you'll make your name."

On Monday Cowley called his boss with the toothache story again and staked out Magdalene College, waiting for the prey to show itself. From the alley alongside The Pickerel Inn he had a clear view of all the college's gates.

He leaned against the wall beside the Suzuki; the motorbike was his most prized possession after the Nikon. After half an hour a light but icy drizzle began and he moved under the overhang of the adjoining building which had been constructed in 1683 in the style of that day, with the upper storey projecting over the ground floor.

By noon he was chilled to the bone and there was no sign of the cream V8. He smoked his last cigarette. The Magdalene rowing club committee, typically loud and beefy individuals in tweed sports jackets, crowded into the pub and Cowley decided to follow them. He could still see the gates from inside.

He ordered twenty Marlboro and a Whisky Mac. The last sip was passing his tonsils when he saw the bulk of Inspector Henshaw disappearing at the far corner of the window. He lunged for the door, hesitated over the bike and decided to leave it, and hit the street in time to see Prince Richard and his escort turn the first right corner.

> *"Pleasures, farewell, and all ye thriftless minutes,*
> *Wherein false joys have spun a weary life."*

Jo hurled herself to the ground, in this case the stage of the Cambridge Arts Theatre inappropriately dressed as a suburban sitting room somewhere in the North of England for the pre-London run of an Alan Ayckbourn comedy.

The three languid men who were conducting the audition for the Marlowe Society's new production of *'Tis Pity She's A Whore* were sprawled half way back in the stalls with their feet up and gave no sign that they had registered her astonishing emotional projection. She sat up and tossed back her hair.

> *"To these my fortunes now I take my leave."*

Her hands flew to her temples as if to prevent her tormented thoughts bursting through her skull and continued in a voice that was almost a scream. Annabella's soliloquy was a real downer, but it was the only long speech she had in the play.

> *"O Giovanni, that hast had the spoil*
> *Of thine own virtues and my modest fame . . ."*

Now she used the softness of voice and slow complacent dip of the eyelashes that she had observed when Victoria talked about Alex, and quivered her lips in what she hoped was a shudder of shameful languor.

Now the business with the letter. She sped in panic to the other side of the stage then fell to her knees for the final couplet.

"Thanks to the Heavens, who have prolonged my breath
To this good use: now I can welcome death."

She stretched her arms heavenward then flung them wide and held the final pose of despair.

There was silence. Somebody out of sight at the back of the theatre coughed. The most etiolated of the triumvirate took his feet off the seat-back, reached into his waistcoat pocket for his fob watch and checked the time.

"How many more have we got to see?" he asked the man on his left, unconcerned that Jo could hear him clearly from the stage as she got to her feet.

"What, girls? Quite a few, aren't there, Jeremy?" The third man consulted his clipboard and nodded.

"Right. We'll have to crack on." He raised his voice without standing up and addressed Jo. "Very interesting interpretation. Have you studied much Jacobean drama, Miss . . . er . . ."

"Forbes," the third man prompted from his clipboard.

"Yes, quite a lot." In preparation for this audition she had devoted a month of the summer vacation to the subject under the affectionate tutelage of the playwright whose son she had dated at school. He had advised her that the Marlowe Society was the most prestigious drama club in Cambridge; all the leading agents and quite a few big directors made frequent talent-spotting trips to their productions.

"I was interested that you took quite such an *athletic* approach. Of course the action of the piece is somewhat melodramatic but too much naturalism of course runs counter to the conventions of the theatre of the period . . ."

"My interpretation has nothing to do with naturalism. This *is* a very emotional speech—Annabella's in love with her brother, she's married a man she doesn't love because she's pregnant with her brother's child and now she's trying to stop her husband murdering him. I did consider a naturalistic approach, going for trauma and having her just blank out, but I felt that would be dramatically wrong and instead I chose to show her as a woman virtually demented in an extreme turmoil of passion. And in terrible fear. I mean, she thinks her brother, who she loves in this absolutely cosmic way, is going to be killed and she knows she's committed incest, and now she's thinking about suicide, which means killing her child as well. Three mortal sins—this woman *knows* she's going to burn in Hell. I mean, people really did believe in Hell in those days. And later there's that awful moment when her brother almost makes a date to see her there . . ."

Jo stopped talking. She had plenty more to say but she sensed she was losing her audience; the three men lounging in the stalls looked paralysed with shock, pop-eyed and rigid like fish frozen as they flapped.

The pallid one in the middle came to life first, nervously shooting his cuffs and realigning his Paisley silk tie. Women who wanted parts in the Marlowe Society's productions usually knew better than to argue with their future directors. "Yes, I see, quite so," he concurred in a faint voice.

A fourth young man sauntered down one of the aisles to sit behind the trio and muttered something to them without sufficient discretion to prevent Jo detecting her mother's name.

The pale man's attitude changed at once from vague bewilderment to polished dismissal. "I think Americans are always *most* original. I really must congratulate you on your accent." He flashed a wide and meaningless smile. "Thank you so much for coming in. The cast list will be posted on our notice board as soon as we've finished auditioning. Can we have the next, please."

Resignedly Jo put on her coat, scarf and gloves. As she left the theatre the next aspiring actress took the stage and launched into the same speech. A large, cow-like girl with a bad complexion, she spoke like an air stewardess announcing the in-flight movie and appeared to have her elbows pinned to the waist of her skirt.

Next on Jo's pilgrimage through the university's great theatrical institutions was a room above a pub where the Footlights Club was located. Around the bar at one end congregated a group of very tall and remarkably lugubrious men and two women; one was a slim, pale creature with eyeshadow the colour of fresh bruises and sprayed-on jeans who perched on a bar stool and caressed the calf of the man next to her with one booted foot. The other female present was the barmaid.

Jo drew a few nervous glances but no greeting. A space was made for her near the bar and she ordered a beer. At least the Footlights seemed to conduct auditions in less formal style than the Marlowe Society.

Three men in green leotards and tights took the make-shift stage at the far end of the room and disentangled the wire antennae strapped to their heads.

"This sketch is called 'The Praying Mantis Wedding,' " announced one of them, who was also wearing a clerical collar and carrying a green Bible.

It was very funny and the jovial murmur around the bar soon broke into laughter.

"You mean I—er—only get one—er—chance to actually make love to my wife?" the bridegroom inquired, aghast.

The preacher nodded with impatience. "Didn't your father tell you *anything*?" Jo remembered seeing the sketch in a fringe revue at the Edinburgh Festival in her summer vacation.

"My father died on his honeymoon. So after we've—er —done it, she kills me, is that it?"

"Yes, you've got the idea now."

"Could I possibly ask *how* the bride usually kills the groom?"

"She bites your head off in a frenzy of ecstasy during her sexual climax."

The groom stepped back in surprise. "I say, I know I'm good but I'm not *that* good."

There was a roar of hearty laughter, followed by congrat-ulation and note-taking on the back of an envelope by the man whose calf was still being proprietorially caressed. His girlfriend's boots, Jo noticed, were a classic Fredericks of Hollywood design, spike-heeled and laced to the knee.

More drinks were ordered and the performers joined the crowd at the bar, squeezing Jo into a corner.

"Are you waiting for somebody, love?" The barmaid was hoping to close up soon.

"No, not exactly, I've come to audition."

"Gentlemen—you've got one more here," the barmaid

informed the drinkers in tones which implied they had better not take too long about it.

"Oh right! Terribly sorry, didn't see you there. And your name is . . . ?" The man with the envelope disentangled himself from his girlfriend and towered over Jo in a friendly manner. She guessed his height at around 6ft 5in.

"Jo Forbes."

"Oh yes, you're—er—yes, jolly good." Jo decided she liked him. He was at least sensitive to the fact that being her mother's daughter was nothing she cared to acknowledge in these circumstances. "And this is a solo spot, right?"

"Yes. It's called 'The Shrink.' "

"Great. Great title. Well—off you go."

Jo walked to the end of the room with her Marilyn Monroe shimmy, the best way she knew to get a room full of men to pay her attention. She pulled up a split red vinyl armchair and did her psychiatrist routine. It went well. They all laughed, nervously at first and hysterically when she fell off the chair at the crunched lollipop gag. She got a hearty round of applause when she finished and the massive man bought her a drink.

"Where's that from—or did you write it?" He put the wet glass in her hand and added "Mud in your eye," as he dipped into the creamy head of his beer.

"Cheers. Yes, I wrote it."

"Based on a shrink you'd actually been to?"

"Yeah, this guy my parents sent me to when I was fourteen hoping they could certify me for smoking dope."

"Oh, *really*. That's terrific, we can always use people who write their own stuff—especially if it's that good." Something in his redoubled interest told Jo they could also always use people with good dope connections, a role in which she was not at all interested. She had quit smoking anything on a regular basis, afraid of ruining her voice.

She decided to change the subject. "I really loved what you did," she told the nearest praying mantis. "I saw someone do it at Edinburgh in the summer but it wasn't nearly as funny—you really put some juice into it."

There was an awkward pause. "Oh, you mean you saw someone else do that sketch?" The large man sounded earnestly confused.

"Parallel thinking," the praying mantis preacher announced swiftly. "Or maybe they pinched it from us. No copyright on a gag, especially a good gag."

The barmaid began locking up the liquor, jingling her keys ostentatiously. Within a few minutes the group sank their beers with a distinct lack of bonhomie and filed out to the street. The large man and his girlfriend were the last, and Jo heard a whispered conversation between them at the head of the stairs.

"Er . . . keep in touch," the large man said to Jo when they reached the pavement. He waved goodbye apologetically as his girlfriend took possession of his other arm and pulled him away as fast as a woman could when walking on six-inch-high stiletto heels.

Jo set off angrily in the opposite direction, threading her way through the cobbled lanes towards The Whim. Out of sight of the café, she paused and fluffed up her hair, using a shop window as a mirror. She took a few deep breaths and tried to forget her disappointment. How could she have been so stupid? She had blown two auditions in two days just by opening her big mouth when she could just as easily have said nothing and smiled sweetly. Just like her mother had always done. Well, that was then and this was now and her mother was another person. There would be more auditions; she found it hard to believe that any of these callow English kids could really have anything to offer her, and even harder to acknowledge that they did not want all the born-and-bred Hollywood know-how she had to offer them.

The door of The Whim was a few footsteps away and she could no longer avoid thinking about that retard who had crashed into her. Now she regretted agreeing to meet him for coffee. Coffee! The biggest euphemism for sex in the Western world. Why was she going through with this charade? She should have turned him down flat the minute he came on to her, the way she did with all the others.

She had told herself that it was for the sake of the Footlights audition that she had chosen to wear her favourite jacket, soft, dusty pink suede, over her only dress, a clinging Missoni sheath that fell in fluid folds of cinnamon, rose and copper to the tops of her high Maud Frizon boots. The outfit was not warm enough and the boots pinched. It was the only ensemble she owned which revealed her feminine curves; she had really chosen it for Richard, and now she wished she could change.

There was something about him that she recognised, some quality of manner with which she felt familiar. That was why she had let down her defence. As she pushed open the door she wondered if she had imagined it.

* * *

HE LOOKED SHORTER than she remembered, and his hair seemed straighter, or perhaps less tousled. There was no mistaking the piercing flash of his eyes and her heart turned over as she sat down at the cramped table.

"Your bike's ready," he told her unnecessarily, made nervous and stupid with excitement. "Shall we have some tea?"

An eager waitress appeared at once, brought the tea swiftly and unloaded her tray with exceptional care. Richard knew he had been recognised and pledged the woman's loyalty with a flicker of a smile. Looking at Jo he felt the same free, exalted irresponsibility that she had sparked before. He felt like a different person, the person he wanted to be, full of the power of certainty. She looked him in the eye, said what she wanted, spoke as she felt. He assumed that this was because she did not know who he was. Common sense told him she would soon find out, but the feeling was so precious that he wanted to make it last as long as possible, whatever the cost.

They talked of nothing and every word seemed full of significance.

"Was I late?"

"No, no—I think I was early."

"Is it hot in here or was it cold outside?" She shrugged off her coat, not anticipating his chivalrous assistance. "This place is always so crowded."

"Are you hungry?" he asked her. "What about cakes? You're not on a diet or anything . . ."

Jo gazed at the plate of amateurish patisserie offered by the waitress suddenly not knowing what she wanted. The emotions of their first meeting had resurged in her also; everything at once seemed to have a sensual significance. One appetite sharpened the other, and she was hungry, but how could she eat?

"Maybe I'm not hungry after all," she said at last, and

watched while he consumed a fat choux bun in two bites. He was sure everyone in the café was looking at them, but no head turned. Cloistered Cambridge had pretended to ignore the covert exchanges of lovers for a thousand years.

They exchanged scraps of information with difficulty in the noisy room. At the next table six male students were telling each other jokes in loud voices and their robust laughter swamped all nearby conversations. Jo and Richard had to lean forward until their faces were almost touching to hear each other speak and he was enveloped in the perfume of her hair. He said whatever came into his head, unable to think of anything but keeping this woman close to him.

"You smell beautiful," he told her, hearing his voice as if it were another man's. "Look at me. I want to look at your eyes."

She raised her head and her long lashes swept up. Obeying this small command was a delicious token of greater submission to come. The effort of holding his gaze made her feel breathless.

"Are they green?"

"What do you mean, are they green? You're looking at them, not me." Men always raved about her eyes. Usually it annoyed her; she tried to be annoyed now, and reduce this disturbing man to the level of the rest, but she could not. She was pleased that he liked her eyes. She wanted him to like all of her.

"They are green, but they're almost blue at the edges and orange in the centre."

"And the black speckles, don't forget them."

He watched her soft upper lip twitch as she teased him and wanted to kiss it. "Where? I can't see any black speckles."

"Maybe they've gone."

There was an uproar of mirth at the next table and two men fell backwards off their chairs. Richard at once perceived looks of censure from the more sober members of the group and caught a few words which told him that half the café now knew that a member of the Royal Family was among them.

He reached for Jo's hand. "Let's get out of here."

An instant later they were walking down the street. She

swayed as they crossed the cobbled roadway, moving it seemed to him to an inner rhythm of femininity.

"Let's cross the river," he suggested. "The shop's that way—we can walk through across Jesus Green." The path across the watermeadows would be almost deserted, now that it was November and the willows had wept their leaves and the grass lost its lushness.

He had captured her arm and felt the supple suede and the infinitely finer softness of her palm. "Your skin is so soft."

"That's because I'm Irish. Well, three-quarters Irish."

"I was thinking that you didn't seem as English as you sound. What's the other quarter?"

"Swedish. But I was brought up in America." It crossed her mind to tell him who she was. That would blow the dream. She half wanted to end it now. This was too strong, too soon. She felt as if she were standing drunk on the edge of a precipice. She felt breathless, claustrophobic, but powerless to break free.

Soon she would tell him. If this meant anything, if what was going on between them was real, he would be able to handle it. If it was just a random eruption, an erotic sunspot destined to die down as quickly as it had flared up, then she would lose nothing. Perhaps he would be able to handle it. People here were not the starfuckers they were in LA, but then again, this man was different.

"You don't seem exactly English, either," she told him.

He glowed with delight, as if she had paid him the compliment he most wanted to hear. "Well, I suppose I'm not really. I'm as much English as you're Swedish, just a quarter. The rest is mostly German with a little Danish. I'm only British officially."

"Just like me. You know, I actually chose to be British. My father was from England so I had dual nationality until I was eighteen, but then you have to choose one and so—now I have a British passport." This decision, made as a formal gesture of separation from Hollywood, her mother and everything they represented, still left her a residue of guilt.

"You're one up on me, then. I don't have a British passport." Well, he told himself, that *was* the literal truth.

"They really don't like you giving up your American citizenship though. You get all these heavy official letters asking if you've really considered the serious implications of your decision."

She was asking for reassurance, and he responded at once. "My father had to change his nationality when he was young. He did it so he could marry my mother."

"And never regretted it?"

"No."

"Just a formality, huh?"

"No—uh—" he was supposed to be good with words but now he could not find the ones he wanted. "In a way it was the most important decision he ever made. It was—well, a question of commitment, I suppose."

There was a pause. Disquiet still in Jo's mind. She sensed that now he was holding something back from her. She *must* tell him the truth now, before any more lies piled up between them. If he couldn't handle who her mother was, he would not be able to handle anything else about her.

It did not happen. As she drew breath and turned towards him, Richard lightly brushed her aureole of curls with his fingertips. "The Irish is strong in you, though, isn't it—especially all this. You've got the reddest hair I've ever seen."

"That's not Irish, that's L'Oréal, dummy."

"You don't delete your expletives, do you?"

"I guess I've got no racial memory of kissing the Blarney Stone."

"What *did* you call me when I knocked you over?"

"Don't you think we should get to know each other better before you ask me to talk dirty to you?"

The way she lowered her voice and let the words murmur over her lips thrilled him. And she was right, of course. He wanted to hear her call him those names again, especially in that voice. "You know me well enough. Come on, what was it you called me?"

"Nothing I'd care to repeat in cold blood but I'm sure it was appropriate in the circumstances." Her blood was not at all cold at that moment.

They were not walking fast. In a quarter of an hour they had hardly moved five hundred yards and now they stopped, by chance below the massive heraldic panel above the gate of Christ's College.

"What is all that?" she demanded suddenly, waving her

free arm at the gilded and painted ensemble of statuary, bas-relief and carved decoration. "That's the kind of stuff that makes me feel totally un-British. What is it all for?"

"It's just a coat of arms." From the corner of his eye Richard noted the presence of Inspector Henshaw, who had followed them from the café, and another man, who kept a less discreet distance. He had a camera in his hand and was purposefully circling them, changing lenses as he did so. Any moment now it would all be over.

"Come on, you're reading History, you can do better than that—whose coat of arms and why . . ."

"There's a better one inside," swiftly he pulled her through the small door in the oak gate into the deep shade of the archway. Keith Cowley cursed, stumbled in pursuit and dropped his lens. Jo noticed him with irritation. Fucking paparazzi. She'd have to come clean now.

"Over there, above that door, do you see?" He pointed to the small replica of the carving on the far side of the grassy courtyard. "It's the coat of arms of Lady Margaret Beaufort, who was the college's patron."

"And what are those animals on either side?" With the same undisclosed aim, they remained in the shadow of the gateway, hoping the photographer had no flash.

"They're yales."

"Yales?"

"Mythical beasts. Silver with golden horns they were supposed to be able to swivel and use to attack from any angle."

"Why are they spotted?"

"Bedight with bezants is the proper term. Ah—because they are."

"What about Harvards? Are they mythical beasts too?" She did not deliver the quip very well and he did not laugh very much. He was desperate now to postpone the moment when the spell would break and all her boldness turn to awed dissimulation as Cinderella's ball gown turned to rags at midnight.

"People believed in yales from the days of the Romans, and they were first used in heraldry by John, Duke of Bedford, the son of King Henry IV." They walked on nervously, and all he could think of to say was what he recalled of a dull afternoon in the library at Windsor with a grandiloquent emissary from the College of Heralds. He could hear the man's pomposity echo in his own voice and was disgusted at his inability to suppress it. Everything was going wrong now. "The Beaufort family descended from his cousin who took the yale as his supporter when he was created the Earl of Kendal. Margaret of Beaufort married four times . . ."

"The Liz Taylor of the Renaissance, huh? What's a supporter?" Jo looked back and was reassured to see that the photographer was not following them. Maybe she had been mistaken. Maybe the man was just a tourist.

"The animals who look as if they're holding up the coat of arms, like the lion and the unicorn, they're known in heraldry as supporters. Every great family had one, like the bull of Clarence or the greyhound of Richmond . . ."

At the end of Milton's Walk she looked back again, and saw a thickset man with blond hair who was definitely following them. She recognised him as the man who had picked up her bicycle in the Market Square. "Go on about Margaret whoever."

A slow burn of rage began. Jo knew a bodyguard when she saw one. Sure, Richard was different, and now she thought she knew why. All this time she had been agonising over the disclosure of her own identity, when he was faking too. No wonder he had seemed so familiar—just another offspring of the rich and famous.

"I'm not boring you, am I?"

"No, no, it's fascinating."

She sounded so sincere that he thought everything would be all right if he kept talking. "Well, Margaret's second husband was Edmund Tudor, a direct descendant of the Welsh royal line, son of Owen Tudor who married the widow of Henry V . . ."

All this time she'd been almost allowing herself to believe that this might just be something big, thinking she was feeling something special when all the time it was just that she recognised that patina of international *jeunesse dorée*. So who the fuck was he?

" . . . and so her son, who became King Henry VII, the first of the Tudor kings, was able to claim descent from the royal houses of England, Wales and France—pretty tenuously, of course, but Richard III had murdered most of the direct heirs to the throne. Although in fact he may not have done. Some people think he was nothing like the dreadful villain Shakespeare made him, but of course history is written by the winners, or the artists the winners employ . . ."

Jo was not listening; she hated the phoney way he was talking. She suddenly recalled that he had left the café without paying any bill.

They were walking rapidly across the field now towards the bridge. More scraps of information from her memory filled in the picture. While he lectured, she took a long, cold look at him. Of course. There was no mistaking him now her mind was no longer fogged by her emotions.

And she had truly worried about telling him that she was a film star's daughter, when he was fucking royalty. What a joke. She tried to laugh but found that she was no longer angry with herself, but with him. What kind of idiot did he think she was?

As they reached the bridge she saw the photographer again, running along the riverbank. He had been tailing them at a distance. The light was not good now, but Jo saw the perfect way to put this egotistical dickhead in his place and reward that sleazeball with the picture of a lifetime.

"Just a minute." She pulled Richard to a halt at the crown of the bridge, where they were clearly visible and there were no shadows. "Aren't you leaving something out here?"

"You mean the Hundred Years War? Well . . ."

"No. You know what I mean. I mean where you come into all this." In her peripheral vision, the photographer approached and raised his camera.

Her voice cut like wire and Richard felt a chill that was nothing to do with the climate. "Oh. That. Well . . ."

"What do you think we're doing here—rehearsing *The Student Prince* or something?"

"No, really, I . . ."

"*Really?* I don't think you have the right to use that word. What do you know about really? If you were into anything real you wouldn't be pretending to be what you aren't." She tried to pull her hand out of his. Infuriated he tightened his grip and pulled her towards him. Her eyes were like chips of glacier and she was rigid with fury.

"Look, please, Jo, don't be angry." This was not possible. Women were never angry with him. "You don't understand. I was going to tell you but . . ."

"But you were having too much fun, right?" She still had one free hand and she raised it slowly, hoping the photographer would pick up the cue. "I guess life was pretty boring and you thought you'd like to while away a few hours playing at being a regular Joe with some chick who was too dumb to suss you out, right?"

She timed the pause perfectly and cracked him across the face as hard as she could. "I was right first time. You are a fucking asshole!"

In shock he let go of her and stepped back. The blow stung across his cheek. He opened his mouth but no words came.

Cowley took shot after shot, as fast as he could get the film through the old Nikon. Two middle-aged women near him squeaked and tittered with excitement.

"Let me give you some advice, sweetheart." Jo pushed her hands into her jacket pockets, pulled back her shoulders and posed as majestically as Joan Crawford. "Next time you want to pass for normal, leave the Aston in the Palace garage and tell your valet not to press creases into your jeans. Then try to remember you're not the only human being on the planet."

She turned on her heel and stalked away. She heard three panic-stricken footsteps behind her, and he caught her arm and swung her back to face him. "What's the matter?" Her lips furled in contempt. She was giving no mercy now. "Did I forget to curtsey or something?"

"Oh, for Christ's sake!" He almost pushed her away. "I thought we were . . . we had . . ."

"Well you were obviously mistaken." For an instant she wanted to rush back and save everything, but instead she turned and walked away.

Had she looked back, which she disdained to do, she would have seen Richard walk back to the end of the bridge, arranging his features to show no emotion. The blond bodyguard followed, with a hint of satisfaction in the set of his heavy shoulders. He had seen the photographer, but his master had not, and in any case the rule was that officers of the Royalty Protection Squad did not harass paparazzi.

By the time he reached Magdalene, Richard was as calm as his face. He had picked the wrong girl, that was all. The wrong sort of girl. She did not know the essential rules. It was not her fault, she had not been brought up in the right environment. Next time he would choose someone more suitable. Next time needed to come soon. He found he did not care for rejection.

Jo walked steadily on to the bicycle shop and reclaimed her transportation. She was mildly irritated by the eager servility with which the proprietor told her that there would be no question of sending His Royal Highness a bill for the repairs, but the discomfort of riding back to Girton in her tight, thin dress soon numbed her mind.

Keith Cowley followed her, and gave the bicycle seller ten pounds to look back through his receipt book for her name. Then he took the next train to London.

Next morning the porter at Girton found a rain-sodden passport lying among dead leaves in a flowerbed and thoughtfully dried it out in his office before returning it to Miss Forbes. The photograph, he thought, was a very good one and he was surprised to learn that she had not had it taken professionally.

The porter at Magdalene chuckled over the copy of the *Daily Post*. Escapades were what he expected of his students, and the more illustrious they were the more outrageous he liked them to be. Prince Richard of Gloucester had been extremely quiet and studious, and a great disappointment to him. This Richard looked much more promising. "Romeo Richard's Smack In The Kisser From A Hollywood Brat." Good lad. Swelling with officious loyalty, the porter crossed the street to the newsagent to buy up every copy of the offending rag, and was disappointed to discover that the owner had already removed them all on his own initiative, except for one copy sold to the Prince's detective who had come in early.

"The bitch! Self-righteous deceitful little bitch! She tears into me for not letting on who I am, and all the time she's doing the same damn thing herself." There was no one to whom Richard could say these things, so he shouted them at the wall of his room, then kicked it and hit the table. He screwed the newspaper into a ball and threw it into the immaculately swept fireplace.

His mind still held the imprint of her face. There had been a large picture of Jo in the paper as well as the paparazzi shot, a studio portrait with her mother, in which something between a pout and a smile made her mouth look luscious.

Richard kicked the table leg, then did what he had intended to do that morning, grabbed the telephone and checked through his engagements with the middle-aged army officer who was acting as his equerry in London. Somewhere in the inner circle, among the long-arranged round of visits and parties that was his social life, he had to find a woman to wipe that picture out of his mind.

CHAPTER IX

"PAMELA SEEMS TO have taken on a new lease of life," Alex remarked, stretching his long, muscular legs across a sofa, in the overfed contentment of their first Boxing Day at Aston Langley. "Don't you get the feeling that she's been waiting to get her hands on all this ever since she married Daddy?"

Alex and Victoria were in the small back sitting room of the house, a cosy sanctuary created by their stepmother with yellow flowered chintz and some of the best-preserved small pieces of furniture, for the family's use during the immense enterprise of refurbishing the rest of their new home.

Pamela was a woman transformed. As a Naval wife she had been energetic in the pursuit of acceptable distractions, but half the person she now appeared as the mistress of Aston Langley. With a sudden bloom in her cheeks and decisiveness in her movements she had begun the long business of transforming the house into a perfect setting for the life for which she had patiently waited since her marriage.

The grander rooms were now in the process of being stripped of all their frayed furnishings and decayed decoration. There were ladders and scaffolding everywhere. Dirty rectangles on the old wallpaper marked the places where the paintings had been. The most important pictures were being cleaned and restored, while the lesser works had been crated and stored. In the library, where the new plans were spread out across six trestle tables, Pamela and her newly employed secretary worked long hours in consultation with the decorator.

Victoria sat on the windowseat, picking at a new piece of gros-point in the steely light of the winter morning. She frowned at her brother's critical tone. "Why are you always so hard on Pamela? You're always trying to make out that she's a wicked stepmother, when really she's just devoted to Daddy and the littles. You've got to admit she's got marvellous taste, and we're terribly lucky that she's got her own money, too, otherwise we wouldn't be able to do any of this without having to sell something."

"Darling Tory, the pure to whom all things are pure. I suppose you even like our cousin Ivo."

"Well I do, he makes me laugh."

"He makes *me* laugh, all right. The man's a joke. I'm sure he wears a toupee." He ran his fingers through his own thick, light brown hair as if to reassure himself that it was real.

"Don't be silly, Alex."

Pamela had produced Ivo like a rabbit from a magician's hat within her first week at Aston Langley. He was a cousin on her own mother's side of the family, which was considered to be artistic. As an interior decorator he was sought after for his understanding of the English country house style, which meant the ability to integrate frayed and battered pieces of junk with priceless treasures.

The brother and sister fell into a companionable silence. Logs from trees freshly felled in the grounds hissed in the grate, and in front of the fire a pair of young Norwich terriers twitched and snuffled, chasing rats in their dreams. Pamela intended to breed dogs. "I shall need an interest," she had declared, as if she were not already absorbed with fabric swatches and wallpaper samples for all her waking hours. "It'll be marvellous to have dogs again. I was brought up with dogs, you know, and I must say I have missed them."

Alex at once predicted that she would choose Labradors and begin manoeuvres to acquire a puppy from the Queen's kennels at Sandringham. Victoria assumed that the dogs would be from some large sporting breed, in keeping with Pamela's general ambitions as chatelaine of Aston Langley. They had both been surprised when the chosen dogs proved to be these small, ginger-haired, prick-eared terriers.

The telephone rang in the distance and Alex pretended

lack of interest. A few minutes later Evans announced that the call was for him, and he swung his legs off the sofa and left the room despite the fact that there was an extension by his elbow.

"Amanda's coming over," he announced to Victoria when he came back half an hour later.

"Who's Amanda?" She continued the calming motion of her needle, trying not to sound hostile.

"You know Amanda, Amanda Meddowes."

"Oh, that Amanda. Have you asked Pamela? There might not be room for her."

"Oh, she can squeeze in with you or something."

Victoria said nothing. Amanda Meddowes was another daughter of the magic four hundred.

"She can't stay long, we're going to Sandringham next week." Prince Richard had invited both Alex and his sister to be his guests during the Royal Family's post-Christmas holiday.

"Well, I'm sure everyone can put up with her for a few days. I thought you liked Amanda."

"Oh, I do. She's rather sweet. I just didn't know she was a particular friend of yours."

"Neither did I until a few weeks ago. We sort of got together at the Snow Ball." Alex bent down to throw another log on the fire and turned to face his sister. He had noticed Victoria was funny about his girlfriends; for a long time she had, in her dreamy way, ignored the fact that her brother was sexually active at all, but since they had been together at Cambridge she had been unable to avoid the fact that he was an attractive young man who was ready to look for a mate.

Alex loved his sister; more than that, he felt responsible for her, and he was beginning to find it irksome. He knew how vulnerable she was, with her persistent innocence and tender heart, but for her own good he had to give up the role of her protector. She was beautiful and widely admired; she was also, in his eyes, a good woman, which meant she was honest, loyal, without ambition and not manipulative. He was not the only man who considered that she would make someone a wonderful wife. Quite a few, indeed the majority of his friends, had taken her to balls or parties, invited her to dinner in London or contrived to partner her on country weekends, and afterwards, puzzled by her amiable lack of response, asked him how best to court his sister. He never knew what to tell them. Victoria just did not seem interested in men. Alex did not connect this with their own relationship. In the understanding of the British upper classes, psychology was bunk.

Victoria looked up from her tapestry, apprehensive and large-eyed. "What do you mean, Alex? Are you trying to tell me you're in love with Amanda or something?"

"It's silly to talk about love so soon, I suppose, but she is very special to me, Tory. You've got to accept that."

"But of course I accept it, why ever shouldn't I?" She stuck the needle through the canvas again, trying to ward off the alarm she felt. "It's wonderful, I hope it . . . you . . . I mean, I hope it works out."

He walked over and put his hand on her shoulder. "So do I. Are you sure you don't mind?"

"What a ridiculous question, why on earth should I mind?" She could not continue to sew without seeming rude, and it suddenly annoyed her to be touched. She put down the tapestry frame and moved away from him. Denying pain was the best way she knew to avoid it.

"We've been always very close . . ."

"Alex, you're my brother, of course I love you and I want you to be happy. I know I rely on you too much to take care of me, but how could you possibly imagine I'd mind if you fell in love? I mean, you're bound to, sooner or later. It's the natural thing, isn't it?"

"But I don't want you to be upset, or feel left out or anything . . ."

"Alex, you mustn't worry about me. I suppose I'll fall in love myself one day. We'll always be V and A, but we've got to grow up and live our own lives, haven't we?"

"Oh, Tory, I'm so glad you understand." He rocked her quickly in a guilty hug. "I'll go and put Evans in the picture. Amanda's catching the two o'clock train so she'll be here for tea."

He whirled out of the room, leaving the imprint of his strong arm around her shoulders and the roughness of his tweed jacket against her cheek. Victoria gazed out of the window. The sky was a blank grey and the light morbid. Fierce flurries of snow, each tiny flake a sharp crystal of ice, blew across the lawn and eddied in the corners of the terrace without settling. She bit her lip and tried not to cry, furious with herself for feeling hurt and angry.

By the time Amanda arrived, full of chatter and gossip, her nose red from the cold and the tips of her blond bob plastered to her cheeks below her cloche hat, she had mastered her emotions and welcomed her warmly. Pamela decreed that they must share a room, since none of the other chambers was fit to be occupied, and so Victoria was obliged to witness the progress of her brother's love affair from the closest possible quarters.

With tiny hints and gestures, blushes and pouts and robin-like dips of her head, Amanda conveyed the proper embarrassment at their blatant state of sexual satisfaction. Since she made this pretty penance, absolution was swiftly forthcoming. Everyone found excuses to leave the lovers alone.

Amanda also did not lose any opportunity to demonstrate her desirability as Alex's wife. There had been a grudging fall of snow, and she bustled out with the two youngest children to build a snowman in the morning and toboggan down the hill in the afternoon. Alex, for the first time in his life, allowed himself to romp with his resented half-siblings.

That evening the lovers were the first to retire. "I suppose they *are* sleeping together?" Pamela looked directly at Victoria.

"Well, Amanda didn't spend much time in my room last night." Victoria's fond smile was a half-second too late for total sincerity, but only her stepmother registered that.

"Well, I shan't change anything. I don't think it would be right to put them in a room together."

"I'm sure that's not what Alex wanted, or he would have asked."

"It is the modern way," her father stretched his legs before the fire. "I suppose they're really being quite discreet and considerate compared to most young people."

"They certainly are." Ivo, standing by the silver tray on which the liqueurs and brandy were set out, mixed a second Black Russian for himself and one for Victoria to try. "Things were different when we were young, eh? Nowadays everyone seems to copulate like crazed weasels and nobody turns a hair."

"As long as they don't do it in the street and frighten the horses," Victoria murmured, accepting her glass.

Horses were not Pamela's concern. She opened a general discussion about Amanda, the better to compute the likelihood of her stepson's deciding to live with the girl. Since he would be at Cambridge for another two years at least, and Amanda was working in an art gallery in London, cohabitation seemed unlikely. Pamela was relieved. She took great care not to betray the extent of her ambitions for the family into which she had married, but they were unlimited. Everyone knew that the Queen did not approve of people living together.

* * *

ON NEW YEAR'S Eve the whole party, divided between Alex's MGB GT, Ivo's Bentley and Pamela's Range-Rover, drove sixty miles across the county to a ball at Morton Beauchamp, the country home of Suzie Chamfer's older sister Jane. Her husband, Nicky Brompton, heir to a dukedom, called himself a farmer and omitted to specify that the estates on whose income his family was maintained comprised three thousand arable acres in Gloucestershire and East Anglia, a hundred times as much in Costa Rica with two gold mines beneath, and a district of London where luxury apartments leased by lesser millionaires rubbed buttresses with 1920s model tenements built by Brompton Trust. From this base a vast pyramid of banking and commercial interests had been erected over the past century. The Bromptons were one of the wealthiest families in England, and Jane's style of entertaining was lavish in proportion.

They arrived early, since punctuality was considered an unquestionable virtue by the rear-admiral. Alex immediately whirled Amanda into the Great Hall, where a few couples were already dancing, and Victoria followed in the arms of her host. Morton Beauchamp had been conceived as a simple, large Palladian manor; as the family's fortunes had prospered so many additions and improvements had been made to the original building that it was now a grandiose grey-stone sprawl of pillars and porticos, elaborated with bas-reliefs and encrusted with statues, a temple in which proportion was sacrificed to pride.

The Great Hall, colonnaded, chandeliered and floored

in gold and white Carrara marble, was a last addition to
this opulent pile. Facing the double entrance doors was a
double row of Corinthian columns whose gilded capitals
supported a musicians' gallery. The entire room was
swagged with evergreen wreaths bound with red ribbons,
whose resinous scent banished the must of six months' disuse and mingled with the perfume trails wafting behind
each newly-arrived and freshly-spritzed beauty.

Every ballroom in England smelt the same that winter.
The females of the upper classes chose their fragrances, as
they selected everything else, according to a rigid common
code; its existence was never admitted but no transgression
ever went unnoticed. The fast young wore Saint Laurent's
new Rive Gauche; juvenile romantics chose Tea Rose. Ca-
lèche was the classic choice, Femme that of those who had
retired to the sidelines of seduction. Unenlightened
nouveaux riches wore Je Reviens, Youth Dew was for shopgirls and Guerlain proclaimed an actress or whore.

Victoria found Rive Gauche overpowering, and preferred to join the Tea Rose faction; she thought it more
natural. Nicky noticed it at once. "Delicious," he complimented her. "Like a garden in June with the morning dew
still on the flowers. And you're looking so grown-up tonight." He had close-curled brown hair and a deep tan
from sailing in summer and ski-ing in winter. His eyes were
wedges of sapphire which put Paul Newman's in the shade
and he enjoyed an appalling reputation with women.

"But Nicky, I *am* so grown up," she told him, aware of
the warmth of his hand below her shoulder blades. She had
chosen a black crepe dress she had bought a few months
earlier but not dared to wear before. The tight bodice gathered into a ring of diamanté below her left shoulder, from
which a triple silk strap ran to a second glittering circle in
the small of her back. It was a very adult design which
played dramatically on the set of her shoulders and the
flawless whiteness of her skin. "I'm nearly twenty. You just
haven't seen me for a year or so."

"Well, I shan't make that mistake again." He pressed her
close to him and looked into her eyes with a question.
Nicky never wasted time.

Victoria looked away at once from force of maidenly
habit. He said nothing, knowing exactly how to time his
moves. The girl had walked in with sexual availability writ-

ten all over her, although Victoria was only aware that the strain of the past few days seemed to have blown away as soon as he took her in his arms. Her life had rearranged itself like the pattern of a kaleidoscope, and in the new design her virginity was suddenly an encumbrance.

Obeying a new instinct, she raised her eyes to his. He rewarded her by brushing his lips against her forehead. "I want to make love to you tonight."

"Nicky!"

"Don't sound so shocked. You know I'm a thoroughly wicked fellow, you can't expect me to overlook you when you're wearing that thrilling dress." He was a beautiful dancer, with the knack of making every woman feel relaxed and graceful in his arms. "You needn't do anything you don't want to. I'd be happy with just a kiss. I'll dance with a lot of other girls like a good chap, and when all the midnight nonsense is over and things start to take off we can slip away for a while. Mm?" He was utterly certain of her agreement, which gave her confidence.

"I've never . . ."

"I know, my love. You weren't ready. I've watched you grow up, remember. Little Suzie's lovely friend. You're ready now, though, aren't you?"

"How can you tell?" She wondered, anxiously, if everyone could see what he could. He held her closer and she felt a faint, visceral shiver.

"I just can. One day a girl becomes a woman and she looks different, that's all. Sooner or later, and for you it was later. I used to call you the Sleeping Beauty. Now, one more dance and I'll hand you over to another lucky devil until our time comes."

He did exactly as he promised and Victoria went in to supper with Ivo feeling both pleased and ashamed of herself. Nicky was so obvious, positively crude with his ridiculous flattery and the way he danced too close. But he was attractive. All the wicked aspects of this adventure seemed completely appropriate. If Alex knew he would disapprove, and if Suzie Chamfer knew she would be furious—so much the better. She drank more champagne than usual, but not too much, having no intention of getting too drunk to behave well and remember everything.

Half an hour before midnight Victoria, growing more excited and apprehensive every moment, was dancing with

Ivo. There was a renewed commotion at the ballroom door and a party of ten unexpected guests entered, with Prince Richard at the centre. Almost everyone affected not to notice. Every woman in the room covertly appraised the Prince. The volume of the conversations in the room dropped then soared again in nervous excitement.

"Hey! Wow! I didn't know *he* was coming," Suzie Chamfer hissed to Victoria from her partner's arms. "God, he's so-o-o-o sexy. Couldn't you just screw the ass off him?"

"From what we hear that wouldn't be a tough assignment," sneered Ivo lightly.

"Oh, don't be such a bitch, Ivo. He can't help being gorgeous. Tory and Alex are friends of his, aren't you?" Suzie, who loved getting her own picture in the *Daily Post*, had been waiting all evening for a proper pretext to get some juicy tit-bits out of Victoria. "Go on, tell us, what was all that about some actress in Cambridge . . ."

"Absolute rubbish, I should think. I know her quite well, actually, and she's never said anything about it." The *Daily Post* was not widely read at Girton. Victoria had heard the story repeated several times, with unlikely embellishments. Since Jo had never mentioned the event, and Victoria could not imagine any woman embarrassing Prince Richard, nor any woman outside the magic circle keeping his attentions secret, she concluded that the whole story was untrue.

"Oh come on . . . he's gorgeous, any girl would . . ."

"Men always look rather dashing in evening dress," Victoria responded, reflecting that she herself was ill-equipped to screw the ass off anybody.

The music stopped. She stepped back, recoiling physically from the unpleasant conversation, at the same instant that Richard moved into the room and the dancers, like iron filings repelled by a magnet, fell away.

In front of him suddenly was the most beautiful woman's back he had ever seen, sweeping from proud shoulders to slender hips, the flesh dimpled over the bones like new-fallen snow on a field. The nape of the neck below her thick, upswept hair was the whitest of all. The black silk cords of the dress lay taut over the skin, cutting into the left shoulder.

Victoria turned around. Afterwards she decided she had been obeying the instinct to meet her destiny. In fact the reactions of the people she could see to the expression on Prince Richard's face had told her he was behind her.

"Why Tory! You look wonderful! How marvellous to find you here." She did indeed look radiant, as if picked out in a spotlight, illuminated by the suppressed sexual excitement generated by another man.

He took her hands and Ivo melted respectfully away. The music began again. "I had to get away, you see. You know we had Christmas at Windsor this year? That was OK, better actually, because it's bigger, but we're at Sandringham now, at least we would be if the parents hadn't decided to knock half of it down, so we're all squashed into Wood Farm and it's not half as much fun. I've just run away for a few days." He was talking fast and she thought he was probably quite drunk, but so was almost everyone else in the room. "And all the guests are in a hotel in King's Lynn, which is probably much more comfortable for them anyway. Oh, but of course, you are coming aren't you, you and Alex?" He smiled widely, delighted with the neat way life had suddenly fallen into place. Lovely Tory. Why had he not thought of her before? If she would have him after he had made such a fool of himself with that American girl.

The bandleader killed the music with his baton, signalling the approach of midnight, and the party formed into circles for "Auld Lang Syne." On the twelfth stroke of midnight she offered him her cheek to kiss; Richard pressed his lips to hers with more than traditional emphasis, felt her startled reaction and then a hesitant but voluptuous response.

Victoria and Richard were sitting close together on one of the leather sofas in the smoking room when Nicky came to find her. She did not notice his discreet glance into the room, and forgot forever that she had even thought of wasting her virginity on him. He pulled a face of cheerful resignation and decided it was time to give his wife's slut of a sister what she had been begging for for years.

Victoria also barely noticed her brother and his beloved Amanda abandoned in an embrace in a corner of the terrace. She saw nothing but the topaz flame deep in Prince Richard's eyes, heard nothing but his voice pledging her to his company at Sandringham, felt nothing but a trance of ecstasy. She had fallen in love.

• • •

THE NEXT MORNING she had a headache and, for the first time in her life, doubts about almost every garment in her wardrobe. She rushed to London to go shopping, in a state of so much anxiety she scarcely felt confident about buying a lipstick. At Belville Sassoon in Beauchamp Place salvation arrived in the unlikely form of Suzie Chamfer, who bullied the shop assistant into producing from the sample room a full-skirted blue velvet evening suit, with black silk braid, a high collar, and a matching loose silk camisole.

"And you can't possibly wear that underwear," she announced, pointing at Victoria's chain-store *broderie anglaise* brassiere. "Next stop Bradley's, they must have some Janet Reger left. And then we'll check out Browns."

"You are kind, Suzie, I just didn't know what to choose," Victoria told her as the smaller woman imperiously hailed a taxi. She was not entirely sincere. Suzie was performing these favours because she, like the rest of the guests at Morton Beauchamp, had seen the Prince make his choice. Already several other old friends had called to renew the ties strained by her term at Cambridge. Victoria was used to being sought after because she was a member of the royal circle, but this renewed interest alarmed her. Being in love with Richard seemed more unreal as every hour passed.

She ended the day with the velvet suit, a brown jersey Saint Laurent dress that seemed modest but clung to every curve and a box full of rococo scrolls worked in pure white lace held together with bows and ribbons, what Suzie called "*real* underwear, darling." Realising at last that she was intruding, Suzie then kissed her firmly on both cheeks, wished her good luck and sent her back to the apartment alone.

Alex and Victoria were invited to Sandringham for the usual weekend, Thursday evening to Sunday night. The royal estate in Norfolk was known to be a sportsman's paradise but a camp-follower's hell, since the day's entertainment for the women whose menfolk set off in Land-Rovers at 9:30 sharp commenced with an hour of quiet comfort before the morning ride, followed by lunch with the guns in a village hall and then the opportunity to walk behind them with the dogs for the remainder of the afternoon. In north

Norfolk in January the wind was vicious and the level fields either frozen hard or thawed to an icy clay which sucked the green Hunter boots off Victoria's feet at every step.

She decided she loved it. Riding she had always enjoyed, although she lacked the finesse and the courage to become more than proficient. She had had a pony at school, and a quirk of Queen's Regulations ensured that every establishment of the Royal Navy kept horses lest all other transport should become immobilised in a crisis. Richard's mother, aware of her timidity and the glorious length of her legs, had her mounted on a twelve-year-old bay gelding normally reserved for visiting statesmen. He was a big, imposing horse known to be infallibly bomb-proof and extraordinarily tactful in taking care of his riders. Victoria adored him.

She had inexhaustible energy for the long tramps behind the guns, her hands in gloves thrust deep into the pocket of her new blue Husky jacket. The freezing air stung her cheeks to their most vivid colour. She had walked with the dogs behind her father and Alex when they had shot grouse in Scotland, wild duck in Spain, and pheasants and partridges all over England. She had listened to the same sportsmen's conversations of how the birds were flying and whose luck was in and whose was not, and the first alcohol she had ever tasted was a sip of cherry brandy from the flask her father carried. Richard's flask contained "chisky," a blend of the sweet liqueur with Scotch, which she agreed was less sweet and more fortifying.

As she walked she could watch only Richard, a lean, tense figure, the quickest to react as the birds left their cover with a clatter of wings. He could almost feel her soft eyes on his back.

Quick as he was, Richard did not have many good afternoons while Victoria was there. He could not concentrate, his normally excellent eye faltered and when Charles and Alex teased him he took it badly.

Since there could be no question of promoting Amanda Meddowes to the status of Prince Richard's regular guests, Victoria had both her brother and Richard to attend her, offering unnecessary help to climb stiles and jump ditches by day, and forming a noisy young threesome in the evening. She found this intensely pleasant, and favoured Richard as blatantly as she dared to pay Alex back for his desertion. The three of them played riotous games of Racing Demon with Andrew and Edward, snatching up the cards and throwing them down with shrieks of triumph.

There was a cheerful, muddled atmosphere about Sandringham that year. Richard's father, full of enthusiasm and grateful for an audience who had not heard his plans before, took them to inspect the work on the big house. Its familiar silhouette of fake Jacobean gables, tall chimneys and mock-Renaissance cupolas was blurred with scaffolding.

"We're knocking down about ninety rooms," he told them proudly. "The place is just too big to run economically. It takes too many staff and the estate only just breaks even as things are."

"But what will you all do at Christmas, Sir?" To Alex the Sandringham Christmas, with the three generations of the family gathered in the ballroom, around a fir tree tall enough to touch the ceiling with presents for the entire household heaped on tables all around the room, was a sacred ideal.

"Windsor's much better, much more room, and the nurseries are bigger . . . I suppose we'll have to think about grandchildren soon. No—you see, Edward VII had this place built for the great shooting parties they put on before the First World War. Scores of guests coming and going all winter, all with their own servants who'd have to be put up. And bags of a thousand or even two thousand birds in a day. It's all over now, people's lives have changed. We never have more than a dozen guests at a time here and the way we run the house has got to be streamlined. I don't believe anybody even wants to live on that grand scale any more."

"Except Nicky Brompton," muttered Richard under his breath.

"Well, that's his business; after all, it's his money and nobody cares how he spends it."

"But this is your private home, too, Sir, and running it involves only your own private funds from the Privy Purse." Alex's instinct for advocacy always led him to argue, but in the detached style characteristic of his father.

"But we're not extravagant people, and we don't intend to set an example of extravagance either. Especially not now. You know, we do actually need an increase in the

Civil List, we can't run a proper show without more money. The Privy Purse has been subsidising public expenses for years and all this inflation hits us as hard as anybody else. So the Treasury have done their investigation and it'll come up before Parliament next session. But naturally we've got to tighten our belts and be seen doing it. They may call our housekeeping money the Privy Purse, but it's not really a private matter, you see."

"*Especially* since the whole country's going bust, inflation's roaring out of control, we've just had the worst trade figures on record and there are over a million people out of work right now," Richard clasped his hands behind his back and gazed across the clipped yew hedges with a sarcastic frown.

"You're not counting the half-a-million who're on strike, then?" Alex fell behind to argue with Richard as Prince Philip led the way towards the greenhouses, where the incessant tinkle of broken glass signified more demolition.

Victoria walked beside him, listening contentedly to his plans but anxiously unable to ignore the argument behind her. Any kind of conflict disturbed her. She was a practised peacemaker for Alex, and her brother was being far more aggressive than was customary in the royal circle. His fight with Richard, however, was really over her, so she did not intervene.

"Men don't go on strike without good reasons," she heard Richard say with vehemence. "They get no pay . . ."

"They get strike pay, half of them are living off the state anyway and the unions are so bloody rich they're buying up more of London than the Arabs," Alex retorted.

"But the fact is that there's no hope for most of those men. Coal, steel, shipbuilding, cars—they're all dying industries. We can't hold our own in the world any more . . ." Richard now had a few public posts, one of which was as patron of a charity concerned with the rehabilitation of drug addicts in the urban wasteland of Liverpool. His day in the city had shocked him profoundly.

"Yes but why? Because our workers are the worst in the world. Idle, apathetic bunch of layabouts. If they pulled their bloody fingers out . . . look at Germany, look at Japan."

"That's not a fair comparison, those countries had billions of aid from the West for post-war reconstruction . . ." Richard prepared to zap his opponent with a two-minute condensation of his last essay on the phenomenon of winning a war and losing the peace, but Alex's choleric recitation of the prejudices of his peer group continued regardless.

"And who gave them the aid? Another bloody Labour government. And now the unions are running the country. The government should never have given in to the miners . . ."

"Oh do shut up, Alex," Victoria did not want Richard to be defeated.

"Don't listen to her, Alex, you tell him." Prince Philip cheerfully slapped her brother on the shoulder. "Anyway, it's good for Richard to have someone stand up to him, he's too clever by half already and Cambridge is making him worse. Perhaps we'll keep you on to argue with Mr Wilson next week. Ah, Fred . . ." He strode across to discuss the progress of the works with the head gardener.

"What the hell do you think you know about it anyway?" Richard demanded angrily of his friend. "What do either of us really know, living the way we do. I saw a boy twelve years old in Liverpool who'd sold heroin in the school playground. Addict himself, of course. Biggest dealer on the street and proud of it—family of six, only his older sister had a job. We can't even imagine what their life must be like. You tell me this, what hope is there for a child degraded by poverty to that level?"

"People can always do something to make their lives better," was all Alex could think of in response.

"You and I don't have the right to sit in judgement on people like that," pronounced Richard with conviction. "We're knocking down ninety rooms we don't need, your stepmother's spending more on Aston Langley than that drug programme could raise in twenty years. It's nobody's fault, there's nothing, nothing really, that we can do about it, it's the way things are—it just doesn't bear thinking about."

Alex lapsed into a disgruntled silence as Prince Philip returned and they walked back to the Land-Rover at the front of the big house. Richard, he reflected, had never displayed so much truculence in an argument before.

The Prince's bad temper increased throughout the weekend. Richard, his three brothers and his parents were staying at Wood Farm, a cosy, undistinguished farm house with only six principal bedrooms. The rest of the family and their guests were scattered through three or four different residences and cars sped to and fro on the narrow estate roads assembling the evening parties. The household and servants were crowded into temporary accommodations and tempers ran short below stairs. Richard became first impatient then enraged as he realised that there would be no opportunity for any kind of intimacy with Victoria.

After dinner on the first evening the room was cleared and the film projector from the big house set up to show *Akenfield*, a film which recreated rural life in East Anglia a hundred years earlier. It was very beautiful and very slow; half the older members of the household fell asleep and Andrew scuffled so much his father sent him to bed. Richard lounged in the corner of a brocade sofa in the second row, so close to Victoria that he could feel the warmth of her arm against his. The film bored him, she obsessed him. He watched her from the corners of his eyes, a beautiful, shadowy profile, her small diamond ear-rings occasionally sparkling in the flickering light of the projector.

He leaned towards her, whispering comments into her ear at every opportunity, trying to make her laugh and succeeding only in making her embarrassed and himself angry. Tory was perfect, so fine and good-hearted, so natural with everyone, everything she did or said so full of her own personal quality of repose. He wanted to court her perfectly, as she deserved, but he had no patience and did not know how to begin.

Their last evening was the gayest, when the young people converged through the estate to dine at Park House, with the amiable Spencer family. The Viscount's dynamic mother-in-law, Ruth Lady Fermoy, had presided here since the departure of his wife seven years ago, and Richard's aunt and grandmother were their guests for the holiday.

The pretty Spencer girls, Jane and Sarah, matched the older royal princes perfectly in age and temperament; the two youngest children appeared briefly to be presented when the company arrived. Shy and plump-cheeked, Diana was tall for her thirteen years and slipped away with obvious relief as soon as her father suggested that she should take her complaining ten-year-old brother away to bed.

After dinner, Richard and his aunt organised the party for charades. Richard gave Alex the unmanly task of portraying Carmen Miranda to pay him back for their recent argument. Before midnight the two grandmothers said goodnight, and Margaret sat down to play the piano. V and A were, by long tradition, excused the duty of singing with her on the grounds that musicality was not among their gifts. Victoria could follow a strong voice, but Alex was utterly tone-deaf and if the two sang together the discord was unbearable. Alex sat contentedly down to listen and Richard at last saw his opportunity.

He took Victoria by the arm and pulled her into the next room, a small salon where they had gathered before dinner, now lit only by the muted glow of two lamps on either side of the fireplace. The logs had burned low.

Instinct told him not to speak. He pulled her to him and kissed her, smothering her gasp of surprise. Her heart was leaping like a fish. The power of his arms was unexpected; they held her like iron bands, although she could feel his hands shake. He tasted of whisky; he had been drinking steadily since the beginning of the evening.

His strength, the dim light and the quietness reassured her and once the first shock was over she softened in his arms and parted her lips. Thoughts eddied slowly through her mind as her senses awoke. The music and laughter from the next room seemed far away; her fears subsided and a languorous heat spread through her limbs.

His arms sensed a heavy warmth in her flesh, the deep, even flow of her breath and he became powerful and patient, sure of everything for which he had yearned. There was a high-sided Knole sofa behind them. He drew her into its shaded depths and pressed her gently back against the cushions.

He left her lips and kissed her chin, her throat, her ear, the angle of her neck where the artery beat under his mouth. The small diamond ear-drops that had belonged to her mother grazed his cheek.

By instinct he found the rhythm of her body, the sequence of advance and retreat, arouse and withdraw, which released her from all anxiety into the full, free flow of passion. New sensations budded and burst with the beautiful inevitability of blossoms opening in their proper season. Soft sighs rose in her throat.

He slipped open the fastenings of her jacket while he returned to her lips, then pushed aside the rich fabric and kissed the ridge of her shoulder. She threw back her head in ecstasy. The combs tumbled out of her hair and it fell down in silken waves. He took it up in handfuls, inhaled its scent and buried his face in its slithering strands, then spread her hair across the cushions, murmuring, "So soft, so soft, darling Tory," before he kissed her again.

He traced her collar-bone, then the edge of her camisole with his fingertips, feeling the fine skin grow even more delicate over the rise of her breasts. At the first brush of his hand against their fullness she felt a jolt of desire so violent that she almost screamed and he knew it was enough, for now. Tension and anxiety began to fill her mind and he soothed her, kissing her forehead and running his fingers through her hair, following its flow from the temple to the tips.

They heard the muffled chords of a finale from the next room and a burst of laughter.

"They'll be wondering where we are," she whispered, suddenly solemn, overpowered by the implications of what they had done.

"No they won't. They're having too much fun. But I wish they weren't there. I want to be alone with you." He nearly added "forever." "Really alone."

"We'll have to be back at Cambridge, soon . . ."

"That's no good. It's not right. We'll be together, of course, but it won't mean anything." Cambridge now seemed more dangerously public than anywhere else in the world. As much as any high-rise kid forced to couple half-publicly in a bus shelter, he was suddenly angry with the whole of creation because it did not contain any private place for the expression of their love. "I want time with you, real time, time to know you, time for you to know me —we've wasted so much already. You've been in my life forever but I never really knew you, don't you see?" He was a silhouette against the lamplight, his shirtfront a wedge of white against the black satin lapels of his jacket. His face was in shadow but she saw the animal-white flash of his teeth as he spoke.

Her right hand lay in her lap and he took it, almost crushing it as he continued with vehemence. "I want us to be away from everything. There's so much I want to tell you. I think . . . I think I've been in love with you all my life without knowing it."

"Richard, don't say that, you can't mean it, all at once like this . . ." She felt cold with panic and sat up, but he would not release her hand.

"Don't you want me to mean it?"

How could she say no? Say no to him? And besides, she did want him to mean it, and to say it, and act upon it. "Yes," she whispered.

He rested his cheek against her bowed forehead for an instant before kissing her again. "Then I'll find a way, Tory, darling, I promise. And soon."

The last half-burned log in the fireplace fell down into the ashes with a shower of sparks. The French ormolu clock whose face was the wheel of Phoebus's chariot discreetly showed them that two hours had passed. As they searched for her combs and hairpins among the cushions they heard that the crowd next door was quietly talking; whoever was at the piano now was not Margaret but a more hesitant player half-heartedly trying snatches of "The Way We Were."

She stood in front of the looking glass and pinned up her hair; he waited behind her until the last lock was smoothed into place then drew her back against him, kissing her neck, her breasts briefly captured in his hands then lingeringly released. Their eyes met in the mirror, then he turned her towards him and held her arms. He was barely taller than she and the sensation of looking directly across into a woman's eyes almost frightened him. "Soon, I promise," he repeated.

They left the room by the main door into the corridor and found the staff setting out coffee and sandwiches in a small sitting room. They found they were hungry and were seated, eating in silence, on either side of the fireplace, their attitudes identical like a pair of statues, when the others joined them.

Alex gave his sister a look of mingled alarm and respect. She smiled at him, feeling the quiet satisfaction of having won a deserved prize.

Richard was as good as his word. Immediately the party left the next day he over-ruled his Private Secretary's protests and cancelled his participation in a trip to France with the university mountaineering club. The family's holiday was over a few weeks later, his parents set off on a state visit to Barbados, and by the middle of February he alone had the use of Wood Farm, barely more than an hour away from Cambridge.

He drove her there himself, firmly suggesting that the two detectives follow in another vehicle. The level fields were blanketed with snow. More snow fell as they rode out the next morning, big soft flakes that turned to ice on their eyelashes as they dared gallops along the hedgerows, and settled on the horses' manes and even on their reins as they walked the animals home.

Every moment he was full of glorious certainty. He could do nothing wrong. He gave his orders to the staff and they carried them out with eager approval.

With Victoria, the perfect actions came from somewhere inside him. She adored him without reserve, all apprehension forgotten. Time had no meaning; after supper they stayed in the drawing room in each other's arms and he found again the resonance of her desire, the spring from which he knew the flood would rise at the right moment.

They separated to sleep, she calmly trusting, he knowing that he was the master of events, and that the great beginning of their love was now very close.

Snow was still falling the next morning, a thick white wall that insulated the house entirely. Its own fences were invisible from the windows.

Her maid brought coffee and toast to her room next morning at eleven. The young woman's face was correctly expressionless but her every gesture was quick with delight. Victoria asked her to draw a bath.

In her underwear and white Chinese silk dressing gown, she perched on the edge of the disordered mahogany four-poster bed to dry her hair. She did not hear him come into the room, but sensed his presence an instant before she heard the friction of his brown corduroy trousers and felt his weight on the bed beside her.

Like an alerted doe she threw up her head and he took her face in his hands. Swiftly he took her again to the exquisite point they had reached a few hours before, then undressed her gently as if she were a child and laid her back against the pillows. The radiance of the snow outside cast faint violet shadows over her white skin. Between her breasts he saw the fluttering pulse of her blood; all her body was alive with the same tremor. Without haste he took off his own clothes, lay next to her and started the last part of her journey to womanhood.

For an instant she anticipated mess and pain, but his touch banished the thought. When he entered her she felt whole, full and complete. When at last he allowed his own passion to take command she held him with dazed tenderness.

Afterwards there were tears in her eyes, and she wiped them away with the corner of the sheet. "Tears of joy." She shook her head. "I thought they weren't real, only something people talked about."

He looked at her as he came to his senses, printing the image of her glorious body in his mind. "I wish I could paint you. I can't believe how beautiful you are. Oh Tory, I love you. Nothing can ever go wrong for us now."

CHAPTER X

"NO, MISS FAIRLEY is not in the college. No, I don't know where she is. She has gone away for the weekend and I have no idea when she will be back. Goodbye." Martha hung up the telephone with a crash that echoed down the Girton corridor and strode back to their room.

"Why don't you just leave it off the hook?" suggested Alex, peering down into the grounds from the window as if he expected a pack of reporters to be baying around the flowerbeds.

"Because every other girl on the corridor is waiting for her Saturday night date to call, that's why. They bitch about Victoria enough as it is." Martha resumed her position at her desk, her left forefinger marking the crucial paragraph in the judgement on the case of Cahill v The Carbolic Smokeball Company. Her right hand began to cover line after line of paper with her neat, even script. "I don't mean to be rude, you know, but this essay's due this afternoon."

"*Nil illegitimis carborundum*, that's the spirit." Now that he knew her better and was no longer dazzled by her exotic fascination, Alex rated Martha as the salt of the earth.

"What's *nil illegitimis carborundum?*" she asked, at once alarmed to think that there might be an important legal term she had neglected to learn.

"Ancient British motto. It means don't let the bastards grind you down."

Martha laughed and, from force of studious habit, wrote the saying down.

Victoria, pushing clothes haphazardly into her weekend case, said nothing and felt wretched. Six weeks of perfect happiness was probably more than most people ever had in their lives, but now it was all over. It was her own fault. She had allowed Richard to persuade her to go ski-ing. In England they had been safe; as soon as they had got to Megève they had only to go out on the balcony together once to be caught by a *Paris-Match* photographer.

After that, European paparazzi had besieged the chalet, camping out in their cars and renting every available apartment within lens range. The latecomers staked-out every ski-lift. In two days the pretty Alpine village was over-run. Three cars were involved in a collision with a dispatch rider on the main street; a doctor's wife from Clermont-Ferrand fell over trying to avoid a group of photographers at the bottom of the resort's fastest run. She tore all the ligaments in one knee and announced loudly that it was a pity Great Britain had never imported the guillotine. Extra police were sent up from Lyons.

They stayed indoors with the curtains closed for a day then decided to come home. That meant a further day's imprisonment while their friends arranged changed flights in new false names. She tried to telephone her father in London, but the line was out of order. She could not reach her brother either.

They flew back separately. She left the chalet at 5 am, lying on the floor of their friend's hired car with a rug over her, feeling desperately vulnerable as soon as she was without Richard. On the plane she saw the blurred pictures of them both, side by side looking out from the balcony. The fringe of long icicles overhanging the chalet roof appeared like knives suspended above their heads.

In London she had to run a gauntlet of reporters in grimy anoraks and sheepskin jackets who waited outside the London flat. They were galvanised when they saw her, took their hands out of their pockets and produced cameras and notebooks, yelled "Vicky! Vicky! Over here, darling! Give us a grin!"

The way into the building was physically barred; behind the closed gates the porter's wife stood waiting with a grim expression, but of the porter or any of her family there was no sign.

Victoria sat helplessly in her taxi until the driver, a beer-bellied East Ender with the air of a man who could take care of himself, put a large, tattooed arm around her shoulders and half-dragged her through the jostling crush, demanding, "Gangway, gentlemen, I thank you, let the lady through," as he shoved the men firmly aside. He seized the gate as the woman opened it, pushed Victoria through and slammed it shut behind her. "Go on up, love," he told her kindly. "I'll bring the bags."

She was too distressed to find her keys and rang the bell. There was a long pause before her father opened the door in his pyjamas.

"You might have told us," was all he said, looking oddly diminished and unhappy.

"I'm sorry, Daddy, it was all so sudden, it just seemed like a dream and I could hardly believe it myself." She walked into the hall and followed him to the kitchen where the housekeeper was setting out breakfast.

"We've had reporters on the phone for days. The first one called at seven o'clock in the morning. I've had to get the calls intercepted. They've been pestering your brother in Cambridge and they're down at Aston Langley. Pamela had to call the police: one of the blighters climbed in the window and was taking pictures all over the house."

"Oh, Daddy, how terrible. And you couldn't get through to us because we couldn't use our phone either."

"I just wish I'd *known*." He sounded weak and peevish, unlike the calm, correct figure of fortitude he had always been. She felt as if she had betrayed him. "And the porter downstairs was taken to hospital this morning, asthma attack. Nothing serious but he's not a young man and his heart's slowing down, so the wife's in a state. You ought to pay her a visit later."

"Yes, Daddy, of course I will." Her voice was a miserable whisper. In the Fairley household justice was the family business and the spectacle of the innocent suffering always outraged them all. Victoria felt so deeply ashamed to be the cause of these catastrophes that she did not count herself among the unjustly persecuted.

In the country she found Pamela preening in reflected glory and the staff imbued with self-importance. Her only solace was little Rose. "Mummy found a man in the drawing room," she whispered. "She got the police to take him away. They came with a car with blue lights. Are you a princess now, Tory?"

With newly cynical eyes, Victoria saw that the spectacle

of the Green Drawing Room at Aston Langley, resplendently refurbished with the three restored Stubbs horse portraits grouped together on what Ivo called the feature wall, splashed across the centre pages of the *Daily Post* had pleased Pamela beyond measure. Victoria realised that her royal liaison was close to the pinnacle of her stepmother's carefully concealed ambitions. She looked back on their family life and saw all the woman's care of her as leading to this end. The nurture of her beauty, the convenient excuses to send her to Aunt Rose or to friends in the magic circle for holidays, even the fact that Pamela had accepted her lack of interest in other men and never pushed her towards a relationship as a truly loving parent would have done, all now seemed contrived to make her the ideal mate for a prince. For the first time Alex's dislike of Pamela seemed well-founded.

Her father's Admiralty driver took her to Cambridge in his secretary's car. She went immediately to see her Director of Studies who, she felt, was politely but not sincerely sympathetic. Other students avoided her eyes as she walked up to her room. A door closed as she approached and she heard a malicious giggle behind it. Her own natural good-nature had so far prevented her from appreciating that the intellectual classes despised both aristocracy and royalty.

She found solace in Martha's warm, formal loyalty and within a few minutes Jo burst through the door, pouring out fury on her behalf.

"We've had reporters all over the college. They've been ringing all the phones and coming in saying they were somebody's brother and God knows what else. And that little scumbag my room-mate actually gave an interview. She's done nothing but call you a dumb debutante for months and suddenly she's really getting off on the whole business and acting like she's your best friend. Can you believe it?"

"Yes," said Victoria flatly. "After this week I think I can believe anything."

Jo flopped down on Martha's bed with a scowl. "Now I know why my mother was so paranoid about all the people around her. And why she had a high hedge, big dogs and people to answer the phone for her all the time." She looked on Victoria's ordeal as a typical act of irresponsible cruelty on Richard's part, exactly what she would have expected of him.

Victoria had never told either of them where she had been going at weekends; unlike her family, neither Martha nor Jo acted as if they had the right to this information, although they had shared every other material fact about each others' lives for months. Jo seemed to regard the reporters as an inevitable verminous infestation such as might occur in the best of homes, and Victoria took comfort from that. Martha treated the whole business with dignified outrage, viewing it as an insult to the Crown more than anything else. The one good thing about these days of assault by the newspapers had been that Victoria discovered who her real friends were.

The telephone at the end of the corridor had been ringing for days. When Jo answered it she simply yelled, "Fuck off, creep!" and hung up at once. Martha's approach was equally hostile but more polite.

"I don't know what the world's coming to." Alex stuck his hands in his pockets. "How can people behave like this? What can they possibly hope to get out of persecuting all of us?" He sat down on his sister's bed and picked up *The Times*, which Martha read each morning for the law reports. "Oh, God, I don't believe it! This is the absolute giddy end!"

"What now?" Victoria felt close to tears. Surely *The Times* could not have joined the hunt.

"Oh, nothing to do with you, Tory, keep calm." The whole business was obviously going to his sister's head. "They've made that woman leader of the party." He showed her the picture of Margaret Thatcher triumphantly taking down her predecessor's portrait from the walls of the Conservative Central Office. For Alexander and his ilk there was only one political party. "That ought to keep the world safe for socialism for the next ten years."

Victoria zipped her suitcase shut and put it on the floor. Her brother had come to drive her to Wood Farm for the weekend, not in the best of tempers. "Martha, I'm leaving these for you. You're not to go out without them." She firmly put her smart, fleece-lined après-ski boots under her room-mate's bed.

"Victoria, you're very kind but they'll never fit me, my feet are huge . . ."

"Put them on and try," Victoria commanded. "You can't walk around in the rain and snow in all this cold with those thin shoes of yours. You've already got chilblains."

This was true, and there was no arguing with Victoria when she put on her admiral's daughter voice. Martha tried the boots and found them a perfect fit.

Without more than a grunt of farewell to Martha, Alex picked up his sister's bag and started down the corridor, leaving her to follow. He had been allowed to drive his car into the sanctuary of Girton, but the photographers were waiting at the gates. An MGB GT with luggage in it offers no hiding place for an adult and Victoria had to sit beside him and endure the cameras knocking against the window and the shouts of "Vicky! Come on, Vicky. Give us a grin!" for an endless thirty seconds before he could accelerate out into the busy road.

"You're mad lending that girl your boots," he said once they were clear of the town.

"It's the least I could do. She's got nothing but a pair of loafers and she hasn't got much money. Alex, why are you in such a filthy temper?"

"I'm not in a filthy temper."

There was a strained silence. "How's Amanda?" she asked at last.

"Pretty well pissed off with this business and I can't say I blame her," he retorted, overtaking a lorry so carelessly that the car skidded in the roadside mud.

"Why—surely it can't have anything to do with her?" Victoria suppressed the unworthy notion that her brother's girlfriend might be jealous.

"Oh can't it? How can we possibly announce our engagement with all this going on? And can you imagine what a wedding would be like with photographers crawling all over the churchyard trying to get a snap of you in your hat? I know it's not your fault, Tory, but this has ruined everything for Amanda and me."

"I'm so sorry, Alex. I never thought."

"Grow up, Tory, get smart. You can't drift through life doing your own sweet thing forever without hurting other people."

She cringed inwardly, feeling guilty of every possible transgression. Alex used to accuse her of being an incurable innocent and too pure to live, but she felt she was no longer pure or innocent. She felt she had sinned once by allowing Richard to make love to her, and again by enjoying it and wanting it, and even more gravely by being proud of this intimate connection with the Royal Family, and most heinously of all by thinking of the future and wanting to marry him.

At the bottom of her heart she also had to admit that she was glad that the world knew she was the woman desired by one of the most desirable men on earth, and in the same murky place she relished the jealousy and the attention and the prurient curiosity of a billion strangers and felt powerful because she, dear, naïve, dreamy Victoria knew well that all those who said they loved her had also taken advantage of her good nature all her life, and could bring those people discomfort.

Her punishment was to have caused pain all around her, to her father, her brother, her friends, her fellow students, her teachers, the whole little French village of cuckoo-clock houses and the doctor's wife from Clermont-Ferrand. Since she herself thought of her relationship with Richard as pure love she saw no material advantages in it, for herself or anyone else, and did not consider that many people, including those over whose distress she was grieving, would benefit from the association.

All these black thoughts dissolved when Richard took her in his arms. "It's going to be all right, darling. My parents have agreed and the press office are going to do a deal with them. Ask them nicely to leave us alone, I'll give them a picture doing something daft and then either they call their people off or there'll be no more passes for the next show for the papers who don't co-operate. We won't put it like that, of course. But they'll get the message."

"I do hope so, Richard. It's been unbearable, I can't tell you." Now she was safe she felt herself begin to break down. She impatiently tried to stop the tears but two large drops burst out beneath her lashes and dropped on to his rough blue Shetland sweater where they hung like dewdrops on a spider's web.

"Don't cry, darling, it's not your fault, it's mine."

"No it isn't, how can it be your fault . . ." Her own words shocked her. How could she possibly be arguing with him? It was a measure of how low the whole business had brought her.

"It is my fault, I should have known this would happen. The idea of any of us getting married sends the newspapers berserk. Look at the hell they put Anne through. I was just living in a fool's paradise, thinking it wouldn't happen to me. Don't let them upset you, darling. We'll just have to take more care."

She took his handkerchief to dry her tears. Getting married. He had asked her to marry him almost every time they made love; he said all kinds of wild things then and she never replied, not daring to believe he knew what he was saying. Now he had mentioned getting married as if in his mind it was all agreed and would inevitably happen.

She loved him so vastly she could not question anything he said, but sometimes now he frightened her. He was often in a boiling fury of ambition, and impatient with any restriction. "I'm sick of always being told what I can't do, I want to get on with my life," he told her after a particularly bitter argument with his Private Secretary. But she knew that, unlike his sister, he had no direction. He wanted to achieve, but did not know what. In the meantime he seized small victories. Avidly he pursued every token of independence that was within his grasp, and a wife, like his car, his bank account or the home to call his own for which he was pressing his parents, was one of these. Victoria had a young woman's sense of the marriage as an awesome commitment, and when he talked of it so lightly unease undermined her joy.

A few days later Prince Richard posed for a formally invited and properly accredited group of photographers with the university's fox hunt, with which he had never ridden before nor had any intention of joining. He threw back a tot of sloe gin and patted the hounds at the meet. A group of anti-bloodsport demonstrators arrived unexpectedly to add excitement; when Jo saw the pictures the next day, she recognised the pasty face of her room-mate and deduced that the girl had been eavesdropping on Victoria's quarters.

In answer to the reporters' questions Prince Richard replied that of course he knew Lady Victoria Fairley, that they had been acquainted since childhood, but that talk of romance was ridiculous and he considered himself far too young to get married. To do the job properly, he then contrived to fall off his horse into a good wide ditch for the benefit of the dozen particularly intrepid pressmen who followed the hunt.

After this the national newspapers withdrew their staff photographers from Cambridge. Keith Cowley, dispirited after a fortnight of being patronised, elbowed aside and once physically trampled underfoot by the fat cats from Fleet Street, took a telephone call one evening in the small flat he had rented with the proceeds of the smack-in-the-kisser shot.

"As you know," Phil Addams' adenoidal voice informed him, "the Palace have asked us to take it easy and the editor's agreed. You, of course, are not on our staff and so we have no control over your actions. I trust you get my drift?"

"Absolutely, squire. You can count on me."

"I thought I could, laddie."

"It'll take time, of course. I'll have to put myself about a bit. If I had a retainer, I could jack in my job and do the thing properly."

"I'll see what I can do, laddie. Have you got a figure in mind?"

Cowley thought of his rent and beer money and doubled it.

"Done," Addams said without hesitation, and Cowley cursed himself for not asking more. "Sharon will take it out of the petty cash. That way there's no names, no pack drill, if anyone asks I never heard of you, OK? And we'll expect you to cover everything else that comes up in your area as well."

He agreed and jubilantly gave notice at the shop the next day. His last actions were to fake a sales note and walk out with the most expensive telephoto lens in his jacket pocket. This was going to be a piece of piss. He was on his way at last.

The prey had grown cunning. He scored plenty of shots of the Prince walking to and from lectures or driving away from Magdalene with his detectives. He got pictures of Victoria doing very much the same thing. He spent long hours straddling his Suzuki in the cover of a hawthorn bush on the Girton Road, waiting for the little red Renault which Victoria had now been permitted to emerge from the gateway. He became familiar with the other passengers, especially the skinny black girl who was often with her. The American chick, he noticed, stuck to her bicycle in all weathers, and he took a few shots of her for luck, which came out very well.

What he could not get was a picture of Richard and Victoria together. He took long hours of telephone briefing from the *Daily Post*'s gossip columnist. He put together Richard's departure for Sandringham on many Thursdays and Fridays with Victoria's exit on the same road a few hours later. He bought maps, and field glasses and a camouflage jacket at an army surplus store and set off across the Norfolk fields to penetrate the estate, but was caught at once by two detectives in a Land-Rover and politely escorted back to the public highway.

With the same equipment, he climbed the walls into the grounds of Girton College in the grey hours of dawn and crouched behind the hedge watching the narrow windows light up one by one as the students awoke. The thought of so many women in nightclothes and underwear began to excite him. He climbed into the lowest branch of a chestnut tree to get a better view, and scanned each window, occasionally rewarded by a glimpse of a body or a brassiere.

When the police came Cowley was intently stroking his hard-on with one hand and gripping the field glasses with the other. The taller constable pulled him to the ground. They kicked him in the balls, stamped on his face and dragged him to the gate with no sympathy for his broken collar-bone, then returned to inform the college porter that the pervert had been escorted off the premises, summary justice had been done and the opportunity of breakfast with the young ladies in the hall would be most welcome.

At the end of the day Keith Cowley left the hospital with his arm and half his chest in a plaster cast. Alone in his flat he drank a bottle of Bacardi and swore he would get Prince Richard and his tart if it was the last thing he did on earth.

•   •   •

"YOU CAN'T HIDE out in here forever, Victoria. Come on, it would be good for you to get out and enjoy yourself. I know you like Monty Python. Come on, come to the cinema with me, just this once."

Victoria shook her head. "You're very kind, Jo, but I really must catch up on my reading."

Jo shrugged and began wrapping herself in the layers of

woollen garments 'necessary to insulate her body for the journey into town. She knew Victoria would spend most of the evening in a romantic trance, making desultory notes on the Florentine school and filing her already perfect fingernails. Anyone so much in love was, in Jo's opinion, asking to get hurt. Especially if they were as naïve as Victoria and in love with an arrogant shit like Prince Richard.

"You've never asked me about that picture," she said, intending to plant a seed of suspicion.

"You said he ran you over or something." Victoria remembered her feeble defence when Jo sat down beside her at dinner that evening, angrily demanding, "What is it with your Royal Family, anyway?"

"Does he always drive like a maniac?"

"Well, he drives too fast sometimes, I must say." This, from a member of the courtier class, was an immense indiscretion, but Victoria counted Jo as a trustworthy confidante. In fact, she found she needed the American girl's sophistication to open her eyes to the nasty new world in which she lived.

"I saw the photographer, you know, I knew he was there and I lined up the picture on purpose. I was so angry."

"Richard's never mentioned it," Victoria's tone was reassuring. She thinks I'm trying to apologise, Jo realised, winding her thick purple scarf several times around her neck. She decided to kill the conversation. What was there to tell of any significance? That they had flirted a little for half an hour? The truth, damn it, was that she still found the man attractive and she was about to act like a jealous bitch.

She set off for the cinema alone with a clear conscience.

Two hours later in a high good humour she stepped out into the icy April night and a leaflet was thrust into her hand.

"Join the Lumière Society! See all the dirty movies!" A student whose combination of obesity, spectacles and bristly ginger crewcut gave him the look of a highly intelligent but bad-tempered pig stood on the cinema steps accosting everyone who passed. "*Last Tango in Paris!* Our next presentation! Cream your jeans and call it art! Roll up, roll up! Get your feelthy pictures here."

"Where? This doesn't have an address." Jo turned back and waved the leaflet under his snub nose.

"Oh, Christ, I knew I'd left something out. We're in Victoria Street, over the King's Head. There's someone there every afternoon."

"Do you make films, or just show them?"

"Of course we make films, but they're crap and nobody would pay to see them. Gotta get the mugs to give us their money somehow, ain't we?"

He glared from under his low copper-coloured eyebrows and she decided he was a total wacko but not without genius potential. She had heard of the Lumière Society, but never considered that there might be advantages for her in joining it. But if she was not going to be the star of the Cambridge stage, there was still the screen. So what if it was her mother's turf?

The room above the King's Head was tiny, awash with paper and dominated by original-language posters for the works of Bertolucci, Antonioni, Pasolini, Truffaut, Polanski, Ichikawa and Samuel Fuller. An inflatable King Kong hung from the ceiling light. When Jo entered the pig-like one grunted from behind a primitive copying machine.

"He's the head honcho," he told her, indicating another man with his feet on an old green metal desk. He was a beautiful specimen of masculinity, on the lines of a Botticelli angel but with a more serious expression. When he saw Jo he swung his snow-stained black boots to the floor and stood up to greet her.

"You're Jocasta Forbes, aren't you?" He shook her hand. "Daniel Constant. I'm supposed to be the president, whatever that's worth. Bazza—this is Bazza . . ." another grunt from behind the copier, "said he'd seen you yesterday. Look . . . er . . . do have a seat," he put down his cigarette, a reeking maize-paper Gitane as favoured by Jean-Luc Godard, and removed a heap of film magazines from a chair.

The telephone rang. Bazza swept a tangle of 16mm celluloid off the apparatus and answered it, then clamped his fist over the mouthpiece. "*Merde, alors!* It's the licensing office at the council, Dan, wanting to know if we're showing the uncut version of *Last Tango* and if we are they want to see it first. Shall I tell him to stick it up his ass?"

"Christ, no. Here, let me talk to him, I'll butter him up," Daniel raised an ironic eyebrow at her and took the telephone. "Can I help you, sir? I am the President of the Lumière Society."

She watched him while he adeptly reassured the official on the line. Drop-dead good-looking was the only fair description. Straight nose, square jaw, clear olive skin, black hair that sprang in thick waves from wide brow. He was broad-shouldered but lean, well-balanced and graceful in a way that made her think of a fencer. His shirt and jeans seemed deliberately nondescript, as if he had been careful not to gild the lily.

The chat he was giving the man on the telephone was really something. She had not heard such skillful bullshit since she last listened to her mother's agent. This man was clever, confident and ambitious, but something was missing. The vibe she got from him was masculine but not aggressively sexual.

". . . of course, we're very much aware of the by-laws regarding the public exhibition of offensive material, and I can assure you, sir, that if we were fortunate enough to acquire an uncut print including any sensitive material we would submit it for your approval immediately. But that isn't the case with *Last Tango* at all. What we're showing is the regular exhibition print passed by the censor. Not at all. Any time there's anything you want to check out, do give us a call. Thank *you*, sir." He passed the black bakelite receiver back to Bazza with satisfaction.

"Eh, Cisco!"

"Ah, Pancho!" They slapped each other on the back and shook hands.

"That was all lies, right?" Jo pushed up the sleeves of her Peruvian sweater and leaned her elbows on the desk.

"Absolutely, madam," growled Bazza, wiping ink from his stubby fingers with a rag. "And nobody does it better."

Daniel came back to his seat. "I invited Bertolucci to come and lecture on the film next month and I just asked him if he had a complete print we could show. Of course, he'd rather talk about the picture the way he made it, any director would. Just in case some nerd from the council comes to snoop we got a regular print and stuck the censorship certificate from that on the beginning of our version. Simple."

"What's the difference?"

"The uncut version is even more pretentious. But more

bums on screen equals more bums on seats. We need the cash. The last president ran a Warhol season."

"Total audience three men and a dog. They thought the dog was asleep but they found it had been bored to death." Bazza finished cleaning his hands with solvent then sniffed the bottle appreciatively. "Hey, you can get quite a buzz off this stuff—want some?"

Daniel stood up and reached for the black leather jacket on the back of his chair. "The pubs are open—coming for a drink?"

"Don't I have to fill up a form to join your club?"

"I think in your case we can skip the formalities. I'll make you an honorary member or something. You ready, Pancho?"

"Let's went, Cisco."

Some hours later, after Daniel and Jo had drunk most of the King's Head only bottle of tequila and Bazza had kept pace with Guinness, they emerged into the frozen night. It was so cold and the air was so saturated that Jo felt as if she were breathing vaporised ice.

"Anybody got any drugs?" Bazza glowered at them both.

"Your drugs are at the flat, remember."

"Oh, yeah, right. Let's go."

Jo had no gloves and began to wrap her hands in her scarf. Daniel thoughtfully extricated the right one. "*Te gelida manina.* Come on Baz, be a gent, take the other one." Her hands in theirs in their pockets were warmer, though occasionally Bazza swayed off-course and threatened to dislocate her shoulder.

"Do you know," Daniel said solemnly. "My mother had a crush on your father when she was young. She was always saying what a pity it was he never made any more films."

"He said when he came back from the war it didn't seem like a man's job any more."

"She'd have loved that. She thought he was the perfect English gentleman, even better than Leslie Howard. She actually named my older brother Robert after him. If that was what she admired, God knows why she married my father."

"Why?"

"Polish, very. Our name should have been Kopczewska. Wartime romance, he was a navigator, she was a nurse." Bazza vocalised a few bars of the Warsaw Concerto. "Then he became income tax collector. Had dozens of other women. When he did come home he just got blind drunk and passed out. Or else sat in his chair crying and singing to himself in Polish. Fell under a train when I was twelve, thank God. She couldn't have found anyone less like your father."

"Maybe he looked good in his uniform. Dad always said that was the secret of his success."

He gave a bitter laugh, his breath like clouds of steam in the air.

Being in their second year at the university, Daniel and Bazza were permitted their own apartment in an approved lodging house. It comprised two high-ceilinged rooms on the raised ground floor of a Victorian villa. The hall was almost completely obstructed by parts of a motorcycle. Bazza's room was stacked with crazy pillars of books rising from the floor like stalagmites around a mattress and an ancient Remington. On the windowsill was a chromium Art Deco teapot from which he pulled a small plastic envelope of capsules.

He tipped six of them into his palm and swallowed them without water, then sat down heavily on the bed.

"What are they?"

In his own room, Daniel drew the once-opulent curtains of wine-coloured plush and lit the gas fire. "Speed. He hates sleeping, says he gets nightmares."

"But . . ."

"Don't worry. He'll throw up in a minute, always does. Then he passes out and sleeps like a baby." She gave him her coat and scarf and he put them over the chair by his desk. Everything in the room was precisely aligned. The books were stacked on black industrial shelving. The floorboards and the fireplace had been painstakingly lacquered black. The sagging mahogany bed was made up with plain white linen. There was a white wool rug in front of the fire, and prints of four Paris street scenes by Cartier-Bresson on the wall above the mantelpiece.

"Excuse me, I feel the need to park a custard," Bazza announced as he proceeded past their door towards the bathroom, stepping carefully over the disassembled carburettor. They heard a door slam, then nothing.

"He'll be OK, honestly," Daniel reassured her. "This is routine."

Jo shrugged. It was none of her business, except, discounting the effects of the tequila, Daniel seemed like an interesting proposition. "Were you two buddies before you got to Cambridge?"

"No. We met at the Lumière Society. I know you think he's loco, but he's a brilliant, brilliant writer. He thinks like a camera. We shot a script of his last year, and a London agent wants to take him on already."

She looked at him sideways, hoping to hide the shrewdness of her questions. Daniel already had the aura of power around him, but since her instincts about men had let her down recently she wanted hard evidence before she made any decisions. "How did he meet this agent?"

"We ran a season of her writers' first films and plays, and then invited her to lecture."

"I get it. And what about you? Why didn't she take you on?"

His tone was matter-of-fact but his face showed tension. "I'm good, Bazza's great."

"Great but wacko."

"And I can get my head together and get the show on the road. I'm a Diaghilev, he's a Nijinsky."

There was a muffled thump from the bathroom. They went to investigate. Bazza lay unconscious like a beached whale by a brown lake of vomited Guinness in which floated intact the six speed capsules. It was a ridiculous sight and they laughed.

"Should we put Nijinsky to bed?"

"Question expecting the answer 'no.' *Could* we put him to bed? He weighs around 14 stone, you know."

They returned to Daniel's room and passed some hours sitting on the floor drinking coffee, listening to the Pink Floyd and talking movies until the tequila burned itself out and sobriety descended in the drowsy warmth of the fire. Vicious sleet began to fall at midnight and she dismissed the idea of reclaiming her bicycle and riding back to Girton. If he jumped her she'd deal with it. Somehow, she did not think that he would.

"I suppose everyone tells you that you look like Jacqueline Bisset?" he said at around 3 am.

"No, actually, they don't." Here it comes, Jo told herself regretfully, here comes the pass. "You don't really think I do, either."

"I don't know . . ." he got up and fetched the lamp from his desk. "You have got the same sort of fragility . . ." he was looking intently at her features, moving the light as he did so. "Maybe it's the nose . . . oh, wow, do that again."

"Do what again?"

"Whatever you did."

"I didn't do anything."

"What did you think of?"

"How I hate my fucking nose and if you actually like it you must be totally weird."

"Then think that again." He pushed her hair back from her cheek and she felt her face start to break up into a smile.

"I can't, you're making me laugh."

"You know what's great about your face?" He put down the lamp and sat on the rug again. "It's absolutely transparent. Everything you feel just shows right through it."

"I think it's just a nothing face."

"But that's it, don't you understand? It can be whatever you want, say whatever you want. It's the perfect face for the camera, the perfect face for an actress . . ."

"What about the bone structure, Momma always said you had to have bone structure . . ." She did Madeline Kahn in *Paper Moon.*

"Honey, you got bone structure but it's the soft tissue that counts."

An hour later she was drooping in a doze, and he suggested that she take his bed while he slept on Bazza's mattress. She stripped off her jumpsuit and her sweater, unhooked her bra but decided to keep on the white woollen lace underwear that was a cyclist's final protection against the Cambridge cold. Six feet away from the fire the temperature dropped, so she decided not to turn off the gas.

She lay wakefully under the clean white quilt reflecting that no one had ever talked to her about her father before. He had not mentioned her mother at all, but somehow implied that he knew she was an embarrassment as a parent.

The room glowed red-gold in the firelight. She got up and went to the desk, which was completely bare except for a pencil tray. One drawer contained writing pads, another essay notes. The drawers on the other side of the desk held what she was looking for, a stack of drafts and treatments in longhand and a typed screenplay. She read them all.

"So what do you think?" He was standing in the doorway in his black underpants, the firelight glowing on the muscles of his chest.

"I think you're putting yourself down. I think you're great." She could not make out from his face whether he was angry or not. He walked into the room and stood in front of the fire. "I think you couldn't sleep either." Half his face was still in shadow, but what she saw was anxiety and a sort of helplessness that touched her. "Am I right, so far?"

"Well," he pulled his hair back with one hand. "I couldn't sleep. And I guess you're entitled to your opinion."

"Now tell me if I'm right about something else." She walked slowly towards him, aware of her breasts stirring as she moved. The pink of the nipples was just distinguishable through their filigree covering. His eyes dropped.

She came to stand close in front of him and took one of his hands. Despite the warmth of the fire she could feel the heat of his erection and see it rise even in the deep shadow between them.

"Fucking me would be a good career move, which is why you're not doing it, is that right?"

He grinned. "How can I say 'I love you' when cars love Shell?"

"Answer the question."

"Maybe I could ask you the same thing."

"Maybe I'm not going to give you the chance." With an unhurried, economical movement she pulled off his underpants, letting her hair brush against his belly; she grasped a penis that was already hard and in the same ideal proportion as the rest of his body and kissed the tip. Then she reached up and wound her free arm around his neck and willed him to the floor.

He dragged a pillow from the bed, put it under her shoulders and began to kiss her. Daniel made love with the same perfectionism that he did everything else. His lips were firm, dry and mobile, his tongue hot and quick as it teased hers. He tangled his fingers in her hair to pull back her head and kiss her throat.

She waited for him to move to her breasts but he delayed so long that her nipples were aching when at last he pushed up the warm lace and took the fullness of her breasts in his hands. Slowly, as if obeying him, the smooth petal of each areola contracted. He grazed the tight buds with his teeth, first one, then the other, and for the first time Jo felt something from the miraculous tissue that before had excited everyone except herself.

She still held his penis and felt it swell and twitch as she stroked it, but he took her hand away, moved out of reach and spread her thighs. She felt herself already slick, but caressing fingers parted her lips and his tongue began to find her secrets. Every dart and flicker was timed so that he gave her the touch she craved an instant after the craving became unbearable. He wanted complete control and there seemed no reason not to cede it. She stopped waiting, questioning and figuring his angles and let the waves begin to build. When the first foaming caps were breaking he pulled her on top of him and abandoned himself, whispering her name between clenched teeth.

Afterwards he pulled the quilt over them and offered her a Gitane. She took it with fingers that would not stop trembling, and saw that the proof of her pleasure pleased him. If he asks me about my mother and Hitchcock now, I'll die, she thought, then wondered from what deep self-destructive vein of her subconscious the notion had sprung.

He asked her six months later. "He's coming to England and I want to invite him to lecture—do you know him? I mean, well enough that I can use your name?"

*   *   *

WHEN SUMMER CAME to Cambridge the cold horrors of the winter became a memory. Sitting with Beale, Bishop and Furmiston on Contract on the daisy-scattered lawn at Girton, Martha stretched her bare legs in the sun and noticed how pale they had become. She wriggled her toes in the fragrant grass, hardly able to believe that a few weeks earlier she had been suffering the agony of chilblains.

Every day Jo cycled down a drive scattered with the June drop of immature chestnuts, tiny spiked spheres like the battle maces of miniature mediaeval knights. She waved happily at the porter, who stood surveying his roses with satisfaction.

In the town the warmth finally penetrated the ancient walls, driving the chill from the alleyways. Sunshine sparkled on the gilded arms of Lady Margaret Beaufort. Trinity became gaudy with geraniums, and the gardener at Magdalene planted out his display of dahlias with pride.

From the window of his rooms Prince Richard saw the willows trailing their leaves in the slow weedy waters of the river. The boat houses relaunched their punts, freshly caulked and varnished, with the damage of the past year repaired, and the new intake of undergraduates handed their girlfriends into the flat-bottomed craft, picked up the ten-foot poles with the greatest possible confidence and pushed off into the crowded waterway. Punting was an essential part of doing Cambridge properly.

"Punts suck," Bazza glared at the idyllic scene. "Punts are for toffs. Let's get a rowboat."

Daniel glanced at Jo, feeling sure she would be yearning to recline in a punt trailing her fingers in the cool water. He had mastered punting in his first year as easily as he mastered everything else, and wanted to show off his skill. He lived in dread that Jo would cease to love him, and overlooked nothing that might please or impress her.

"Let's get a rowboat and go up to Byron's Pool," Bazza pulled a crumpled £5 note from his back pocket and hired a skiff without waiting for argument. Daniel took off his T-shirt, lowered the oars into the water and pulled them swiftly upstream between the reedy banks of Grantchester meadows. It was a marvellous exhibition of manly power and strength, done in the characteristically self-deprecating way which was both typical of Daniel and particularly British, and which irritated Jo. Half the ability of this arrogant little country seemed to be lost in the prohibitions of its social divisions; thus Daniel, although he probably rowed better than many of the men in his college boat, would never consider joining the rowing club because the sport was the preserve of upper-class philistines, not artistic refugees from the petty bourgeoisie.

The champagne, Jo's contribution to the picnic, was tied in an old net shopping bag and trailed in the cool water behind the boat like a sheet anchor. Bazza lay down in the bows, dropped some psilocybin and put his hands behind his head with a contented sigh. Dragonflies skimmed his face shaking rainbows from their glass wings.

With a skilful opposition of his oars, Daniel turned the boat into the shady backwater below a small weir that was their destination. Bazza tied the boat to the overhanging branch of a tree with exaggerated care. "The trees are blue," he announced. "Goodbye, young lovers, I'm going for a walk." In a few moments he had disappeared in the wood and the cracking of twigs beneath his boots died away.

Daniel is going to make love to me, Jo predicted to herself even as he walked towards her in the narrow, rocking boat. He knows that the smell of fresh sweat turns me on, so he's going to do it right now. It will be delicate, languid and romantic, as befits this occasion, but with just enough urgency.

He knelt on the ragged velvet cushion beside her and did exactly as she had foreseen. Her body was always ready to accept the exquisite pleasure he gave her, and she could always let her mind float away.

Afterwards he opened the champagne so gently that nothing but a wisp of vapour followed the cork, and handed it to her for the first drink.

"I think you've got charmed hands," she raised the bottle to her lips and let the cool foam run down her throat. "Everything you touch obeys you."

"Then take off your blouse." She passed the bottle back to him and slipped the brief white cotton shift over her head, shaking out her hair. They sat in silence, half-naked in the warm air, and finished the champagne. She knew Daniel wanted to look at her breasts as much because he adored her as because he wanted to study the way they looked in the dappled, liquid light of the riverside. He spent hours looking at her body, and because she knew his interest was at least half technical she had become able to see herself in the same detached way. She was thinner, and the British climate suited her delicate skin. Her cheeks blushed pale pink and the ivory whiteness of her breasts showed the faint tracery of blue veins.

The weir roared in the distance. After a while he made love to her again and this time her whole being responded and they lay still in each other's arms afterwards.

"You'll have to find a flat for next term," he told her. "I've got to move back into college and I'm not doing this in a miserable little bed and sending you back to climb into Girton in the middle of the night."

"To feel is to obey," she told him.

Later she considered the idea carefully. She did not want to live by herself; Daniel's devotion was so intense she sometimes felt smothered by it. She wanted the defence of other women around her. A year in the convent atmosphere of the college had allowed her to discover that she liked the companionship of her own sex. Who else would join her to sit up half the night discussing whether she would love Daniel more if he loved her less?

•   •   •

IN LONDON, PRINCE RICHARD had a diary meeting with his Private Secretary at Buckingham Palace, then drove to meet Victoria at her apartment. She made him tea in the kitchen and took it up to the compass alcove.

"I wish I could just come round and have tea with you like this every day." He gazed wistfully out of the window across the Thames. Every remaining weekend of the term was now committed to what he called family business, which meant either official engagements or time spent with his family; his secretary had demonstrated with an officiousness which Richard found detestably patronising that both classes of commitment needed to be scheduled more than a year in advance.

Friends had thoughtfully invited Richard and Victoria to Spain in early August. Afterwards he would join his father and brothers on the royal yacht, then go on to Balmoral, where Victoria would join him again for a week, and then they would go back to Cambridge. He could see her for exactly three weeks in the next four months.

"You could if I moved out of Girton next year." She had already made the same miserable calculation. Furthermore, although Martha and Jo were loyal to her in their way, most of the other women in the college were not anxious to be her friends. Victoria had counted it her birthright to be socially acceptable. Awareness of this rejection was slow to dawn but bitter when it had finally arrived.

"Darling, you couldn't possibly . . ."

"Yes I could, and I think I should. I could get a flat in the town. I've already talked to my tutor and she's agreed."

"But won't you be lonely?" He loved her for her softness, which coupled with her height and her imposing looks often made her seem like an overgrown child. There were no other women from the magic circle at Girton. He was afraid she might decide to move in with her brother.

Richard was discovering that a young man with personal glamour and exceptional good fortune in life was not universally popular with his own sex. His brother Charles, at the same age, had been much less prepossessing and the Cambridge establishment firmly believed that the logistical problems of his love life had been solved by the Master of Trinity College, Lord Butler, who allowed his girlfriend to stay at the Master's Lodge. The feeling at Magdalene, where the fellows' wives and the students' girlfriends all twittered admiration for Richard, was that this prince was a playboy who had already bedded two of the most beautiful women in the university and needed no help from anyone to keep his excessive libido satisfied.

"Well I might, but I was thinking that perhaps the other girls would come in with me. I know Jo Forbes hates living in college." She looked at him with grave grey eyes and he thought he saw an unavoidable question in them. If he objected now, he would raise the suspicion that there had been something between himself and that Hollywood brat. Which, he told himself, there had not been, not at all.

"I didn't know she was a particular friend of yours."

"She knows the score. I can trust her. And Martha, of course. She's been such a brick."

"Yes, hasn't she? Jamaicans are wonderful people." This was a notion he had received almost from birth; his great-aunt, Princess Alice, Countess of Athlone, loved the place and had adopted the cause of Kingston's university in the mid-Fifties. His sister had chosen Jamaica for her honeymoon, and the Palace offices had been littered with high-flown official communications with the island for more than a year as a consequence of the Commonwealth Conference.

"You've got all this planned already, haven't you?" he asked Victoria, amused at her initiative.

She blushed and busied herself pouring a second cup of tea. "I think there's quite a rush for the nice places. We'll have to get organised pretty soon. If you think it's a good idea I'll talk to the others as soon as I get back."

"It's the best idea I've ever heard. Good for you." He

took her hand and kissed it, thoughtfully grazing her knuckles with his teeth. It flattered him that she was prepared to be so daring and so practical for his sake.

Martha was also flattered out of her mind by the proposal, and bit her tongue before she could say that her parents could not afford it. Her book bill was already hundreds of pounds, and she dared not write home about that. Jo and Victoria lived in worlds in which the possibility of something being too expensive did not exist. She decided to stay in England in the long vacation and find a job.

Jo immediately located an ideal apartment, the upper half of a tall, early-Victorian terraced house in a peaceful street lined with birch trees. It was an easy walk from Magdalene. There was a first-floor drawing room that was positively elegant by the time Victoria imported some of the furniture and pictures relegated to box-rooms at Aston Langley by her stepmother. The rest of the accommodation was arranged so that each girl could choose a bedroom on a different floor. The two men renting the apartment below turned out to have attended the same school as Victoria's brother.

Best of all, there were three exits; by the front door, by the back door into a mews behind and by a fire-escape from the roof of Jo's attic bedroom to the small enclosed garden at the end of the street.

The only person not delighted with this arrangement was Keith Cowley, who regarded Victoria's change of address as a personal insult. He now looked on her as his particular professional property. How dare the cow disappear without a word to anyone?

Cowley had finally scored the perfect picture of Victoria with the Prince at the university polo match against Oxford in the summer. By the time the *Daily Post*'s process department had painted out Alex and Amanda it had come out quite intimate. Victoria was a difficult woman to photograph, her face had too much character, but that time he had caught her gazing up from her chair at her lover with a perfect look of blank adoration.

He wormed his way into the regular pack of royal photographers and scored again at Royal Ascot in June. Prince Richard was paired with Lady Leonora Grosvenor for the Royal Family's traditional ride down the course before the first race, and most of the ignorant Fleet Street mob were satisfied to get him with one of the country's greatest aristocratic beauties. Cowley had already seen Victoria in the Royal Enclosure, in a fluttering cream silk dress and a small hat trimmed with an apricot silk rose. She hated hats, especially large ones, which was lucky for Cowley since nothing ever shaded her face. He waited patiently for two hours and caught Richard, now resplendent in morning dress, holding her hand on the walk back down to the winners' enclosure.

Phil Addams refused to pay for him to follow them to Balmoral, and sent a local boy instead. He got nothing, but a German freelance stalked the couple successfully and got a charming shot of them sitting simply on the river bank. The romance was now almost nine months old and the hottest story in Fleet Street. Addams screamed down Cowley's telephone like a madman every morning.

Cowley was not as bothered as he might have been. Being a press photographer was a tough life. He did not care for the long hours or the company, and had his sights firmly fixed on fashion. Meanwhile, money and status had improved his sex life considerably. He was running a couple of girlfriends, both of them real lookers. He was putting together a portfolio of fashion shots which he intended to send up to Jim Kelly at *Vogue*. And he was making useful cash on the side with some nude stuff. Nothing hardcore, more the artistic market, *Playboy* and *Penthouse*; well, he sent them stuff but so far he'd only sold to the smaller magazines. The girls loved it. Great little exhibitionists, both of them. He was thinking about talking them into doing a session together.

The *Daily Post* was his bread and butter, and they were putting on the pressure. He had to find Lady Victoria fast. He now had a red Alfasud, nippy and not too rusty, but although he haunted the Girton road he failed to catch her. The spade chick had vanished too. He tried telephoning as a friend of Jo Forbes, but the college secretary gave nothing away.

Then the spade simply stepped out in front of his car one morning. No mistaking her, the only six foot negress in town. He let her cross the road and watched her stride away under the yellowing birches, slow and deliberate like a giraffe. He parked the car, combed his hair and grabbed his new Pentax.

"Excuse me, miss," his accent had also moved several rungs up the social ladder. "I'm doing a feature on student fashion for *Vogue* and I wonder if you could spare a few moments to let me take your photograph?"

"What, *me*? You want to photograph me?" She was laughing. Great. Make 'em laugh and you'd got 'em. The *Vogue* line always worked.

"It will only take a few moments, I promise you."

"You're sure you want to risk your camera—my face might crack the lens, you know."

"Come on, you can't mean that, a beautiful girl like you —you've been photographed before, I betcha . . ."

"Well . . ." She *had* been photographed several times by the *Gleaner* back in Kingston, but so had almost every other girl in Beverly Hills. It was a very small town.

"Of course you have." He rapidly backed away and began lining up the first shot. "You're practically a professional, I can tell. Don't smile. I want some serious ones first. Just a bit to the left, against that tree, that's the ticket . . . lick your lips . . . look in here," he pointed at the blank glass aperture of the lens, "lovely, lovely." In fact, she didn't look half bad. Huge eyes, and she was wearing some kind of scarf around her head so her neck looked endless. The silver birch bark showed her up well, too. "Put your hand up to your face now so I can get that bracelet. Beautiful, just beautiful, oh yes . . . now look up, over there . . . lick your lips again . . . terrific." He knew he could make any woman look good; it was a knack. Get 'em relaxed, tell 'em they were beautiful, accentuate the positive and retouch the negative. Simple.

He reloaded the camera and she kicked up some dead leaves, feeling awkward. "*That's* great! Really great! Do that again! Terrific! Smiling now!" She picked up the little yellow birch leaves in handfuls and threw them into the air, thinking that she ought to feel silly but, since this man was concentrating so intensely, not at all self-conscious.

"Fantastic. Those are going to be great. Now, tell me what you're wearing and where you bought it . . ." He pulled out his notebook from his jeans pocket. Martha obligingly told him that her plain, ladylike beige shirt-waister came from a chain store, that she had decided to wear the dress's fabric belt to tie up her hair, and pull the waist in with a wide plaited leather belt bought in one of

Cambridge's best-known boutiques. Her silver bracelets came from the same shop, and her sturdy laced brogues, worn with brown wool ankle socks (Martha was taking no chances with chilblains this winter) had been hand made by Manolo Blahnik for her flatmate who was now bored with them.

"These are going to look fantastic. *Vogue* will be over the moon when they see the prints. You've got real style, you know. You really know how to put a look together and how to act in front of a camera. Are you sure you've never done any modelling?" Easy boy, he told himself. Don't lay it on too thick.

"Quite sure," Martha picked up the heavy canvas bag in which she carried her books. "I'm only a law student."

"Well, I'm really grateful to you, thank you very much for giving me your time," he told her with his most plausible smile. "You ought to think about it, you know, modelling. Let me send you some of the prints."

"That would be nice, my mother would love to have them. I think she'd die of joy if she saw her daughter in a fashion magazine."

"Give me your address, then."

"You can send them to Girton, that's my college."

"I thought you said you lived in town, somewhere."

"Anything you send to Girton will reach me," she said firmly. Of course this was just another newspaper scam. They'd all seen her with Victoria and figured everything out. "I really must go now. Goodbye."

She strode rapidly away from him, angry with herself for being so vain. She should have known better. Nobody could possibly want to photograph her.

CHAPTER XI

"I KNOW YOU think that fashion is about clothes," Jim Kelly's meaty hand picked up three transparencies by their edges and deposited them in a straight line on the light box. "But I am here to tell you that fashion is all about cunt, and that," he pushed the scraps of coloured negative across to the small, thin woman opposite him, and handed her a magnifying glass, "is the most amazing cunt I've ever seen."

Auriol Meredith hunched her shoulder blades inside her beige Emanuelle Khanh crochet sweater and peered at the pictures. Jim Kelly was in a very delicate emotional state. He fell in love with a new face approximately every five years. Usually, it was a very new face, a girl he'd pick out from the constant stream of models which flowed through the sixth floor studios of Vogue House. This girl often had no experience, often she had no ambition; she always had an extraordinary body and a look which was absolutely fresh, absolutely now and absolutely right. She would come to Jim as nobody and leave him as a star.

They always left him in the end. Jim's relationships had built-in obsolescence. He called his models air-heads, dodos, and birdbrains, among many other insults, but his women were always smarter than him. Once he had made them into exquisite icons of style, he worshipped them and always in the end, they grew bored with modelling and bored with him, and drifted regretfully away.

Isabelle Latouche had lasted four years and ten months. Having arrived in London with fifty pounds and a spare T-shirt to crash on another model's floor, she now never travelled with less than twenty-two pieces of Vuitton luggage. She was currently at the Pierre in New York getting cosy with an ageing rock star. Isabelle pouted sullenly from sixteen of the twenty-four *Vogue* covers tacked to the wall behind Jim. She was Mauritian, honey-skinned with up-swept eyes, hair like twining black snakes to her waist, a mixture of Tamil delicacy and French arrogance. Jim always went for women who projected contempt, and his taste was becoming more exotic.

"Where did these come from?" Auriol looked at three pictures. They were amateur stuff, totally banal, but the girl fitted Jim's specification exactly. Automatically in her mind Auriol identified, priced and dated every garment the girl was wearing: Marks & Spencer dress, this season, £27, Mulberry belt, last autumn, £40, Manolo Blahnik shoes, two years old, about £120, bangle by Corocraft last spring, £2, ankle socks by Pex, £1.50. The socks were nice.

"Some berk in Cambridge, keeps sending me stuff and asking me for a job."

Auriol wrinkled her tiny pointed nose with disdain. From *Vogue*'s perspective, all chic stopped a mile from their own doorstep. Any serious fashion contender contrived to live within this radius, even if they had to crash on a different floor every night.

"I want to get that long tall nigger in here for some test shots," Jim announced. "Next Thursday. Get some stuff together. I want to do some make-up shots as well. Just look at that face." He rubbed his hands together with anticipation. "Well, say something, then."

She raised a perfectly pencilled eyebrow. "What is there to say? You've obviously made up your mind. What about Kenzo's Inca look—bright colours, layers . . ."

"You're the boss. Right, you ratbags, back to work . . ." He bounced across the corridor to his studio where a team of shoeless assistants were fussing around two models in pastel Dior suits who stood without enthusiasm in the centre of a sheet of grey paper.

Auriol lifted the telephone with resignation. As an assistant fashion editor at *Vogue* she might, in theory, be Jim Kelly's boss, but in practice he turned out over four hundred pages for them every year—British *Vogue*, French *Vogue*, Italian *Vogue*, American *Vogue*, Australian *Vogue*, every shot was different, every shot was perfect, every detail of every garment was displayed, every colour of every cosmetic was exact, every jet-lagged celebrity was radiant, and every couturier, manufacturer and fashion store in every country around the world was satisfied and they all rebooked their advertising every season. Jim was one of the few photographers in the world who could stand the heat.

They paid him as much as they could, which was peanuts. He got a million a throw for TV commercials, did a few every year, called them his pension and said advertising was crap. Jim Kelly worked for *Vogue* for love. If he wanted the nigger next Thursday, then Auriol Meredith would arrange it.

"We think your pictures are very interesting and we want to use them in the Directions section in the January issue," she lied fluently down the telephone to Keith Cowley. "We will need your models to sign our model release forms authorising the use of their pictures. If you will just give us their addresses . . ."

Cowley immediately obliged. He could just picture the look of bedazzled gratitude those scrubbers would have on their faces when they got an official letter from *Vogue*. They'd do anything he wanted. That stuck-up spade might just ask him round for a cup of tea.

. . . .

"POSTMAN, POSTMAN, DON'T be slow, be like Elvis, go man *go*!" It was Victoria's turn to fetch their letters from Girton and Jo watched her from the window gliding swan-like down the street with a complete lack of urgency. "She's always so slow. What do you think would persuade Victoria to move her ass?"

"Tell her Richard's here?" Martha took off her spectacles and rubbed her eyes. The room had large windows but the grudging light of the November morning was not good enough for hard study.

"She wouldn't believe it. He never just comes by, does he? It's like the conjunction of the planets with those two, totally predictable, moving in fixed orbits. Anyway, there's no gorilla parked down there." Jo was waiting to hear from the agent she had been to see in the long vacation. She had taken a fifteen-minute film made by Daniel and agreed to get her nose fixed. The man had seemed tepidly positive.

Martha was waiting for a cheque from home. Her family

was well off by Kingston standards; she had much less money than her flatmates. Her holiday job had paid her debts but now she was broke again.

Victoria did not know about waiting for mail. All she ever yearned for was Richard's phone call every morning and his visits in the afternoons, when his detective stayed outside in an anonymous Rover and Jo and Martha tactfully found reasons to be elsewhere.

"Bills, bank statements, here Jo, that looks like your mother, and yours, Martha . . ." Victoria drifted through the door, producing letters one by one from her Hermes hunting bag. Handbags were her particular extravagance. She reached for her silver paperknife to open the envelopes. She extracted two engraved invitations, the first of the flock that would crowd the gilt-framed looking glass by the beginning of December, then settled down to read a letter from one of Aunt Rose's daughters. All Victoria's female relatives and friends wrote faithfully. They considered it important to "keep in touch." Each letter was a strand in the social web woven by Englishwomen for centuries, an indestructible matrix which held the élite together however thin it might be stretched through counties, colonies and postings overseas.

Victoria's friends wrote on thick paper from Bond Street, their envelopes lined with crackling tissue, their writing large, even and rounded. Most had no news apart from the doings of other friends, but Victoria's status as a royal consort, however informal it seemed at present, made it more than ever important to correspond with her, although, of course, Prince Richard was never mentioned.

Jo ripped her two letters open with eager fingers. "*I wish I could be with you, sweetheart, to break this news,*" her mother wrote from Bel Air on her familiar peach stationery, "*but there is so much to do here . . . Your father and I have regretfully decided that we must sell our home. Now that both our little birds have flown the nest we have no need of such a large place . . .*" she skimmed the rest of the letter without interest. She knew her parents were broke. Lorna had not worked for a year. Her father was always talking of people he was seeing, real estate deals he was about to do, businesses he was setting up, but the truth was he was as helpless as a turned turtle. She knew they would have to sell the house. She opened her second letter.

"Good news?" Martha asked, waiting for Victoria to pass her the paperknife.

"Good news and bad news. Yes, he'll take me on, but I have to get an Equity card."

"Well, can't your mother arrange that for you?" Victoria did not appreciate that there were certain differences between the actors' union and an exclusive nightclub.

"I'm sure she could, I doubt very much that she would and I'm certainly not going to ask her. Daniel's got a plan, anyway."

"Daniel's always got a plan, hasn't he?" Careerism was something else which the English girl was not culturally conditioned to understand. She had been bred to believe that ambition was the resort of people with no connections.

"Sweet Jesus!" Martha suddenly stood up, her last letter in her hand. "After this I'll believe in Santa Claus!"

"What happened, somebody send you the head of Rudolph the Red-Nosed Reindeer?"

"Oh, for heaven's sake, Jo!" Any suggestion of cruelty to animals upset Victoria.

"Sorry, sorry! So come on, Martha, what's happening?"

"You know I told you some creepy little photographer guy told me he was doing pictures for *Vogue* and tried to get this address?" Jo nodded. Victoria was puzzled. They had decided not to mention the incident to her.

"Well, he really was with *Vogue*. Look—they're asking me to come to their studios."

Victoria took the letter. "It must be a joke."

"Why must it be a joke?" Jo snatched it from her with irritation. Lately Victoria was sometimes unbearably patronising to both of them. "It looks perfectly genuine to me. We can always check it out."

Victoria shrugged her shoulders, gathered up her post and went upstairs to her room.

Martha sighed. "She didn't mean it that way."

"This is a dream come true. An invitation to go to *Vogue* studios for a session with *Jim Kelly*. Do you know who Jim Kelly is?"

Martha laughed and threw up her hands in a gesture of helplessness. "I've never heard of him—who is he?"

"Well, if he isn't the most famous photographer in the world he's certainly in the top ten. Just about anyone would be dying to have him photograph them. He does all the Beautiful People—look . . ." From the untidy pile of magazines on the ringmarked butler's tray she extracted a *Vogue* and flicked through it. "Here—Kelly's Heroines—The Fifty Most Beautiful Women In The World. Catherine Deneuve, Jerry Hall, Lauren Hutton, Loulou de la Falaise, Faye Dunaway, Natalia Makharova, Charlotte Rampling, Maria Schneider, Cybill Shepherd, Claudia Cardinale, Princess Grace, my fucking mother, Farrah Fawcett, Paloma Picasso, Gloria Steinem, Mother Teresa, Marisa Berenson, Jeanne Moreau, Simone de Beauvoir, Lauren Bacall, Grace Jones . . . and half a dozen models including naturally Isabelle Latouche because she's his girl-friend."

"But I don't even know who most of those people are."

"So what? Don't tell me you're going to turn this down?"

"Well . . ." Martha glanced guiltily at her books.

"You can be late with one essay once in three years, Martha."

"There's so much to do this year, Jo . . ."

"Being black means you have to try harder, huh?"

"Go on, hit me where it Hertz." She sat down again and her face dissolved into a grimace of guilty delight. "But they can't be serious, Jo."

"Why not? You're a great shape for wearing clothes."

"But I'm not beautiful." In disbelief, she framed her face with her hands, inviting her friend to consider it.

"Well, as it happens, I think you are. You're just not into being beautiful right now. But that doesn't matter. They'll just make you over in the studio."

Martha shook her head and tossed the letter on to the table. "I don't know, I feel foolish just thinking about it—if I go, will you come with me?"

"Just try to stop me!"

Martha reached out for the telephone, hesitated, then, her mind made up, took the receiver and began to dial.

She spent the rest of the day walking distractedly from the mirror to her desk, wondering if she had done the right thing. Martha was mentally exhausted. All she could see around her was work, fat tomes to be read, notes to be organised, essays to write. The mock court hearings, called moots, which she had enjoyed at first, were now an ordeal, because her confidence deserted her and her mind blanked as soon as she had to speak.

Her intellect, the basis of her pride, was no longer strong and supple, eager for new challenges. Studying grew harder and harder; each time she sat down with her books she had lashed her weary mind to its task with visions of the disgrace of failing her degree. The future seemed to hold nothing but a mountain of information which she no longer had the courage to attempt, stored in daunting books she could barely afford to buy.

Her work was excellent, her tutor praised her, but Martha had lost all sense of perspective about herself. She had no emotional resources to restore her spirit. Every weekend she seemed to have so many essays to write that she could finish them all only by working solidly from first thing in the morning until late at night. With little money, she lived on toast and chocolate bars.

Sometimes she would agree to go out to dinner with one of her admirers, but the novelty of being considered desirable had palled. Her dates were nice men, she would have liked to like them, but they could see her only as a sexual conquest. She had to be cerebral, cold and sarcastic to deter them, and the strain of being that way when what she wanted was a few hours of warm, relaxed companionship was almost worse than staying in alone. Her only true friend was Neville Green, the plump and sweaty scion of a famous family of Jewish lawyers from London. Neville never hassled her. They were convenient partners at the few formal social events of the Cambridge year. He was brilliant, unpopular and unattached. Martha had quickly learned the ways of the ancient civilisation in which she was living and she acknowledged with sadness that whatever Neville's sexual tastes were, they probably did not run to adult women.

She paused in front of the mirror, an elaborate gilt-framed loan from Victoria's family, whose depths seemed cobwebbed with antiquity. It was weeks since she had worn make-up. She scraped her hair back into a pleat and wrapped her head with scarves, because it was months since she had set or straightened it. Straightening meant a trip to London, expensive and time-consuming, because no hairdresser in Cambridge reckoned to deal with negroid kinks. She could not possibly be photographed by this Jim

Kelly with two inches of curling regrowth springing out of her scalp.

She pulled on her boots and went out, first to bank the cheque from home and then to buy some perming cream. Mild panic suspended her common sense. She was unable to decide which brand was the strongest, and so bought three. When she got home she decided she might as well mix them together. Her mother had warned her that products meant for European hair were never strong enough for black hair.

"My God, what's been happening here, it smells like a laboratory!" Jo caught the chemical aroma as soon as she opened the door. In the bathroom Martha was sitting on the edge of the bath with her hair stretched tightly over large wire rollers, anointing it with neutralising solution. "Here, let me do the back for you. God, this stuff stinks! How long do you have to leave it on for?"

Martha reached for the nearest packet and consulted the instructions. "Half an hour."

"Can we open a window?" Martha obligingly opened the narrow casement and sat in her ragged white towelling bathrobe flicking through a new issue of *Vogue* and consulting her wristwatch at intervals.

Jo was reclining on the chaise-longue in the drawing room with a volume of Jane Austen when a wail of despair sounded from upstairs. She threw the book aside and ran up to the bathroom.

Martha was clutching the rollers at the sides of her head. The four holding her back hair had already fallen into the bath, taking the hair with them, and as Jo watched the one remaining above her forehead slowly broke loose and fell to the floor. "It hurts!" she wailed, turning her head from side to side in agony, "it's burning all over my scalp."

"You've got to wash that stuff off right now." Calmly, Jo stepped over Martha's legs and turned on the taps in the washbasin. "Go on, put your head right in."

"But all my hair will come off!"

"All your hair's going to come off anyway, Martha. I think you just about napalmed it."

"But . . ."

"Stay cool, hang loose. There isn't a problem. You can wear a wig. Diana Ross wears wigs all the time."

Obediently Martha dunked her head in the water and

felt relief as the chemicals were washed away. "Thank God you were here, Jo. You're so calm."

"Not always, but right now, yes." Jo took a towel and carefully dried Martha's head. "Your scalp looks OK, I don't think it's going to blister or anything." Tiny circles of frazzled hair fell off at each touch. She made Martha soak her head again to get rid of them and then assessed the damage. All that remained of Martha's hair was a fine fluff like the down on a brown chick about half an inch in depth. "Don't look in the mirror until I've finished," she commanded, and rummaged in the cabinet on the wall for some scissors to trim it as much as she could to an even length all over.

"Well actually, I think that's an improvement," she said at last, stepping back to admire her work and let Martha see herself in the mirror. Martha immediately burst into tears and sat down on the edge of the bath again. "I think you look like an African princess. All you need now is some ear-rings."

Jo ran up to her own room and brought down a pair of big silver hoops threaded with a few semi-polished lumps of pink coral which she had bought in Marrakesh, and made Martha put them on.

"It's no good," she moaned in front of the mirror, "I can't see anything now I'm c-c-c-crying so much." She wiped the tears from her swollen eyes with a towel.

"I promise you, you look absolutely great," Jo said firmly. "You think it's a disaster but this was meant to happen. You'd never have had the courage to do this yourself but it looks amazing. Trust me. In the morning, you'll see I was right. Now come and have a large vodka."

The evening went from bad to worse. Victoria returned an hour later, to get ready to dine with Richard and her brother at a small and as yet little-frequented French restaurant Alex had discovered. She was always in a state of tension when she was going to meet Richard and the sight and smell of the bathroom infuriated her. "You might have cleaned the bath out—how could you use my towel?" she complained angrily, appalled at the alien mess.

"Martha had an accident, don't be angry, she's terribly upset . . ." Jo swept the rollers and the remains of Martha's hair into a waste basket and sluiced down the bath.

"Terribly drunk, you mean. And the smell in here. The trouble with you two is that you've both had maids to pick up after you all your lives and you haven't the faintest idea how to live with other people . . ."

Jo ignored her and ran downstairs and out of the back door to throw the reeking remains into the dustbin.

What Victoria said was true, but she saw no reason to make a fetish of domestic trivia. Neither she nor Martha could cook more than toast and coffee. Without the benefit of Victoria's boarding school lessons in washing, ironing and tidiness, Jo's room was a perpetual tangle of expensive clothes, sprinkled with a layer of Dior face powder, tinkling with odd ear-rings and lumpy with unpaired shoes. Like a Christmas pudding this fragrant jumble concealed coins and all manner of lucky charms, lipsticks, cassettes, items of underwear, a book of Byron's poetry lovingly inscribed by Daniel, a shark's tooth set in gold, a Polaroid camera and at the very bottom a photograph of her mother, father and sister in a tortoiseshell frame. Jo looked at this disorder as if it proliferated of its own will. Everything that was truly important, the key to her bicycle lock, the only jeans which had ever fitted her, her Sonia Rykiel sweater, the books she was studying, Daniel's new script, her Terry de Havilland shoes, and the handbag fashioned from seven exquisitely dyed colours of baby python skin by Nigel Preston, she used every day. The rest was irrelevant.

Martha could not achieve such fine careless disdain, and tried always to do what Victoria expected of her, but like Jo she had been brought up to consider the use of servants to be a crucial privilege which distinguished you from lesser folk, and so she often fell short of the English girl's ideals.

To compound the night's ill luck, Prince Richard arrived to collect Victoria when she was still in the bath. The vodka bottle was three-quarters empty. Jo answered the door.

"Listen," she whispered fiercely in the hallway. "Something terrible has happened. Upstairs is a woman we love who has just burned all her hair off and is totally freaked out. For Chrissake tell her she looks great or I'll . . ." she hiccuped, lost for inspiration.

He wanted to laugh but her ferocious expression forbade it. "OK, you don't need to tell me, I hate to think what you'd do. This is obviously a serious situation."

"It's a total catastrophe for her and you've *got* to make her feel OK about it—you know you can do that for her, don't you?"

"Yes, yes—lead on, then."

"And if you laugh I'll kill you."

"I won't laugh, I promise."

"Because actually it looks great but she's very straight and she doesn't think so."

"I understand."

"Good." Maybe he was not a total asshole after all.

Richard followed Jo up the stairs, preparing to play his part in this ridiculous feminine melodrama.

He had arrived early and unannounced precisely because he hoped to confront Jo and put away the unfinished business they had. It was nothing in reality, after all. It was obvious that the Hollywood brat counted her brush with royalty as insignificant; she had said nothing to Victoria about it. Maybe there was nothing to say. All the same, he wanted no shadow from the past in his new life. His love affair with Victoria was moving towards its inevitable conclusion.

Now Jo had swept everything aside and recruited him into a new conspiracy for two. He watched her walk up the narrow staircase ahead of him. Victoria had long straight legs and self-effacing hips. Jo did not. She seemed to be all curves and ellipses, articulated in a way that could not be ignored.

"Have you met Martha Harley?" With commanding grace, Jo presented the tall, tearful Jamaican who stood unsteadily in the middle of the worn red Afghan rug from Aston Langley, holding her bathrobe around her with an expression of total panic on her face. "Martha is at Girton with us, reading law. She won the Commonwealth scholarship from Jamaica. She is being photographed by *Vogue* this week and," another hiccup, "until an hour ago she had long black hair like Sophia Loren."

Richard took Martha's slender brown hand. "But you aren't really upset, are you?"

Martha gulped. The world was becoming extremely fuzzy at the edges and she did not believe that this was happening.

Richard looked her over carefully with sincere admiration. Victoria had presented both her flatmates to him before, briefly and formally. Martha was already a familiar sight to him as she was to the whole of Cambridge, with her elongated limbs and café-au-lait complexion. "I remember exactly what you looked like with long hair and this," he passed his hand over her head, brushing the traumatised tips, "looks fantastic. Magnificent. You look wonderful."

"R-r-r-really?" she stammered, finally reassured by this laying-on of hands.

"Really. You look absolutely stunning. You look like a Masai princess."

There was a silence. Martha's face suddenly went all ways at once and the three of them started to laugh. Jo sat down heavily on the club fender in front of the fire. Richard felt Martha sway, and chivalrously handed her to the chaise-longue.

"Truthfully, Martha . . ." he could not stop laughing, "even if it was an accident, you really look beautiful. How did it happen?"

Martha looked at him with huge, wondering eyes, her fingers shyly covering her mouth. With an effort she mastered the vodka and held back the giggles. "It was such a shock, it just all came away when I went to unpin it and now all my hair is out there in the dustbin and . . ."

Another gust of laughter swept through the three of them. Victoria appeared, pink and flustered in a grey angora dress.

"Why are you all laughing?" she demanded. Richard jumped up and went to her side immediately, throwing back the resigned grin of a man being tyrannised by a woman he otherwise loves.

A few minutes later he was handing Victoria into his car in the street outside, and looked up to see Jo at the window unsteadily waving her thanks.

Martha sat on the chaise, touching her head lightly all over with her delicate fingers. "Isn't he the sweetest man?" She smiled foolishly at Jo, then slowly swayed across the chaise and passed out.

Jo fetched Martha's quilt and tucked it around her, then went to bed herself. In the morning they asked each other what had happened, but neither had any clear recollection. To their immense surprise, Prince Richard telephoned to ask if Martha was all right and Victoria, by now restored to benevolent serenity, assured him that she was fine.

•   •   •

JIM KELLY SHOOK Martha's cool, narrow hand in his broad, hot paw and looked her over. "This is first time for virgins, isn't it?"

"Excuse me?"

"I mean, you've never done this before?"

"Oh no, never." Martha nervously flicked back the ends of the long, straight black wig which Jo had reluctantly taken her to Harrods to buy that morning. Jim Kelly had a round face with down-turned, deep-set eyes whose colour she could not make out. His russet hair was short, and the gold hairs on his forearms were exposed by the rolled-up sleeves of his denim shirt.

"Well, there's nothing to worry about," he told her flatly. "If those ugly old toerags can do it anybody can." He pointed at three models swathed in black jersey evening dresses by Karl Lagerfeld who stood in the centre of the studio and giggled. Martha thought they were the most beautiful women she had ever seen.

"What's your name, then?"

"Martha Harley. And this is Jocasta Forbes."

"OK, Harley, tell you what we'll do, you and your friend go and park your backsides over there while I get on with trying to make these bleeding gargoyles look like something and then you'll know the drill."

He directed Martha and Jo to a dais at the side of the studio and they sat obediently to watch.

It was late in the afternoon and the floor behind the photographer was littered with discarded film wrapping and overflowing ashtrays. Every face was taut with concentration.

The studio was a large, stuffy room whose six windows were covered with black blinds. From the ceiling at the far end hung rolls of coloured paper ten feet wide. The white paper was in use for this shot, pulled down to cover the wall and most of the floor; around the edges stood a forest of lights crowned with silver umbrellas. The margin of polished wooden floor, pockmarked from three decades of high heels, was covered with a tangle of power cables.

Auriol Meredith, who had introduced herself first before

presenting them to Jim Kelly, sat on a bentwood chair by the door, her small nose pointing like an eager dog's in the models' direction. Her severely bobbed black hair fell to her sharp jaw; scarlet lipstick gave her thin mouth the look of a crayon line in her pale face.

At the back of the studio the photographer's two assistants busied themselves loading magazines and polishing invisible specks of dust off the lenses that fitted into the foam recesses of two silver camera cases.

Kelly leaned over his Hasselblad, his shirt straining over his thick waist. "You, pigface," without looking up, he pointed at the haughty blond on the left, "get your arm down. Further. And stick your bum out. Not so much. Right. Pigface on the other side." The brunette smiled, stretching her perfectly glossed copper lips over her alabaster teeth. "Turn your shoulder more towards me. Bit more. Stop. You in the middle, gimme a bit more tit." The luscious creature tossed back her Titian mane and squeezed her elbows to her sides to push her vestigial breasts together. "More. Gimme more, you old bag of bones."

"That's it, Kelly, this is all I've got." She had a broad Australian accent.

"Two flea bites on an ironing board. Pathetic. Can't you get pregnant or something?"

The three of them shrieked with laughter. "For heaven's sake, Kelly, don't *encourage* her!"

He stepped back from the camera and gestured to a colourless young man with half-a-dozen make-up brushes in the back pocket of his jeans. "Do something, will you? And fix that ratbag's eyes, they look like two pissholes in the snow."

"Lovely turn of phrase," Jo whispered ironically in Martha's ear. The Jamaican did not realise it but her mouth had dropped open with amazement at the outrageous cabaret proceeding briskly before her wide eyes.

Expertly the make-up artist brushed contour powder over the Australian's shallow cleavage. The blonde turned her face to him like a flower seeking the sun and he deepened the rich purple shading in her eye sockets.

Kelly stepped back to the camera and the girls resumed their poses. "That's more like it. Pigface over there, your gut's hanging out. Lay off the pizza."

"You know I hate pizza, Kelly."

"I know you're a lying cow. You look like Moby bleedin' Dick. Suck it in, girl. Kill three and four." This was to an assistant, who crouched over a power unit and switched off two of the lights. "Gimme three again. Right. Polaroid." The other assistant stepped forward with the Polaroid camera and the shutter clicked. There was a release of tension while he waved the print in the air, waiting for the picture to develop, then peeled it apart and handed it to Kelly.

He looked at it, scratching his chin in thought. "OK, here we go." He leaned over the camera again and began to release the shutter, muttering a stream of instructions. "Keep that arm down, up a bit, pigface stay where you are, shoulders, *shoulders*, away from me now, pigface over there look up, *up* . . ."

The lights popped and flashed incessantly, then suddenly Kelly stood back and an assistant ran forward to change the film and he began again. "Turn right around now, watch that arm, gimme something a bit dykey now, not too much, heads closer in, closer, look back to me . . . lips, pigface, more lips, come on girl, get those cocksuckers working, that's better . . ." The girls moved around, varying their poses slightly as he directed.

In a quarter of an hour it was over. A girl brought Kelly coffee in a plastic cup, the assistants extracted the exposed films and labelled them.

" 'Bye Kelly," the models called out as they trooped toward the door.

"Ta-ra, you ratbags," he responded, lighting up a Camel.

"Hi, Kelly," called two more girls in Saint Laurent panne velvet, wine red and emerald green, who were immediately ushered in by a team of junior editors. Scrupulously they all wiped the dust off their feet on a small piece of paper beside the white background roll then tiptoed barefoot into position in front of the camera before putting on their shoes. The editors, on their knees, began pinning, tweaking, and taping the dresses to hang correctly for the next shot.

"Right, whatsyerface, Harley, now you know how it's done. You go off with Auriol here," the tiny woman in black stepped forward, "and I'll have you on next. And you can stuff your Inca look. Auriol, stick her in the riding gear we did this morning." He stubbed out his cigarette, slugged back the rest of the coffee and stepped forward to the camera. "Right, you ratbags, show me some shapes."

Auriol led them down the long corridor to a room almost filled with loaded dress rails. The red-haired Australian was there, picking at her nail varnish while a girl unpinned her dress.

"Welcome to the glamorous world of *Vogue*, kid. Not like you imagined, is it?"

"It certainly is not," Martha shook her head. She did not know what to think. "I don't know what I imagined, everyone just floating around being beautiful somehow."

"Well, nobody floats around here. They're out on their ass the minute their feet leave the ground. This place is a factory. A production line, you'll see. Kelly's one of the best. You don't mind the way he talks, do you?"

"Is he always as rude as that?"

"Most of the time he's a lot worse. It's just his manner. No one takes it seriously. It makes a nice change. Everyone else you'll ever meet in this business is all darling this and darling that and it doesn't mean shit. Kelly just gets on with it." The last pin was removed. She shrugged her lovely shoulders and several hundred pounds' worth of Lagerfeld fell to the floor, leaving her completely naked except for the thick layer of make-up which covered all the freckles above her tiny waist. "Don't worry kid, you'll be all right. Everyone was a beginner once. You're lucky, you're starting at the top."

"Let me try this against you," Auriol extracted a yellow checked blouse from the end of the rail and held it against Martha's face. "No, too much—where are the Burberry things we did this morning?"

"I think they're next door." The assistant picked up the black dress as the red-head stepped delicately aside.

With a click of annoyance, Auriol left the room and the redhead took Martha's arm. "Just stay on the right side of that one. A real Muffia godmother. If Kelly didn't have his eye on you she'd soon make you an offer you can't refuse."

"What do you mean?"

"The Muffia. The dykes who think they run the fashion business. They don't, but you want to keep on the right side of them. If they decide you're dead, you might as well start choosing the music for your funeral."

"Thanks," said Martha cheerfully, "I'll remember that."

She was beginning to enjoy herself. This whole business was like a ridiculous game of make-believe. And everyone took it so seriously.

Auriol darted back into the room like an angry hummingbird, a pile of country woman's clothes in her arms. She compared a tweed jacket to Martha's skin and gave another click of satisfaction. "Right, let's go to make-up."

Jo followed them, with the Australian who casually whirled a blue kimono around her nakedness as they walked. "Are you with an agency?" Jo asked.

"Uh-huh, Models One." The dark girl, in platform sandals, a pair of jeans and nothing else, walked across the corridor in front of them. "Is your friend signed up?"

"No, but I think she'd better be, don't you?" Auriol and Martha were now a few paces ahead of them.

"Too right. Isabelle's with Models One so they probably won't take her because there'll be such a fracas, she's so big-headed . . . I'd go to Marianne, the other girl's with them, she'll have a card." In front of the open door of another room the blond model sat in a ragged red G-string grimacing as she pulled off her false nails. "Sabine, do you have a Sed card for the agency number?"

The blonde reached into the pocket of a large carpet bag that gaped open by her feet and pulled out a card printed with three contrasting pictures of her, her measurements and the agency's details. "This for your friend? They'll just love her, they're always complaining there aren't enough really good black girls around. Say I sent you. They're bastards for paying, but then so's everybody."

In the room at the far end of the corridor the pallid young make-up artist had spread out his equipment.

Nakedness was obviously no big deal around this place, and so without being asked, Martha unbuttoned her Marks & Spencer shirtwaister, unhooked her new white Marks & Spencer brassiere, bought specially for the occasion, and sat down in front of the mirror in nothing but the matching broderie anglaise panties. She caught Jo's startled eye in the mirror and winked. She saw Auriol trying to pretend she was not looking at her. And this Jim Kelly was supposed to have his eye on her? Martha Harley, alias Sticks, the ugliest girl in school? This was all just too silly for words.

"Can we take off the wig? Are we using the wig?" The artist turned to Auriol.

"Let's see how she looks without it."

He removed the curtain of patent-black hair from Martha's head. Auriol nodded immediately. "Much better without."

"It's a nice wig, though, some of them are so kind of lifeless," he checked the label as he laid it aside then turned to her face in the mirror. A girl appeared with a set of false nails painted scarlet.

"Oh my, those eyes . . . you remind me of that story, the cat with the eyes like saucers . . ." The artist swept coffee-coloured foundation across her face and neck with a sponge.

"Where did you get that?" Martha turned the pot around to see the manufacturer's name.

"The theatrical cosmetic shop in Covent Garden. It's the only place you can get good make-up for black skin."

"We went to Harrods this morning and it was hopeless."

"Darling, don't tell me! It's a *nightmare*! Natural beige, rose beige, peach beige, coral beige, ivory beige—any colour you like as long as it's beige, am I right?" He fluffed a cloud of fragrant powder around her with a large soft brush.

"That's an artist's brush?"

"Badger hair, the best—it's so-o-o-o soft, doesn't it feel soft? You can get a really even effect with a soft brush. Your neck is so lovely, it just goes on forever . . . now let me see . . ." He hovered over the array of cosmetics laid out on the counter at his side. "I don't think the eyes need too much, do you?"

Auriol shook her head. "Kelly wants to do the new Saint Laurent colours on her afterwards."

"OK, we'll keep it simple—I just wish somebody would *tell* me. Just maybe a little slick of violet, I have the most *divi-i-i-ne* violet, Lancôme, it goes on so beautifully . . ."

From make-up they went to hairdressing, where an overweight blond woman spent half an hour spraying and fingering Martha's traumatised frizz until it relaxed contentedly against her scalp in tight, gleaming curls like the fleece of a pampered lamb.

In the next room Auriol helped her into jodhpurs, a silk shirt with a stock and a suede waistcoat. There was a spontaneous murmur of approval from the onlookers. The classic English clothes, interpreted by a French designer, fitted like a second skin. Against her darkness, their formality looked almost perverse.

"VKN, darling," the Australian girl informed her.

"VKN?"

"Visible Knicker Line. You'll have to take them off."

Martha hardly dared touch the glorious garments; by now she was far more concerned about damaging the clothes than her modesty. On the other hand, she did not want Auriol's assistance. She swiftly unzipped the trousers and dispensed with the last of her underwear.

"I see what you mean about the production line," she said to the Australian as they proceeded to the next room for shoes. "They'll never have my size, I have terrible trouble finding anything to fit me."

"Don't we all? It's because all the big sizes are up here at *Vogue* not down in the shops. If you're smart you'll ask if you can buy them afterwards, that way you get them half-wholesale. By the way, my name's Corinna. You're Harley, aren't you?"

"I suppose I am." With immense satisfaction, she stepped into a pair of exquisite chestnut kid boots with double straps around the ankles. They fitted perfectly. They made her feet look sexy, rich and elegant. They looked as if they had never tripped over, never felt a chilblain, never run around in the dust of poverty. If those feet belonged to someone called Harley, then that was who she was.

The next room was jewellery. Auriol picked out a stock pin and pearl ear-rings. Martha fixed the pin in the cascade of silk below her chin and everyone nodded approval.

"Right, monkeyface, up there and look mean." The studio had been changed. The background paper was now grey and covered the dais, which was in front of the camera. Martha wiped her feet on the paper, tiptoed forward and stood while Auriol arranged the silk into perfect folds. She brushed one of Martha's nipples with her fingertips as she did so. It could have been an accident.

Jim Kelly looked through his camera and fell in love. He did not see a woman. He saw shapes: planes, angles, contours, textures, shadows, all exciting. He saw chocolate skin, rich and smooth, gleaming over the high cheek bones, the firm swell of the muscles, the tapering legs, the fine wrists and ankles. He saw long bones, delicately articulated but strong as girders. He saw a small skull carried on a slender neck with the steely grace of a woman bred to carry heavy loads on her head. He saw a mouth like a hibiscus flower, a tiny chin, ears like little shells from a coral beach, eyes full of innocent animality. He saw all this without analysing it or even putting it into words and as he adored it he worked.

"Turn your hips towards me, not so much, good, now look up, stick that arm up . . . put something on her cheeks, can you?" The make-up artist scurried forward and swept some pearly powder across her face. She giggled as the brush tickled. "Don't laugh, monkeyface, this is haute couture, this is serious business."

She cracked up. The silk shivered in its folds.

"I said, don't laugh." His voice was not angry but it silenced her. "Right. Polaroid."

A quarter of an hour later she was back in the make-up room where the artist blended rays of pink, bronze and violet across her eyelids, murmuring admiration for the arch of her brows and the perfection of her skin. She went into the studio wearing heavy gold hoop ear-rings and Corinna's kimono.

"I need the shoulders," Kelly said and Martha, now perfectly comfortable in her new, uninhibited personality, was about to drop the garment carelessly to her waist when she caught Jo's eye and saw her friend violently shake her head. She pulled the kimono down to expose the upper part of her chest.

"More, gimme more," Kelly never raised his eyes from the camera. Now Martha felt uncomfortable.

"This is it," she told him, remembering the drill. "This is as far as I go."

"That's as far as she goes," Kelly repeated, standing back with a feral grin. "Right. Polaroid."

It seemed very late when he walked Jo and Martha down Bond Street towards Langan's Brasserie. " 'Ullo, Andy," he greeted the handsome manager. "This is Andy," he introduced them, "he'll give us some horrible table by the kitchen door."

"Michael's here tonight," Andy pointed discreetly to the large table near the entrance where Michael Caine was sitting with a fat, noisy man in a white suit whose fist was clamped around a bottle of Krug.

"Nah, I'll say hello, but I don't want to do the business with Langan tonight. Looks like he's rat-arsed as usual." Kelly wanted to impress the girls but not to overawe them, nor to expose his precious new find to the Irish restaurateur's notorious drunken caprices. There were always famous faces in the bright cavernous bustle of the brasserie, but the place was also big enough for two people to have a private conversation in comfort.

Caine noticed Kelly and amiably waved his cigar in greeting. The photographer called, "Cheers, Mike, good to see yer," but made no move towards the top table. Peter Langan fixed the women with his glassy, drunken eyes.

"Why, it's little Jocasta, isn't it? You have grown up, haven't you?" The brown-bear voice behind her was unmistakable.

"Hello, Uncle Jimmy." Jo turned around and stood on tiptoe to swap kisses with James Stewart. "What brings you to London?"

"I'm talking about a play, dear. This is the only place for the theatre, you know, the real theatre . . ."

While they talked waiters scurried to re-lay the table that the great star had just vacated and in a few moments the three of them were seated. Both women noticed that the edge of Kelly's aggression was blunted now that he realised that Jo was some species of celebrity.

"I knew I knew you," he said to her, extracting the Camels from the pocket of his blue-jean jacket. "Who are you?"

"My mother is Lorna Lewis."

"You nearly said 'was,' didn't you?" Jo blushed, a rare occurrence. "I've photographed her, I remember. Not too raddled for her age. Maybe I'll do some snaps of you one day if you're around."

"I'll hold you to that." The waiter poured champagne into tall flute glasses and she sipped it with caution. Martha tipped the contents of her glass down her throat; she was thirsty.

"You will, and all. I can tell. Right, what are we eating? Forget the menu, it's all in French. What's good tonight?" This was to the waiter who stood patiently beside him and began a rapid recitation of dishes. "Do you like sausages?"

Kelly demanded of Martha. She nodded. "What about quail's eggs?"

"I've never had quail's eggs, what are they like?"

"Small. Forget quail's eggs. You're hungry. I know you birds with ribs like park railings, you all eat like pigs." He finished ordering for them all with the same practical rapidity that he had taken sixteen photographs that afternoon.

"Have you got a boyfriend?" he asked Martha after she had disposed of a spinach soufflé with butter sauce followed by two fat *saucisses Andalouses* on a bed of green lentils with potatoes and onions, and was about to embark on a large slice of *tarte tatin* which glistened with caramel and swam in cream.

"It's none of your business," she told him as haughtily as a woman can with her mouth full. The second bottle of champagne was almost empty and Jo had drunk little. In a few hours Martha seemed to have flipped into a new dimension. The anxious Third World scholarship student was unrecognisable in this sassy creature who sat with perfect equanimity in a slip of borrowed red Halston, surrounded by shiny 22-carat celebrities, eating fine food, drinking good wine and holding the greatest fashion photographer in the world at arm's length.

"It soon will be my business." Kelly swirled his Armagnac around the glass and gulped it down, looking defiance at Martha. "My advice is to get rid of him. You're a woman who needs to be treated right."

"And you're telling me you know how to do that?"

"I've treated you right so far, haven't I?"

"How should I know? That was first time for virgins." Martha looked coquettishly away and Jo decided to sit back and fade out of the conversation; whatever instincts had been liberated in Martha that day were not leading her into danger.

"What about this Isabelle woman, isn't she your girlfriend?"

"She's gone," he admitted frankly. "We'd got to the end of the old frog and toad anyway."

"The end of what?"

"Frog and toad. Road. That's rhyming slang. Like whistle and flute, suit. Or jam-jar, car. They don't talk like that where you come from?"

"No, man, in Jamaica everyone talkin' nice-nice, slow-slow, like de reggae music, man, you know?" The accent was outrageously broad; Martha was surprised she could remember how to speak that way after months in Cambridge.

"Oh yeah, I know. So that's where you're from. Bob Marley, 'No Woman No Cry.' We'll put that on in the studio next time you're in." Jim Kelly had been born in an affluent but unfashionable portion of the London conurbation called Pinner, miles away from the Cockney homeland in Bow. He talked like a Cockney only because, since *Vogue* had taken on David Bailey, Terence Donovan and Brian Duffy in the Sixties, it had become the London photographers' dialect.

There was a commotion at the far end of the noisy, crowded room and one of the assistants appeared, weaving between the diners towards them with a folder under his arm. Kelly motioned to the waiter to clear the table and opened the folder. It contained dozens of black and white pictures of Martha in the riding outfit, contact sheets and prints which were still damp from the laboratory.

Kelly spread the prints out and considered them, frowning.

"Oh, let me see!" Eagerly, Martha jumped up and leaned over him, draping her bare arms across his broad shoulders. "Oh, they're fabulous! Just divine! Aren't they, Jo?" She had even the fashion vocabulary, Jo noted. And there was no doubt about it, the pictures were stunning.

"Well," Kelly pulled on his Camel and swallowed the smoke, hiding his exultation, "I've seen worse, I must say." Other people gathered around, mostly Kelly's acquaintances. Sean Murray, a new gossip writer with the *Daily Post*, was pulled into the group by the coked-up debutante he was dining. With a squeak and a clatter and a jangle of her outrageous necklace hung with silver lockets, Corinna the Australian pushed her way to the front and began exclaiming over the pictures. "Which one are you going to have for your card?" she asked Martha and then, without waiting for a reply, picked out the most dramatic pose. "This one! She can have this one, can't she, Kelly?"

"You catch on quick, don't you?" The photographer resignedly put the print in Martha's hand, then added two more. "Who are you signing up with?"

"Marianne," Jo supplied the name and Martha, who had no idea what the conversation was about, smiled acquiescence.

Kelly scrawled his name on the bill and stood up. The group of onlookers dispersed. Sean Murray hastily made his way to the telephone in the coat room. "I suppose I'll have to call them if I want to get you in again. In about a month's time. Maybe before, if you can get away."

"I'll see what I can manage." Martha dipped gracefully to let the waiter help her into Jo's old black redingote, which skimmed her knees although it had been calf-length on the original owner.

Outside the restaurant a flash popped in their eyes. Langan's was always haunted by paparazzi. The two women settled composedly back into a taxi which drove off towards Kensington where Jo's mentor the playwright had placed his London flat at their disposal.

Martha sat back in the corner of the cab and squealed with laughter. "It is too much, Jo! It's all too much! I walk into that place like I did and I walk out like that! Like this!" She pulled apart the coat and looked incredulously at the dress, the shoes and the beautiful, glamorous creature into which she had changed. "I mean, it's past midnight and the dress hasn't turned into rags yet."

"But Martha, you were acting like you'd been modelling all your life! What in the world happened to you?"

"I don't know—something just snapped in my head and it was all so easy, just a game, a kid's game played by great big children. It was all so different, and that girl—Corinna —was so kind, and everyone just assumed I was Kelly's new discovery and so I thought why not? You were watching— you tell *me* what happened."

"I don't know what happened. You just knew how to do it all, like ducklings know how to swim."

"I was so tired," she said, "I think I got drunk on it all, like you can get drunk on almost nothing when you're exhausted." The illuminated façade of Buckingham Palace whirled past outside the window. "Which room do you suppose is Richard's? I can't believe I've really met him, you know. Or all those people in the restaurant tonight. This is all a dream."

"Do you want to go through with it? Do you sincerely

want to be a model, Martha? Because it's not just for to-night, it's all there if you want it."

"You're such a good friend, Jo. You've always known the drill, haven't you? I couldn't have done this without you here, I just knew I was safe if you were around."

"But I can't always be around—Kelly wants you, he wants you badly. He can make it happen. It's all yours for the taking, Martha, if you want him."

"Well, darling," the champagne finally hit her and she leaned her face against the window, rubbing her forehead against the soothing cool glass. "All I can say is, it sure beats working."

The next day they arrived at the tiny offices of Mari-anne's agency. "Jim Kelly has already called us for you," Marianne herself informed them. She was a taller clone of Auriol Meredith, same bob, same lipstick, same Sonia Rykiel black knitted dress with a spotted bow at the neck, same high-heeled black laced brogues. The receptionist, the accounts clerk and the two other bookers in the room were all wriggling in their chairs with excitement. Getting Jim Kelly's new girl meant a lot. In the restless, fickle world of fashion it meant that Marianne's would automatically become the top agency in town.

"Kelly says since *Vogue* are using the pictures he'll pay you for doing the test yesterday, and he thought you might like some of the money in advance. To go shopping. He said you'd just arrived in London or something."

"Well, yes," Martha admitted, "I suppose I have."

She left with an invoice book and instructions to collect her card the following week. Jo inquired what Martha's daily rate would be, and Marianne pursed her thin scarlet lips and quoted a figure. Martha calculated that a week's work would be equivalent to her scholarship grant for a whole year. For that she had worked like a dog since child-hood. For this she had done nothing. It was absurd, impos-sible. All she could do was laugh.

She returned to Cambridge with a Vuitton grip crammed with new clothes. Her mind, miraculously refreshed by the adventure, ate up the work that awaited her with its old energy and a new confidence.

"Good heavens—you're in the papers," Victoria ex-claimed, her breakfast toast dribbling marmalade over the *Daily Post.* "What on earth were you doing at Langan's?" It was a place Victoria would have dearly loved to visit with Richard, but he avoided it because of the photographers.

"Having dinner," Jo replied shortly.

"A picture of us—how amazing, let me see!" Martha looked over Victoria's shoulder. The picture showed her leaving the restaurant with Jo and Kelly " 'Dusky beauty!' Too much! 'Legendary lensman's exotic companion . . . !' Oh wow! 'And meanwhile in New York Kelly's former love Isabelle Latouche is consoling herself with ageing rocker Ron Rivetts.' So he *was* telling the truth about her . . ."

"You can't believe that stuff," Jo instructed her immediately. "Never believe anything in the papers. Reality is anything you can hit with a hammer, remember?"

"I mean, look at all the nonsense they're always writing about Richard," Victoria dusted the toastcrumbs disdainfully from her fingers as if each one were a newspaper lie.

"I thought they were leaving you alone more now?" Martha gave the newspaper back to the English girl.

"Yes, they are, thank goodness." Victoria pulled the tortoiseshell comb out of her hair and swept it back into place again, bending down to look in the long Empire mirror in the corridor. "Well, off to the library . . ."

A week later Martha was back at *Vogue*, whirling across the studio in yards of embroidered ice-pink chiffon by Zandra Rhodes in the company of two other models.

Kelly watched her move, fascinated by the precise way she placed each narrow, pink-soled foot on the floor. She had changed in seven days. Her face was even more luminous, her eyes wider, the shadows of fear no longer lurking in their depths. The Garden-of-Eden innocence was gone with the Marks & Spencer dress.

He booked her twice more at *Vogue*, but each time Martha felt she had known him all her life. "You must be bored to tears with this crap," he announced. "Come to my house at the weekend and let me do real pictures for a change."

Kelly's house was squeezed between two grander dwellings in a steep street in Hampstead. Every possible piece of furniture was covered in Afghan rugs, madder red, dark brown and indigo. There were low sofas and floor cushions, plantation blinds permanently closed across the windows and oriental brass pots containing plants that needed more light. The effect was lavish and dark but, when she looked closely, it was not very thoroughly dusted.

His housekeeper, a Philippino with long hair braided into a pigtail, was directed to take Kelly's pair of greyhounds out for a run on Hampstead Heath. Kelly made tea and brought it into the first-floor sitting room. The studio was on the floor below.

"You know your trouble, monkeyface," he handed her the tea in a wide French café cup. "Your trouble is, you don't know what it's all about. When you do, you'll be all right." He said this with absolute authority, but did not believe it. Sexual initiation was not going to change her as far as the camera was concerned; in fact, it might take away that wild-animal look of openness in her eyes. He had a feeling that this one was going to be like Goya's naked *maja*, physically available but locked up inside.

"No," she agreed, kicking off her shoes, "I don't know what it's all about. I suppose now you think you're going to show me." She felt totally comfortable with this man. He was in control, he knew what he was doing. He was even sexy, in his tousled, workmanlike way.

"Well then, don't hang about, take your clothes off."

By now well accustomed to nakedness, she swiftly unbuttoned her skirt and jacket of shining black leather, pulled off her tights and her white cowl-necked cashmere sweater, and threw her clothes in a heap at the side of the room. He took off his own clothes without haste.

"Now lie down and let me look at you."

He spent a long time looking at her naked body, as if trying to imprint every detail of it in his mind before he changed its status forever. Her long, thin upper thigh lay casually forward over the lower one, casting a deep shadow over her flat belly and the secrets beneath.

After a while he moved over and began to kiss and caress her very gently. She liked the feel of warm hands but his touch was so light it was almost irritating.

He parted her thighs and she felt his fingers separate her lower lips, but there was very little sensation. Patiently he teased the reluctant flesh and in time there was something, a gentle, delicious thrill seeping slowly upwards. He pushed a finger inside her with the surprising delicacy his big hands showed when handling film, and drew more sensations from her, but as the thrill grew her confidence ebbed. She lay tensely in his arms, afraid.

"This is not going to be easy," he told her, holding her firmly. "I can get you drunk, I can get you stoned, or we can carry on regardless and put it all down to experience."

"Is it going to hurt?"

"Maybe. You're very tense. I can't get two fingers into you, and there's more than that to give you." He pulled her hand down to let her feel.

"Well, you're the gaffer, Kelly, you're the one who knows the score, whatever you think . . ."

"I'm not the gaffer now, darlin'. Not when I'm with you." She looked at him wonderingly and understood something Jo had seen immediately, the fear that beautiful women inspire in the men who make their living from them. Now she understood the insults, the nicknames and aggressive, no-bullshit manner. He needed her, he needed all of them.

He fetched a bottle of champagne and two glasses and made her drink one while he cupped her tiny breasts and licked the hard nipples. She was still frozen with apprehension. He poured a second glass for her and kissed her neck and shoulders, feeling the tension ebb a little.

Suddenly he pulled her back on the cushions with a growl, poured a lake of the sparkling golden liquid into her navel and began to lick it up.

"Stop it, you're *tickling*, Kelly, stop it, I can't bear it," she was giggling and pushing him away but he persisted to the last drop, kissing and licking the sensitive skin until she was weak from protesting. Then quickly he pushed himself inside her before she could stop laughing, feeling the heave of her diaphragm in her narrow body like the distant beating of butterfly wings. There was a little pain, which made her catch her breath, but he kept moving and she began to feel warmth, if not exactly pleasure.

Then she got hiccups, which made him laugh, and he finished quickly while he still could.

"That wasn't too bad, was it?" he asked as soon as he dared.

She shook her head and smiled at him sorrowfully. He held her close and kissed her forehead. The long, tender homage he had planned to pay this glorious body would have to wait.

CHAPTER XII

IN HIS SECOND year at Cambridge, Richard decided to study with a tutor from another college. Quentin Boyd taught a history course which all his students found inspiring. He was, however, a man who had little understanding of emotions, particularly his own.

He was blind to the fact that he disliked his royal pupil, and completely unaware of the primitive reasons. Quentin Boyd was far too high minded to consider himself capable of being jealous of such petty good fortunes as youth, good looks, wealth, winning social ease and unequivocal heterosexuality frequently indulged. After teaching the Prince for a few months, Boyd found that his pupil also had a good mind to add to his physical blessings, a discovery which had wounded him more severely than any of the many injustices of an academic's career.

In consequence of this dislike, Quentin Boyd outwardly praised all his pupil's attributes and drove the young man pitilessly in the name of duty. He pressed him remorselessly with the multiple questions for which he was famous, seeking the weak spots in his intellectual functioning. He loaded him with work. Having found the areas of study for which the Prince had the least taste, he directed him towards them without hesitation.

Hour after hour, Boyd leaned his lined, greyish cheek against the wing of his chair, looking down at the swell of his belly as if seeking inspiration from the buttons of his old green cardigan, chain-smoking, unsmiling, launching across the unswept fireplace a stream of questions designed to pierce the Prince's mental armour. Richard invariably left Quentin's tutorials feeling humiliated.

He read and wrote in a fury of frustration, determined that his next essay would not be deluged with contempt in the same way as his last. The irony of their relationship was that Richard worshipped his tutor.

"He is a brilliant man, brilliant," Richard informed Victoria with solemnity. "God, the bastard makes me work, though. He won't let me get away with anything—lazy thinking, secondhand ideas . . . he just keeps on pushing until I come up with the goods. I am so lucky he's teaching me."

Victoria could not share his enthusiasm. Their relationship was a year old and seemed to her to be cooling. Richard was as ardent as ever when he was with her, but the intervals between their times together stretched from days to weeks as he pleaded essays, or piles of reading, or the necessity of a trip to Windsor to raid the library there for a book he was sure Boyd did not expect him to have read.

When official engagements or family business took him away, all that reached her were his morning telephone calls, often strained and hurried, and the pictures, inevitably of Richard surrounded by beautiful women. She could accept the laughing girls in crowds trying to kiss him, but the women who were their friends or acquaintances, who were always captured with lowered eyes guiltily trying to dodge the camera, were harder to ignore. She felt she would be lowering herself if she quizzed him about Lady Katriona, or Lady Annabel, or the Hon. Miranda, or Suzy or Jane or Caroline, so she said nothing. Victoria told herself that these women were just Richard's friends, formal partners invited for the occasion, that there were too many of them to be significant, but she could not heed her own good sense and felt less and less secure.

She had no one with whom to share her misgivings, and no position from which to negotiate for more of his company. "You don't mind do you, Tory darling?" he would enquire if he postponed a date, with a momentary flash of that look which sank into her heart, and she would acquiesce uneasily. Sometimes he withdrew from arrangements they had made together at the last moment and she would have to set off for a country weekend with their friends by herself, feeling lonely and abandoned. Without Richard she felt fragile, as if she were made of glass. The suspicion that he was being unfaithful possessed her mind completely.

She probed the conversation and analysed her friends' behaviour towards her, searching miserably for clues to her lover's disaffection, and often found the tell-tale signs she was seeking because, without the star attraction of her better half, she was a distinctly less welcome guest. "Of course we'd *love* to have you on your own," her hosts assured her, but in this Noah's Ark world all animals went in to dinner two by two, and there was always a frantic scramble to find a new partner for her, ensuring that she arrived to be greeted awkwardly with masked resentment.

An intellectual fascination was something she could not understand. She found her own work agreeable and took pride in doing it adequately, but the passion with which Richard was now pursuing his studies was beyond her comprehension. His love for her was the most important thing in her life, and now she felt that his neglect must be her fault.

Victoria looked around at the other women who had been in Richard's company. For the first time she regarded Jo with suspicion, and wondered why men found her so sexy, and what she did in bed with the beautiful Daniel, whom Victoria had dismissed as pushy and rather odd.

She remembered all the criticisms she had received in her life, and decided she was not thin enough, not erotic enough, not smart enough, not witty or modern or switched-on enough to hold Richard's interest. As if the magic qualities could rub off by closer association, she courted the affection of Jo and Martha again, but as she could not confide the source of her insecurity the renewed friendships struggled to bloom. With Jo, she went on the Beverly Hills diet, and filled the refrigerator with pineapple and papaya, which Martha said tasted so different in the miserable Cambridge climate that they were not worth eating. Alone, Victoria made trips to London to buy new, more daring clothes and lunch with her London friends, assiduously trawling gossip both to entertain Richard and discover if he was known to have seen another woman.

Richard sensed her uncertainty but did not feel the pain it caused her. "You are my whole life, Tory," he told her, again and again after making love, "you're the sun in the sky and the air that I breathe. Don't ever let me lose you,

Tory. Promise me you'll never leave me." He held her closely to him, feeling her heart still surging from her climax, infuriated by her cast-down eyes and melancholy expression.

"I promise," she whispered. "Of course I'll never leave you—how could you think such a thing?" And all the time she wondered if his sudden possessiveness betrayed his own intention of leaving. The certainty of their early days had gone. Their love had become a dark field in which they both blundered into obstructions they could not see.

Even in her company, Richard lived more and more in his new interior world, entranced by its glittering attractions. His latest project for earning Boyd's approval was always in the front of his mind, but it was an impossible task. Faint praise was the best he ever won, and it was followed with an elegant excursion to discover what Boyd clearly saw as the pitiful limitations of his thinking.

"An *interesting* essay, quite well expressed, but I wonder what exactly you were getting at when you bring in Montesquieu's remarks about the place of commerce in England in the eighteenth century?" Boyd taught a course which examined the colonial achievements of Europe in the eighteenth and nineteenth centuries. As Richard was excited by the grand interplay of nations, and bored by social history in general, his tutor had asked him for an essay contrasting the supposed national characteristics of the colonial powers.

"I think Montesquieu argued that the monarchy in France had barred the nobility from commerce, whereas in England the nobility were free to do business and so to plough the wealth they had originally derived from the land into enterprises in the Empire," Richard's reply was fluent. He was determined this time not to be cowed by his tutor's superiority.

"And Montesquieu was writing when?"

"1769."

"Yes, and he concluded, did he not, that the power of the monarchy in Britain was weakened as a consequence? History has proved him wrong. I can see that this passage had a certain resonance for you."

"But his argument was about the English character though . . ."

"You need to learn not to indulge your subjective tendencies quite so extensively, Richard. I find your essays are always composed with a lack of balance and perspective . . ."

This was true. In another student Boyd might have praised the originality.

As the academic year drew to its end the bright fragments of his ideas fell for the first time into a pattern as if someone had placed them behind a kaleidoscope lens. He emerged from months of intensive study of his country's past with a radiant, inspiring sense of what it was to be English. Generations had toiled under the vile climate of this tiny scrap of land to create a prosperous and well-ordered society in which each man considered himself to be a monarch. These hardy, adventurous individuals had issued forth to conquer the world. He saw the English as a uniquely free and self-reliant tribe, who may not, understandably, have ascribed the same need for liberty to their subject races in the early days of colonialism but who eventually propagated their ideals of individual self-determination across the globe.

He also began to formulate an analysis of his own family's part in the development of the nation, a role characterised by humanitarian reason and restraint rather than the greedy addiction to hierarchy displayed by foreign tyrants. "Well, at least they've taught you to think," his mother approved, with the implication that what he thought was another matter; but although she smiled with undisguised condescension when he tried to explain his ideas to her, he knew she was pleased with him for attempting to rationalise his world.

Victoria noted the new elation of his mood and, knowing that she had not inspired it, was now certain that another woman had. She arrived at Balmoral in August feeling sure her invitation was only a matter of polite form and that it was the last time she would be there as Richard's companion.

She flew to Aberdeen in a small shuttle plane full of men going to work on the oil exploration rigs in the North Sea. They were mostly very drunk and the flight was turbulent. She approached the Range-Rover that waited for her at the airport with shaky legs and the smell of vomit still in her nostrils, and almost fell into his arms in shock when he appeared beside the vehicle.

Her fragility, her trembling hands and the pallor under her summer tan, moved him at once. He was full of concern, and insisted that they drive a few miles down the coast road and stop to let her take in the cold, clean sea air. She stood on the pebble beach beside him feeling foolish and breathing deeply at his command.

"I have missed you so much, you can't imagine how much," he said, taking hold of both her hands. "I don't ever want us to be apart for a long time again."

"You always say things like that," she protested, made irritable by the journey.

"Only because they're true. Don't you want me to say that I need you, Tory?"

"Oh, don't be silly." She smiled crookedly, ready to weep with relief. A tear glistened in the long lashes at the corner of her seaward eye, and he brushed it away with a fingertip. "It's the wind making my eyes water."

From that moment the clouds seemed to lift from their love and they understood each other again. Richard scarcely left Victoria's side and every day found a new excuse to keep her to himself away from the rest of the party; he came to her room every night, returning to his own in the mornings far too late to avoid running the gauntlet of discreet cleaners and maids in the corridors. Victoria recovered all her former serenity; her complexion bloomed and her shoulders resumed their proud carriage.

Their companions remarked these events warmly. The couple were the very picture of young love and since the family, their staff and most of their guests had known both Richard and Victoria since childhood their affair had a general blessing. Knowing glances were exchanged around the table at dinner whenever Richard laughed loudly at something Victoria said, or when the company rose and the lovers, caught unawares, were the last to stand, delayed by their affectionately tangled feet.

The family and their guests attended the morning service at Crathie Church on Sunday as had been the custom for a century. The cars of local sightseers crowded the roadside, and by previous agreement a small group of photographers was permitted to wait at the foot of the steep path to the church. Keith Cowley had finagled a place among them. By now he knew Victoria's face rather better than that of his own girlfriend; she looked, he thought, better than she had for ages; she had, he thought, the self-satisfied look of a chick who was getting fucked flat every night. She had not looked like that for some time.

Cowley declined his editor's orders to return south to Sunderland to photograph a mass demonstration by unemployed former shipyard workers and stayed on in a pompous Victorian hotel up the valley in Braemar.

Victoria had been invited for a week, but Richard cajoled his mother into agreeing that she might stay for a fortnight. His mother looked anxious, but then, he told himself, she often did.

After lunch on Sunday, the rest of the guests departed and a temporary peace settled on the castle, animated by the distant bustle of rooms being prepared for the new visitors.

"Let's go out for tea," Richard proposed, and they set off into the heart of the estate in an open-topped Land-Rover. There was no need for close security here. Unseen in the distant hills overlooking the estate half a dozen men tramped through the heather, enjoying the pure air and the mellow afternoon heat. Accompanied by dogs and occasionally scanning the landscape with field glasses, they blended unobtrusively into their surroundings. Two of them flushed Keith Cowley out of the woodland overlooking the castle, and conducted him back to his car.

"I can't believe this weather," Victoria shook her hair in the wind as the vehicle bumped off the sandy track and halted in the sparse shade of a group of pine trees. "If only it was like this every year. No one will ever forget this summer, will they? It's been like the Mediterranean."

"I'll never forget this summer," he said, helping her down from the Land-Rover and stealing a kiss as he did so. "But not because of the weather."

A rosy blush spread under her tan and he held her tightly in his arms for a few moments, wanting to make love to her immediately on the fine green grass under the trees. An instinct warned him to be sure of privacy, now at this moment more than any other, and he set her slowly down.

"You're so strong," she murmured, marvelling as always at the power in his slim arms. Through the rolled-up sleeves of his checked cotton shirt she saw the sinews flicker. He had more strength than much bigger men. He had picked her up as if she weighed nothing.

They pulled off their shoes and sat on the bank of the stream with their feet in the icy water. The rest of Britain roasted contentedly in drought. Streams had dried up, the fields were parched and golden, and farmers, their harvests already prudently gathered, worried about fires and delayed burning the stubble. On Deeside, however, the cool streams still ran swiftly down from the mountains and the fine grass grew lusher and greener than ever before in living memory.

He had taken her to a tiny cottage of grey stone built in the crook of a clear stream that meandered over the floor of the valley. A glade of pines surrounded it. Victoria and Albert had chosen the site for its natural romanticism. No other person or habitation could be seen in the wild hillside that stretched beyond the small wooden bridge to the horizon, and there was no sound other than the chuckle of the water and the clatter of a single disturbed capercaillie on the far bank.

They watched the ungainly black bird flying low over the heather.

"I think it's unfair to shoot them, they get up in the air so slowly." Victoria lay back on her elbows, admiring her long, lightly tanned legs below her spotless white shorts and splashing her toes idly in the water. She wore a thin navy blue cotton sweater with cap sleeves and looked, he thought, like an absurdly feminine parody of a matelot.

"There's no fun in capercaillie. Not much in grouse, either," Richard agreed, throwing a pebble of pink granite into a tiny pool downstream. He was seething with impatience to get on with his plan for the hour.

"Fun," she teased him, "I can't see the fun in killing poor silly defenceless birds that can't look after themselves."

"Do you mean you want me to give up shooting when we're married?" He held his breath, waiting for her reaction.

"Yes. And that ridiculous James Bond car, and drinking whisky, and riding in point-to-points, and climbing silly mountains and you can forget about learning to fly helicopters, too. And any combination of the foregoing. I want to know that my husband is going to come home every night, not have to pace up and down worrying about whether he's killed himself."

"Why do I have to give up whisky?" Did she realise that this was serious? He leaned back beside her and turned her face towards him.

"Because it tastes revolting when you kiss me."

"Well, I suppose that's a good enough reason. And how many children are we having?"

"Well . . ." thoughtfully she pulled up a handful of grass and let the fresh-smelling blades fall through her fingers. "Not lots, because I want to be with you all the time not messing around having babies. Maybe two. Or three. Three, let's say."

"OK, but they've got to look like you."

"No, they've got to look like *you.*"

"But I want them all to be tall like you."

"All right, tall like me but otherwise to look like you."

"Great. Is it a deal, then?"

"What do you mean, is it a deal? Dreadful American expression. Is what a deal?" She was giggling and tugging at the grass, half-hoping he was not serious and half-hoping that he was. She had squashed her fantasies of marriage. The concept raised too much anxiety and it seemed disloyal even to picture in her mind's eye marrying into the Royal Family.

"I mean, we *are* getting married, aren't we?"

"No, we're lying on the grass talking about it."

"Please, Tory, I'm not kidding. Please say you'll marry me, please." It seemed to him suddenly an awful thing to ask, a life sentence of duty and restraint, the last thing any normal woman would agree to do, the last thing he ought to ask of this beautiful gentle creature who was so much less robust than she appeared.

"I . . ." she swallowed, her throat tight with emotion.

"I haven't talked to anyone about this. Please, Tory. I can't imagine living without you." He put his brown hand over hers, willing her consent.

"But what about . . ."

"I only want to know about you, Tory. Do *you* want to marry me?"

She lifted up her head at once and answered simply, "Yes. I want to marry you more than anything in the world."

"Then we are getting married."

Animated by the thrill of triumph, he jumped up and pulled her to her feet for a long, formal kiss to seal the pledge. Apprehension shivered in her lips. "Don't worry, darling. As long as we've got each other, as long as we can be together, everything will be all right. And if ever it isn't, I'll make it all right, I promise."

"Are you sure, Richard?" The enormity of what she had agreed to was slowly coming into focus.

"I'm sure that I want to spend the rest of my life with you, Tory. I've never been more sure of anything in the world."

Invisible in the brilliant sky above them, a skylark tipped its song over their heads like a blessing. Victoria sighed, and sighed again, suddenly breathless. Happiness and fear were struggling for dominion inside her.

"Won't they say we're too young?"

"Yes, of course they will, but I'm three years older than my father was when he made up his mind, so my parents can't very well make a fuss. Anyway, they love you, Tory, everyone loves you. I know they'll be delighted." He began to walk her slowly up to the cottage. "I'm so happy, Tory. Everything's going to be wonderful from here on, I just know it. Come on—let's see what there is for tea."

He opened the low door into the cottage and she gasped as she saw the tiny room crowded with huge gaudy summer flowers. The staff, obeying his impatient instructions to "just fill the whole room," had pillaged the gardens for lurid dahlias, gladioli, and delphiniums. The close air was full of the delicate scent of sweet peas.

The next instant he swept her into his arms and carried her over the threshold. "Just practising," he set her down again, his hands lingering over the softness of her breasts beneath the supple knitted cotton. "Let's hope the champagne's still cold."

In the centre of the white tablecloth the ice bucket was dripping with condensation. Inexpertly he popped the cork, splashed the chilled wine into the pair of crystal glasses which he had specified, passed one to her and linked his arm through hers for a lovers' toast. "To us, and our future, darling."

She finally looked at him with her solemn grey eyes. Holding her gaze, he kicked shut the door and spread an old plaid rug on the floor. In the dimmed light she thought he looked almost menacing as he returned to her and began to kiss her, pulling the thin sweater over her breasts and dragging her towards the floor. He was careless and urgent, driven by the fear that she would slip away into doubt unless he overwhelmed her with sensations.

Afterwards he was tender, then suddenly hungry. All the requisites of a Scottish tea were arrayed on the table and only slightly splashed with champagne. He carved chunks of fruit cake and they ate it with some small strawberries which had unusually been added to the spread.

"Do you realise we've been engaged before? Open your mouth." He pushed one of the tiny, gritty fruits between her lips.

"What on earth do you mean?"

"Someone told me." He took a strawberry himself. There was one left. "Apparently we got engaged here when we were tiny tots."

"I don't remember anything about it."

"I do, just. I remember thinking you were the most wonderful girl I'd ever seen. You were absolutely blond and you had a blue dress. Here, we're sharing the last one." He held the last strawberry between his teeth and gestured to her to come and take her share of it. Laughing at last she leaned avidly on his chest and tried to bite. His lips closed over hers and her breasts fell into his hands. "Why did you go and get dressed? Now I've got to take everything off again."

They were late for dinner, which surprised no one. Very pink, embarrassed and delightful, Victoria slipped last into the room with her hair still damp. By the time she left the castle at the end of the week most of her acquaintances in the magic circle had heard that Richard had proposed. Keith Cowley had captured her sitting lost in thought on the riverbank while Richard, knee-deep in the water, cast for salmon. She arrived at the London apartment to find photographers once more crowded in the street outside, and her father looking grave.

•   •   •

"WELL, WE AREN'T in a good position to tell you that you're too young, are we?" His mother sat in the corner of the lumpy green linen sofa, her hands tightly folded in her lap.

"Definitely not. And I know you'll tell me I'm always falling in love, but all that's been over since Tory. I just know I couldn't live without her. Do say it's all right, Mother." Richard checked himself from laying on the boyish charm with the one person who was impervious to it.

"I know that if you've made up your mind there is absolutely nothing any of us can do to change it."

"You sound as if you're accusing me of something." Neither of his parents was smiling and for the first time Richard suspected that his plans might not be as perfect as they looked.

"I am not accusing you of anything."

"But don't you like Tory?"

"She's a lovely girl and I've always liked her very much." She glanced nervously up at her husband, who stood beside her leaning against the mantelpiece.

"Well then, what's the matter?"

"Let's be sure we've got this right." His father walked slowly to the far side of the room and turned back towards them. "You have proposed to Victoria, I take it?"

"Yes, I have."

"And she has accepted you?"

"Yes she has. And if you like her, I don't see what the trouble is."

"Did she say anything?"

"Say anything?"

His mother shook her head. "Philip, she may not know. She was almost a baby when it happened."

"Of course she knows . . ."

"I wouldn't count on it." His mother pinched her lips together, cutting off a harsh judgement of Victoria's family before she could give it voice.

"Knows *what* for heaven's sake?"

"Richard, your father and I have talked about this between ourselves already. You were so obviously in love, you're so . . ." she paused, searching for the words to express her son's passionate impatience to seize life and live it to the full. "Well, you are impetuous. But . . . there's something we can't agree about."

"Mother, you're driving me crazy, what *is* all this?" She lifted her chin to give herself courage and told him. Richard immediately prepared to take the night train to London.

• • •

"OF COURSE, I am absolutely delighted, Victoria. For you and for both of you. I know you love him. He's a delightful young man. You're both very young, but I know that you realise what a great responsibility is involved and you're very brave to accept it." Charles Fairley patted his daughter's arm, and she noticed that the skin of his hands had grown thin and dry, with the faint brown blotches of advancing age gathering on the back. His hair was still thick but completely white; even the untrimmed fine hair at the back of his neck was like swansdown.

"I'm so glad you're here alone, Daddy. I can hardly take it in myself. I just can't believe it. I couldn't bear the thought of talking to Pamela and all the littles just now." The rest of the family were at Aston Langley, while Alex and Amanda were still away in Portugal.

"Well, there's no peace for the wicked, the Admiralty sees to that. I'm glad I was here to get the news first. I knew something was up the minute those blasted photographers descended again. I think this calls for a celebration. Perhaps I should take my daughter out . . ."

"No, Daddy, please. I just want to be here quietly with you, tonight. I don't want to have to fight my way past all those people again."

"Well, you'll let me have a drink at least, while you tell me all your plans." He rang for the housekeeper to bring ice, and poured himself a large whisky from the decanter on the silver salver presented by the officers' mess when he left Hong Kong. Victoria found that she wanted a strong gin and tonic. The plan, outlined breathlessly by Richard, was for them to talk to their families in the remainder of the vacation, announce their engagement formally at Christmas and marry in the spring.

"You are quite, quite sure, my dear?"

"Yes, of course I'm sure. I love him so much, Daddy. I know it'll be difficult at times, but then all marriages are, aren't they?"

The next day, to her surprise, he returned from work early and asked her to sit with him in the compass alcove. The thick, dusty haze of a late summer day in London hung in the air above the stream of traffic along the Thames embankment. The dry foliage of the plane trees lining the riverside highway obscured the sunlight from the west and the view of Big Ben beyond the laden branches.

"This is something I had intended to tell you before you got to the point of thinking about marriage, but you've beaten me to it, rather. Or perhaps I put it off longer than I should have done." He was trying to achieve the omniscient judicial manner which always helped him pronounce on difficult matters, but in the face of his daughter it eluded him. "Your brother has guessed most of it already—has he ever talked to you about your mother?"

"No." Instantly, foreboding leaked into her mind, the suppressed doubts of her whole lifetime welling into a cold flood. "We never seem to talk about her, although I suppose he can remember her."

"You know that you said yesterday that all marriages have their difficulties?" She looked so intensely fearful that for a moment he faltered in his purpose.

"Yes. Do you mean that you and our mother . . ."

"Our difficulty was rather out of the ordinary, Victoria. After we had been married for a few years, and your brother had been born, your mother's personality changed. She had always been a very up and down sort of person, either frantically gay or—well—quite miserable really. What happened was, she stopped being happy. I kept thinking she would recover and turn back into the same merry little Pet, but she didn't, she got worse."

He paused, wrenched by the innocent bewilderment in his daughter's eyes. "I didn't know when I married her that quite a few of her family were like that; they kept very quiet about them. One of them's still in a hospital in South Africa and no one's seen him for years. I stopped off once, when we were posted to Hong Kong, to make sure everything was all right." He was wandering from the point and she did not bring him back to it, afraid of what was to come. "But, in the end we had to call the doctors in."

"Do you mean she was ill?" Victoria heard herself ask the question as if she were a stranger very far away.

"She was mentally ill. They said she was schizophrenic. I didn't believe them at first. She was just . . . quiet, not like herself. She went into hospital for a year, and then one day she turned up at our house and she seemed quite all right. And then you were born, and it all began again." He could not bring himself to tell her everything. The details would have to wait.

"But," again, her voice seemed faint and distant. "I'm all right, aren't I?"

"Yes, my dear, of course you are. They told me that although it was clearly a matter of inheritance with her, you two might be perfectly all right and as far as we know you are. Perfectly."

"But how can you tell? I mean, she was normal when you were married, wasn't she?"

He sighed. He had stood back for years, watching both his children with acute anxiety, alert for any sign that the fatal flaw had been passed on to them. Every childhood tantrum, every adolescent mood had been observed and analysed without giving any sign to the children that might in itself predispose them to neurosis. After almost twenty years of such dissimulation, Charles Fairley felt empty in his heart. It was his duty to acquaint his daughter with the facts of her lineage, the more so now that she was to marry into the Royal Family. It was even possible that one day she might be Queen.

"She seemed normal. I really can't understand her family's attitude. I'm afraid the only interpretation really is that they wanted her off their hands. She had had episodes before, and they certainly knew what was wrong with her. She had a complete nervous breakdown when she was seventeen. Perhaps they just thought she would get over it."

"Who were they?" Suddenly she realised that she knew almost nothing of her mother's relatives. In their restless, nomadic childhood so many connections had been strained. A vivid, pretty woman with a lot of lipstick had once appeared during a posting in Plymouth and been introduced as their aunt, but Pamela had not made her welcome and she visited only once.

"They were . . . they are scattered all over the world. An old Navy family. I think it was all a bit beyond them. Both the parents are dead now, of course. There's a sister in Somerset. Some of them went to Australia. Brazil, Rhodesia . . . they don't really keep in touch." She remembered the exotic stamps which Alex had proudly steamed off their Christmas cards for his album. "My dear, I expect this is all a bit of a shock and I'm going to leave you now to think things over. I'll see you at dinner and if there's anything you want to ask me I hope you will do it then."

They sat down two hours later at the corner of the long mahogany table in the dining room, with a tasteless cold soup before them and the housekeeper's Irish stew in a chafing dish on the hotplate. Victoria could think of nothing to say. Her mind was paralysed. It seemed rude to sit with her father in silence, so she tried to talk about inconsequential things, but every topic she fixed on seemed unexpectedly loaded with relevance. Pamela's dogs, or her friends or her latest plans for the house always passed the time, but it seemed wrong to talk about Pamela at that moment.

The noise of the door opening in the hallway broke into their fitful conversation. There was a crash of cases being dropped and Alex appeared, suntanned but not cheerful. He had not been expected. The sun had bleached his hair to the colour of straw and the grey Fairley eyes looked almost blue against his reddened skin.

"Amanda and I have had a row," he announced bluntly. "There was no point in hanging around so I've come back. Going to take a shower—I'm absolutely shagged."

"Well," her father observed with a mild, rueful smile, "I suppose it never rains but it pours."

Victoria watched with detachment as the two men contrived to talk quietly downstairs after dinner was over. She felt weary of being the centre of so many people's attention, the object of so many covert operations. Eventually her father looked in shamefacedly to say goodnight, and after him Alex came up to the drawing room and plumped himself down in the fat pink chintz armchair by the fireplace.

"Dad's been getting the family skeletons out of the cupboard, has he?"

"Is it a skeleton, Alex? He said you'd guessed it all."

"So would you have done if you hadn't always been determined to smooth things over and pretend everything was as nice as pie when it bloody well wasn't. Want some of this?" He had brought a bottle of whisky and two tumblers up with him.

Victoria shook her head. He ignored her and poured a hefty shot of liquor into both glasses, then held one out for her. "Take it, you need it. I know I do."

Silently she got up and walked to the bathroom to add some water from the tap to the drink. "I'm sorry about Amanda." She crossed her ankles as she sat, spreading the skirt of her white and blue dress with automatic care to look elegant.

"No you aren't, you two never got on. Why don't you admit it?" He gulped his drink, and poured another one.

"But for your sake, Alex . . ."

"Fuck my sake. Why are you always doing things for other people's sake, Tory? It never works, does it? Did you agree to marry Richard for his sake?"

"It's none of your business."

"Sorry. I'm a bit hacked up right now. That was what did it for Amanda really."

"What, me and Richard?"

"No, the skeleton. She couldn't handle it. She said she could, she said it was fine, but no girl wants to think her kids are going to grow up and start slitting their wrists, does she?"

"Is that what . . . what our mother . . . ?" Why had she imagined it was over and she already knew the worst, when there were still parts of the picture in darkness? Of course there was more, and of course it was worse. That was why Alex had come up to talk to her now. A sense of predestination was breaking through the shock. This was something she had known without knowing it all her life.

"Didn't Dad tell you?"

"He's got you to do it, hasn't he?"

"Don't blame him, Tory. He's suffered all our lives and it can't have been easy for him."

"It's not easy for me either, or you, is it? Particularly not for me, not even knowing. My God, what must they think of me?" Tears suddenly rushed painfully into her eyes and she gripped the glass so hard that he saw her knuckles turn white. "Come on then, you might as well tell me all the sordid details. What horrible things did she do?"

"It's not so bad, Tory, don't let your imagination run away with you."

"I'm not supposed to have any imagination, am I?" She sniffed bitterly and drank. The taste of whisky made her think of Richard and she felt like throwing the glass away and screaming with pain. Behaving like a madwoman, in other words.

"She was suicidal, that's all. It was that story about the ghost at Aston Langley, the grey lady, that put me on to it. She tried to drown herself. The first time they found her in the middle of the Round Pond in Kensington Gardens. Dad said I was on the edge playing with my toy boats, you were asleep in your pram and she was out in the deep water saying she wanted to die. That's when they realised she wasn't quite the full quid."

"Well, I suppose a little thing like that would give you away rather. Frightening the ducks and so on." She looked at the drink with distaste and took another mouthful, trying not to taste it as she swallowed. "What else?"

"It sounds as if she tried almost everything. That was why they had to put her in hospital. When she died, you know, she'd got out and stolen one of the doctor's cars and just driven it into a bridge. Bang, all over."

"So she was actually . . ."

"Committed. Yes, she was. I went through all the papers, just to see for myself. She had been committed to a mental hospital before you were born, before they thought she'd recovered. Obviously she went over the edge again after . . . afterwards. The inquest verdict was accidental death though, I suppose Dad had to work hard for that."

"What exactly do you mean by that?"

"It should have been suicide while the balance of the mind was disturbed, that's what they usually call it when someone goes off his head and tops himself."

"Oh, I see. Legal niceties are a bit wasted on me tonight."

"Don't be bitter, Tory. We're OK, both of us, that's the main thing."

"How can you say that?" She tried to get up from the depths of her low chair, but she had already drunk too much to achieve the indignant spring she wanted and so she swayed unsteadily forwards. Alex was now quite drunk, his face flushed and his wet hair hanging untidily in his eyes. "We can't be sure. We can never be sure. And how can I possibly . . . possibly . . ."

"Marry Richard? It's his choice. I hope your luck's better than mine." He drained his glass and refilled it without looking at her.

"*Luck!* That's just like you, Alex, thinking of nobody but

yourself. Do you realise he must think I tried to hide all this, they all must think that."

"No, Tory, everyone knows you're straight as a die. You couldn't con a penny out of a schoolboy. And he's not the heir, after all. If Richard's as mad about you as he says, he won't mind." Her face distorted with pain at his ill-chosen words. "Sorry, sorry, didn't think what I was saying."

She stood up. "I'm going to my room. You're being absolutely unbearable. Just because everything's gone wrong for you, you're trying to make me as unhappy as you can. I just won't let you."

She swayed along the corridor to her bedroom, shut the door precisely behind her and lay down on the bed. The room seemed to swing from side to side. She wished she had drunk enough alcohol to pass out instead of having to endure this unpleasant sensation and the painful confusion of her thoughts.

There was a feeling of inevitability about the whole affair. As soon as she had realised that Richard was asking her to marry him this dark uncertainty had opened up in her mind, like a concealed pit whose shape was only clear now that she had fallen into it. It had been foolish to think she had ever been meant to be happy with him. She had tried very hard to be good, to do and think everything a daughter of the courtier class should, but at bottom she had known she was unworthy and now she understood why. The notion that her pride in having a royal lover had violated a taboo, and that this disaster was the consequence, refused to yield to common sense. As the night hours lengthened, she began to marvel at her own presumption. The institution to which she had proposed to ally herself was almost holy and it was part of her trust to protect it. If she added her tainted blood to theirs it would be a betrayal.

Richard himself receded in her imagination, ceasing to be a man and becoming a sacred creature who had to be protected from his own folly. She began to feel noble as she accepted that it was her duty to give him up. A measure of calmness returned and at last she slept.

The next morning the telephone rang before breakfast and her brother answered it. "Here she is," she heard him say as she came downstairs in her white cotton night-dress.

"It's him," he handed her the receiver and made off to the kitchen, shutting the door behind him.

Richard's voice was so emotional that she hardly recognised it. "I've got to see you," he said, "will you be alone there?"

"I don't know," she said miserably. "My father will leave for the Admiralty soon but Alex . . ."

"You can tell Alex to get lost for a few hours, surely. I must see you, darling."

The words forced themselves through her lips. "I didn't know, Richard."

"I'm sure you didn't, Tory. But it doesn't matter, it isn't important . . ."

"Of course it's important, Richard . . ."

"We'll talk about it when I see you. Get rid of everybody." He hung up and she stood without moving, the purring receiver in her hand, with tears running down her face and falling on her night-dress. After a while Alex came out of the kitchen and made her sit down and drink a cup of tea.

"He says he's coming over, Alex."

"Good. Well, you'd better get dressed, hadn't you?"

"I don't want to see him."

"Don't be silly, you must see him."

She shook her head, and fumbled for a tissue to mop up the tears.

In the event, she did not dare to carry out her intention of evading him. They had a long, bitter meeting; he tried and failed to persuade her that what had come to light was of no consequence. She was withdrawn and refused to talk about her feelings. Instead she simply repeated that she could not marry him.

CHAPTER XIII

"GOOD EVENING, LADIES and Jellyspoons! Yes, you are in the right hall, you've come to see Various Artists in their earth-shaking production of 'Tarantula, the Eyebrow that Ate Manhattan,' a satirical revue which will commence in a few moments." Costumed as a magician's handmaid in a pink satin basque and fishnet tights, Jo threw her arms wide to indicate the company's spangled banner at the back of the stage, then clutched her side with her black-gloved hands. From the marabou-trimmed neckline she extracted a furry black spider, threw it fearfully to the floor and stamped on it with a stilettoed foot. "Well, whaddya expect?" she demanded in an acute Bronx accent. "He wanted his name above the titles."

A girl tittered. Jo scanned the interior of the Morning-side Masonic Lodge. There were five people in the hall. One couple were holding hands and appeared oblivious of everything except each other. A dishevelled man in a raincoat who looked like a tramp sat in the second row. The two other men were only a little more prepossessing. One of them she recognised as an official from the Arts Council whom Daniel had approached for a grant to make a film. The other she did not know, but she wished he would stop picking his nose.

On the back wall of the hall a bas-relief carving of a single eyeball held between mason's tools glared back at her. "We are sincerely proud to be here in Edinburgh participating in the largest arts festival in the world . . ." Three more couples slid into the back row as she finished the introduction. "But first, 'Great Moments in Physics.' Professor Wittgenstein is going to reconstruct for you his legendary experiment to discover the tensile strength of brassiere elastic!"

At the word "brassiere" the three men in the back row laughed loudly. More drunks. Still, this audience was a hundred per cent larger than the one they had achieved the night before.

Bazza appeared in a Dr Kildare white coat, with multiple stethoscopes around his neck and an enema bag trailing from his trouser pocket. He wore an overlarge green fright wig held in place by a baseball cap, and trousers rolled up to reveal black sock suspenders.

"I have here fifty metres of ordinary brassiere elastic!" He glowered at the audience, holding up a large roll of elastic, lifeless pink in colour and frilled at both edges; they had discovered it in a dusty old-fashioned haberdasher's shop around the corner. "It is a most remarkable substance! In fact, one of the strongest substances known to man! My assistant, the lovely Miss Masochista Devine . . ." Jo tottered forward on her high heels and curtseyed to the audience with a wiggle . . . "is going to hold one end of this elastic in her teeth—so!" She clamped the edge of the elastic in her jaws. Behind a screen at the back of the stage, Daniel provided a drum roll.

"Are you all right, Miss Devine?" She nodded vigorously, unable to talk without dropping the elastic. The pink ostrich plumes in her hair swayed with the motion.

"In my famous experiment to determine the strength of brassiere elastic I demonstrated that, when extended to its full extent . . ." Bazza, holding the roll aloft, jumped heavily off the stage. "The tensile strength of this, ordinary brassiere elastic, is around *five thousand* tons per inch which, in layman's terms . . ." He unrolled the elastic, keeping it stretched tight, as he walked slowly through the central aisle between the benches to the back of the hall. The meagre audience turned round on their seats to watch him. Three girls dressed in identically long black skirts slunk into the hall and he bowed to them as they took their seats. ". . . enough to propel an average sized elephant the length of a football pitch or, if you would prefer a more brutal analogy, enough to launch a small intercontinental ballistic missile. Are you *all right,* Miss Devine?"

Jo nodded, smiling around the mouthful of elastic. The three girls tittered in unison. Bazza reached the end of the hall and the pink line stretched tightly between his hand and Jo's teeth. Maybe all that torture from the orthodontist had been worth it.

"Miss Devine is a woman who has devoted her life to science." Jo rolled her eyes and nodded again. "In order to demonstrate to you the incredible kinetic potential which is locked up here in this ordinary brassiere elastic, I will now let go of my end and Miss Devine will take the full force of the recoil in her face." Jo clutched her heart in shock, rolled her eyes furiously, squeaked in terror and made her knees knock.

"Do not be alarmed, ladies and gentlemen. We have an intensive care ambulance standing by ready to take Miss Devine immediately to Edinburgh Royal Infirmary, where one of my colleagues, an eminent world famous plastic surgeon who is giving his services free in the cause of science, is standing by to repair this lovely woman's face."

"Mnergh! Mnerrrrgh! Arrgh!" Jo gibbered and gesticulated in fright, jumping up and down on the stage. The fourteen members of the audience were tittering and sitting on the edges of their seats.

"I must ask you gentlemen in the front row please to stand back now . . ." as the front row was empty this was an unnecessary command, "and if any vital organs, eyes, nose or perhaps a tonsil, should come your way please pick it up immediately in a clean handkerchief and hand it to me. Thank you." Bazza gestured for silence. He was a highly charismatic performer and despite the empty seats the hall was spellbound. Even the three tittering latecomers suddenly looked grave. "Now we shall perform the experiment. Are you ready, Miss Devine?"

"Mmmmnngrh!" Jo shook her head violently.

"I said, are you *ready,* Miss Devine?"

"Aarrgh? Aargh!" She shook her head again and stamped her foot.

"Come, come. Think of your place in the history of science. Think of your name as a footnote in all those textbooks. *Are you ready, Miss Devine?*"

"YES!" bellowed Jo. The elastic, released the instant she opened her mouth, recoiled the entire length of the hall and Bazza fell flat on his back. The tiny audience roared with laughter and one of the drunks tumbled off his seat.

Jo curtseyed and tripped swiftly off the stage. Her place was taken by Colin Lambert, a handsome blond man in Elizabethan black doublet and hose, carrying six fencing foils, a plastic sheet and a bottle of stage blood. Colin's party piece was a sketch written by Daniel, the death scene from *Hamlet* as a monologue.

She joined Daniel in the makeshift wings. He watched with approval as Colin bounced around the stage with swords flailing in both hands, spouting Shakespeare's lines in half-a-dozen different histrionic voices. The tiny audience were giggling.

"Hams it up a treat, doesn't he?" Daniel leaned down to whisper in her ear.

"Yeah, but he's like that when he plays it straight too. I'm not surprised they kicked him out of the Marlowe Society."

"Their loss was our gain." Colin collapsed, writhing in multiple death throes and the drunk in the back row again fell off his seat with laughter. "Though somehow I don't think they threw him out for overacting."

Colin had found his way to the Lumière Society shortly after Jo. He was then already notorious for his raging ambition. He had understudied several minor parts in the Marlowe Society's last production; as the first performance approached the actors suffered all manner of dirty tricks, from phoney telegrams announcing deaths in the family to the heavy come-on from Colin's bedraggled girlfriend. It was some time before he finally understood that his presence was no longer welcome. Colin was not a sensitive man.

He immediately transferred what he considered to be his loyalty to the Lumière Society. "I think film is really the best medium for an actor," he had announced to Daniel with the cool of a polar ice-cap. "Stage work has more prestige, of course, but that's just snobbery. All the really exciting directors are working in film. Take you, for instance. You're a star already, everyone's talking about what you've done here. Personally, I would feel privileged just to say I'd met you, let alone worked with you."

"Well—uh—we're glad to have you on board," Daniel had replied at once, seeing great possibilities in Colin's Greek god physique and slightly crooked features. In private he said to Jo, "Watch your back, kid—that's one mean mother. If Lady Victoria thinks I'm a pushy bastard she'd better not meet him." He underestimated Colin, who had Victoria cooing over him immediately and glibly discovered half-a-dozen acquaintances they had in common. He could not bear to be disliked by anyone.

At the end of the show the man from the Arts Council bolted for the door like a scared rabbit. The man who had been picking his nose got wearily to his feet and shuffled forward to approach Jo. "Is there not any nudity in this show?" he enquired.

"No, there isn't." Daniel at once appeared protectively at her side.

"Did you just not do it tonight then?"

"This is a satirical revue," Daniel told him in crisp tones. "Nobody takes their clothes off."

"I was told that Miss—ah—Miss Forbes, is it? That she, er you, has a—ah—topless scene with—ah—another actor and . . ."

"Who are you?" Daniel ran his hands through his hair with a weary gesture.

"I'm from the *Daily Post*, actually. We were informed . . ."

"You were misinformed, all right?"

"Okay, okay, just doing my job . . ." The man shuffled away, muttering excuses.

Daniel sighed and squeezed Jo's shoulders protectively. "What on earth was he doing here?" she asked him.

"Sounds like somebody induced him to believe there was a hot story down here. Nothing to do with you, Colin, by any chance?"

Out in the corridor the aspiring actor was brushing dust from his Hamlet costume with undue care. "Was what anything to do with me?"

"Come on, Colin. It's me, Daniel, remember. I'm one step ahead of you, always. You called up the *Daily Post*, didn't you?"

"Well I was only trying to get us noticed, for fuck's sake." He stuffed the costume into its protective cover, tossing his golden curls in annoyance. "Nobody else seems to have thought of publicity."

Daniel stood over him and spoke with muted menace. "Publicity is my job. I don't want you worrying your pretty head about it, all right? And lay off Jo, will you?"

"It's all right for her . . ."

"She wants to make it her own way, not by trading on her mother's name the whole time. That's her decision and we all have to respect it."

Colin glared at Daniel and for an instant Jo thought he would hit him. Then he shrugged his shoulders and turned away. Daniel shook his head and glanced at her through the open door with resignation. Variations on this scene had been enacted daily between the two men since they decided to take a show to Edinburgh. Before Jo's eyes Daniel had become more and more sophisticated in techniques of domination, but every time Colin lost a round he redoubled his efforts.

Bazza appeared at the end of the corridor. "The bog's choked again," he announced.

"I know just how it feels," Daniel replied, pushing past Colin to investigate.

The next performers, an experimental dance group, arrived to take over the hall. They clustered in a corner limbering up and massaging their feet while Daniel and Bazza struggled to unblock the lavatory. Jo, Colin and Colin's girlfriend, who was now their stage-manager, crawled across the stage on their hands and knees picking up the peanuts which had been spilt during the Jimmy Carter's Oval Office sketch.

"There must be an easier way to get an Equity card," she tipped the last few dusty nuts into the paper bag.

"There is for you, dear, so I don't know why you're doing all this. It's poor nobodies like us who've got no choice." Colin's natural expression was sulky. Now it was murderous. He stood up, twisting the neck of the bag to close it with a vicious gesture. The bag immediately burst, scattering the peanuts anew over the dusty boards. There was a hiss of annoyance from the dancers. "Sorry! Sorry!"

"At times like this I don't know why I'm doing it either." Resignedly, Jo began picking up the nuts once more.

Rachel, Colin's girlfriend, looked around for a new bag and, not finding one, took off her shapeless black felt hat for a temporary container.

"Excuse me," the tramp looked up from his seat, where he had been sitting unnoticed scribbling in a small dog-eared notebook. "I'm from *The Scotsman.* I seem to have lost my programme. I wonder if you could give me your names?"

The dancers pricked up their ears and fixed the actors with a look of pure hatred. For the duration of the Edinburgh Festival, *The Scotsman* was the most influential newspaper in town. Jo ignored the hostility behind her and gave the man the information he wanted.

People began to trickle through the Lodge's imposing light oak doors and take their seats for the next performance. There was a shout of triumph from the end of the building and the noise of the lavatory working. Daniel and Bazza appeared, drying their hands on a ragged towel, and the five members of Various Artists swiftly vacated the venue in good order according to their contract. They were not prominent among the 300 theatre groups which had come to perform in church halls and school assembly rooms all over Scotland's capital city, and a daily performance in the early evening at the Masonic Lodge was the best Daniel had been able to achieve.

"If we can go to Edinburgh," he had predicted at the beginning of the year, "you and Colin will qualify for your Equity cards, I can do a bit of wheeling and dealing and we may even make some money if people actually come and see us. It's the best possible shop window. Everyone goes to Edinburgh—all the agents, producers, directors, casting, everyone. All we need to do is raise enough money."

"But Daniel, we haven't got anything to take to an arts festival. Just a couple of student films, that's all. Nobody would cross the street for two ten-minute epics on Super-8."

"Get your lines right, Jo. What you're supposed to say is 'we can put on our *own* show, right here!' " Bazza tap-danced a few steps and struck a pose.

"You can't dance, he can't sing and I'm not Judy Garland—we apologise for this fault in reality." Jo shrugged, wondering why she was suddenly so pessimistic. I'm chicken, she told herself crossly. This is the first real opportunity I've had to stand up in front of an audience, and the mere idea scares me.

"It's quite simple," Daniel continued, ignoring them. "We can do a great classic of the English theatre in punk costume and bore everyone to death, we can write a three-hour polemic about the Soweto riots and find that every other fringe group has had the same idea, or we can knock up an outrageous revue in really bad taste calculated to offend everyone but not quite get banned and make our fortunes."

"I vote for the last one you said," Colin spoke before he realised that Daniel was not entirely serious.

"You would." Bazza gave a hog-like snort. He and Colin had an unspoken agreement to co-operate only until one or both of them was rich and famous.

"And I suppose you want me in a tits'n'ass costume with my mother doing a star cameo?" enquired Jo in an unpleasant tone.

Daniel refused to be needled. "Costume yes, mother no." He pulled open his desk drawer and began to sort out some sketches the three of them had written for fun the previous year. "We can use your psychiatrist monologue, that'll be great. And that thing you did with the Queen and Agatha Christie . . . let's work that up into something, that was great too."

When Jo realised that Colin was quite prepared to massage the necessary finance from the Lumière Society's cash flow, she decided that it was time to break into the plastic surgery fund. It paid for the hire of the hall, their keep, and a rattling old station wagon which could transport them all with their props. What the hell, she decided. She could always tell her mother she needed more money. Perhaps she didn't really need plastic surgery after all, now her face had grown up a little.

With Jo clutching Daniel's arm for stability in her high-heeled boots, they walked downhill to the centre of the city in the luminous northern twilight. She watched her reflection in the shop windows as they passed, and liked what she saw. Her hair was pinned up in curls, with a few tendrils escaping down her neck. She had decided to let the henna fade out, but the tips still had a faint gleam of chestnut. She wore a black Mexican cotton skirt and a blouse brightly printed with red and pink roses which Martha had brought back from London and insisted on giving her. An antique silk shawl around her shoulders dripped fringes to her hem.

The idea that she was ugly no longer obsessed her. Despite the time they had been together, a day never passed without Daniel telling her she was beautiful. He worshipped her body and her face with such intensity that she stopped denying his praise and began to look in the mirror with less critical eyes. She joked that she was just his portable shrine, but at the bottom of her heart she began to accept herself.

She had learned a few tricks, a dozen different ways to pin up her hair, a thousand ways to put her clothes together to look however she wanted—a gypsy for Daniel, an earnest student for her tutor, a decorous example of *jeunesse dorée* for her mother's flying visits to London. Disguising her shape was no longer the over-riding priority; she enjoyed dressing-up. If she was pleasing herself, she liked to look like a pre-Raphaelite muse, in clothes which trailed and fluttered and felt good against her skin. The sensuality of suede, silk, and cashmere beguiled her, although she felt uncomfortable in expensive garments and thought it vulgar to dress richly when none of her companions could.

Her body had also changed. Wretched miles of cycling to and from the college had made her fit. The lingering layer of puppy fat had finally disappeared; her tits had been the first things to go. They were still pretty, but they had lost some of their adolescent volume and now men looked at her face first. She had rounded limbs, and a body that was slender but retained an appealing, characteristic softness. She still had too much gut; Daniel loved it. He told her she had a belly like a heap of wheat.

The damp, sunless English climate seemed to suit her complexion, which was now creamy and pale with a light dusting of freckles over her nose; Daniel called them angels' kisses. Although she had reluctantly accepted that she would never have the endless flamingo legs she admired on other women, the proportions of her body had changed as she matured. The nose still looked like a ski-run, but with everything else refined it no longer seemed such a catastrophe.

They stopped at an art gallery in Grassmarket for an exhibition by one of Bazza's friends, then, re-animated by his lukewarm white wine, skirted the foot of the castle, crossed the railway and panted uphill along Hanover Street.

For a month in the late summer each year Edinburgh lost its grey-stone primness and lived up to its title of the

Athens of the North. The air was warm, the nights long and light. Thousands of artists of every discipline thronged the steep, windswept streets. They saw and were seen, did business and pursued pleasure and seldom went to sleep before the dawn. The burghers of the city went to a few of the plays themselves, and pursued their daily business full of pride in their superior Celtic sensitivity.

Halfway up the hill four actors dressed as gorillas capered across the steep pavement, thrusting handbills for their play at every passer-by. From the floodlit castle forecourt, clearly visible across the low-lying streets between, drums and bagpipes announced the beginning of the evening's Military Tattoo.

They made their way to the pillared entrance of the Assembly Rooms, where Daniel counselled they should see Lorcan Flood's company play Sophocles. Flood was a god to Daniel. He firmly believed him to be the greatest director alive and lectured them all about his re-discovery of the ancient magic of the stage. Although any of the great national theatre companies would have welcomed him, Flood chose to roam the world with a company of actors whom he handpicked for their extraordinary talents. He chose classic plays and dismantled them, searching for the kernel of human truth under centuries of tradition and veneration. Daniel found everything Flood did thrilling. Colin, well aware of the limitations of his own intellect, agreed with Daniel. Jo was uncertain; the Sophocles, simply performed as a prehistoric myth, interested her but seemed peculiarly passionless. Bazza sat down heavily and went to sleep. He considered that Lorcan Flood was a charlatan.

Colin and Daniel checked the audience as they took their seats. At an important production like this there was bound to be someone worth hustling in the hall. Sean Connery was hard to miss; even when seated he was head-and-shoulders above everyone else and several shades more deeply suntanned. Colin promptly scraped acquaintance with the pale, nervous man beside him, the director of Connery's last film. When the play was over he joined them without a backward glance. The three men turned into a nearby pub, with Rachel following grimly in their wake, still clutching her hat full of peanuts.

The darkened streets were still crowded with people, milling from one show to another. The gorillas had gone, but a whitefaced mime troupe in harlequin suits was turning cartwheels in the same prime pitch.

Jo heard the final crashing chords of the Tattoo echo in the cool night air across the heart of the city, followed a few minutes later by a fusillade of explosions. The fireworks filled the black sky with their magnesium glare, to the astonishment of two elderly ladies waiting at a busstop. They raised their eyes from the pavement with reluctance.

"The Festival," one of them announced by way of explanation.

"Och, aye, the Festival." Her companion nodded, as if remarking a change in the weather.

"Jesus H. Christ," Bazza muttered as they passed the indifferent pair. "Bloody geriatrics wouldn't know it was the end of the world unless a nurse came round to explain it to them."

They bought baked potatoes from a stall on a street corner, and devoured them as they stood in line for admission to the midnight television broadcast from a large circus tent in one of the parks. In the excited crowd jostling under the hot lights Jo saw *The Scotsman*'s critic, looking untidy but less like a tramp without his raincoat. He caught her eye and gestured that she should wait while he battled through the crowd to join her.

"Have you people got a telephone number?" he demanded, reaching for his notebook. "The producer's just asked me to present the Fringe highlights tomorrow and I'd like to include your show—can we send a crew down in the afternoon?"

"Of course," Daniel took over the conversation, "which sketch do you want? The Oval Office would be good . . ." Jo listened as the two men began fevered negotiations. Bazza stood apart, clutching a can of Guinness protectively to his barrel chest.

At 2 am they were on the street again, arguing about their next destination.

"I think we should go home and get some sleep," Daniel said firmly. "We can't foul up on television, we need to be on top form and we've got to pick up the costumes from the hall first thing in the morning."

"God, you're getting boring. It's early, for Chrissake. What about medication time? I'm not even decently smashed yet." Bazza stuck his hands in the pockets of his trailing greatcoat and glared at them.

"My feet hurt, Bazza, I want to go home," Jo complained. It was uncool to take the car into the city, and impossible to park it, anyway.

"Well you two lovebirds go home, then. I'm a big boy, I can take care of myself." With his pug nose in the air, he started defiantly down the street.

"That'll be the day," Daniel followed with resignation, knowing that if he let Bazza out of his sight he was perfectly capable of disappearing for a week.

The Traverse Theatre had been dark for hours, but the bar was jammed with people. Bazza immediately disappeared to do business with a skinny, fox-faced young man who had appeared at his elbow, impelled by the dealer's mysterious instinct for a sale.

Rachel appeared out of the noisy crowd, her thick black makeup smudged across her corpse-white cheeks. "You'll never guess who Colin's oiled up to now," she took a vicious drag on her cigarette and swallowed the smoke. "Lorcan Flood. He just came over when we were all in the other place with Connery. Colin hit on him right away. Sometimes he really embarrasses me." She took another drag, swaying on her high platform soles. She was drunk, but then so were most of the other people in the room.

"We'd better join him," Daniel put his arm under Jo's elbow and steered her through the crush. Bazza bulldozed his way to join them from the opposite direction.

"Fuckin' useless place," he grumbled. "Nothing to score but a bottle of amyl and he wanted a tenner for that." He showed Jo the brown glass chemist's bottle tucked into the inner pocket of his raincoat. "I hate fuckin' amyl, it gives me a headache."

"Then why did you buy it?" Jo was not in a good temper. Someone had trodden on her cramped toes.

"Maybe I can trade it for some decent drugs later."

Lorcan Flood was radiantly sober. He stood quietly in the corner of the bar, a half-empty glass of lemonade beside him, deep in conversation with a visiting Hungarian film director. Despite the press of people, the two men were in a space apart. Flood's pale blue eyes never left the man's face and he seemed oblivious of Colin hovering ingratiatingly beside them. Daniel suddenly faltered as he approached, overcome with the presence of a man he revered.

As if he sensed their arrival, Flood turned his intense gaze towards them and Jo, still hanging on to Daniel's arm, felt a surge of energy sweep them both towards him. Lorcan was like a puppet-master controlling them by the force of his will. She saw annoyance on Colin's face as he stepped aside, and heard Daniel introduce them.

"Ah yes," Flood nodded his close-cropped head, "I hear you're one of the most interesting new companies this year. You're stuck out in the Masonic Lodge, aren't you? We were planning to come and see you in a couple of days."

For a minute Jo thought Daniel was going to faint. She felt a tremor right through his body, but Flood suddenly extended one of his fine white hands and took Daniel's arm. "I'd really like to talk to you. They're closing up here, won't you all come to our house for a while?" He smiled, benevolently despite his pointed teeth, to include Bazza, Colin and Rachel in the invitation.

As if given a cue, the barman unceremoniously turned the lights full on and yelled, "Away wi' all o' ye, now. Ye can all jest fuck off. Drink up and get awa' to your beds." To emphasise the point, he began collecting glasses, clinking them noisily together.

"We are each other's family. We all live together during a production," Flood explained as he led the way to a pillared house in one of the finest squares on the hilltop, where a tall, dark-haired woman in black harem pants opened the door.

The upper windows blazed with light; quiet laughter and the growl of Patti Smith floated down the graceful half-spiral of the stairs. Lorcan led them into the sitting room, where the furniture was pushed back against the walls under dust sheets and mattresses covered with Indian bedspreads were arranged in a semi-circle on the bare boards.

Jo wondered if Lorcan lived more together with the dark woman than with the others. Somehow he did not give that impression, although she had a wifely air as she padded off to the kitchen in bare feet and reappeared with coffee in a Moroccan silver pot, then sat very close to his side while he talked to Daniel.

Bazza, still in his raincoat, tramped curiously upstairs. Rachel lay down on the farthest mattress and went to sleep; Jo rescued the hatful of peanuts as her grasp relaxed.

At intervals, several other members of the company appeared quietly in the room. The conversation widened to include them all and Lorcan, she noticed, did less and less talking. He looked at her directly while he listened to the others but instead of feeling uncomfortable under his strange light eyes Jo found herself sitting taller and feeling calm.

There was a lull in the conversation and Lorcan got up and walked out of the room. He returned with a book which he leafed through until he had found the page he wanted and then handed to Jo. "Why don't you read for us?" he asked. He had a very gentle voice.

She focused her eyes on the page, and saw that it was a poem.

> My spirit dwells in this vile body
> Like gold wrapped in a filthy bag,
> Or like the reflection of the moon in a muddy pond.
> With such disparity between mind and body,
> No wonder the foolish despise me.

The words died away and there was a long silence, broken by murmurs of appreciation from two of the actors. Lorcan nodded, obviously pleased that he had found a text which was significant for her. Jo was so moved by the sound of her own voice she felt as if she wanted to cry. Daniel was looking at her with awe; she hated the look on his face, it was slavish, full of love and pain, like a kicked dog. Colin almost snatched the book from her hands and read the next poem in it, a crass gesture which dispersed the disturbing magic of the instant. A few minutes later the group broke up in gentle embarrassment and Jo found Lorcan by her side showing her the rest of the house.

"I love this house," he told her. "It belongs to an old friend of mine and I try to take it whenever I come to Edinburgh. Come here and look," they had reached the topmost rooms, and he led her to the dormer window, open to the still air. "When it's clear you can see away across to the other side of the Firth of Forth. There's a beach at Cramond on the Firth which is very beautiful at this time of year, the sea is quite warm. Perhaps you would like to go down with me one day when the weather is fine."

"Daniel promised he would take me to Cramond when our run finished," she told him at once.

The dawn was about to break, a faint glow of gold behind ribbons of dark cloud. He leaned against the high windowsill. "Daniel knows you will leave him, doesn't he?"

"I don't want to leave him." She watched the sky, stubbornly evading his eyes.

"You will have to leave him, you know it and he knows it. That's why he's afraid. You are stronger than he is. Your destiny is important, I can sense that about you. The time will come when you have to leave. You aren't happy with him now, are you?"

"I am . . . secure with him. I feel like we're going in the same direction." Lorcan said nothing. She felt herself pout, annoyed with him for pulling into the open a truth she had been trying to hide; she had attached herself to Daniel because he was safe; he adored her, she could control him, and while she was with him she could damp down all the dark forces within her. He was a place to hide for herself.

Lorcan turned and walked towards the door, as if she had disappointed him, but Jo followed without speaking. On the next landing he halted. "When you are ready to leave, you can come to me," he told her. It was a bare statement of fact, not an invitation, although his low voice made her spirit vibrate like a harp string.

There was a smell of bacon from the kitchen where the dark woman was making sandwiches, her mouth tight with jealousy.

At six they roused Rachel, collected Bazza and walked back to the tenement flat which they had borrowed.

"You're so right, Daniel. Lorcan really is a truly great man, isn't he?" Colin never knew weariness in the presence of success. "He's just—well, human, isn't he? Just himself, completely natural, and yet he's probably one of the most important men in the whole world in the theatre, isn't he?"

"Yes, Colin," Bazza reassured him with heavy sarcasm, "you can sleep soundly in the knowledge that tonight you met one of your most unforgettable people."

"Oh, fuck off. You all think you can get away with taking the piss out of me and I won't know it but I'm not that dumb, Bazza. You'll find out some day."

"I can't wait."

"I liked that poem he made you read," Rachel yawned as she spoke to Jo.

"Well, I was disappointed, frankly," Daniel cut in at once. "I didn't expect Lorcan Flood of all people to be into all that designer Buddhist crap."

"Is that what it was?" Jo suddenly wanted to defend the poem, if not yet the man who had chosen it for her.

"Of course. Pathetic. Second-rate Japanese philosophy translated by people who probably compose birthday card verses on the side. I expected better. That was when I really saw his feet of clay, I'm afraid."

"Well, at least his people had some quality gear. I managed to unload that bottle of amyl on them." Bazza reached into his inner pocket and showed Jo a small plastic bag of capsules with a satisfied smile. Jo said nothing and sighed inwardly. Lorcan had been right. He had already won her; she had never given herself to Daniel, and now it was just a matter of time before the relationship died.

Their lodgings contrasted unfavourably with Lorcan's light, spacious house. Someone had been sick in the stone-flagged stairwell. Four flights up, they opened the door on an untidy room, chilly despite the summer atmosphere, which smelled of the stale smoke of the men's cigarettes.

Only Colin slept. Bazza snarfed a fistful of speed and sat down to write. He began every day with a large notepad, emptying his head on to the paper. Jo lay wide-eyed beside Daniel, thankful that with five of them crowded into one room there was no possibility of sex. Whenever he felt insecure Daniel always made love to her, with a passion so pitifully desperate that it repelled her. She tried to disguise her feelings, but it was becoming more and more difficult.

After an hour she went to join Rachel, who was methodically sorting through their costumes and properties for the day. Daniel brought the newspaper in at nine, rejoicing over their small but excellent review in *The Scotsman*.

That afternoon the Masonic Hall was more than half full. Lorcan Flood did not come, but four of his company sat in the front row, basking in the hot television lights. Halfway through Colin's *Hamlet* monologue Jo saw one of them extract the brown glass bottle of amyl nitrate from his jacket pocket and pass it along to the others. Colin surely saw it also; he judged his first fall to perfection, catching the bottle with the tip of a foil and splashing the exciting spirit liberally over a whole section of the audience.

His applause was rapturous, but Jo, who took the stage next, to do the Queen and Agatha Christie, had as much of an ovation as twenty people can manage. Every line she spoke was greeted with riotous laughter. A cloud of the drug then reached her, and she felt herself gulping air and flushing scarlet as she struggled against an overwhelming urge to screech like a parrot. Her eyes seemed to be blazing like fireworks. The television cameraman, crouching in the centre aisle, was nearly knocked over by the mirthful crowd.

"Great, that was just great. Terrific. God, they loved you, didn't they?" The reporter was fortunately innocent of the real reason for the crowd's euphoria, although the telltale chemical reek still lingered in the air and the dancers were sniffing suspiciously.

"It was a complete accident, Daniel, I swear," Colin babbled as they quit the building. "You've got to believe me, I had no idea . . ."

Daniel simply smiled at him, too tired to argue. "Why not go home and catch some Zs, Colin?" was all he said.

Once the bright blond hair had disappeared around the corner Bazza thoughtfully informed them that the night was young and he had enough speed left for all of them to enjoy. They each swallowed a capsule, and set off for a cinema downtown to see Robert Redford and Dustin Hoffman uncover the Watergate affair. By midnight they were back at the television tent, watching themselves on the monitor while the audience around screeched and hooted with laughter.

When Lorcan Flood himself arrived at the Masonic Lodge the following day, the hall was already full and Daniel had to find an extra chair. Various Artists had been discovered.

A month later the man from the Arts Council wrote offering Daniel half the money he needed for his film. Bazza's agent introduced them to a producer who put up the rest.

Colin, who had also left Cambridge that summer, withdrew from the film three weeks before shooting was scheduled to begin because he was offered a part in a television series. "I do think all the really important work is being done in film now," he told Daniel. "Film has more prestige, of course, but television is really where the money is and—well—needs must. You do understand, don't you?"

"Of course we understand, Colin," Daniel told him. He had fought for months with the producer over the casting of the male lead. Bazza rewrote Colin's part for the minor Hollywood name the producer had originally wanted without a word of complaint.

Very soon afterwards Jo found herself stepping in front of a camera to face an actor whom her mother's agent Selwyn had scathingly referred to as "one of those know-nothing New York kids hung up on the Method who doesn't know dick from shit about this business except how to ask for a million a picture." This seemed an unfair judgement. He gave Daniel far more respect than Colin had ever done, walked around the set in a concentrated daze talking to himself, and made the costume designer angry by rejecting thirty-six shirts as unsuitable for his character. Halfway through the shoot he was nominated for an Oscar for his previous film. For the first time since she had known him, Daniel went out and got drunk.

"What's the matter with you?" Jo demanded, laughing as she tried to stop him rolling off the bed.

"Nothing's the matter with me, don't you get it? Or with you. There is absolutely nothing either of us can do now to fuck this picture up. Our—hup—our future is secure. Our fortunes are made. Our names will live forever. I now believe in God, the Easter Bunny and re-incarnation. Amen." He passed out, smiling like a cherub. Jo turned him on his side in case he threw up and went back to study the script for tomorrow's scenes.

CHAPTER XIV

"VICTORIA! YOU LOOK like a new woman, you've lost so much weight. God, you make me feel guilty. You've been dieting all summer, I bet. You look marvellous!" Jo flopped down on the chaise-longue in their sitting room and made a fuss about pulling off her boots to disguise the shock of her flat-mate's appearance. It did not suit Victoria to be so thin; with her large bones, her face looked gaunt.

"Oh, I just didn't feel like eating very much. It was so hot this summer." The smile did not reach her eyes.

"I suppose you've had better things to do than pig out." Victoria was plainly steeped in unhappiness, but Jo now knew her better than to believe that she would confide the reason.

"Yes, we were rather busy. Travelling and so on." She drifted across to a battered Regency console between the windows and tucked the late roses she had brought up from Aston Langley more securely into their vase. Jo looked at her back and wondered if she should persist, but decided against it. Talking to Victoria about herself was like talking to a stone wall.

"Do you know what's going on with her?" she asked of Martha when the Jamaican girl finally flounced into the hallway, in a white Jap miniskirt and leggings, two days after the official start of the term.

"Do you mean, has she *told* me?" The cab driver struggled up the steps with three Vuitton cases and Martha tipped him generously. "Pigs might fly, Jo. Since when does Victoria tell us anything any more?"

"Are there any rumours in London, then? You hear all the gossip, don't you?"

"Oh, well that's different. Have I got some hot gossip for you. Oh boy! Is she . . . ?" Her huge eyes, expertly enhanced with a thin line of blue kohl, glanced upstairs to ask if Victoria was also at home.

Jo shook her head. "It has to be something to do with Richard, doesn't it? I mean, he's all she cares about."

"*And* how. You'll just die when you hear. Let's get some coffee. Is there anything to eat? I'm starving." They retreated to the kitchen, and Jo found some chocolate biscuits.

"Well, darling, the word is that Lady Victoria has been holding out on all of us." Martha tossed a huge grey Thierry Mugler coat over a chair and tore open the biscuit packet. "You know her father's wife is not the mother of Victoria and Alex, don't you? And she never talks about her real mother. Not surprising! What happened was when Victoria was just a baby her father was having an affair with that woman he's married to now. Victoria's mother was just *distraught* and she tried to kill herself, so to get her out of the way they had her committed to an insane asylum where she had a little accident—know the kind I mean? Of course the whole thing was hushed up, the inquest was rigged, and when all the fuss had died down Daddy married the new Mommy. Well, none of that would have been too bad, only Richard apparently proposed to Victoria this summer and then . . . well, you can imagine, when the Queen found out . . ." She giggled cheerfully, her mouth full of crumbs. "And Richard is just crazy in love with Victoria, I guess we know that. So, when he told his mother he wanted to marry her, naturally she just flipped her wig! Said no way, *no way*. They had a terrible row. And Philip read the riot act, too. So Richard's really mad and talking about getting a divorce from the whole family, dropping right out like the Duke of Windsor, right? And she's—well, how is she?" She took another biscuit and ate half of it in one bite.

"Awful. She looks like a ghost. But no talky, not a word."

"Isn't that just typical? We'll have to get her to open up somehow, I promised the girls I'd give them the story from the horse's mouth the minute I got here."

Jo made the coffee, wondering what was becoming of them all. Victoria had seemed such a straightforward British girl, a perfect specimen of the Empire-building race, but in the year she had been in love with Richard all her strength had drained away, leaving a withdrawn shadow. And Martha, the primly loyal Commonwealth student of their first year, had become a chattering parrot whose intellectual faculties were exercised most by the relative merits of Revlon Superlash or Lancôme Maquicils mascara. The more modelling she did, the less anchored Martha seemed to be to anything. Not, Jo corrected herself, that I can hold my head up so high. I have covered my agenda, I am an actress, I have an Equity card, an agent, some good reviews and a film to make, but all that came from Daniel and I cannot accept it with a clear conscience because I cannot give him what he wants in return.

She moved towards the table with the coffee and Martha scooped the beautiful coat out of her way. "Careful, I haven't paid Thierry for this yet! Isn't it to die for? Feel how soft!"

Jo obediently touched the luxurious wool to her cheek. "Yes, it's beautiful. Where have you been all summer—apart from Paris?"

"Well, and where *haven't* I been? Oh, Jo, I've had such a fantastic time. Take a look at this." She dipped into her bag and produced her stout British passport, now battered and bulging with new visas. "I have actually been right around the world. And don't look at me like that, Miss Prism! I know what you're thinking and you're wrong. I got all my reading done and I'm halfway through my thesis already, so there! I just lay out by the pool in Pattaya scribbling away and calling up another *piña colada* every hour. Now you can tell me all about you."

Jo told her, thinking it sounded very flat beside the colourful excitements of Martha's summer. "So Daniel's hassling with this producer because he wants Colin to play the lead and the producer wants a big bankable name to make sure he gets his money back. And if he gets his way, which he will because he always does, we'll start shooting right after Christmas."

"Oh, wow! Incredible! Isn't it all just like a fairy story, Jo? Here we are, I'm a model and I've just been around the world, you're going to be a famous film star and Victoria's a princess. Well, almost a princess." She shook her head, still stylishly cropped, and the heart-shaped diamonds set in her big gold hoop ear-rings twinkled.

Jo pointedly said nothing. Martha understood at once. "It's not a fairy tale to you, I suppose. You grew up in all this. But it is like a fairy tale to me, you know?"

"I know." Jo decided she was being uncharitable. Martha had stepped so naturally into the role of beautiful person and world-class celebrity that it was easy to forget that she was new to it all. "You're just bedazzled, aren't you?"

"Yup." She grinned broadly and ate the last biscuit. "I feel like I'm dreaming and I never want to wake up, *ever.*"

Later, when the contents of the suitcases had been crammed into her cupboard Martha noticed the uncharacteristic muddle in Victoria's room and felt a pang of guilt about the dirt she had dished. "Is Victoria really cut up?" she asked, adding a litre of duty-free vodka to the drinks set out on the tray in the drawing room.

"Yes," Jo confirmed with an expression of warning. "She doesn't look at all like a princess-in-waiting. Something's gone wrong between those two, there's more going on than we know yet."

Victoria passed the week striving for normality, being tightly pleasant to the others. Inside, she felt as if she were about to collapse. She was eager to go through the motions of student life, looking for comfort in routine and work, but finding only that when she applied herself to her studies she had lost a terrifying amount of ground in the care-free year behind her. She felt utterly alone. Seeing her brother only reminded her that they shared bad blood and were therefore outcasts.

Richard called her every day but she tried not to do more than reassure him that she was all right. Since her voice was constricted with misery and her replies mechanical because her mind, rigidly separated from her turbulent emotions, could not supply the words, she did not convince him.

"I must see you, Tory, I have to see you," he demanded, walking up and down the worn carpet in his rooms with the telephone.

"Richard, there isn't any point. We've been through this. You've got to leave me alone now."

"But I don't want to leave you alone, I love you and you're in terrible pain . . ."

"I must deal with this myself. I have to make a life without you sooner or later, and the sooner I start the better."

"You don't, you can't . . ."

"I must, Richard, surely you understand? We've talked about it, haven't we? I can't marry you, I can't. It just isn't possible. We have no future together, we must just get on with our lives." She sat in a tense heap in the corner of the sofa, biting her lips and blinking back tears. "Please, Richard, don't upset me any more. This is the best thing in the long run, you must see that."

Eventually she would make him feel guilty, and he would let her go, and take up the threads of his day in a black temper. His happiness had fallen to pieces in his hands. He tried to tell Victoria that her suffering was unnecessary, that what seemed so shameful to her was of no real consequence, that he loved her none the less, that his parents put his happiness above all other considerations, but she would not listen. He agonised over her distress and cursed her for her perversity in the same breath.

Victoria was no less confused. She dreaded the daily call, but felt happy the moment she heard his voice. She knew she had taken the right, the most rational, the best decision, so why then was she boiling with rage against fate? She was doing what was correct, but all her instincts screamed violation.

She struggled through a week, but on Friday, with the empty weekend stretching ahead of her and no invitations extended to a woman who was now well known to be in a delicate situation with the Royal Family, desolation conquered her. The others were out. She imagined them happy in their lovers' arms, admired and fêted, and, most covetable of all, full of purpose and hope for the future.

Panic roared in her ears. She stood up from the sitting room sofa and felt as if she were going to fall. There seemed to be a flash like lightning outside the windows, but she knew it was an illusion, there was no rain, no thunder. Maybe she would go mad after all.

If she went home, she decided, she would be safe. Her little half-sister Rose would distract her, insulate her from this agony by her childish innocence. She went upstairs at once and began to pack before it occurred to her to check the train timetables. The last connection to Aston Langley was long gone. She dared not drive. She was trapped in Cambridge until the morning.

The hours gaped in front of her and she found herself running downstairs and darting from room to room as if trying to find a gap through which to escape the black despair ahead. All the time her higher consciousness, a bitter, rational voice in the top of her head, observed that her behaviour was crazy.

Images of all the unstable kings of England revolved in her mind in a ghastly diorama, George III talking to trees, Canute defying the sea, Edward VIII abdicating for love of a middle-aged American divorcee. From the recesses of her memory emerged the stories she had half-heard and loyally ignored all her life, of subnormal or afflicted members of the royal lineage who had lived their sad lives in obscurity. Wood Farm, she recalled, had been a home for one of them; the place she had felt hallowed by her own happiness was now part of the sinister pattern. She shook her head violently to shut out the notion, and grasped the door-knob for support as she swayed off-balance.

Directly in front of her the drinks tray, a replica of her father's salver, gleamed in the lamplight. It held three bottles. The Vladivar vodka, large and vulgar, loomed over the slim pyramid of Galliano and the half-empty cognac. A drink, just to steady her nerves.

You could drink vodka straight, the Russians always did, she remembered her father telling her. There might have been some ice, but she was too impatient to look. She poured the spirit carelessly and drank it without tasting it.

Jo and Martha returned together at midnight.

"Victoria's up late," Martha remarked, seeing lights shining from every window.

Upstairs they found her sitting still on the floor beside the empty grate. She did not look up when they came into the room.

"Victoria—are you all right?" Jo was quite sure she was not.

There was no reply.

"Victoria?" She shook her shoulder. Victoria slumped sideways and they rushed to catch her before her head hit the brass fender. She was unconscious.

"My God, I can smell something—it's liquor!" Martha

wrinkled her nose in disdain and turned to the drinks tray.
"The vodka. Good heavens, look—she's emptied the bottle!"

Jo sat on the floor, wedged uncomfortably against the
fender by Victoria's shoulders. "That's a hell of a big drink,
especially for someone who doesn't put much away. No
wonder she's totally zonked."

As if to belie her Victoria's eyelids trembled, then
snapped open and she sat awkwardly upright. "How do you
feel—are you OK?" Jo asked her again.

Victoria waved her hands airily. "I'm so sorry," she
lisped. "Do please forgive . . . I . . . I . . ." she gulped
and looked helplessly from one to the other.

"Are you going to throw up?" Jo enquired in a calm
voice.

"I don't think . . . yes. I . . . I . . ."

"Let's see if we can get you to the john in time." Martha
knelt to help and between them they struggled upright.
Victoria had no control over her legs and they dragged her
to the bathroom, her arms held firmly over their shoulders.
She collapsed on the black and white tiled floor in front of
the lavatory, then did her best to sit upright.

"Actually, maybe I'm not going to be sick," she announced in a more distinct voice. "I'm so sorry. This is just
a . . . a temporary sense-of-humour failure." As if personally offended by her understatement, her stomach
heaved and half a litre of vodka tinted with yellow bile hit
the porcelain. Jo thoughtfully pulled her hair back from
her face as she retched.

It seemed as if she sat spewing all night, until finally
there was nothing but mucus to expel in the spasms of her
traumatised gullet. Martha and Jo washed her face and
hands, stripped her soiled clothes and dressed her in a
clean night-gown and cleaned up the bathroom.

"Can I have some water?" she asked meekly, the burning taste of vomit still in her mouth.

"You may not be able to keep it down—just rinse your
mouth out." Jo handed her a glass of water. Victoria immediately gulped it and half a minute later leaned over the
lavatory again to throw it up.

"I'm sorry," she whispered, tears trickling down her
cheeks. "I . . ."

"Don't worry, you'll be OK now, you've got the alcohol out, that's the main thing."

They put her to bed. It had happened rarely in Victoria's life that anyone had tucked in her sheets and prepared to stay with her while she slipped into sleep. "Do you know," she said, enunciating carefully because she was drunk, "the best thing about going to bed with Richard was having someone there when I went to sleep? You know that awful moment between being awake and asleep, when you feel as if you might never wake up or something?" She started crying again and Martha put the tissues by her hand. Gratefully she pulled out a handful. "You know it's all over with us, don't you? I told him I couldn't marry him. You must know why, everyone knows why . . ."

"I've heard things but I don't know if they're true. You don't have to tell us anything if you don't want to." Jo sat on the edge of the bed and waited while Victoria struggled to control her voice.

"I've got to tell somebody," she said between the painful convulsions in her chest. "I haven't got any friends, I can't bear it, you're the only real friends I've got now, everyone else just looks shifty the minute they see me. Isn't it funny how everyone is all over you when they think you're going to join the Royal Family and the next minute doesn't want to know you because you're not?" Slowly, with many pauses while emotion choked her, she told them what had happened and Martha felt doubly remorseful about the gossip she had been so enthusiastic to trade.

"And that's it really, over, finished, kaput. I can't do it, I'd never forgive myself. I know it's the right thing. But I feel so . . ." She dissolved in weak sobs once more and Martha patted her hand. "I won't see him," she continued. "I know if I see him I won't be able to resist, so all I can do is just keep him away."

Eventually she fell into a heavy sleep. Jo carefully turned her on her side and took away some of the pillows, then she and Martha left the room.

"Poor kid." Victoria often seemed much more than one year younger than Jo. "I don't understand it. Why is she putting herself through all this? If all they want is for him to be happy, why doesn't she just go ahead and marry the guy. God knows, she loves him."

"It's more than love, though, isn't it? He's everything to

her. She just can't believe she's good enough." Martha shook her head.

"Her story isn't the same as yours."

"Not mine, just what I heard." All the same, she condemned herself, you made that story yours when you repeated it.

"If her father had been having an affair, he'd hardly be the one to tell her, would he?"

"I guess not. You're right, the poor child. She's really taken it hard."

"And where's Prince Charming? If he really cared for her he'd come around and break down the door, instead of letting her drown herself in misery like this."

"Right—what a shit, eh?"

Neither of them spoke with complete conviction. They were both a little bit in love with Richard. In his absence, Martha felt that he was semi-sacred; in his presence, she found him dazzling, not just as a man but as someone whose untarnishable fame eclipsed all the tawdry glitterati among whom she now moved. When she reviewed this extraordinary year in her life, it seemed as if his presence had released the deluge of good fortune which followed.

Jo wanted very much to dislike Richard, she told herself she found him arrogant, without the modesty appropriate to a man who had done nothing to earn his immense worldly status. But her heart refused to follow her judgement, and the memory of their first meeting lingered. Their paths crossed infrequently, but every time she felt a charge of energy in his presence. Lorcan Flood, who believed in re-incarnation, had solemnly told her that he felt they had known each other in a past life. When she saw Richard, Jo knew what the theatrical magician meant. There was a lingering sense of recognition with the Prince which she could not explain.

Neither woman had acknowledged this attraction; now both transmuted their feelings into a determination to see the obviously ideal marriage of Richard and Victoria take place.

Victoria was in a deep sleep the next morning when the telephone rang and Jo darted downstairs to answer it before the noise aroused her. It was Richard.

"Listen," she began in an impetuous half-whisper. "You

have to get over here. Victoria needs you. She's absolutely miserable . . ."

"What do you mean? She hasn't tried to do anything silly, has she?" There was no need to ask who was speaking; Jo's American accent had made a comeback under emotional pressure. Afterwards Richard wondered why he had allowed himself to fall immediately into a conspiratorial conversation about his most intimate preoccupations with an outsider.

"No, she just got totally smashed last night and told us everything. The whole thing has just knocked her sideways. We have to help her get over this."

"I . . ." he hesitated. He had no words to say what he felt and the habit of concealing his feelings from all but the closest intimates was now long ingrained.

The pause annoyed her. "Look, how soon can you be here . . ."

"I can't."

"What the fuck does that mean, you can't? You've been seeing Victoria over a year, you say you're in love with her, she's certainly in love with you, you want to get married and now when she needs you, you can't make it? Terribly sorry, Your Highness, this must be some ancient British custom I don't understand."

He was angry, which was what she had intended; angry enough to come clean and talk reality. "Look, I'm at Windsor, I have to be here. There's a great family council of war on. You may not realise this, but next year my mother celebrates her Silver Jubilee, that means . . ."

"I know what that means. Queen Victoria had one, didn't she?"

He took a deep breath and tried not to lose his temper. "It means the 25th anniversary of her coronation. Now the whole country is planning massive celebrations, I have to play a part in them, this is one of the very few weekends we can get all of us together for a meeting and I have to be here now."

"Why? You can telephone. You can get someone to fix your diary for you—you do have someone to do that, don't you?"

"Yes I do, but he is not my mother's son."

"Oh, for Christ's sake . . ."

Standing in front of his bedroom window looking out

across the private garden at Windsor, Richard willed her to understand. He could not possibly tell an outsider how tense his mother was becoming, how the more elaborate the Jubilee plans became the less certain she was that they were appropriate. She saw the whole year as a test of public feeling for the institution she represented, and for once in her life was visibly unsettled. Richard, who needed to be loved almost as much as he needed to breathe, had never sympathised with his mother's reasons for doing her duty without courting public affection, but now that public feeling was to be put to the test, he understood exactly her acute apprehension.

"Look," he said simply, "this will be the most important year of my mother's life, next to the year she became Queen, and I must be with her. Just today, just at this moment, she is the one who needs me most."

Jo sighed, trying to think of one final clinching argument. With her intense sensitivity, she could hear everything that Richard was afraid to say. Victoria's misery seemed insignificant, almost a personal indulgence, when compared with his commitment to his mother.

A long silence echoed down the telephone line. Richard's mind was full of tormenting possibilities. He wanted very much to confide in Jo. The world, even his corner of it, seemed to make sense when he talked to her: otherwise it was becoming less and less comprehensible. He could not understand why Victoria had changed before his eyes from a woman who had seemed to him always serene to a shrinking, disoriented creature who suddenly, in a whispering voice full of shame, insisted she wanted to repudiate everything that had been between them. With the unshakable arrogance of his age and sex, he felt this was merely a woman's caprice. He was both irritated and grateful that this American had intervened between them.

"I rang to speak to Victoria," he told her apologetically. "If she's there, I'd like to speak to her now."

"She's asleep," Jo answered bluntly.

"Perhaps when she wakes up you could tell her that I'll see her on Monday. Now I really must go, I'm late for a meeting already." He hung up and did his best to clear his mind before joining his family.

"The shit," Jo muttered, slamming down the receiver.

Victoria woke up an hour later, pale and puffy-eyed. Jo

brought her tea in bed, and relayed Richard's promise in an encouraging tone. "But I can't possibly see him," Victoria countered immediately. Her eyes darkened with dismay. "I can't. You don't understand . . ."

"No, I don't." Jo sat on the end of the bed and crossed her legs. "Nobody understands, Victoria. Martha came back from London with a mass of gossip—I won't repeat it, I've never heard such garbage, but people are passing it around. How long do you think it will be before the newspapers notice that you aren't with him? You say you love Richard, so why are you humiliating him like this? Do you think he even understands what's going on with you?"

"I've told him, I've tried to explain."

"You must think of who you are," Jo argued gently. "And who he is. You can't hide, you know. It's not your fault, but this is part of your life you have lived in public and you can't try to disappear now."

Victoria suddenly looked up, her eyes huge with unshed tears. "That's just it. I can't think of who I am, I don't know who I am any more. It was something I never considered, something I took for granted, but now I've just been told that I'm not who I always thought I was, not a . . ." she paused, unwilling to voice the thought. ". . . not a normal person . . ."

"Of course you're a normal person."

"Maybe I am, maybe I'm not, nobody knows really, do they? I've just got to live with that. But all the same, I can't possibly marry him, maybe I can't ever marry anyone . . ." She swallowed gulps of air and tried to be calm but the grief was too violent. Her chest felt as if it were tearing down the middle. She began to scream and raised her hand to her mouth as if to stop the noise. Her knuckles crammed against her teeth, she battled in vain to control herself and Jo saw panic in her eyes as she failed. Victoria's teeth broke her skin; blood ran down her hand and stained the white lace cuff of her night-shirt. The American appreciated at last that Victoria's characteristic serenity had not been a genuine state. Her inner being was wounded and in turmoil. She had drifted into adulthood in a prolonged trance of post-traumatic shock. This new pain was awakening old emotions.

Martha, now a habitual late sleeper but roused by the noise, came running up the stairs. "Just stay with her," Jo commanded, and went to the telephone, her mind racing uselessly. The imperative of discretion seemed to block every action she could have taken to help.

She called Alex, but he was not in his college. She called Daniel in London, and left a message on his answering machine. She saw Victoria's handbag, tipped it out and found the small, well-used address book; there was no entry at all for Richard. In the end Jo called her tutor and, without giving any reason or, indeed, being asked for one, obtained the number of the college doctor.

The physician came within the hour and prescribed tranquillisers and sleeping pills. Victoria looked wonderingly from one face to another as she swallowed the first dose. After half an hour of tearful conversation, she slept.

The next day she passed in a deep chemical apathy. The others helped her get up, bathe and wash her hair. In the afternoon, when the heavy drizzle seemed to have settled in for the rest of the day, she suggested a walk. Martha looked at her quizzically. "It's raining," she said, "you can see that, can't you?"

"Oh yes. But I like walking in the rain. So does Richard. The whole family goes out in such bad weather that people think they're mad, you know."

They shrugged their shoulders and took her to the botanical gardens. Martha cooked dinner for them all and Victoria, now deadly calm and apparently reconciled to Richard's arrival the next day, went to bed at nine.

"I feel so much better now," she told them as she left the room. "Those pills are marvellous. You've been so kind to me, both of you. You've really saved my life."

Richard came at his usual hour in the late afternoon, guilt adding lustre to his charm, and even Jo was won over by his concern. Victoria, her senses deadened by the drugs, accepted his attention with pathetic gratitude.

Privately, he noted her dull eyes and shaking hands, her thinness and slow responses, and was appalled. He decided to ask his personal physician to call on her. Alex, who appeared the next day, was equally alarmed, and took her to another doctor. Twisting a tissue in her hands and talking in a low, monotonous voice, Victoria acquired over a hundred sleeping pills without any conscious intention of doing so.

She tipped them together into the scratched silver cigarette box she had brought from home but never filled, and decided that the sight of the blue and green capsules was comforting. In her new world of utter uncertainty, they were something of which she could be sure.

Numbers seemed to mean very little, and so she forgot the dosages which the doctors prescribed. She hoarded the tranquillisers in their little brown bottles and slipped one into her mouth whenever she felt overpoweringly helpless; this was several times a day.

Every night she chose one sleeping capsule; after a few days she began to wake in a blurred panic before dawn, and so began to take two, and then three. She enjoyed sitting up in bed with the box full of coloured pills and stirring them around with her fingers. One night she fell asleep with the box still open on her lap. It tumbled to the floor with a noise loud enough to alarm Martha, who was studying downstairs.

There was no way of knowing how many of the hoard Victoria had taken. Martha immediately called the college doctor, who had more experience of young suicides than most other physicians in the country and ascertained at once that Victoria was in no immediate danger.

"Get rid of these," he told Martha, indicating the capsules scattered all over the bedroom floor. "Where do you think she got them? Is another doctor treating her?"

"I think so. Her—um—brother's doctor, I know she saw him . . ."

"Try if you can to get his name and address, and I'll write to him and let him know what's going on. I warn you, people in this condition can be very devious, and they can also have no clear idea of what they're doing. She'll probably deny even having the drugs when she wakes up so perhaps you can find out where she got them indirectly . . ."

Martha nodded, her eyes large and grave behind her spectacles. Victoria's condition and the need to settle down to her last year of work had knocked a great deal of the fashion fizz out of her. In the morning she left a message for Alex at his college, intercepted Richard's telephone call and by noon had given the college doctor the information he needed.

When Victoria at last woke up she was, as the doctor predicted, too confused to respond to Martha's gentle but persistent questioning about the sleeping pills. She was dismayed, however, to find that she had none left and immediately made an appointment to see her brother's doctor that afternoon and ask for a new prescription.

"She ought to go cold turkey on this now," Jo said when she returned from London that night. "If she starts messing around with drugs it'll only make things worse for her, not better. God knows, I've seen enough people wreck their heads that way."

Martha nodded. "I've seen a few for myself, now. Victoria hasn't, she just doesn't know what she's doing. I kept asking her what she was taking and she just looked at me."

"When she gets back we'll just have to see if we can get the stuff off her."

Victoria resisted help with unsuspected ferocity. "I know you're only thinking of me," she said, with a hollow echo of her old social smile, "but I really am quite capable of reading the label on a medicine bottle and taking two tablets a day or whatever it says."

"I think the fact that you had over a hundred different pills in bed with you last night argues against that." Martha slipped automatically into her cross-examination manner.

"I don't believe you," Victoria answered at once. "I couldn't possibly have had that many. I had none left this morning."

"That's because I threw them all down the lavatory last night. Look, we're not doing this to persecute you, we're doing it because we're your friends and we care about you. Call the doctor and ask him if you don't believe me."

"Right, I'll do just that." Victoria pulled her address book out of her handbag and dialled the telephone with angry stabs of her finger, turning her shoulder discourteously towards the others as soon as the surgery answered. The conversation lasted nearly half an hour. At the end she carefully replaced the receiver and said, "I'm sorry, I seem to have made a mistake." Then she lay back on the chaise-longue and closed her eyes.

After a few moments tears glistened in her eyelashes. Martha moved over and hugged her. "He wants me to see a psychiatrist," Victoria whispered. "I can't possibly do that." To her mind the suggestion was doubly shameful; to the Fairleys and their class, psychiatry was an option for cowards and weaklings, a fig-leaf which failed to disguise personal inadequacy. Now Victoria saw it also as a confirmation that she bore the stigma of madness.

Her resistance was gone, and she fumbled in her bag for her new tablets. Jo woke at six in the morning, and found her sitting on the top step of the fire-escape in her scarlet night-dress, oblivious of the icy mist which lay over the rooftops.

She seemed quite lucid. "Don't worry," she said to Jo with a rueful smile, "I'm not having another sense-of-humour failure. I was just hot so I came out to get cool. That awful photographer can't be about this early. I'm coming in now." She reached for the iron banister rail to pull herself to her feet; her grip slipped on the damp metal and she almost fell thirty feet to the ground, but Jo grabbed her free hand and pulled her back into an awkward heap in the doorway. "That didn't look very convincing, did it?" she asked with a feeble laugh.

Jo made her coffee, and they sat in the kitchen. "You look a bit better," she offered, hoping to get Victoria to open up at last.

"Am I looking awful?" Her hands flew to her hollow cheeks. "I suppose I must. I ought to wash my hair."

"How do you feel?"

Victoria considered. How she felt had never been important before. She obediently probed her consciousness, trying to find emotions, but discovered nothing. "I don't know. I feel sort of blank." There was a long pause, and Jo said nothing. "Do you know what I really can't bear?" Victoria put down her coffee suddenly and it splashed on to the table. "I'll always love Richard but I don't mind not being able to marry him because it would have been frightful, he told me so himself and he ought to know. What I really can't stand is being not told, being lied to, by my father, everybody. I feel as if they all cheated me by not telling me."

Jo nodded, hoping for more. "You're angry with them," she confirmed.

"Yes." Victoria straightened her shoulders. "Yes I bloody well am. And so is Alex, you know. But he's taken it better." She saw the comforting, familiar path into which to deflect her unbearable feelings, and went on talking about her brother until Martha appeared.

By ten she felt able to wash, dress and set off for a

tutorial. "I found her out on the fire escape at six this morning," Jo told Martha, "I don't think she was planning to jump but . . ." she shrugged her shoulders, "I don't think she knows what she's doing."

"There are two of us," Martha proposed, "if we take it in turns we can watch her around the clock."

There was a thoughtful silence in which both women considered their personal accumulations of neglected work. Martha stood up, tossing her spectacles on top of her notepad with a decisive gesture. "It's the only way. I'm going to call Kelly now and tell him to do without me for a week or two."

By the time Cambridge was held in the dead, cold clutch of mid-November Victoria was going through the motions of her life like a sleepwalker. Against her will she found herself walking by the riverbank or straying off the pavement in the busy streets, sly, dramatic gestures calculated to prey on her friends' concern for which the small part of her mind that remained clear hated the involuntary majority.

As the end of term approached, Victoria's tutor wrote to her family and suggested that she needed to go home and stay there until she had recovered. Martha's tutor bluntly threatened to send her down and made bitchy observations about Commonwealth scholarship students who wasted opportunities which thousands of more worthy candidates would have seized. Jo's tutor, who had already dismissed her as a brilliant girl determined to waste herself as an actress, marvelled at her ability to skimp reading, sleep through lectures and turn in essays which were more original and better constructed than the work of her conscientious fellows.

Richard was desolate. He saw the woman he loved, in whom he had invested his whole self and his entire future, slipping away into a dark chasm. At first he tried to save her. He telephoned every morning without fail, to be answered first by one of the others and then by the flat, drowsy voice of Victoria roused from narcotic unconsciousness. He wrote notes, sometimes two or three in a day. He sent flowers every week.

Every afternoon he called at the apartment and sat alone with Victoria for as long as he could. He talked nonsense, told her jokes, saved news of their friends and fashioned tiny incidents into little stories to amuse her.

"Bear up, Tory, we'll get you through this," he reassured her, crushing her thin shoulders as if to force his own strength into her weakening frame. "I love you, darling, I'll always love you, and you love me, and nothing else matters, nothing at all."

He feared that he would lose her, or that if she survived this inner ordeal she would be overcome by the trials which their marriage would bring, and a lifetime of loneliness opened up before him. More disturbingly, he felt angry with her, and sensed that she was angry with him, as if her rejection were his fault. He suppressed all these feelings with displays of optimism. He passed long, alcoholic evenings with Alex in his room, talking of everything but the future.

"I don't know what to do," he admitted, sitting on the rug by his cold hearth as another drunken midnight slipped past. "I feel I'm the one who's hurt Tory the most. If it wasn't for me she wouldn't feel the way she does about . . . about your mother. I just make it worse for her."

Alex hiccuped quietly and poured out the last of the scotch. He had his own conflicts to reconcile. Disloyalty to Richard could not be admitted, but he half-hated the man for the very reason he was now confessing.

"And the worst," Richard drained his tumbler in a gulp, craving sanctuary from his torturing thoughts, "is that she's suffering so much because she's such a good person. If she was one of those ambitious little bitches that tries to grab my balls at every cocktail party—oh yes, they do, let me tell you, the word's out that I'm going to be back on the market any day now—well, if Tory was like that she wouldn't care, she'd hush everything up and lead me on for all she was worth. It's because she's *not* like that . . ."

Alex made a gesture of apology and rose on unsteady legs to go and vomit in the bathroom. Richard watched him with glazed eyes.

He felt bitter frustration. A maddening burden of obligations lay before him. The court was still engulfed in the task of organising his mother's Jubilee Tour of Australia, New Zealand and the Pacific, and then of the whole of Britain. He was committed to accompany his mother, and the other members of his family, to all the major reviews, pageants and processions arranged for the celebration. In addition, he had undertaken to visit Africa with his brother Charles in March, and to be installed as a Royal Knight of the Thistle in St Giles' Cathedral in Edinburgh in May. He was to ride with his grandmother and his younger brothers in the Jubilee procession through London in June.

His uniforms for all these occasions were made after two fittings only, instead of the usual seven, to the loud disapproval of his tailor who was alarmed at the speed with which the muscular bulk of the Prince's shoulders was increasing.

The IRA issued an official commitment to a blitz of bombing for the Jubilee; extra security meetings were called, his detectives were summoned for special training and he used the general alarm as an excuse to cut down his less official engagements. The handful of charities which he had agreed to patronise had each asked for his presence. In Cambridge the Magdalene hierarchy had to be allotted their proper quota of dinners and teas in his last year. Every quasi-official society in the university laid claim to him for just one occasion before he quit the university and to refuse them would cause offence. Only his tutor, taking a perverse pleasure in the Prince's increasing distress, benignly advised him to do what he needed to and not concern himself too much over half-a-term's work in his final year.

He cancelled his social engagements ruthlessly, leaving a score of disappointed hostesses to curse; a wit among them called him Rich the Bitch and the name ran up the grapevine so fast that overnight it reached his aunt, who relayed it to his mother in their regular morning telephone conversation.

She gave a short, sarcastic laugh. "Well, I suppose somebody had to think of that sooner or later."

"He really has been playing fast and loose. All kinds of people are upset." Margaret decided to say nothing further. To her, and to all those with memories of Petronella Fairley, there was a strong element of predestination about the couple's present anguish, as there had been about their initial joy.

Others were less sympathetic. His Secretary enraged him by resisting daily orders to refuse commitments and rearrange his diary. In the magic circle, the opinion that

Prince Richard was a fatally selfish young man quite unworthy of his position gained strength, particularly among older people.

Fortunately the press interest in Richard and Victoria was temporarily overshadowed, not only by the impending Jubilee but by a rumour that his brother Charles was to announce his engagement to Princess Marie-Astrid of Luxemburg. At Christmas a French magazine snatched a picture of Victoria looking gaunt and vacant as she went to church with her family at Aston Langley, and contrasted it with the happy picture of them both at Balmoral in the summer, but the British newspapers paid little attention. Hungry freelances continued to send in photographs of Victoria, but the editors wanted smiling blonds on the pages, not a tense, dishevelled woman wearing neglected clothes.

At home Victoria's health improved. Pamela, not pleased to see her ambitions in danger of being thwarted by the sheer weakness of their neglected vessel, treated her with more solicitude than she had ever shown before. She could, as her husband had discovered long ago, be an irresistibly sensitive companion when she chose, and Victoria was now elected the new focus of her energies.

"Don't go back to Cambridge, Tory darling," she counselled. "There's such a bad atmosphere, so much pressure, all those neurotic students. You're just not up to it at the moment. Stay at home and rest, and then in the autumn if you really want to finish your degree you can go back. Though I think a little job is really what you need, something to take your mind off things. Maybe something to do with pictures, so you can use your training, hmn?" She patted Victoria's lank hair with a bright smile.

"I'm being such a bore and a nuisance . . ." Victoria hated her step-mother touching her but never resisted it.

"Nonsense. This is what families are for, propping each other up in the bad times. I do blame myself, really, I should have made your father tell you the whole story much earlier. You just grew up rather quicker than we expected."

Since Navy tradition required the senior officers' wives to take an interest in preventing nervous breakdowns among the spouses of the men in their husbands' command, Pamela felt that she had plenty of the right kind of experience to restore Victoria's spirits. She was a perfectly sensible girl who had had a ghastly shock. All she needed was fresh air and exercise, and encouragement to take an interest in herself again.

A kindly old hunter was borrowed from neighbours, and Victoria took to the invigorating habit of a morning ride. There were shopping trips to London during which Pamela praised her slimness, ensured that she was equipped with a glorious selection of clothes from the new season's collections and encouraged her to dare a sleek new haircut. Houseguests, including Jo and Martha, came and went in a carefully chosen cycle, selected first for their comforting intimacy, later for their stimulation.

Victoria did jigsaw puzzles and read books to Rose. In the house, immersed in the reality of her family rather than the haunting facts of her past, she regained strength. She drifted from room to room each day, looking at the newly cleaned and displayed pictures. The portraits of her ancestors, their homes, their horses and their dogs, their possessions and their servants helped her to strengthen her new sense of herself. It was a mere sketch beside the robust identity on which she had rested before, but she felt it was at least genuine, not built upon a lie. The portrait of her mother she could not find. The trunk room was smartly painted in dark green, but the case with her mother's things was no longer there; it seemed disloyal to ask to see it.

Richard visited almost weekly, and Pamela was encouraged to find that he was determined to over-ride all Victoria's misgivings about their marriage. She left them alone as much as possible, more than might be considered polite, and he was grateful.

Victoria no longer shrank away when he touched her; one evening he began to kiss her and she responded. Her movements were tentative, but so sweetly familiar that his blood caught fire and he tried to make love to her immediately, pulling her down to the hearthrug without seeking consent. He caressed her thighs exactly as he had always done, and for a moment she acquiesced but as soon as his fingers found her opening she became tense and awkward. No amount of tenderness could rouse her. Although she longed to feel again the irresistible flush of desire, her senses remained obstinately asleep. Eventually she began to cry. The sound was like a shower of cold water bringing him to his senses and he felt shame so severe his skin prickled. He apologised over and over again, almost weeping himself.

The incident hardened her attitude. At odd moments she recognised that she hated Richard. He was trying to impose his will on her and now that her spirit had returned, scarred and weak as it was, she began to resist. "The bastard," she whispered to herself with guilty satisfaction as she walked her horse home the next morning. "He's only thinking of himself." Saying the words aloud, watching her breath steam in the raw, wet morning air, made her feel less anxious, but not calm enough to do without the little cream capsule of Valium she took every night with the family doctor's blessing.

At the beginning of February Richard returned to Windsor for the family celebration of the day marking the 25th year of his mother's rule. They walked in the raw cold to their church for morning service to the sound of a single bell, like thousands of other families all over the country. Long practised at covert observation in public, Richard watched his mother as the chaplain pompously announced that the nation's debt to her was incalculable, and saw tension narrow her lips and deepen the creases below her eyes.

The university mountaineering club claimed him a few weeks later for an expedition to Switzerland. The intoxicating combination of physical danger, isolation and comradeship with a few men from the world outside the royal enclosure cleared his mind and gave him new energy. He reneged on a promise to stay on with friends to ski, and returned to Victoria.

He found her composed and more beautiful than ever with the girlish softness gone from her face. She had long rehearsed what she intended to say to him.

"Nothing has changed," she warned him, now without regret. "You must understand that. I will always love you but I cannot possibly marry you. It would be a terrible thing to do. You know that yourself, you know that this is for the best in the end. I'm sorry, but I have made up my mind and you must not try to change it for me."

"What do you want me to do?" he asked, hearing his own voice from the distance of shock.

"I'm not going back to Cambridge, I'm going to Florence to do an art history course in the summer and then I expect I'll get a job. But—we must finish it, Richard. You've got to set me free."

"You don't want to be free." He found he could hardly look at her. He wanted to shake her, slap her, punch her and the impulse shocked him.

"No I don't, but I must move on, don't you see?" He nodded in silence, howling inwardly as the wound opened up in his heart.

He left the house with a show of tender politeness and a sense of relief. Once his disturbed emotions settled, he realised that their relationship was over and was glad; however passionately he had sought intimacy with Victoria, there had always been a heavy sense of loneliness with her. He had loved her serenity, but never succeeded in penetrating it. When he got close to her, he found there was no one there.

· · ·

"WHAT ARE WE doing here?" Daniel glowered elegantly around the rose-red brick walls of Magdalene's first court.

"You're here for the movie, I'm here for my friend Victoria. Now shut the fuck up and smile."

Daniel arranged his arm affectionately around Jo's bare shoulders and gave the photographers his best boyish grin. Above the ancient tiled roof of the courtyard, black clouds were drifting across the gilded sky of a midsummer evening.

"You're the lucky one. I've never gone out in a monkey suit before in my life and after tonight I'm never doing it again." Jim Kelly ran his finger around the collar of his white dress shirt to loosen it. He was not born to wear a tail coat and all the trimmings. He looked like an amateur butler and he knew that most of the other guests at the Magdalene May Ball belonged to the class that could detect an amateur butler from first-hand experience. "Bloody ridiculous, making everyone dress up like this."

"They do it to keep the gatecrashers out." Alex was on the ball committee and privy to all the secrets. "Buck up, guys," he told the scrum of photographers whose whirring lenses almost drowned the distant music of the steel band.

"Almost done, sir," the servile new man from the local

paper reassured him, while the big boys from the nationals fell over each other trying to get the best shot.

"I thought that the napalm on the walls was for keeping undesirables out." Daniel felt Jo quiver with the apprehension that he was going to ruin the evening. Why did women set so much store by all these outward displays? He hated any kind of party; he was frankly jealous of Victoria and Martha and whatever had gone on in that apartment for two years. That year they had spent anguished hours discussing why and what she was holding back from him, why she hurt him when she did not intend to, why she could not change. It had got them nowhere. His film had won the critics' prize at Cannes. All Europe was raving about Jo and her *sensualité rare et raffinée.* He had everything he had wanted and it seemed like nothing because she was out of his reach. He felt cheated, and when he stopped smiling his face was thunderous.

"Napalm!" Alex snorted cheerfully. "It's only blue paint, stains their clothes so the bulldogs can spot them."

"Harley, love, I'm losing you, gimme a shape," pleaded Keith Cowley from the *Daily Post.* "That's a girl, show us that lovely frock."

Obediently Martha wound herself into a sinuous curve at Kelly's side, pulling down the shirred neckline of her violet silk jersey Saint Laurent to reveal one polished chocolate shoulder.

"Anyway," Daniel went on with malice, "why bother to keep people out? This is meant to be the terminal debauch, last great freaky circus, the Saturnalia before we're all set free into the wide world. A few gatecrashers just liven things up."

"People who've paid a hundred pounds a head for the tickets tend to get miffed if they know others can get it all for free," Alex explained amiably, missing the real hostility behind the film director's words. He had been pouring champagne down his throat at garden parties all afternoon. At his side was his new girlfriend, Charlotte Pitts, only sixteen and delectable in a pale blue flounced gown of the kind Jo said looked like a boiled sweet wrapper. Alex was on the up again.

In the centre of the group Richard and Victoria stood side by side in silence and smiled at the cameras. Together in public for the first time since their private parting, they felt uncomfortable. They both considered that they were there for Alex's sake. While Victoria had been overwhelmed by the truth about her mother, Alex had flung himself violently into the considerable social whirl at Magdalene. Since he was on the ball committee, since every May Ball committee is hell bent on making their bash the most extravagant, the most spectacular, the most memorable of the season, if not the decade, he had unhesitatingly asked them both to attend. Victoria could refuse her brother nothing. For Richard it was another unpalatable but inescapable obligation. Alex's notion was to gather them all together for a great farewell to their student years, incidentally ensuring that his own party would be made up of the most glittering names at this or any other May Ball.

"OK, guys, that's it," Alex waved the photographers away as if brushing off a crowd of Calcutta street hawkers. Grumbling, they began to pack up their cameras as a team of bouncers recruited from the rugby club moved forward to escort them to the gate. The party moved off to make their way to the college lawn, where Pimms and champagne cocktails were being served in the candy-striped marquees.

Richard and Victoria were the last. "Your Highness . . . er, excuse me, please, sir, Your Highness . . ." Keith Cowley caught up with them as they approached the Pepys Library. They halted. Henshaw the detective, who had been following at a discreet distance, prepared to intervene if necessary.

"I am most terribly sorry . . ." Cowley now considered his accent unimpeachable, "but the most frightful thing has happened, I've forgotten to put a film in my camera," he had the empty Nikon open in his hand, "and my editor will murder me if I miss this picture. He'll sack me on the spot. Could you possibly let me take just one more, it'll only be a few seconds . . ."

Richard laughed. "You don't mind, do you?" he asked Victoria quietly.

"Of course not, the poor man." She arranged her face as she knew it looked best. Her dress was also of the sweet-wrapper variety, peppermint green taffeta with bows gathering the sleeves. It was an opulent style which only a woman of her height and proportions could wear and stood out clearly against the ancient brick wall. A white rose in full bloom hung over their heads. They were relaxed and animated now that there was only one camera to face.

Cowley swiftly loaded the camera and took ten perfect frames. "I can't thank you enough, sir. It would have been my job this time, for certain." Servility, that was the ticket with the Royals.

"Sure you've got enough?" Richard took Victoria's elbow and they prepared to walk on; Cowley took two more pictures.

"Oh yes, this'll be all I need. So kind of you, sir. I really appreciate it. May I wish you a pleasant evening."

He backed away, almost bowing, then sped to the gate where the paper's dispatch rider was waiting.

"There you are, lad, one dozen of the best royal exclusives—hit the road!" He watched the bike roar away over Magdalene Bridge with satisfaction. The old trick always worked.

"Victoria, wise *up*, darling. You are so *naïve*," Martha swayed gracefully back a half-pace despite her heels sinking into the grass, allowing Alex to hand out the first round of cocktails. "Cowley *always* pulls that trick, didn't you know?"

"No, I didn't." Victoria accepted her drink with little enthusiasm. "I've been away from all this nonsense for a few months and I must say it was very pleasant."

"It was my fault," Richard admitted, trying to lighten the atmosphere. "I was the one who fell for it. I just felt sorry for the poor little sod."

Martha's rich laugh rippled across the river and echoed from the walls of the building on the far side. "Darling, never waste your sympathy on scum like that. Give a photographer an inch and he'll take a mile. I should know." Kelly squeezed her backside affectionately, marvelling that his hand could almost enclose the neat, tight mound of flesh. She twitched away with a squeak. "They're all just animals, darling, believe me."

The light words sank heavily in the air. Kelly and Martha appeared the picture of contented sensuality which depressed the two unhappy couples in the group and intimidated Charlotte, who was barely reconciled to the loss of her virginity a few weeks ago.

"What about this jubilee lark, then?" Kelly demanded of Richard, figuring that it would be some time before he had another chance to get this kind of stuff from the horse's mouth. "People are going bananas, aren't they? They've painted Union Jacks and 'Betty Rules OK' all over the railway bridge in my street. How's the old lady taking it?"

"Rather well, I think. I've hardly seen her, she's been rushing all over the place, but I do believe she's really very moved. And surprised. When we were planning it all she kept saying she was sure people wouldn't be interested . . ." Richard was grateful for Kelly's question. No one had yet asked him about what was uppermost in his own mind. He answered at length while Victoria prickled at the photographer's presumption. One never initiated a conversation with royalty, Kelly should know that.

Daniel abruptly left the group and went to stand by himself at the riverside, regarding a passing juggler with distaste. A cloud of blue smoke billowed across the lawns from the roasting pits where three whole sheep were turning over charcoal. Jo considered going over to sweeten his mood, but only for a split second. She was beginning to hate herself for feeling guilty that she could not love him as he wanted.

The steel band gave way to a pair of medics singing a comic song about sinusitis and trying to fapdance in frogman's fins. The more easily amused half of the gathering laughed raucously.

They ate salmon and roast lamb. Kelly amused himself coating individual strawberries with cream and feeding them to Martha, watching the miraculous flower of her mouth open to enclose each fruit. He had decided to put together a portfolio of erotic photographs of her; he had a few already, taken when she was hardly aware of what he was doing.

The crashing chords of a pop group resounded from the discotheque tent.

"Let's go." Daniel tossed his napkin on the table and reached for Jo's hand. She gave an imperceptible shake of her head and indicated Richard with her eyes. Royalty had to make the first move, she knew Daniel knew that. God, why was he being so offensive tonight? "I said, *let's go*," he repeated, standing up and trying to pull her to her feet.

"Daniel, what's happening with you? They're just a bunch of noisy punks, you hate that kind of music . . ."

"The Adverts," Alex supplied obligingly, "we were very lucky to get them. They're supposed to be very popular."

"They *are* very popular and *very* sick," Martha informed them cheerfully. She was becoming an expert on everything ephemeral.

"Right, let's go," Richard stood up suddenly, flashing a devilish smile around the table. "I can't miss this, I may never get the chance to hear anything sick again in my life."

Victoria obediently rose and took his arm, feeling positively unhappy. All through dinner people had been noticing her presence with the Prince and whispering behind their hands. This, added to that awful photographer's trick, made her feel as if the whole of England was gossiping about her.

As they left the dining tent another camera flashed in her face. At once four muscular oarsmen from the security team ran forward to flatten the photographer. They threw him and his camera into the river and returned to apologise to Alex.

"Better do a sweep and check he's the only one," he ordered pompously. "We can't have the paparazzi turning the ball into a bloody circus."

"Surely you don't need the paparazzi's help?" Daniel muttered under his breath.

Jo pulled him aside at once. "Stop it, Daniel, for God's sake. Why are you being so offensive?"

"You know damn well why."

"No I don't. You can't say it's anything to do with you and me . . ."

"Can't I? I'm only here for you. A few pictures in the society pages aren't going to get any more people to see the movie, you know that."

"Well if you're here for me, why are you trying to spoil everything?"

"Because I know there's no point—whatever I do for you it will never be enough, will it? You'll never give me what I want."

She clenched her fists in despair and sat down on a white wooden bench. Behind her the first of the fireworks lit up the charcoal sky. "Daniel, I don't know what you want. We've been through all this a million times."

"I want you, that's all."

"But you've got me."

He seized her arm roughly and she resisted him with all her strength. In anger he pushed her away and she almost fell to the ground. "Lying bitch. I want what you give them, your precious girlfriends, I want your time and your attention and your tender concern," his mouth twisted as he spat out the words, "that's you, that's all of you, that's what I want and you'll give it to some brainless arrogant little tart of a Sloane Ranger and you won't give it to me."

"You get everything I can spare," she told him with bitterness. "Don't talk about Victoria like that."

"You think she's your friend, don't you? Those people never make friends out of their own class, don't you understand? This isn't America, this is the old world and things are done the old way, and that crew are there to see that it never changes, they make sure the upper classes still have the upper hand. They keep a bunch of idle parasites to act out all the pageantry and round them they operate a system that's got no place for you. And you've fallen for it, you dumb little sucker, you're flattered silly because you're buddies with a royal fuck . . ."

"For Christ's sake, Daniel, she could have killed herself this year . . ."

"Too bad she didn't succeed. One less . . ."

Jo jumped up and hit him, the noise of the slap reverberating across the distant river. In case he returned the blow, she ran towards the crowd outside the discotheque tent, stumbling in the darkness over the empty champagne bottles that littered the lawn.

At the door of the marquee she paused and looked back. Daniel was walking quickly towards the garden wall.

She saw him start to climb but a commotion from inside distracted her. There was a convulsion of the tightly-packed crowd and Victoria, with Alex holding her close, and half the security team pushing back the people, emerged in tears. Heads turned as she half-ran into a free space on the dark lawn. The rest of Alex's party followed, and Richard ran to join the brother and sister for a short, intense discussion.

"What happened?" Jo demanded of Martha.

"Some fool photographed her—just some oaf with an Instamatic taking happy snaps—and she thought it was another goddam paparazzo and totally collapsed." The Jamaican stood with her hands on her narrow hips, watching as the distant trio moved off towards the gate into the Master's private garden. "Looks like she's going home." Victoria was staying with them at the flat, not only for the ball but to supervise the removal of her furnishings.

"Do you feel like getting smashed?" Jo realised she had drunk very little and now, angry at Daniel, decided it was time to start.

"No, but I'll keep you company while you do it."

Jo procured a bottle of champagne and they sat on the grass by the riverside and watched girls in crumpled silk dresses squawking and giggling as their escorts handed them into punts. They discussed their futures, their careers, the apartments they were buying in London and the foolishness of men. The throb of the band ceased and the disco took over the music tent, its strobes flashing through the striped canvas and lighting up the heavy foliage of the chestnuts.

The wine hit pleasantly and Jo reclined on her elbows, gazing aimlessly at the night sky.

Some time later they were dancing, Martha with Kelly who was teaching her to rock-and-roll despite the disco's preference for Donna Summer, and Jo with Richard. It seemed the correct thing to do, since they had been left partnerless. They were both good dancers, they had been taught well, and Jo found it pleasant to spin across the floor and show off her dress. It was tightly-draped, with a fuchsia-pink skirt gathered to a bustle behind and a black bodice with silk ropes instead of straps. She had worn it at Cannes but never had the pleasure of it until now.

He watched her twirling adeptly, her silk skirts snapping in the slipstream like sails in a breeze. The creamy fullness of her breasts above the bodice rippled at each step. Nothing seemed changed between them since the instant he had collided with her bicycle three years ago, although he felt older, much older, worn and disappointed; and she was going to be a great actress. She had vowed that she would do it, and it was happening.

"Sir! We're going to Grantchester, are you coming?" One of the oarsmen from the security squad, his blond beefiness now relieved by a tiger lily behind his ear, hailed the Prince familiarly.

"Do you want to go?" He looked down at Jo and their

eyes locked momentarily with a jolt. He was, she realised, very drunk but not showing it.

"What's at Grantchester?"

"Breakfast. Come on."

Another man and two girls in crushed taffeta flounces were already in the punt. With six of them aboard the craft was low in the water. Jo trailed her fingers in the coolness, encountering a floating bottle and an abandoned corsage. Lights blazed from every college and as they slipped under the bridges Jo watched the watery reflections on the stones. Inspector Henshaw returned from driving Lady Victoria to her flat in time to see them disappear in the shadows below the Bridge of Sighs.

Richard pulled off his jacket and tie and seized the punt pole, although he had little experience of these awkward vessels. He almost ran into other craft twice, and then nearly lost the pole when it stuck in an unexpected patch of mud. He wrenched a muscle in his shoulder pulling it out. The pain and the exertion sobered him slightly. Jo smiled at him from her seat in the stern. Beside the other thick-waisted, bedraggled girls she looked cool and defined. This was not the mere appearance of composure, like Victoria's fragile façade. There was something centred about this woman that made him feel safe, but at the same time a thrill of danger ran through him every time she looked at him.

At Mill Pool the level of the river changed; they disembarked and the men hauled the punt over the iron rollers to the higher channel. Richard relinquished the pole to one of the others and settled beside Jo, enjoying in silence the long glide through the meadows.

The clouds thinned and the moon, three-quarters full, appeared to silver the squat, pollarded willows. Jo suddenly felt breathless, as if her dress were too tight. She inhaled deeply, catching the smell of the water and the rank scent of nettles from the river bank.

The old web of enchantment fell on them again, but this time there was no deception, no awkwardness, no wrong-footing. Pain and anger floated down the slow stream with the debris of the night's celebration. They said nothing, and did nothing, mutely conspiring to keep their secret from their boisterous companions.

The meadows gave way to gardens as they passed

through the village, and then they sighted the café where a group of crumpled revellers was already assembled at the rickety tables under the coloured lights.

The others stumbled drunkenly off the bow of the punt and scarcely noticed that Richard shoved off again from the sagging landing stage. He took up the pole and pushed on upstream, his shirtfront gleaming in the moonlight. Jo watched him, letting the languor of lust flow through her. Would it be disloyal to Victoria to make love to this man? She thought not. Victoria had rejected him. At the bottom of her heart Jo also acknowledged that Daniel was right about the Fairleys; they cared only for their own kind. Loyalty to them would never be reciprocated.

The satiny water rippled after them. There was no sound other than its liquid whisper and the sudden shriek of a hunting owl in the middle distance.

Tall trees overhung the river banks, and beyond them stretched a flat field of wheat. Richard saw a good landing by an uncultivated corner that stood shoulder high with the white flowers of Queen Anne's Lace, and pushed the punt towards it.

As he helped her out of the boat he pulled her into his arms and the clouds covered the moon. They fell among the frothy leaves, kissing hungrily. The dress seemed unbearably constricting and she pulled at the zipper, releasing her breasts into his hands with a sigh.

His touch was so sweet it felt like a pain. He heard her breath catch as he held the soft fullness, and then rasp in her throat as he kissed the nipples and felt them pucker from rose-petals to raspberries under his tongue.

She reached out to caress him and met that artfully tailored impediment to passion, the Savile Row crotch. "Jesus, I do not believe it—button flies!" Whispering and laughing, there was a flurry of fingers, a tangling of his cream brocade braces and at last she found what she was looking for, taut and hot for her wet lips.

Perhaps his tailor was wiser than they thought. Their fatal urgency was checked. She was confident and loving, and he sprawled on the fragrant carpet of vegetation and let her tease him as much as she wanted.

They made a decadent picture, a half-naked woman and a man in evening clothes more exquisite than mere money could buy, lying in the meadow flowers making love. A luxurious consciousness of the moment took hold of them both and they savoured the darkness and their solitude to the full. His fingertips roamed her skin, so soft that it seemed merely a warmer contour of the windless night air.

He wanted her breasts again and pulled her close where he could nuzzle them; as she moved she parted her thighs with a gesture of invitation. Soon there was nothing to do but lie in his arms anticipating the moment of his entry, a rich, drowning sensation engulfing all her body.

It ended sooner than either of them wished, because once inside her he could not hold back. They lay together talking; neither of them remembered what they talked about. They were truthful but had no desire to probe each other's thoughts. They both recalled afterwards the closeness, the smell of the water and the dry honeyed scent of the flowers, and above all these, the feeling that they had briefly existed in a different dimension, a parallel universe into which they had passed together.

At length Jo noticed that the dawn light was strengthening behind the clouds and felt self-conscious. She saw her dress a few yards away and sat up to retrieve it, and with her clothing they resumed the cares of their separate worlds and remembered that he was to fly to Liverpool the next day to rejoin his family, and she was to fly to Paris with Daniel; their new film was to begin shooting the following week.

As they drifted downstream through Grantchester he noticed the familiar square shape of the police Range-Rover at the roadside. "There's my detective, and he's brought the car."

"Do you want to stop?" she asked, her body twisting voluptuously as she sat up to look.

Richard considered. It was a long, slow, exhausting journey back to Cambridge. In the back of the car he could hold her for a few precious minutes more. He should not have evaded Henshaw, the man's job was to protect him.

"No," he said, "I want to be alone with you as long as I can. Do you mind?"

She shook her head. "I was hoping you'd say that. I like being with you." She was about to open her heart and pour out her strange confusion of feelings, but Henshaw saw them, called out, vaulted a gate and ran across the meadow to the bank, and there was nothing to do but return with him in the Range-Rover.

She saw Cowley's fraudulent portrait of Richard and Victoria in the *Daily Post* the next day and felt guilty. Rod Stewart on Daniel's car stereo belted out "The First Cut Is The Deepest." She tried to feel mature. An actress famed for her *sensualité rare et raffinée* should be capable of taking casual ecstasy in her stride. That was all it had been, after all.

For days afterwards Richard could almost feel the living hot silk of her enclosing him, but then the memory began to fade. He endured another month of ceremonies, feeling increasingly uncomfortable each time he dressed in formal clothes, walked out to validate the expectations of another group of strangers and posed for one more photo-opportunity. When he returned to Balmoral he felt as if he himself were flat and one-dimensional like a photograph.

As they receded in his memory, the few hours on the river bank began to seem as if they had been his last few moments of being fully alive.

One morning he yearned to hear Jo's voice, and called Harley for her number, to find that she too was working abroad for the summer. That was surely for the best. Jo was so ambitious, so independent, she would never let herself become entangled with him.

CHAPTER XV

"LA-LA-LA-LA-LA-LA, MONTEGO BAY!" Corinna sang along with the crackling car radio, fanning herself with her straw hat. Kelly's assistant swooped the rented Mercedes violently across the road to avoid a large pothole, throwing the three models in the back of the car together into a corner. "Take it easy! I'm too hot to die!"

"I'm only driving like a Jamaican," the youth protested.

"Darling, Jamaicans drive on the left hand side of the road, not both sides at once." Harley, in a corner of the back seat, rearranged herself and smoothed down her white drill shorts.

"They're worse than fucking Italians, bopping all over the road. If you ask me they're just trying to waste us so they can steal the cameras."

Harley—no one called her Martha any more—gave a lazy laugh and gazed out of the window. Abuse of her countrymen did not offend her, since she now felt little in common with them. Kelly was more sensitive on the subject than she was.

"Shut up," he ordered his assistant in an amiable voice. "This is her country, she ought to know."

"Oh, are you really from Jamaica?" Ulrike, the deeply tanned German model sitting next to her, turned her cropped head with a tinkle of ear-rings. "I didn't know, I thought you were from somewhere in Africa."

Harley gave a small purr of amusement. Most of the international fashion élite probably thought Jamaica was a place in Africa anyway. A large proportion of them were seriously convinced that she was an Ashanti princess. They also thought that she was fabulously beautiful. She did not care. Her soul, starved of attention for so long, still lapped up their adulation as greedily as she had consumed all the gourmet dishes which had been put before her in half of the finest restaurants in the world. Why should she care how stupid people were? She was a star, a sensation, a phenomenon, a queen, one of the most famous models in the world, with ten *Vogue* covers to her credit. She had now been round the world three times, she earned two thousand dollars a day and she owned, among other jewellery, a pair of diamond ear-rings that had belonged to Marie Antoinette. At that rate of doing business, they could be as foolish as they pleased.

Besides, however cheap and ignorant their flattery, it had made her a better person. Harley was embarrassed to recall the arrogant, sarcastic girl who had quit the island four years ago with her nose in the air, covering up her pain and loneliness with ridiculous ideas of her own superiority. She was confident now, and less inclined to harsh judgements of other people. Her caustic humour had mellowed into delicious wit. She no longer hung back from people, she was open and friendly. If the price of all this was that she must put her mind out to grass and take herself at the world's estimation, it was worth it.

"So where are you from, Harley, are you from Kingston?" the German girl persisted.

"I lived there before I came to England, yes," she admitted, not wishing to be rude. Location trips were usually fabulous fun and she did not want to sour the atmosphere, but she was acutely uncomfortable in her homeland. She did not want to be identified with this small, rundown island where the roads were pot-holed and lined with ragged people begging rides and hawking trashy souvenirs.

The glitzy north coast was a Jamaica she had not really known. Denzil, her stepfather, had designed many of the pillared villas tucked away in luxuriant gardens above the turquoise sea, but Harley had never considered this area as part of the island. She had flown into Montego Bay as a foreigner, and like the other aliens from rich worlds she was embarrassed by the poverty and appalled at the slow, inefficient room service in the hotels.

In addition she was outraged by the policeman who had brazenly asked for "something for me" when he stopped them for speeding an hour earlier, and had to bite her tongue on a speech about bribery corrupting the rule of law and degrading the principles of justice. She was shamed by the hustlers who lounged around fringes of their hotel's private beach flexing their muscles and flashing their gold jewellery; they hissed at the white women, furtively murmured the names of different varieties of ganja at the men and when she passed they gave low whistles and called her "Sister." She did not care to be related to them.

"Are you going to see your family?"

"Well, I don't know . . ."

"Kingston's terribly dangerous, isn't it? Aren't you afraid of getting shot if you go back there?"

"Of course she isn't," Kelly interrupted. "She's ashamed of me, that's all. Won't take me home to meet the folks. She's staying on to see them after we fuck off home."

"My family live over this side of the island now, anyway." Harley smiled vaguely at the distant sparkle which she presumed was the sea. Her contact lenses were back at the hotel; on the whole Jamaica looked better without them.

"Oh, I see." Ulrike slicked back her cornsilk hair and lost interest. Harley glared at the back of Kelly's head. She had no desire to see her family on this trip. She had visited when she graduated, and toiled through the required round of parties, being shown off by her stepfather and, in a rather distant but still well-meaning way, by her mother also. She had posed for formal photographs in her gown, and given a talk at the University of the West Indies. Every conversation had centred on her great achievement, but the glorious legal career had stopped dead, and now she would have to deal with the curiosity and the criticism, explaining why suddenly she was a fashion model not a lawyer. She knew a lot of people would be disappointed in her.

Her mother, on the other hand, was now ecstatic about her success and wrote regular, gushing letters which made her feel more guilty than any reproach. Harley did not care to acknowledge that she had stepped through the looking-glass into her mother's frivolous, exterior world.

Kelly frowned over the map. "Where did you say this waterfall was?"

Harley barely suppressed a sigh and scrabbled in her bag for her spectacles. "Around here." She leaned forward and traced the road vaguely with one pearlised pink fingernail. Kelly had decided he wanted to shoot the swimming costumes at a waterfall; a natural, remote, unspoiled waterfall was his specification, not one of the well-trodden tourist sites. She recalled her stepfather showing her one about an hour away from Montego Bay, but now they were on the road nothing looked familiar. "I think the small roads aren't marked on this map."

"I suppose you will know the turning when we get to it?"

"I don't know, Kelly, I haven't been to the North Coast for so long it all looks the same to me now . . ."

"Birdbrain. Maybe one of these people will know," he indicated a small group slumped in the shade of a tree at the roadside. "Pull in, let's give somebody a ride."

"No don't, Kelly."

"Why not? Take that girl there, she might know where the hell we're going." The assistant swooped the car into the roadside and opened the door for the nearest person, a round-faced young woman in a washed-out pink dress. She got up inelegantly and came towards them with hesitation, dragging her feet in their broken plastic sandals and glancing nervously back at her companions who followed her with envious eyes.

Kelly moved to the back seat to let their passenger ride in the front and direct the driver, and the models crushed together to make room for him, protesting about the heat and their clothes.

Her voice a respectful, heavily accented whisper, the girl showed them the turning uphill from the coast road. Her eyes lingered covetously on Corinna's new Sony Walkman. The Australian passed it to her for inspection, and she fingered it at length, disbelievingly listening to the music from the tiny headphones. Harley, disgusted, shrank down in her corner and pulled her hat over her eyes. Much about the girl reminded her of her childhood companion, Hyacinth, but they were a long way from Rush River and, she told herself, Hyacinth would have been older.

Very soon she asked them to stop and let her out.

"Is this it, is this where you live?" Kelly was surprised that she had waited so long for a lift when her journey was so short.

"Dis me mada yard heah," she lisped, tentatively trying

to open the car door. "You got to keep on de road dis side a mile an' half, den you see de place you lookin' for."

Kelly reached forward and opened the door for her. "We thought you must live further away if you were waiting for a ride."

Harley noticed a small wooden shack a few yards back from the roadside, surrounded by spindly shrubs and rusting pieces of automobile. A young pig rooting by the doorway trotted off with a squeal as a man stepped out and pissed against the house wall. Harley shut her eyes and hoped none of the others had noticed.

"Me can't walk up, me shoe broke." With studied pathos, the girl showed them her plastic sandals, standard Third World footwear, which were torn and had rubbed her skin raw in places. "Me can't get money for new shoes yet. Do you perhaps have any small change that you could spare?" Kelly stuck five American dollars in her hand before Harley could protest.

They found the waterfall easily half-a-mile further up the valley, and spent an uncomfortable day shooting around it, the white girls wearily slapping mosquitoes and complaining of the cold water. Kelly was unusually hard to satisfy and when the afternoon had worn on and the light was failing, his assistant dropped a film magazine in the river and they had to do the last shot all over again.

"Roll on Paris," Harley said when they were at last back in the air-conditioned comfort of their hotel.

"We're not going to Paris," Kelly told her, stripping off his sweat-soaked shirt. "So you can get that idea out of your head right now."

"But we always go to Paris," she protested.

"*I* always go to Paris. You do what I tell you. This time I'm not going. The Pret's just a fucking circus. Auriol's getting the dresses sent to London—we'll do 'em in the studios in half the time without the Chambre Syndicale breathing down our necks."

He was referring to the governing body of the Paris fashion week, a ferocious bureaucracy whose aim seemed to be to prevent any garment ever appearing in the press at all.

"But I promised Yves . . ." Harley felt strung out with frustration. The feeling was becoming familiar. In October Corinna, who always did his show, had taken some of her pictures to Yves Saint Laurent, who had asked to see her immediately. "What are you, really?" he asked her seriously from behind his spectacles. "Are you a goddess, or a gazelle? I think you were born to be on my runway. You are nothing like a mannequin but you make my clothes look superb." He halted the rehearsals for his show to make a place for her, but *Vogue*, or rather Kelly, needed her on the same day and she had been forced to refuse.

"Never mind—you will join us in the spring, yes?" The great couturier had called his assistant over then and asked her to book Harley. She had flown over for fittings and was living for the moment when she stepped out on the catwalk for the first time. Standing in front of a camera all day was getting very, very boring.

Paris in fashion week was definitely a circus. The other girls had told her everything: the chaos, the crazy hysteria that took hold of everyone, the dizzying excitement of each collection, the mad scramble in and out of fabulous garments, the breakneck sprints to and from legendary fashion houses. It was obviously sheer insanity and she longed to get out into the thick of it, instead of being cooped up with Kelly all the time. She yearned to be one of the glorious girls who flocked around Yves or Thierry or Emanuel or Claude at the end of every show under the gaze of a thousand lenses, swaying on high heels, their soft hands applauding with the noise of beating dove wings. And afterwards she wanted to join the noisy parties in the brasseries and the clubs, instead of going straight from the hired studio to the Plaza Athénée with Kelly every night.

"You had no right to promise Yves anything," he said bluntly, going into the shower. "Your contract with *Vogue* says you can't do anything without their permission."

"Oh but how could they possibly object if Yves wanted me . . ." He turned on the water at full force and drowned her voice. ". . . and anyway I know there isn't any contract with *Vogue*, they just pay me by the day like anyone else." He had not heard. Perhaps it was just as well. She was afraid to let him know that she had been checking out her position.

Since leaving Cambridge, she had been photographed exclusively by Kelly and it was not until the great Snowdon had approached her almost diffidently at a party and asked her why she refused to work with him that she discovered Kelly had ordered her agency to turn away all other offers.

This intelligence had come through a friend of Corinna's who worked in Marianne's office and who confided that they had even refused a television commercial for her. Marianne herself had denied any special arrangement.

Even when *Newsweek* had run a cover story on her, Kelly had insisted on taking the picture. "I don't want you getting ripped-off," was his explanation, so affectionate and reasonable she at first accepted it. Now she felt his protectiveness was sinister. On this trip, as on every other, he had the tickets, the passports, the money, the itinerary and the credit cards. He said he liked to take care of her, that she needed him to do these things.

She wanted to break out, but three things held her back. She was fond of Kelly, and did not want to hurt him. She was grateful to him, and the suggestion that he had implanted of her incompetence made her afraid she could not manage without him. And then there was the sex. More than anything, that crippled her will. It was all her fault; she had never been able to get into it, and on this trip, things were getting worse.

She went to the next bungalow to talk to Corinna. The best thing about this business were the friends you made.

That night was the unhappiest she and Kelly had ever spent together. She saw him go light on the booze at dinner and her heart sank. When Kelly did not drink he was getting ready for a big number in bed. Because she was being difficult, he was going to try to screw her into submission; he would say he was trying to give her pleasure or help her relax, but what he wanted was total control. Being incurably analytical, she understood this; she also knew that Kelly was unaware of the primitive way his mind worked.

In the sweaty, anxious small hours of the morning, she endured as long as she could then pressed her fingertips in the special place in the small of his back where the right touch always made him come. He pulled out and rolled off her at once, as if he were angry, then pulled her to his chest and crushed her to him with affectionate desperation.

"Let's be honest, kid," he kissed the smooth dome of her forehead. "You are a fabulous looking chick and you are absolutely fucking useless in bed. You're so skinny it's like lying on a bed of nails and you've never had an orgasm yet, have you?"

Was he going to leave her, she wondered, without much

feeling except a distinct relief that his cock was no longer rooting in the bruised folds of her flesh. "I'm sorry," she whispered.

"*You're* sorry." It was the only time he had ever spoken to her with rancour. "Not half as sorry as I am. I don't know why I bother, I really don't. I've done everything I know to do, you get turned on all right but half the time I think you get more of a buzz from a good dinner. What's the matter with you, anyway?"

"I don't know. I just can't . . . I don't . . . I can't ever relax enough, I suppose." She shrugged her shoulders. "I do love you, Kelly, and I wish I could, I really do but I just can't feel the way other women feel."

"What do you know about what other women feel?" He reached for his cigarettes and in the flare of his lighter she saw the humorous lift of his eyebrows and guessed that he was smiling. It made her feel worse. He was so patient, so unselfish; why wouldn't her body do what he wanted?

"Well, I asked them, you know. I thought maybe I was doing something wrong."

"I don't want you talking about me, OK?" There was an edge of anxiety in his voice now.

"I wasn't talking about you, Kelly . . ."

"Well, don't. Ever. This is private, it's between us. I don't want you discussing it. Promise?"

"Promise." There was a silence. She listened to his heartbeat, slowing down as his excitement subsided. The blood in her veins never surged like that. Making love felt pleasant but, damn him, he was right, it was just about as nice as a good meal. Whatever it was that made Corinna prance like an excited horse when she had a new boyfriend, whatever brought that dark languor into Jo's strange eyes, whatever had wrapped Victoria in a golden dream for months, whatever that was, she knew she had never felt it.

Harley felt no deprivation. Her frigidity was just the final dimension of the glorious joke of her life. Wise in the ways of her decadent new world, she knew she was a symbol of all the savage urges in human nature; the fact that she herself could not feel the animal lust she was so well paid to project was a deliciously amusing irony. Laughter was her great protector. Laughing stopped her thinking. While she laughed, she could enjoy being a fake. She did not mind cheating the whole silly world, but she did not care to accuse herself of cheating Kelly.

At the far side of the bed, he drifted towards sleep with a sense of failure that was painful but also comforting. He did not really want the final surrender from her. Her huge almond-shaped eyes were still veiled when they looked at him. Her body was the most erotic creation on earth, but the windows to her soul were shuttered and it was that tension which gave Harley her unique magic. Without that, she would be just another black chick; perhaps it was all to the good that he could not break it.

The shoot went badly. Kelly fussed and fretted, re-photographed clothes in different locations and was never satisfied. He searched for what he considered wonderful locations, country villages of palmetto-roofed shacks, a rusting, derelict sugar refinery, a long beach of grey pebbles used only by fishermen, and Harley, for once not understanding what he wanted, grew more and more mulish, feeling that he was picking the ugliest views of her country on purpose to humiliate her.

Part of his problem was that in her own landscape she no longer appeared exotic. He could pose Corinna against a field of yellow-flowered okra and the contrast was dazzling. Ulrike could sit on a mossy tombstone in an old churchyard and look like some pale colonial ghost. Harley looked like part of the scenery; she sensed it, she was acutely uncomfortable, and the more she sulked the more she looked like an idle field hand with ideas above her station. She struggled for her dignity and lost it. Her ability to display clothes evaporated. Whatever she wore seemed to hang off her bones like rags.

He was unable to put any of these feelings into words. All Kelly said was, "I'm not getting the real Jamaica here." Then he decided to move to Kingston, which she took as a punishment. Scarcely speaking to each other, they quit the spacious luxury of Montego Bay and moved to a tacky concrete hotel in the new quarter of the capital, where the light fittings were ready to fall out of the ceiling and the TV was chained to the wall. The men went out on a recce, and next day to Harley's horror drove across the stinking gully into Trenchtown.

"Kelly, you can *not* shoot here. You'll be using cameras and they'll be using guns! It isn't even safe for a white person to drive here, there are riots all the time, the place is just carved up between the gangs . . ."

"*Shut up.*" He did not even look at her. Corinna squeezed her arm in sympathy.

They drove slowly up the dirt road. There were few cars, and it was quiet. The blistered concrete houses with small yards and dusty, stunted trees gave way to tin shacks separated by crooked alleys. Torn posters and slogans covered the walls. Two apathetic women sitting on wooden stools in the shade of a half-built shanty followed their car with blank eyes. In the doorway of a bar a young warlord flicked back his dreadlocks and watched them with emphatic hostility. Somewhere behind the houses a fire was burning, and smoke and sparks drifted upwards in the hot air above the sagging rooftops.

They stopped at a long wall of concrete blocks covered in graffiti and scarred with bullet holes. It was, Harley knew from the talk in her mother's house, the boundary between the territory of the two gangs which disputed control of the ghetto. The largest, latest and most distinct slogan read "Welcome to Seaga City" in uneven letters of red paint.

"Aren't those kids just adorable?" Corinna raised her camera and snapped a trio of infants in ragged vests and shorts who were playing in the dust at the roadside.

Instantly the urchins ran to the car. "One dollar! One dollar, miss! One dollar, just one dollar! Please, for me, one dollar!" Six eager brown hands reached through the open window.

"You have to keep the window shut or you'll blow the air conditioning," Harley announced in a tight voice, leaning over to hit the switch which closed the windows.

"Oh, wait, I wanted to give them something. They're so cute . . ." Corinna was scrabbling in her purse for some coins.

"They're not cute, they're idle. They ought to be in school, not begging on the street. Don't give them money, they don't deserve it," Harley advised, coldly brushing the urchins away.

"Come on, you slags, get the show on the road," Kelly ordered, scanning the wall for the most interesting section to choose as a background.

The clothes were simple white sundresses, and they

changed in a lopsided wooden shack that might have been a bar if the proprietor had been able to buy beer. There were some broken crates and flattened, rusty Red Stripe bottle caps lying around to testify to better times.

A silent crowd gathered. The assistant continually shooed away boys who tried to touch the cameras. Kelly lined the girls up against the wall and began to shoot. At last he was getting something worth having from Harley. She was now projecting sheer fury, but in a curious, passive mode that robbed her limbs of energy and her face of expression. She was in a trance of rage. It almost frightened him, but, professional to the last, he merely changed lenses and took some face shots while she was unaware.

Harley, holding herself defiantly aloof, heard the gunfire before any of the others. Machine guns, more than one, and then a distant outburst of shouts and screams. One party's posse was out to shoot up the enemy neighbourhood. She decided to say nothing. If Kelly caught a bullet or two it might improve his temper.

The crowd scattered when a pickup loaded with gunmen turned into the street at the far end.

Ulrike yelped in alarm.

"For Chrissake, Kelly, something's really up—let's get out of here!"

"Hey, ratface . . ." He would not even turn around.

Corinna was already pulling at the locked door of their car. Ulrike and Harley ran after her. The assistant frantically stuffed cameras and film together into the cases, then began to pat his pockets, feeling for the car keys.

"I got 'em," Kelly announced without moving, a fresh cigarette between his lips. For an instant Harley thought he was going to force them all to stay and be shot, robbed—or worse—just for the hell of it. Then, to her relief, he picked up his tripod and strolled towards the car. He had scarcely taken his seat when the assistant hit the gas and they drove off, skidding and bucking over the cratered track. Harley looked back and saw two vehicles crowded with armed men behind them, weaving violently across the road spraying the shanties with bullets.

. . .

"I DON'T KNOW why my wife wants to live in Miami. She flies there twice a week to get her hair done as it is." Below a cascade of purple bougainvillea, Harley's stepfather surveyed his family and friends and was content.

His wife was not. "Honey, everybody's moving to Miami. The Paleys, the Changs, all our friends, they've all gone already. This island is finished. Martha, you tell him, you've travelled, you've got a good education, you can see the way things are going, can't you?"

Harley sat on the old wall at the edge of the terrace with her endless legs elegantly crossed. She was gazing across the emerald valley to the peaks of the Santa Cruz mountains in the distance. Coming home with Kelly had stripped her heart, but now he and the whole *Vogue* circus had flown back and she had time to heal. The trance of longing in which she had passed her early childhood echoed like *déjà vu*. It was a poignant, almost luxurious sensation to recall from her present position of worldly eminence.

"It doesn't have to be Miami, but I don't see any good reasons to stay." She smiled at Denzil to take the sting out of her disagreement. Now that they could talk to each other as adults, she discovered that her stepfather, a benevolent shadow in her youth, was a person she liked very much. He had all the soft qualities of manhood, patience, tolerance and generosity. He was a good husband and a fine father; her mother often said she was lucky to have found him, and Harley pushed aside the question of whether she herself would ever enjoy the same good fortune.

Denzil's patriotism, she considered, was a sentimental indulgence. "What exactly are you all waiting around in Jamaica for?" she asked, with a half-laugh. "It seems to me Manley's taking this country to hell as fast as he can. You could have a good life almost anywhere else in the world. It looks like it's time to get off the rock." She sipped her lemonade; she had forgotten the rich, oily aroma of freshly-picked lemons.

"We want to have a good life here, Martha." Denzil nodded, knowing she expected his reply.

Her family had prospered. Her stepfather was the most sought-after architect on the island, currently engaged in building an immense hotel in his famous Creole-classical style. Their own home was a showpiece, a long, narrow plantation house dating from the eighteenth century; the old building had been extended, enclosing a wide, flower-hung terrace at the rear. It was almost 1,000 feet above the azure sea; the air was fresh and the views from every cunningly constructed vantage point were breathtaking. Harley was surprised how happy she felt looking at the mountains.

"We have a good life here with the guards and the dogs and all the rest of the security, but that's not how a family should live. Martha, honey, you are *so* right." Her mother had now acquired the faintest American accent. "I'm telling you, people are either waiting to get out or waiting for Castro to march in. Jamaica's got nothing now for people like us." She pouted with annoyance, folding her shapely arms and looking down at her smart white shoes.

Harley found it easy to look on her mother with charity, and see her as a crass, slightly pathetic woman, driven by anxious social ambition, with a certain inborn grace but a complete lack of style. She wavered between naïve joy at her daughter's fame, her husband's success and the expectation of further glory reflected from her twin sons, and greedy determination to have more.

"But for the boys' sake, honey, for Spencer's sake, don't you agree we just have to move? He's talented, he needs training, and he needs it now. His coach says he should have gone years ago. What right do we have to hold him back? And the only place he can really learn tennis is in America."

Spencer, to everyone's delight and surprise, had been taken on to a tennis court by a hotel pro three years ago and was discovered to have exceptional ability.

"He's fourteen and the last thing he needs is his family around him, pushing all the time." Denzil's normally patient tone sharpened. "I am not going to be one of those fathers who puts all his own ambitions on to his son and robs him of his childhood. I've agreed that Spence can go to Florida next month. He can go by himself and we'll see how he makes out."

"Fourteen is much too young to be alone in a foreign country," his wife protested without much conviction. She knew that this battle was already lost. "He still needs his mother. You're just afraid that he'll go away and stay away, like Martha."

There was an embarrassed pause. "All along Jamaica's been a place people leave." Denzil turned to look at the hazy mountains, his hands extended to touch both sides of the ancient stone archway which framed the view. "I don't care to join that exodus. How can this country ever amount to anything if its citizens walk out on it? Especially people like us. I don't think it would be arrogant to say that we're the leaders of this society; it's people like us who should stand firm and set an example." Their guests murmured assent and he turned back to acknowledge them. "And don't forget, not everyone is leaving. Our friends, the Campbells here, have no plans to go anywhere, isn't that right?"

The four Campbells, parents, son and daughter all alike in their tawny skin tone and fine, aquiline features, nodded agreement. "We were hoping to get Claude off our hands when he was offered a place to do a post-graduate degree in Montreal, but he says he's inclined to stay put now," the father explained with pride. Claude tried to catch Harley's eye, but she pretended to be absorbed by the hummingbird that was hovering over the creepers on the far side of the terrace.

Claude Campbell was another surprise. She had expected to see him as urbane as ever—urbane for Jamaica, at least, a tacky gold watch, one of his silk ties and the sharp, lightweight suit that was practically a uniform for young Caribbean lawyers; instead he wore washed-out jeans and a sports shirt, and his hair, which had begun to recede prematurely at his temples, was cropped very short.

"From what you're saying, Martha," he cleared his throat nervously and she gave him a mildly disdainful glance, "it sounds as if you're not planning to come back here to practise."

"Practise? Oh, practise *law*, you mean." A gay little laugh, implying she had forgotten her ridiculous teenage ambitions. "Oh no, I couldn't come back to Jamaica now. I'd go crazy on this little island. What on earth could I do here?"

"Oh, you might find something to fill up your days."

She did not care for his tone. "Claude, I have a different career now, and I am at the top of it. Modelling gives me everything I want."

"Does it really?" His pose was stiff and his tone conversational; all the Campbells had a slightly formal social manner, but Harley was satisfied to see that his interest was more than merely polite.

"Yes, Claude, it most certainly does. I go everywhere, I meet everyone, I make good money, I've got a good man, I enjoy my work and I'm happy. Modelling gives me everything I ever dreamed of, more than I ever dreamed of, if you want the truth."

"But what do you give it?" He dropped his voice, trying to shift the conversation into more personal territory.

Harley laughed again, making sure the whole group heard. "Darling, I just give it everything I've got!"

"And she has a wonderful life, don't you? Wonderful. I see her in all the magazines, she's been all round the world, she's making so much money. You must be a millionaire already, aren't you? Well, you will be soon, I am sure of that. Honey, you are a star, a re-e-eal jet-setter. Did you see her on the cover of *Newsweek*? My little girl, our little Martha? And she's met Queen Elizabeth's son, he's one of her friends, isn't he? My daughter is a star and now it looks like my son's going to be a champion as well. I am so blessed in my children, I tell you I can hardly believe it." Her mother fluttered to Harley's side and embraced her, and Harley put on her most opaque face and noted that her mother had never called her "little" before in her life.

The party set off down the hillside and drove to the Crescent Beach Club, one of her father's first tourist developments, a sprawling complex of bungalows and swimming pools attached to a well-equipped tennis centre. The courts were dusty from disuse, since the projected influx of sports-crazed tourists had never appeared. The club was about to go into receivership, but the evil day had been postponed long enough for the Tennis Championships of the West Indies to be played there that year.

Spencer was the favourite for the junior title. Harley saw her brother jogging nervously from one foot to another on a warm-up court, and strolled across to watch him.

"What's new, Shel?" she asked his twin, who was sitting waiting in the shade with spare rackets and a towel, "is he going to win?"

"No question! Spence is going to walk it. You know, there's no boy on this island to touch our brother on a tennis court."

She sat down beside him. It was most agreeable to find that one of her annoying kid brothers was going to amount to something in life. It made her own achievements seem less freakish. Maybe success was in their blood.

The twins were growing less alike as they matured. Spencer, she thought, had something of her own looks, with his long limbs and long neck, although his skin was very dark. As he trained and approached adolescence he was also becoming heavier; his legs, once as etiolated as her own, were developing athlete's muscles. Sheldon was like his father in his compact build and small features, with the same businesslike demeanour which was amusing in a thirteen-year-old.

Her brother's partner was his coach, a lean, blond American who systematically put the boy through his paces before an attendant came to call him for his match.

Harley and Sheldon walked back across the scorched turf to the shaded spectators' stand. She nodded graciously to her parents' friends as she took her seat. In Jamaica now she was a person of great consequence, more than a mere celebrity, and she found herself exaggerating her Cambridge accent and behaving with regal dignity to fulfil the community's expectations. She had left her outrageous Claude Montanas and her understated Calvin Kleins in her suitcase and found an elegant pink silk Chloë suit which some subliminal premonition had made her pack knowing that it would be exactly the thing her mother's friends imagined a top model would wear.

The match, as Sheldon predicted, was a walk-over for her brother, despite the fact that his opponent was a young champion from the Bahamas who was already talked of as a world-class player. Spencer could use his long limbs with astonishing speed; he spanned the court like a spider and there seemed to be no corner beyond his reach.

Afterwards there were the congratulations and photographs, for which Harley was also called out, and then a reception on the Club's verandah, a charming area open to the sea breeze, which would have been considerably more attractive if the paint had not begun to peel on the white filigree balustrade. The cushions on the bamboo loungers were faded and the smell of neglect lurked in the corners despite the lavish buffet, the immense flower arrangements and the ice-sculpture of a swan imported to impress the guests.

She made gracious conversation to the British High

Commissioner and his wife, the American Ambassador and his wife and the Minister for Tourism and his wife. She was then presented to an endless stream of prominent West Indian citizens who bored her until she stood among them like a column of pure disdain with a smile painted on it.

Claude, she noticed, was also ill at ease and as the gathering grew noisier they found themselves standing apart at the edge of the crowd.

"I suppose," he said, being careful to keep accusation out of his voice, "all this seems terribly naïve to you now."

"Well . . ." she smiled, searching for a diplomatic answer.

"Well, yes," he replied for her. They laughed. "You're used to the real hot spots, aren't you?" She nodded and shrugged apologetically. Something about this new, low-key Claude made her reluctant to boast. "Tell me some of them," he urged, leaning one hand against one of the slim wooden pillars supporting the shingled canopy. "Tell me some of those grand places you've been."

"What kind of request is that?" she countered, embarrassed.

"I get the feeling that this is just another picturesque corner of the Third World to you now, isn't that so? Just another exotic background?" he persisted.

"Oh, Claude, you're not going to lecture me, are you?"

"I apologise, that was unfair."

"Yes, it was."

"But it *is* true, isn't it?" He had always had a maddeningly superior smile, which now insinuated itself across his finely drawn lips.

"No, it is not true, it is a judgement based entirely on supposition." She folded her arms, recovering for a moment her best debating style. "You have no evidence for suggesting that that is my opinion."

"I think I do. I think the way you look down your nose is all the evidence anyone would need. And the support you gave your mother this morning. 'Just get off the rock'—wasn't that what you said?"

"I was just talking simple common sense, Claude. People are murdered in Jamaica every day; you're on the edge of civil war and the place isn't safe—I don't want to read in the *Gleaner* that my family have been shot dead in their beds."

"You don't want to do anything about the political situation either, do you?"

"Oh, for heaven's sake, what could I do?"

"Not much from the cover of *Vogue*, that's for sure. For God's sake, Martha, you were a really bright kid . . ."

"And a long way it got me," she awarded him the sneer outright for that one. "I could tell you really admired me for my brain, Claude. All you boys did."

He had no idea what she meant. "If this country doesn't amount to much in your eyes, think about what people like you . . ."

She decided that attack was going to be the best method of defence. "What are *you* doing about it, Claude? I don't see you running for office. I don't see you even fulfilling your potential. You had your chances, that post-grad fellowship in Canada and what did you do? You passed on it. You ran out."

He straightened his shoulders, affronted. "That was a considered decision. I was offered a job in a good firm here and I decided that right now was not the time to leave."

She was wearing high shoes, which allowed her to look down at him with an expression of sublime contempt.

"We started equal, don't forget. You were a brilliant student, you had every opportunity I had. At least I took up my scholarship, I got my degree, I went all the way with it. All I can see you doing is sitting here in this little island finding reasons not to get off your ass."

He turned abruptly and walked a few steps away from her to control his anger. Harley smiled and decided to show no mercy.

"You think you've really achieved something, don't you?" He almost shouted the first few words, then dropped his voice to a harsh, over-controlled hiss. "You know your problem? You think you're white."

She released a peal of laughter. "Darling, I look in the mirror all day long . . ."

"You don't even understand, do you? You think you're white, you really do. You think you're one of them. You think you're the same as they are, that the world turns the same way for you as it does for them. You aren't and it won't, and one day you'll wake up from this ritzy dream you're living in to find that out."

"Well . . ." she tossed her head, leaning back against

the balustrade. "If thinking you are white means getting out and going to work and making the most of your opportunities instead of just sitting down and bitching about what you haven't got, then yes, you're right, that is what I think."

"Yes, but you can't make the most of opportunities you don't get . . ."

"You *can't*. Me *c-y-a-a-a-a-n* do dat. Me *c-y-a-a-a-a-n* do nuttin' about it . . ." she mimicked the broad accent of the country people. "You know, that is *the* most characteristic Jamaican expression. English kids are taught that there's no such word as 'can't.' The way we raise our kids, that's the first word they learn."

They glared at each other in silence for an instant.

"Whatever happened to you?" She saw his eyes roam momentarily over her face as if he were looking for traces of the awkward girl he had taken to Bridget Chang's dance. "I used to think you looked like a queen, you looked so tall and fine, you spoke so well, you were just head and shoulders above all the other girls and you were always serious and they were always stupid. If anyone had told me Martha Harley would turn out this way, I would never have believed them."

She was tempted to ask him why he had never expressed this profound admiration when she had needed to hear it, but decided to let it go. Claude's opinion was now of no consequence. "Nor would I," she giggled, taking his arm to walk back to the rest of the party. "Life is just full of little surprises, isn't it?"

Claude returned to Kingston that evening, which made it easy for her to avoid him during the rest of her stay. She went to the beach with Spencer and Sheldon, satisfied her mother and her friends with stories of her glamorous life.

Denzil tactfully offered to drive her over to Rush River to see her grandmother, and sat between the two women like a referee while they drank lemonade and made glacially polite small-talk. The old woman seemed smaller and darker than Harley remembered; her false teeth were very obvious. Nothing in the tiny shack had changed. It had been freshly painted the same washed-out yellow. Next door she noticed Mada Joyce's yard more unkempt than ever, with a new infant playing in the dust and another man idling away a few hours pretending to chop kindling sticks.

"You have not enjoyed this trip, have you?" At the foot of the hills, her stepfather made a circumspect turn on to the coast road between two large holes.

"It's been good to see you all. It's just . . . the country's in such a mess. I don't know how you can be so unconcerned. It must be affecting you, too."

"Of course. I've been lucky but there's no doubt people are staying away from Jamaica now. I have faith that they'll come back, that's all. There'll be an election, there has to be an election. Manley's just an actor; he can offer the moon and make people believe it really is within his grasp, but I think they know the truth now. Things will get better. And you can help, you know."

Not another pitch, she thought angrily. "How can I help?"

"You can bring them back, when the time is right."

"Them?"

"Your people, the rich, the jet-setters, the beautiful people, isn't that what they're called now? Jamaica used to be their special paradise. When I was a kid everybody came here. The Kennedys had a house here. Errol Flynn bought a whole little island. Ian Fleming created James Bond here. You've got that disbelieving look of yours, Martha, but you know it's true."

"Yes, but all that's gone now." The idea of herself as a style leader nevertheless intrigued her.

"Let me show you the house I've just finished."

He halted at the roadside and swung the car around, heading back around the wide bay and up over the headland. He turned down a side road which had been newly metalled, and followed its twisting course down the steep cliff.

The road ended under a wide, shingled porch, shaded by dense vegetation. The blank white walls gave no indication of the splendour of the villa behind. He pushed open the double hardwood doors and led her into the cool interior, offering his hand as she stepped over the unfinished section of the floor.

"I bought this land years ago, when I was working on the Changs' place. Somehow putting a Greek temple up in Kingston didn't seem right to me. What I wanted to do was build a house in the traditional style using only local materials, and make it more beautiful than any other house I'd ever designed."

Beyond the vestibule was a wide courtyard shaded by three royal palms. In the centre a simple fountain stood in the middle of a hexagonal pool that was already crowded with white water-lilies.

"All the water comes from the mineral spring up there," he turned and pointed high above the roof to a small cascade spouting from the cliff in a mist of rainbows.

The villa was only two storeys high, with balconies on the seaward side of every room. There was a sombre, high-ceilinged drawing room for which he planned a parquet floor of native hardwoods. The master bedroom was built on an outcrop of rock which fell directly down to the sea.

"There is no air-conditioning," he explained in his even, soft voice. "The windows are shuttered and the movement of the sea cools the air naturally and stirs it so it moves continuously through the house and is always fresh."

On the leeward side an elderly gardener was watering a smooth sweep of green lawn edged with a row of topiary conifers. Paths of the same simple, earth-red tiles used for the terrace led to the swimming pool and the white wooden staircase down the cliffside to the sea.

"Isn't that the most exquisite beach you have ever seen? That even you have ever seen? Hmm?" Her stepfather's oval face, normally almost oriental in its reserved expression, was creased with pleasure. The beach was a tiny crescent of beige sand, fringed with grey volcanic rocks, lapped by shallow, turquoise water, and overhung by aloes and oleanders. It was late in the afternoon; the sun was behind them and every leaf cast a long shadow across the pale sand. The spring water splashed down between the vegetation at one side of the bay, and he had built another lily pool, and a small terrace with a fanciful pointed canopy beside it, halfway down.

A few metres from the beach the colour of the water became deep sapphire, dappled darkly with rocks below the surface.

"It is absolutely perfect, absolutely. Lovelier than Goldeneye. See out there, where the waves are breaking?" She followed his pointing finger and saw a disturbance in the water about a hundred metres from the shore. "That little reef keeps the sharks out, they can't swim over it. And

I have not seen one sea urchin on those rocks. There's something in the spring water they don't like."

Harley stood still, watching the water fall and the shadows lengthen. The sea was not her element. She could not swim, and shared a cultural mistrust of the vast living jewel that hid so many dangers and displayed such a capricious temper. With all that, she was awed by the beauty of the tiny bay, and the little palace her stepfather had created with such sensitivity that it seemed to rise from the rocks as naturally as the spring or the grass.

"It's the most beautiful house I've ever seen," she told him. "People will fall over themselves to buy it when it's finished."

He nodded, pleased with her praise. "I don't really want to sell it, but an Englishman called Nicholas Brompton wants to buy it and he's offering a lot of money . . ."

"I know Nicky Brompton." Harley was noncommittal. "He likes beautiful things."

"You seem to know everybody," he laughed. "Well, I guess he's the kind of beautiful person we need here."

They walked back, a pair of pea-doves fluttering over their heads to roost somewhere in the eaves. She understood that Denzil, in his turn but in his subtle, sympathetic manner, was trying to awaken her loyalty to her native land. He had calculated that luxury and flattery would touch her where moral appeals had failed; that implication affronted her, although he had almost succeeded.

Harley left the next day feeling calm and a little ashamed of the distress she had experienced on re-encountering her homeland.

She had not flown for years with her own passport and her own ticket in her hand; Kelly always took care of those things. At London airport she hesitated and checked the signs before joining the short, fast-moving queue of British passport holders rather than the large crowd of other nationalities. She was drifting through the customs hall, postponing the moment when Kelly would take possession of her again, when two uniformed men approached her.

"Would you mind coming this way, Miss?"

"Is this your luggage?" The younger man took charge of her suitcases.

"Yes, of course it's my luggage. What's all this about? I haven't got anything to declare."

They did not reply, but took her to a small windowless room where another two officers, one male and one female, were standing behind an empty desk.

"Could I see your passport, please?"

She handed it to the man with hesitation. All her life the figures of authority had stressed the value of this document. A British passport had been presented to her as one of the greatest possible privileges, to be treasured and guarded always, never surrendered.

"Sit down, please."

He leafed through it with what seemed to Harley was exaggerated slowness, paying close attention to every stamp. "You seem to be a well-travelled young lady."

Feeling uneasy and diminished, she said nothing.

"And this is your signature?" He turned the page towards her.

"Yes, of course it is." She noticed that they were both looking closely at her clothes and jewellery. "And you are six feet tall?"

"Yes." Why was he asking these stupid questions?

"And you are a student?"

"Not any more." He made an illegible note on the blank writing pad in front of him.

"Ah, I see. What is your job now?"

"I'm a model."

"A model." He said it as if humouring a child in a fantasy. "What kind of model?"

"A photographic model."

"I see. Do you have any photographs with you, by any chance?"

"No. You can ask my agency for my card."

"Oh can we? And what agency is that?"

"I'm with Marianne's." The name of one of the most famous model agencies in the world clearly meant nothing to either of them.

"And have you been in Jamaica on business?"

"Partly and partly to see my family."

"Your family live in Jamaica?"

"Yes."

"All of them?"

"Yes, all of them. At least," she paused, remembering that she had no idea where her father might be, "all of them as far as I know."

"As far as you know."

He continued to question her about every detail of her life, until the notepad had a column of hieroglyphs on it. The two officers then opened her suitcase and asked her about every item in it. Her large make-up bag was taken away. She herself was taken into another room which had an examination couch like a doctor's surgery in it. The woman officer asked her to take off all her clothes, then made her spread her legs and touch the floor with her hands while she walked around her and inspected every crevice of her naked body. With brisk gestures and an impersonal apology, she asked Harley to lie down, put on a pair of plastic gloves and pushed two fingers into her vagina and then one finger into her anus. Afterwards she peeled off the gloves with her fingertips and dropped them into a wastebin as if they might be contaminated.

"You can put this on," she said, handing Harley a short robe of white plasticised paper. Then she scooped her clothes off the floor and prepared to leave the room.

"What on earth is all this about?" Harley demanded.

"We are from Her Majesty's Customs and Excise," the woman replied. "The other officer is from Immigration." She closed the door behind her and Harley heard a key turn in the lock.

Harley at once tried the handle and found that it did not move. She sat on the couch. She wanted to curl up her knees, but the robe was so short she could not do so without revealing herself indecently to anyone who might be spying on her through a hole in the wall. There must be holes in the wall, she thought, although she could not see any. Instead she crossed her legs. The room was completely bare and silent apart from the background noise of the airport muffled to an indistinct hum.

After a while she began to want to cry, and distracted herself by trying to remember the details of some of the immigration judgements she had learned. She tried to recall the 1971 Immigration Act. Surely it did not affect her status? Her memory was vague. She tried to recite the principles of *habeas corpus* and found that she could recall them with an effort.

How much time had passed? They had her beautiful 1955 Jaeger le Coulture watch, so she did not know. A long time, certainly. Kelly had promised to meet her, but they had parted so coldly she was suddenly afraid that he had changed his mind.

She got off the couch and banged on the door. She wanted to shout for attention as well, but could not think of what to say. "Excuse me," hardly covered the situation. "Help!" was too much. Perhaps nobody would hear her anyway. She hit the door so hard her fist hurt, then almost fell through it as the woman officer opened it.

"What's the matter?" she demanded, her eyes expressionless.

"I want to see a lawyer."

"Why?"

"I have the right to see a lawyer."

"You have no rights at all, dear. We are not police officers and you haven't been charged with anything." She pursed her thin pink lips, suppressing the word "yet."

"Then you have no right to keep me here."

"We have the right to detain you while we investigate your status."

"You have my passport, what else do you need?"

The woman wrenched her mouth in a sarcastic grin. "That is for us to determine. Do you need to go to the toilet?"

"I don't know, how long are you going to keep me here?" Harley remembered stories of whole families of Commonwealth immigrants being detained for months at the airport. She had read them in the newspapers with vague liberal sympathy, never dreaming that anything similar could happen to her.

"I can't tell you. If you need to use the toilet, you can bang on the door again only there's no need to make so much noise. We can hear you perfectly well."

She stepped quickly backwards and slammed the door.

Harley walked slowly up and down, feeling more powerless and more frightened at every moment.

Suddenly she heard several sets of footsteps in the corridor outside and the door opened quickly. Kelly stepped through it and took her roughly in his arms, an inelegant move since the top of his head hardly reached her chin, but she felt weak with relief at once.

"What a bloody cock-up." He stepped back and motioned to the woman officer, who put Harley's clothes on the couch with respectful care. "I had to raise bloody hell to find out where you were. Come on, darling, get dressed and let's get the fuck out of here."

The woman officer nodded at her. "We don't need you any longer. You can go now."

Harley was about to thank her but checked herself. No thanks were due for the liberty that was rightfully hers. The woman left and Kelly tenderly helped her into her clothes. In the outer office her bag was waiting for her and he seized it with one hand, propelling her towards the door and the freedom of the customs hall with his other arm around her waist.

Back at his apartment, she opened her bag to find that her every tube of make-up had been cut open, and the creams squeezed out so that half her clothes were ruined. The heels had been cut off all her shoes, and the lining of the bag itself was slashed in several places.

"Pigs. They just thought you were carrying." He handed her a glass of very cold Bollinger and she drank it so fast she choked. "They saw a black woman in expensive clothes and figured she couldn't have paid for them by doing anything legal."

"One of them was Immigration. They probably thought I was a Ugandan on a false passport."

"Well, ratface, any more of that nonsense and I'll marry you. Then you'll be as British as I am. That'll put a stop to that little game for good and all."

She could see he was enjoying the role of rescuer and protector more than ever. "Thank God you were there."

"I'm always here for you, you old toerag."

CHAPTER XVI

"TINA AND ELLIS really wanted a quiet wedding and since most of their friends are back East now they decided they would prefer to have the ceremony there." Lorna sat at her new white wicker desk touching the edges of a stack of freshly addressed wedding invitations with her fingertips, as if keeping the pile neat would compensate for the embarrassment of not being able to marry her daughter from her own house. "We would have had some difficulty fitting even a small party in here, as you can see." She dipped her head apologetically, indicating the modest proportions of their new home.

"But it is a pretty house. You seem as if you are really happy here," Jo consoled her mother with sincerity. The sun room in which they were sitting was bright with flower-printed cushions and tall plants growing in blue-and-white Chinese pots. Calico blinds half-drawn across the glass roof screened the strongest light. "It's more your style of home, somehow. I can see you're really comfortable here."

Her mother sighed. "The old house was rather gloomy, I suppose. I think your father liked it more than I did. He likes being out here in Pacific Palisades, though, he likes being closer to the ocean. We've been such gypsies the last few years it's just good to have some kind of home, even if it is small."

The rest of the house was equally airy and pleasant, decorated in her mother's favourite shades of fresh blue and white, but it was not large. Jo's lack of interest in real estate prices was profound, but the cramped rooms, charming as they were, told her eloquently that her parents were broke. It was a Spanish-style home which was less incongruous among the Californian cypresses than their old mansion, but Jo felt that it had an impermanent quality, as if her parents could not really accept that their fat years were finished. The furniture was all modern, much of it bamboo or wicker, difficult to relax in because it seemed too light and frail.

They ate supper as a family for the first time for four years, around a cold, glass table, with Lorna gently introducing the new housekeeper to the way she liked things to be done. Tina kept up a self-involved litany of her wedding arrangements, in which the words "Ellis thinks we should," "when Ellis's brother got married," "Ellis's father advised us," and "Ellis's mother says," recurred frequently.

Jo observed that her sister's blond hair, even and natural in hue and without a suspicion of a curl, was drawn back and held in a velvet bow at the nape of her neck and not a single strand looked as if it would ever dare to break loose. She wore a demure pink cotton dress with a white Peter Pan collar and seemed to be making an effortless transition from the perfect preppie to the perfect young Scarsdale wife. She looked strikingly like her mother, although it was the young Lorna she resembled, not the anxious middle-aged woman who presided nervously at their reduced table.

Her mother had aged in Jo's absence. There were shadows under her ultramarine blue eyes and the laughter lines had become deep wrinkles. Her complexion had the exhausted texture of wilted poppy petals; she had tied a jaunty blue and white spotted scarf around her throat, which disguised the crepey skin but unfortunately accentuated the stubborn beginning of a double chin. The veins on her hands were corded and Jo noticed that she wore a loose white shift which still did not hide the substantial breadth of her hips. Her father, who had always appeared older, was not showing his advancing years so much.

"Such a pity you can't stay longer, sweetheart," Lorna observed, making as if to touch Jo's hand but suppressing the gesture. "I really am so proud of you, making all these pictures and doing so well."

"Only two films, and neither of them made it over here, did they?"

"No, but we got some prints sent over and you were very, very good, darling." Her mother was talking with an authority Jo had never heard before, her blue eyes reinforcing each point with a steady gaze. "I think you are quite marvellous on screen and I have no doubt you have a brilliant career ahead of you."

Jo refused to let this pass. "I thought you didn't want me to be an actress."

"I wanted you to be happy. Acting is a hard life, you have to take a lot of knocks, you're at the mercy of people who perhaps aren't the nicest or the kindest in the world and I just didn't want you to suffer the way I had to. The way I do still, let's be honest. But you're young. And maybe things are different in Europe. And you are talented, sweetheart, never let anyone tell you different."

"And you've got your degree. If things don't work out you can always teach, can't you?" Her father had clearly intended this inquiry to sound theoretical, but Jo picked up his meaning at once.

"Yes, I can always teach. Are you working up to telling me I'm too old to need an allowance?"

"Well, Jocasta, you are an adult, after all . . ." He sat up in his chair in a pathetic attempt to give himself the stature of a real *pater familias*. "The plain truth is we can't afford to keep you on the payroll any longer."

"That's OK. I can see the way things are." Jo wound a strip of lettuce around her fork, projecting unconcern. There was a pause in which the only noise was the desultory scraping of steel cutlery on amusing Mexican ceramic plates and Jo recalled the silver forks and handpainted bone china they had used at the old house.

Her sister was obviously following the same train of thought. "Ellis's grandmother is giving us her own wedding silver, isn't that wonderful? It's called the King's Pattern, really old and ornate, and she has kept it all the years since her husband died, every single piece, in little chamois leather bags in this wonderful silver box in the attic that it took two men to carry downstairs."

"That's lovely, dear, I'm so happy for you both," Lorna acknowledged quickly. "But Jocasta, I want you to know I really am serious when I talk about your work. I've been in this business a long time and I have never, ever, seen anyone with such . . . with your . . ." she paused, again lost without a script.

"Mother, you're very sweet, but all I do is what Daniel

tells me to do." This was something which had been nagging unmercifully from the back of Jo's mind for a year. She had a persistent sense of inauthenticity about acting. She had certainly made two films, her agent had a folder full of laudatory reviews, she had given interviews, been lunched by producers and posed for a seven-page *Vogue* fashion spread with Jim Kelly in Forties satin ballgowns of the kind she had worn for the second film, but she did not feel like an actress. Hearing her own mother call her that discomfited her.

Both her films had been written and directed by her lover. He had told her where to look, how to move, even how to dress. He had invited her into his own immensely sophisticated interior world, dismantled his plots and characters, and explained them to her. More than that, Daniel's films were a homage to her. He looked into the mysterious depths of her eyes and dreamed of the woman she was in her essence, the woman he accepted he would never truly know. He hated the dream and worshipped it, and from this torment created goddesses, dominating, fascinating and treacherous.

Daniel had gained an instant reputation as a male writer who could create great parts for women. The roles were crafted with the full power of his intelligence and terrifying devotion. Jo found them exhilarating to play, but also dangerous. Her own self was submerging; she was becoming his vision. This was Daniel's final throw, his last attempt to possess her. Her opportunistic seduction of him had finally reaped its whirlwind.

She had to break free, but it was not that simple. Their sex life had dwindled to kisses and embraces, hesitantly sought on his part and reluctantly endured by Jo. She lived in her own apartment, but independence was not easy. He called her, or saw her, every day, talked through every decision with her, was already planning their next picture. She had done her best to tell the small world of British filmmaking that they were no longer a couple, but, to the many creative minds who might have wanted to use her, the sheer intensity of their past relationship was an intimidation. Her London agent received few scripts for her, and none of them of any quality.

Her father cleared his throat. "This Daniel. He's doing well, is he . . ."

"God, why are men so primitive? You think because you're not paying for me now some other man has to. If I'm not your possession, then I must be someone else's. I'm not going to marry Daniel, if that's what you're working up to."

Offence gleamed in her father's weak grey eyes. "That is not what I intended to say at all, Jocasta, you will please apologise."

"Oh, for heaven's sake! That's exactly what you intended to say, you were checking out the possibility of getting both your daughters off your hands this year. Well, relax, Dad, I don't consider myself your business any more, you are free to louse up your life and spend your wife's money without feeling any responsibility towards me."

"Jo! How can you say such a cruel thing!" Tina immediately sprang up and ran to her mother's side, and to her surprise Jo saw Lorna flick away tears from the corners of her eyes.

"I'm sorry," she said, disturbed by the effect of her words. "This is all—unexpected. Everything happened while I was away. If I'd been here I suppose I'd have understood better."

Her mother's small hand found hers on the cold glass and pressed it. "I understand, sweetheart," was all she could manage to say.

Having inflicted such regrettable pain on her parents, who had proved so much more vulnerable than she had always believed them to be, Jo was unable to resist when her mother insisted that as a family they attend Selwyn's legendary Thanksgiving party.

"Selwyn agrees with me about you," she whispered, taking Jo's arm as the parking jockey disdainfully drove away her old Corniche down the palm-lined drive. "He's going to see what he can do for you here, if you think that's a good idea, of course."

"Sure, why not?" Jo smiled, her feelings mixed. Doing any work in LA would put her back in the bag of being Lorna Lewis's daughter; however, it might be a way to jump off the professional pedestal to which she had been confined by Daniel.

The aroma of roast turkey mingled with a cloud of marijuana over the pool. The caterers had tented the garden so colourfully that it looked like the encampment of some

Italian renaissance army. Every woman over the age of thirty-five was wearing a swathed white silk something; her mother's was a new Adolfo and Jo had to admit she looked better than all of them. The younger women drifted around in what Harley would have dismissed as fancy-dress clothes, cowboy boots or harem pants, loaded with jewellery of one ethnic derivation or another. Jo complacently shook out her bias-cut tunic of mint-green embroidered chiffon that floated to thigh level over a Fortuny-pleated skirt and congratulated herself on at least learning how to dress while she was in Europe. Her hair had a new light henna which gave it life without looking too positively red; now that her complexion was a permanent creamy-white, subtle colours suited her best.

Selwyn was obviously flourishing. She checked Jack with Anjelica towering gracefully over him, Travolta looking uneasy in black leather, Ryan and Farrah head-to-hairdo in a fierce argument while the rest of their table looked embarrassed. Elizabeth Taylor was seated in state with Selwyn and his wife, her sapphires blazing in the sunlight, allowing lesser luminaries to approach and pay court. "I just hope she isn't going to get up and break into 'Send In The Clowns,'" Jo's father murmured, steering them to their places a considerable distance away.

Her mother worked the room with consummate style, cheek kissing among the wrinkled faction, Kirk, Ronnie and Nancy, dear Uncle Jimmy. Jo watched and listened, noticing the way she greeted everyone with a little shriek and a flutter, creating enough discreet commotion to let the nearest two hundred people know that she was still big enough to be bussed by the best.

Jamie Lee swooped down on her. "My goodness, it's Jo-Jo. You look just gorgeous. You really have slimmed down, haven't you?"

"Well, what about you? You used to have hair you could sit on! It looks really great short . . ." and she was drawn away to meet up again with all her old school friends. Most of them, she noted wryly, hardly recognised her without her tits, and talked about nothing but bodies, their diets, their personal trainers, their gyms, their classes, and their running schedules.

"Is Ryan still around?" she asked after a while. There was an embarrassed pause.

"Oh, Jo-Jo, didn't anybody tell you about Ryan? He was drafted and, well, of course he went to Vietnam and he was one of the very last boys not to—uh—come back. Not exactly killed, his father doesn't know absolutely, but he was reported missing in action and that's the same thing isn't it?"

"But . . . he went to college . . ." She remembered his letters, although after about a year they had both stopped writing.

"He got into dope and dropped out. It was kind of fatalistic of him if you ask me, he knew better than to do that. I mean, dope really screws up your body . . ." The group murmured agreement and returned to its favourite topic.

Jo shivered, but not from the air-conditioning under the pink-striped canvas. Ryan was part of her history; she stopped herself calling him her first love, the emotion was too mild for that name, but they had shared precious things, time, their fiercely tender young emotions, their own dual view on the rest of the world. She had welcomed his body into hers; now it no longer existed. It had become part of the mud of a distant country and there was nothing to mark where it had once been except this ghostly, chill imprint on her flesh.

She wandered inside the house, running her fingers over the serpentine white leather seating unit because she wanted to touch something solid.

"Jo! How marvellous! This is great, just great! Fancy seeing you here."

The richly insincere voice was unmistakable. "Oh hello, Colin," she said, as he strode towards her, the turned-back cuffs of his white shirt and suede jacket flapping. The kiss was ominously a little more than merely thespian. "What are you doing in La-La land?"

"The same as you, I should imagine, hustling work, dear. The Big Orange is the place to be if you're in our business, isn't it? And they *love* the old English accent. I've got an agent and he's got me some TV already. I'm here with him today, actually. And what about you? I saw you earlier with your mother, that was your mother, wasn't it? You've done so well, I saw some of your notices, they were marvellous . . . I thought you were doing another picture with Daniel."

Jealous, ambitious, desperate, Colin did not change. If

anything, being in LA trying to break into the biggest time of all just made him worse. Jo could not despise him now, only pity him. "I don't think I should really do another film with him. Daniel and I . . ."

"It's all over, is it? I heard that it was, I must say, but I didn't like to ask."

"Working with him is difficult," was all she wanted to tell him. "And Rachel?"

"Wh . . . oh, er, Rachel. Yes, she's in London, she's doing terribly well, terribly well, starting her own theatre, sort of an off-off-Broadway kind of thing . . ."

"Off-off-Shaftesbury Avenue . . ."

"Yes, yes, ha-ha, you've always had such a marvellous sense of humour. It really is good to see you, Jo. I was feeling kinda homesick, this place doesn't really agree with me yet, but it's home to you, isn't it?"

"Yes, but it never agreed with me either." It was also good to see Colin, even if he was a congenital shit. The inner chill she had felt for Ryan faded. Colin somehow connected her back to life.

They sat down on the shiny.white leather and talked over old times for a while, which meant that Colin talked about himself and she listened and smiled and let herself relax, so that it was a shock when she heard him say, "I've always felt we would be together one day, you and I, there's something special between us, isn't there?" and his lips descended on hers and his large, clumsy tongue flickered inside her top lip.

She jumped backwards in alarm, half falling off the slippery leather. "Colin!"

"I'm sorry, I'm sorry, you're just so beautiful I guess I couldn't help myself." At once he helped her to her feet with the elaborate old-fashioned courtesy she despised because she was starting to learn that it always preceded gross behaviour. Colin was concerned only to leave his options open. "Maybe not now, not here, but one day, I just know, you're so gorgeous . . ." He pulled her briefly to him and let her feel the hot bulge in his jeans, releasing her before she pushed him. "But you're right, not now, let's forget it, it never happened, OK?"

They went back to the party and passed a bar; he insisted on getting her some champagne. She heard the two gay bartenders resume their conversation as they passed on. "If you want my opinion, Lorna Lewis is still the best looking woman in Hollywood."

"Nah, she's too short. Angie Dickinson really does it for me. I'm getting a pass on to the set of 'Policewoman' next week."

"But her *clothes*. Look at Lorna, that's another new Adolfo, just right for her, so simple."

"And s-o-o expensive, seventy thou' at least, and she's s-o-o broke."

"But I think that's just divine about her. If Lorna Lewis was starving and she had just one egg left she'd use it to wash her hair. Now tell me that isn't real style."

Jo looked around for her mother. She would introduce Colin to her, that would keep him quiet.

A few days later Selwyn took her to lunch at Ma Maison and laid it on the line. "I could get you a few parts because you're your mother's daughter, although that doesn't count for much any more."

"So why . . ."

"Because everybody likes a family, that's why. They see Lorna Lewis's daughter going into the family business, it gives them a nice warm feeling and they forget they can't communicate with their own kids any more. Your mother's name will get you through any door in Hollywood, but what you come out with is up to you."

"And you don't think there's much for me here?"

"Don't get me wrong. I've seen your pictures, I'm not saying you're no good, but you're not the kind of actress I'm being asked for. You could get your nose done, lose ten —maybe twenty—pounds, get your hair bleached, they only want blonds, remember even Meryl Streep's a blonde, and then I'd still have trouble. You just don't have the right look. Can you do anything, can you dance? Everyone's making dancing pictures now, you taking ballet classes or anything?"

Jo shook her head and stirred her shrimp salad.

"I don't mean to be unkind, kid, but you're not right for this town. You haven't got that all-American look, and you're not sexy and ethnic either. Look at Carrie Fisher, Hollywood brat like you are. OK, she did *Star Wars*. And where did she do it? London. Take my advice, kid, go back, you'll make out better over the other side of the pond."

He paused to gaze around the room. "Tell me about my mother," Jo said suddenly. "Is she having a tough time?"

"You're asking *me* about your mother?"

"I've been away so long, I feel I don't really know her."

"Since you ask, yeah, she's had a tough time. She's brought a lot of it on herself, she's been choosy when she couldn't afford to be, but what the hell, it got her a good name in the end. You can't eat on your reputation, that's all. Hey, maybe you can do me a favour here."

"Certainly, if I can, but what . . ."

"Moses Spielman's putting together a new TV series; it's going to be really new, really different, really big, family story about a newspaper millionaire, calling it 'Heritage.' They want your Lorna for the mother. The money's OK, could be good if it takes off, very good. She won't do it, says TV is just where old actors go to die. Talk her round for me, can you? Frankly, I don't see where else she has to go."

"All right, Selwyn. I'll do what I can."

Colin did the job for her. He became a regular visitor at the new house in the week before the family flew East for Tina's wedding, spouting outrageous flattery which Jo saw refreshed her mother a great deal. "A TV series would be perfect for you," he announced with the full expanse of his spurious authority. "In Britain TV is really where it's at. It's so exciting, being able to touch people like that, reach out to them in their own homes . . ."

Before they left, Lorna called Selwyn and accepted the part.

Jo spent six months in New York taking acting classes. When she returned to London, she called her own agent. Nothing. Alone in her apartment, she took off all her clothes and looked in the mirror. The body is the actor's instrument—maybe Selwyn was right. If all she could do was look voluptuous when Daniel was calling the shots, she could not expect any alternatives.

The months dragged on and her savings dwindled. She took ballet classes, jazz classes, Tai Chi, movement classes for actors and, when she could see the faint outline of muscles in the rounded softness of her thighs, she took her courage in both hands and went to see the legendary Dreyas Reynecke.

"Can you do anything with this?" she asked tentatively,

standing in his studio feeling horribly exposed in her black leotard.

"The question is not what I can do, but what you can do," he answered in his soft Dutch accent. "I can't do anything with anyone who isn't prepared to work."

"Oh, I'm a worker, don't worry."

He made her stand in front of the mirror, then against a grid of movable wires which measured the alignment of her bones.

"You are a woman who is meant to be soft, my advice is not to lose any more weight or it will show in your face. But everything in your body is collapsed here, in the upper spine," he explained, firm fingers stroking between her shoulder blades as he showed her her profile in the mirror. "Your chest is concave, your pelvis tips forward which throws your stomach out . . . maybe you were the first girl in your class to wear a bra, yes?"

"However did you guess?"

"Everything about your body says you are trying to hide your breasts, that's all. It's quite common. We have to teach you to stand straight and be proud of your body. Then your stomach will come in, your shoulders will be square, and if you work hard, then soon you will have a figure to be proud of."

Her frequent companion in the studio was a slender woman with an oval face who wore her black hair scraped back severely like a ballerina and tore through her hundred sit-ups in a blur of speed.

"What is she, a dancer?" Jo asked after she had thrown a rather worn fox coat over her grey leotard and left. "She's in great shape."

"Isn't she just." The studio assistant handed Jo her ankle weights. "Now look, check your body, make your waist long, the foot is turned in, that's right. No, Joan's been coming to us for years. Just another out-of-work actress, doesn't know when to quit. Jackie Collins's sister, you know, the writer? Made more bad movies than you've missed hot dinners, but she never gives up. She's going to LA to test for Aaron Spelling next week, so who knows? Maybe life begins at fifty."

"I'll settle for something starting at twenty-five," Jo sighed as she began her pliés. At least all the toil was paying off. She was definitely a better shape and her belly, at last, was flat.

She hung out a great deal with Rachel, her new boyfriend Simon, and Bazza, who shared an apartment on the top floor of a decaying stucco mansion around the corner from her own place in Holland Park. After a few months they were joined by Roland, a shy Alain Delon lookalike who moved in with Bazza, steadying his behaviour considerably.

Free from Colin, Rachel emerged as a dynamic woman whose bird-like alertness and fragility hid formidable administrative skills. She developed a penchant for laced ankle boots and old black-and-white crepe dresses. Jo watched her grow in strength week by week, boldly soliciting grants, courting the critics and convincing the theatrical establishment that her enterprise was to be a crucible of young talent. The Queen's Arms Theatre, at the rear of the pub of the same name, opened to great acclaim the following spring with Bazza's first play.

Jo returned from the first-night party late, with the unhappy impression that everyone was a success except her. There was a message from her agent. "Lorcan Flood called to see if you would be free for a tour with his company. I didn't know how you'd feel about that. Three months rehearsal, six months on tour. Wonderful professionally, of course, but he pays peanuts."

She sat up for the remaining few hours of the night, turning the proposition over in her mind. Working with Lorcan meant learning, growing, finally turning out her spirit and finding out what she could do with it, finding out what acting was all about. Would working with Lorcan also mean an affair with Lorcan? He frightened her. She was also broke.

In the morning she called her agent. "I'll go with Lorcan," she announced. "Maybe I'll learn something. And let's face it, what else do I have to do?"

* * *

"WHERE ON EARTH has the Sartorious got to? I saw it here yesterday, right at the front of this table." Victoria gazed sternly around the dusty basement of Sotheby's in Bond Street, looking among a hundred haphazardly-stacked gilt-framed paintings for the most valuable of them all, a portrait of George IV's Derby winner Sir Thomas. "Now come along, it's the most important painting in the sale, we can't possibly have mislaid it, it must be here somewhere."

The workmen in their brown overalls grudgingly searched the room. Victoria consulted her sale programme again. "And the Rowlandson prints—ah yes, I can see them." They were correctly labelled so she ticked them and continued. "Four aquatints of the Leicestershire Covers, over there, all numbered, fine."

The telephone rang and she answered it with difficulty, reaching over a small Victorian genre painting of a blacksmith at work. "Oh must I? I'm so busy down here. Oh, very well. You must excuse me," she turned to the workmen as she replaced the receiver, "I've got to go up and see somebody who's come in with a painting. Keep looking for the Sartorious, it really must be found."

She checked her appearance in the ormolu overmantel that was waiting to take its place in a furniture sale the next week, smoothed her hair and loped up the stairs two at a time, arriving at the customers' counter with a pretty flush in her cheeks and a smudge of dust on the shoulder of her white blouse.

A tall, fine-featured man with very blue eyes and straight blond hair was waiting for her. "My mother wanted to see if these were worth selling," he told her, unwrapping two pictures in heavy gold frames which had sustained a few chips.

Victoria turned on the desk light and examined the pictures quickly. They were oil paintings of hunting scenes from the mid-nineteenth century, not particularly well executed but charmingly composed with some amusing details. The signature of the artist was clear on both.

"These are by E. B. Herberte, he's quite popular at the moment, and although the frames are damaged the canvases are all right. I would say they're worth about £500, maybe up to £1,000 each." She was brisk. This was always the worst moment, when you had to tell people their priceless family heirloom was in fact an undistinguished piece of junk. And people seldom brought things in to sell unless they needed the money.

To her relief, he seemed pleased. "And if we asked you to sell them for us . . ."

"Well, it's a bit unfortunate really, we've got a very big

sale of sporting paintings in New York in a few weeks, but we're just crating them up now and the programme's been printed so it's really too late to put them in that. We could put these in one of our smaller sales of Victorian oil paintings earlier, but I think you'll get a better price if you can wait for the next specialised sale."

"Well, no hurry, let's do that then. My mother's just moved to a new house and there's no room for these. I expect they'll be safer in your storeroom than in our attic."

"I wouldn't bet on that. I shouldn't tell you this but I think we've just lost the most important painting in the sale."

"I thought you were looking pretty hacked-off about something. Hold still a moment . . ." He reached forward and pulled a cobweb out of her hair, with a tiny spider abseiling from it on a gossamer rope.

"Oh goodness, I didn't even notice it, I was so distracted." Her hands flew to her temples, smudging dust on one cheek. He thought her combination of competence and confusion delightful. Patrick Hamilton knew Victoria Fairley worked at Sotheby's now, had half-hoped to meet her, and had recognised her immediately, but for all this calculation he would not have dared approach an ex-girlfriend of Prince Richard had she not been wearing a distraught expression and a cobweb in her hair.

"Look, why don't you take a break, let me buy you lunch? Nothing grand, just a bite around the corner, hmn?"

"I couldn't possibly . . ."

"I'm sure by the time you get back they'll have found that picture and you won't have another thing to worry about."

"Well, it's very kind of you but . . ."

"Yes, isn't it? Now, do you need a coat?"

He was irresistible, very correct in his manner, nice-looking and considerate, so she agreed. She went to get her jacket, suddenly regretting the grime on her blouse and the whole period she had passed at Sotheby's wearing neat, inoffensive clothes in the gloomy storerooms. All she had to make herself look more appealing was a slick of lipstick in a rather unassertive pink.

He took her to a pompous oyster bar, around the corner as he had promised.

"I think everyone in here is either a property developer or a man who sells second-hand Jags, don't you?" He had a good, frank grin, the kind that made people trust him. "House champagne and lobster salad? That should put the roses back in your cheeks."

"I don't think you're in property, or old Jags."

"I'm in the Foreign Office. You don't remember me, do you?"

"Oh dear, how awful, do forgive me, I'm so bad at faces . . ."

He was encouraged by her willingness to be in the wrong. "Patrick Hamilton. We've met at a few dances. I knew your brother at Cambridge."

"Oh yes, of course, how silly of me." She was too well-mannered to admit she did not remember him.

Patrick motioned to the waiter to pour the champagne, pleased to have succeeded in adroitly placing himself socially. It was something of an exaggeration to say he knew her brother; he had managed half-a-dozen brief conversations with Alex in the two years during which they had coincided at university but, as a keen student of the Fairley fortunes, he knew that her brother had rejoined the Navy and was now safe.

"So why sporting paintings? Is that your special interest?"

"No, I really like watercolours, but they aren't so fashionable and there's no room in that department at the moment. They're terribly busy in the sporting sections because everybody wants them for the boardrooms, so I'm starting there."

There was a general feeling that a career at Sotheby's or Christie's, or perhaps one of the grander Bond Street galleries, among the artistic detritus of Britain's great houses, was ideal for a well-bred and reasonably intelligent girl who was marking time until marrying and setting up her own home. Someone like Victoria, supposedly surrounded by *objets d'art* all her life, always had the right kind of manner; although she did not know it, Victoria's own thoroughbred looks had directed her to the sporting paintings section as much as the effects of the market.

Patrick returned her to her work at three, pleasantly buzzing from the champagne and with an agreeable sense that a man had been interested in her for herself alone.

The Sartorious had, as he predicted, been discovered immediately after she left, which made her feel that he brought good luck. It was about time she had some luck, she decided.

He courted her with the greatest possible sensitivity, choosing French restaurants where the food was exquisite and the atmosphere calm, and none of the waiters augmented his wages by tipping Keith Cowley of the *Daily Post*. He invited her to the ballet although it bored him, and to Glyndebourne for the opera, which bored them both, and she took him to a succession of art gallery openings and explained the pictures to him in a confidential whisper.

Ambitious men being driven alike, Patrick guessed correctly that a slew of opportunistic suitors had paid court to her since her liaison with Prince Richard had ended, all wanting to capture the royal glory at second hand. His motives were exactly the same; his method a good deal more subtle.

He himself had a large measure of insecurity, for Patrick's mother had committed the social misdemeanour of divorcing his father without securing adequate wealth to maintain her status; instead of marrying again, she had devoted herself to her brilliant son, whose ambition was now to regain the position of which they had both been cheated. He could sense how much Victoria felt diminished in the Prince's shadow. It charmed him that she did not seem cynical or bitter, just serenely accepting of the baseness of human nature.

He allowed her to introduce the subject of Richard when she felt comfortable confiding in him, and at once gently dismissed it, saying, "I think those boys all have a lot of trouble growing up. I mean, they do try, but it's not a normal life, is it?"

A few hours later at his small, silent house in Battersea she willingly allowed him to draw her head into the hollow of his shoulder and hold her protectively in his arms for a long while before beginning to kiss her. Patrick had cold-bloodedly acquired plenty of experience with women, most of it discreetly with shopgirls picked up in a King's Road wine bar, preparing himself for the time when he needed to arouse the sensuality of the woman of his choice. His ambition was to be the youngest ambassador ever appointed, for which position he needed the best possible wife.

He let her set the pace. He complimented her endlessly, on everything that stressed her individuality—her taste, her conversation, her opinions. Confidence soon settled on her like a radiant cloud, making her bold and tantalising. Kisses, even as elaborate as he made them, were soon not enough; he noted her dilated pupils and hot, fast breath, felt the pulse in her neck quick and uneven under his lips and knew she was impatient. On the pretence of their early calls for work the next day, he drove her home with an elegant show of regret.

"Victoria, I want to marry you," he told her simply, the next time they entered the familiar intimacy of his house. "I can't go on like this without telling you how I feel. I'm not the kind of man who plays the field, you know. For me, this is something very, very serious." He was holding both her hands in his, willing her downcast eyes to look up.

She seemed almost disbelieving. "I love you, Victoria, I love you." Fool, he should have said that first. He pulled her gently into his arms. "Please, I must know . . ."

"I love you too," she whispered uncertainly. "I feel . . . safe with you, Pat."

"We'll be abroad all the time, of course, you know that, don't you? And I can't offer you much, only . . ." he kissed her hand.

Judging that it was time not to talk any more, he walked her slowly upstairs to his bedroom, reverently removed her clothes and began to make love to her. Victoria threw herself into the hot tide of desire with an avidity which surprised him and saved the enterprise from disaster.

As he prepared to enter her, the realisation that he, Patrick Hamilton, to all intents and purposes a nobody, was to put his cock in the sweet pink orifice before occupied only by royal flesh, and pour his juices into a woman who had received that essence of the oldest ruling house in Europe, fell on him like a ton weight and he felt his erection fail.

Victoria had anticipated as much and was as desperate as he to beat the hex. To his surprise her languid white body recoiled towards him; he felt her hands, clumsy but eager, caress his shaft and her lips fasten awkwardly around the head. It was all inexpert and she had clearly never tried to suck a penis before; that realisation alone sent his blood surging back so violently that he almost came in her mouth.

They set a date for the wedding a year later at the village church in Aston Langley. Victoria felt as if a cold, wet blanket had been lifted from her shoulders. She decided she was happy, and did not need to take her pills any longer, but after a week without them she became so alarmingly weepy and emotional that she changed her mind, and resolved that the pressures of the wedding were too much for her to bear without chemical assistance.

Her father was unalloyedly delighted. Pamela made the best of it. Rose began squabbling on the telephone immediately with her seven selected cousins and acquaintances over the colour of the bridesmaids' dresses. The Royal Marines granted Second Lieutenant His Royal Highness, the Prince Richard, weekend leave for the occasion. His present to the happy couple was a plain silver tray.

"I suppose you realise that everyone thinks this man's an utter shit?" The Navy had granted Alex a week's leave. It was the first time they had seen each other for eighteen months. "I don't know him, you know. He tried to scrape an acquaintance with me; it wasn't hard to guess why, so I gave him a wide berth. The man was on the make."

Patrick had skillfully prepared this ground. "Going to the kind of intellectual school which I went to is a bit of a two-edged sword," he had told her with an elegant gesture of self-deprecation. "You're always thought of as clever and devious, just because that's the school's reputation. But this country needs good brains, especially in the Diplomatic Service. I'm rather against this English tradition of disparaging cleverness, myself."

"I'm sure you were mistaken," Victoria told her brother with perfect confidence. "Pat has a direct way with him sometimes and he makes no secret of his ambitions, but I rather like that. I mean, why should he pretend he doesn't want to get on? We're not all born with silver spoons in our mouths."

Both Harley and Jo were among the house guests at Aston Langley, Harley more glamorous than ever, Jo slender and preoccupied.

They duly admired Victoria's dress and exclaimed over the packages from Thomas Goode and the General Trading Company which arrived each day. They agreed that

Patrick was a wonderful man and that Victoria was too lucky for words. They also remarked to each other that the transfiguring adoration which Richard had inspired was absent.

The night before her marriage Victoria could not sleep. She went down to the kitchens in her night-gown and found her two old friends already there, making coffee with care among the massed apparatus brought in by the caterers.

The three of them sat down and gossiped, enjoyably picking over their lives and their past until Victoria suddenly said, "You don't really like Pat, do you?"

"Which of us are you talking to?" Harley laughed, trying to keep things light.

"Both of you. You don't like him, I can tell."

"Victoria, darling, we aren't marrying him. If you love him, that's all that counts, isn't it?"

"She isn't sure she does love him, isn't that it?" Jo crossed her legs with a slither of blue silk kimono.

"Oh, Jo, nobody can hide anything from you, can they? You always know exactly what's going on." Victoria felt her eyes ache as if she was going to cry but no tears came. "I don't know, I don't know how I feel, I don't know what I'm doing . . ."

"Well I know, my sister was just the same," Jo smiled as she recalled Tina collapsing in a tearful heap on the end of her bed the night before her wedding, all self-possession wrecked. "All you've got is good old-fashioned stage fright, for which we in the theatrical profession recommend a large Irish coffee and as much sleep as you can get. Sir Laurence Olivier used to bang his head against a wall, but I don't think you need go that far." She got up and searched for a saucepan, then opened the nearest of the two massive but elderly refrigerators.

"Pat is a wonderful man, you know. He's so kind, so sensitive, he's made me feel like myself again. And he says he doesn't mind about . . . you know, the family thing."

I bet he says just that, Harley and Jo thought silently and simultaneously.

"But he doesn't make you feel like Richard made you feel?" *Nobody* could make a woman feel like Richard had made her feel, Harley and Jo agreed in silence.

Jo poured cream over the spoon and pushed the rich

alcoholic brew towards her friend. "No," Victoria lowered her head, gingerly pulling the saucer towards her.

"The first cut is the deepest, honey. You can't expect to feel the same way twice." What the hell do I know, Harley asked herself, keeping the twisted grin off her face.

"I suppose not. You're both right. We will always be friends, won't we?"

"Of course." One white and one brown hand closed over hers. "Wherever you are in the world, there'll always be a telephone."

"Where are you going off to?" Harley stifled a yawn. The kitchen clock said 3 am.

"Patrick's first posting is Athens, we're going directly from our honeymoon. It's a very good place, apparently, he's very pleased."

The next day she was married in a glorious sweep of ivory taffeta with her paternal grandmother's lace veil. Patrick looked and acted immaculately. The local constabulary called in reinforcements to keep away the crowd of fifty local people and one hundred and eighty press photographers.

Prince Richard arrived with the Bromptons, with whom he was staying at Morton Beauchamp; he looked magnificent in his dress uniform, and was charming to everyone, although when he kissed Jo on the cheek she caught the scent of drink; not the mere smell of whisky on his breath, but a spiritous aroma which seemed to emanate from his pores. Her godfather used to smell the same. Richard must have been drinking heavily and habitually for some time. They had an inconsequential conversation which made her feel unexpectedly regretful.

•   •   •

THE FOLLOWING EVENING Captain Clive Fairbrother of the Queen's Own Victoria Rifles walked into the officers' mess at Royal Naval College, Greenwich with a long, powerful stride. Like most men confident of being the tallest in any company, he reached the centre of the room before he halted to look around for his objective.

Richard was lounging in a shabby red wing chair in a far corner, reading *The Field*.

Every head in the half-empty room turned as the Captain passed, partly because at 6ft 4in, white-blond and deeply tanned, he was an arresting figure, and partly because however stoutly his brother officers maintained that Second Lieutenant HRH the Prince Richard was just an ordinary bloke, gut fascination with all his actions was endemic among them.

Alerted by this slight stir, Richard looked up from the account of brown trout fishing in New Zealand which had been adequate to capture his attention for ten minutes while he awaited his guest. He rose and ironically threw a salute so perfect that it would have warmed the vestigial heart of his old colour sergeant.

Fairbrother reacted sharply with surprise, and the two men shook hands.

"You do outrank me, after all," Richard apologised as they sat down.

"Not much and probably not for long, the way I hear it." The chair groaned under Fairbrother's fourteen stone. "And only if we pretend rank's all that counts."

"It's all that counts around here. What'll you have?" An orderly stood silently at his elbow.

"If you say so. I'll have a beer if it's cold." The orderly stepped smartly away, evidently knowing that Richard wanted another Scotch. "Why have they sent you back to school?" He waved a large square hand to indicate the splendour of the Wren palace beyond the shabby confines of the building which served the Navy as an instructional institution.

"NATO course. This is my third bloody stint. They've had me doing strategy and a special weapons course already."

"Is it as bad as all that?" The drinks were deferentially deposited on the ring-marked table.

"I only joined the Marines to keep my parents quiet and get some climbing in. I didn't bargain with them sending me back to school."

"You let 'em know you were bright, that was where you went wrong. You ought to act dumb, that's the way I play things."

"Tough act to keep up, is it?" Richard had become adept at pitching the first ritual insult; too mild and it could be taken seriously, too strong and his partner would catch the smell of condescension. Get it right and the whole encounter flowed.

"Oh, I can manage if I put my mind to it, Sir." Clive's smile showed all his teeth. The cap on the incisor broken at school now did little credit to the Elgin dentist. "Of course, I'm not lumbered with a degree like you. That is a bit of a give-away."

Richard wondered how closely his old adversary had been following his career. He had left Cambridge with a 2:1, a better degree than anyone, including himself, had expected. "So what brings you to London?"

"Orders, same as you. But while I'm here I thought I'd see if you'd care to renew acquaintance. Not entirely on a social basis, Sir, I admit."

"Oh, yes?" Richard liked directness, but was now wary of his instinct to put too much trust too easily in people who spoke their minds. He had invited his old enemy out of curiosity. Fairbrother had sought the meeting formally through his Palace office, but with no stated purpose; in doing that he had presumed outrageously on their past relationship, a year of the intense intimacy of adolescent hatred followed by awkward reconciliation.

"Yes. The way things seem to be with your—er—set up, you might be planning to stay in the service a few years, but from what I've heard since I've been here you've set your heart on being the youngest climbing officer the Pongos have ever had. Is that right?"

"I did say that, I shot my mouth off in a radio interview before I joined up, but yes, that's the goal I've set myself. You've got to have something to aim for, haven't you?"

The two men paused to appraise each other, under cover of ordering fresh drinks and exchanging small talk. The room was slowly filling up as men who had been away for the weekend returned. Four officers of the Fleet Air Arm occupied the circle of chairs next to them and began the classic Sunday night interrogation of one of their number who had enjoyed a weekend in pursuit of a woman who had parted with her telephone number in an encouraging manner at a cocktail party.

"So go on, man, what happened?"

"What do you mean, what happened?" The seducer savoured his beer, clearly in no hurry to entertain his hosts.

Fairbrother had matured well, Richard considered. His confidence felt securely founded, instead of the empty bravado he had displayed as an adolescent. "You're climbing too, I understand."

"Yes, but the Army's a means to an end for me as far as mountains go. You've been on service expeditions, you must know what I'm talking about."

Richard nodded cautious agreement. "I've only done a couple. The standard was pretty poor."

Behind him a boisterous voice riposted, "You know bloody well what I mean, I mean, did you fuck her?"

The adventurer took another pull at his beer. "Yeah, of course I fucked her." There was a general roar of approval and two more men strolled across to join the circle.

Fairbrother was oblivious. "Mountains are the only thing that do it for me, you know. It's gambling, isn't it? Nothing's sure on a climb. It's you against the impossible, all the time. And when I know I'm standing higher than any other man in the world at that moment . . ."

"Or when you're standing somewhere no one ever has before . . ." They drew closer together, partly to hear each other against the rising volume of ribaldry. "So you're planning to get out of the Army and make out on your own?"

"Yes. I've got a seven-year stretch and when it's over I'll start putting my own expeditions together. Which of course is why I'm here. I was wondering how you'd feel about coming in with me on a climb in a few years' time." He paused to let Richard assimilate the implications of his suggestion.

The conversation beside them continued at accelerating pace.

"Good goer, was she?"

"Got a few in, did you?"

"A few? I should say. Bangs like a shit-house door, that one. Couldn't get enough." There was another wave of approving laughter and new drinks were ordered all round. "And the mouth on her . . . talk about centrifugal force! I tell you, it felt like a couple of Gs coming down the spout."

Richard, in uncharacteristically distractible mood, mentally answered the catechism on his own behalf. Did you fuck her? Yes, I fucked Jane Brompton, what else can you do when you've just seen the only woman you've ever loved get married? At least I suppose I fucked her, I usually do when I stay with them, Nicky makes himself scarce on purpose.

Got a few in, did you? Probably. I was pretty drunk, I can't remember exactly. Good goer? You couldn't call her that. She's a nice woman, a nice lay, sweet, affectionate, Nicky gave her a good education before he lost interest. She's always willing. And grateful. She didn't cry at least, which she has before, but she always looks at me with those bloody devoted-bitch eyes. I hate that look. I hate having to fuck Jane Brompton, if the truth were known, I'd rather just talk to her, but at least it keeps me out of trouble.

The men lowered their voices for the next phase of the conversation. Richard knew the sequence by heart. There were a few stories about him, too, he knew: he'd wormed them out of one of the boys on a survival training exercise. Flattering, but all invention, which he regretted.

Fairbrother noticed that he had lost Richard's attention. "Is that what the Navy boys call a run ashore?" He nodded in the group's direction.

"That's the ideal, I think."

"Do you ever get into bull sessions like that?" It was a daring inquiry but Clive had less than twenty-four hours left in London and was determined to reel in his catch before he left.

"Sometimes. You have to, really."

"I suppose it's unfair on the others, you being such a playboy and everything."

"That's a load of crap." Richard was stung, and at once regretted showing it. Fairbrother's speculation was the exact truth. He could tell a few dirty stories to show he was one of the lads, drop a few hints to keep the shine on the image, hold his own against Andrew, let the boys make him almost a mascot, but honest disclosure was impossible.

The truth was that Richard could score any woman he wanted. He had proved that to himself immediately he left Cambridge. Outside the protective walls of the university he found himself adrift in utter loneliness. He felt full of potential, but unable to use it. His parents, in the calm, omniscient style which enraged him, had for a year tried to steer him towards the Navy. His brother Andrew was spontaneously inclined to this traditional course, but all Richard saw in it was the painful inevitability of encountering Victoria's brother or father.

"I need time to think," he announced, with a marked lack of grace.

"Well, don't take too long about it," his father ordered with equal acerbity.

Ambition, like a formless monster, hounded him until his mind scattered in panic. He wanted to do so much, and saw no opportunities. He accepted a score of invitations to become the chairman, president or patron of organisations as diverse as the Royal Historical Institute of Great Britain, the Society for the Preservation of Inland Waterways, the Commonwealth Youth Education Council, the National Film Board of Scotland, Alpine Conservation Year, and the Liverpool Lifeline Project for the rehabilitation of drug addicts. His instinct was to accept every approach made by such bodies in a desperate attempt to fill up his days; he rejected his Private Secretary's counsel of moderation so rudely and so often that the man resigned.

Every morning in that period of restless limbo he awoke in a stew of nervous tension which by the evening became a fever of lust. He took every woman who offered herself to him, and seduced so many others until he frightened and disgusted himself. The joke—he tried to tell himself it was a joke—was that he did not want any of them. He drank a great deal, at first for comfort, then to insulate himself from the knowledge of what he was doing. Drinking and fucking quickly became interlinked compulsions. He believed no one noticed, but the women gossiped and he quite often appeared in public in a state that was obviously alcohol-enhanced if not exactly drunk.

He buried his emotions; all that drove him was a need for challenge, and so he engineered more and more dangers within the confines of his sanitised social round. He found himself at last being reintroduced to a woman he had casually separated from her fiancé at a country dinner party a fortnight earlier and screwed a mere six feet away from the diners, in the cloakroom among the Barbours and the muddy boots. The pathetic way she looked up at him, the adoring whimper in her voice were mildly familiar; he had been so drunk he might as well have dreamed the entire incident; his strongest recollection was the smell of wet waxed cotton. He vaguely remembered her face, did not know her name, had no idea what he had said to her and was horrified to hear that she had broken her engagement on the strength of some understanding he had induced.

"I am most terribly sorry," he heard himself articulate the words with great care and difficulty, as if his mouth were full of broken glass, "I've done something absolutely unforgivable. I can't expect you to understand, I don't know that I really understand myself, but I . . ."

"You were drunk," she said with gentle resignation.

"Yes, I was. I just . . . I couldn't . . . I don't know what came over me . . ." he hung his head, consciously playing the shamefaced little boy, an act that had got him out of trouble before, though nothing on this scale.

"Don't worry," she gave a game toss of her head. "It's nothing I can't smooth over. I did wonder if you weren't a little cut up, about Tory and everything."

In this manner he had learned of Victoria's engagement.

Charles had intervened to save him. At least, that was how he saw it now. At the time his brother's invitation to join him on his annual summer fishing holiday with Lord and Lady Tryon in Iceland seemed a casual afterthought. Once in that elemental landscape Richard felt his soul cleansed and his mind clear. He also found himself shamefully unfit, and facing a commitment, as the honorary chairman of the Cambridge University Climbing Club, to climb Mount Blanc by the Goutier route before Christmas.

His life fell into place. Climbing was the only thing that offered him the scale of challenge he craved and the discipline he acknowledged that he needed. He could pursue it in any of the services, but there seemed no reason to fight his parents on the issue; he elected to join the Royal Marines.

During his training, he found the Bromptons' hospitality at Morton Beauchamp convenient. Jane, ten years his senior and the dutiful wife of a man whose power of seduction almost equalled his own, had offered something of a challenge; the affair was a comfort, a sexual release but for both of them it carried the sad stain of compensation for another love.

Fairbrother drank his beer slowly and appraised his target. Something new about the Prince was familiar to him. One type of man joined the services because he fancied he looked good with a gun; he drove too fast, drank too much, and usually signed up when he realised that as a civilian the only activity which satisfied his craving for sensation was breaking the law. This good sense, and a sound but sadistic training officer, usually saved him, but every man of this kind had a certain look. He acted to hide pain and deny passion, fronting-up mean and guarded. To most people, he looked tough. It was the aspect of a man who, but for the grace of God, would end up in jail, which many of them eventually did. The Australian was surprised to see that look on Richard.

"I don't know, Clive," the Prince responded suddenly, as if aware that he was being harshly judged. "If I'm still in the Marines when you get this expedition together I'd have to get leave to do it. Obviously they make exceptions for me as it is. It might be tricky. Keeping it quiet isn't what you had in mind, I take it."

"No. I'll need sponsors and they'll obviously be in it for the publicity. Shall I tell you what I've got in mind?"

"By all means, go ahead."

"A Japanese team have just cancelled their permit to climb the West Ridge of Everest from the north in '84. I reckon we could have a go." He saw the bronze glint in Richard's eyes and knew success was within his grasp. "I want to make it a lightweight, Alpine-style operation, as far as I can. It's more of a crack if you go for the necessary minimum, don't you think?"

"Yes. Yes, I do." Richard had already discovered that climbing was as dangerous, and by the same token as satisfying, as people chose to make it. Somewhere between safety and suicide, climbers picked their own level of risk. As technology and equipment made things easier, mountaineers made them more difficult. "I've got a bit of Alpine experience now . . ."

"I know you're doing the Eiger in a couple of years . . ."

"You've been doing your homework. Yes, I am. And there should be time for me to get some Himalayan climbing in . . ."

"That would be useful, Sir, but not absolutely essential. I'm hoping I won't be the most experienced climber in the party by a long way. And plenty of blokes have taken on Everest as their first expedition in the Himalayas."

"I wonder how many succeeded." He saw Clive recoil at the intensity of his tone. "Don't forget, if I make a prat of myself, the whole world knows about it. Win or lose, I do it in public."

"I wasn't planning to blow it, Sir."

"Good. Look, I'm keen, but I'll have to talk this through with a few people first. I'll let you know in a week or so, OK? Do you need a car, by the way?" Fairbrother found himself deftly parcelled up in the Prince's charm and dispatched on his way. Being driven back to his billet through the wet London streets, he wondered if he had been wise after all. If his scheme got the royal approval, his future as a professional climber would be assured; he would also be committed to putting his life in the hands of a man who seemed not to care for life at all very much.

Richard went to bed with a light heart, suddenly beguiled by the strange pattern of his destiny as he saw it unroll, ferociously determined that neither his commanders nor his family should cheat him of the prize of Everest.

The next day he went to see a senior officer at Whitehall. "We have been invited to send some officers to visit the Irish Army," he began, making a tent of his fingers. Richard distrusted the gesture. It was supposed to convey consideration but he associated it with bad news. "The purpose is to foster increased understanding and goodwill between the two forces, and it has been decided to send two officers to the battalion attached to the United Nations mission in Lebanon. This is an opportunity for us to learn about peacekeeping in a particularly difficult theatre, from a force which has considerable experience, having contributed to UN contingents for almost thirty years. We're sending you because you're the best and brightest we can spare at the moment."

"Yes, sir." Richard assumed the correct mask of obedience.

"Although the greater good that could be achieved by yourself in particular in terms of understanding between the nations rather than the armies is naturally something we would be foolish to ignore. However, there are obvious hazards in sending you to Lebanon so there will be some security personnel accompanying you."

"Yes, sir."

"I expect you were hoping for something a little more challenging?"

"Yes, I was, sir." Damn it, they praised his leadership qualities enough—was he never to get the opportunity to use them?

"Next time, I'm sure. You won't be short of excitement. The UN boys get their share of shot and shell. We're not deliberately keeping you behind the lines, don't be concerned on that score."

"No, sir."

The officer opened his file, pushing it a few inches forward on the desk top. "You're a first-class officer, you won't be wasted. They say you've got that quality President Kennedy described as 'grace under pressure' and we value that above all else in the Royal Marines. Experience, that's what you need. Look on this as a learning opportunity."

"Thank you, sir, I will. If I might make one point, sir?"

"By all means . . ."

"I think grace under pressure was Hemingway's definition of courage, in fact."

"Ah, yes. Hemingway. Always get American Presidents mixed up."

A few days later Richard dictated a letter to Clive Fairbrother formally to confirm his commitment to the Everest expedition in 1984. He scrawled a postscript. "It's good to know I've got this to look forward to—they're packing me off on a bloody PR exercise now."

CHAPTER XVII

"SUZIE, IT'S TOO awful, they're sending him to the Lebanon and there's practically a war there. I love him so much. I can't bear even thinking that he might be . . ." Jane Brompton flinched away from the word "killed." She blinked hard to stop the tears escaping from beneath her thick dark lashes and took a large sip from her third gin and tonic of the evening.

Suzie Chamfer thought her sister was pathetic, but had a good reason not to say so. "Do be sensible, darling. If there was any real danger they wouldn't dream of sending him. He'll be back in four weeks without a scratch on him. It'll be the best possible thing for you—absence makes the heart grow fonder and all that. I mean, he's not going to fall for someone else in an army camp, is he?"

Jane sniffed and looked around for tissues. Suzie pulled a grimy wad from her handbag and watched her sister wipe her long narrow nose. "It's bad enough loving him and knowing we can't ever be together."

"But you couldn't really want to marry him, could you? Have the Palace run your life for you? Do think, darling, it would be absolutely pissing awful. You've got the best of both worlds as things are. I think you're terribly lucky."

"I shouldn't have told you, really."

"Of course you should, I'm your sister, I care about you. I'm really quite insulted you didn't tell me before." Suzie patted her hair and glanced at her reflection in the windows of the winter garden at Morton Beauchamp. She was now blond, with half-an-inch of regrowth in evidence, and the most expensive scissors in London could not make the unruly tufts fall the way they should. Still, reflected in the algae-dimmed glass by the weak light, she did slightly resemble Debbie Harry of Blondie. Suzie looked at her sister's orderly dark chignon with distaste wondering how much more of this pitiful recital she would have to hear.

"You were the only person I could trust. I couldn't bear not being able to talk to anyone and thinking he might . . . but you mustn't tell a soul."

"I swear. Not a word. Listen, I really must . . ."

"Of course, your party, I forgot. I've got the money all ready." They retraced their steps along the mosaic floor between dusty tree palms to the door which led to Jane's small private sitting room, Suzie in jeans with her quilted purple satin jacket over one shoulder, her older sister already dressed for dinner in coral-pink taffeta.

"It's a first night, darling. It's terribly important to be seen at these parties if you're serious about being an actress. Producers and people just forget you if you don't get your face in the papers pretty often."

"Of course, I do understand." Jane looked at her sister properly for the first time and decided she was looking unhealthy and her behaviour was jumpy. Suzie talked constantly of being an actress but, apart from a small part as a pert serving wench in a Regency romp last year and an audition for the new James Bond film which had come to nothing, her career was mostly spent at parties. The struggle was obviously taking its toll. "So selfish of me, maundering on about my silly problems. Look, here it is, two thousand, that was right, wasn't it?"

She handed Suzie a thick blue envelope full of £20 notes. Her younger sister gave her a quick kiss and a hug. "Bless you, Janie, you're wonderful. I need this film course desperately, they're always telling me I need more camera experience. You're sure Nicky won't mind?"

"He won't even notice. I took it out of the house account, he never looks at it. You sure you can't stay for dinner?"

"Love to, but I've got to fly. Keep smiling. And don't *worry*, darling, he'll be absolutely A-OK. And I won't breathe a word."

She flogged her rattling little Fiat back to London with her foot on the floor and went straight to the outer fringe of Chelsea, looking for a retired rock'n'roll roadie who had found a less strenuous way of earning a living. In the third pub she tried she found him, blue-chinned and slouched against the bar. He pocketed half her sister's money in exchange for a packet of cocaine, imaginatively packaged in a floral plastic washbag.

At her apartment in a mansion block around the corner she sampled her purchase and changed into an Anthony Price sheath in electric blue. Her escort, otherwise her agent's boyfriend, arrived and accepted a line also. They got to Langan's at exactly the right time, slightly before the big stars so the photographers were trigger happy and inclined to snap any pretty girl who caught their eyes.

Inside, she saw Sean Murray, a gossip writer on the *Daily Post*, champagne glass cradled against his well-padded chest, methodically working the room. A few peals of what Suzie considered her delicious silvery laughter and his bulk loomed beside her; he was a tall man, which took the cherubic edge off his rosy-cheeked good looks.

"Darling!"

"Darling!"

"Mmmgh!" Over her shoulder as they kissed he noted Rod Stewart arrive with Alana Hamilton.

"Mmmngh!"

"You look superb!"

"Darling, how sweet!"

"What's new?" Who *was* that cross-eyed beefcake with Olivia Newton-John?

"I'm up for an American TV thing next week, I'm so excited I can hardly breathe, darling. They never tell you, but I'm pretty sure it's for 'Heritage.' Megabucks if I score."

"Oh well, we'll have to see what we can do, won't we?" He wound an arm around her waist and pinched a protruding hip-bone reassuringly. Ringo and Barbara. And Colin Lambert! He was supposed to be in LA. Obviously life as Lorna Lewis's toy boy had lost its lustre. "Anything else?"

"I can't *wait* to tell you, darling, but *not here.*"

"This must be a biggie!"

"Abso*lute*ly!" She winked one china-blue eye and passed her hand over his crotch, a gesture firm enough to be felt and fast enough not to be seen. Murray was a terrific lay, drunk or sober, not that Suzie or anyone else could ever remember having him sober. Still, it was nice to be able to mix business with pleasure when one had the opportunity.

They went to Tramp, and encountered Keith Cowley making a rapid exit with an expression of disgust. "Nix," he muttered, "see you at Tokyo Joe's."

Tokyo Joe's was also quiet. Being launched by the brother of the ex-lover of Princess Margaret was more than a new nightclub needed to get off the crowded ground within a stiletto's totter of the Ritz.

Murray being a man who loved his job, they took a cab down to the far end of King's Road to a new nightclub opening that very night and destined, Murray announced as he checked the carpet already peeling from the walls, the hole in the ceiling through which rain was dripping and the sound system barely sophisticated enough for the massed vocals of Village People, to close by the end of the week.

Dawn found them at Murray's home, an apartment on the fifth floor of a red-brick Belgravia mansion, two low-ceilinged rooms under the roof originally intended to accommodate the housemaids. Murray had taken the advice of Aristotle Onassis seriously and bought the best address he could afford, even if it was too small to kennel a dog in comfort.

"So what's the big news?" The sofa groaned under his weight. He ran his hands through his over-long brown hair. "Your sister giving Nicky the big E, or what?"

"Better than that, darling." She opened her silver leather purse and tipped out its contents on the fingermarked glass coffee table. "Blade, sweets?"

"Bathroom."

She returned with the business section of his razor held delicately between her fingertips and laid out two lines on the table top. He leaned lazily forward to snort his share.

"Ah! Hmnh! Shaken not stirred! Well, what then? Your old school chum Vicky found out she's married a 22-carat prick and done a runner?"

"Nope." Suzie rubbed the last grains delicately into her gums.

"Rich the Bitch, then, it's got to be."

"Third time lucky, darling."

He sat up, galvanised as much by the scent of the story as the chemicals penetrating his nasal membranes. "Go on, girl, don't tease, tell me all."

She did so. He shook his head in delight.

"Wow! Your dear old sister. Sweet girl. I've always liked Jane." Suzie bridled momentarily. Everyone said they had always liked Jane. "Hasn't got an ounce of your pzazz, though." He rolled off the sofa and sat down heavily beside her on the shaggy wool carpet that had once been white. "How's old Nicky taking it? The biter bit at last, eh?"

"She says he's really pissed off. Can you believe it? After the way he's treated her."

"And where's he off to?"

"Lebanon. Something about the United Nations and Ireland, she said. I didn't understand but I'm sure you'll be able to make sense of it."

"More than sense, darling, a page lead, if not a special spread . . ." Visions of glory entranced him. For Murray, glory meant his name in very large letters with his picture beside it and the increased certainty of taking over the gossip column when the next new editor of the *Daily Post* ordered heads to roll. It was also Sunday, and he had full command of the column because his boss liked weekends in the country. He lay back on the rug, one hand behind his head, and smiled broadly at Suzie. She really was a delicious little article, in every respect.

"Now you won't forget me, will you?"

"Darling, while Richie-boy is fucking your sister you'll be on my mind night and day." He dipped his fingers into the tight bodice of her dress, trying to work out how it unfastened.

"No, I mean about the Americans and everything."

"Keith got some shots of you tonight, didn't he?"

She nodded, standing up to pull down the concealed zipper.

"Consider it done, darling. What are you wearing under that?"

"I could ask you the same question." Holding the dress provocatively in place, she slipped one high-arched foot out of its shoe and wriggled her toes under his belt.

"Oh, this is too much. I don't know what goes on with women today. You don't expect to get laid just because you've given me a line of coke and a great story?"

"Oh, well, if you're not up to it . . ." she shrugged, zipped, resumed the shoe and made as if to gather her possessions and leave. Two seconds later she was pleased to find herself lying on the rug with the dress around her waist and his tongue applied confidently between her legs.

"I hope the day never comes when I'm not up to you, sweetheart," he mumbled happily an hour later. "Christ, is that the time? Gotta get motoring—can I drop you anywhere?"

Suzie was up to her ears in Badedas at her own apartment when she heard a squeal of tyres outside. From the front window she saw a tasteful dark blue Mercedes parked casually across two-thirds of the pavement and a slim young woman in riding breeches and a Gucci shirt leaning impatiently on her door-bell. Her brown hair was held back in a plain tortoiseshell clip.

"Here you are," Suzie said brightly as soon as the girl was inside and the door shut. She handed her the floral plastic washbag with three-quarters of its original contents intact. The girl accepted it with a flicker of disdain.

"I hope it's better quality than what you had before." She had a faint French accent.

Suzie smiled warmly and held out her hand for the money. The girl pulled a roll of notes from her shoulder bag. "Thank you *so* much," Suzie said, with the exquisitely calculated degree of frost only the best-bred English women can command. Maybe the cow would like it better packed in a Gucci purse. "I *do* hope you like it. So nice to see you again."

The interloper departed. Suzie counted the money, ran some more hot water into her bath and plunged under the foam. A hundred-plus per cent profit, her picture in the *Daily Post*, lots of dope, lots of champers and an absolutely epic screw—what more could a girl want in twelve hours? She decided to sing. "You Don't Bring Me Roses" was the first tune that came to mind and it sounded horrible. So Streisand need never worry on her account. Maybe she should go roller-skating in Hyde Park. Maybe not. Couldn't possibly test for "Heritage" with a broken leg. Maybe she should call up good old Col and pick his brains. He must have all the inside dope from Lorna Lewis. Yes, that was what an actress ought to do at a time like this. But she definitely wasn't going to screw *him* again, far too much like hard work.

•   •   •

"STEADY. STEADY WITH your right." Nicky Brompton's hand descended firmly on the Barbados-gold forearm of Princess Louise of Meinenbourg to still it. "Do a bit more of that butterfly stuff under the tip, that was great." Sprawled across the dark blue quilted chintz of the bed in his Knightsbridge house, he was instructing her to give head to his exact satisfaction.

"I can't help it—it's so beautiful," she murmured, her lips poised to descend on him again. "I l-o-o-o-ve it so much." She swept aside her sleek curtain of brown hair and went back to work. Princess Louise was a pleasure to teach. She had decided early that her best chance of getting the attention she deserved was to become a world-class sexual athlete. Naturally, serious training was essential.

Nicky was known throughout the rich and English-speaking world as Needle Dick, and sucking him off did not present a great physical challenge. Psychologically, however, he was an important exercise. The man she married might be the same, or even smaller, and Princess Louise knew it was important to make a man feel confident of his virility no matter how mean nature had been in constructing its physical manifestation. Otherwise, as her mother had pointed out when Nicky Brompton's sapphire eye had first fallen on her daughter across the rim of the Meinenbourg Cup for individual distinction on the polo field, he might seek consolation by trying to stick the stupid thing into every woman he met.

Louise teased him delicately for another ten minutes then sat on the turgid protuberance, wedged it into the narrowest angle she could achieve between bone and muscle, threw some rapid pelvic crunches and finished him off.

He seemed well satisfied, gasping like a landed fish before rolling over and patting her on the backside. He reached for their half-finished balloons of cognac on the night table.

"Just—the best," he murmured, wiping a trace of VSOP from his lips across her nearest nipple and watching it pucker. "Wonderful, darling. What can I say?"

She draped herself along the far end of the bed and let him look. Princess Louise had none of the sentimentality which might be expected of a nineteen-year-old. She had decided that too much post-coital affection made a lot of men nervous. It put them under pressure. Her strategy was just to display the goods and let them make the choices.

It also helped fix their minds on what they had just sampled. She and her mother had worked hard on her body all her life and both were properly proud of it. She had had surgery, at the perfect time, three years ago, when her bones were still growing, so that the patrician straightness of her nose, the nubile tilt of her nipples and the athletic narrowness of her thighs now looked utterly natural.

"Would you like to go to Annabel's?" he asked. Proposing the smartest nightclub in town always seemed a gracious way of ducking the second round in bed.

Louise was alarmed. They were bound to meet people she knew, or people he knew, and tomorrow everyone in London would be talking about them. Appearing in public with a high-bred low-life like Nicky was the last thing she needed. Princess Louise had slept with more men in four years than most women enjoy in a lifetime, but as far as anyone knew her experience was limited to a teenage romance with the son of an Austrian steel millionaire.

"But what about your wife?" she countered, alarm in her blue eyes. "People are bound to see us."

"My wife. My dear, faithful wife, Jane." He hung his head as if in severe sorrow. "Louise, you're so innocent. You must be the only person in London who doesn't know that Prince Richard has been screwing my wife on a regular basis for months. She's only too pleased to get rid of me and she doesn't give a damn what I do."

"Poor Nicky, how _terrible_ for you."

"It's a real fix, isn't it? I can't very well kick up a fuss, I can't possibly divorce her—do you know, I've even had people think I ought to be pleased? Honoured, for God's sake. The bastard. I mean, we're related, you know."

Louise knew very well. The kindred and affinity of the royal houses of Europe, to which she herself was attached by the single, brief union of her mother and father, was engraved on her memory.

"I've heard the most awful things about him," she prompted.

"Well, they're all true. And worse. I could tell a few stories . . . he's another playboy, just like the Duke of Windsor, if you ask me. Except Uncle David was just stupid and I really do think Richard must be mad sometimes.

All that mountaineering business. I feel sorry for Jane, really. She's the one who'll be hurt in the end. I love her, you know. You're very, very sweet, Louise, but sometimes I . . ." a deep, phoney sigh swelled his chest, "I just can't bear it any longer. I just have to find ways of getting it out of my mind, that's all."

Quel shit, Louise thought to herself. God, he must think I'm dumb. Still, there are angles to play in that.

She embraced him as uncarnally as she could. "Darling, I couldn't possibly go out dancing when you're so sad. Couldn't we just have a quiet supper somewhere? You can talk to me about it. I know I'm too young to understand, but maybe I can cheer you up a teeny little bit if I sit and listen for a while."

●   ●   ●

WHEN SHE RETURNED to the privacy of the friends' apartment where she was staying, Princess Louise waited until the hour when she normally telephoned her mother. Early on Saturday evening, just before Princess Marie-Agnès went to Mass, she relied on a call from her daughter.

The elder Princess of Meinenbourg drifted around the world in an approximately predictable course according to her current sources of income, but whether she was in Paris, Rio or Palm Beach she liked to maintain a proper display of devotion.

Marie-Agnès was more sincere than appeared, and prayer was a genuine comfort to her. Sometimes she still asked God to reveal his purpose in sending Prince Leopold into her life to marry her, give her a baby and an incurable addiction to social eminence. She had been thirty when they met, a handsome but unsatisfied woman running her father's orthopaedic clinic, at which the Prince arrived with a broken neck after a fall playing polo.

Five years after their marriage another accident killed him outright, leaving Marie-Agnès with the child, the title and very little else. The castle of Meinenbourg had been destroyed in World War I; her mother-in-law had reintroduced enough wealth to the family to keep up their position for several decades, but her husband's passion for the most ruinous sport in the world had reduced the estate to a little house near Deauville, a few pictures and a trust for Louise's education.

God's intention in taking Marie-Agnès to a high place to show her the world and then snatching it all away was never clear, however many priests attempted to help her understand it, but after Mass she could return with new heart to the task of making the best of what she had. This meant accepting fees for the discreet social flotation of nouveaux-riches, hiring her name and presence to commercial enterprises of impeccable tone and funding, and ensuring the best possible marriage for her daughter.

She herself would also have liked another husband, and had received several proposals from wealthy and tolerable men, but on marriage she would lose her title and when the chips were down the idea of ceasing to be a Princess was unbearable. Marie-Agnès preferred to be royal and live precariously to having security at any lesser rank, and so she kept her figure trim and her credit good.

"But of course he can't possibly marry you, you realise that? None of the English can marry a Catholic, there's a law against it." She anxiously questioned her daughter, cradling the telephone in her shoulder as she checked her manicure. Receiving the body of Christ with chipped nail polish was in very poor taste.

"But that is the question, *maman chérie*. Do you think it would be advisable simply to have an affair with him?"

Princess Marie-Agnès was silent while she weighed the consequences. British royalty, for all most of them were ludicrously inelegant, were the biggest prize of all; they had everything—breeding, titles, power, the biggest palaces, the smartest guards, the most elaborate ceremonial and the largest personal fortune of any ruling house. What made them truly dominant, however, was their integrity. They were not like the Dutch or the Scandinavians, proud to jostle in the supermarkets beside their subjects. They were not like the Grimaldis, letting their children run around nightclubs with *n'importe qui*. The Queen of England knew how to behave like a queen.

Her son Richard, however, was too attractive for comfort. Suppose Louise fell in love? Suppose he fell in love with her, and she renounced her religion like that Austrian girl? Marie-Agnès shuddered, then tried to reassure herself. Her daughter had a steely concentration which was convenient, although she often asked herself from where in their families she had inherited it. She would never make a mistake like falling in love.

"After all, I'm only nineteen." Louise also lacked the imagination to understand her mother's real fear. "Two or three years couldn't possibly do any harm . . ."

"As long as you make sure it's two or three years. I think it would be a mistake just to pass through his life for a few months. It would look as if you were not a serious woman, Louise."

"Don't worry, if I can keep him a month I can keep him as long as I like."

Marie-Agnès smiled at this youthful boast.

"You think I can't promise, but I can, I know exactly how. You know the world has changed since you were my age."

"Some things never change, darling."

"And some things do. So what do you think?"

"If you are sure you can control him . . ."

"Completely. Trust me. I can't meet him for a month because he's on some army thing but then I've got the introduction all arranged. I love you, darling *maman*." The telephone receiver in London clattered as Louise impetuously dropped it into place. In Paris, Marie-Agnès picked up her handbag and her veil and decided to say a special prayer for her daughter.

• • •

"KEITH, WE'RE GOING to get that shit if it's the last thing we do!" Murray pinned a snatch shot of Prince Richard leaving Annabel's looking dissipated on the wall of his office at the *Daily Post* and started drawing red target rings around it. "The man's a cad and a poodlefaker! I want his head on a plate and his balls in a nutcracker! Money no object, Keithie-boy, that scum dies!"

Cowley paced a wary circle round the end of Murray's desk, thinking that his nibs was looking exceptionally chipper this morning. Sundays, when Murray got his chubby paws on the column, were becoming a whole new ballgame. The guy was a real mover, even if he was an utter piss-artist.

"Yeah, well, so Rich the Bitch rides again, so what? Haven't they sent him off to Israel with the Marines or something?" The entire Middle East was one undifferentiated sandy war zone to the photographer.

"Lebanon. Gives us time to get our act together, Keithie-boy. Stake him out, dontcha-know!" He stabbed the photograph with an accusing finger. "A bounder who wears braces like that deserves no mercy!" Murray's speech was sprinkled with pseudo-aristocratic archaisms culled from P. G. Wodehouse and Noël Coward. The springs of the editor's chair squealed as he sat down and put his feet on the desk; Cowley retrieved ten prints of the glitterati at Langan's as the photos slipped off the pile of papers on the desk-top.

The clock of St Bride's sounded across the Sabbath silence of Fleet Street. "Aha!" Murray immediately stood up again. "The noon-day gun! Time for a spot of lunch, I think. Tally-ho for Hacks, what?"

"Colin Lambert wants you to call him back." The newest recruit to the column, a colourless New Zealand girl with a bad complexion, handed Murray the number on a message slip.

"I'm sure he does, Sandy. Be a good girl, get on with those calls to Buck House and the Ministry of Defence. Use your charm, darling, see what you can get out of them. And while we're out get Rod Stewart's file for me."

Hacks wine bar was an annexe to the gutter press of the world. Its brass-studded leatherette door opened to thirsty journalists from midday to midnight. By three o'clock in the afternoon Murray's cheeks had a fine St Emilion glow and the whites of Cowley's eyes were pink, making him look more than ever like some species of rodent.

"Do you know why I'd really like to nail our Richie?" Murray carved the end off a half-corona from a batch he had been awarded by a grateful public relations woman. "He got my brother sacked from school, that's why. Little shit made out that my brother, *my brother*, stole one of his letters to sell to *Die Stern*. David never got over it. They were supposed to be friends. Ruined his life. Just about killed my father." He sounded as if he were about to burst into tears. His own material role in the drama had been submerged in his memory for years.

"Disgusting," Cowley sympathised.

"David couldn't get a job here because of all the scandal. He's a car salesman in Rhodesia now. Weighs about 20 stone. Married a black. Couple of pickaninnies." Cowley offered his gold Dunhill lighter but Murray mournfully waved it aside, sighed and struck a match. "I never use a lighter with good cigars—spoils the taste."

Murray sucked and blew smoke with a tragic expression. His father had died of cardiac arrest shortly after the Inland Revenue began to investigate his offshore bank accounts, and his brother was extremely stupid and perfectly happy with his lot, but Murray's notions of family loyalty excluded these considerations. He required righteous indignation to fuel his fire, and the facts could be adjusted to provide it.

Cowley hunched his shoulders with eagerness. "Yeah, old Richard, he always acted like a right royal bastard at Cambridge. He's a randy little sod, no error. So now he's banging hell out of Nicky Brompton's wife, is he? Where's their pad exactly?" He felt exceptionally cheerful at the prospect of doing ill to a man who, as he saw it, had caused him a broken collar-bone and three months' wages in consequence.

"Gloucestershire. Old Janie's taken to the bottle, too." Murray always referred to the subjects of his stories as intimately as possible, by nicknames or first names, even if he had never met them.

"Yeah, well, her husband always would screw anything with legs. I'm surprised she hasn't hit the sauce before."

Murray frowned, not wishing the swell of his moral outrage to be punctured. "I like Nicky, he's a good chap. What gets me is—this is the sort of thing the Duke of Windsor got up to all the time, carrying on with married women. It's an appalling way for a member of the Royal Family to behave. They're supposed to set the example, uphold the moral standards of the country. It's disgraceful."

"Yeah, I agree. We'll catch him at it, don't worry."

"That's our job, isn't it? Keep society up to scratch by exposing the wrong-doers. Trouble is, we'll have to be clever . . ."

"It shouldn't be too difficult, Sean. All I gotta do is nip down to Glos when His Royal Highness gets back from the trenches and catch him in the act—should be a piece of piss with this new lens I've got . . ."

"We couldn't use that kind of picture. We can't run the story, if you think about it."

"Why the hell not?"

"Adultery's a bugger, old boy. Story never stands up. Both parties always deny it outright and sue on the spot. I mean, the Royal Family can't sue, and Janie wouldn't, she's too sweet, but Nicky might . . . no, we can't do Richie yet." He took another pull at the cigar and watched the ash cool, his thick eyebrows contracted in thought. "We'll run something on the Lebanon angle and bide our time. Poodlefaker like that'll trip over his own cock one day and *then* we'll have him."

Back in the office by half-past four, Murray glanced over the notes his assistant had typed for him, rolled some paper into his own machine and began tapping. He led the column on "Hero Prince Goes to War," splashed a fetching photograph of Suzie Chamfer over "An Honourable Heritage," announced "Alana Heartbroken Over Marriage-Shy Rod," killed the King's Road nightclub in three lines and returned Colin Lambert's two further calls for the final story, "Au Revoir Hollywood Says Baronet's Cousin."

By eight his work was done and all that remained was to wait for a final check when the page was set in type. "What would you say to a spot of dinner, Sandy?"

His assistant looked up from her desk as if a bullet had ricocheted over her head. "We could grab a bite around the corner and be back by ten to see the page off the stone."

"Sounds like a good offer to me," she announced, suddenly looking almost cheerful. Murray briefly considered the advisability of giving her one. Sandy looked as if she had never had a decent fuck in her life, but that type were inclined to turn nasty afterwards and he needed someone to hold the fort in the office. Besides, even with a bag over her head he would still know she had a complexion like cold porridge.

Keith Cowley stayed at Hacks, drinking black coffee to sober up before setting off for the evening's assignment, a gala performance by the Royal Ballet in aid of the Dancers' Benevolent Fund, in the presence of Her Royal Highness, Princess Margaret. He knew in advance the occasion would be a total waste of time. Nobody liked pictures of Princess Margaret because nobody liked Princess Margaret. She was another one who did not play the game. Still, it was better than going home.

He signed the bill and picked up his camera bag, wondering how he had got lumbered with a family. It seemed as if one minute he had freedom and hope, an Alfa Romeo and this great little exhibitionist with fabulous tits, and the next she was telling him she was pregnant, her Dad was going mad, and what was he going to do about it? Now he had a wife and a son, a staff job, a company Ford, a small house and a large mortgage. If he went home he had to watch one of the fabulous tits, now twice its normal size, being stuffed into the baby's mouth, a sight which totally turned him up, while his wife whined that she never saw him and they weren't a proper family. Standing in the rain waiting for Princess Margaret was definitely the smart choice.

* * *

"ROAD COMMUNICATION BETWEEN Beirut and the South of the country has been highly dangerous for some months now," the British military attaché bellowed in Prince Richard's ear as the helicopter rose in a cloud of dust from the landing pad on the hillside overlooking the city. "We are going to fly north first, Sir, over the Christian part of the city, then turn around to head south over the sea."

"Why is that?" Richard enquired, mechanically showing interest.

"Because down there are several thousand militiamen with SAM-7s who can't resist a helicopter, no matter who's flying it." The diplomat was a tall, sinewy man with dark hair cut very short; with the ease of people far from their roots, the two men were forming a particular sympathy.

"I see," Richard replied and fell silent, an acceptable response in view of the noise inside the craft.

"How long have the Irish Army been in Lebanon?" inquired his companion on the visit, a ruddy-cheeked army major. It was an elementary question the man should not have needed to ask. Richard judged him to be a little crass and found his company irritating.

"Just over a year," the diplomat replied. "The UN forces were sent in after Israel invaded, in response to raids across the border by Palestinians based in the south of the country. But it's all a bit of a cock-up, as you'll see. Half the factions haven't signed the UN agreement, the Israelis are arguing about the territory involved . . . nothing's simple in this country."

Richard's preparatory briefings on the situation in Lebanon had alarmed him by revealing gaps in his own understanding. He felt chastened by the shallowness of his knowledge, even after three years studying his country's history, and the privileged information which had inevitably come his way in a family where the red dispatch boxes detailing world events were his mother's daily chore.

After twenty-four hours in the country, his mind was beginning to balk at the task of making sense of his impressions. Already, he felt disoriented. He had been unprepared for the beauty of the land when seen from a distance, the blue-white snowy peaks of the Mount Lebanon range and the verdant hills below them. No sooner had he registered that impression of ancient serenity, than it was obliterated by the close-up view of the wounds of three years of civil war.

The mountains endured in the distance, while in the foreground he saw only half-destroyed buildings, staircases cascading into sudden void, walls pockmarked with bullets, rooms ripped open to expose the modest secrets of their inhabitants' lives to the baking air of high summer.

They had been received and briefed by the Irish commandant in his office overlooking one of the largest refugee camps in the city, visible from his windows only as a vast huddle of low concrete and breeze-block houses. Their conversation had been accompanied by the tinkle of ice in their glasses and the continuous rattle and rumble of distant firing, and illuminated occasionally by the red flare of bombs.

"Do excuse the mess in here," the commander had indicated crates of papers on the bare concrete floor, "my old office was hit by a couple of RPG 7s yesterday. Fortunately I was out to lunch at the time. At night of course," he added as if anxious not to give the impression that he had not taken this random assault in good part, "we enjoy the fireworks, especially when the power's cut and the men can't watch television."

The helicopter flew down the coast and landed them at the United Nations headquarters in the south of the country, where the Irish were deployed with contingents from the armies of Finland, Fiji, France, Nepal and Norway to keep the peace.

Their objectives, according to the Security Council Resolution which Richard dutifully recorded at the beginning of his notes, were to determine the cessation of hostilities, confirm the Israeli withdrawal, restore international peace, assist the Lebanese Government in regaining its authority in the area and render the population humanitarian assistance.

For several days they toured the Irish battalion's territory, wearing borrowed flak jackets and helmets and accompanied by a large escort in armoured vehicles. In small compounds under dusty trees, they were greeted by bagpipes playing Scottish airs, in tribute to the major whose regiment was from that country. They inspected guards, visited observation posts, stopped at checkpoints and listened to the Irish NCOs explaining, as they stood rigidly to attention, the intricacies of continuous tit-for-tat attacks made by the Israeli invaders, the Christian militia they sponsored, the Lebanese forces and three separate Moslem militias who accepted no authority but that of their own leaders.

Richard wrote up his notes nightly, struggling to put into military language an analysis of what seemed to him to be war passionately justified by all parties but in the last analysis waged for its own sake. He had seen operations described as "route-clearing" or "searching a village where terrorists are known to be hiding" which were nothing more than an excuse for gun-happy soldiers to spray the ground with bullets.

The Irish battalion, like the other United Nations forces, had frequently been shelled in the outbursts of indiscriminate fighting, and several men killed, one even as he set off the flares meant to inform the attackers that they had hit a UN position. Statistics explaining how many tank rounds or how many mortars had hit the peace-keeping force in any given period seemed to express the essence of futility, but he dutifully incorporated them.

His training officers had briefly recited the theory of a peace-time army as a deterrent to war and given emphasis to a fighting man's basic function of killing. His agile intelligence had no difficulty in parroting, even embroidering, the line in the few command opportunities he had enjoyed.

Now he found himself talking to men younger than himself whose decorations announced real experience in keeping peace by force, men with a precocious maturity he admired and an irrepressible Celtic sense of humour which accorded with everything in the enterprise he found bizarre.

In the villages, he looked with increasing curiosity at the people across whose homes the battle raged, who went about the business of living without protest, taking account of danger and accepting tragedy. When people were shot the dead were mourned with high emotion that seemed a reason for living in itself. He noticed boys in their early teens comparing and admiring guns like toys.

"What will happen here?" he asked the military attaché towards the end of the trip. They sat inside the Irish headquarters enjoying the sharp cool of the evening, listening to a new outburst of firing close by and trying to assess the identity of the aggressor.

"Who can say?" The diplomat raised his hands and let them fall on his thighs in a gesture of despair. "I've been here four years. Every day I think it can't get worse and every day it does."

"It's the Palestinians who're the troublemakers really, though, isn't it?" the major interjected with confidence. Richard clicked his teeth in annoyance.

The diplomat nodded. "When I came here first I had very little sympathy for the Palestinians. I was in Munich when they massacred the Israeli athletes at the Olympics; terrorism was a crime I could not understand. Now I'm here, and I can see where it comes from, I can't see things in black and white any longer. Now it seems to be the last resort of people in utter despair. They have no hope, nowhere to go, no action they can take. Some manage to get out. For those who stay, everyone more fortunate than them is an enemy and they figure their best chance is to take a few out with them."

"That's just crazy," the major retorted. "I can't agree with that. I've talked to chaps in my regiment who're in Northern Ireland and . . ."

"If you lived in Beirut I promise you it would start to seem perfectly logical." The diplomat lit a cigarette.

"Palestine is a country which no longer exists, except in the hearts of its people. It disappeared, due to an accident of history. Those villages we visited are as much Palestine as anywhere. That refugee camp in Beirut we could see from the commandant's office. When the country was partitioned in 1947, when they created the state of Israel, the Arab portion of it was immediately taken over by Jordan."

The major pulled the ring on another can of beer. "The French are responsible for this mess, though."

"I think we are," Richard told him. "After all, the British administered Palestine between the wars. We decided to cut it in half, and the rest of the world agreed with us, but nobody agreed on the borders. This bloody mess is of our making."

"Not *entirely* . . ." the diplomat interjected with caution.

"No, but it seems to me we've got debts here we've just walked away from. Another part of the world where Pax Britannica wasn't all it was cracked up to be." He noticed a look of shock on the military attaché's lined but pleasant face. "I'm not supposed to say things like that, am I? I'm supposed to arrive, and nod and smile and be interested, tell you you're doing a fine job and carry on, and then leave. I'm not supposed to think, let alone say what I'm thinking. Don't worry, I won't do it again."

The next morning they set off for the last time in a convoy of armoured personnel carriers for the final inspection visit of the tour, to a hill which had been an Israeli position and was now occupied by the peace-keeping forces. The new Israeli position was clearly visible half a mile away, with a Sherman tank, heavy mortars and machine guns behind earthwork walls.

The journey back to the coast took them through a busy checkpoint where a group of militia men were demanding the identity papers of every vehicle passenger.

"They're Amal," the attaché said with confidence, "reasonable on the whole." Richard privately questioned the judgement. The soldiers stopping the cars looked to him to be about fifteen years old, with hair so short they were virtually shaven, and Kalashnikovs welded to their sides. Their actions had an aimless agitation.

"What are they looking for?" the army major inquired.

"Trouble, if you ask me. And if they don't find it, they'll make it." Richard was tired of looking on and doing nothing. He opened the door and got out of the vehicle. The others, alarmed for their royal companion's safety, followed him.

The Citroën ahead of them was punctured with a line of bullet holes and was so dirty that it had been a few moments before he realised it was an ambulance. The blue light on the roof had been smashed and the Red Cross on the door was half-obscured by a rusting dent.

He walked boldly forward and looked inside as the driver, a middle-aged woman with short blond hair, handed the militia guard a sheaf of identity papers. Richard saw the now-familiar blue of Palestinian documents and, to his surprise, the green of an Irish passport among them.

The militia men began to inspect the papers with malicious over-attention and, although he could not understand their discussion, the tone of it was an unmistakable crescendo of hostility.

He leaned down to the window to talk to the driver. "Which one of you is Irish?"

"I am," she replied in a firm voice, registering no surprise.

"What's the matter?"

"They're looking for somebody, I suppose. We're all women and children in here, they can see that." The low interior of the ambulance was crowded with five women and several children. On a stretcher in the centre of the vehicle lay a boy of about twelve. His legs were taped with bandages to makeshift wooden splints. There was the sweet smell of infection in the stuffy interior.

"Where are you hoping to get to?"

"We are going to Beirut," the woman affirmed immediately. "The boy was shot yesterday and I believe his pelvis at least is shattered if not his spine. Our clinic was hit last week and we can't even get him X-rayed here so it's hard to tell. Their village is all but destroyed now, the rest of the family are in one of the refugee camps, I want to get him to the Gaza hospital . . ."

Two of the militia men prowled around the ambulance, peering through the grimy windows. They raised the tailgate and motioned for the people to get out.

"The road to Beirut is supposed to be highly dangerous."

"I don't know who you are, why you're wearing that uniform or how long you've been here, but the whole country is highly dangerous and if we let that deter us we would never get our work done." Her words were harsh but spoken in such a sweet tone that offence was impossible. He registered something about her that was very womanly but not feminine as he was used to appreciating that quality.

The Irish officer escorting them approached with hesitation, but Richard spoke before he opened his mouth. "I think this comes under the heading of humanitarian assistance, don't you? They're planning to take this boy to Beirut to hospital—we can make room for them in the chopper." It was a statement which was a hair's breadth away from an order.

Seeing the four armoured vehicles of the UN forces, and the willingness of their occupants to be involved with the situation, the militiamen's attitude altered. After more discussion the papers were returned with an excess of formality and the augmented convoy was waved on its way.

"You realise there's not enough room in the chopper for all of them," the attaché pointed out in tones of mild amusement.

"I do. I realise that this probably exceeds the mandate, too. We'll just have to leave half the security escort behind and send down another helicopter to get them."

"Yes." The man smiled in mild admiration. "I think we will. But I hope you're not planning to leave me with the second party, because someone ought to be keeping an eye on you, Sir."

"Will we take care of the ambulance until you get back?" the Irish officer enquired as four of his men carried the boy on the stretcher to the helicopter.

"That would be most kind," the woman shook out the creased skirt of her plain pink shirtwaister dress. "It was actually hi-jacked last week—you wouldn't believe people could hi-jack an ambulance now, would you? Fortunately they abandoned it just a few miles away and it was more or less in one piece when we got it back."

"I'll get some of the boys to check it over," the officer promised.

Richard assumed command of the resources he knew were available, and when the helicopter landed on the hillside at Beirut another ambulance was waiting. "We'll come with you," he told the woman, raising his voice to inform the Irish Army escort party of his intention. "There's nothing to do here tonight that can't wait."

"The ambassador has planned a small reception," the attaché muttered with a light smile.

"The major will be delighted to attend it, I'm sure."

They passed through five military checkpoints on their way to the hospital, where the traffic was narrowed to a single file by lines of old tyres on the rutted roads. At each one the party produced their papers, the militia men noted Richard's borrowed Irish Army fatigues and reluctantly waved them through.

The injured child was semi-conscious when they passed the final inspection and arrived at the refugee camp. The devastated streets outside seemed orderly and substantial by comparison with the dirt roads and open drain which ran between the concrete and breeze-block huts. The Gaza Hospital, a large, modern building with insignia of the Palestinian Red Crescent Society over its door, stood proudly in the midst of the squalor.

The news of their arrival had been telephoned ahead and the boy was immediately transferred to a trolley and wheeled away to be X-rayed. The rest of the party wearily prepared to wait in the emergency department; there were not enough chairs and in the end, after much offering and refusing of seats, they all sat down on the floor, the attaché quietly shaking his head and murmuring, "The ambassador will love this when I tell him."

The blond woman bustled away, returning with water to drink and some boiled sweets for the children, which seemed to revive them. The child closest to Richard pulled his sleeve and asked him a question.

"What is she saying?"

"She's asking your name."

He told the girl, and she tried seriously to pronounce it, halting over the "ch" sound. A little boy joined her and asked another question.

"He says, how old are you?"

"Tell him I'm twenty-four."

The girl asked another question.

"She says, have you got any brothers or sisters?" The woman was watching Richard carefully as he answered.

"I've got one sister and three brothers."

There was some general discussion between the children

and the oldest of the women. The girl, her dark eyes wide with curiosity, asked something else.

"She says, are you married?"

"Tell her no, I'm not."

The next question came from the little boy.

"Are any of your brothers and sisters married?"

"Only my sister."

The old woman said something which made the whole group laugh, obviously a pitying observation on the plight of a family with four brothers on the shelf. Richard found himself smiling; the shield of artificiality behind which he had walked for weeks had been lifted. Name, age, wife, family—life was very simple.

"What about your husband, where is he now?" he asked the blond woman, having noticed a narrow band of gold that was her only jewellery.

"I am a nun," she replied evenly. "A bride of Christ, you see. Sister Bernadette, I'm called."

He held out his hand to shake hers, wondering how to introduce himself. "Oh, I know who you are now, all right. I knew I'd seen your face somewhere and this gentleman," she indicated the military attaché, "put me in the picture. I suppose you did not realise what I was?"

"I think of nuns in long black clothes and veils, I suppose."

"And I think of a prince in grand court dress with a few orders with diamonds and a sash. So we're both wrong there. Ours is a working order, we work with the Nansen Trust, an international charity concerned with refugees, so I don't have to go around all dressed in black or anything like that. I am a nurse, also, at least I am supposed to be, although what I really do is begging."

"Begging?"

"On a grand scale and in a dramatic way, but that's all it is really. Begging for money or for medicine or for permission to drive a few miles further up the road. Whatever I can get for the people I am here to serve."

"And sympathy, I suppose." The attaché straightened his spine against tiredness.

"I do *not* ask for that. Ever. It's no use. The only place you find sympathy is in the dictionary between shit and syphilis."

"You're trying to shock me," Richard protested amiably.

For no reason, the memory of Jo Forbes escaped from the place in which he had imprisoned it.

"And I'm not getting very far, I think." She caught his eye and he wondered how a woman pledged to chastity could have known the working of his mind at that moment.

In an hour the X-rays were ready and the doctor, a bulky Lebanese with nicotine-stained fingers and in a spotless white coat, arrived to confirm that the boy's pelvis and lower vertebrae had been shattered by bullets and that he was being prepared for an immediate operation that would take several hours.

"There's nothing we can do here for a while," Sister Bernadette said, adding something for the family's ears only. "I'm going to try to find the rest of these people's relations. Would you care to come outside?"

It was almost dark as they left the hospital, picking their way across water pipes and ditches, the military attaché stumbling doggedly in silence beside his charge. Warm yellow lights glowed from the doorways of the houses and occasionally Richard caught the smell of freshly-baked bread, incongruously wholesome in the close, foul air.

Sister Bernadette had conversations with people sitting outside their homes, and eventually found her way to a house occupied by two couples and their children. The news of the arrival at the hospital was greeted with joy and excitement. They were invited inside, seated on upturned wooden crates and given mint tea and fruit, while neighbours crowded into the tiny building to share the celebration and children were dispatched to borrow glasses. Richard found his hand shaken and kissed repeatedly.

Eventually they were outside again, walking with a large group back to the hospital, taking a different route past the two-storey, towered building which the Sister told him was the camp mosque.

"It all looks very permanent," Richard remarked.

"It is very permanent. This camp has been here since 1947." The military attaché was walking behind him.

"At first it was tents, now they've built these little houses. Would you mind if I took your arm? I can't see my way with all these people around." He felt her cool, dry hand on his wrist. "The Palestinians are a problem the world wishes would go away, but they won't. They can't."

"What do they live on?"

"Some of the men get permits to work in the city. There are all sorts in here, doctors, architects . . . And some of the families have relatives who're working in other countries who send them money. Many more would go, but they've no passports. No country, no passport. There it is. Have I told you how that boy was shot?"

"No, I don't believe you have." In the midst of so much senseless killing, it had hardly seemed important.

"He was playing a game with his friends we've called Lebanon roulette. A lot of the kids are playing it, it's a kind of craze. There was a sniper covering their street, so they took turns to run across and see if they would get hit."

At the hospital the operation was still in progress.

"You don't have to wait, you know," Sister Bernadette announced as if dismissing him.

"I think I will, if you don't mind."

"No, I don't mind at all."

Eventually the doctor reappeared, his olive skin grey with fatigue, and announced that he had done his best and that time would now tell if the child would be able to walk.

The Sister escorted the two men to the edge of the camp where their transport was waiting, the driver asleep behind the wheel.

"Well, I thank you," she took the Prince's hand. "Thank you for everything you have done today. I am truly very glad you were sent to help us."

"So am I," he replied, pressing her fingers and searching for what he wanted to say. "I would like to do more—you know . . ."

"I know. Well, I'll pass the word onward and upward and we'll see what comes of it. Now I wish you both a safe journey."

He climbed into the car, mildly annoyed that she obviously doubted his sincerity. The attaché gently shook the driver awake and they set off, weaving slowly across the dark street between shell holes.

"And thank you," he turned to the diplomat, who looked surprised.

"Whatever for, Sir?"

"Don't sir me, for God's sake. For not being a pain in the ass."

"Well . . ."

"I went over the wall on this one, I know, and you'd have

got the blame if anything had gone wrong. I wanted you to know I—ah—appreciated your attitude."

"It seems there's no harm done. Anyway, I think you enjoyed it."

Richard paused and examined his feelings. He had intervened, commanded, done what he felt was right and succeeded. One tiny piece of help had been given, a minute drop of charity lost in the huge ocean of injustice around them. He was not tired, although the adrenalin surge of his first decisions had long faded. Now he felt very alive. "Yes," he agreed slowly, "I suppose I did enjoy it. I feel— almost clean, somehow."

"Well you certainly don't look it," the diplomat pointed at his dusty, sweat-stained shirt. "We'll have to smarten you up before you say goodbye to the ambassador."

CHAPTER XVIII

HARLEY LAY CURLED in a ball in the centre of the red-draped bed, telling herself that this was the last time she would wake up to see the mid-morning light shining through the carved wooden shutters and smell the stale tang of Kelly's cigarettes.

Last night, in the Caprice, while he was automatically ordering the three-chocolate pudding for her, she had decided to leave him. Not that she did not like, or want to eat, three-chocolate pudding; she loved it, but it was time somebody took the trouble to ask what she wanted. Today she had a God-given opportunity to escape. The laboratories had ruined a whole batch of film from yesterday's session, and Kelly had gone to the studio early to reshoot. She was not needed.

The telephone rang and she checked her watch in surprise. It was 8 am. Nobody in fashion ever called anyone at 8 am. Curiously, she rolled across the crimson sheets and answered it.

"Martha? Is that you?" It was a man's voice. She was puzzled; only her family now called her Martha.

"This is Martha Harley, who is that?"

"This is your brother, Sheldon."

"Shel! Where in the world are you calling from?" The deep, masculine voice had not sounded like one of her kid brothers.

"From Florida, but we're coming to London in a few weeks. It's really exciting, Martha, Spence is going to qualify for Wimbledon. All he needs is one more tournament and he's sure to do it. But he's just got to play more on grass so we thought . . ."

"I don't believe this! You sound as if you're calling from the next street! Yes, of course you can stay with me but wait a minute, wait a minute, just hold on . . ."

In blind confusion she scrambled for the disordered dressing table and groped for her spectacles. They were tangled in the six-inch diamanté ear-rings she had worn the night before; impatiently she freed them and rammed them into place. Kelly's bedroom came into focus.

She returned to the telephone and spoke in a low voice. "Now listen. Of course you can stay with me but I'm moving, OK? I'm moving today. Can you hear me? Here's my new address." She read it out. "So when are you coming?"

"I don't know yet." He sounded so adult and efficient Harley smiled to herself in wonder. "Spence is playing in Australia next week, and depending on how that goes we'll either come back here or go directly to London. But I'll be in touch, OK? And thanks, Martha. It'll be great to be with you." The line was precisely severed the instant she had finished her own goodbye, and Harley put the telephone down, encouraged. Having her brothers in town would make things much, much easier. Leaving Kelly had been on the cards for a long time, but she was dreading it. She decided to call Corinna and see if she could come over to help.

Two hours later a taxi driver looked aghast at the ten suitcases piled in the hall of Kelly's house.

"This is it, is it?"

"I've just got a few more small things upstairs and my coat . . ." Harley looked distractedly around the gloomy interior, feeling sure she must have forgotten something important. She had her make-up box, she had her address book, she had her very own, brand new and as yet unused American Express card, she had her gorgeous new pink Calvin Klein coat to keep out the raw March cold: she reassured herself she had everything she needed.

A large pink orchid in a brass pot appeared at the head of the stairs with Corinna's exquisite legs below it. "You can't possibly leave this behind, darling, it's gorgeous. And there's the carved horse you bought in India, don't forget."

"Well, I don't know if I can get it all in one cab. We might have to come back for some of it . . ." The driver stuck his fists in his fat waist as if the women were piling up possessions on purpose to annoy him.

"Oh no, no coming back," Harley announced immediately. She was afraid that if she had any opportunity to change her mind about leaving Kelly, she would. Heavens, how that man had undermined her. Running out this way was cowardly and she hated herself for doing it, but somehow they had got into a situation where nothing she said seemed to get through to him and every week he found a new reason why they ought to get married.

They had a bare hour in which to leave before the housekeeper returned from walking the dogs. Not that she had any reason to avoid him, but she did not want to get involved in too many explanations. "We can put some stuff in my friend's car and if we can't get it all in I'll take two cabs."

"Suit yourself. You really need a truck for all this." With bad grace, the man picked up the smallest two cases and walked down the front steps. Harley walked empty-handed after him and supervised the cramming of the vehicle with her belongings. She went back into the house for a last look around, re-read the letter she had left for Kelly under the teapot in the kitchen, and then left for the last time. She and the orchid squeezed into Corinna's dearly-loved classic Karmann Ghia.

"Where are we going, love?" the driver enquired.

Harley directed him to her apartment in Nine Elms, for so many years just an address on the small collection of bills she paid each quarter, and an hour later the porter carried the last of her cases through her own front door.

"Looks like you're here to stay, miss," he ventured, since the other residents would undoubtedly be asking him who the black woman in number 116 was and whether she planned to be in permanent residence. Number 116 was one of the more expensive duplexes overlooking the river; the cheaper apartments on the south side had enjoyed a good view of the race riots in Brixton, barely a mile away. Watching petrol bombs and barricades of blazing cars had unsettled the occupants of the luxurious new high-rise.

"Yes, I'm here to stay," Harley confirmed, looking with determined satisfaction at her panoramic view of the river from the fifteenth floor.

"You seem to have travelled quite a bit, if you don't mind me saying so, miss." He eyed the airline labels which she had not bothered to remove from her bags.

"I'm a model, I travel all the time," she informed him, pressing a ten pound note into his hand with a gracious expression. Dressed for moving in grey sweatpants and a T-shirt, she knew she did not look like anyone's idea of an international model, but money always talked to this type. He was a solid, grey-haired man who filled out his uniform with the pompous air she had come to associate with retired army sergeants.

"Well, er, thank you very much, miss. Quite a lot of our residents travel, as a matter of fact. Any time you're off just let me know and my wife and I'll keep an eye on the place for you, water the plants . . ."

"Thank you so much, you're so kind." Harley had learned from Victoria the art of establishing social superiority in a few well-enunciated words and sweeping menials graciously out of the door once they had served their purpose.

"Who decorated this place?" Corinna demanded in disgust, picking up an oatmeal tweed scatter cushion with the tips of her fingers.

"Heaven knows. The developer's interior design team. They used this as the show apartment and I couldn't face the hassle of buying furniture so I just said I'd take it as it was." Harley surveyed the tasteful all-white interior without enthusiasm. It smelled stale and unloved. "I just liked being able to look down on the city." She walked across to the wall of plate glass and looked for a way to let in some air.

"It must be just magical when it's dark, with the lights on the water and everything." Corinna joined her, considering that this would be the first time for years that Harley would sleep alone. Together they found the locks and rolled back the doors to the balcony. "Would you like me to stay with you, just tonight, in case you wake up at dawn with the blue meanies?"

"Corinna, I have done the right thing, haven't I?" Harley was not sure if she wanted company or not.

"Honey, you should have done it years ago. You've got money in the bank, Marianne's on your side, you're booked for the Pret, you've got that coffee commercial to do, you've got the test for the James Bond film, you've got wonderful friends . . ."

"But all that came through Kelly."

"Don't put yourself down. Kelly may have opened a few doors but after that you did it yourself. You'll be right, you'll see. Now let's get these bags unpacked."

An hour later the porter, now beaming with goodwill, delivered a huge arrangement of lilies in a basket from Marianne. Shortly afterwards he called up from his desk in the building's marble atrium to announce Miss Jo Forbes, who brought a very large bottle of champagne.

With clothes in piles all over the bedroom, and the carved Indian horse standing expectantly in the middle of the living area floor, they popped the cork and discovered that there were no glasses. The porter, by now thoroughly intrigued, called up at that moment to see if anything was needed and loaned his own cut crystal champagne flutes, acquired free with every four gallons of Esso from the neighbourhood garage.

They sat on the thick white carpet by the window and Jo proposed the toast. "To freedom! To a new life! To success!"

"And fuck men!" Corinna added.

"Or not," Harley drained her glass.

"Or not," Jo agreed.

"So how *is* Lorcan?" Harley smiled wickedly as she reached for the bottle and refilled all round.

"Lorcan—well, that's a head trip, you know."

Harley reflected that she did not know. Perhaps all those dinners she had enjoyed with Neville Green in Cambridge added up to a head trip, but she doubted it; he had been good to talk with but not exciting. Maybe a head trip was what she really needed. She certainly could not imagine ever doing anything personally significant with her body, except working, of course.

Jo was talking on regardless. "He did something really strange to me. He's convinced we're fated to have an affair, but he said I needed to explore my sexuality, and that if I got involved with him now I never would, I'd just use it. The play he toured was *Antony and Cleopatra*, only stripped down to nothing, the way he does, and he made me play Cleopatra, first understudy another actress and then alternate the role with her, and . . . well . . . I think that was his way of making love to me."

Corinna looked sceptical. Harley looked blank. Jo saw

that neither of them understood. She was not sure she understood herself.

The Australian threw down the last of her champagne. "Did it work?"

"I don't know."

"What do you mean, you don't know?"

"Well, I'm not seeing anyone. I feel different in myself, but I guess I won't know if I really am different until I get involved again."

There was a silence and Harley filled the glasses once more. "You know what I'm really looking forward to?" she said, admiring the pastel spring sunset through the golden liquid, "I'm going to really enjoy never, ever, having to apologise for not having an orgasm *ever* again in my entire life."

"Let's drink to that," Corinna endorsed.

"You're not worried, are you?" Jo suddenly appreciated that her friend was almost quivering with nervous tension.

"Oh no," Harley assured her airily. "Living with Kelly's been such a nightmare these last few years I know I've made the right move. It's just . . ."

"You've got used to being taken care of, to the attention, to the paparazzi, to the pictures in *W* and the *Vogue* covers and now you think you've walked out on them too?" Jo picked at the frayed bottoms of her jeans and looked up with raised eyebrows.

Harley nodded, with a philosophical expression. "That's it, Jo. Right as usual. I think you were born with a built-in bullshit detector."

"Maybe. Don't forget it's my job to put myself in other people's skins. That stuff doesn't bother me, because I was born into it and I think it's worthless, but if I were you that's what I'd be worrying about—who I am now I'm not Kelly's girl."

"I don't think women should look to men to give them status," Corinna announced in a pious tone. There was a silence. Nobody liked to point out that Corinna, cute as she was, was becoming one of the world's most committed starfuckers.

"You need to put that horse over here by the window," Jo announced suddenly, jumping up to move the statue herself. "And the orchid has to go out of direct light or its leaves will scorch."

"Jo, Jo! How do you know all this stuff!" Harley marvelled as her friend moved her only two domestic possessions, adjusted the position of a couple of chairs and suddenly made the impersonal apartment look like a home.

"I don't know," Jo shrugged as she stood back to consider the effect. "My mother's always fretting about her orchids so I suppose I just picked it up. Isn't that strange? I never thought I had anything of my mother in me."

"You know what will really make you feel like this is your own home at last?" Corinna could never bear to be out of the limelight for long. "Giving a party. Why don't you give a great party for all your friends and as soon as you see everybody here all round you, you'll feel terrific!"

Harley nodded immediately. "Darling, that's a *fabulous* idea. Now who shall we ask . . ."

They searched for paper and a pen, sat at the blond ash table, opened their three fat Filofaxes and made a list. It was past midnight when they finished and Harley, recognising that she was desperate for comfort, encouraged both Jo and Corinna to stay the night.

Some time later in the darkness the ivory telephone by her bedside rang and Harley automatically answered it.

"You fucking bitch." It was Kelly and he sounded drunk. "You lying fucking bitch. Do you really think you can walk out on me like that . . ."

Jo, at the far side of the bed, awoke and sat up rapidly, sensing Harley's fear. "Who is it?" She groped for the lights.

"I'm not going to kill you, I wouldn't waste my time. I'm not even going to do your face in, because if anyone else photographs you you'll look like shit anyway. I'm the only person who'll ever take a good picture of you, you skinny black tart. You are finished, girl, finished, *finito, kaput* . . ."

"Put the phone down," Jo ordered, seeing Harley wide-eyed and paralysed with fear.

"In this town you will never work again. Or in any other town. I'll put the word out on you. You're dead meat, you cunt . . ."

Jo reached across the bed, pulled the receiver from Harley's hand and slammed it down. Harley burst into tears. The telephone rang again and Jo angrily seized it, cut the connection, then threw the receiver down on the table. She took Harley in her arms and soothed her.

"Was he angry?"

"He—he was drunk. He said I'd never work again. He said I was finished . . ."

"Well, what the hell, you've always got the law to fall back on." Jo took care to pitch the remark short of a reproach, appalled as she had been to witness the erosion of Harley's self-respect. "Forget what he said. He was bound to be angry. He'll get over it, you'll see. In a month he'll have found somebody else." Harley sniffed, uncertain. "How did he get the number?"

"I don't know."

"Who did you give it to?"

"Only you, Corinna, Marianne and my family. There wasn't time to tell anyone else."

"He got it from Marianne then, didn't he?" Dumbly, Harley nodded. "Time to change your agent, don't you think?"

"I couldn't, Marianne's the best. I mean, we can't be sure it was her. Maybe he just heavied one of the girls in the office."

And maybe Marianne figures his business is more important to her than yours, Jo thought, but kept the notion to herself. They fell into a restless doze, until a thin howl came from the displaced receiver and Harley, reasoning that Kelly must have passed out, or at least abandoned the idea of threatening her over the telephone, decided it was safe to replace it.

Immediately, the telephone shrilled once more. Jo leaped across the bed, snatched it up and yelled, "Fuck off and leave her alone, you bastard!"

The echoing drone of an intercontinental cable sounded in her ear. "Excuse me?" A faint, courteous voice spoke after a moment of hesitation. "I think I may have called the wrong number. I was trying to reach Martha Harley."

Jo hesitated for an instant, wondering if it was a trick, reasoning that Kelly was too crude to be capable of such sophistication. Then she handed the telephone to her friend. "I think it must be your family."

"Hello, who is this?" Harley asked with apprehension.

"Martha? This is Spence, Martha." The line had a long, delayed echo.

"This is me."

"Are you having trouble?"

"Nothing serious. Where are you?"

"Australia. Listen, I've blown this one, so we're going to France, and we'll be with you in about four weeks, OK? Can you hear me?"

"Yes, I can just about hear you. See you soon, kid. And hurry up. I need my family around me, OK?"

They said goodbye and Harley handed the telephone back to Jo, who placed it carefully in a corner with a pillow on top of it. "And in the morning," she instructed in severe tones, "you will get your number changed and have a serious talk with Marianne."

"Yes, *ma'am!*"

*   *   *

HARLEY'S PARTY TOOK place a month later. The porter took great pleasure in admitting thirty women who were beautiful beyond the bounds of his imagination, along with assorted scruffy-looking men, some of whom his wife was sure were pop stars. They both recognised Ringo Starr. They knew Jo Forbes very well by then, but did not care for the strange-looking older man who escorted her. About half the men were dressed with reassuring formality, in dark suits and striped shirts, including Corinna's escort, Nicky Brompton, whom the porter acknowledged with obsequious discretion because he had visited another lady in the building on previous occasions. Suzie Chamfer wore the corduroy knickerbockers recently made fashionable by Lady Diana Spencer, the girl whom the *Daily Post* had nominated as the country's future Queen. Suzie arrived with Colin Lambert, although neither had been invited. They left quickly when they realised that no one was going to photograph them. Her part in "Heritage" had made Suzie a big star in America, but as the series had not yet been seen on British television she was irritated to discover that she was not yet famous in her own country.

Marianne arrived in the Muffia's new uniform, top-to-toe black Chanel; with her came most of her staff, who wore black copies of Chanel, in obedience to the boss's dictum that she alone was to wear the genuine designer items and anyone who didn't like that could find another job.

Auriol Meredith, about to leave *Vogue* where she felt frustrated as one fashion editor among many, and become the editor of a newer, glossier and, she announced, infinitely more stylish magazine backed by a French publisher, came alone, and also in black Chanel, but with a white blouse.

"This magazine is going to be *up!*" she announced in a high excited voice to everyone at large. "Aware! Visual! We're so visual now we don't even know how visual we are —rock videos, TV all the time, reading two magazines at once—everything's about image now, it's subliminal, it just hits you, like that! Pow!"

A circle formed around her, murmuring agreement.

"Auriol is such a *fabulous* editor," Corinna purred, snuggling proprietorially against Nicky Brompton's shoulder. "She makes you feel so special. Even the way she hands you a hat or something makes you feel just beautiful."

"What we want is a magazine to psych us out, give us clothes that really relate to our lives, tell them about breast cancer or what's happening in Brixton, or Belfast . . ."

"Auriol is *the only* fashion editor," breathed a diminutive designer, his cigarette raised with a camp flourish. "She doesn't know about style, she *is* style."

"All that pink-for-spring, get in a few dresses, do a few snaps . . . that's out. Forget designer-junk dressing, two-dollar socks with Gucci loafers! Integrity, immediate, image—that's the mood of the Eighties." Auriol pawed the air like a frenzied terrier as her audience listened with reverence.

"Have my brains turned to Buck's Fizz or is she talking absolute garbage?" Jo muttered to Lorcan Flood.

"I think your brains are fine," he confirmed.

"Auriol's just had a marketing meeting too far," Harley's face was as motionless as a Yoruba carving. Jo tried to penetrate the mask.

"Where do you put your head when they talk like that to you?"

"On another planet, darling. But they don't usually talk to us. Nobody cares what a model thinks as long as she's pretty, sober and at the studio on time." She glided away to check on the barman, protectively scooping up the opulent false sash of her peacock-blue chiffon sheath. At the back of her mind, Harley was still surprised every time she crossed a crowded room without knocking something over.

"But, darling, what about commercial?" Marianne was paying Auriol close attention, mentally running through the new faces she had seen in the past week, wondering if any of them had the look that said integrity, immediate, image.

"Commercial is an emotive concept in fashion . . ." Auriol launched into another speech; the circle broke up and the two women sank to the sofa in an obsessional discussion.

They were still there at 2 am, with a few of Marianne's girls in respectful attendance, when the last of the revellers were kissing Harley goodbye and the hired staff had restored the apartment to a state of pristine cleanliness, and departed.

"Darling, darling Harley," Auriol stood up and checked her appearance in the gilt-framed mirror which dominated one wall of the room. "Simply divine party, fabulous apartment, I really don't want to go home but we really must— can your little man call us a taxi?"

A few minutes later the porter called up to say that the cab had arrived.

"Will you just check with him that it really is outside?" Marianne draped a black wool wrap around her shoulders and fluffed up her hair. "Sometimes they say the car's there and actually it isn't and I do so hate having to wait around . . ."

"Of course." The internal telephone was fixed to the wall in the kitchen. As she dialled the porter's number, Harley heard a flurry of movement from the hallway. "Yes, the car is right by the door, waiting for you," she called out, but got no answer. The apartment was empty.

"Bye, darling. Talk to you tomorrow but not too early, huh?" Marianne looked around the front door and blew her a kiss. Muffled giggles sounded from the corridor outside as the door closed.

Alone in her home at last, Harley felt calm. All her fears had melted. She had been afraid none of her guests would come, or that the party would go terribly wrong and everyone would sneer about it for weeks. Her worst fear had been that Kelly would show up and make a scene. He could easily have done so, judging from the gratifying proportion of gatecrashers which confirmed that the date and the address of her party had been on the grapevine for weeks.

She slipped a Police CD into her new stereo system, finished a plate of hors d'oeuvres and most of a half-bottle of champagne, and wandered up and down the room, listening to Sting and gazing out over the river, feeling deep satisfaction. After a delicious ten minutes she drifted up the spiral staircase to her bedroom.

"There you are at last, darling," Auriol Meredith was lying on her stomach across the bed. The bathroom door was open and the traces of scented steam in the air suggested that she had showered. Her clothes were nowhere to be seen and she was wrapped in a small pink towel which barely covered her buttocks. Her white skin looked the colour of lard against the cream coverlet. "I thought you were *never* coming—to bed, I mean." She gave Harley a meaningful look from beneath lowered eyelashes. "I brought a little something for you to take care of all the other problems, don't you worry. It'll be absolute bliss. God, I'm so glad you finally left that brute, Kelly. I don't know how I bore it, seeing you with him all that time, knowing you were making a terrible mistake . . ."

Harley, shocked but not comprehending, walked up the last few steps and stood at the top of the staircase, her back against the iron guard rail.

Copies of *Vogue* were scattered all round the bed, some of them open at Harley's own photographs. Auriol pointed disdainfully at them. "I mean, it's all there, isn't it, in the pictures? You're exquisite, darling! You're wildness, savagery, the blood, the senses, but he just couldn't reach you, could he? He didn't understand. Men don't really understand women's bodies, do they? It isn't their fault . . ."

"I don't understand either, Auriol." Harley heard herself speak in a low, cold voice while her mind was a whirlpool of questions. One of the most influential women in fashion in the country right now was trying to make a pass at her. Had Kelly set this up? Maybe Marianne . . . maybe she thought this would be a smart career move. What exactly did lesbians do to each other, anyway? And whatever Auriol was planning and whoever had fixed it, how the hell was she going to get out of it?

"Of course, you don't but that's it, don't you see, part of your specialness." Auriol rolled over and stood up; she held out her hand and walked towards Harley with a bright, excited smile. "You're so innocent, so primitive— you are *Africa*, my darling, the dark continent, the . . ." she saw Harley's expression of anger and swiftly changed direction. "That's why I *admire* you so much. Ever since I discovered you I've watched you learn, change, so fast! You've just eaten up the world, haven't you? But underneath you are a child, my darling, aren't you? You don't know yourself, you don't know what you want . . ."

"I know I'm not gay, Auriol." She tried to keep her voice level and reasonable.

"But you do know that a man can't really give you pleasure."

"I wouldn't say that. I loved Kelly and I enjoyed being in bed with him in the beginning . . ."

"Darling, everyone knows he couldn't give you an orgasm. Don't you think that the body is the ultimate truth?" Harley promised herself that she would never trust anyone again, never confide any material information about herself and never, ever gossip again in her life. "Come and sit down," Auriol perched on the end of the bed, her naked legs primly crossed.

Harley folded her arms and did not move. "Now, Auriol, please . . ."

"Just come and sit here with me and talk about this." Her voice was rising to a cutting whine. "Don't insult me, Harley. Come and sit down. I can hardly rape you—men are the ones who rape, aren't they? I am a woman, I am your friend and all I want is your happiness, believe me. So come, sit." She patted the bed and Harley reluctantly moved to sit upright beside her.

"Such good champagne, darling, I do admire your taste." From the white marble night table, Auriol picked up a full glass. "Want some?"

"No, thank you. What do you want to talk about?"

"You! You are what I want to talk about. You are my favourite subject, my absolute obsession, my inspiration! I can't wait to get this magazine off the ground just because its whole look is just utterly *you*! It's so exciting, so fabulous! But I do want to know how you feel. If you think you'd like another man in your life, then tell me what you want, what you're looking for." Auriol tipped the glass playfully against her gleaming red lips.

Harley was about to retort that another man was the last thing she needed at that moment, but bit back the words before Auriol could turn them to her own advantage. "What an interesting question." She played for time, keeping her eyes down.

"I mean, if you really loved Kelly, what went wrong?"

"He wanted to control me and I resented it. He invaded my whole life, and I let him. I was too young I suppose. I thought he was kind, but he wasn't, he was cruel really. I wasn't a person to him, just something to look at."

"So now you'd like a lover who's different? Kind, gentle, sympathetic, who'll allow you, encourage you, to be yourself . . ."

"I don't really want a lover at all."

"But no one has ever really loved you, have they? Loved *you*. You don't want someone whose idea of love is just to penetrate and dominate, of course you don't. And that's all men can do. But a woman doesn't love like that." She gave a sigh and looked wistfully down at her tiny, scarlet-tipped toes.

Harley stood up, determined to put an end to this nonsense. "Auriol, it's late and everybody's drunk so much champagne—I don't want to get into all this now. Let me just call you a cab . . ."

"No, darling, no. You're right, talk isn't right now. Let me just show you . . ." She moved suddenly forwards and Harley tossed back her head like a startled horse, blessing the fact that she was too tall to be kissed unwillingly by anyone of less than her own height.

Then she felt Auriol's fingers crawling up her thighs. *"Don't do that!"* She snatched at her skirt, pulling it even tighter and pushing Auriol's hand away, jumping backwards out of reach and stumbling over the trailing corner of the bed-cover. "Stop this, Auriol! Stop it at once and get out of here!"

"Darling, what's the matter? Don't you trust me? Oh, I've scared you, I am so, so sorry . . ."

The internal telephone shrilled from downstairs; the noise checked Auriol in mid-sentence and Harley seized her opportunity.

"I must get it—somebody must have left something behind." She almost fell down the stairs and ran for the sanctuary of the kitchen.

"I've got two young gentlemen down here for you, Miss Harley." The porter sounded sleepy, doubtful and irritated. "Are you expecting your brothers tonight?"

"Yes! Yes! Are they there, can I speak to them?"

Sheldon was babbling in jet-lagged excitement, and she cut him short. "Thank God you're here, I need your help. Now listen, did you take a cab and is it still there?"

"Yes, Spence is just paying him . . ."

"Stop him, stop the cab and I'll be right down. Whatever you do, hold that cab."

She ran to the lift and a few moments later flew across the gleaming void of the atrium into Spencer's strong arms.

"Listen, boys," she began, as soon as the greetings and the hugging was over, "you have arrived at exactly the right time. I have been giving a little party and upstairs is one guest who has had rather too much champagne and doesn't want to leave." Her poise was returning quickly; the porter, with his uniform greatcoat over his pyjamas, was standing behind his desk, now alert and officious as always, and she smiled to include him in the plot. "She is rather a difficult woman and I'm going to need your help to persuade her to go home, OK?"

"Sure thing!"

"No problem!"

"If you gentlemen are going up, I'll have a word with the driver, shall I?"

Outside the brightly illuminated building Harley saw a non-descript Ford saloon at the kerb, with a man in jeans, who was presumably the driver, leaning into the boot, busily rearranging its contents.

"I'm in a real fix here," Harley told her brothers as the lift glided upwards. "This woman just about runs the fashion business in this country, and when you arrived she was lying around my bedroom trying to seduce me."

"Don't worry about it. She'll take one look at us and revise her itinerary immediately," Sheldon promised, confidently adjusting his shirt-cuffs and settling his tie.

The warbling cadences of the duet from "The Pearl Fishers" sounded from the bedroom as they entered the apartment. Obviously Auriol had decided to put on some mood music.

"Wait here, kids, I'll go up and see if I can persuade her to get dressed and leave quietly." Harley climbed the staircase, feeling irrationally confident that the mere presence of her brothers would divert Auriol from her purpose. The illusion evaporated as she entered the bedroom. The lights had been dimmed and the bed artistically disarrayed; Auriol, now completely naked, lounged against a pile of pillows fingering one of her dark nipples. She flashed Harley a coquettish smile.

"You took *such* a long time I decided to start without you. Now why don't you come here and let me introduce you to a girl's best friend?" Beside her on the rumpled sheet Harley noticed a cylindrical device of surgical appearance, at least eighteen inches long, with a padded white rubber head. Her eyes widened. "It's only a vibrator —instant orgasm, never, *ever* fails."

Harley took a deep breath to control her anger. "Auriol, will you please get dressed and leave now?"

"No, I will not." She sprawled across the bed with a pout of defiance. "You know I'm your only true friend, Harley, and you don't really want me to go, you're just . . ."

"Auriol, my brothers have just arrived to stay, and if you don't put on your clothes and leave immediately I shall ask them to . . . to help you out."

"You're being absolutely ridiculous . . ."

"No, you're the one that's being ridiculous . . ."

"And I don't believe a word you say. Brothers! Very convenient. What brothers? You've never talked about any brothers."

"OK, kids, come and get her," Harley shouted downstairs. In a moment the spacious room was filled by the muscular presence of Spencer and Sheldon, who took one look at Auriol and began to laugh.

"She won't get dressed so you can just wrap her up in a sheet," Harley ordered, spying the Chanel suit hanging inside the wardrobe. Swiftly, she found an empty plastic bag and tossed the garments into it, followed by the vibrator.

"I shall scream the minute we get outside," Auriol announced as Sheldon, picking up the sheet with disdainful fingertips, and wrapped her tightly so she resembled a giant maggot. Spencer threw her over his shoulder and started for the stairs.

"Oh dear, yes, I can see you have had some difficulty, Miss Harley," the porter was dead-pan as he escorted the strange party from the elevator to the doors. The cab driver, a young black man, jumped up with a broad smile to open the rear door of his vehicle when Auriol, true to her word, began to struggle inside her white cocoon and shriek at the top of her voice.

"Help! Help! Police! Rape! Kidnap! Help!" She opened her red mouth wide and bit Spencer's arm, causing him to half-drop her with a shout. Harley let out an involuntary scream.

There was an echoing pause. Auriol struggled so violently that they could not hold her. A cruising police car on the far side of the road slowed down and turned quickly. The wail of a siren drowned all other noise. The vehicle swooped towards the kerb and halted with a screech of brakes, a number of constables leaped out and within a few seconds three men were holding Spencer and another was helping Auriol to her feet amid the tangle of sheeting. Harley yelped as she felt her arm twisted by another cop, and saw Sheldon and the driver forced against the car.

"It's all right, officer, it's all right . . ." The porter, more pompous than ever, came wheezing towards them, the heavy skirts of his greatcoat flapping and his breath puffs of steam in the cold air. "Don't jump to the wrong conclusions here. I can assure you that nothing untoward is taking place."

The police, responding to his manner, his uniform and his colour, at once relaxed their grip, and allowed Spencer to stand up. The porter's duties included presenting the local constabulary weekly with a brown envelope of cash to blind official eyes to the parking offences of his residents.

"This young lady lives in my building," he pointed at Harley, "and these gentlemen are her brothers. She has given a party and I understand one of the guests was reluctant to leave. They were merely escorting her to a taxi."

"You know her, then?" The senior policeman looked reluctantly from Harley to the porter, noting her expensive clothes.

"Certainly. A very respectable and—uh—well-connected young lady."

"May I ask why this woman is not dressed?"

"I gather she had taken a drop too much, officer, and refused to put on her clothes."

"I see. Very well then." The policeman did not approve of women who got drunk. He surveyed the group and stepped back with reluctance. Deciding that if an arrest was not forthcoming, a little titillation might be extracted from the situation, he suggested that his men could drive Auriol home, an offer she accepted with poor grace, hobbling barefoot towards the nearest car with the sheet held awkwardly around her body and the bag containing her clothes in one hand.

The next morning Harley brought the porter a large bottle of his favourite single malt whisky. He glowed with the satisfaction of a successful knight-errant. "I hope you weren't offended, miss. I think the police just saw, er—all of you—and got the wrong idea. You can't really blame them, with all the riots we've been having."

"No, of course not, I quite understand," Harley reassured him. "I am just so grateful to you and so glad you were there to speak up for us."

"It's a lucky thing your brothers arrived when they did. Are you a large family?" The porter, who had always maintained that all sooties looked the same to him just like the Chinese, was positively proud that he had discerned the resemblance between Harley and Spencer. She was the first black person he had ever spoken to on a regular basis and on the whole he regarded her as a charming young lady, but there were the other residents to think of and he believed blacks always had large families.

"Oh no, the twins are all the family I've got," she was unaware of the purpose of his enquiry. "I hated them when they were little, but now they're grown up and they're here they're really a great comfort."

She needed comfort a few days later, when Marianne abruptly informed her that the agency could no longer represent her. The contract for the coffee commercial was already signed, but Harley was recalled for another test for the part in the James Bond film, and lost it to a noisy eighteen-year-old from Sierra Leone whom Marianne had just signed. Her name was Cherie, she was several shades darker than Harley and she made no secret of her professional ambitions. "In a white world there's only room for one black model at the top, and that's me," she told the studio at large. "I think it's because I have the right look for now, the look says image, immediate, integrity." She patted her wedge-cut coiffure and gave Harley a glare of contempt.

"So, you just go down the road to the competition," Sheldon counselled calmly.

"The news has been out for days," Harley shook her head, puzzled. "The competition ought to have called me by now. Maybe Kelly . . ."

"I never want to hear that name on your lips again," he replied in the magisterial tones of their grandmother.

It was fortunate that Harley took his advice, for when she walked into the offices of Models One the receptionist convulsed with amazement. The head of the agency showed Harley that day's edition of the *Daily Post*, which carried one of her most celebrated *Vogue* cover shots over a story that the world-famous Jamaican beauty was dying of a mysterious cancer which had hideously bloated her once-lovely body and caused all her hair to fall out.

"Don't worry," the woman reassured her coolly. "That's just Marianne being a bad loser. The more successful you are, the more enemies you'll get, it's natural. Sue them, get some more publicity. And get ready to go to Venice in August—we're sending all our girls to the International Red Cross Gala and the occasion would not be complete, believe me, if you were not there."

CHAPTER XIX

TO BE CARRYING her first child in Athens in the spring seemed very satisfactory to Victoria until her husband called from the Embassy to say he would be late for dinner.

"There's a terrific flap on," he explained, in the voice of studied impenetrability he employed to remind her that every diplomat had to expect his telephone to be tapped, "I'll tell you all about it when I get back."

"You won't be too late, will you?" She was having a wonderful pregnancy, but it was becoming more and more difficult to stay awake after ten in the evening.

"I can't give you a time, this is a big one." He rang off abruptly.

Victoria was determined to be the best possible wife to Patrick. He expected no less, and the Diplomatic Service had envisaged no other career for her. If he worked late, which he often did, she was always alert and smiling when he returned, ready to pour him a drink and listen to the account of his day. She quickly gave up the awkward business of cooking evening meals for them both, noting that Patrick was irritated by the obligation to eat and praise her offerings, but she kept his favourite snacks in the refrigerator in case he should unexpectedly announce hunger.

She rejected coffee as bad for the baby, and warded off sleep with her latest piece of tapestry, which had progressed rapidly since the baby had slowed down her days. It was an easy geometric pattern in two muted colours, copied from the shredded original covering of a long footstool from Aston Langley, which it was intended to replace. She was assembling her own collection of small, easily portable tokens of ancestral standing; the gracious life of a British upper-class nomad was second nature to her.

At almost midnight, when she had resorted to pacing wearily across the small living room, Patrick came in, pale but excited by the day's events.

"The Prince of Wales is getting married." His embrace was perfunctory and his tone portentous. "Coded note in the bag this morning, then a call from London to say there was a press leak and to get a move on with spreading the word. Ambassador still away for the weekend, half the Embassy running round like chickens with their heads cut off . . . still, I managed to get them all calmed down and we rounded everybody up in the end."

"How wonderful. They must be terribly pleased." Victoria had a special tone of voice in which she said "they" when she meant the Royal Family. "It is Diana Spencer, I suppose?"

"Yes, of course."

"Poor little thing. I do hope she's up to it." She knew he was watching her reactions carefully. Once out of England, Victoria had noticed shades of emotion in her husband which had escaped her before. Although he tried to hide his feelings, she became aware that he was acutely sensitive about her relationship with Prince Richard. Moments of deference, odd suppositions which he made about her or cutting remarks which he instantly bit back all betrayed the ambiguity of his attitudes. She was unsettled to find her husband so vulnerable, but decided to smother her own doubts and try to boost his confidence. "What a good thing you were there to take charge, Pat. You always know exactly what to do."

He glowed and patted her arm before asking for a drink. She brought him a stiff vodka with the absurdly expensive English brand of orange juice which he preferred to the syrupy Greek alternative.

"The date's at the end of July, so you'll be in London for the wedding."

"I certainly won't be invited," she said sharply.

"That's not what I meant at all." His jaw tightened with momentary anger; Patrick understood well enough that trading on royal association was a mortal sin, and was annoyed that his wife should suspect him of committing it—

albeit justly. "But they're going to put on a tremendous show and you'll be there to see it all."

"Yes, I suppose I will." She was to leave shortly for England, to stay with her family until the baby was born and she had recovered. Since her delivery date was in high summer, and Athens was oven-hot and crammed with tourists at that time, Pat had urged the sense of staying until September at least. "But I'd much rather be here with you, Pat."

"Now, Vicky, sweet, we've been through all this. And I'll be with you, they'll give me the time off, I'm sure."

"I know, and of course I'd much rather have the baby at home, but I hate having to be away from you for so long. Why won't the stupid airlines fly women after the fifth month of pregnancy?"

"Because they don't want any mid-air deliveries. You can't blame them. It will seem like no time, you'll see. And Athens is hell in the summer."

"Yes."

In bed he made love to her, very gently and quickly, as if afraid to disturb the modest swelling that would be their child but needing to reassure himself that she was still available to him. Afterwards Victoria felt too warm and could not sleep. She lay still, listening to his breathing and the night noises of the city, thinking about the youngest of the Spencer girls. Her recollection was of a plump, shy teenager, sweet, directionless and occasionally wilful. Diana seemed frighteningly young, five years younger than she was, much too young to know what she was doing.

The flutter of the baby inside her, a new and thrilling sensation a few days earlier, intruded on her thoughts. She felt hot now, and was sweating even though she had thrown off the sheet. So far she had enjoyed a perfect pregnancy, regaining the sheen on her hair and clotted-cream bloom of her complexion which she had imagined lost forever after Richard. She put on only a little weight, and drifted past the crammed windows of Athens' infant boutiques with a pleasant sense of serenity that for once was not chemical. She had given up taking her pills on the advice of the Embassy doctor.

A light rain fell on the city, making the air oppressively humid. The apartment was air-conditioned, but the equipment was old and noisy, and unnecessary in February; if she got up to turn it on, she might wake Patrick. She touched the slope of her belly and wondered how large it would swell in the months to come. The inevitability of giving birth descended on her like a black sheet. She felt trapped, deceived, angry that the only way back to youth and beauty was through suffering.

At three it was still raining and she was more awake than ever, turning over and over in her mind the question of taking a sleeping pill. The certainty of oblivion called longingly to her and in the end defeated the vision of embarrassed nurses hiding her deformed child from her eyes. She went to the bathroom, retrieved the store of drugs from the depths of a cupboard and took one.

When Victoria arrived at Aston Langley a week later, exhausted to tears after seven hours of travelling, she had the old, familiar and cruel experience of walking into her family as a stranger. The littles had grown, Pamela was busier, there were more dogs, and the furniture had been moved. "Her" room was as usual a place in which she had never set foot before, identified by her old blue rabbit but alien in its chintzy newness.

For the first few days she automatically took part in the polite and futile ritual of picking up threads of the others' lives and offering scraps of information about her own; when the family's doctor called she was slipping rapidly into weepy confusion. He gently stressed that finding an obstetrician and attending ante-natal classes should be her priorities. He added the pointed advice that the cottage hospital in Greater Aston had no resident anaesthetist. Pamela, who implied by all her actions that Victoria had once been a tiresome responsibility but was now of no concern to her, suggested that shopping for the nursery was best done in London, and so Victoria was glad to accompany her father to the capital.

The apartment was full of memories, and again her moods lurched frighteningly. The best she felt was numb, the worst an all-enveloping distress. She was deadly tired in the evenings, but woke in the small hours of the morning and could not sleep again. The obstetrician insisted that she take no unnecessary drugs, but the midwife, catching her desperation, reassured her that the occasional 50 milligrams of Valium could do no harm and that the sleep would do mother and foetus good. Victoria felt better as soon as she had the prescription in her hand.

Thus stabilised, she began to take pleasure in keeping house for her father. It was the first period in her life which she had enjoyed alone with her only biological parent, and now that she in her turn was beginning a new generation and moving up one step in the progression of life it seemed comforting and correct to be his temporary partner.

Sometimes she accompanied him to friends' houses for dinner, or took his arm proudly at Admiralty functions and engaged the other wives in small-talk. Her father exhibited his famous daughter with a simple pride which she found a relief after Patrick's carefully contrived reticence.

At home, he talked over his day's work with her, pushing aside supper plates to draw maps of the North Atlantic illustrating the contentious fishing grounds and pulling out classified reports from his old black document case to quote statistics. After supper, when they were both tired, he would sit in his deep wing chair and smilingly enquire after the baby before drifting into reminiscences of her own birth and childhood.

Pamela had no interest in their London home, but Victoria, while buying a wicker crib and the recommended supply of layette clothes for her child, also took pleasure in rearranging the other rooms, adding flowers and cushions to relieve their masculine austerity. She found much to do in the way of getting chimneys swept and furniture restored. All this industry calmed her, and diverted her attention from the massed Royal Wedding souvenirs on sale all over London and the cheap copies of Diana Spencer's wedding dress given pride of place in every bridal boutique.

One day, in a taxi on her way to Peter Jones's store in Sloane Square for a few more baby essentials, the vehicle swerved violently and she was thrown to the floor. A pale blue Volkswagen Polo shot past, with a crowd of photographers running in pursuit.

"There she is," the excited driver informed her, pointing at the little car as it took the corner ahead at dangerous speed, "there's Lady Di! I thought we might see her, her Mum lives round the corner here somewhere. Of course, she used to get around on her little bicycle but these photographers are making her life a misery so she drives everywhere now. Shame, isn't it?"

The conversation was of Charles and Diana wherever she went, and it annoyed her to have her opinion on the match solicited not only by people like the porter's wife, who could not have known better, but her own friends and relatives.

"I don't know why they're all asking me," she complained, "I haven't met the girl since she was twelve and I hardly know Charles at all."

The wedding provoked a new delineation of royal favour in the magic circle. Her father and Pamela, Aunt Rose and her husband, had all been invited to the vast reception before the wedding at Buckingham Palace. Victoria felt piqued at her exclusion, and annoyed with herself because she knew the feeling was unreasonable. She was justifiably uneasy among her own peers, oversensitive to their coded enquiries checking the family's status and aware that pairing her off, as a heavily-pregnant unaccompanied young woman, was a headache for her hostesses.

A storm of ugly emotion threatened on the horizon of Victoria's consciousness. The frustrations of late pregnancy combined with anger and jealousy, and were all denied, for she knew she had no reason to feel rejected, or to envy Diana, and that pregnancy was a natural state in which women of her class were supposed to be as energetic as ever and not to make a fuss.

Too much tension would harm the baby, but the Valium helped, and she positively enjoyed spinning the same yarn to the midwife, the obstetrician and her family doctor, and taking each prescription to a different dispensary so that her deception would not be discovered.

Escape from the world's fascination with the royal wedding was essential, but hard to achieve. Victoria gave up reading the newspapers and avoided the television news. She began to look up girlfriends outside the magic circle who might be able to divert her attention.

Suzie Chamfer treated her, and most of the other diners under the artificial apple blossoms at Mortons, to a noisy account of her season in "Heritage." "And would you believe," she confided, enthusiastically sucking the last fragment of meat from a crab claw, "that Jo Forbes's mother is just the sweetest person imaginable? Everybody just adores her. On my first day on the set she had lunch with me—not that she actually had lunch, just a few carrot sticks, that woman has such discipline—and was so charming and did everything to make me feel at home. I mean, LA is a frightful place—really she was absolutely like a mother to me and when she found out I knew Jo, she just talked about her the whole time. How *is* Jo, by the way? I saw her at some party a few weeks ago and she looked sort of sad."

"I must look her up, I haven't seen her for ages, either." Victoria rarely thought about her former housemates.

In her present state of suspended rage, Jo and Harley suddenly acquired a forbidden glamour. She called them both and, because Jo was rehearsing a play at the Queen's Arms all day, invited them to dinner.

The evening was stilted from the start. Jo arrived in a grey sweat shirt and trousers, slimmer than Victoria recalled her, with grubby hands from the dusty rehearsal room. Harley arrived late in a simple black dress which made it evident that there was still not a milligram of spare flesh on her bones. She was graciously attentive to Victoria's father, who responded to her with a twinkle of the same fascination that she had aroused in Alex years earlier. Both her old friends chattered freely of their hopes and ambitions, swapped news of contracts and whines about their agents, told witty stories about their colleagues and gossiped about common acquaintances, and Victoria felt excluded. Harley, now a favourite with several of the other photographers at *Vogue*, launched into the story of how a certain magazine editor was choosing Lady Di's entire wardrobe for her, but seeing the broken look come on to Victoria's face she dropped the subject.

"I can't believe you're pregnant," Jo said suddenly after Victoria's father had left the table on the pretext of reading some papers. "How do you feel?"

"Fat." Victoria smiled ruefully and put her hands on her stomach. "And hot. And tired, most of the time. But it won't be long now."

"You're going to be a mother." For all her prodigious empathy painstakingly trained, Jo could not imagine how that state would feel.

"Don't go on about it," Victoria pleaded in a fretful voice.

"You must be so nervous."

"I wish . . ." She struggled for words for the feeling she could hardly recognise. "I wish my own mother wasn't dead. I want someone to tell me what it's like. Daddy just says we were both caesareans because Mummy was so small."

"My mother always told me it was the worst pain in the world, like hot iron in your stomach, but when you had the baby in your arms you forgot it immediately," Harley tested her coffee, made a face and added more sugar.

"It can't be that bad or people wouldn't have six. But nobody will tell you. I asked Jane Brompton and she just said she had so many drugs she couldn't remember. I asked Pamela and she just said it was so long ago."

"Sounds like a conspiracy." Jo pulled one knee up to her chest and hugged it thoughtfully, reflecting on the hard-won flatness of her own belly. Bearing a child seemed an awesome responsibility for which she would never feel sufficiently adult.

Half-an-hour later Victoria's strength suddenly failed and she apologetically asked them to leave. She went to lie down on her narrow bed immediately and the baby began to move, at first gently then more and more violently as if it were trying to kick its way frontally out of her stomach. She turned from her back to one side and then the other, in pain and distress, wondering fearfully if this could be the beginning of labour and acutely conscious that there was no one to turn to for comfort or advice. She reached for her sleeping tablets, but the baby convulsed so powerfully that she was forced to fall back and wait out the struggle.

The next morning she looked so grey and hollow-eyed that her father, alarmed, called the doctor, who found nothing wrong. Pamela was summoned from Aston Langley and bustled about the apartment making a show of concern.

Three weeks later Victoria felt a tentative spasm while leaning awkwardly over the bulge to brush her teeth, and by that evening she was reclining, comfortably anaesthetised, in the labour room talking to Patrick in Athens on the telephone. The baby, a girl, was born as midnight approached. She did not cry, but fixed Victoria with a glassy gaze that seemed reproachful.

The birth had been lengthy, and the next day passed like a hallucination. At her first moment of genuine consciousness she saw a dazzlingly handsome man in uniform appear at the foot of her bed and thought for an instant it was Richard. She rubbed her eyes and struggled weakly to sit up. He put a bouquet of pink flowers in cellophane on her table and she realised it was her brother.

"Alex!"

"Well done, darling. How are you?"

"Fine. I'm fine."

"You look beautiful."

"Don't be silly, I must look a mess."

"I've never seen you look so beautiful. You were born to be a mother, Tory darling. I got leave the minute I heard. I'm so glad I'm here with you."

He held her and kissed her; a fog of happiness rolled in and she shed a few tears.

Guiltily, she was less delighted when Patrick arrived shortly afterwards, with a larger bouquet and champagne which he insisted be broached immediately, although Alex was plainly not anxious to spend time in his company. He cooed over the baby, who slept on regardless, and held her with surprising confidence.

Sarah Jane Charlotte was the quietest baby the nursery nurse engaged at Aston Langley could remember. She did not feed very well, which annoyed Victoria who felt that if she was prepared to suffer the indignity of breast-feeding the child ought to be grateful. At the age of six weeks, the baby's mood switched abruptly to severe irritability. Sensitivity to her mother's milk was the local doctor's diagnosis, which suited Victoria's mood ideally. Both Patrick and Alex danced attendance on her, circling each other like duellists as they vied for her attention, until Patrick had to return to Athens at the end of a month and Victoria and her brother passed the golden days of August in each other's company.

"You are all right, aren't you, Tory?" he asked as he prepared to depart for Gibraltar.

"Why does everyone keep asking me that?"

"Women are supposed to get a bit down after giving birth, that's all."

"Well, not me. Especially not with you here."

He looked at her as if he were about to say something important.

"What on earth are you gaping at me like a goldfish for?"

The moment passed and he shook his head as if to clear an unwelcome memory. "Nothing. Just—take care, Tory."

"Of course I'll take care, I always do, don't I?"

* * *

PRINCE RICHARD LET himself into Princess Louise's apartment and found the stage set as he expected. Their relationship was becoming a series of rituals which she believed to be the spells which would bind him irrevocably to her.

He entered the room always with the mingled anticipation of excitement and disgust, a sensation which had become an aphrodisiac. Automatically, he began to undo the gold buttons on his scarlet jacket. The place had been the scene of his darkest secrets; he was drawn to it because the two small rooms contained the dimension of himself never revealed elsewhere, and at the same time he wanted to escape and deny everything that happened here as soon as the unique atmosphere enveloped him.

The wealthy Iranian for whom Louise worked as a social secretary owned the apartment; he had paid for all the silk and ormolu furnishings and allowed her to use her own taste. The drawing room was small, heavily draped in gold and softly illuminated by a pair of candle lamps in mirrored sconces on the wall.

Richard went straight to the glass-topped table by the double doors into the bedroom, where a small reading lamp cast a pool of light over two ruler-straight lines of cocaine and a gold straw. She had made the drug their sacrament. He leaned down and sniffed it quickly and carelessly; as always it was set out on a circular silver photograph frame containing her own picture with the words "Richard, I love you" written across one corner in her even, ornate script.

The chemical taste cut into the lingering sweetness of after-dinner cognac at the back of his palate. The bedroom door was six inches ajar, and he heard a soft rustle of her clothes from within.

As he pushed open the bedroom door he heard another sound of disturbed clothing and a soft, inarticulate exclamation made under Louise's breath; she was standing against one of the bedposts, smiling, her arms crossed over the bodice of the red dress she had worn to dinner. As he walked towards her she unfolded her arms and let the gown fall to the floor in a crackle of taffeta. Her body was offered to him in an opulent white satin basque. Richard smiled inwardly, already more acute under the drug's influence; some kind of bridal number was exactly what he would have expected, if he had for once allowed himself to think at length about Louise's tricks.

She held her crimson sash out to him, her head pleadingly on one side. "Tie me up, darling, you know how I love it."

The pronounced sibilants of her accent added to the unreality of the scene; as soon as he was with her, he felt like a figure in a tableau. She had perceived and exploited his sense of theatricality, bringing true all the prophecies of doom which his youthful vanity had elicited.

He paused to touch her breasts, wanting to get to the final pitch of excitement quickly, then took the sash, bound her wrists and tied them to the mahogany bedpost. Sinuous and deliberate, she arched her back and presented herself; she had firm, high, muscular buttocks like a polo-pony, the golden skin banded white with a bikini-mark.

In the mirrored door of her cupboard, artfully left open at the perfect angle, he saw her eyes darken and her eyelids close as he touched her. A pink flush appeared on the fine skin of her neck and tiny drops of sweat broke through her make-up. For all she held her poses at the extreme of ecstasy, Louise's orgasms were unmistakable when she was tied. At other times they were noisier but less convincing. He suspected that she rationed herself, and he was correct. Louise had not planned to feel genuine desire with him; it threatened her self-control and so she fought it.

The drug was making him feel omnipotent, and he was tempted to prolong the scene, but as she recovered and pushed efficiently against him he was reminded that he was obliged to dance at his brother's wedding, that his temporary absence had caused disapproval and that Louise herself would be determined to extract the last inch of advancement for herself from the occasion. In the mirror he could see that her lips, sensuously blurred a few moments earlier, were falling into their characteristic petulant droop.

He withdrew without coming, untied her hands and allowed her to fuss over him for a few minutes. Then he watched as she sat down to refresh her make-up. Her hair was beautifully pinned around a small diamond tiara, and not one lock seemed to have been disturbed.

"So how was your dinner, darling? Was it terribly boring?" Her hands moved fast and efficiently among the feminine impedimenta of her dressing table.

"No. Not as bad as all that. Did you have trouble getting away from your party?" After the storm of rage with which she had greeted the news that she was not to be invited to the pre-wedding supper, Louise had ungraciously agreed to join one of the dinner-parties of young people who were to join the two families for the ball afterwards. Richard had then considered the logistics of the situation more carefully, and realised that unless he accompanied her there would be no opportunity to get down the ideal quantity of coke on which to pass the night.

Not for the first time, he had found himself darting across London in the night to the two high, narrow rooms near Eaton Square, impelled by a need for the white powder which gave him the illusion of mastery over life.

An hour later Richard was dancing with his mother in the ballroom at Buckingham Palace. In the blaze of light and hubbub of conversation his charm was at its most vivid. He took care to make her laugh, and ignored the cynical voice at the back of his mind which observed that his own mother liked him better when he was coked-up and animated; it was an understandable mistake. He drank less, he seemed happy, and although every morning he climbed out of a slough of melancholy it was nothing that a couple of lines could not fix and Louise kept him well supplied.

"What *is* that thing she's pinned on her dress?" his mother asked suddenly, and through a gap in the dancing couples he saw Louise, partnering his father, touching the little diamond-framed portrait on a blue and gold ribbon which was her only jewellery apart from her tiara. She had changed to a very simple dress, a column of ice-pink chiffon with a trailing scarf, typical of the restrained simplicity she affected around his family.

"It's some order or other—St Michael and St Somebody, Stephen I think, she did tell me but I've forgotten. It's the family's hereditary decoration, anyway."

"Oh, yes."

"Oh come on, Mother, don't do the silent disapproval bit with Louise. I know she's not your sort but she can't help being who she is."

"She does make you happy, doesn't she?" She had a way of commanding his gaze, even though she had to look up to him, but Richard was beyond feeling uncomfortable under her sudden stare.

"Yes, she does, but you won't be marrying me off for a long while yet so you can relax."

"Well, that's a great relief. I'd hate to have to go through this again too soon."

"What you mean is that it's a great relief I'm not in love with her because you don't like her." He said it lightly and smiled warmly so that the harsh truth seemed like a private joke.

"That's not fair, Richard. I don't dislike Louise, it's just . . ."

"You have to admit she's good for me. I've got over Victoria at last." Did the guilty excitement show on his face, he wondered? It exhilarated him to deceive his mother like this, to talk about his good spirits while he knew their source was purely chemical and she did not.

She frowned, unwilling to voice the explanation for her unease. The suggestion that her son had a drug problem, and that it was Belgian, Catholic and brown-haired, had been tactfully introduced to her several times in the past month. "Yes," she admitted reluctantly, "you do smile more when she's about."

"Come on, Mother. I can't get serious about Louise or anyone while the Marines are sending me all over the place. I do spend half my life freezing to death in Norway, after all."

This was undeniable and she nodded briefly. "But for a girl about whom you're not serious, you seem to see an awful lot of her."

"You used to complain that I fell in love constantly. Now you're complaining because I don't."

"That isn't what I meant at all."

"You'd just prefer me to find a sweet girl like Diana?"

"Don't be silly, Richard. I think Louise is rather sophisticated for us, that's all."

"Perhaps I'm rather sophisticated for you, too? Have you thought of that, Mother?"

"Quite often, actually." She smiled with determined good humour, deciding tonight of all nights was no time to start an argument with any of her children.

The dance ended and they changed partners. Richard watched Louise, still dancing with his father. He leaned down to listen as she talked to him, then threw back his head and laughed. Prince Philip liked Louise. Most of the men in his family did.

Andrew called her tremendous fun. Edward thought she was sensitive and intelligent, and his father openly admired the dignity with which she managed her testing inheritance of high birth and low income. In fact all three were, like Richard, mesmerised by Louise's intangible aura of sexuality. Charles, being in love, was immune to it, and joined their mother in instinctive mistrust of her. Nevertheless, even he felt he was judging his brother's chosen companion unfairly. There was nothing wrong with Louise that any of them could see; true, she was not English, but that was no cause for condemnation. Her behaviour was perfect. She acted with ideal grace and modesty; she could never be faulted or laughed at, except for the calculation which was the cause of her perfection.

The ball ended in the small hours of the morning and Richard accompanied Louise back to her apartment. They drove through the flashlights of a crowd of photographers at the Palace gates and Louise artlessly let go of the balloon emblazoned with the Prince of Wales feathers to give them a clear view of her face.

In the Mall the most dedicated onlookers were camped in sleeping bags and on the scaffolding around the Victoria fountain the first of the cameramen were laying their cables. Through his diminishing high, Richard was reminded that in thirty hours he would have to play his part in the great pageant of his brother's wedding.

Louise sat apart from him in the back of the Rover as Henshaw drove them smoothly through the empty streets. A tension developed in Richard's mind. It would be a few days before he could see her again, an interlude in which he had to stand up with his family in public, a part of the picture of perfection on which the country needed periodically to gaze. As far as he was concerned it was a false image, and he hated to be part of it. With some coke, he could breeze through the ordeal impersonating his normal self. Without it he would plunge directly into a pit of depression.

Cocaine was not addictive, Louise told him that often enough, implying that a real man would not be so weak as to become habituated. It just made life temporarily bearable. When he returned to the Marines he sweated out the overmastering doubts that followed its withdrawal in violent action and physical ordeals. The cadre itself was like a family. Being close to men with whom he had been bonded emotionally with shared pain and exhaustion gave him the strength he needed.

Away from them, he was as vulnerable as a crab that had shed its shell, until the drug gave him the illusion of control. He would have to ask Louise for a supply, and before she gave it him she would demand something of him in return. This too was a ritual. She would ask for a public token of his devotion, he would resist and then they would argue. She knew it and he knew it. They were only waiting to be alone to begin the struggle.

Once inside the apartment, she made her terms clear at once. "Oh darling, I forgot, my mother asked me today if you were coming to Venice."

"You know I can't, Louise. I told you so when you first asked me, didn't I? I've only got a month's leave."

"But you said you would ask for more. The Marines can hardly refuse you. Your father is their colonel-in-chief, after all, isn't he?"

"Captain-General," he corrected her automatically.

"Well, whatever. Doesn't it mean they give you whatever you want?"

"No, it does not. It means I can't ask."

"That's a lie, Richard. Don't lie to me, please. It makes me angry." She sat down on the slippery white brocade sofa, her face expressionless. The gesture was a negotiating move. She kept the drugs somewhere in her bedroom.

Had he said he would ask for more leave? He talked so much when he was high he seldom remembered what he said.

"It's not a lie, it's the way things are. Why can't you understand?"

"All I understand is that you've always got an excuse why

you won't do anything that's really important to me. The
Red Cross Gala is the largest event she has ever organised,
Richard. There will be more than a thousand people, film,
television, reporters, everything. She does not expect me to
attend alone. You never think of other people, Richard, do
you? Or really of me? When the whole world knows we are
a couple, it is impossible for me to appear in public without
you." Her flat blue irises glared with the force of her will.
He knew she was ruthless in these battles; she was like a
witch who changed shape constantly. Now the pleading,
playful depravity of a few hours earlier was impossible to
imagine.

"Louise, I couldn't ask for more leave. I've already had
more than I should this year."

"That's because you want to climb your stupid mountains. Are they really more important than me?" Her tone
was glacial; Louise never troubled to be seductive when
she had the upper hand.

"You're a bitch," he said suddenly.

She gave him a look of contempt. "I don't think so. But
if that is your opinion, then you can leave."

Fury burst in his mind like a shell and he decided to take
her at her word. He turned swiftly and in silence, slammed
the apartment door behind him and ran down the stairs,
feeling lighter and more free at every step.

The elation was short-lived. He found he did not want to
go home, and instead directed the detective to a small
house in a mews on the far side of the park. On the way he
stopped at a telephone box and, using the coins which
Henshaw passed him, he called to wake the woman who
lived there. She was a relic of his promiscuous days, one of
several good-humoured creatures who would welcome him
to their beds at any hour if they were sleeping alone, and
give him hot chocolate, decent whisky, aspirins, good advice and whatever else he might need if they had it in the
house.

After ninety minutes of warmth and comfort he felt
guilty about taking so much and giving nothing to a good-
hearted girl except the crested balloon which Louise had
disdainfully abandoned in the car. At the Palace he slept
for a few hours, drank a pint of strong black coffee and
passively endured the final wedding rehearsals. Everyone
was strained and irritable. Diana looked as pale as paper.

Richard watched Charles fuss over her and felt something malevolent which he refused to acknowledge as jealousy.

A dark void was opening in his mind. His brothers and parents seemed like strangers. He could not concentrate on anything. Charles talked to him and he heard but could not listen. He played nervously with his cuff-links, a habit which irritated everyone, and forgot half the instructions which he was given. Snap out of it, he told himself. Get a grip.

At noon his inner distress was so great that he felt nauseous. He escaped to his bedroom and telephoned Louise, cursing when there was no answer. She was playing games. He tried to put himself in her place and reason as she would, as if this effort of imagination would cause her to materialise and respond.

At three he tried again and she was there.

"I'm sorry. I will come to Venice." He was so angry with himself for this surrender that he could not say any more.

She said nothing and he heard a sigh of annoyance. "Please forgive what I said." The words had to be forced between his teeth.

There was still a silence.

"Louise, please, please . . . say something." He recognised pure fear trickling through his consciousness. She knew she could do anything with him now.

"You hurt me very much," she responded at last in a small, distant voice.

"I'm sorry, truly I am."

"It's not like you, Richard. I think you are taking . . . I think you are eating too many sweets. You should stop it." Since the *Daily Post* had tapped Charles's telephone calls to Diana, they had all become adept at talking in code.

"Louise, not now, not today, please . . ."

There was another pause and another sigh. "I suppose you want to send a car over for it?"

"I can't leave, we're still going through the arrangements for tomorrow."

"Very well. But soon, Richard. I'm going to the airport in an hour."

"The airport . . . are you going away?" He could not disguise his anxiety.

"Only for a week. I'm going to Paris with my boss. Don't

worry, I'll give you enough. I just can't stand to be in this country right now."

He ended the conversation and hung up, feeling weak and dirty.

CHAPTER XX

JO DIPPED A TINY brush in the black eyeliner, rested her elbow on the counter in the dressing room to steady her hand and slowly painted a line from the inner corner of her eye to the outer, flicking it out along the line of her lashes. The cheap, gritty cosmetic clogged the brush and she regretted the bottles of Dior and Saint Laurent that she had thrown away half-used when she was rich. Perhaps she could take a chance with her Visa card when the play opened. You could not really play Elizabeth Taylor with Woolworth's eyeliner.

The eyeliner was the key to the character. Once she had her eyes ringed in black, drawn down and closer together at their inner corners, the rest of her face seemed to arrange itself. Her nose looked sharper, her upper lip set in a spiteful bow, her chin lifted and she became the image of a great beauty spoiled by selfishness. Then came the fluttery, phoney voice inflections, the pouter pigeon bosom, the cinched waist and the insinuating ass, the hobbled walk and the business with her hands which she remembered her mother doing whenever she felt on display in public.

"I won't be a minute," she called to the others through the open door. The Queen's Arms theatre was so small you could shout to the stage from any part of it.

"No sweat," Simon, the director, was chalking marks on the boards. "Bazza and Roland haven't shown up yet. They called to say the bike won't start and they can't get a cab. We must be the only people in London working today."

Jo stuck the famous Taylor beauty spot on her right cheek and began to pencil in the heavy black eyebrows. She heard Bazza's heavy tread, followed by Roland's feline footfalls, in the corridor which connected the theatre to the pub.

"Fucking hell—you'd think the world had come to an end just because Charles and Di are getting hitched. It's like a nuclear disaster out there—no cars, no one on the streets. Everyone's glued to the television already."

"Leave it out, Baz. You two have never been on time for a rehearsal yet." With good humour, Simon stood up and dusted off the knees of his jeans.

"The bar's packed out there," Bazza went on with a gesture of contempt. "They're all crying into their beer already. Disgusting. At least it's fucking raining. God's on the right side."

"I see you've been shopping?" Simon indicated the heavy black leather jacket which Roland was wearing.

"Oh, yeah—we got it in a market yesterday. It's a US airforce flying jacket, the real McCoy, son, no error. Show 'em, Roland."

The younger man stepped forward and posed, glowering, pulling the collar of the black leather jacket around his ears and flicking back his greased forelock. He had the mean, vulnerable, humorous look that was exactly right for his role. If Bazza had written a play about James Dean principally to celebrate his lover's exquisite looks, nobody was complaining. *Too Fast, Too Young* was a brilliant piece of work, without a surplus word or an untrue line.

The other members of the company peeled themselves off the hard wooden benches and went to work. Jo had to speak the opening lines from a wheelchair at the front of the stage. Renting this equipment for the play's run of four weeks was the biggest item in the props budget, and had been the subject of much discussion among the company. Jo, after a year with Lorcan Flood, was used to improvising anything, but Simon insisted that he wanted Liz wheeled about in a clanking metal contraption.

"The thing I really remember about *Giant*, the thing I'll never forget, was the night of Jimmy Dean's death," Jo began in an affected, husky drawl.

"Brrrrm, berrrrmmmm, berererrrrrr, eeeeeeeeeouou-ououow, *blam!*" Simon supplied an approximation of the sound of a Porsche Carrera crashing on Highway 46.

"I just can't believe this awful thing has happened," Jo

wailed. "Not to Jimmy—he was so young, so full of life . . ."

"Kill the spot, Jo turns around to Rock . . ." Rock Hudson was represented by a blown-up photograph. Bazza, playing *Giant*'s director, stood over her.

"My face is a mess, I've been crying all night," she pleaded.

"Too bad. You gotta movie to finish. Hell, the kid just got what he wanted, after all." There was a distant roar of voices from the bar and Bazza glared in that direction.

"How can you say that?" Jo shouted, making her hands into fists and half-rising from the chair.

"If she can't control herself we'll have to shoot over her head," he ordered, motioning to invisible cameramen.

"You're a callous bastard," Jo screamed, leaping to her feet ready to storm off the set. "I hope you rot in hell!"

"Lights down, everybody off, spot on Roland in the coffin, and . . ." Simon turned the page of his script as Roland lounged forward, chewing on a toothpick. In the bar, someone turned up the volume of the TV and cheering crowds and the crashing music of military bands resounded through the walls.

"Death is the only thing left to respect," Roland half-whispered. "It's the one inevitable, undeniable truth. Everything else can be questioned, but death is truth. In death lies the only nobility for man, and beyond it only hope."

From the bar came a surge of cheering voices, in which a few shouts of "Isn't she lovely!" were discernible.

"Must be the dress," one of the actors muttered to another, gazing curiously towards the closed door.

"Oh, for Christ's sake," Bazza muttered, stamping angrily off the stage.

"If a man can bridge the gap between life and death, I mean, if he can live on after he's died, then maybe he was a great man," Roland pressed on, his face set. He was acutely aware that the role was the chance of his lifetime.

"Can't we tell 'em to keep the noise down?" demanded Bazza.

"No. We can't beat 'em, we'd better join them, don't you think? It's only a couple of hours." Simon had opposed Bazza's insistence that rehearsals should not be suspended for the day of the royal wedding from the start. The event had given them an extra week of rehearsal time anyway, because Rachel had decided that there was no point in opening a play and hoping to attract attention while the rest of the country was dazzled by gold coaches and confetti.

"I'd quite like to see it, see her dress anyway." Rachel spoke for the first time from the back of the theatre, where she was patiently clipping the press tickets to programmes and stuffing them in envelopes.

"Pathetic. Some nineteen-year-old virgin with the IQ of a slug marries a jug-eared prat who's never done a day's work in his life and you go all gaga." Bazza spun on his heels with the precarious grace of the paunchy, snarling at the actors who had willingly left their places to head for the bar. "Well, I'm going to drop a Mandie and lie down. You can wake me when it's all over."

The rest of them squeezed into the pub; the patrons of the Queen's Arms were enjoying the public holiday with the utmost exuberance. People sat with bright sentimental smiles, crowned with paper hats, festoons of red-white-and-blue streamers around their necks, downing drinks with the characteristic urgency of British merrymakers when temporarily freed from the licensing laws. It was hot in the bar, despite the sulkiness of the weather outside, and a dense haze of cigarette smoke blurred the giant video screen hired for the great occasion.

Jo and her companions found perches at the end of a banquette just as the commentator was reverently informing the audience that the wedding ring had been fashioned from the same nugget of Welsh gold which had supplied the metal for the rings worn by the Queen, the Queen Mother, Princess Margaret and Princess Anne.

"Oh my goodness, look at that train," Rachel marvelled, her eye fixed on the TV screen.

"Silk taffeta, 25 yards long it is." A plump woman with an Irish accent and eyes awash with beer and emotion made room for them on the bench. "Embroidered with sequins and pearls. And the ear-rings are her mother's— that's the something borrowed." She began to dab her eyes with her napkin and the man sitting beside her turned and took it from her to continue the task clumsily with his large, work-torn hands.

"Here is the stuff of which fairy-tales are made." The

Archbishop of Canterbury was beginning his address by the time Simon and Roland returned to their table with beer and cheese rolls.

"I wonder if Victoria Fairley's watching this," Rachel flashed her sparrow-quick smile at Jo.

"I'm sure she is. She's Victoria Hamilton, now, of course."

"Oh yes, of course. Did you go to that wedding?"

"Yes." Jo let her eyes drift back to the TV, unwilling to talk about her friend. She felt a strange pang of loyal sympathy, knowing that however deep Victoria might bury her feelings, she would be inhuman if this huge spectacle did not arouse some regret for what might have been. Jo herself was searching the screen for the familiar figure of Prince Richard, and cursing the cameras as they offered her Nancy Reagan, the King of Tonga and the adorable infant bridesmaids instead.

"I remember my own wedding now," the Irishwoman began as the bride and groom swept slowly down the aisle of St. Paul's Cathedral on a flood of Elgar. "The singing was lovely and I had my mother's shoes which pinched like the devil." It was somehow clear that the mountainous man at her side was not her husband.

"Were you married in Ireland?" Jo, ever curious, was glad to be distracted. She had seen Richard at last, sitting in an open carriage, sword-straight in his blue uniform. He seemed like an unreal thing, not a man whose warm body she had once held in her arms under the night sky. In the thick of the noise and smell of the bar she could not even summon the quality of that memory.

"I wanted to be," the Irish woman responded, "but we were living in Liverpool so all my family came over. The house was full for a week . . ."

"Nothing's going to happen now—they're all having lunch." Simon stood up as the last of the coaches clattered through the gates of Buckingham Palace and the crowd surged forwards to fill the roadway. "Come on—back to work."

"Oh no," Rachel over-ruled him at once. "We've got to see them wave from the balcony."

"They'll be hours," Simon protested.

"No, they will come out directly," asserted a young Asian woman sitting at the next table with a red-haired youth who wore the same denims and tattoos as the rest of his hard-drinking friends. "They always do that."

A roar from the crowd outside the Palace confirmed her opinion and Jo looked up to see the various members of Richard's family appear on the balcony. He himself stepped out quickly after his two younger brothers, looking ill-at-ease.

"She's crying, look, the Queen is crying," the Irish woman insisted.

"She is not," said an older woman standing beside her.

"She is, too, at least she looks as if she might any moment. And why shouldn't she pipe an eye? Her own mother did the same. And Charlie's been long enough finding the right girl."

Jo watched the figures on the screen arrange themselves into the multiple icon which she had discovered that the British people needed to see every Christmas, every summer and at every significant event in the Family's life. Richard leaned forward to say something to the pageboys which made them laugh, and as he straightened up and smiled directly out into the camera she had the absurd illusion that he was looking at her.

"Go on, Charlie boy, give her a kiss, kiss the bride!" Loud voices from the far side of the bar echoed the urging of the crowd.

"Kissing the world goodbye," Roland observed with a sour smile as the bride and groom turned towards each other.

"They're in love, I'm sure they think the world's well lost for that," Rachel suddenly looked sad and fiddled with her empty glass.

"Can we please get back to work now?" Simon stood up again and this time, reluctantly, the company followed him. Bazza, true to his word, lay on the floor in a doped slumber, and Roland thoughtfully draped a coat over him. They stood awaiting instructions from Simon, feeling awkward and ill-at-ease because they had left the ceremony before it was finished. None of them would admit it, but they felt alienated and suddenly lonely, condemned by their art to be apart from the warm common run of humanity. Jo had a keen sense of being excluded, which she recognised with irritation. What did I expect, she asked herself crossly, a personal message from the Palace balcony?

"Do you suppose it is a dreadful life?" Rachel asked Jo as they closed the door on the merrymaking. "I mean, worse than your mother's, for example?"

Thanks to the success of "Heritage," Lorna Lewis was now an international screen matriarch. Six months of the last three years had been devoted to shooting the glitzy soap opera which had caught the entire world's imagination, and the rest of the year Jo heard from her family only briefly, although wherever she went she saw interviews and photographs of her mother on the news-stands.

"I don't know, my mother never talks about pressure or anything. I think she thinks it's unprofessional."

"I bet Princess Di's going to have it really tough," Roland jumped up on the stage and resumed his pose. "All those palaces and servants and diamonds and things. Absolute fucking buggering hell. I *really* feel sorry for her."

Jo thought of a cold Cambridge afternoon when Victoria had sat in their kitchen, her arms outstretched on the table in a pose of utter defeat, turning a teaspoon over and over and saying, "I'm just not up to it, that's the truth. I just couldn't cope."

"It is goodbye to normal life, that's for sure." She stepped up on to the stage, collecting her thoughts.

"Goodbye!" she declaimed, striking a tragic attitude:

Goodbye to red sandals with stiletto heels,
Goodbye to ever looking as rough as you feel,
Goodbye to saying whatever you like,
Goodbye to riding the streets on a bike,
Goodbye to real friends and hello to duty,
Goodbye to freedom, to feeling, to beauty,
And hello to flunkeys and hello to flattery,
And paparazzi and gossip and cattery.
Nineteen years only to belong to yourself,
Now you are owned by everyone else.

There was a moment of silence and then a round of applause.

"Did you just—make that up?" Roland enquired in wonder.

"Yes. Well, I read something in a magazine like it." Jo herself felt surprised that the verse had bubbled out of her mind so spontaneously. She looked uncomfortably at Ra-

chel, who returned her glance with a knowing expression.
"I suppose you're right, it is a bit the same for people like
my mother."

"And for you," Simon said in a quiet voice.

"No, I'm safe, nobody knows who I am, not really. Can
we get started now? It's late, isn't it?"

Too Fast, Too Young opened a week later. Half-an-hour
before the limp rust-coloured velvet curtains of the theatre
were due to part Jo stood in a quiet corner behind a pile of
plastic beer crates running through some voice exercises, as
much to calm her nerves as to work up the seductive neo-
Texan drawl Liz Taylor affected in *Giant*.

Rachel appeared, her face pinched and tense, framed
prettily between her best jet ear-rings. She held out a
bunch of blue anemones made into a posy with paper lace
and a velvet ribbon. All the members of the company had
considerable expertise in making touching gestures on a
low budget.

"I just wanted to say again how much Simon and I appreciate you doing this." She blushed and dropped her
head, her dark ringlets falling across her cheeks, embarrassed at having to make a declaration of emotion.

"Rachel, they're lovely! But really, I'm the one who
should be grateful." Jo kissed her warmly, feeling immediately cherished.

"We argued for ages about whether to ask you. I mean,
it's not a big part, and we can't pay very much, and it's so
wonderful for us. I know you're very modest and you hate
being who you are, but just because you're in this show
people will come and see it or take notice of it, at
least . . ." In the normal way, first-nights at the Queen's
Arms seldom attracted more than a couple of critics.

"But this is a wonderful part and it's great to be able to
work with you. And I love being with you all, Rachel, I've
known you so long, we've been through so much together,
you and Simon and Bazza, I mean, I feel I belong with you,
somehow." She forebore to add that she had nothing else
to do anyway. The year with Lorcan Flood had taught her
more about acting than she had ever realised there was to
learn, but it had not brought many scripts to her agent's
office. The empty days ran into each other; her life was a
dreary routine of staring at the apartment walls waiting for
the telephone to ring until the solitude and silence were

overpowering and she ran out to the gym, or to some classes, or to see other out-of-work friends and have long, envious conversations about what their more successful acquaintances were doing. Being an actress had begun to seem like a wretched fantasy on the Sunday afternoon when Rachel had called.

She saw Roland, white with nerves, running over his big speech under his breath and cracking his knuckles, and went over to propose that they spend the final ten minutes before they were called doing some breathing exercises.

The performance flashed past like a hallucination, as did the awkward hour passed with warm white wine and congratulatory friends afterwards. Unable to face the emptiness of her own home, Jo stayed over with the rest of the company, lying sleepless on the floor beside Rachel and listening to the cars pass by in the night on the street below.

The second night was better, and the third day brought the newspapers.

"By Jove, we've done it!" Simon announced, tossing the *Daily Post* down on the desk in Rachel's crowded office. "We are a hit. We are all a hit. We are each a hit separately and we are also a hit together. Listen to this. *Basil Wright at last fulfils his early promise and emerges as the new white hope of London theatre . . . a smouldering debut* from you, Roland . . . *masterly direction*, that's for me . . . *but the show belongs to Jocasta Forbes . . . a sensational performance . . . lustrous sexuality . . . an actress with a noble Heritage* (sorry, Jo, but that's what it says) . . . *laser-force emotional projection . . . the quintessential tragedy of wasted beauty . . .*"

"Christ, to think they get paid for writing that crap!" Even Bazza could not put on a convincing show of disdain.

"*The Times* is even better, and the *Mail*, and the *Standard* . . ." One by one Simon spread the rave reviews across the desk and the company crowded around to read them.

"Pinch me, I think I'm dreaming," Roland whispered to Jo and she nipped his forearm affectionately.

"You're crying." Huge tears like crystals hung on his thick lashes.

"I did used to dream about things like this," he whispered, suddenly turning his back on the others. "I wish I could tell my mother."

"Well, can't you?"

"She hasn't spoken to me since she found out I was living with Bazza."

"You could call her, couldn't you?"

He shook his head and Jo decided to let it drop. "Are you going to call your mother?"

"I don't know where she is—on location with 'Heritage' somewhere. She'll find out soon enough, it'll get through on the grapevine."

The telephone rang and Rachel, struggling with the cork on a bottle of *méthode champenoise* reached over to answer it. For the next week it seemed as if she took calls without stopping. Bazza was interviewed by all the fringe press and most of the Sunday heavyweights. Jo was interviewed by the *Daily Post* and *People*. Roland was invited to model leather jackets for *Vogue*, and auditioned successfully for a jeans commercial.

The tiny theatre was crammed every night. Jo was touched when half a dozen fans, kids of sixteen or seventeen, hung around after the performance to ask for autographs and see her to her car, although Simon immediately insisted that she drive home with Rachel and himself. "They may look pathetic," he said sternly, "but those types can get pretty weird."

She began to get fan letters, and then someone left a bunch of flowers, wilted offerings plainly stolen from a suburban garden, outside the theatre's door with her name on them each day. Her admirer was never seen; he took care to visit before the pub staff arrived for work.

The charm of this gesture vanished when the flowers had a smudged note on them which read, "I am your king, You are my queen, I love you as no other man can love you, the full moon will unite us forever." The signature was illegible, but Bazza declared it to be the name of a heretical Egyptian pharaoh.

"It's a sicko," he said gleefully. "Totally bananas. Do show me if he writes any more."

"Who's a sicko?" Rachel demanded sharply, noticing Jo's look of revulsion.

"I'd have thought she'd be glad to have such an ardent

admirer," he stuck his hands in his pockets in a gesture of defiance.

"Well I'm not," Jo told him with anger. "It makes me feel sick and slimy and if this dump had a shower I'd take one, OK?"

"OK, OK!" Bazza threw up his hands. "Who can understand women, anyway?"

"Anyone with the proper motivation." Rachel pinched her lips in reproof. "Do you think we should report this to the police?"

Jo shook her head. "What's to report? I'm upset, but upsetting an actress isn't a crime. Let's just forget it."

After a few nights the memory faded. Rachel took care to get to the theatre early every day and throw away the dying flowers and whatever was with them. On the night of the full moon she asked Jo to sleep over at their place; Simon alerted the landlord of the Queen's Arms, who invited some of his more muscular regulars to look in on the theatre and make sure that the company left the theatre safely. These preparations were disguised from Jo, but she scanned the audience with particular care that night, wondering if any of the pale, work-weary folk crowded expectantly in the shabby auditorium was imagining himself as a reincarnated pharaoh. It seemed unlikely.

As the month's run approached its end a musical unexpectedly folded in the West End and the theatre owners suggested to Rachel that *Too Fast, Too Young* should transfer for a further six months. The next day, Jo's agent called her at midnight when she returned from the theatre.

"Have you signed your contract for the transfer yet?"

"No, why?" Her heart sank. She had been foolish to imagine that success could really be so easy.

"Charlotte Rampling just got sick and pulled out of a film with Julian Samuel. They want to know if you're free —what am I going to tell them?"

Jo caught her breath. Julian Samuel made exquisite, evocative, slow-moving films that were widely admired, not least by her. He was one of the directors she had hardly dared wish to work with some day.

She took a deep breath, feeling her back ache from two hours of thrusting out her breasts like Elizabeth Taylor. "That's a wonderful offer, of course, but I can't run out on Simon and Rachel now—they're like family."

"Six months in the West End for peanuts, six weeks on location in Morocco—they're offering top dollar, Jo. A director of Samuel's stature, this is what you need now, in my opinion. I don't have to tell you, with Samuel you could be talking Oscars. This is no time to get sentimental. You've done everything you need to do with *Too Fast*, you've got the notices, you'll get the awards. Time to move on."

"No. I couldn't possibly. I know they can't re-cast me without the show losing something. And they were the only people who believed in me when I was down and they need me now and I'm going to stick by them."

"You won't get this chance again, Jo."

"No, but there will be other chances, and better ones."

Her agent hung up, cursing her for an arrogant, stupid, sentimental, loser bitch.

At the theatre two days later, Rachel and Simon stood together over the *Daily Post*, in which Sean Murray had splashed a story headlined "Hollywood Brat Snubs Oscar-Winner Samuel." The accompanying picture of Jo, pouting over cleavage enhanced by Liz Taylor's push-up bra, was printed over two columns, in obedience to Murray's rule that the nation liked nothing better than a nice pair of tits to look at over its cornflakes.

"Is this right, Jo, did you really turn him down?" Simon's mild grey eyes were wide with respect.

"Uh-huh. I'm with you guys, aren't I?"

"But Samuel's one of the all-time greats. You love his films. You said that Chekhov thing he did was the most beautiful movie you'd ever seen."

Rachel suddenly showed the steel force of will which her myopic mannerisms and fragile, thrift-shop glamour normally belied. "We can't let you do this," she announced. "This is a big, big break, Jo. We all know you've been praying for something like this. I simply couldn't look at myself in the mirror in the morning if you turned it down because of us."

"Neither could I," added Simon. "You're a brilliant screen actress, Jo. You're great on stage, you're the best thing in this show for sure, but film is where you belong and you cannot pass this up."

There was an awkward silence. The office door crashed open and Bazza lurched in, half-filling the small room with his bulk. "Is she being a stupid cunt?" he demanded, giving Jo his most porcine glare.

"Yes," Rachel sighed and twisted a finger in her hair. "We've talked about this, Jo, and we're withdrawing your contract. You've *got* to go with Samuel. We'll find someone else."

"But you can't possibly recast in time?" Jo looked doubtfully from one stern face to another, feeling exhilarated and rejected at the same time.

"Nobody will play Liz the way you have, Jo, but don't you see that because you've made the role into a star vehicle every actress in town will be after it now?" Simon put his arm around her shoulders. "Now call your agent, get your typhoid shots and be like Webster's dictionary, Morocco-bound."

"That's such a silly song," Jo smiled foolishly at them all, trying not to cry, "I never saw any Webster's dictionary that really was Morocco-bound."

Rachel picked up the telephone and planted it in front of her. "Dial," she commanded.

Jo sniffed, wiped her nose on the sleeve of her sweatshirt and did as she was told. "You're the best friends in the world," she told them.

"Yeah, well don't think we care about you or anything," Bazza retorted at once.

The first three weeks on location with Julian Samuel in Tangier were everything Jo imagined they would be. He was a gentle, painstaking man who poured praise over her like buckets of warm honey. Her co-stars, a distinguished French actor and an English actress in her seventies, treated her initial nerves with generous respect. The crew quickly fell into an almost wordless harmony. Occasionally the producer, an elderly Polish-American who had backed several Samuel pictures before, visited the set and sat smiling benevolently in the shade of a large umbrella, watching the shooting.

The fourth week was spent in a deserted hotel, an oasis of luxury in open scrubland south of Casablanca, where they sat in the jacuzzi watching the moon rise behind the palm trees, feeling the hot night air on their damp shoulders. The Englishwoman told outrageous stories about Noël Coward, the Frenchman launched intense discussions on the function of the classical theatre in modern life, Julian recounted tall tales of the casino in Marrakesh and Jo found herself for once willing to talk about her mother.

The production manager was the first to lose his seraphic smile but then, as Samuel acknowledged with a helpless wave of his hands, the Moroccans were not reliable. Their next hotel, in a tiny town in the Atlas foothills, was a spartan establishment originally built as a French Foreign Legion fort. The lavatories were temperamental and the lamb stew smelled of goat.

One by one, the crew began to fall into ill-temper. The Englishwoman discovered from her hairdresser that the producer had not followed them south and wages had not been paid for two weeks.

The schedule required them to move on three days later, but no transport, no tickets and no instructions arrived. Samuel set off to drive to Casablanca, where the producer was supposed to have a temporary office, to investigate. He did not return. They passed a desultory day in blazing sunshine around the lukewarm tank of water sunk in the former parade ground which constituted the hotel's pool. In the evening half the crew were ill with diarrhoea and vomiting.

"Oh dear," the English actress said at last. "I thought Julian had stopped doing this kind of thing. He's a wonderful man, but hopeless with money. He gambles, too. I'm very much afraid he's run out on us and we're stranded."

The hotel manager had reached the same conclusion, and locked their luggage in his office. With great reluctance he allowed them to use the telephone. Jo's agent, in her controlled, bite-the-bullet voice, confirmed that not one dollar had been paid.

"How am I going to get home?"

"I'll wire you a ticket, dear."

"The nearest airport is Casablanca—that's seventy miles away. The hotel's holding all my luggage, I've got no cash at all . . ."

There was a deep sigh from the distant end of the line, as if Jo were being wilfully tiresome. "Don't you have an American Express card?"

"Yes, but I don't think they've heard of American Express here. They're a little backward, they want cash." Jo's sense of humour was strained. She had a permanent, violent pain in her abdomen.

"I'll see what I can do," was the weary reply. "I suppose there's no bank in this town?"

"One hotel, one café, one taxi and a market twice a week."

The next day the police arrived, quickly followed by the British, French and American consuls. There was a great deal of shouting in several languages, at the end of which the weary film-makers were transported, without their luggage, to Casablanca airport and escorted aboard a flight to London at gunpoint. Jo knew nothing of this. She travelled to Casablanca in an ambulance, semiconscious with a high fever, and was taken to hospital straight from the airport.

"I told you to get your typhoid shots," Bazza lectured, eating the grapes he had brought her himself.

"It isn't typhoid, it's some virus. How's the show doing?"

"Sold out to the end of the year." Simon had cast an older actress who had just left a long-running soap-opera as Liz Taylor. Jo tried not to feel jealous, but every newspaper in the hospital was carrying the woman's pictures and interviews. "But I don't look in, now. I can't stand hearing that raddled old tart saying your lines."

"I'm sure she's very good."

"Oh, come off it. You were terrific. She's only on three months' contract. Get well soon."

Recovering took Jo all of six months, and she was still thin and weak. She went home alone to her apartment and remembered the mood of careless optimism in which she had bought it; the large, high-ceilinged sitting room was on the first floor, at the same level as the leaves on the plane trees in the street outside. The plants in her window boxes were dead, and so was the huge weeping fig tree which used to separate the morning light into flickering curves in summer when a breeze blew through the long windows.

Rachel had contrived to rent the apartment to a visiting German academic, so Jo had money in the bank but the peculiar sense that her home was not quite her own. Rachel had also superintended the cleaning, and there were fresh daffodils in vases on the white marble mantelpiece and a fire laid ready for lighting in the ornate iron grate. Her favourite pastel kelim rug looked fresh and spotless. There was no dust in the corners of the stripped board floor, and upstairs the smell of fresh polish lingered over the French cherrywood bed. She sat down on it wearily, noting the ornaments out of place and the pictures not quite straight, the tiny traces of someone else's occupation. She shook out her lace pillows and rearranged them, suppressing the superstitious dread that she was destined to sleep in this bed alone forever.

She was trying to decide whether to treat this fit of the blues with some cautious shopping or a run in the park when Simon called to invite her to the final party for *Too Fast, Too Young.* "The houses are still packed, it could run for years, Rachel's been going demented trying to find another theatre, but no luck," he explained.

"So it's back to the Queen's Arms."

"Yes. But we're going to take a break first. Oh, and one other thing, Rachel and I decided to get married."

"That's wonderful, congratulations. I thought you didn't approve of bourgeois social institutions."

"Yeah, well, we're a bit older now. I mean, she's not pregnant or anything. We just decided we wanted to make a public commitment. It's going to be on Saturday on Parliament Hill, too cold for a picnic but we thought everyone could fly kites or something."

"What a beautiful idea." Jo felt restored to an unstable cheerfulness.

The blues returned when she woke alone in the silent apartment the next morning, and then the telephone rang. She heard the echo of a bad transatlantic line. When the voice was at last audible, she realised that Daniel had been holding his breath.

"I thought I'd call," his attempt to sound casual was a failure. "I've written something I want you to see."

"That's nice," she responded, guarded. "Do you mean it's something you want me to do?"

"Well, yes. Another film. The biggest thing I've ever done, actually. We've got the money. I wrote it for you, of course. I hope . . ."

"I'll read it," was all she could say. She did not want him to talk any more. She felt powerless. Her life seemed like a dark maze full of blind alleys. The only paths she could follow led in the wrong direction.

•   •   •

"WELL, IT MAY be Venice and it may be August and it may be hot and it may be stinking and there may not be any air in here, but this is a still lot easier than working on the ranch." Jerry Hall stood patiently while the hairdresser crimped the last six inches of her hair into Botticelli waves. "And there are so many shiny people out there. I counted Paloma and Mercedes and Loulou and Yves and C.Z. and Jacqueline and more Gettys and Mellons than I have ever seen in one room in my entire life, I swear."

"The Princess is just totally blissed-out—I think she's been having a multiple orgasm since 6 pm," murmured the make-up artist as he dusted Harley's shoulders with gold.

She chuckled wickedly. "Mellons for ecstasy, huh?"

"Too right!"

"What about my sister?" Stephanie scowled at herself in the pier glass, twitching the draped skirt of her first dress about her ankles. It was a flamboyant Krizia, impossible to wear and particularly unflattering to her square-shouldered, athletic shape.

"Oh yes, and Princess Louise and Prince Richard and Gloria Thurn und Taxis and Yasmin Aly Khan. Where the hell is Thurn und Taxis anyway?"

"Who cares? Hey, watch out, Corinna!" Harley swayed backwards to avoid a pot of strawberry yoghurt in her friend's careless hands. The International Red Cross Gala at the Palazzo Zenobio was the social event of the season, but behind the ruched silk screens which hid the entrance to the catwalk the models' changing room was as cramped, crowded and malodorous as tradition demanded.

"Sorry, darling! Here, I can't eat any more—anybody want some? It's fat-free."

"Sweetheart, nothing in life is fat-free," the parrot-house chatter of the room rose in an appreciative crescendo as Harley whisked the pot out of her hand, "but I'll finish it anyway, I'm starving." From the corner of her eye she saw Cherie scowling into her hand-mirror. Miss Integrity-immediate-image had been featured in every issue of Auriol's new magazine, but it had been pitifully obvious at rehearsals that she had never stepped on a runway before.

The hairdresser, spraying conditioner over Harley's curls, caught the direction of her thoughts. "Funny, Cherie doesn't look so right-on since they cut her dreadlocks for James Bond. You know she wanted me to give her extensions. Can you imagine! Extensions! Just a nightmare! And with these clothes."

"She's just a kid," Harley decided to be gracious.

"And she's put on so much weight! Everybody thought she was going to be such a sprauncy little mover and now she's just a joke. She should go find herself a tapeworm, and fast."

"Oh no!" Corinna objected. "Cruelty-free dieting, if you please."

"She's really got it in for you, though, hasn't she?" Nimble fingers coaxed Harley's hair into perfection. "Poison daggers in every look." "Toxic waste, darling. She'd be better off looking where she's going when she's out there—she just bumps into everyone, the choreographer's going demented."

"But she can't move," the girl lowered her voice to a confidential hiss, tweaking the last few disobedient curls. "I mean, I hate to bitch but she's black, isn't she? How come she can't do anything with her body?"

"She's just shy. This is her first big show."

"If she's shy then she's in the wrong business." The hairdresser moved on and the make-up artist sat down to paint Harley's eyes. The humid, reeking atmosphere of synthetic perfumes and cigarette smoke was making them water, and she decided to take out her contact lenses for a while, leaving them in their little blue plastic case on the ledge in front of the mirror.

"Close your eyes for me," the artist requested, wholly absorbed in the task of gilding her beauty. The feel of the small, soft cosmetic brushes on her eyelids was soothing. From the ballroom she could hear the string quartet and conversation, evanescent like the sun reflected off the little waves in the lagoon.

"Hold *absolutely* still now." She scented the artist's breath, sweet, with a trace of spearmint, as he tipped each eyelash with paint. Behind her, Jerry was telling a story about Mick and the Princess. A little drop of melancholy fell into her thoughts.

Every one of the models chosen for the Gala had her own place among the company of pre-eminent celebrities assembled in the ballroom: when the show was over they would trade the gowns they were showing for their own equally glamorous dresses and rejoin their escorts for the rest of the evening. Harley was with an Argentinian tennis champion whom she had met through her brothers. He was amusing, stupid and handsome. They had perfected a divine tango, but when the party was over she would have to face another night with him. He prized her as a possession in public, and in private took her frigidity as a personal insult; first there had been criticism, then fury, now he had rapid, perfunctory sex for his own satisfaction only, devoid of intimacy. She dreaded his touch, and dreaded moving on to another bed, another disappointed man, another cycle of sad conversations in the night.

"Can I borrow some of your hairspray?" It was Cherie's voice.

"Sure, it should be there on the counter," she waved a hand in the general direction of her make-up box without opening her eyes.

Again and again, Auriol's persuasive words came back to her. Maybe she *was* gay. She liked women's company, she enjoyed the fragrant, giggling, harem world of modelling, she admitted she felt excitement displaying herself out there on the runway. Maybe Auriol was right.

"There you are, all done," the artist pronounced. She opened her eyes and saw herself as a blur in the mirror. "Don't you like it?" he asked anxiously, noting the dullness of her response.

"It's divine," she reassured him, leaning closer until she came into focus. "Fabulous. I love it. Let me just put my eyes in and see it properly." She groped along the ledge for her contact lenses.

"OK, let's go, *avanti, avanti, rapido* . . ." the choreographer shouted over the room. "Everybody places, *numero uno*, ready please . . ." With squeals and curses, zippers were pulled, feet crushed into shoes, lips glossed and earrings clipped. The dressers were elbowed to the walls as the models took up their positions for the battle.

"My eyes! Anyone seen my eyes?" Harley patted the counter in front of the mirror, desperate to feel the little cylinder which contained her lenses.

"They were right here, honey," Jerry assured her.

"They're not there now," the hairdresser asserted, beginning to search the adjoining space, turning out cosmetic boxes and lifting dirty Kleenex. Slick chords of George Benson sounded from the ballroom.

"Silence! *Silenzio!*" the choreographer commanded,

beckoning the first two girls, Corinna and a blond American, to the entrance.

"I can't find my contact lenses!" Harley wailed in desperation.

"*Silenzio!*" The choreographer gestured violently. She felt Jerry take her hand.

"Just follow me, honey. Keep your eyes on my back and turn when I turn."

"I'll keep looking while you do the first number," the hairdresser patted her other hand.

Together the two women negotiated the stairs, holding their heavy skirts clear of their high-heeled shoes. Harley fumbled frantically into her long black gloves. George Benson gave way to Sister Sledge, which was their cue; Harley took a deep breath and followed Jerry Hall's cheetah-printed Hanae Mori back out into the dazzling glare of the lights.

She could see nothing for about four feet. The pink and grey ballroom, with its huge gilt-wood chandeliers and bas-relief of negro gueridons was beyond a mist. Because the runway had been built at head-height, the guests were a moving sea of indistinct shapes at her feet. The photographers, corralled by the upper stage, were invisible but she heard their camera shutters like hailstones on a tin roof.

"Jerry! Over here!"

"Harley! *Avanti!*"

"To me, to me!"

"Smile, darling!"

"*Bella, bella! Bellissima!*"

Jerry, a shimmer of paillettes, was in view ahead of her. The runway was only fifty yards long and as the music swept through her Harley relaxed and began to groove. Her dress was a tight black velvet Saint Laurent with a deep red silk flounce at the hem, hot and hell to dance in, exquisitely tailored but needing a lot of movement from the model to look interesting.

She reached the end on cue, twirled and dipped, extending her right arm with its muff of red feathers and holding the pose. There was applause.

"Hang in there, kid, you're doing great," Corinna encouraged in a whisper as she swept past in a long slither of iridescent Thierry Mugler silk.

Jerry's shape emerged from the blur of light and colour,

stalking towards her. They crossed at exactly the right place and Harley prepared to turn again at the opposite corner of the runway.

Suddenly she trod on air and heard screams all around her as she fell. Faces came into focus. Someone stepped forward to catch her but she slipped from his arms and hit the polished wood floor with a painful thump, her limbs bent awkwardly in all directions and her back twisted. She heard a noise like a gun being fired.

"Stand back," commanded a man's voice and she sensed the flurry of onlookers checked and space around her. Flashlights blinded her and she heard the click of shutters from every side. Her right leg felt burning hot. She tried to straighten it but it refused to move.

"Don't move, Martha, you've broken your leg." The man's voice was matter-of-fact, almost humorous. "Did you hear the noise? It snapped like a twig. Just lie still, there's a stretcher coming through for you."

Above her head, she heard the pulse of the music and the swish of skirts as the fashion show continued. The jabber of the crowd diminished, but the heat from her injured leg was becoming unbearable.

Harley knew nothing more until she regained consciousness in a modern hospital ward and found her leg imprisoned in an arrangement of steel splints and wires. The pain was excruciating, but the nursing nuns were quick to notice her recovery and bring her an analgesic which made her feel weak and dreamy.

An hour passed uncomfortably before visitors began to appear. First came the Princess, sincerely sympathetic, with an armful of carnations. The Argentinian brought roses and behaved as if she had contrived the entire accident expressly to embarrass him. Corinna came last with a selection of newspapers and a large box of chocolates.

"Well, if you're going to break a leg, kid, that was the way to do it. Do you realise who you fell on?"

"Who the hell was it? Do you know, he called me Martha? He must know me . . ."

"How's this for *flagrante delicto?*" The Australian held up an Italian newspaper with a front-page photograph of Harley, wide-eyed with dismay, apparently falling into the arms of Prince Richard.

"Oh, my God!"

"He was right underneath, you fell smack bang on top of him."

"Oh, God, how embarrassing! How awful!"

"I mean, I know women fall for little Richie every day, but not literally. Couldn't you have found a more discreet way of getting his attention?"

"Corinna, this really isn't funny. I feel such an absolute klutz. The whole world must have seen this by now. I think I'm going to die."

"Well, don't die before he pays you a state visit."

"What!" Automatically, her hands flew to her face and hair.

"He should be here any minute. Do you want me to fix your face up?" Businesslike as ever, she dipped into her purse for tissues and began to remove the remaining traces of gold eyeshadow from Harley's eyelids.

"The Princess wants to know if you'd mind just one photographer."

"Why didn't she ask me herself?"

"You know her style, she always gets someone else to do the dirty work. And it is in a good cause. And Princess Louise is spitting broken glass, she's so jealous. Here, I brought your own make-up, do you want to do it or shall I?"

"I can't, my right hand's bandaged. Why should Louise be jealous, for God's sake?"

"Because she's a nose-job, that one, and you know they get paranoid, and she's trying to get her hooks into Richard and marry into the Royal Family."

"That's just gossip."

"Nicky Brompton told me, and if he isn't the horse's mouth he's the horse's cousin at least."

"Horse's ass, more like." They giggled; Nicky had not been particularly gracious when he threw Corinna over for another model. "So is it OK about the photographer?"

"Oh, God. I can't say no, can I?"

"Uh-huh. Better give in gracefully." Corinna tenderly pressed powder into the finished maquillage, tidied the sheets and tucked them in, gave Harley a broad wink and made for the door at the end of the ward.

The doors re-opened a few moments later to admit a flock of white-coiffed nuns, Princess Marie-Agnès, Keith Cowley in white drill and a panama hat and four men in dark suits, of whom one was Prince Richard. As the party approached her bed Harley remembered their first introduction and felt her mouth begin to twitch with irrepressible amusement.

"We can't go on meeting like this," she smiled, holding out her uninjured left hand for him to shake. The Princess gave a visible shudder of horror at the breach of protocol.

To her surprise, he kissed her hand. "It's very good to see you again, Martha. How do you feel?"

"Awful. I'm so sorry, I . . ."

"Please don't apologise. I love it when old friends drop in."

There was a round of delighted laughter and Keith Cowley stepped forward, mumbling for permission to take his hard-negotiated exclusive picture.

They posed and then Richard heard himself ask the rest of the party to leave for a few moments. A clear corridor of escape from his emotional prison seemed to open up before him. Martha Harley, laughing and bright-eyed, looking absurdly prim in her hospital gown of coarse white cotton, had wiped out the intervening two years in a few unaffected sentences and his only objective was to obtain a pledge of her company before he left.

"Will you have to stay in traction long?" he asked, scanning the bouquets on the table beside her to see if he could read any significant signatures on the cards. The red roses looked ominous.

"At least a week. Maybe longer. They're trying to get the bones realigned. I twisted everything when I fell."

"But everyone else is going home now the Gala is over. Wouldn't you rather be in London with all your friends?" His mind, normally so agile in solving strategical problems, was stalling as he searched for an excuse to see her again.

"Oh yes, but they can't fly me back like this, I'd take up a whole row of seats. I'm insured, but I don't know if I'm covered for that."

"Will you let me see what I can do to help?"

She blinked at him foolishly, at last understanding through the screen of shock and drugs.

"How terribly kind of you, sir . . ."

"You'll have to do two things, though."

"I will? I mean, of course I will."

"Call me Richard and have dinner with me when I'm on

leave again. I'm afraid it won't be until the winter, some time."

"At least I'll be off crutches by then, I mean, I hope . . ." She reached out, looking for wood to touch, and tapped the back of an old chair at the bedside.

"Crutches or not, it's a deal, yes?"

"Oh, yes. I'll look forward to it." This is not real, this is not happening, she told herself even as her ears registered the exchange and her eyes told her that he was sitting casually on the end of the bed talking just as if he was—anybody. She felt again the dizzying sensation of fate hauling her upwards to a destiny so glorious she dared not even dream of it.

Half-an-hour later, when Prince Richard departed, Keith Cowley took some more pictures of him outside the hospital for luck, and noted the unmistakable expression of suppressed excitement on his face with amazement. Not that skinny spade chick, surely, he pondered as he headed for the telex office, torn between racist dismay and enthusiasm for a dynamite story.

Two days later the doctor agreed that Harley could travel, and she flew to England in a Royal Air Force plane from the Queen's Flight, with Corinna, and a thickset and highly amused army nurse in attendance. In a week her leg was set in a cumbersome plaster cast and she was allowed to return to her apartment, where a bouquet arrived every week with a card which read simply "Richard."

He considered severing his relationship with Louise by a letter, but in a fit of distaste and hostility decided to do nothing. He could live without her and he could certainly live without all the temptations she represented. He did not call her, and instructed his office that calls from her should not be accepted. In due course a letter from her arrived, several pages of violent scrawl reproaching him for his bad manners and hinting that she would take revenge, a tasteless, vicious communication which he read with perverse satisfaction before dropping it into the shredding machine with his own hands.

CHAPTER XXI

"WHATEVER IS THE matter with you, Vicky? You never used to be such an up and down sort of person." Patrick's chiselled lips twitched with annoyance as he tied his white tie. In the early days of their marriage Victoria had delighted in doing this for him, but now it seemed her fingers had lost the knack of getting the bow as perfect as her husband required.

"There's nothing the matter with me," she put the lid on her powder box with an emphatic tap. "Nothing that getting out of this hell-hole won't put right, anyway. I can't stand it being so disgustingly hot and sticky. It makes me feel ill."

"I thought you said they were coming to fix the air-conditioning today."

"Don't blame me for the Jamaicans, Pat. I thought they were coming today, but they didn't. It's always the same in this bloody place. They always smile and say no problem and then nothing gets done." She stood up from her dressing table in an angry swirl of floral chiffon, avoiding her reflection in the mirror. To her dismay, she had grown large much more quickly in her second pregnancy and now, at five months, her appearance horrified her. "I'll never understand why you couldn't have organised another job in Europe, you're always saying that's where the action is."

"You know this was an enormous step up for me, Vicky. If I'd turned it down, the FO would have wondered if I was really serious about my career at all. I don't enjoy Kingston any more than you do, but we'll just have to grin and bear it."

"Is it such a big promotion really?" A few days ago he

had casually disclosed the fact that Jamaica was to expect a visit from the Queen in a year's time. She immediately wondered if he had known that when he accepted this posting, and seen an opportunity to advance himself through her. Another such opportunity, because by now Victoria knew her husband.

"Yes, it is. It's within my abilities, I think, but I haven't got the right experience . . ."

"You've got the right wife, though, haven't you?"

There was an icy silence, then he turned, took her hands, and fixed her with his pale blue stare. "The right wife for me can only be the woman I love." The synthetic cinnamon tang of breath freshener emanated from his lips. He squeezed her fingers, as if the gesture would make her believe him.

Sometimes she thought his greatest gift was lying. Patrick's lies were so elegant, so precise, so perfectly engineered for their purpose that the sheer mastery of their creation intimidated her. "I'm sorry, Pat, I didn't mean it to sound the way it did."

He kissed her forehead. "Of course you didn't. Let's go, we'll be late."

As they reached the front door of their villa she paused, feeling again the sensation of the ground sinking beneath her feet like an old, soft mattress. She halted, fearful of falling, and was tempted to run back upstairs to the bathroom on the pretext of forgetting her lipstick and take a pill from the bottle she once again had banished to the back of the medicine cabinet. Just one will make me feel all right, she tempted herself; Pat's upset me, but I'd be letting myself down if I made a scene. It can't really hurt the baby. Sarah was fine, after all.

"Do come *on*, Vicky," Patrick called from the car door, and she collected herself and walked to join him. Consciously sedate, their driver negotiated the steep avenues of Cherry Gardens and cruised through Kingston's diplomatic district. Victoria eyed the garish streets with distaste. The new buildings in Kingston were ugly concrete slabs which managed to be massive and yet have an air of impermanence as if at any time a new régime might send in the bulldozers to sweep them all away. The British High Commission, set back behind forbidding grilles, was the most brutally hideous of them all, despite its smart white paint and the lion and unicorn supporting the gaudy coat-of-arms. The sprawl of low-rises reminded her of the utilitarian architecture of service buildings; subconsciously she expected to see a dockyard or a guard-post at each corner to justify the aesthetic offence.

They joined the queue of vehicles proceeding at a snail's pace across the scorched park around King's House, and eventually alighted between the royal palms at the grand entrance. More from habit than care, Patrick steadied her arm as they mounted the steep, red-carpeted steps.

On Commonwealth Day there was a traditional reception at the former colonial governor's residence. This was greeted with equally customary demands from the opposition that the Jamaican government should symbolically reject all connection with the planter-enslavers and use the occasion to affirm their country's freedom; but it took place just the same.

Patrick set off like a searching gun-dog as soon as they entered the reception room. She had for a long time believed that he needed to circulate at these events but now suspected simply that she bored and irritated him and he preferred to talk to his colleagues without the impediment of a wife at his side. She had been content to make her own way and find her own friends among the other diplomatic wives in the same situation, but lately she had been in a more fragile emotional state; she now kept an anxious eye on Patrick as he progressed through the crowd. At her height, it was easily done.

His habit was to make smiling duty calls on his immediate superiors, the American first secretary, and perhaps the Frenchman with whom he played tennis. Then he would join a blond woman with large gold ear-rings and a leathery suntan who invariably collected a noisy group around her; she was some kind of tourism consultant, and a fixture at most of the island's social gatherings. Her name was Susannah McLeod, and Victoria was sure Patrick was having an affair with her. She knew it from the excessive degree of patronising chivalry he used towards her, and the loud, barking laughter she saved for his witticisms.

Patrick returned to take his wife in to dinner. He was unflaggingly entertaining through the long, formal, mediocre meal, and listened with close attention to the ceremonial reading of the Queen's message, as though he had never heard before the suggestion that year by year, Commonwealth Day was a reminder that this unique family of nations stood for tolerance and co-operation, a distinctive element in the troubled world deprived of benevolent British influence. In fact, Victoria knew that Patrick himself had checked the text a few hours earlier.

He danced with her briefly, then once with the High Commissioner's wife, and then several times with Susannah McLeod. Victoria drifted into conversation with the wife of the Bolivian ambassador, a dynamic woman about ten years her senior who had elected to promote Jamaican artists and was always arranging gallery shows for them; her energy sometimes revived Victoria but now simply made her feel more tired. The soft-ground sensation was returning; she really should have taken a capsule.

"I don't think you've met my cousin . . ." A conspicuously well-dressed man with smooth brown hair and a taut, rectangular smile approached them. "Mrs Victoria Hamilton, may I present Ruben Santiago?"

For an instant she thought he was going to kiss her hand, but he merely took it with dry, cool fingers and bowed slightly. "Delighted to meet you."

The Bolivian woman fluently reinforced the introduction with information about them both, but Victoria half-heard her as if from far away. She felt nauseous and weak.

"Do you feel quite well?" The newcomer did not release her hand and implied with a drop in his voice and a movement towards her that he had noticed her pregnancy and was concerned.

"I think I'm too hot in here," she said.

"How thoughtless we are, keeping you talking and standing up. Is there somewhere outside we can sit down?"

"The verandah, out there . . ." Together the two of them escorted Victoria outside. Santiago was half-a-head shorter than her; she felt a nervous tremor in his hand as he guided her.

The rear of the building was on a smaller scale than the imposing façade and undecorated. It might have been the pavilion of any village cricket club in England, with a ragged lawn and parched rose beds arranged around a ridiculous stone bird-bath in the moonlit middle distance.

Ruben promised to find iced water and returned soon with a waiter carrying a tinkling pitcher and three glasses.

He extracted an ice cube from the water and rubbed it on Victoria's wrists, explaining, "I do this for my mother sometimes. She feels the heat very much." His accent was quite strong, but he spoke slowly and was not difficult to understand.

The cool water dripping from her wrists and this unexpected care from a stranger were soothing. He patted the skin dry with a handkerchief discreetly monogrammed in dark blue. She tried to say something about his kindness but the words jumbled awkwardly together.

"*There* you are, Vicky." It was Patrick, an odd note of alarm undisguised in his voice. Susannah McLeod was walking behind him, her stiletto heels sliding on the polished stone floor. "We saw you leave suddenly, are you all right?"

"Perfectly all right, Pat. Go back and enjoy yourself. It's just too hot for me in there. You know . . ." She introduced the two Bolivians and, after a few minutes of awkward small talk, Patrick and his partner returned to the ballroom for what they promised was one last dance.

Ruben watched them with particular attention. "Don't you think there is something that looks quite ill-bred in a woman with such very short legs?" he asked bluntly.

She recognised the social insecurity of a Third World aristocrat, but the bitchiness of the remark enchanted her.

"I don't know who she is exactly but I'm sure she can't help the length of her legs," she said with spurious magnanimity.

"But I thought you knew her?"

"My husband knows her." Ruben said nothing but his quick sidelong glance showed that he had picked up her implication immediately.

"In Bolivia a woman like that would not be invited to a reception like this."

"Ruben is the most dreadful snob," the ambassador's wife interjected, nervous of the turn their conversation had taken. "He talks about people as if they were horses. He is obsessed with breeding."

"I would deny that," he smiled, drawing tactfully back. "But our family is one of the oldest in Bolivia and we like to adhere to certain standards. There is such a thing as natural good breeding, of course, but that woman does not have it."

"What about me, have I got it?" Victoria judged his entire conversation to be grossly ill-bred, but the sheer crudeness of it delighted her.

"Most definitely. But I think your family is quite good. Certainly better than your husband's, am I right?"

She felt herself blush and wondered if he knew who she was. It seemed likely that he did not. She had noticed that most people who enjoyed high status in their own countries were usually so wrapped in their native social obsessions that they were oblivious to foreign gossip.

"How can you tell what kind of family I come from—by the length of my legs?"

"By everything about you." He tossed his head, unsmiling.

"I think you are embarrassing Victoria," the ambassador's wife patted his arm with affection but he withdrew it, offended.

"I just say what I think, that's all. For me, a woman should have some refinement about her."

"Refinement is rather wasted in a town like Kingston, isn't it?"

He laughed, showing all his blue-white, even teeth. "Can you really call it a town? I call it a hole. A revolting hole full of stinking, stupid people. The best thing that could happen is another hurricane should blow it all away. I'm only happy here for a few moments each morning when I wake up, before I remember that I'm in Kingston, and then I despair."

"Ruben!" the ambassador's wife hissed with horror.

"Don't you feel the same?" he said to Victoria. "You must hate this place."

"Well, it isn't very comfortable for me just at the moment."

"You should get out up into the mountains. Preferably of course one should get out of Jamaica altogether, but since we are stuck here we can make the best of it. Why don't you both come with me tomorrow—let me invite you for a picnic. That's what English people enjoy, isn't it?"

The ambassador's wife looked doubtfully at Victoria, who agreed at once. She went home with Patrick shortly afterwards in a soft good humour which she concealed in case he interpreted it as an invitation to have sex. This time the rich sensuality of the middle months of pregnancy was not something she wanted to share with Patrick. He was making love to her with punctilious frequency nowadays, either to demonstrate that he was not the kind of uncaring husband who spurned a pregnant wife or to convince her that he was not having an affair with Susannah. She now knew that nothing Patrick did was ever spontaneous.

She began the next day with coffee, a week-old copy of *The Times* and the post brought to her bedside by their maid. Harley's handwriting stood out among the routine printed envelopes; she opened the letter eagerly but read it with distaste. *I feel that I must tell you this myself for the sake of our friendship* . . . She saw Richard's name with a stab of shock and read the letter again with more application to be sure that she had not mistaken its meaning.

"How could he!" She almost shouted the words aloud, then squeezed her hand over her mouth to silence them. Painful enough to be so horribly, doubly betrayed without the world knowing it.

Later her fury gave way to a sense of emotional claustrophobia. An hour with a tactless stranger had shown her that she lived with others in a prison of their expectations. Although in her own interior world her love for Richard was a dry, faded memory, it was a public event which would define her life forever. She could do nothing, and even he himself would be powerless to move her out of his shadow.

It was stuffy inside the house and she went outside, but the bright sun reflected from their small swimming pool stabbed her eyes and the purple of the bougainvillea on the patio seemed to shimmer like a flame. Without her drugs, the beauty of Jamaica was becoming an unbearable glare of raucous colours.

Hopeless sorrow attacked suddenly and she sat down on the lounger on the terrace, waiting for tears. The telephone rang. Victoria took a deep breath, stood awkwardly upright and went to answer it.

"I thought Ruben was simply talking last night," the ambassador's wife sounded nervous and apologetic. "But he says he will be here to pick me up in a few minutes and we should be with you in half an hour."

"That's wonderful—so we're going on a picnic?" Her mood immediately changed to childish excitement.

"So it seems, if you really feel . . . I mean, I can always say you need to rest . . ."

"No, no, I'd love it, it's a lovely idea."

"Ruben is quite unpredictable. He isn't really my cousin, you know, his sister is married to one of my cousins so I just call him that . . ." Victoria understood that her friend was declining to sponsor any relationship the two of them might develop, and communicating grave misgivings about the man's character. She felt again the impulse which had almost made her give her virginity to Nicky Brompton, the urge to pay back evil destiny by a sin of her own. Well, she asked herself, why not? And anyway, what harm can come of this, a chaperoned picnic when I'm obviously pregnant? The man is just being kind.

They arrived in an embassy Mercedes and Santiago directed the driver up into the hills. The road was soon winding between jungle-covered peaks with the occasional orange accent of the flame-of-the-forest trees among the green. The car was spacious and cool, and the tinted windows reduced the glare of the sun comfortably.

High in the mountains he ordered the driver to stop, and led the two women into the unsuspected peace of an ancient arboretum, where rare trees stood in silent majesty by the banks of a clear, cold river.

"The English have a passion for gardens, don't they?" He slowly conducted them along a pebbled pathway to the water's edge. "Can't you just imagine, two hundred years ago, some crazy little English botanist giving his whole life to these trees?"

"And ever afterwards people making sure the park was cared-for, almost forgotten, right away up here on the mountain where nobody ever comes." Victoria looked up at the smooth grey trunks and the canopy of foliage high above them. Nothing moved in the gardens except the river and the small green dragonflies which hovered over it.

The driver brought the picnic in a basket and Victoria was amused to see that Santiago had taken the trouble to contrive cucumber sandwiches, a local smoked fish that was strong-tasting but almost as pleasant as salmon, and a tartan rug to spread on the clipped elephant-grass of the river bank. He was childishly anxious to do everything in what he saw as the correct English fashion, which she found soothing; most of Kingston society affected a crass pseudo-Americanism.

The next day he invited her for lunch to the home of

another South American, an immense modern villa in the hills with a refreshingly cool swimming pool. She discovered that Ruben spoke seven languages and had intended to become a lawyer, although why he had changed his mind and what exactly he did in Kingston was not clear. His thoughtfulness wrapped her up like a child's blanket. When she left for London the following week it was Ruben, not Patrick, who took her to the airport and, brushing officials aside, escorted her through such channels of privilege as the establishment possessed right to her seat on the plane.

In Britain she found herself again assaulted by gossip and newspaper reports, this time about Richard and Harley. "Did you know this was going on?" Pamela enquired in a glacial tone, implying that Victoria had had a responsibility to prevent this shocking liaison. She at once focused her anger.

"Of course I did and I think it's perfectly wonderful for them," she glared at family and friends, daring them to test her loyalty. "She's a super girl and I'm sure she'll be terribly good for him." Despite her brave words she steeled herself to share a strained lunch with Harley and then considered duty discharged.

After the months of uncomfortable waiting, the birth of her son was routine, and almost an anticlimax. Everyone seemed to have a first-class reason to be uninterested. Patrick found himself too busy to leave Jamaica. Alex was at Portsmouth, and managed a scant weekend's leave. Pamela pleaded commitments to the littles and visited once only. Two lavish bouquets arrived, the first from Suzie Chamfer in Los Angeles, the second from Harley. She left them both behind at the maternity hospital, feeling obscurely angry.

The baby was boisterous and noisy. After a week with her father in London, watching his determined patience as she and the nurse took turns to walk the screaming bundle up and down the narrow corridor leading to the nursery, Victoria decided to return to Jamaica at once.

She was about to announce the change of plan to the nurse when a key turned in the front door and her father reappeared, an odd lack of expression on his face.

"What happened, Daddy? Have you been to the office?"

"Yes. Yes, I was there for about half an hour."

He walked slowly towards the drawing room, pausing in the doorway and catching hold of the frame as if he were going to stumble.

"Whatever is it, Daddy? Are you all right?" She silently motioned the nurse to leave them and take her temporarily silent son with her.

"Yes, yes. I'm fine." He went on into the room and paused by the fireplace.

"Did you have an accident, or something?"

"It's your brother, Tory." He suddenly resumed his normal air of resolution and she followed him into the room as if drawn by a magnet.

"Alex?"

"I got a call as soon as I went in. He was with some people on the Isle of Wight for the weekend and apparently went windsurfing." He paused, looking up at her with a pleading expression, and she realised for the first time that with age her father had been losing his height.

"He said he'd taken it up . . ."

"He hasn't come back. This was yesterday. They're searching now, couldn't go out at night of course."

"You mean he might be . . . he might have . . ."

"They haven't found anything yet. Not the board, nothing."

"Oh, no . . . You mean . . . Poor Daddy, don't say any more." He opened his arms and she came awkwardly into his embrace. She had grown up with stories of the savagery of the sea, and knew that it was foolish to hope. "You're a sensible girl," he said, in effect telling her not to cry.

By noon there was no more information. They sat in the drawing room listening to the lunch-time news bulletins on the radio and hearing of Alex's disappearance. The word "missing" hit her like a muffled weapon but she felt very little. Her father began to weep in the afternoon, which made her feel acutely anxious although she did her best to express sympathy. In the evening Pamela arrived, officious and flustered as if the death of her stepson were an inconvenience rather than a tragedy.

Their doctor arrived the next morning and Victoria accepted with relief a new prescription for tranquillisers and sleeping pills.

After the inquiry and the funeral she saw the last letter

of condolence acknowledged, including, to her muted but comforted surprise, a black-edged card bearing an elegantly phrased expression of sympathy from Santiago. Her brother's possessions were committed to a trunk in the cellar of the great house, and his sword was hung on the wall of her father's study in London. At last, three weeks after the tragedy, she began to feel the pain of her loss. Her moods swung from brittle confidence to fearful panic. She doubled the doses of tranquillisers, craving peace from the chaotic jumble of events around her, and without a single conscious thought obtained another prescription from the doctor at Aston Langley.

She tried to choose a significant object to remember Alex by, but nothing spoke to her and in the end she packed four of his old rugby shirts with her luggage and returned to Kingston.

Patrick welcomed her, offered sympathy and admired his son with something she could not differentiate from genuine sincerity. The maid avoided her eyes; she found an empty Estée Lauder cosmetic bottle and some cotton wool pads stained with make-up in the garbage, several long blond hairs in the bedroom and bathroom and dozens of lipstick-stained cigarette butts in the tubs of oleander beside the pool.

Santiago waited four days before visiting. Politely, he dismissed the baby, and talked about her brother. Numb as she was, the feeling of freedom in his company returned, stronger than before. He questioned her about Alex with an awkward reserve which made her feel that he sensed the cataclysmic scale of her own emotions. He began to call for tea every day, at a tactfully chosen time when both children were usually asleep. He said he was thinking of renting a weekend house in the hills, and a few days of particularly oppressive weather provided the excuse for a drive to inspect it.

She found herself lying under him in a cool shuttered bedroom that projected from the steep hillside over the treetops, smiling and content, feeling his shaking hands on her legs, smelling his acrid sweat and sweet aftershave against the musty background of the mattress. He whispered "beautiful, beautiful" and made love to her with brashness which disguised a touching, almost childish, anxiety.

Patrick detected nothing, but the maid soon understood the change in Santiago's status in her affections. From sulky avoidance, her manner became boldly confidential, and Victoria dismissed her with a pleasing sense of having some control over her life at last.

•   •   •

"WHAT ABOUT THIS one?" Jo pulled a short red dress with gold buttons out from the untidy pile of clothes in the centre of Harley's sitting room.

"What, the Chanel? It makes me look like an air hostess." Harley held the dress against herself and looked at it in the mirror without enthusiasm.

"*Nothing* could make you look like an air hostess. It's a great colour." Jo suppressed her irritation and wished she could find a way to get Harley to relax. They had been trying to choose a dress for this occasion for half an hour already, and Harley was in such a stew of confusion that the longer they talked and the more garments they tried, the further they seemed to be from a decision.

"No. Chanel was never my cup of cocoa, you know." They started to giggle and Jo pulled another dress off the pile. It was a dark-blue bandage-like Azzedine Alaia.

"Oh, God, no, it makes me look like an alien after a body transplant."

"Where did you get all these things anyway?"

"I'm only borrowing them. They just pulled them off the rail at the studios when I said I hadn't got a thing to wear."

"Did you tell them who you were going to dinner with?"

"No, of course not. Well, not exactly. I just sort of implied it was a heavy date, you know." Her beautiful mouth twitched with excitement; sitting cross-legged on the floor in her underwear, Harley looked like a giant brown grasshopper.

"Well, try this then." Jo pulled a black silk sheath from the pile and threw it casually in Harley's direction. She pulled it over her head and scrambled upright.

"Oh God, it's awful."

Jo had to agree. "You look like a schoolteacher."

"Or a missionary. Or a born-again Christian doorstep evangelist or something." She quickly slithered out of the offending garment and looked at the designer's label with distaste. "Born-again Christian Dior, yuk. God, I'm s-o-o-o nervous, Jo. I can't get my head around this at all. I can't believe it's happening. Prince Richard is coming to take me out to dinner. Why? Why me?"

"Why not you? He's been sending you flowers for six months, and calling you up every week."

"I don't know—it just seems so strange, first Victoria, now me. What was it about that house in Cambridge?"

And me, Jo added silently. Out loud she argued, "It isn't so strange if you analyse it. Whatever brought the three of us together must also be what attracts him."

"But I'm not his type."

"Aren't you putting the guy down, here? How do you know he has a type?" Jo considered what she knew of Richard, which seemed like nothing and everything at the same time. "Look Harley, the one thing you can be sure of is that no dress in that pile can make you look like an English rose, and that's exactly why he's interested in you. I mean, he likes you, you like him, you communicate really well but the bottom line is that you like him because he is who he is and he likes you because you're . . . different. Isn't it?"

Harley sat down again on the floor, suddenly calm. "Yes. That's exactly what's going on. Do you think maybe I shouldn't do this?"

Jo smiled, pleased that she had managed to crack the tension. "What *you* think is what's important, isn't it?"

Harley nodded doubtfully. "But I don't know what I think. I *can't* think. My whole life is so insane and this is just the next crazy thing. Maybe next year they'll want me for the Space Shuttle programme, it wouldn't seem any more crazy than this. I'm just zapped."

"He's just a guy," Jo said gently.

They pondered this thunderous understatement for a minute in silence and then began to laugh. They laughed until they were breathless and Jo's pale face was almost red. Quite what was so funny, neither of them could understand.

"If different is what I have to be, then that's easy, I know how to do that," Harley said at last, reaching for a tissue to wipe away the tears of mirth from her eyes. She went up to her bedroom and brought out a Lagerfeld dress from the year before, tailored black silk with a deep white cuff across the shoulders. It was a severely classic design which she knew accentuated her personal exoticism. Plus, of course, the plain pearl and diamond ear-rings, which looked positively witty against the brown shadows of her ears.

"Perfect," Jo agreed when she came down for approval. "Now, my dear, you *shall* go to the ball."

They hugged at the door and parted. Harley sat down to do her make-up and Jo drove back to her apartment. She had a dinner invitation from Bazza, and intended to go out, but time dragged and she could not find the right mood to be sociable. She was restless and apathetic simultaneously, resisting a melancholy inner voice which demanded an explanation for her frozen heart. For months now she had been Harley's confidante, and yes, her friend needed someone she could trust now, but Jo accused herself with bitterness of trying to love Richard vicariously and cheating everyone all round.

The Prince drove himself through the icy March rain, wanting every possible token of command to give him confidence. He had been in Belfast for three months and although the peculiar adrenalin of that tragic city still ran in his veins he felt close to mental exhaustion.

It was difficult to step directly from one artificial world to another, and even harder to leave his protected social reserve for the dangerous unknown beyond its boundaries. The long frustrating months of separation now made Harley seem like an impossible conquest. She must, he thought as he crossed the Thames by Chelsea Bridge, be used to men who were smarter, wittier, and certainly taller, than he, men with more time to court her, able to offer her participation in their useful lives, promising untroubled, committed relationships, not the public ordeal which was all his company implied. She had only agreed to have dinner with him out of good manners. In his mind's ear he already heard her explaining that she was flattered by his attention but in love with somebody else.

"Who shall I say, sir?" the porter barely looked up from his desk. He seemed obviously accustomed to announcing her suitors.

"Richard," he said, his voice cracking with nerves.

"Richard . . ." the man at last looked up, about to demand a surname, and recognised him at once. "Oh yes, yes of course, sir, do forgive me. Let me show you the way, sir."

A few minutes later the white lacquered door of her apartment opened. He looked up into her huge brown eyes and could think of nothing to say. For an instant they stood still in mutual panic and then Harley laughed, a low, rich, warm flow of noise which soothed his nerves, and held out her hands to him.

"Well—how nice to meet you after all this time."

They went to a small, new restaurant in Kensington which he favoured for its style and discretion. The tables were well-distanced and the lighting soft. If any of the other diners noticed them they were too polite to indicate it. Detective Henshaw, awarded the customary small table by the kitchen door, ordered the venison steak and found it excellent.

Harley saw at once how tense Richard was and set out to entertain, telling bright stories about the Red Cross Gala, the nuns in the hospital, the trials of modelling with her fractured leg in a plaster cast and the commercial she had done for which she had to be shot from the waist up. He listened and laughed, regretting that all he could call to mind himself were scraps of savage Royal Marine humour which did not even seem funny in the elegant make-believe world she created around them.

"You know all about my family," he said at last, searching for a way to get closer to her. "But I don't know anything about yours—tell me."

She did so, again embroidering a scintillating tapestry round the figures of her grandmother and mother, her stepfather and her brothers. The tight line of his brows began to slacken and she saw warmth in his eyes, the unmistakable burn of desire. He began to tell her how beautiful she was. How right Jo had been; he was just a guy. She could tease him into bed the way Kelly had done with her. The voice of self-preservation told her to beware, but she ignored it. She was flying now, ready for adventure.

Perverse daring took hold of Richard also. He felt like a stick in the stream of her laughter, swept gratefully along on careless eddies which washed away the hours, the distance back to her apartment, the awkwardness and the fear of fear. Louise and her depravities became an irretrievable memory. She undressed him with fingers as skilled as a mother's with buttons and knots, shed her own clothes and rolled into his arms, warm and supple, her lips soft on his skin.

Something like danger goaded their senses. His hands caressed her, held her, crushed her to him despite her sharp bones and he poured incoherent endearments into her ears between kisses. For a few moments she thought that a feeling she had not experienced before was rising in her body, but as soon as she acknowledged it, the shy sensation reached a plateau and swelled no further.

A moment later he cried out as if hurt and it was over. Harley wrapped him in her arms and decided that if the Big O was not going to happen with Richard, nobody was going to know about it except herself. She'd seen people fake orgasms in the movies. No way was this precious affair going to be soured by her insignificant little female failure.

By unspoken agreement, they flaunted their relationship as publicly as they could. Richard derived acute enjoyment from the storm of publicity which broke around their ears, the pack of paparazzi who attended them and the sanctimonious newspaper editorials trumpeting a further step towards the new, multi-cultural Britain. The shock which underlay the attention was quite apparent to him, and highly pleasing. Nothing else he had done in his life had struck back so effectively against the forces which limited his life. They had wanted him to conform, and now he could defy them and defeat them with their own hypocrisy. He also felt absurdly proud to be photographed with a dazzling woman half a head taller than he was, who could plainly have had her pick of the world's most exciting men.

Through Harley, he could also test his family's moral strength. He brought her to Windsor for lunch and watched with satisfaction as his parents employed excessive politeness to mask what he saw as unease. Harley's own tension increased her appetite, and his mother could not disguise her fascination as she consumed a large portion of rich caramel dessert.

"However do you manage to keep your figure?" she enquired with audible respect.

"I'm very lucky, Ma'am," Harley responded at once, feeling on familiar ground. "I don't have to think about it. My figure keeps me instead."

Everyone laughed, his mother most of all. Afterwards

she announced her approval. "What a very jolly girl, Richard. I do hope we'll see her again."

Summer began, and he joyfully paraded Harley at Ascot in a very simple hat with an undulating brim of semi-transparent pale yellow voile which delighted the photographers. After Ascot came Wimbledon and as she sat beside him in the royal box and watched her brother, the forty-ninth seed, defeated honourably by Jimmy Connors, Harley told him with total sincerity that she had never been so happy in her life.

"Nor have I," he answered at once when she told him again that night. "You've made me feel like a new person, Harley. When I'm with you there seems to be some point to my life. You won't ever leave me, will you?"

"What kind of thing to ask is that?" she countered, suddenly formal and serious for all she was naked and wrapped in a corner of her quilt. "You're the one that leaves—you leave me all the time. Your job, your family . . . I know you have to do it, but you can't talk to me about leaving when you're never here and when you are here you have to go home before breakfast."

To her surprise he looked hurt. She folded him in her arms at once. "Darling, I'm so sorry. I never meant to upset you."

"I know. I suppose I feel it too. I hate having to leave you."

"You don't hate the Marines." It was almost a question. She had picked up on his ambivalence and he was ready to talk.

"No," he said with caution, probing his feelings. "Once I'm back I just become part of the machine, I can forget what's really on my mind. But being with you makes me see things differently. I keep thinking about the future and wondering what the hell I'm going to do. I can't stay in the Royal forever—there's a whole side of me that is just submerged in that life."

"Well," she said in a reasonable tone, "what do you want to do?"

"Anything that's worth doing. You know, I used to wish I'd been the son of an unemployed miner, so at least I'd have somewhere to go in life."

He had tried for so long to hide his tenderness that he felt ashamed at times like this when she pulled out of him feelings he wished he did not have. Because their time together was fragmented, they threw themselves into intimacy with a driven urgency that moved their relationship on in vertiginous leaps.

Such physical passion as they achieved at the start cooled to the level of a comfortable companionship. Her muted responses did not disappoint him; she made him feel clean again after Louise's corrupting excesses. He was so unworldly, and at times so childish, that she felt strong and maternal with him and began to treat him almost as another brother. They passed many nights simply talking, teasing and testing each other in exhilarating mental play-fights which were a delight to him and a relief to her.

He was the only man she had ever encountered who seemed to appreciate her innate chastity, and if this was good for her soul it was bad for business. Work seemed less and less exciting. Her old magic rapport with the camera seemed like a cheap trick and she was bored with performing it.

Her bookings soared, but had to be carefully scrutinised because the agency received many enquiries which were obviously phoney. At the Pret, no less than four designers coyly announced that she was to wear the wedding dress, the traditional conclusion of the show. The pictures were on the front page of every newspaper in the world, she was called the Queen of Paris and the prospect of her marrying into the British Royal Family was discussed in acres of newsprint. Richard was amused. Harley was annoyed.

The rest of the country did not wholly share their enchantment with each other. At the Palace letters arrived demanding how Her Majesty could contemplate the pollution of the royal house with the blood of an inferior race. "How would His Royal Highness feel if he woke up one morning and found a coffee-coloured imp sitting on his pillow?" demanded the most memorable hate letter, written in shaky capitals on cheap blue paper from an address in London's southern suburbs. At first these letters were thrown away. When their volume swelled significantly, the two Private Secretaries tactfully apprised Richard and his mother of their existence, and were brusquely ordered to continue destroying them.

Almost every morning the porter at Harley's home did the same service for her, consigning to the dustbin envelopes which, from their aroma, contained banana skins or dog shit, or from their contours enclosed six-inch nails. The razor blades had a convenient propensity for cutting through their packets anyway.

He caught two skinheads daubing National Front slogans and swastikas on the front of the building, but missed Sean Murray and an acquaintance, disguised in the overalls of the window-cleaning company, who succeeded in drilling a hole in the wall of Harley's bedroom and inserting a radio transmitter. With nothing to obstruct the signals in the clear space of the river embankment, the reception in the van parked on the carriageway through Battersea Park was perfect, although their content disappointed Murray intensely.

One icy night in April, Richard telephoned Harley at midnight. "Thank heavens you're there. Listen, I can't explain on the phone, can I come and see you?"

"Of course. I'll be waiting—aren't I always?" He had spoken so abruptly that he sounded for a moment almost like his father. "Where are you now?"

"I'm on my way."

An hour later the porter sleepily announced him. He was in uniform and as she looked him up and down in surprise he told her, "I shouldn't be here but I had to see you. They're sending us to sea, Harley. I'm going to be away a long time."

"So what else is new?" She eyed him with gentleness, wondering if she ought to ask. His whole manner told her that he was involved in something of great consequence.

"The whole regiment's being sent to the South Atlantic. We're sailing in a couple of days."

"Is it this business with the Argentinians and the Falkland Islands?"

"Yes. The Argentinians are invading. The cabinet are going to be asked to endorse a combined forces task force today. It's going to be the biggest show since Suez, if not bigger." He put his arm around her. For once, she was unable to think of anything to say. This was not the right time for the gay, teasing style of her normal conversation with him. She felt disoriented. She had not been prepared for this occasion; only tearful wives in black-and-white films saw the men they loved go off to war.

"Surely it will all be over in a few weeks? They'll negotiate . . ." She knew as she spoke that it could not be possible.

"Can I stay for an hour?" he asked, holding her close.

CHAPTER XXII

"HE WAS UP THERE with that jungle bunny for four hours last night, he's going off to get killed, and all they did was talk." Murray tossed the transcripts across his desk with disgust. "You'd think he'd forgotten what it's for."

"Maybe it got frozen off up some bloody glacier." Keith Cowley shook his head to dispel his hangover. "He must be going soft—she's gotta have a great sense of rhythm, know what I mean? I thought you reckoned they'd be getting married?"

"Don't I wish? Now there's a story for you. Queen's son weds six-foot coon, Royal Family in the Brown Windsor soup, questions in Parliament, riots in Tunbridge Wells, the nation mourns . . ." Murray took his feet in their handmade brogues off his desk and looked at the night's haul of photographs. "For Chrissake, Keith, we can't use these. What were you shooting on, porridge?"

The images of Richard and Harley leaving Langan's the week before with a party of friends were blurred, as if taken in a thick fog.

"I thought I'd try a different film," the photographer explained in a weary tone. "She's as black as the ace of spades and half the time she just fades into the background. If I can't get her against a white wall or something you can hardly see her."

"Any normal man would have that up against a wall as soon as look at it—I wonder what's going on with old Rich the bitch and the skinny spade. Jim Kelly's offering us some nude shots of her but they're too porny for a family newspaper." He pulled the transcripts back and looked through them again. "They're on about Plato, should Gibraltar go back to the Spanish and will she get him some Scott Crolla brocade braces—the vanity of the man! A fine romance, I don't think."

"I reckon your operator fell asleep on the job." Cowley packed up his cameras and prepared to leave. "I know old Rich—he'd shag anything with a pulse. Whoever listened to the tapes missed the action, that's all. You want to get some professionals down there. OK, folks, see you in a couple of days."

"I was really sorry to hear about your father," Sandy looked at him from behind her old Remington with earnest sympathy. Cowley had asked for a few days off to attend his parent's funeral.

"Good riddance if you ask me—silly old sod."

"You don't mean that really." Her grey skin looked even duller and her eyes were too close together, he thought.

"Yes I do. Went soft in the head when he retired. Fancy playing with guns at his age, serve him right, should've known better."

He winked at Sandy as he left the room and strolled through the *Daily Post*'s open-plan office, sparsely populated at ten in the morning. Anxious to keep his clothes clean, he avoided the heaps of smudgy proofs and the congealed plates of fish-and-chips left over from the previous night and stepped daintily around the overflowing waste bins and the pots of mouse-poison placed at every corner. Cowley now fancied himself as an impeccable dresser. He shopped at Burberry, Mulberry and Turnbull and Asser, favouring the casual English sporting look, tweeds, corduroy and handmade punched brogues. He carried his cameras in a reproduction leather fishing bag. If he sank to jeans they were Lauren; he liked the little polo player monogram. Cowley had learned to ride, went out with a notoriously nouveau-riche Hertfordshire hunt when he had the leisure and planned to take up polo as soon as he renegotiated his contract with the *Daily Post*. Anything to get away from his wife.

He drove north alone to his father's funeral, screwing up his eyes against the fluorescent yellow flowers of rape that now stretched away to the foreshortened horizons around the farm. The landscape had changed since he had left. The tumbledown barns crammed with baled hay were gone, and in their place were new, metal-roofed shelters stacked with silage in black plastic and straw, mechanically wound in giant lavatory rolls.

The fields were deserted. The solitary figures of his parents' neighbours, walking slowly over their land, pulling each foot from the mud in turn, were gone.

He wanted to see a scarecrow, a familiar amusement since his childhood, presiding drunkenly over the fields of winter wheat, but there was none. In the far distance a machine droned, scooping beets from the thick earth. The Cowley holding stood out as an unprofitable patch of mud in the mechanised prosperity all around.

In the kitchen he found his mother with two of her sisters, three elderly women with bowed backs who moved stiffly around the table as they set it with plates and cutlery.

"You've come," his mother said without looking at him. Keith's attendance at family gatherings had been erratic since he left for London.

"Are you expecting a lot of people?" he asked, wrinkling his nose at the smell of pilchards which an aunt was decanting from their tin.

"Just your relations." His mother's tone was accusing.

There was a tap at the front door, so hesitant that for a moment he thought he had imagined it.

"That'll be somebody now, I expect." She pointed towards the door. "You can answer it, you're the head of the household now." He went with reluctance, reflecting that his new title was no particular cause for pride. The farm had been mortgaged heavily and was deep in debt.

At the high doorstep stood a thin, middle-aged man in a grey suit and a young man with a thatch of blond hair, and muscular arms revealed by rolled shirtsleeves and blue Barbour jerkin.

"If it's convenient," the older man began ingratiatingly, "this is Mr. Stone from Brompton Agricultural and he'd like to take a look around."

Cowley looked at them without understanding. The blond man shook his head.

"Brompton Agricultural are negotiating with the bank to buy your father's farm," he explained with the instinctive tact of a decent man, which Keith at once resented. "We're a division of Brompton Holdings and we are the major landowners in this area. From our viewpoint, there is a natural logic to the acquisition of this property, if we can agree on a price."

Mrs. Cowley ventured from the kitchen, wiping her hands on a cloth. She broke into a feeble smile. "Oh, it's you again, Mr. Stone. I thought it must be the man from the insurance. Take a look around, yes, do. I'm afraid we can't entertain you, it is the funeral today you see . . ."

"Of course. I do understand, Mrs. Cowley. Don't bother about us, we'll try to keep out of your way." The two men set off for the fields. Pausing at his Range-Rover, the man from Brompton Agricultural produced a lap-top computer which he held comfortably in the crook of his arm, tapping in calculations as he walked.

"Nice young man," his mother commented as she shut the door. "He told me he could make this whole farm into a 200-acre field and a storage facility. Of course, farming's a business nowadays. His firm spent more on fertiliser last year than your father earned in a lifetime."

Cowley decided to say nothing about the family's finances. His mother suddenly plucked at his sleeve and straightened up her bent back as if to whisper in his ear.

"The insurance are being difficult, Keith." He was alarmed at her conspiratorial tone. "They'll be coming soon to talk to me and I don't know what I've to tell them." The lines in her face ran grotesquely into each other and she folded her arms as if to hold in her distress.

"Why, what's up?"

"They're saying it wasn't an accident. They're saying your father . . ." Articulating the words was beyond her. "And they're refusing to pay. We'll be bankrupt. The bank's taken the farm as it is, there's nothing left, not a penny. I don't know what I shall do, I don't."

"Don't worry, Mum, it'll sort itself out." He put an arm awkwardly around her shoulders, feeling guilt that for all he earned good money in London he spent it as fast as he made it and had nothing to spare for her. He despised his mother, but did not like to think of her living out her last days as a lonely inmate of an old people's home.

She sniffed resolutely. "Yes, I expect it will. Look on the bright side, that's all we can do. The vicar's been very good. He was agreeable to bury your father although I know he does prefer cremations, but he said your Dad had spent half his life in the churchyard and deserved a place in it now he's gone. That's important. Consecrated ground, you see. They don't bury you in consecrated ground if your death wasn't natural."

Back in the kitchen she moved to a drawer that was rarely opened and took out a black case. It contained twenty-four silver-plated fish knives which had never been used. She looked proudly at them lying side-by-side on their synthetic satin pillow and began setting them out.

"Do we have to use these?" Cowley picked up one of the ornate implements with disapproval.

"They were our wedding present from my aunt Doris. I've been keeping them for a special occasion."

"People don't use fish knives any more."

"Don't talk such nonsense, Keith. The Queen uses fish knives at Buckingham Palace, I read it only last week."

"Fish knives are common."

"Nothing's ever good enough for you, is it, young man? Your own family aren't good enough for you, are they?" She was slamming down the knives angrily as she spoke. "You think we're nothing, don't you? Rubbish, that's what you think we are. Well we may not be grand like the folk you know in London, but we count for something all the same. You should have listened to your father. He had it right. We're yeoman stock, he used to say. The backbone of England. Yeoman stock. That's something to be proud of, Keith."

Six hours later Cowley was back on the road. Once Cambridge was behind him he pulled into a country house hotel and ordered a bottle of champagne and some smoked salmon. He warmed himself by the open fire in the bar and let luxury blot out the memory of his origins.

• • •

SPENCER DROVE HIS sister's little white Mercedes through the drab streets of London's western outskirts without enthusiasm, reflecting on the sin of taking a performance car through a suburban high street in the afternoon. The ugly grey thoroughfare was choked with jaywalking shoppers, red buses and mothers driving children from their schools. High-rise apartment blocks rose in the grey sky, the wind sweeping garbage in eddies around the shopping precincts at their feet. This was the twins' first taste of a British winter and they were not enjoying it.

"Pull over, Spence, I want to get some cigarettes." Sheldon tossed an empty packet out of his window.

"You smoke too much."

"You're right. But I can't see this tennis centre around here and maybe we can ask in the shop where it is."

Seeing the logic of this, Spencer nodded and began to scan the mean, single-storey shops which huddled at the roadside. Eventually he noticed a newsagent which advertised cigarettes on the far side of the road. There was a temporary break in the oncoming traffic, and he casually swung the car across the carriageway and parked it with two wheels on the pavement.

"I'll go," he announced, getting out of the car. "What do you want, twenty?"

"Uh-huh. Benson & Hedges."

"Just because it's their tournament doesn't mean you have to smoke their brand."

"Wrong. I will not be the one pulling out a packet of Marlboros when the sponsors come around to press the flesh. They don't have Kents in England. Not in a place like this, anyway. Now get into that shop and find out where in hell we are."

He lounged back in the corner of his seat and watched his brother's long legs in their green sweatpants eat up the width of the pavement in three strides.

A tapping noise sounded by his ear and he turned angrily around, expecting to find some boys wanting Spencer's autograph. He had a following of British black kids, small but devoted, going-on obsessed.

A helmeted policeman's head filled the window frame. Without the ignition key, Sheldon could not activate the electric windows, so there was nothing for it but to get out of the car, stepping cautiously into the traffic and walking round to the pavement.

"Is this your car?" The officer glanced meaningfully at his companion, who muttered into his lapel radio before climbing out of their police car which was drawn up behind the Mercedes.

"No, this is my sister's car."

"Your *sister*'s car?"

"That's right, my sister's car." The words "something wrong with that?" begged to be added, but Sheldon was always cautious with authority.

"And—er—the property in the back, is that your sister's too?" He bent down to look inside the low body of the vehicle and indicated the haphazard pile of bags, racquets and sports clothes behind the front seats.

"They are mostly my brother's things."

"Your *brother*? Your brother plays a lot of tennis, I suppose." His voice was blunt with sarcasm. A second white police car drew up behind the first, and two more officers joined the group.

"That's right. My brother is a professional tennis player. He is here for the Benson & Hedges tournament, we're on our way to the David Lloyd Tennis Centre and . . ."

"Has your sister had this car long?"

"I'm afraid I don't know."

"*You don't know?* But you're driving it, aren't you?"

"She just lends it to us while we're staying with her. We don't live in this country, we came in yesterday from playing a tournament in Trinidad, only here for the Benson . . ." He told himself to shut up, aware that he was talking too much because he was nervous.

"Do you always park on the pavement where you come from?"

"I'm sorry about that . . ."

"Can I have your driving documents?"

"No, I don't have anything like that with me. My brother was driving . . ." Where the hell was Spencer anyway? It was taking a long time to buy those cigarettes.

"You don't mind if we check, do you?" The second policeman opened the car door and tried to release the lock on the glove compartment, but failed. "No keys," he announced.

"Can we have the keys?"

"My brother's got them."

"Your brother again, eh? All right, turn around and put your hands on the car."

Sheldon looked from one man to another in disbelief, then found himself seized bodily, turned around and held down against the car roof. Booted feet kicked his legs apart and hands began roaming his body, patting pockets and turning out their contents.

"*Hey, what you doing with my brother? Get your hands off my brother!*"

"Get him, lads!" Sheldon heard urgent, scuffling feet

and swearing. He was hit in the face and felt blood in his mouth, then a kick which burned like fire took his legs from under him. Instinctively he curled into a ball, his hands over his head. Some children were screaming. Blows exploded across his back and around his neck; one arm was dragged away and a boot crushed his neck. From the corner of one eye, through a veil of blood, he saw Spencer's limbs flailing on the ground, more blood smeared across the dirty paving stones, and the feet of onlookers.

An instant later rough hands lifted him and dragged him down the street. He heard himself scream as the undamaged side of his face scraped the roof of a car as he was pushed inside it.

He tried to speak, feeling as if his teeth were halfway down his throat and his mouth disconnected from his nervous system. The car drove off, its siren wailing.

"What's happening, where are you taking me?" he managed to say at last.

"Shut up, you fucking nig-nog." This time a fist landed squarely in his eye and the world vanished in a dark red mist.

More than twenty-four hours later Harley returned to her apartment and found four hesitant, whining messages on her answering machine from a man who said he was a lawyer who had been appointed to defend two men who claimed to be her brothers. It was already the evening. The last message included a home telephone number, which she dialled with a smothering feeling of apprehension. The man grew less apologetic as she questioned him.

"They were brought before the magistrates this morning on charges of assaulting a police officer, possessing cannabis with intent to supply others and theft of a motor vehicle," he confirmed.

"They were *what*?"

Professionally neutral, the man continued his recitation of events. "Bail was refused. It would in any case have been several thousand pounds . . ."

"I think I could have found that without too much difficulty." She was unaccustomed to people who assumed that she must be penniless.

"In any case, your brothers have been remanded and they're at Wormwood Scrubs prison."

"Can we get over there at once—I must see them."

"I'm afraid it won't be as easy as all that, Miss . . ."

"My name is Martha Harley," she reminded him in a cold voice.

"Yes, quite. You will have to make an application. In the meantime I should warn you that they did not seem to me to be in terribly good shape."

"What do you mean?" A deep chill took hold of her guts.

"They apparently resisted arrest and had to be restrained by force."

"I bet they did, I bet they did." She searched her memory for the details of court procedure, learned, it seemed, in another lifetime. "Please excuse me, Mr—er—, I'm going to see if I can get some advice on this. Let me call you at your office tomorrow."

She slowly replaced the receiver and began to take off her coat, moving through the apartment like a sleepwalker. She arranged the facts analytically and examined them. Her brothers had been the victims of a racial attack. Such things happened in London every day; the police were worse than the people. She knew this, but had never related the knowledge to herself until now.

She thought of Richard, and thanked God he was thousands of miles away at sea, where the storm she was about to create could not touch him. Her anger was so vast she felt as if she could destroy him with it, like a hurricane indiscriminately razing everything in its path.

The first priority was to get help, and that meant a lawyer, the best. She ran to her bedroom for her old telephone book and found a London number for Neville Green. When she had last heard from him he had joined a firm famous for its liberal alignment. To her joy he answered her call at once, obviously interrupted in the middle of a dinner party but delighted to join the fight on her side. He took the court lawyer's number and promised to speak to her early in the morning.

There was nothing now to be done until daylight, but she could not sleep. Inside her head a dam began to burst. Cracks sprang in the great wall of frivolity which she had constructed, year by year, to insulate herself from what was all around. Then the truth spurted out in ugly waterfalls and made a lake of hatred.

Neville Green, grown plumper and blue-chinned, called

early as he had promised. "I managed to see them this morning," he told her. "It's not good news, Martha. Spencer—that is the taller of your brothers, isn't it? Spencer has quite a bad injury to his arm and we need to get him into a hospital quickly. It will probably have to be the prison hospital, I'm afraid."

"You mean it's his right arm?"

"I do, yes. Now, they've got to go back to court by the end of the week when the police say they will be producing more evidence, and I am reasonably confident I can get them out on bail then. The other side's lawyer doesn't like this one any more than I do."

"I suppose you told him who I am?" She tried to keep her voice cool and even. After all, there were some advantages to being what her grandmother called a concubine.

"It may have slipped into our conversation, shall we say? I think he does appreciate now that if their case isn't watertight this affair could embarrass the police more severely than they could possibly have imagined when they decided to amuse themselves kicking in a couple of heads yesterday afternoon."

Two detectives, embarrassed but pruriently inquisitive, came to question Harley the next day. She put a photograph of Richard in a silver frame on the coffee table and treated them with ironic politeness. At the next court hearing the charges of possessing drugs and stealing the car were withdrawn and the police no longer opposed bail.

She took the boys straight from the court to hospital, where Spencer's grossly swollen arm was X-rayed. Four bones in his wrist were crushed. The surgeon pinned them together and assured him that he would recover the full use of his hand, but as spring turned into summer he sat morosely in her sitting room working his fingers and still could not manage to grip anything smaller than a can of Coke.

One light May night when her brothers were asleep Harley sat on the end of her bed and looked at her photographs. She had sixteen of them framed on the wall. Her eyes were tired and she had taken out her lenses, so she rummaged at the back of a drawer for her old spectacles to look at them properly. They had been her favourites and her pride—works of art, some of them had won awards. Now she saw a different meaning in them.

Her mind raced ahead, free at last to make the connections she had suppressed for so long. Kelly's pictures in particular told the story with their accentuated curves and suggestive symbolism. Sexuality—that low, taboo and primitive instinct with which whites were so uncomfortable in their assumed superiority—she had been their image of sexuality and had been well rewarded for it. This was the niche for which she had willingly been moulded, the place she was permitted to occupy in a white world.

The pictures were lies. They denied her personal truth. She knew she was a creature of the mind; sexually she barely functioned. Perhaps her own sexuality was something that had vanished along with the rest of her true identity.

I'm a victim, too, just as much as Spence, she told herself, but her conscience argued. She was not innocent. She had colluded with the enemy, connived at her own debasement. Well, now she would stop.

She considered taking the pictures down, but decided to leave them for the moment, to fuel the fight. She called her agency the next day and told them she did not want to work any more. They were angry and did not understand.

A few photographers loitered outside the apartment building but with the newspapers increasingly full of the news from the war in the Falkland Islands there was no space for lighter topics and they soon disappeared. Harley and her brothers observed the people and the press become more and more passionate.

"Are you worried about him?" Sheldon asked as the three of them watched the news coverage on the television. It was a day when the facts were thin and the officers being interviewed were particularly terse, indicating that the fighting had reached a crucial phase.

"Yes," she said, uncertain. "But I can't relate to this. All these men are being killed for the sake of some tiny islands on the other side of the world. I don't understand."

"The whole country's gone mad," Spencer added morosely.

She became aware that her feelings for Richard now seemed as insubstantial and deceptive as the light reflected from the surface of a lake. Occasional piercing anxiety for his safety struck her, but with it came anger and a sense of betrayal. She could not avoid including him in the aversion she felt towards Britain itself. He had been a small part of the long, subtle conspiracy to deprive her of her inheritance.

A few days later the news came of the Argentinian surrender and the war was over.

She had a strained, barely audible, satellite telephone call from Richard. "I'll have a whole month's leave when we get back," he told her. She said nothing. It was followed by a few letters. One disturbed her, a page of "I love you" written over and over again in handwriting which grew more and more angular with each line. It crossed her mind that he might be suffering, perhaps even wounded, but the idea seemed remote and insignificant. I ought to care, she told herself. Why don't I care? She did not even look forward to seeing him.

The newspapers were now ready to make an entertainment out of their misfortune. When their case was to be heard, Harley and her brothers struggled through a huge crowd to the court, protected ineffectually by one of Neville's clerks.

In the corridor she met Neville and their barrister, an intense woman with long black hair whom she recognised as another of her Cambridge contemporaries. The woman leafed through the duplicated sheets of evidence with a confident smile.

"I'm going to call a linguistics professor," she announced. "You'll see here from the police notes that you," she nodded at Sheldon, "have made a lengthy statement and you are also supposed to have abused the police in your native Trinidadian dialect, which is all very carefully recorded." She showed him the relevant passages. "Since I understand that you're a Jamaican and have travelled to Trinidad only on business as your brother's manager, it seems unlikely that you even know what half these expressions mean. This is all the result of giving the police race relations courses. They teach them West Indian dialects and this is the use they make of the knowledge. We're getting more and more of these cases."

Harley sat in the public gallery reflecting that if she had not been so ready to throw away her gifts for the sake of vanity she might now be in the well of the court herself, bobbing her bewigged head and clutching the lapels of her gown, saying "m'learned friend" with the ease of long practice and earning the approving attention of the judge as she successfully operated the machinery of justice to release two innocent men.

After the linguistics expert gave his evidence the police conferred with their lawyer and withdrew from the case.

"You'll sue for damages, of course," Neville Green spoke to Spencer as the triumphant defence group reconvened in the corridor.

"I just want to get out of this fucking country and start my life over," he growled, mechanically massaging his disabled wrist.

"Spence, you must," Harley urged him.

"Who says I must?"

"I do. You must claim what's rightfully yours. They owe you. They've done wrong and you have to make them pay. It's your duty, Spence. Listen, kids in this country look up to you. If you let yourself be kicked around, they'll go on letting themselves be kicked around too. Like it or not, you're up there, you're a leader."

He looked at her with a curious expression and raised one eyebrow ironically. "I'll sue if you'll take the case, sister."

"I won't be able to take it, because I'm going home. Stick with Neville, he's OK."

"What do you mean, you're going home? When did you make this decision?"

"Just now. As long as I stay here I'm just keeping other black women down. I'm going home, I'm going back to the law, and I'm going to serve my own people. If they'll have me, that is."

The twins took an elbow each and walked her away from the others down the grimy vestibule of the court building.

"But what about—you know, lover boy?" Sheldon was embarrassed to raise the subject.

"I'm leaving him, too. I don't feel anything for him any more. He's part of the whole thing, don't you see? If I hang out with him, I'm just perpetuating the whole lie. He stands for Britain. I stand for Jamaica. Our nations aren't part of any great family. Family are there for you when you need them, right? Sure, we've got history, culture in common, the crap they teach us in school. Answer me, you two, what did you learn in school that prepared you for this?" She glanced with hostility around the room; at the far end the police witnesses were deep in a furtive consultation with their counsel.

"Britain just made our country up," she went on, the bitter realisation of the past months crystallising as she spoke. "A little bit of sugar, a little bit of strategy, trade routes, infrastructure, a few thousand Africans, a few Indians and Chinese, education, religion—cook up for a couple of hundred years and when the economics don't work any more you give the people who're left their independence and call them a new country. But the British aren't *there* for Jamaica. We're just an accident they had along the way. And all that garbage about the Commonwealth is just a way to retouch the past and make it look a little less despicable than it really was."

They glanced at their sister nervously, half pleased and half concerned.

"This is a big change of head, Martha." Ever businesslike, Sheldon prepared to argue the downside. "You'll be giving up a great deal."

"I've thought it through," she countered at once. "I've written to Claude Campbell and he thinks he can get me a job with his firm. I won't be giving anything up, Shel. I'll be getting back a part of me that I threw away years ago because I thought it was worthless."

"But won't you miss London?"

She had not even considered the possibility. Now when she did so the only reason for regret seemed to be her friends. "I'll miss the people. Especially Jo. I wish she wasn't away making this film, I'd like to see her before I leave. Right now she seems like the only good thing about this country."

• • •

"WHY ARE YOU so nice to me?" Victoria pulled the sheet around her as she sat up. Having two children had exhausted the resilience of her breasts and she preferred to hide them.

"How can you ask me that? I love you. I can't help being nice to you—it comes with the territory." Ruben came out of the shower room, a towel around his waist, and crossed the bare board floor to sit on the bed beside her. He kissed her shoulder. After two years the bedroom of his house in the hills was as anonymous as it had been when they first

saw it, furnished with a banal bamboo suite. All he had
added was new bed linen, pastel American percale sheets
printed with tropical flowers. "Are you angry that I gave
you jewellery? Will it mean trouble for you with your husband?"

She glanced at her blouse, discarded at the foot of the
bed, with his gift pinned through the collar. On the plain
gold bar five graduated opals, the largest almost as big as
her thumbnail, gleamed in the shuttered light. Seven diamonds were set between them. Opals were bad luck, she
remembered Aunt Rose telling her that when she was
given her mother's jewellery on her eighteenth birthday
and had gazed in fascination at the chips of blazing colour
in the milky stone of a ring.

He reached for the pin himself, turning it between his
fingers and watching the stones. "They are from our family's estate, we own the mines. In my country, it would be
unthinkable not to give jewellery to the woman you love.
Don't you like it?"

"Of course I like it. I'm just not used to being given
presents, I suppose."

"You should be used to it. Beauty for beauty. But nothing I could give you would be more beautiful than you
are." He never delivered his compliments without looking
deep into her eyes as if to make sure they had found their
mark. Immediately she felt softer; her parched spirit drank
up his flattery and was avid for more, even though in another part of her soul she squirmed with shame.

Their affair was interrupted occasionally when Ruben
said he had to travel. He left Jamaica for a month at a
time, sometimes sending her letters full of formal requests
for news and accounts of his family's affairs in La Paz.
When he was gone she craved him desperately; as soon as
he returned she despised herself even as she strained her
body against his. Every reunion was more passionate than
the one before, followed by a more intense backlash of
self-disgust.

All her moods now oscillated violently. The babies
looked at her with large, wary eyes, never knowing whether
she would smother them with affection or irritably push
them away to their nurse. Her servants followed her caprices with sullen hostility. In public her temper and her
grooming were erratic. She was no longer the flawlessly

gracious diplomatic wife. Patrick showed no annoyance in company but was frankly impatient when he was at home, which was less and less often.

While Ruben was almost obsessively discreet, her husband's affair with Susannah McLeod was common knowledge. One or two of her closer acquaintances among the diplomatic wives had spoken to her about her behaviour, and its consequences for her marriage, but the alarm these warnings aroused only made her feel more anxious. She felt herself out of control, careening downhill into emotional collapse, and the only route back to normality was to take more drugs. She had a sense of fatalism about her life, as if her bad blood were bound to come out, and that this tortured existence was her destiny.

"Did you really go home?" she asked him suddenly. "You never say why you have to leave. Sometimes I feel that I don't know anything about you."

"I went back to Rio to see my family. You know they expect it. Then I went to Florida for some business meetings." When she asked him what his business was, his replies were always vague.

"Now you're back." Her tone was brittle.

"I hate to be away from you." He pulled the sheet away and took one of her breasts in his hand. "I wish you were not married, Victoria."

"That's easy for you to say." His presumption, the mere idea that she would ally herself to him, outraged her.

"I know, but I must say it. I must say what I feel." His accent, his alien, unctuous politeness, the touch of his soft olive skin, everything she disliked about him, excited her. Ruben was not a good lover. He imagined that the more violent he was, the more satisfied she would be, and when she timidly asked for gentleness he seemed not to hear her. As a result she was often angry after he had made love to her. Unable to identify the cause, she pinned her feelings elsewhere.

She pushed his hand away and moved to the edge of the bed. "I've got to get back, it's late."

"Of course. Let me help you." He was extraordinarily deft with women's clothes and she enjoyed the luxury of being dressed by someone else. The opal brooch was ceremoniously returned to its black velvet box and she put it in her handbag.

"Do you have your little pills with you?" he asked with concern. In a flash of malice, hoping to make him feel guilty, she had confided that she needed to take tranquillisers to endure the strain of their affair; he had accepted the information with gratitude, as a token of affection, and now treated the drugs as part of their conspiracy.

"Yes, look," she showed him the small silver pill box in which she carried a few capsules in case she needed them unexpectedly. "All safe. Have you still got the keys?"

He pulled them from the pocket of his blue doublebreasted jacket and showed them to her. "Are we going now?"

"Yes, we must." He escorted her to her car. They had driven to the house in her own little Ford.

"So many keys. There aren't that many doors in your house." The large bunch jingled as he turned the ignition.

"Some of them are my husband's." She spoke with longcherished annoyance. She hated carrying Patrick's spare keys. Any of his possessions was now a focus of annoyance.

"When can I see you again? Can I take you to the races the day after tomorrow?"

She sighed. The prospect of driving out to the dusty, pretentious little racecourse at Caymanas was not enticing, but the island offered few better amusements. "Why not?"

"I'll call for you at ten, yes?"

"Half-past." She was finding it hard to get up in the mornings at the moment. Ruben, unlike most of the other South Americans she had encountered, was a punctual person.

He drove slowly down the winding mountain road without talking and finally turned into the steep driveway of their villa. The garage was narrow, and he suggested that she get out before he drove the car into it. Behind the screen of the bougainvillea he suddenly pulled her to him and kissed her.

"I'm sorry, I must be crazy," he released her as unexpectedly, so she staggered for an instant. "I need you, Victoria. I can't bear living this way but . . ." he raised his hand to stop her protest, "I know this is all you can give me. I have no right to ask for more. I'm sorry. Forgive me. Don't worry, I'm going now." Although his head was cast down, she had the impression of tears in his eyes. He turned and walked briskly to the iron gate and she watched him in dumb confusion.

On the notepad by the telephone was a message in the maid's laboured handwriting noting that Martha Harley had called and left a Kingston number. She looked at it for some minutes without understanding. Her dulled reasoning considered motives for such a call, but produced no conclusion. In the end curiosity, and the desire to see the one woman in the world with whom she now shared the determining fact of her life, impelled her to dial. When the rich, chuckling voice she remembered answered from the offices of a well known law firm, she invited Martha to the villa for drinks immediately.

They sat on the verandah and made cautious small talk for half an hour. Martha admired the babies and played with them awkwardly, addressing them almost as adults.

"Why did you come back?" Victoria asked as the nurse took the children away to bed. She was nervous of the answer.

"I decided it was time to come home," Martha responded with care. "It wasn't anything to do with Richard, if you need to know. I don't expect you'll believe it, but we were friends more than anything else really. It wasn't a love affair. The media just blew the whole thing out of proportion." She saw relief on her old friend's face and knew she had been right to be economical with the truth.

"But—does he know you're here? Isn't he still in the Falklands?"

"On his way back. I left him a letter, it was all I could do."

The dusk was falling rapidly, enhancing their new intimacy. "Is he happy?" Victoria asked, raising her clouded grey eyes.

"I don't think so. He can't see any future."

"He's a marvellous person. It's a shame he is who he is."

"Yes."

There was a companionable pause. Victoria straightened her shoulders, feeling refreshed. "Aren't you going to miss all the excitement in London?"

"No. Not yet. I've had more excitement in the last few years than most people have in a lifetime, after all. My old life was destroying me, Victoria. You have to be what you are, don't you? Otherwise the effort of translating yourself just exhausts you, doesn't it?"

"I suppose it does, yes."

"Where's your husband, is he late coming home?"

"I expect so, he often is." There was no need to explain to Martha. In the aftermath of their separate distress, the two women knew each other's hearts by instinct.

A few hours later Victoria sat at her dressing table and considered her situation. Her vision was temporarily clear, as if a shaft of sun had pierced the clouds obscuring her thoughts. Like Martha, she had to be who she was. She was a Fairley. She was Patrick Hamilton's wife. She was born to set an example; her husband had deceived her and betrayed her, but her duty was to behave according to her own standards, not to take licence to the same moral deficiency.

Patrick came home so late that she was asleep, and left early in the morning before she awoke. She decided to drive down to his office at lunchtime and confront him, but could not find her keys. For a few minutes she accepted this excuse to avoid taking action, but steeled herself and called her neighbour, a businessman's wife, and borrowed her car.

"This *is* a surprise." Looking embarrassed, Patrick stood up behind his desk as she walked into his office. A flash of alarm hardened his eyes, but he suppressed it at once.

"We have to talk," she said, walking around to stand behind him with her back to the window. Outside, New Kingston's traffic crawled past the High Commission's iron fence.

"Darling, is this the right place? I'm very busy."

She looked at the papers spread out on his blotter with disbelief. "Is it so urgent you can't spend half an hour in conversation with your wife?"

"I'm drafting some notes to send to London for the Queen's speeches." The royal visit was only three months away. She picked up the nearest sheet of paper and read his regular, hieroglyphic script.

"*A nation which enshrines the greatest British values . . . unique strength and wisdom of the Commonwealth have derived from the rich diversity of races, peoples and cultures which have united to serve ideals which outweigh our individ-*

ual differences . . . what about our individual differences, Patrick?"

He settled the knot of his tie, a gesture she knew pre-saged hard persuasion. "Well, to tell you the truth, Vicky, I was hoping this was just a phase you were going through, these moods and so on. I know you don't like Kingston. I was pretty much counting on you being right again when we move on. London knows I'd like to leave as soon as they can spare me here."

She gasped in annoyance. "I don't mean *me*, Patrick. I mean you. You're having an affair with Susannah McLeod. I know it, the whole town knows it, you can't deny it . . ."

"Now, Vicky . . ." He stood up, glancing nervously at the door to make sure it was shut.

"No—listen to me. You're to stop it. Break it off. You're betraying me, ruining our marriage . . . do you want me to divorce you? Because I will. I won't live this way a day longer, Pat. If you don't give me your word never to see that woman again I'll fly home tomorrow and make sure the world knows why." She threw his notes on to his desk. "You got this promotion because of me and you'll lose the next one the same way if you don't come to your senses."

"I don't accept that there's a word of truth in anything you're saying." He squared up to her as if he intended to hit her, but she stared him down, full of cold fury.

"If you don't start to act like a husband to me and a father to your children, you won't have a family, Pat. You'll be a pushy little nobody, just as you were before you met me. All you'll be is the man who danced with the girl who danced with the Prince of Wales's brother. It's as simple as that. Since you're making notes, make some more. Here . . ." she reached across the desk for his notepad and put it in front of him. "I'm sure there's a form in these matters. How about 'Dear Susannah, my wife has found out about us and so I regret . . .' no, why regret, this isn't anything you'll regret, darling, is it? Go on, you finish it, you're clever with words."

"Don't be cruel, Vicky."

"What should I be, kind?"

He finally looked away, conceding defeat. "I'll see to everything, I promise. Immediately, today. You're right, of course. I've been very unwise."

"Yes," she agreed in a crisp tone, "you have, haven't you?"

He came home at eight that evening, slightly drunk and obviously disturbed, but insisted on taking her to dinner at a very expensive restaurant a few miles up into the hills and ploughing through a reaffirmation of love for her. Feeling pleasingly powerful, she told him that when his actions bore out his words, he would be welcome in her bed, but until she had such proof of his sincerity they would sleep apart.

Ruben appeared the next day, bearing her keys which, he explained, he had inadvertently put in his pocket.

"I can't come to the races with you today," she told him in a level voice. "And I can't see you any more. What we're doing is wrong. I want to save my marriage and . . ."

"You don't love him," he countered immediately, taking her hands.

She pulled them away. "I did once and I want to again. He has promised to break off with this woman, and I must play fair too. Surely you can understand that?"

To her disgust, he collapsed into a white iron chair on the terrace and wept. The last shreds of guilt in her heart vanished. "Stop it." She almost spat the words.

With what seemed to be a great effort, he mastered his feelings and stood up again. "Will you let me at least see you as a friend?"

"No. It's impossible. I'm sorry." He looked up at her with his soft black eyes and she saw that he was taking comfort from her fear that if she met him again she would be unable to control her feelings. He held her gaze long enough for her to feel a quiver of desire, and broke it at the precise moment at which her senses threatened to overwhelm her resolve.

"Then we must say goodbye." This time he kissed her hand and the soft imprint of his lips lingered. "I will always consider myself fortunate to have known you, and blessed to have loved you. Truly." He stepped back, almost with a bow, and departed.

She did not see Ruben again in Kingston. His instant disappearance pained her slightly. Patrick was as good as his word. Despite a burglary at the High Commission a few days later, in which his office and several others were ransacked and a large number of classified files removed, he came home every evening in time to see his daughter and son before their bedtime. All his considerable energy was devoted to healing the breach with his wife, and in a month she gave in to his pleading and they slept together once more.

The royal visit was a great success, and a few months later the word came that they were to be transferred to Dublin. With a light heart, Victoria began to plan the packing of her household and looked forward to shaking the dust of Kingston off her feet forever.

CHAPTER XXIII

THE RED ROSE WAS bruised and wilted. Richard paused by his desk and considered throwing the flower away.

The Secretary noticed his hesitation. "Shall I get someone to put that in water, sir?"

"Why not? Good idea." A florist in Croydon had supplied every man aboard HMS *Canberra* with a flower as a token of the nation's gratitude for saving some 1500 British citizens of the Falkland Islands from foreign domination. He had received his along with more than six thousand comrades and he found that he cherished it as a badge of belonging with them. It was also a remembrance of a month in which the foundation of his life had permanently settled.

The praise of the brigadier still rang in his ears. "You took whatever was thrown at you, you went on and did the job, you used your imagination, your initiative, and your leadership as a Royal Marines officer should. You kept your men up to scratch in the freezing cold and the pissing rain on bloody terrain against a difficult enemy. In those conditions it's the ability to endure that wins the battle, and that's just what you gave them."

"I think our training counted for everything, sir." He had at last learned the value of modesty. "It was all down to fitness and fieldcraft, really. Going by the book and being sharp enough to know when to throw the book away."

"What you did at Mount Charlotte was a piece of absolute tactical genius." The older man had looked at him almost angrily. They had been faced with the problem of taking the hill, which was covered with heavy machine gun posts, at night, with rockets which had no night sights.

Richard's solution, propounded almost immediately, was for one company to set up a diversionary attack, drawing the enemy's fire, so that their exact positions were revealed. The remainder of the force, coming down from an unexpected direction, had used mortars to illuminate the hillside so that the rockets could be aimed with precision. The capture of Mount Charlotte had already become part of the war's mythology.

"We'd been using anti-tank weapons to clear enemy trenches—it seemed the logical thing to do. The Loggies were magnificent—all we had to do was ask for the kit we needed."

The Logistical Regiment had supplied crates of rockets almost as soon as this improvisation proved successful, despite the fact that over most of the battlefield there had not been a tank in sight.

"Yes, Logs came into their own, no doubt about it. But Mount Charlotte was classic lateral thinking in the field. Your personal courage was an inspiration and I am in no doubt that the speed and aggression which your men showed in the attack was at least in part motivated by you. You may as well know I've put you forward for a decoration."

"Thank you, sir."

"And I believe I should congratulate you on becoming an uncle." Richard recalled the ripple of sentiment that had softened the man's weatherbeaten features, a strange sight after weeks of looking at resolute faces pinched with cold and blackened with camouflage cream. "I'm delighted for them, of course, sir, and it's a great relief to me as well."

"How's that? Don't you—ah—get moved down the line of succession now?"

"Exactly, sir. I can hope for a bit less attention."

"No harm in hoping, I suppose."

He had at last a solid sense of inner satisfaction and on the long sea voyage home it did not diminish. Together with his shipmates he heard the Prime Minister proclaim that Great Britain was great again, and a few days later red-white-and-blue balloons and banners greeted the Royal Marines' triumphant entry into Portsmouth harbour. His parents, with Andrew who had returned himself a few days earlier, had sailed out from Spithead to meet his ship, and they had driven back to Windsor together.

That had been yesterday. He felt strange in his own home again after so many weeks of sleeping in icy mud or in a claustrophobic ship's cabin with four other officers. For all they were overjoyed to welcome him, he was beginning to feel his family were also suffering unusual stress. One of his mother's detectives had resigned; and the IRA had bombed the Household Cavalry in Hyde Park, almost within sight of the Palace, killing men and horses indiscriminately.

He had called Harley and got no answer. There was a pile of unopened personal letters on his desk and he picked out hers immediately, already angry as he opened it.

He read it twice without understanding anything except that she had left the country, and left him. After weeks of living on nationalistic fervour, the idea seemed ridiculous. His first instinct was to fly to Kingston immediately and make her change her mind, and he went as far as to order British Airways tickets, but the tired look in his mother's eyes made him reconsider. Everyone told him and Andrew how much older they looked after the war, but his mother seemed also to have aged.

The family travelled to Balmoral a few days later and the clear air and dramatic landscape began to work their healing magic. His thoughts cleared but he was still reluctant to accept rejection.

"I can't understand it," he told his mother one day when he was her only companion for tea on the lawn. "She says she doesn't belong here and that being with me makes her feel like a traitor. Of all people, Harley was the last ever to talk about being disadvantaged because she was black. She was quite scornful of people who pleaded that sort of thing. I asked her once and she said she had never experienced racial discrimination herself." He sat down heavily on the tartan rug beside her.

"But I'm sure that what happened to her brothers made her see things in a different light. Blood is thicker than water, after all. It was a very nasty case, Richard, I followed it quite closely. Her brother will never play tennis again and he's right to be taking it further. The whole thing is blowing up into a scandal and the only good that can come out of it is to make people more aware that society just cannot work if people aren't more tolerant. And the police must be above suspicion."

"Do you think she's upset and she'll come back when she's got over it?"

She looked at him with the cool expression that she always used to reduce his heated emotions. "What do you think? Is she the kind of person to change her mind like that? How would you feel, if it was your brother?"

"Very angry and very bitter," he said at once.

"Well, then."

His father and Edward came out to join them. Prince Philip was less sympathetic. "Jesus Christ might have described himself as an under-privileged working-class victim of colonial oppression," he announced. "It isn't what happens to people, it's how they choose to react to it that's important. Pity. She seemed like a sensible girl."

"And good fun, I really liked her," added Edward, unaware that he was making Richard feel worse.

Richard refused to acknowledge jealousy, but the whole family and Charles in particular were so wrapped up in the new baby that he felt excluded. Andrew's girlfriend arrived the next week, with a pack of reporters following, apparently frenzied at the prospect of the Queen's son having an affair with an American actress who had once appeared naked in a film. The estate staff were edgy and the story of Keith Cowley being pushed into the Dee by an elderly retired school mistress who caught him on the riverbank amused the company only briefly.

Desolation stole suddenly in on him again like a mountain mist. He had no appetite for anything, except shooting, which for the first time in his life seemed appealing. Waiting in the butts for the whirr of wings and the raucous call of the grouse, breathing the clean scents of peat and heather, was a distraction in the daylight hours.

In the evenings he was withdrawn. No woman attracted him, although many tried, but he had no appetite for petty adventures now. He had closed down his emotions, and even the prospect of conquest had no thrill.

In the dark of a sleepless night, he resolved to take hold of his destiny. Life had cheated him, teased him, led him on, given him energy, strength of will and courage and failed to offer any purpose for these superior gifts; he was not obliged to accept that. "When you are doing nothing you are doing wrong," was an ancient piece of advice from his great-uncle's polo manual which had been quoted at him since childhood. He decided to act upon it and returned to London.

"Work," he told his startled equerry. "I might as well find something to do. Go and get the file on the Nansen Trust." He was the patron of the Trust's operation in London. News of the Israeli attacks on Beirut, and massacres in the refugee camps had been in the newspapers for days and had pricked his conscience. He had now seen enough of death to imagine the sights, and the slaughter of such pitifully defenceless people angered him.

One rainy evening he was called to the telephone and heard Harley's voice again, clear but with a delayed echo. "I couldn't just leave you with a letter," she sounded calm and happy. He remembered how she could occasionally switch on all the dignity she had suppressed.

"I hope you understand, Richard. It wasn't you. It was everything."

"Of course I understand." Understanding did not make it hurt less.

"And you must come to Jamaica and see me one day."

"Yes," he agreed, trying to sound as mature as she was.

The face of Sister Bernadette, streaked with dust, her blue eyes narrowed against the Middle Eastern sunlight, her nun's complexion pink and clear but leathery in texture, came into his mind's eye frequently. She herself was no longer in Lebanon, but at the Trust's headquarters in New York. He remembered her last letter, suggesting that they might meet, but it had arrived when he had no free time.

"Get her on the telephone," he ordered his secretary, and when the call came through a few moments later he simply said, "I've a few weeks' leave, Sister, and I thought we could meet. Shall I come to New York?"

"I don't know where you would want to stay," was her doubtful reply. It made him laugh.

"I expect I'll find someone to take me in. Just don't tell me there's nothing I can do for you now."

"Oh no," she replied, anxious that he might have taken her seriously. "Now that would be the day, when there's nothing to do. Could I tempt you to become a film star, for instance?"

"Do I get to play opposite Jacqueline Bisset?"

"Do you not think she's too old for you?"

Within three weeks he had flown to New York, agreed to present a television documentary about the Lebanon refugee camps for the Trust, raised the finance with one terse telephone call to Nicky Brompton, flown directly on to Beirut with the video crew for ten days' hectic shooting and returned to London with a renewed sense of purpose.

"In future," he instructed his office, "any requests from the Nansen Trust get top priority."

"There's another one here," his secretary said at once, passing him the letter. "Will you attend their charity film premiere in February. It's very short notice . . ."

"Let's look at the diary, it may not be possible . . ." His next posting with the Marines was to be to Hong Kong, but he had to attend two more special courses near London first and there was the possibility of leave between them. They consulted the planner, and saw that he would be in London. "Tell them yes," he ordered. "What's the film?"

"Ah—something called *The Hour of Dust*," he consulted the information sheet included with the letter, "a love story set in India in the last days of the British rule, starring Jacqueline Bisset, Colin Lambert and Dame Peggy Ashcroft, directed by Julian Samuel."

"Splendid." He wondered if Sister Bernadette had advised on the choice. She had a great deal of worldly good humour, even for a nun.

A month later he was shown an apologetic letter from the Trust announcing that *The Hour of Dust* was not going to be available in time for the event, and the film to be shown was to be *Claudette*, a wartime espionage thriller starring, among other famous names which he did not register, Jocasta Forbes.

Richard's secretary looked at his face and saw a violent reaction, like distant summer lightning, in the depths of his eyes. "It is partly a British production and the director is English too. I understand the other film was held up by some financial problem," he offered by way of explanation.

"And it probably wasn't very complimentary about Uncle Dickie either." After the initial shock, the news seemed to have cheered His Royal Highness. "Good. Tell them I'm looking forward to it."

When February came he dressed for the premiere in a

mood of heavy indecision, unable to choose between two different, new shirts, between gold or pearl studs and white or yellow braces, while his valet's patience was eroded to something close to irritability.

Jo set off for the theatre with Daniel in a corresponding state of mental turmoil. She visualised meeting Richard in detail to calm herself, but her blood seemed to be fizzing and her concentration was poor.

"So," Daniel remarked sarcastically, "fate has taken a hand and sent us a royal hero of the Falklands to bless our endeavours. Isn't that grand?"

She sighed and did not reply to the taunt. It echoed her own thoughts with sinister accuracy. Daniel was in a black depression; in this mood he was oversensitive to the point of being almost psychic. While they had been making the film he had been able to behave normally, but now she was frightened by the changes in him.

In the last few days when he had been in London, he had appeared lethargic and had spoken very little. Whatever he did say was bitter and negative. *Claudette* was a masterpiece, but the film seemed almost to have cost Daniel his sanity. While success seemed to have stabilised Bazza, who was now two stone lighter, rarely used drugs and got to all his appointments on time, it had undermined Daniel's entire personality.

The responsibility for Jo was oppressive. Their love affair was long over, but working together had forced them into each other's company; one evening he had asked to hold her hand and clutched it for hours, eventually saying, "You won't ever really leave me, Jo, will you? I know I'll die if you ever really leave me."

Richard sat through the film in a trance, watching the face that was hers but not hers, jealous of the entire audience for sharing the simulation of her emotions with him. Was she still with Daniel Constant? Was she living in London? He had been too embarrassed to find out but now these seemed like the most important questions in the world.

He saw her at once in the receiving line at the reception afterwards, half-way down, in a very simple grey dress with a divided overskirt and tight sleeves. Constant was several yards away, which gave him hope.

Distance gaped and time dragged until the Trust's director presented her. "Of course, I know Miss Forbes." The first words that came into his head, so banal he wished he could take them back. She was executing a very deep curtsey, no doubt to mock him. "How are you? Where are you living now?" *Please* look at me, he asked in silence.

She raised her eyes at last. He saw the strange rays of colour in the irises clearly. She was speaking but he did not hear the words, only their sense.

Her hair was light brown now, as it had been in the film, but longer, curling and pinned up with a jewelled comb. With her white shoulders and softly modelled face, she looked like a Gainsborough. "What a beautiful dress." What an unbelievably stupid thing to say.

"Thank you." He *is* nervous, she realised. A tiny butterfly of delight unfolded its wings somewhere under her ribs.

"I'm told this is what they call a *film noir*." He was desperate to prolong the conversation.

"I think that's what they say about any film with a sad ending shot through a lot of Vaseline." Intimacy was enclosing them like a curtain, shutting out the crowd of people all around them.

"And . . . so . . . what are you working on now?"

She mentioned that she was to make another film in a few months' time. "I haven't any commitments at all until then," she said slowly, willing him to decode the message. He was still holding her hand and he pressed it, questioning. Her smile was an agreement.

•   •   •

"IT'S SOMEBODY FROM Heathrow Airport, Sean." Sandy put the call on hold and looked doubtfully across the offices of the *Daily Post*'s gossip column. "She says you'll know what it's about."

He raised his bloodshot eyes from his copy of the rival *Daily Mail* without enthusiasm. "I haven't a clue, you ask her."

"Can you tell me what it's about?" Sandy had permed her hair and taken to wearing a black pseudo-Chanel suit with a split skirt, but he thought she looked as unprepossessing as ever. The voice on the end of the telephone chirped with excitement. "Sean, I think you should talk to her. She says Prince Richard has booked two tickets to Jamaica under a false name."

"For God's sake, woman, why didn't you say?" He snatched the receiver from her. "Uh-huh. Uh-huh. Can you give me the flight numbers? And the seat numbers? Are the flights fully booked? Are you absolutely sure? What about stand-by? OK. Listen, thanks. Give my assistant your address for the cheque." He almost threw the instrument back at Sandy and rolled joyfully out of the door, heading for the editor's office, snatching up a small hunting horn which he had taken to using to announce his biggest scoops. The few other journalists populating the office at 11 am sluggishly raised their heads as he lumbered past, blowing discordant blasts on the horn and yelling "View-halloo-o-o-o-o! Tally-ho!"

"Keithie, old sport!" he yelled down the telephone half an hour later. "Wake up, grab your cameras, your Gold Card and the old Ambre Solaire and get down to Heathrow pronto!" The photographer slurred sleepy protests. "We've got Rich the Bitch stitched up at last! I've got someone down there already trying to get stand-by tickets. The wife's packing the bags, accounts are breaking out the dollars, Thunderbirds are go! Come on, man! When we get there, there'll be time to nail the bastard and sink a few Zombies too, eh? I'll pick you up in an hour." He tossed the receiver down in triumph. "Sandy—we'll lead today on Lorna Lewis quitting 'Heritage,' you've done the notes already. She's just angling for more money. And there's Suzie Chamfer's engagement to Colin Lambert. And get my expenses done up-to-date while I'm gone, OK, doll?"

Murray had conceived a special hatred for Jo Forbes. She was an American, which in his eyes automatically made her a scheming vampire lusting for royal blood. She was also one of those pretentious actresses who refused to give interviews except to the quality papers; in his book gang-rape was too good for that sort.

Murray's newest electronic toy was a bug which could tap car telephones. A few years after it had been decided, for security reasons, to equip the royal cars with telephones a former Palace employee had sold Murray the numbers, and by this means he had learned that Prince Richard and Jo Forbes had something going.

When the *Post* jubilantly broke the news, the woman had had the nerve to call the police to disperse the crowd of more than a hundred photographers who collected outside her apartment. She had also had the gall to call in a debugging company to search her apartment for devices, and remove the radio transmitter in the wall. She had hired Neville Green, the notorious pinko lawyer, to prepare a file accusing the *Daily Post* under some obscure point of law relating to telephone tapping. She had gone to these lengths when all his bug had relayed were dull conversations with her agent and the noise of the actress practising her morning yoga.

She had now left her home and disappeared. The woman had no sense of the obligations of life in the public eye, and the arrogance to pretend that she could court publicity when she wanted it and evade it when she did not. The prospect of Keith's camera catching her topless on a beach, or even naked through a bedroom window, satisfied them both immensely.

* * *

JO LISTENED TO the churning of the sea in the rocky inlet twenty feet below the open window and felt the cool currents of air on her skin.

"Like the breath of mermaids," she said.

He laughed. "How do you know mermaids breathe?"

"They must breathe, they've got noses."

"That's completely illogical. You can't assume that they have lungs because they've got noses. How do you know they haven't got gills?"

"I've never seen a mermaid with gills, have you?" He was running his fingertips idly across her back, circling each vertebra in turn, and it was difficult to think.

"No, but . . ."

"Look, it's a fact, Richard," she rolled over luxuriously and guided his head to her breasts. "Mermaids are able to breathe either air or water and if they're breathing air it must be cold and salty and full of ozone, like sea spray. Any fool knows that."

He kissed the fragile areola, feeling it swell against his lips like some exquisite little sea creature. Her skin indeed tasted salty, from their mingled perspiration; they had been making love the whole long tropical morning, beginning when they awoke together at the first light. Now the full bright heat of the day blazed outside the window. On the shaded ceiling drops of light thrown up from the waves below danced like sparks. The sound of their urgent breathing echoed in the room, a heated counterpoint to the roaring of the sea.

Afterwards she lay across his chest and listened to the thundering of his heart. His responses were so volcanic that she was almost frightened, but with him she at last found the licence to release her own demons. His body was hard and fit, and it thrilled her to entice him through the long erotic dance to the point where they consumed each other without restraint. They met so seldom, and under such strain, that they were always famished for pleasure. Jo also acknowledged to herself that it was easier to make love than to talk.

He was hanging blissfully between sleep and wakefulness, playing with her hair, fanning the damp strands out across her shoulders. "Why do we argue so much?"

"I'm a contrary bitch, that's why. Anyway, it turns you on."

"No, it doesn't."

"And you're a liar, that's another reason."

"I am not."

"This isn't an argument, this is a contradiction. Listen, fella, I didn't come all this way for an argument to have you change the ground rules. Either you argue or I'm going home, understand?"

They laughed, feeling each other's guts shake companionably together.

"Where shall we have breakfast?"

"How about out on that little pavilion by the lily pool?"

"Do you think the peacocks will come over that far?" The birds, accustomed to sole possession of the pleasure dome, had raised a family of handsome young whose plumage was just growing in, and Jo had enjoyed feeding them the leathery white toast that Nicky Brompton's staff considered essential for a proper British breakfast.

"They need the exercise. They're putting on weight. The way those birds are going, they'll be too fat to roost on the roof by the time we leave. We'll be doing them a favour."

He picked up the telephone to order the meal, then headed for the shower. She slipped on a plain blue seersucker robe and followed him, sitting on the edge of the tub to talk. These simple presumptions of intimacy devastated him. Not since he was six years old had anyone carried on a casual conversation with him in the bath, or assumed the right to hold him in her arms all night. Everything she did intensified his sense of being.

Their affair was six months old and had progressed from a passionate state of tension to something rich and strong which, for the moment, nourished them both. Their dual identity had taken on a life of its own which gave their individual lives new dimensions.

Although her self-possession was daunting, Richard had invited her into his life and tested her. She had spent a raw weekend at Sandringham, and several weeks at Balmoral. He was reassured to see that although she was undoubtedly intimidated, she naturally adapted her manners to the company and in time grew relaxed with his family. She was also thoughtful with the staff, who at first viewed her with suspicion. The legend of Mrs Simpson keeping the cooks up half the night to make bacon sandwiches in the American fashion was resentfully cherished at Balmoral.

After Harley, however, she was disappointingly quiet and serious. They had expected an actress to be more entertaining. His brother Charles had been the first person to warm to her.

"Are these all heather?" she asked one day while the men were shooting. "I've never seen so many different kinds of plant. Why are there so many?"

"They are all heathers," Charles replied, "and there are so many because this is almost an untouched eco-system. This is how things are meant to be. Apart from burning off the heather in some places to get more young shoots for the grouse to feed on, we don't interfere with it. And the land is too poor to farm and always has been."

She immediately appreciated the vast difference between the rich carpet of vegetable species in the hills around the royal castle and the impoverished landscapes she was accustomed to seeing in the rest of Britain. Within a few minutes she and Charles were engaged in a long discussion to which Richard listened with amusement.

If he was testing her, she also put him on trial.

"Sometimes," she told him lightly, indicating the luxuriously neglected landscape outside and the Scottish baronial furnishings of the drawing room, "I get the feeling that this entire estate is the British national theme park and that you are a hologram of gracious country living revolving endlessly around in it." She picked at his Shetland sweater in mock disapproval.

"That's exactly how I feel about it sometimes, too. If you were a hologram, what would you do?"

"It's different for me," she answered, "I get paid for it, I don't have to do the stuff I don't like and I'm allowed to choose the form."

"Well, I get paid for it too. Maybe I could choose the form as well."

"Do you really think so?"

"Yes," he answered, thrilled that she was obliquely probing the possibilities of his future. "When I'm with you I feel as if I could do anything."

"Be serious, Rich, damn you."

"I am being serious. And if I don't do everything I can to make my own choice, I can't be worth much, can I?"

She nodded, satisfied. She thought of him as the same kind of challenge. He was a foreign country, profoundly different from anyone she had ever known before, and yet he seemed so familiar.

Annoyingly, the only person to sense her feelings was her mother, who arrived in London immediately the news of her daughter's new affair had broken.

"I just felt I had to be with you," she said by way of apology. "How are you?"

"I'm OK," Jo replied, unwilling to confide. The idea of her mother basking in *her* celebrity did not charm her, but there was no one else she could talk to and she ended up talking confusedly for some time. "The whole thing makes me feel as if I'm standing on the edge of a cliff and I could fall off any time. I love him, but I can't imagine sharing his life," she said at last.

Her mother nodded and produced the sweet smile that signified maternal understanding for millions of "Heritage" fans. "If you ever need me, just call, won't you? I'm finishing with 'Heritage' after this series and then I'll have more time."

Jo had smiled and said nothing. Her mother had been promising more time in the future all her life.

In the full brilliance of the late Jamaican morning, Jo and Richard, in swimming costumes and T-shirts, made their way barefoot down the board stairway to the shade of the canopy halfway down the cliff. The peacocks, now alert to the dilatory habits of lovers, fluttered heavily down from the villa's roof; with personal offence expressed in every step of their arched feet and turn of their long necks, they assembled by the lily pool, beady eyes scanning the silver dishes on the table.

"This really is the ultimate fool's paradise, isn't it?" Jo stretched in the warm air, enjoying tiredness, the strained joints, the grazed skin and bruised tissues which constituted the agreeable aftermath of making love.

"Couldn't it just be paradise?" He wanted to tell her he loved her, but she was gazing out to sea with a clouded expression that warned him not to force the pace.

"No. No, it couldn't. In a week we'll have to go back to it all and this will just be a dream."

"I want it to be like this forever."

She had such overpowering senses of sadness and anger that for an instant she could not draw breath. At length she managed to say, "Richard, every stenographer from Des Moines dripping Coppertone on her Danielle Steel on the beach at Montego Bay wants it to be like this forever."

"What's the matter?" He reached between the coffee cups and took her hand.

"Why must there be something the matter because I'm being realistic?"

"No, there is something the matter."

She held his gaze for an instant, angry that she was about to weep. "Yes, there is. I love you."

"Is that so bad?"

"You know it is, it's a disaster. I want to be happy, Richard. I want my life, I want a man who shares it, I want a family. For me, this is a disaster. For you it's probably quite pleasant."

He had been about to insist that she had misunderstood, that he wanted what she wanted and he wanted it with her, but the cruelty in her voice angered him violently.

"You really can be an absolute bitch sometimes." He released her hand.

•   •   •

"GOTCHA." STANDING IN a speedboat beyond the reef, struggling to support his camera with its long lens, Keith Cowley fired shot after shot. His lurid Hawaiian shirt, wet with spray, flapped damply in the wind. He felt considerably more positive about Jo Forbes than Murray. The woman was a dream to photograph. He'd never taken a bad picture of her, and whatever she was thinking was always written all over her face. It looked like the lovebirds were having a row, too, which was the best kind of picture. One of these should be worth a million. The wind was brisk and the sea choppy. Balancing in the boat was difficult but he could not get the shot if he sat down. He was using the fastest film and the quickest exposure, but there was so much light about that the chances of the pictures being too blurred were undeniable.

"I'm not happy, bobbing up and down like this," he muttered to Murray and the boat owner, who sat in the shade of the craft's small canopy. "Can't we land and get some stuff from the cliffs?"

"You c-a-a-n't land here, see the reef all around?" The boat owner's pink-tipped finger pointed out the barrier of white foam through which black rocks projected like shark fins.

Murray scanned the shore with his field glasses. "Can we sail on around the point and come in at the other side, then climb back over the top?"

The man nodded, fingering his torn T-shirt. "The estate is almost an island. You can come in safely on the landward side, but you have to climb through the bushes if you don't want to be seen."

"No problem. Take her in." The idea of crawling up on the enemy like a commando appealed to Murray at once.

• • • •

"I'M TRYING TO explain." Jo wondered if she should be explaining at all. How could she possibly hope for understanding from someone so far from ordinary human experience that he might as well have come from another planet?

"Keep trying, you might make it." He was hostile now, as well.

"Please, Richard, this isn't easy for me." He turned away from her but she jumped up immediately and curled into his lap. The warm aroma of her skin seemed to fill him completely.

She stroked his hair in silence, trying to analyse her feelings. As long as they were together away from the world she felt safe, but she knew that as soon as she got into a car and left this enchanted sanctuary the relentless assault on her would begin again. The price of this happiness was high. The separations, the loss of her home, the miserable nights in other people's bedrooms, when she hugged a pillow for comfort and tried in vain to find the faint scent of his hair, were wearing away her spirit.

Her family, her real family, the friends she had assembled over the years, were now separated from her because she had to keep secrets. She felt herself being ground to powder and blown away, while he, she could see, thrived on their love and grew stronger as she grew weaker. It was as if he were a vampire taking all her life force.

Part of her poured it out willingly. Now she knew him, she understood that he was a man who could have been great were he not confined in a small cage by the accident of his birth. She had the power to liberate his spirit and it seemed to her that this was a fine service to perform, but she herself was diminished in the process.

When she tried to tell him these feelings, the words slipped away like frightened fish and all that came out sounded like jealousy. There was nothing to do but hold him now and let the future bring what it would.

Footsteps sounded emphatically from the stairway and they looked around. It was Detective Henshaw.

"I think you ought to know, sir, the sensors have picked up some intruders on the other side of the estate."

"Damn." They stood up. "How many?"

"Two. They're moving together in this direction. The ground's so rough the guards are being quite slow in getting to them. We've let the dogs out. It might be better to go inside the house, sir."

With regret, they returned to the villa and dressed. In the guardroom they saw the images from the infra-red cameras, blurred shapes that indicated two people climbing around the cliffs.

"They must have landed from a boat, sir. This looks like it here, on that little beach on the east."

"Let's take a look."

"Is that wise, sir?"

"They're only paparazzi, Chickie."

"Yes, look," Jo pointed to one of the screens linked to the closed-circuit video system. The blurred face of Keith

Cowley was distinguishable as he made an ungainly descent towards the beach. "It's that little shit who followed you in Cambridge. Damn, damn, damn. How can they do this to you? I hate all photographers everywhere. I wish they were dead."

One of the dogs, a German Shepherd, appeared, leaping down the rocks to seize Cowley's arm, and a silent struggle filled the screen.

"We mustn't have anybody injured," Richard said at once, alert to the way the situation could develop. "Better just get hold of them, put them back in the boat and tell them to push off."

With Henshaw, they made their way down to the pebble strand where the boat was beached. The owner had disappeared at the first sound of the dogs barking. The detective searched the camera case he found in the small cabin and exposed all the film in it.

"They took enough booze with them." He indicated two litre bottles of Mount Gay rum in a plastic cooling bag.

"Have they drunk any of it?"

The detective showed him one bottle which was two fingers down. "Not much."

"Good. Let me deal with this by myself." Richard turned to Jo, wanting to protect her even from the eyes of the men who were trying to destroy her. "Why don't you go back to the house?"

"Sure," she agreed too quickly, resenting his assumption of control.

A few minutes later Murray and Cowley appeared, walking shamefacedly between two guards armed with rifles. Richard smothered his distaste and summoned all the charm he could to persuade the men of his right to privacy.

The boat was relaunched, the engine started and the two men obliged to re-embark. The guards pushed the little craft off and Richard gave them a perfunctory wave.

"The fuckers have opened all your film," Murray announced, passing Cowley the bottle.

"Doesn't matter." He grinned, baring all his grey teeth. "That was all unexposed. The stuff I've shot's here, if they haven't found it too." He rummaged in the cooling-bag below the ice packs and produced a nondescript package of transparent plastic. When unwrapped, it contained three rolls of Kodak, still furled in their cases. "All present and correct. Mission accomplished, if you ask me. I'll have a drink on that." He tilted the bottle against his smiling lips.

The boat was heading slowly out to sea, and Murray narrowed his eyes against the glare of the sun to make out the line of the reef. "Water, water, everywhere, who needs the filth to drink?" He took the bottle from Cowley. "Are you sure you know how to steer this thing?"

"Never driven one before in my life, but how difficult can it be if that little sambo can do it?"

They settled down to enjoy themselves in a mood of triumph. The spirit worked quickly in the sun and when the boat left the lee of the promontory it was a long time before they were aware that a fierce current had swept it along the coast.

Early the next morning, the coastguard from Port Antonio, self-importantly hoping for ganja boats, saw a John Crow dive towards the shoreline. Within thirty seconds, three more of the big black birds wheeled in on the same flight path. Others swooped over the hazy green hills, the instinct of carrion-eaters telling them that if one bird dived and did not rise again it must have found food.

The body of Keith Cowley, battered by the sea and torn by the vultures, was recovered later that day. The boat, with Murray semi-conscious in it, was found drifting at sea almost twenty miles away. He was still too drunk to remember that he had ever had a companion at the start of the voyage, but the next day sobriety returned.

The films were still untouched in the cooling bag. Murray had them developed and the pictures wired to London before he could be persuaded to identify the body.

The *Daily Post* splashed the shadowy images as large as possible and devoted even more space to lauding the heroism of its reporters. The rest of the world's press scrambled into action. A flotilla of hired craft put to sea and surrounded the villa, while three helicopters roared overhead. The photographers aboard found that the prey had gone to ground. Richard and Jo had decided to leave as soon as the news of Cowley's death was broken to them.

•   •   •

RICHARD HAD NEVER seen his mother so angry. Her face was white and her mouth pinched with tension.

"So it was an accident, as far as we know?"

"I saw them sail away all right. What happened after that I don't know." Richard held Jo's hand protectively. Her fingers were stiff. She was sitting beside him on the small white sofa in his mother's office, her back absolutely straight and her face set with tension.

"Perhaps you feel that it served the man right?" He felt Jo shudder. The Queen looked at them both.

"I feel terrible because I actually said . . . I wished he was dead," Jo replied at once.

"Well, they have given you a terrible time, haven't they?"

"Don't they give everyone a terrible time?"

"I never think that makes it any easier." She gave a small sigh. "The office will have to issue a statement. You mustn't feel too badly, either of you. It's terrible but the man exposed himself to the danger through his own actions and it was nothing to do with you." She gave a small nod of dismissal and a tight smile.

Richard escorted Jo down the long Palace corridor. She was tightly wrapped in her own feelings. They had done nothing but fight since leaving Jamaica, but he felt the eye of the storm passing and decided to try to reach her.

"You look angry," he said gently.

"I am angry. With everything. With you as well, if you want to know. I just feel—trapped."

"Darling, it won't always be so hard. When this is over . . ."

"Spare me the pep talk, please. This will never be over—you've seen the newspapers. They're making out that that man was a saint, just because he was one of their own. They'll never forget and they'll hold me responsible for his death."

They drove in silence to the house in a graceful crescent off Brompton Road which belonged to the director of her last film. He was in Los Angeles, and she shared the building with his two teenage sons, who returned only rarely from their girlfriends' homes.

He passed a sad, sleepless night convinced that she would soon end their hopeless relationship. Pride took hold of him. The thought of another rejection was intolerable. Perhaps, he argued with himself, it was for the best. This tragedy was another test, and she was failing it. If she could not ride out her feelings over something like this, she would never stand the strain of sharing his life.

In the morning, his temper was vicious. "I know what's really bugging you," he accused her. "You just can't stand sharing the limelight with anyone else, let alone anyone who's a bigger public figure than you are. You couldn't stand it with your mother and you can't bear it with me, either."

Instead of hitting back with fury, as he expected, she agreed in a tone of icy objectivity. "I think you're absolutely right," she said, standing cradling her hot coffee in the kitchen. "I feel as if my life is being completely wiped out and I can't stand it. You should see the sort of scripts my agent has been getting—I mean, I suppose I should be glad she's getting any at all, but they're absolute junk now. Nobody takes me seriously. Everything I've worked for has just gone."

He was temporarily checked in his purpose, but reason drove him on to the end he had planned.

"Look, this isn't fair to you." He took her in his arms by the front door, telling himself it was the last time. "I'm going to be away for months now. It's got nowhere to go, has it? Let's make a clean break now and call it a day."

She looked at him carefully, searching for a sign that he did not mean what he said, but his face was for once closed and impenetrable. "You're right," she said lightly, "I think that would be the best thing."

After he had gone she sat down on the staircase and cried until her face ached.

He had left as late as he dared in the morning, with scarcely enough time to pick up his kit and be driven to the service airfield for his flight to Hong Kong. His mother had asked to see him as soon as he returned and he ran down the corridor, cursing.

"Do you want to marry that young woman?" she asked as soon as he was inside the door of her office.

He was momentarily struck dumb.

"You always want to marry them, so I suppose you do?"

"It isn't as easy as that."

"She's honest, she's brave and she knows what counts in life, I think. You could do a lot worse."

"You've decided *you* want me to marry her, then, you and Father?"

"Richard, do try not to let this one get away." The little dog at her feet groaned in its sleep as if to underline the injunction.

"Don't tell me what to do—I'm old enough to manage my own life," he snarled at her suddenly, slamming the door as he left the room.

Jo endured the empty house for a week, then, meeting Rachel by chance on the street, she had a tearful cup of coffee with her in Covent Garden and accepted her offer to move into Bazza's old room in their apartment for a while. "At least now we know what's going on with you." Rachel's fragile smile warmed her a little.

"It's all over now," Jo replied with resignation. Rachel and Simon exchanged a glance which she did not miss. "No, I mean it. He ended it, not me."

She needed her friends about her immediately. Daniel Constant killed himself in Los Angeles; his maid found him hanging from the balcony of his house. There was a fare-well letter for Jo, written in chaotic, smudged lines of pencil that were nothing like his characteristic precise style. "*I know you will despise me for being so weak and loving you so much, and no doubt your contempt is all I deserve,*" she made out, "*but I cannot bear knowing that you are with another man, particularly one who stands for everything about England that I despise.*"

"You *must not* blame yourself," Rachel lectured her sternly in their messy, gingham-curtained kitchen. "This is just a bad twist of fate, but you didn't create it and you mustn't let it get to you."

"No, you're right," Jo answered, without much convic-tion. She had a terrible, cold, withering sensation in the depth of her body, and a crackling telephone conversation with Richard, formal in tone and strained around half the globe, could not assuage it.

The next production at the Queen's Arms was a mime play performed in masks. Although she felt as if she could bring no one anything but misfortune, Jo hesitantly asked for a part in it, knowing she would not be refused, and for a few weeks of rehearsals managed to recapture some bal-ance.

The theatre was the most fashionable fringe venue in London now, and no longer had difficulty in attracting the attention of the press. A few days before the opening night there was a photocall in a small park nearby, but her heart sank when she saw twice the usual number of photographers waiting.

The eight actors posed together in their masks and costumes, but after only a few minutes someone called out:

"Come on, take the bloody masks off."

"Come on, Jo, we know you're there, give us a grin, there's a good girl."

Simon had prudently parked his old Volkswagen nearby with the keys in the ignition and they had agreed that if disaster struck they would simply run to the car and drive away. He put his arm around her shoulder and they bolted between the municipal flower beds, the pack of photographers running after them. One of them grabbed at her mask, missed and pulled her hair hard and wrenched her neck painfully.

One man had been way ahead of them. Simon reached for the keys and found that they had gone. In front of the car a photographer stood grinning, waving the keys in one hand and unzipping his fly with the other.

"Don't panic," Simon patted Jo's arm. Rachel, seeing what was happening, pushed through the crowd and gave him her own key. He turned it, but the old car's engine coughed and refused to start. He released the handbrake. "We're on enough of a slope to get her moving."

"For God's sake don't hurt anybody," she prayed in silence.

By now there was a noisy crowd all around them, some hammering on the car roof and others joining the jerk-off party barring their way with an unprepossessing array of waving penises. The car rolled faster under attack, the engine caught as Simon let in the clutch and they drove away down the hill. As they turned out of the park Jo felt a violent spasm of nausea and pulling off her mask she wound down the window to be sick.

"I can't do this to you all," she said when they got back to the theatre. "If that was just for starters every performance will be chaos and nobody will be able to get near the place."

"We can stand it, if you can," Rachel assured her in a gentle voice.

"I can't," she announced decisively. "I can't take any more. Lorcan Flood has suggested that I go down to his place in the country for some peace, and I think that's the only thing I can do now."

CHAPTER XXIV

LORNA LEWIS WATCHED her husband step stiffly up to the mounting block outside their stables and wondered how much time they had left together. In her imagination he was still as vigorous as the day they met, and as handsome, but she could not deny that now he moved more slowly every day, and forgot things; and his conversation meandered. It seemed as if one day she had left their house as usual at dawn, and come back at dusk to find that old age had captured her husband while she was at work. She had decided right then that she was working on her last series of "Heritage."

They were dressed alike in jeans and chequered shirts. Lorna was trim now, if not as slender as she had been in the years of her early blooming. Her hair was in fact as much colourless as blond, but she had it tinted a warm honey shade which lifted her tired complexion. Her skin had few lines but they were deep ones, and although she regretted them she acknowledged that they gave her face the authority which it had lacked in her youth. For a woman past the age of sixty, she was a radiant inspiration. Her fan mail, still hundreds of letters a week, told her so.

Robert took the reins in his arthritic fingers and motioned away the groom who had led out his big chestnut. He preferred to ride with an English saddle, which concerned his wife, who saw no safety margin in the small stirrups and slippery leather. Robert always listened with courtesy when she tried to change his ways, then carried on exactly as before. He rarely gave way to the irritation of an old man brought face to face with his weakness. His atti-

tude to ageing was sweet resignation. Lorna thought that
she loved him all the more for that.

As a young wife it had taken her many years to discover
that the man she thought so sophisticated and wise was in
fact gentle to a fault; in mid-life, when they had hit hard
times, she admitted she had resented his passive nature.
Now that their last years were still sweet, it seemed a fine
and manly quality.

They rode out in the thin morning sunshine, enjoying the
resinous scent of the pine trees which stood about their
favourite trail. The farm—Robert seemed reluctant to call
it a ranch—was high in the hills and the air was full of
energy. Their land bordered on the Angeles National Park,
but although it seemed like the centre of the wilderness the
nearest town, Applewood, was only ten minutes down the
road.

As they walked their horses uphill, Lorna stood up in her
stirrups and looked down on the red tiled roof of the ranch
house. It was a sprawling Spanish building, originally a hollow square with a central courtyard. The oldest walls dated
from the past century and the succeeding generations of
occupants had added their own improvements. With time
on her hands, Lorna was considering continuing the tradition.

"Honey—do you think we should build another terrace
out on the east side of the house? It would be so nice to be
able to sit out and have breakfast in the morning sun, don't
you think?"

He answered her with an amiable grunt.

"And maybe a pergola leading from the terrace down to
the pool? With climbing roses? I'd love to grow some of
those lovely classic roses again, you know, Malmaison, Feli-
cité et Perpetué, the ones you liked so much at the old
house? And some camellias, I believe this is wonderful
country for camellias. With something low and evergreen
underneath them. Do you think Confederate jasmine
would take up here?"

They reached the crown of the hill, where the trees gave
way to long grass speckled with daisies, and the horses
picked up their heads and scented the breeze.

Lorna pushed her docile mount on to catch up with her
husband.

"So tell me, darling, what do you think?"

"I think the house is just fine the way it is, sweetheart."

They cantered quietly between the swaying grass and flowers until the trail led into the forest once more. The sun strengthened, making pools of brightness on the clean red earth sprinkled with pine needles.

"Do you think," she began again as the horses ambled onwards, side-by-side, "we should give a benefit dinner to raise money for a new museum in Applewood? They really have a wonderful collection of Indian art down there and it just isn't displayed in the best way. It needs a whole gallery to itself. Maybe if some of us girls got together . . ." Lorna Lewis was happily not the only Hollywood veteran of her vintage to have holed up in the mountains to enjoy her prime.

Her husband gave a visible shudder. His idea of hell was a house full of women with time on their hands and charity on their minds.

"Sweetheart," he said slowly, looking at her sideways under the brim of his hat, "do you really want to know what I think?"

"Of course I do . . ."

"I think you are bored witless up here and you should go back to work."

"But I don't want to do anything that will take me away from you ever again," she told him with vehemence. "You know how I hated having 'Heritage' take over my whole life for all those years."

"It doesn't have to be like that. You could just make a little movie now and then, couldn't you?"

She smiled, half to herself. Her reward for what she called seven years in the salt mines on "Heritage," shrewdly invested by herself from the beginning, now amounted to almost twenty million dollars, and because she loved her husband it charmed her that he still talked about her work as if it were a feminine pastime like needle-point or macramé.

"Maybe if . . ." she was about to say "I," but another idea suddenly occurred to her. "Maybe if *we* had control, maybe if we produced it . . ."

"What do I know about producing movies?" He had caught her meaning at once and she saw the glint of excitement in his sky-blue eyes.

"About as much as I do, sweetheart."

A month later they sat by the hearth in their library, the firelight flickering over several piles of scripts. Lorna sat on her heels in her favourite place, with her back to the blaze, with another script open in her hands.

"This is it, Bob, this is the one. *The Dawn of Dreams.* I just know it. As soon as I read it I forgot about all the others. Isn't it a great story?"

"What's it about?" His voice was sleepy. Robert had trouble keeping his eyes open after 7 pm.

"This girl who has an illegitimate child when she's sixteen and puts it up for adoption. Twenty-five years later she sets out to find the child, who's in a mental institution because she's supposed to be subnormal. The woman kidnaps the child and they set out on this wild journey through small towns in the country, with the state police after them. Then they take to the woods. Gradually it turns out that the girl is perfectly OK, she's just been drugged and institutionalised all her life. They meet all these weird people in the forest, a kid firewatching, a bunch of hippies, a Vietnam vet who can't adapt—the deal with them all is that they aren't crazy, society is. It's based on a true story. And in the end they come out of the forest and she sues the State. Isn't that terrific?"

"Absolutely terrific." He seemed momentarily more alert. "A story to touch the heart of every mother in America, eh?"

"Hey, that's great, let me write that down." She snatched up a pencil from the English Jacobean table she was using as a desk and scribbled on the top of the title page. "Do you think people still care about mothers in America? Maybe we should say 'every woman in America.'" There was no reply. Her husband dozed.

The next morning she leaned eagerly across the breakfast table in the bright white morning room and carried on the conversation as if they had not stopped talking. "And you know who I think would be perfect for the daughter?"

"Huh?" The emphasis in her voice was unmistakable and Robert put down his orange juice in alarm.

"Jocasta. Perfect for her, absolutely perfect. At this point in her career she ought to get up and really show 'em what she can do."

"I don't like to be too negative, but do you think she'll do it?"

"I can only ask her, can't I? I mean, if I can't ask my own daughter, who can I ask? I know she's been very difficult and distant and everything . . ."

"But to a cockeyed optimist like her mother that's nothing at all."

She smiled at him kindly and looked around the pretty room with a sigh of satisfaction. Ever thrifty and equally sure of her taste, she had brought up all the wicker furniture and the blue and white Chinese pots from the house in Pacific Palisades for the breakfast area.

"But what about the kind of company she's been mixing with? She may have changed her ideas quite a bit . . ." He spoke with the naked hostility of a father whose daughter has been dating a man he considers unsuitable.

"I know Jocasta, Bob. She is an actress to the core, she's a fighter and she's a complete individualist. Whatever that Prince Richard may have done to her, he won't have broken her spirit. Nobody could do that. Jocasta's a winner."

"It hasn't been that easy for her . . ."

She knew he thought she was being unreasonable. They had had the same conversation a hundred times. "Only because she made things difficult for herself, and I admire that. She will triumph, trust me." The cheap and cheerful possessions of their lean years reminded Lorna that she had overcome every other obstacle to happiness in her life. Making peace with her daughter was the only challenge left. "Could you spare me for a few days, Bob? I think I'll fly straight to London and give her a surprise."

• • •

CLIVE FAIRBROTHER'S EVEREST Expedition was made up of thirty climbers from the combined services of Britain and Australia, with a British television crew in addition. They were scattered across the roof of the world in seven camps. Fairbrother himself would go no higher than the third of them, from which the final assault on the summit would be made by a team of four.

Richard held the Video 8 camera awkwardly in his chill hand. It was difficult to operate it with gloves on, but impossible to take them off for long. The film crew, not climbers and now down at the base camp, expected them to record the vital moments of the adventure themselves.

"Well, Clive, this morning we're going to make the first attempt on the summit. How do you feel?"

"Oh, for Chrissake, Richie, what kind of a fucking question is that?" Formality had become a hindrance after the first thousand feet. Fairbrother was the leader of the expedition; Richard, as much by his abilities as by his status and most of all by his gift of natural authority, could have been an alternative focus for the other men. From the outset of the expedition, on their long trek through Nepal, he had persistently supported the Australian's command, and in doing so had won the man's unaffected friendship.

"That's what interviewers are supposed to say, isn't it? Come on, my fingers are freezing. Answer the question, how do you feel? Confident? Shaky?"

"Ah—you'd be a fool to be confident about an attempt on the summit of Everest. You have to acknowledge that there have been far more failed attempts on all the Himalayan peaks than successful ones. There are so many things you can't predict, especially the weather. It's brilliant now —" he gestured at the sparkling landscape of snow and ice, already glittering in the sun of the early morning, "but as you well know cloud or snow can come over any time without warning. Last night was terrible, wind, violence, flying ice. And you can't predict how the oxygen will go, how the loads people are carrying will affect them as they get higher."

"And what about the plan?" His fingers were completely numb. He would have to stop obliging the TV team soon.

"Well the plan's bloody marvellous as you should know since you worked it out with me, but the best plan in the world won't get you to the top if everything else is against you."

"And tell us about the four men you've picked for the summit."

"Well, I've picked each man for his lucky face. Seriously, I can't think of a tougher, more robust or better qualified group—we've got the three best mountain men in the party and His Royal Highness Prince Richard who's the most vain, stuck-up, opinionated little shit I've ever . . . mmnf! I've ever had kick snow in my face, I should think the rest'll go hell-for-leather just to get away from him . . . mnff!" Richard kicked snow at him again then turned off the camera and set about warming-up his hands.

"Hey, turn it on again. There's something I've forgotten."

"Oh hell . . ." Richard had his gloves on and decided to struggle with the camera as he was rather than expose his hands again.

Fairbrother's voice was deep with emotion. "This expedition is the culmination of two years of planning and supreme efforts by the whole team over the last eight weeks to get as far as we've got. And as we're launching you guys up the hill, we want you to know that all our thoughts and prayers go with you."

The four men set off a few minutes later. Above them the support team were already dug into snowholes. Ambitions for an Alpine-style climb without oxygen had been abandoned. The plan was to gain one camp each day, until they were below the most difficult part of the whole climb, where four men would push on to the top.

Richard's predominant emotion was a solemn elation. To have been chosen for the summit party honoured him beyond expression. He was too experienced now even to guess his chances of being one of the final pair, but the acclaim of the rest of the group was, he told himself, enough. At that moment it seemed to him there was nothing more that he could do in his life.

The legendary landscape of the Himalayas spread out below them, snowy peaks breaking through cloud like vast waves on a frozen ocean. Everest was a realm of enchantment for every climber, but particularly so for him. The mountain had been conquered first in the year his mother became Queen, an achievement which the whole country had experienced, however irrationally, as a blessing on her times.

The beauty of the mountains, the fantastic shapes of the snow and ice, the dazzling monochrome tapestry occasionally splashed with the vibrant yellow or ochre of lichen, never failed to exalt him, sometimes almost to madness.

Physical existence at these tremendous altitudes was unpredictable. Every man had his ceiling, a height above which his body would simply refuse to function. He had seen several of the others collapse, their legs bending helplessly like those of a baby trying to walk, when their thick blood refused to flow any further through their arteries.

Every man who had gained this height had individually surpassed personal limits of exhaustion.

Here normal standards of comfort or energy were as meaningless as the day of the week. Richard himself had experienced blinding headaches and flashes of hallucination lower down the mountain, but they had ceased now.

They made good progress in the morning, moving along the ropes fixed by the support party, but at mid-day heavy snow began and they arrived at the next camp tired and very late.

The hard going meant that they were using more oxygen than they had planned. The members of the support team, who had brought up the bottles and supplies and dug out the snowholes after each fall, were grey and silent with fatigue.

There was a lot of wind and spindrift in the night. The next day they worked along a ridge with difficulty in deep, fresh snow, and then began to climb through a deep ditch; there was less snow there, and it was not technically difficult, but because the sun did not fall into the area to warm it until the afternoon, it was bitterly cold.

A storm raged in the early hours of the morning, the wind screaming over the mountain like a monster. They all slept badly and in consequence set off late in the morning, with ice crystals driving into their faces. Richard felt as if his head was full of mist. Each breath he took bubbled in his chest. His feet and hands were tingling painfully.

An hour later his limbs began to obey him reluctantly. The going was vilely difficult, over boulders and ice, and his pack felt heavy enough to crush him to the ground. All sensation had left his hands. There was no snow and the wind had dropped, but the cold was deadly.

A voice in his head commanded him to give in and go back, but he pushed on, the first of the party. Raising his head to look ahead was an appalling effort and he began to see double. After an incalculable time he felt a heavy touch on his shoulder, but decided it was an illusion born of oxygen starvation.

Again, his shoulder was touched, this time not gently, and he turned round.

"All right, mate?" asked the man behind him.

He hesitated, not wanting to accept the truth, then forced himself.

"No," he admitted. "I'm blown. I've got to give in."

His companions, muffled in their layers of insulating clothing, nodded and he knew his condition must have been obvious for some time. He blundered past them and began the wretched descent back to the camp, stumbling and falling. Cloud covered the hill as he struggled alone, aware of nothing but the rope guiding him and the breath rasping in and out of his lungs.

Within a few paces of the snowhole he collapsed, and remembered nothing more. The support team poured hot orange squash down his throat and dragged him under shelter, where he lay gulping oxygen for a full day and night.

The rest of the summit party returned, one of them almost as exhausted as he was. They returned together to the lower camp in a mood of bitter disappointment.

"We have to pick up everything we can from this and learn from what went wrong so that the next party have a better chance." Clive spoke with resolution, but Richard could see that he too was desperately downcast. They talked of the weather, undercharged oxygen bottles and the exceptionally deep snow the others had encountered higher up, and revised the plan for the next attempt.

Since no one else was going to mention them, Richard raised the particular psychological pressures set up in a team of three, which always split into a pair and one alone. He also took the blame for failing to divide his load of equipment between the others before turning back, so that they were short of some important items. Then he lapsed into a morose silence. He knew he was a fair scapegoat for the disaster.

The next team went up two weeks later, by which time Richard was at the base camp. Fairbrother came to talk to him when he was reading in his tent.

"I hope you're not trying to hog all the responsibility for what happened," he began.

"I hope you're not going to try and tell me it *wasn't* my fucking fault," he countered in anger.

"I'll let you figure that out for yourself."

"I'm not made of the same stuff as the other guys."

"We're all made of the same stuff. Every living organism has its limits of endurance."

He shook his head. "It wasn't a physical thing, it was in my mind. I just could not do it."

"Whatever you want to believe, Rich—I can't stop you. Actually I didn't come to cry over spilt milk, I came to tell you something and ask you something. I wanted to tell you that this has been the experience of a lifetime for me and I wouldn't have been able to do it without you. So thanks."

"I should thank you. It's the greatest thing I'll ever do, I know. You know—well, you don't know but you can guess —there's not much ahead of me now."

"Nor ahead of me." Both men were technically still in the services, but would quit soon after the expedition returned. The mountain had straddled their lives for so long that they had been unable to form any other ambition.

"Well that brings me on to my next point." Fairbrother scraped his bearded cheek. "Getting you all up here may be the last thing I'll ever do. I had a pain the other day, the doctor looked me over and my heart's jumping around like a prawn in a frying pan. He grounded me. Two guys are taking me down tomorrow and they're going to fly me out of Nepal. However it goes, this will be my last mountain."

Involuntarily Richard reached out and hugged the man clumsily through many layers of clothing and sleeping bags. There was a silence in the chill interior of the tent which seemed unbreakable.

"Well, take care," he said at last. He was suddenly aware that Clive was almost as dear as a brother to him.

After Clive had gone, the weather restrained its fatal caprices; the climb was successful and in the general jubilation Richard felt his own failure less acutely.

After he returned to England the heavy inertia of oxygen famine seemed to persist. To make him feel worse, Jo's face stared at him all over London, from hundreds of posters for her last film. He had forced himself not to think of her, and while he had been away, physical danger had wiped even her memory out of his mind. Now that he was both tired and idle, she was a vision who occupied his mind nightly.

He moved through the days like a sleepwalker, carrying out the actions required of him as he accepted the nation's praise for his achievement, returned to the Royal Marines headquarters to finalise his departure. He saw great pride and pleasure in his parents' faces and tried to react to it but his responses seemed inadequate. The knowledge that his courage had failed oppressed him thoroughly, and since the expedition overall was judged a famous victory there was no one to whom he could talk. He had intended to take a holiday, but enjoyment seemed to have no meaning. Jo had once accused him of climbing mountains to escape from life. He heard her voice clearly now.

Eventually he confided in Sister Bernadette, with whom he now had the leisure to plan a second documentary, this time about the Vietnamese refugees in Hong Kong. She listened for a long time, and made some observations about the nature of vocation with immense certainty.

"Now, I've no place to be saying this sort of thing," she concluded, "but as I never got anywhere by doing what I was supposed to do I'll forge ahead. I don't know what plans you've got for your life, but if you ever feel that you would like a job, the Trust is in severe need of a Director."

He looked at her in amazement, sure that he had misunderstood. "Mind you," she added in a conspiratorial tone, "they don't pay much."

•   •   •

THE CELLS BELOW the famous Criminal Court in Kingston were stiflingly hot. The small, cream-walled interview room had no windows. No air moved anywhere in this underground place of confinement, where prisoners were held before being taken up to the courts above. Since taking a job in the public prosecutor's department, Martha had spent many uncomfortable hours in these subterranean ovens.

The woman she had come to question was still in the police station on the other side of the street. All the cells were crowded, and until the men before the courts at present were dealt with, the next batch of accused had to wait. Outside, the loosely assembled crowd, made up of those with a close personal interest in the cases being tried that morning and of people who regarded the Criminal Court as a source of free entertainment, milled around on the sidewalk, fanning themselves and carrying on idle conversation.

She looked through her notes, trying to make sense of them. The woman, who seemed to have had several names but was known as Ella Cassidy, had been arrested as an accessory in one of the biggest drug trafficking investigations the island had ever seen. Martha had been informed that the American and Canadian authorities were also involved; half the suspects were to be extradited if found guilty.

Ella Cassidy did not seem to have been a large part of the story; she had been deathly scared at the arrest and had immediately offered to turn Queen's Evidence. Since her lover was a kingpin in the operation, her testimony was considered important.

Martha sighed and took off her spectacles to rub her eyes. The woman had fried her brains with crack and what she said barely made sense.

There was a crescendo of shrieks from the street above. The prisoners were being brought across to the court building and their women, who had been waiting patiently in their most alluring dresses for the sight of their men, knew the form for this event was wailing and crying and catching hold of the men's shirts with gestures of desperation until the constables pushed them aside.

A few moments later an impassive wardress, her blue striped blouse miraculously fresh, opened the door and Ella stole through it. She wore a red satin gown which was now severely creased; the arrest had been made at a party.

"Sit down," Harley indicated the chair, trying to sound encouraging. "How are you today, Ella?"

The girl cleared her throat nervously. She was short and fleshy, with surprisingly pretty legs. "I am very well, thank you." She had the oddest way of talking, one minute in American slang and the next with expressions that would not have been inappropriate in an English drawing room.

The door opened again and the girl's lawyer, a young man in a brown suit, came into the room with a blue-uniformed constable and stood awkwardly against the wall.

"I would like to go through what you've told me, Ella, to make sure I've understood everything and written it down correctly." Martha read through her statement slowly, pausing with patience to make the many corrections the girl requested. It wasn't much, but it was enough, with the rest of the evidence, to get at least some convictions.

"They not going to send me to prison now?" It was more of a statement than a question.

"You must understand, Ella, that is not the way the prin-

ciple of Queen's Evidence works. I know you see lawyers
doing deals on television, but that isn't how things are in
real life. We can tell the judge how helpful you have been,
and we most certainly will be sure to tell him, but what
happens to you is up to him."

The woman's murky eyes enlarged with fear. "Hey,
that's not fair, I don't buy that."

"It's the law, I'm afraid. I explained that to you in the
beginning."

"She can't do that to me?" Ella turned around and appealed to her lawyer, who stepped forward and confirmed
what Martha had said.

"I ain't goin' to prison, no way."

"Is there anything else you want to say, Ella?" Martha
checked herself in closing the file; maybe the woman would
add something. Dumb as she was she must know more
than she had told.

The woman twisted indignantly on her seat, straining the
seams of the red dress dangerously. Finally she announced,
"OK. OK. You want to hear something? Then listen up.
You ain't gonna belie-e-e-eve what I tell you." With many
self-aggrandising details, the woman told the story of how,
as a maid in a fine house in Cherry Gardens, she had been
paid by the lover of the mistress of the house to report to
him everything she could about the husband.

"It seemed like he was that stuck on her, he wanted to
know every little detail about that man. He even had me
thief his diary. Go through his pockets when you brush his
clothes, he told me, bring me everything you find. He
wanted me to thief his case that he took to work but I said
no, that would get me fired for sure."

Martha tried not to sound impatient. "Well, that's very
interesting, Ella, but I have to concern myself with crimes
committed and the only person who committed a crime
there seems to be you."

"I ain't finish. After a year or so, the woman she finish
with this man and he take up with me." She patted her
chest with pride, rearranging her gold chains. "And that's
when I learn a thing or two and I begin to understand
what's really coming down. I thought he was fussing about
the husband because he love the wife, but no! All the time
he was romancing the wife because he interested in the
husband! And the reason, you're asking me." She paused,

well aware that she had her audience's close attention. "The reason is that the husband work at the British High Commission, and this man is a big hit man, and he is planning to hit Queen Elizabeth herself when she come to visit Jamaica. And I, I know everything about it. Now, they can't send me to jail, can they?"

Martha reached wearily for her note pad, not believing a word of the fantastic recitation. This was a day when debriefing dope-crazed low-life had definitely lost its charm.

"Most interesting," she said, her pen poised. "Let me take down the facts. First of all, what was the name of this family?"

"The name is Hamilton," she told her with pride. "Mr. and Mrs. Patrick Hamilton. They were fine people. Mrs. Hamilton, I believe she was a personal friend of Queen Elizabeth. Did I say something wrong?" Martha's head had snapped up at the sound of the name.

"Not at all, please continue." She recorded the story with growing amazement, her hand looking like a spider as it raced across the paper, the pen between her long fingers. She remembered Richard saying, "There's a limit to security. Of course, anyone could kill any of us almost any time and they've certainly tried. But to do it right, to get away and do it dramatically, that would be a terrorist's real objective and that would be much more difficult than buying a good rifle and learning how to use it."

Ella Cassidy was not pleased to find herself remanded again and taken back across the street to the police station, although Martha took pains to explain that she was still an innocent woman and in time it might well turn out that there was insufficient evidence to convict her.

Six weeks later three detectives representing different countries met in her office, where the ceiling fan worked if it was not particularly effective. They stole covert glances at the picture high above the door of a girl in jodhpurs and a cashmere sweater and with huge, antelope eyes, who bore a small resemblance to the woman of the law in a black business suit who now sat behind the intimidatingly tidy desk. Martha kept the photograph to remind herself of how easy it was to be seduced.

The Jamaican officer opened the conversation. "The man called Ruben Santiago turns out not to be Bolivian at all. The embassy couldn't help us and I thought the trail was going nowhere until his name came through on an Interpol alert." He passed Martha a photocopied document and a photograph. "We'll have to see if the woman Cassidy can identify him, but if this *is* the man he is a Palestinian who spent part of his childhood in South America. He has a number of aliases of which Ruben Santiago is one. And there was a theft of documents reported at the High Commission at the time this woman says he was around."

"But is there any evidence of an assassination plot against the Queen?"

The British detective cleared his throat. "There were threats made at the time, but nothing unusual. However, we have just heard something else that may be significant. The diplomat in question, Patrick Hamilton, was posted to Dublin, where *he* has just been assassinated. And the Irish police have evidence of another assassination plot—against Prince Richard."

.   .   .

LORCAN FLOOD'S HOUSE in the country sounded idyllic when he talked about it. It looked adorable when Jo saw it, a grey stone cottage on a hillside with an orchard and a small plantation of larches behind it and a walled garden in front. Huddled at one side were a small barn and a hen house, from which some particularly pretty fowl with grey and white speckled feathers emerged to parade around the front path. A line of washing blew in the breeze. It was spring, and the hills were crowded with sheep and lambs.

For the first two weeks of her stay, the house was as perfect as it had been painted. Three other people were staying there, including Lorcan's current lover, a boyish, black-haired French girl. The cottage was situated in a wild, de-populated area which had been in dispute between the Welsh and English for centuries and was still scattered with the remains of mediaeval castles.

He took her for long walks over the hills, and listened while she poured out her heart. It was Lorcan's policy never to judge anyone, but she had the feeling that his view of her destiny was from a different perspective than hers.

"I just have to heal," she told him, "to get away from all that craziness and find myself again. Then I'll be OK."

"Poor little flower," he remarked, "so tired of standing

in the field by yourself. Time to go back into the earth to gather strength for the spring."

"Thank you for being the earth, Lorcan. You're very wise, I'm lucky to have a friend like you."

By way of acknowledgement, he inclined his head with a god-like graciousness that always needled her. Lorcan could be intensely pompous at times. Then he said, "And when you're ready to bloom again, what?"

"I don't know. Whatever comes along, I suppose."

His silence suggested that this was not the right answer. She knew it, too. A cold numbness filled her mind and she could neither distinguish her emotions nor express them.

The French girl cooked erratic vegetarian meals for them all, and Jo had again the calming sense of belonging to a family.

The old black telephone rang one morning and Lorcan was summoned to London to see a casting director. He returned ten days later, having been to Los Angeles, and left again immediately to begin work on a film.

"Don't worry," he told them cheerfully as he climbed into his car on the sloping stone track. "If you need any help with anything just ask the people at the farm—they're terribly kind."

Shortly afterwards the French girl decided to go home, and the other two members of the household went with her. Jo was alone.

She luxuriated in solitude at first. It was not the same as being in London suffering the familiar death of a telephone that did not ring, either with work or love. She walked for hours in the hills and revelled in the rare pleasure of a British landscape with no people in it. She read Lorcan's books voraciously, chopped firewood until her fingers were blistered and watched junk programmes on the television. She scattered corn for the chickens and pegged out the washing when the weather permitted.

After a few more days alone, her emotions began to bleed through her blank mind and identify themselves. Anger came first, and she found herself suddenly full of furious energy that she had to burn off by climbing the steepest hills and digging over Lorcan's garden for hours.

One night she made a doll out of flour and water paste, gave it a crown of larch needles, called it Richard and stuck pins in it. Anger was a cleansing emotion, she told herself sternly when she felt guilty. She would never get over him unless she expressed her rage.

After that she felt swamped with sadness. Being always honest with herself, she could not deny that she had lost the only man she had loved fully in her life, and she had lost him through not daring to trust the strength of their love. Without it now she felt half-dead, as if a limb had been amputated or part of her mind cut out. Her only comfort was that being in so much pain at least proved she was alive.

It rained heavily every day, which was more of an inconvenience on a windswept hillside than in London but she comforted herself that, if there were any paparazzi lurking in the Iron Age earthworks on the opposite hill, the daily downpours would discourage them. Alone, she began to become nervously suspicious and lock the door at night, although there was no sign that anyone had followed her.

In isolation, her strength ebbed. The countryside began to take on a more sinister aspect. She noticed the buzzards forever hovering over the hillsides, alert for injured sheep; the springy turf was scattered with the bones of animals which had fallen off the precarious rocky paths or lain down in the rain with a full fleece and been unable ever to get up again once the wool was wet. The magpies, which she had considered a cheerful sight in the greening hedgerows, pecked out the eyes of newborn lambs. Soon she felt a fool for seeking beauty and missing the inherent savagery of nature.

The fox was the first disaster. She heard a commotion in the hen house at night but assumed that the poultry were squabbling about their pecking order and nothing was amiss. In the morning she found one hen moping hysterically under a bush and the rest dead and mutilated, lying in a mess of their own blood and feathers in their well-appointed little home.

The gruesome sight gave her nightmares. She thought it was the shock that made her feel weak and shivery the next morning, but by the evening she knew she was feverish. She decided she would find a doctor the following day, and went to bed.

When Lorna Lewis drove her hired car up to the cottage an instinct told her she had to go inside immediately. She had telephoned, cabled and written to her daughter's last known address, and eventually learned from Rachel of her whereabouts and her low state of mind. Knowing very well what her daughter must be suffering, Lorna feared for her.

She noted that there was only one car, Jo's modest little Renault, beside the building. The only noise she could hear was the moan of the wind in the larches. The lone chicken, half its tailfeathers gone, watched her apprehensively from under the decorative frill of feathers on its head. The building was icy cold and gave no sign of having been heated recently.

"Is anyone home?" she called out politely, stepping into the low-ceilinged room that made up half the ground floor. She heard a voice murmur upstairs. "Jocasta? Is that you?"

She found her daughter in the big brass bed, her face dark red and her lips cracked. The room smelt of sickness. Jo was plainly burning with fever and although she opened her eyes and looked directly at her mother she obviously saw nothing. Words were coming out of her mouth but they were jumbled nonsense.

Remembering the virus Jo had caught in Morocco, Lorna called a doctor. He administered antibiotics, prescribed more and looked the American woman over. She seemed a capable sort, even if she was an actress, so he decided that hospital treatment would not be necessary unless the condition refused to respond.

When Jo regained consciousness she was alone and the bedroom looked different. Her clothes had been put away, the furniture had been moved and there were some early roses in a water glass on the night table. The window was open and she wanted to close it, but every movement was an effort.

Small sounds came from downstairs and she wondered if Lorcan had returned early. She stood up, swaying, and walked painfully to the head of the stairs. There below, in front of the fireplace, a woman knelt with newspaper, kindling wood and coal, making up the fire with the skill of much practice. She wore jeans and a very clean pink sweatshirt which was not the ideal attire for this dirty job, but Lorcan's masculine blue-and-white apron protected her clothes. There was a long interval before Jo realised that this was her mother.

"What are you doing here?" she protested in a weak voice.

Lorna turned with a shining smile. "Is that my daughter speaking?"

"Who else is here?"

"I'm so glad you're OK." Her mother brushed the ash from the apron and came up the stairs to hold her. "Your fever's all gone, I can feel that." She pushed Jo's sticky hair back from her forehead. "Would you like to take a bath while I make up your bed? Clean sheets would be more comfortable, wouldn't they?"

Extreme tiredness settled on Jo's shoulders like a heavy bird coming to roost. All she could do was nod.

Her mother nursed her for a week, bustling around the small house with obvious enjoyment. She shopped in the village, washed clothes and cleaned out the neglected rooms energetically.

"You'll have to forgive the way I cook," she told Jo, producing another meal of meatballs in cream sauce with potatoes. "I never learned anything but Swedish home cooking from my grandmother."

"I never knew you could cook," Jo answered, reflecting that this person busying herself with simple domesticity was someone she had hardly known at all.

She would not let Jo get out of bed for several days, and came in to sit with her and watch the television. Colin Lambert appeared twice a week in a historical romance set in Kashmir in Queen Victoria's time. He was making a useful career out of playing British army officers in India.

"Isn't it strange how someone so beautiful can be so stupid?" Lorna remarked as they watched the rich rays of a sunset gleaming on Colin's golden curls by a lakeside.

"I wouldn't call Colin stupid, exactly. For an absolute shit with no talent whatever, he's done pretty well."

"Yes, he's not dumb exactly, he's . . ."

"Just dumb about what's really important. His values are all wrong."

In their new mood of companionship, Jo ventured to put into words something about which she had been thinking for several days. "I always wondered if he tried to hit on you?"

"Darling, when you're married to a man twenty years older who hasn't made a great success of his life, *everyone* tries to hit on you. It gets really tiring keeping out of their way." She laughed. Jo was beginning to understand that she had misjudged her parents. It was perfectly obvious now that her mother loved her father deeply.

"When I was a kid, I used to think you must be having affairs all over the place."

"Yes, I know you did."

"Didn't it make you angry?"

"At that time everything you did made me angry. I guess I wasn't exactly the mother of the year. You had a hard time growing up, didn't you?"

"Uh-huh. But it's over now."

Her mother suddenly put her arms around her and held her very tightly. "It's never over, darling. Look at me. I finally grew up enough to be a responsible parent."

"Don't cry," Jo wiped the tears out of her mother's eyes with the cuff of her nightgown. "It's OK, Mom. We made it through all right, didn't we?"

"I suppose we did."

A few days later Jo's strength returned and Lorna, with becoming embarrassment, mentioned that she had had a purpose in seeking out her daughter, the actress. She produced the script of *The Dawn of Dreams* in her hands and said, "I think that no one could play this part as well as you, Jocasta. But don't let me tell you how to run your career . . ."

"In the circumstances, Mom, I think that's pretty funny."

Jo curled up in the windowseat with the rough stone wall digging into her back and read the script through.

"This is a dream," she told Lorna, her eyes bright with excitement. "This is the kind of part I always wanted but no one ever offered me. Do you really . . ."

"Yes of course I do. You don't think I came all this way just to get my long lost daughter back, do you?"

"Thanks, Mom," was all she could say, clutching the script to her chest.

Afterwards Jo looked on the next six months, when they made the film together, as the happiest time of her life. After the first few days of shooting, Jo found that she had access to a depth of feeling she had never been able to use before. Her performance moved to a higher dimension; she felt it, and when the technicians burst into a spontaneous round of applause at the end of the day, she knew that everyone else was feeling it as well.

The pleasure of getting to know her mother as a person

for the first time was as acute as the joy of being in love, except, as she told Lorna late at night at the ranch house, it was better because you knew this love was forever.

"Who were you really in love with?" She was accustomed, now, to her mother's oblique shrewdness.

"Richard," she answered in a low voice, staring into the fire. "But I couldn't handle it."

"Why don't you tell me about it?"

Jo considered. Even after almost a year her feelings were so huge she could hardly see them clearly, but she began to talk and gradually reduced them to a size that could be encompassed by words.

"Well, do you want me to tell you what I think?"

"Yes—I mean, what's a mother for?"

"Exactly. I think you should try again."

"Mother, he threw *me* over, remember?"

"Only because you asked him to. It takes two to screw up a good relationship. Don't you feel differently now?"

Jo paused and considered. "Yes," she said, "I feel like a different person, the person I was meant to be all along but got distracted from. But it's nothing to do with him. It's to do with being with you, knowing I was wrong about you— it's as if I had to come back here before I could go forward."

"So—why don't you just call him?"

"It's not that simple. How could we ever make a relationship which worked?" She twisted a lock of her hair around her forefinger, a childish gesture which Lorna observed tenderly.

"Probably the same way everyone else does. You're assuming he's a different kind of person from you, that he has different feelings. He isn't that different, is he?"

"No," she replied carefully, feeling a new door open into the future.

"So—what are you, afraid that he'll turn you down again? I mean, what's the worst thing that could happen if you call him?"

"You're just betting that if you call me a coward I'll be angry enough to do it."

"Well?"

Lorna urged, nodding at the telephone on the Jacobean table. "You do have the number, don't you?"

CHAPTER XXV

"WHATEVER ELSE THE future has in store for me, I'm never going to pack up my whole life and move house again." Victoria watched with unsmiling satisfaction as the removal men carried the first of her packing cases into her new home.

"I remember your mother saying that every time we moved." Her father was walking up and down the empty sitting room, turning stiffly to look around the bare space. "Everything's very well finished—now I see what they mean by smart as paint."

Eager to return to London after her husband's death, Victoria had bought the house from a developer before it was fully refurbished, and had it completed to her own specifications. After decorating three of her own homes in five years, she knew exactly what she wanted, and with Patrick's insurance to add to her own income from her family, there was no need to stint. She had demanded several major pieces of furniture from Aston Langley, as well as some of the pictures which Pamela had consigned to a storeroom.

Upstairs the children's feet resounded through the carpets as they ran from room to room, followed by their new nanny.

"Are you sure you'll be all right here tonight, Tory?" He looked at her from below eyebrows that were growing thicker and whiter each year. Alex's death had moved him suddenly closer to old age. "You can all come and squeeze in with me while things get straight here . . ."

"We'll be fine, Daddy, don't worry. It's terribly kind of

you but I'm so keen to get on with life, with my *new* life, I can't bear to waste a second."

"You're much too young to be saying things like that. Too young and too lovely." He smiled, relieved. Talking to Victoria had been more difficult for him since her brother's death, and now that she had also lost her husband she seemed less accessible than ever. She looked normal, indeed, she looked very well, her father acknowledged that her beauty had matured strikingly in the past few months, but her responses were distant. The elderly man kept his thoughts to himself, accepting that everything nowadays was more of an effort than it used to be, now that he had lost his relish for living. He had decided to take early retirement from the Admiralty the following year.

By the evening the new home was arranged, lacking only details of decoration and personal clutter to look as if Victoria had lived there all her adult life. Her father stayed for a supper of scrambled eggs with his grandchildren in the kitchen and was driven sleepily back to his own home content that his daughter had surmounted this latest in a succession of traumas with all the competence he would have expected.

Victoria's competence now resided in a collection of drugs which she arranged carefully in her bathroom cabinet before going to bed. She was no longer exactly clear what she was taking, or what she was supposed to take. She had several tranquillisers to calm her, anti-depressants to lift her mood, narcotics to help her sleep and a painkiller for the knife-like ache in her neck which had appeared after Patrick's death.

Her husband's assassination had instantly made her heart lighter, although she admitted that to no one, least of all herself. From her point of view Pat had made an ideal death, quick, dramatic, with overtones of patriotic martyrdom; it had freed her from a marriage which she knew had been a terrible mistake. It had also been perfectly timed.

The reports of Richard's love affair with Jo had disturbed her. Press stories and paparazzi pictures she ignored, unable to equate the dignified, unsmiling woman in the pictures with the Jo she remembered, an untidy student in outrageous clothes. The gossip which Patrick had related, maliciously but with tact, she also dismissed. Far more serious was what she heard from her family and friends.

"They fight like cat and dog but he simply can't keep his hands off her," Suzie Chamfer confided, visiting on her way to a location in Connemara.

"It's just sex, then?" Victoria inquired, carefully shielding her expression.

Suzie had been breezily open as usual. "There's no such thing as *just* sex with him, is there? God knows what he's got but when he falls for somebody he just devastates them. Hurricane Richie. My sister's never recovered, she's becoming a *total* alcoholic. I mean, you should know if anybody does."

"We were so young, I can hardly remember." Victoria flinched from the thought of Richard sharing with another woman the precious intimacy they had once created together. She had sensed intuitively that Princess Louise was a temporary erotic fascination, pursued as much to annoy his family as for its own sake; knowing Harley as she did, Victoria never doubted that Richard had been a diversion for her. Jo was different.

From another hidden corner of her mind, Victoria recognised that Jo was uniquely dangerous. She had watched the American woman forge her own identity from the flux of her inheritance and her ambition. Jo had created for herself an immense inner power, and that was a dangerous example to a man like Richard, who was himself drawn to the same struggle. Victoria saw it as a futile enterprise for him. Richard had his background to define him, just as she did, and questing outside it was a perversity, satisfying to the individual, perhaps, but potentially fatal to the social system which he represented. Jo, Victoria considered, would bring out the worst in Richard.

More disturbing news followed.

"The Queen really likes her," Pamela told her when she visited Aston Langley in the summer. Her stepmother's habitually bright manner was dulled. Both women felt the gravity of the prospect of another disastrous American alliance for the Royal Family. "Of course, it isn't so crucial now, who Richard marries—now Charles and Diana have had another boy he's way down the line of succession, but all the same . . . The Queen is the very last person you'd expect to be starstruck, isn't she? Even after that awful business with the photographer drowning in Jamaica. She's supposed to be furious that he broke it off."

"How very odd," Victoria responded. "Still, it's all over now, thank goodness. Do you suppose he'll ever settle down?"

"I think they're getting rather worried. Andrew isn't going to waste any time, by the looks of things."

When Victoria's husband died just a few weeks later, it seemed almost shockingly fortuitous to both women. They said nothing to each other as they acted out the rituals of mourning, but cherished a shared purpose.

After years of chemical manipulation, Victoria's mind was separated into several parts. A tiny portion in the far depths of her consciousness clung to reality. The rest, fragments of wishes, fantasies and suspicions, swayed like waterweed in the stream of her will. What Victoria wanted to be, she saw. Whatever conflicted with her desires, she could not perceive.

Her conscience was an obedient function which she could mould at will; it readily agreed that her duty was to marry Richard. She was strong now, and he was the one who had become susceptible and confused. She alone could give him the strength to play his part in the world. Furthermore, she was owed this happiness, by destiny, by the world and by Britain itself. They had conspired together to take away her mother, her brother and her husband. Richard was her just reward.

In addition, she concluded that he also owed her his love. He had taken the unrepeatable first flush of her emotions and marked her for life, his own identity stamped upon hers like a brand. She was his already, she would always be his, and taking full possession of her was now his duty. The distant voice from the bottom of her heart told her that what she really wanted was revenge, but she could not hear it.

To encounter him again was simplicity itself. Pamela set the machinery in motion with a ball at Aston Langley for the joint coming of age of Thomas and Aunt Rose's youngest son. It was a natural occasion to fill the house with five hundred young people, and Richard was invited as a matter of course. Victoria, in a carefully chosen low-backed black dress, was dancing with her young brother when she felt a hollow in the crush behind her and turned, with a thrilling sense of *déjà vu*, to face Prince Richard once more.

He looked considerably older. He was broader and his face was still roughened and bronzed by the Himalayan weather, but more than these his eyes showed it. They were no longer lucid with emotion, but shuttered and dull. She thought he looked hard.

When they danced she used all the conversational skills polished through years of diplomatic entertaining to relax him, and in time succeeded.

"You've changed your scent," he said suddenly, in the midst of discussing nothing in particular.

"Yes, I have—do you like it?" she asked, fanning the spark with a soft smile.

"It's sophisticated. You used to wear a rose perfume, didn't you?"

"How clever of you to remember."

"Of course I remember, you always smelt of roses."

He was not exactly smiling, but Victoria was satisfied that she had touched him. Richard was simply pleased to see her poised and confident. Although Victoria had ended their relationship, he felt now that it was his impetuous ardour, and his selfish desire to marry and acquire a man's estate thereby, which had drawn her into the situation she was unable to tolerate, and so she weighed on his conscience. He felt nothing else for her. His sensibilities were cauterised. It seemed to him unlikely that he would ever feel anything for any woman.

Their apparent rapport had not gone unremarked elsewhere in the room, and since the consensus among the magic four hundred was that Victoria Hamilton was a good thing and a safe bet, more invitations pairing her with Richard followed in brisk succession.

In London, during the week, she shopped and lunched assiduously, learning all she could of his state of mind. The general opinion was that Richard was profoundly unhappy, drifting without any purpose to his life and beguiled by unsuitable ideas.

One day a basket of spring flowers arrived at her house, with a note saying simply, "Welcome home. Ruben." She felt mild surprise, then a faint frisson of forbidden excitement, and she immediately squared her conscience once more. Santiago, after all, was the only person in the world who had sought her friendship for herself alone. It was a happy coincidence that he was in London. His behaviour was always correct, she could control him easily, and his attention flattered her—so what harm could there be in enjoying it? The glow of another man's admiration would help her with Richard.

He telephoned the next day, and called for tea, bringing a small pink box containing soap made from English rose oil. She knew, because she had laughed over it in Harrods with Pamela, that it was the most expensive soap in the world. It was the kind of extravagant, perfectly chosen gift she knew she would never get from any Englishman. He was vague about his business in England and exquisitely well-dressed. She marvelled at the freshness of his striped shirt and the fit of his dark blue suit. His cufflinks were lapis lazuli and she caught the faint, familiar tang of *vétiver* from his aftershave.

Half hidden in the crackling marbled tissue wrapping the soap was a jewelled butterfly, its wings panes of topaz and its body set with tiny emeralds. She handed it to him with firm regret.

"I can't accept this, Ruben. Even though I am a widow now, I don't want to . . . to . . ." Words failed her. There was no delicate way to express it.

"I understand," he said quickly, obviously trying not to show disappointment. "It's too soon . . ."

"No, not that. You know what my marriage amounted to." She wanted to tell the truth and get things on to a firm footing. "There is someone else in my life now." He looked so downcast she was afraid he was going to weep. "But we could perhaps be friends, Ruben, if you would accept that."

"I would be honoured," he answered at once, and she allowed him to kiss her hand to seal the agreement.

A friend proved something she needed. A sense of not belonging still nagged at Victoria in the narrow confines of her social life. Her mind had once been half-awakened, and, manipulative as he had been, Patrick had been a stimulating companion. The role of a Kensington mother bored her intensely, and the world beyond her children was scarcely more interesting. She was not ready to relapse forever into social small-talk, stories of ski-ing, shooting or hunting and accounts of the doings of mutual friends edited to fit the bounds of good taste.

Ruben happily took her to art exhibitions. She decided to begin collecting herself, and he accompanied her to auctions with enthusiasm. She found his eye excellent and his taste faultless. He occasionally took her to concerts, or the opera, entertainments she had never felt the licence to enjoy fully before.

His adroit comprehension of a woman's mind was also balm to her lonely soul. She took him shopping, finding his reactions helpful as she dressed the new part of a young widow. Discreetly, he continued to give her presents, always so thoughtfully chosen that she could not refuse them. Sometimes they were trifles, like a rose-scented candle in an engraved glass. Sometimes they were things he had plainly gone to a great deal of trouble to acquire. She positively treasured the Chanel handbag, opulently quilted and trimmed with gilt, which he brought her only a few days after the shop explained that there was a six-month waiting list for this particular status symbol.

"Wherever . . . ?" she asked in amazed delight as she unwrapped it.

"My cousin imports Chanel into Bolivia," he explained, equally pleased with her reaction. "I simply asked her to send it in the diplomatic bag."

"I think you're a very wicked man," she said with a pretty toss of her head.

"I know," his glance, Latin and liquid, implied a judgement on all their past relationship. She felt very comfortable with him.

As her renewed relationship with Richard progressed, she confided in Ruben without, of course, telling him the identity of the man in her life.

Soon there was much to relate. Officially the Prince was enjoying an extended holiday after leaving the Royal Marines. In fact, he was locked in a battle of wills with his parents and their advisers. His sole ambition was to accept Sister Bernadette's invitation to become the director of the Nansen Trust. His mother and father were divided over the issue, and had decided to call what he referred to as a council of war, a dinner party to which the Prime Minister, a senior civil servant at the Foreign Office, Britain's United Nations representative, and directors of two major charities had been invited, and briefed beforehand on the topic to be discussed.

The consensus favoured his father's view that a British prince had no business meddling in international politics, let alone as the agent of an institution founded in Norway and based in New York. Richard responded to the assembled worthies with an excess of charm which his mother knew was simply a tactical screen behind which his position was the more stubbornly entrenched.

The following weekend Victoria was invited to lunch at Windsor, a privilege into which she read a great deal more than was intended. It was one of the small gatherings at which the Royal Family appeared for all the world like the clan of a Victorian country squire, entertaining the pillars of their small community beside their friends and relatives after Sunday morning church.

Prince Philip and the Dean of Windsor fell into an earnest discussion about evolution.

"Dad's riding his hobby horse again," Richard's tone to Victoria was half humorous and half critical. "He thinks he can reconcile science and religion if he goes on about it long enough to the right people."

"I'm afraid I encourage him," the Dean admitted tactfully. "It's good for us churchmen to listen to ideas from people who have the capacity to stimulate."

"Don't you find also great attraction to evolution from the moral point of view?" Prince Philip continued as if his son had not spoken. "The adaptive process works on man's behaviour, doesn't it? Those who live by the sword die by the sword, while prosperous, civilised communities live in peace which is usually inspired by a high religious philosophy. The whole system encourages improvement."

"I think that's a nonsense," Richard broke in with a marked lack of courtesy. "It's against all evidence. History's full of instances of a country's high religious philosophy simply degenerating into fanaticism and producing nothing but death and destruction. Look at . . ."

"You've missed the point," his father snapped. "Fanaticism or fundamentalism are precisely the kind of excess which dies out because of the evolutionary process." There was an involuntary intake of breath by the Dean, who was aware that the two men were already in conflict.

"But it doesn't actually die out, does it?" Richard pressed on while the rest of the table fell into an uncomfortable silence and the footmen cleared the plates. Victoria felt her skin prickle with alarm at his harsh tone. "And an excess of peace and prosperity is what causes a society to fail. At bottom people are idle and self-interested and that's what brings about their downfall—and nothing changes. Your theory is just a Utopian daydream."

"There you are," his mother smiled wickedly at the Dean. "That'll teach you to come here for stimulating ideas; the whole family seems to be full of them this morning." There was general laughter and conversation resumed around the table. The confrontation had been averted. Prince Philip gave his son an aquiline glare before taking up his argument again in a quieter voice.

After lunch Richard and Victoria walked down to the gardens at Frogmore, where the spring flowers naturalised around the artificial lake were at their best. He was obviously still agitated and walked rapidly.

"I didn't know your father was so interested in evolution," Victoria said in a soothing tone.

"I can't stand him arguing in that pompous way when he doesn't know what he's talking about." Richard had his hands deep in the pockets of the old Barbour jacket he wore over his navy sweater. "God help me if I ever get that far removed from the real world."

"*Richard!*" She was shocked to hear him so forthrightly critical.

"Of course, we're not arguing about his theories at all really, you know that."

"What are you arguing about? He seems in a terrible mood."

"What the hell I'm going to do with my life." They left the lakeside and followed the path which led to Queen Victoria's mausoleum, a massive building whose copper roof gleamed green in the optimistic spring sunshine.

"I was wondering about your plans," she prompted with caution.

"I haven't got plans, Tory. I've got one plan, one ambition, one obsession, and I won't be talked out of it."

"You mean the refugee idea?" She too found the prospect inappropriate, not least because Richard would probably live in New York and travel constantly.

"Yes. What my father can't understand is that I *can* do this, and I've *got* to do it. If you only knew the things I've seen, Tory. There are thousands—millions—of refugees in this world with no country, no home, nothing but their ideals, hoping for a better life, victims of forces they can't begin to comprehend. Nobody wants them. They don't live, they exist—on charity. But they need more than that, they need somebody to speak out for them. God, if some Irish pop singer can go on television and raise fifty million pounds for Ethiopia, I can at least try my hand, can't I?"

They were walking slowly between two hillocks formed from the earth excavated to make a lake. The contrived contours of the park which had been his mother's childhood playground always irritated him.

"You're not a pop singer," she pointed out, delighted that he was eager to discuss his future with her.

"No—I'm an excessively privileged person with a first-class education and the feeling that I ought not to be wasting it all."

"You're not wasting anything, Richard. You can find a marvellous job . . ."

"Showing my face, pressing the flesh, looking interested, lending my name—it doesn't seem like a proper life for a man, Tory." He paused in front of the enclosure where his immediate family were buried. Set some feet apart from the other graves was the plot where the Duke of Windsor lay. The clumps of forget-me-nots planted around the graves were at the peak of their flowering, knots of sentimental blue enclosing each white stone.

"But think about it, Richard," she urged in a lower voice while the penalty of rebellion lay illustrated before them. "It'll be hell in security terms, travelling round the world like that. You could easily be—assassinated." She dropped her voice to remind him that the experience was close to her. "And you can't avoid getting tangled up in politics."

"That's exactly what my father says."

"Well, I do think he's right."

"What does everyone else think?" He was searching for a lever to change his father's mind.

"You'll be angry."

He stopped walking and took her hands. "No I won't, I promise. Tell me what everyone else is saying. You must, Tory. I know I can rely on you to tell me the truth." His eyes, she noticed, were clear now and looking frankly into hers.

"They think you're completely mad," she said firmly.

"You belong here, in Britain, Richard. You're part of this country."

He nodded. She interpreted it as acceptance. In fact, he had confirmation that Tory was of a piece with the forces that restrained him. Her courtier's instinct was to resist change at all costs. She would dare nothing, risk nothing and preserve him, and his family, like mammoths frozen in the arctic ice, for the sake of their vision of Britain. Without the companionship of his fellow Marine officers, he was increasingly aware that such folk hampered his best qualities. He had already resolved to dilute their influence by inviting Clive Fairbrother to join his staff. At least, that was how he rationalised it. He would not confess his loneliness even to himself.

"Besides," Victoria ventured as they turned and walked back between the avenue of budding chestnut trees towards the castle, "it would be a terrible life for your wife."

He shrugged, then gave her a look of momentary bitterness. "I can't seem to find a woman to put up with me as it is."

"She could be right under your nose," she suggested, falling into her old half-joking tone.

"Maybe you're right." His answer was abstracted; he was wondering where in the vast, anonymous real world Jo Forbes might be at that moment.

Of such misunderstandings Victoria built her fantasy. He talked to her often, knowing she was a true touchstone of her caste, hearing her arguments so that he could defend himself against them when they surfaced again in the mouths of his parents' advisers. She logged every conversation, every dance, every routine compliment, every ordinary courtesy on the side of her progress.

The notion that Prince Richard should have married his first love was an increasingly popular one among the magic four hundred. Hostesses all over Britain co-operated to keep the wayward Prince within their own extended family and save both the man and the country from his dangerous passion for foreigners. Victoria and Richard were paired constantly at dinner parties and house parties throughout the winter. She persuaded herself that these meetings had been sought by him in order to further their new closeness. The exhaustive explorations of his possible course in life were to sound her out for her own role as his wife. This time, she would be equal to the challenge.

She told Ruben she expected to receive a proposal soon. A few weeks later, she told Pamela, as if announcing the expectation to a third person would make it into a fact. Pamela eagerly but obliquely broadcast the news. One afternoon Victoria took a telephone call from Sean Murray of the *Daily Post*, but she denied everything as a matter of course. A small group of photographers appeared outside her house. She was gracious to them, feeling restored to a kind of glory by their presence.

* * * *

MARTHA FOUND BEING cross-examined a disorienting experience. She was accustomed to second-guessing her victim's thoughts and asking the questions which would give her the right answers. To suffer the same manipulation herself was unpleasant.

The fact that her inquisitor was a British policeman made her the more uncomfortable. She found that the most violent emotions she had were hatred and contempt for any representative of the institution which had allowed her brothers to be victimised. She told herself that this man, cold, formal but astute, was not responsible for his corrupt colleagues, but could not suppress her feelings.

"Did Mrs Hamilton discuss her relationship with this man?"

The Inspector probably looked younger than his age, with pleasantly regular features, soft brown hair and a prominent Adam's apple; his white skin confirmed that he had rejected the pleasure of his hotel swimming pool and applied himself to his work diligently in the weeks he had spent in Kingston investigating the Santiago affair.

"She didn't—at least, not in so many words."

"What do you mean in so many words?"

"I mean . . ." She searched for a way to explain the empathy of female friends to a man, knowing that however acute he might be, he could have no real understanding of it. The strange collusion between two women who had loved the same man, agitated by cross-currents of affinity and jealousy, was something she hardly comprehended herself. Nor was she sure that the past tense was correct; she still loved Richard although she opposed what he represented. She was enduring this man's inept questioning because Richard was in danger, and he was dear to her.

Victoria loved him just the same. The Victoria she had most recently known had been a confused, bitter woman but that force was alive in her. Martha was inclined to consider that love was like energy, neither created nor destroyed, but able to change its form. It was a compulsion which directed and compelled them all. She wondered if the pale, humourless Inspector inspired the same quality of emotion; she doubted it.

"I mean that Mrs Hamilton gave hints that her marriage was not happy but she never said anything specific," Martha said at last.

"What k-kind of hints?" He had the vestige of a stammer, which irritated her.

"She would make disparaging remarks about her husband, or about men in general."

"Nothing more than that?" He was obviously disbelieving. Out of courtesy, Martha had vacated the chair behind her mahogany desk and was sitting opposite him on the tired grey seating units which furnished the conference area of her office. She wished now that she had not been so gracious. She wanted to hide behind the protective authority of the big desk stacked with legal files.

"To me, the implication was quite clear. Where is this getting us, Inspector? You'll forgive me saying this, I know —" she knew how to deliver a cutting smile "—but my understanding was that we were to collaborate in this investigation since the activities of this man Santiago are under investigation both in your country and mine. Now I'm beginning to feel as if I am the one who will be standing trial."

He looked at her with embarrassment. Martha wearily poured out a little more charm. It was now a weapon she could use when it suited her. When she first returned to Kingston her mood had been austere, and she had scorned to smile and make herself attractive. She had been intrigued to discover that if she played down what was held to be her beauty, men resented it, white men in particular. With time her attitude had mellowed.

"Perhaps if you told me what kind of information you're looking for I could be more helpful," she suggested. "My own involvement with Mrs Hamilton was quite a while ago and I had only just returned to Kingston. My memory for personal matters isn't too precise, I'm afraid. Have you reason to believe that Mrs Hamilton was actually implicated in the murder of her husband?"

"I'm sure you appreciate that I can't disclose that kind of information."

"I'm sure *you* appreciate that this so-called collaboration isn't going to get very far if you don't."

They regarded each other with frank hostility.

"You will have to excuse me now." Martha stood up and offered her hand to be shaken. "I am already late for another appointment. If you are going to be in Kingston for a few more days, and you think it would be worthwhile, perhaps we could set up another meeting." She tried to sound positive. She needed the facts that this man was determined to withhold.

Late that evening she sat on the verandah of the Campbells' house and talked over the affair with Claude. They met every week at a free legal clinic in a village inland, and because the Campbell family had their country house a short drive away, it had become a custom for her to dine with them afterwards.

The clinic's clients were mostly one of two kinds; abandoned mothers asking about the right and probability of child support or anxious old people concerned about the titles to their land. Advising them tried her patience, but on this occasion restored her enfeebled sense of purpose.

"I'm wasting my time on this Santiago business," she told Claude, who sat on the steps a few yards away, the glow from the house highlighting his white shirt and the shine on his forehead where the hair was receding. "If he's ever caught, I can't see the British extraditing him to Jamaica to stand trial."

"So why pursue it? The investigation is the police's business, anyway."

"Can't you guess why? It wasn't exactly the Attorney-General's orders but I'd have had a hard time refusing. Since I'm so intimately connected with Santiago's victims, past and future, I have to be involved. God, this is such a small, small island."

"Sorry you came back?" He lit a cigarette and glanced at her humorously over the lighter flame.

"Stop teasing, Claude. I'm too tired."

"You sound like a wife already."

"Everything's always conjecture with you, isn't it?" Claude was approaching thirty, and his parents were anxious that he should find a wife. Every real conversation he had with Martha alluded to marriage. She knew it was his tentative way of assessing her attitude to him, but she refused to pick up his leads. There was the pleasure of revenge in that, and besides, she was not certain that a wife was something she would ever want to be.

"If they can send that fool over from England," she said suddenly, "they can damn well send me to London."

"Oh, come on," he protested, throwing away his cigarette in anxiety. "There's no need for that."

"No need at all. But I'd enjoy it. If I scare up the evidence to nail Santiago first, then the British will have to let us have him for a trial here. Besides, I'll enjoy it. I feel I'm ready to go back."

"For good, or just for a visit?" His attempt to sound casual was not successful.

"Who knows?" she answered lightly. Let him sweat, she counselled herself.

*   *   *

AT THE THIRD attempt to telephone, Jo heard the guarded voice of some member of the Palace staff say he would see if His Royal Highness was available. There was an interminable silence. Alone in her parents' living room, where the ashes of the fire were cold, she waited by the telephone. It was morning in California, night in London, the time he had always asked her to call, when, if he had been at an official function, he would have returned.

"Jo?" His voice sounded eager. Providence had sent them one of those telephone lines that was clearer over seven thousand miles than many which crackle to the next street.

"Hello, Rich."

"Where are you?" Eager and confused.

"I'm at my mother's house. I'm in California." She did not know what else to say. Need for him swamped all her thoughts.

"Are you coming to London?"

She realised that she had no plans at all, and no reason, other than him, to be in London. She thought of her apartment, once such a proud haven of independence, now cold and neglected, defiled by the hole in the wall where the radio transmitter had been inserted. She had filled it in with cement, but it was still there in her mind. How long would it be before photographers gathered outside again, and she would be forced to ask herself which of her neighbours had betrayed her to the newspapers? The place was tainted. It was not her home any more, but the home of the lost, hounded woman she had been before. She never wanted to live there again.

"I . . . I don't know," she said at last.

There was a silence. "Well, if you were in London, maybe we could meet?"

"Yes." The appalling logistics of such a meeting unrolled from her memory. "Maybe you've got a window in your diary the year after next." Damn, she hadn't intended to bitch.

"I'm leaving the Marines, you know."

"Yes. You climbed your mountain, I read about it. What are you doing now?"

"Nothing." His voice was guarded. "Listen, will you call when you get here?"

If I get there. Such nerve the man had. "Sure. Maybe next week."

The next morning she told her mother she was returning to London for a few days. She suddenly felt too nervous even to say Richard's name aloud, although they both knew why she was going back.

"You look tense," Lorna offered on a neutral tone.

"I *am* tense." Something of her old frustration with her mother returned.

"It will be all right, Jo. I know it." She put her arm around Jo's shoulders.

"How do you know, Mother? That's such a silly thing to say. You don't really have any idea what I'm looking into. Nobody here has. I mean, you all elected an actor President, for heaven's sake. You just see the British Royal Family as a Dickens story in a Cartier setting, you have no idea what they're really like, let alone what they're actually about. This is a *real* national institution, not a pretend one like 'Heritage.' "

"You're right," Lorna told her at once. "I know I don't really understand; but you do, and that's why I know you'll be all right. Luckily for all of us, Prince Richard isn't in love with me."

The trace of irony in her voice mellowed Jo's mood. "I don't know that he's in love with me either," she remarked with good humour.

"You're not frightened, are you?" Her mother pushed back the tangle of brown curls from her forehead with a gesture Jo remembered from childhood.

"Of course I'm fucking frightened," she said angrily, and then they both laughed, realising how long it was since she had had any impulse to swear.

The ever sociable Suzie Chamfer, back on the West Coast to start the new series of "Heritage," called on Lorna a few days later and immediately appreciated Jo's disinclination to visit her own apartment.

"Why don't you stay in our house?" she suggested, shooting a shrewd glance at Jo from beneath the tousled hair that all the balsam in Hollywood could not quite tame. Like everyone else in London, Suzie had heard the rumours about Prince Richard and Victoria Hamilton. Unlike most other people, she was reluctant to believe them. If great love was beyond Suzie's emotional range, she knew it when she saw other people in thrall to it, and Richard had had that look only when he was with Jo. Suzie also had an instinct for people who used more drugs or drank more alcohol than was wise. Victoria was not in the same class as her sister Jane, but to Suzie she had the muffled, off-key personality of an addict. "Colin's filming in France for a month. You can have it all to yourself. I mean, I don't know what you need to do in London . . ."

"Nor do I, until I get there." Jo felt guilty about all the times she had called Suzie a blue-blooded bimbo who made the average shop-window dummy look talented. "I don't know how long I'll be there, either. I'd really like to live near my parents now. Even if I can't work in LA, I want to spend some time with them. Maybe I'll just be in London for a couple of weeks to arrange for everything to be sold."

Lorna, who had been taking a telephone call in the study, appeared suddenly, almost dancing with excitement.

"I think you'll have to be back by April, sweetheart. That was Selwyn and he says it's almost certain our picture is going to be nominated."

"Nominated?" Jo's mind was elsewhere.

"The Oscars, you dummy!" Suzie shrieked with joy and jumped up to kiss Lorna. "How utterly utterly divinely *fabulous*! Oh wow! I think I'm going to cry." She kissed Jo, who was slowly taking in the news. "Now listen, darling, off you go to London quickly and get whatever you have to do done and get back here right away. And our house is your house, all right?"

It could not really have been anyone's house but Suzie's, in a grey brick terrace in the most fashionable part of Fulham, its narrow rooms decorated in a scaled-down version of English country house style. Multiple ruffles of brightly flowered chintz frothed around every window, table and cushion; deep silk fringes hung from the sofas and every time Jo crossed a room she almost fell over a brocade footstool. Every flat surface was cluttered with silver photograph frames; most of these held glamorous pictures of Colin and Suzie, but some of them contained old black-and-white pictures of the Chamfer dynasty, with pride of place going to a group including Suzie's grandfather and King George VI posed with their guns in front of fifty dead pheasants at Sandringham.

To Jo the house was unreal but not unpleasant. She recognised it as a pretty exercise in British self-mythology. It seemed like a stage set and she began to feel the jittery energy of performing. With a bold adrenalin sparkle on top of her new confidence, she called Richard, who sounded more composed, indeed, rather formal. He invited her to dinner the next day, which surprised her.

She could not guess that he was almost shaking as he put down the telephone. He at once told his Secretary to cancel a dinner with the Royal Rutland Regiment, of which he was now honorary Colonel-in-Chief. The man stood open-mouthed in petulant amazement. Such engagements were never cancelled under any circumstances.

"I'm ill," Richard told him with an ironic rasp. "I've got 'flu. I'm weak and feverish. A heart complaint is a possibility."

"But, Sir, it's very short notice . . ."

"Then you'd better not waste any more time."

Richard set off in a stew of confusion, not knowing what he wanted from the encounter. He argued the possibilities of her call around and around, not daring to think directly

of renewing the affair, in case she was unwilling, although
there was nothing he desired more.

Jo answered the door herself, wearing a plain ivory dress
several years old which always gave her confidence. The
shock of his presence paralysed her for an instant; she had
forgotten his spell. It was an aura of intense life; she felt
drawn towards him, impelled into the unique world which
the two of them created together.

Moving automatically, they exchanged tense greetings
and social kisses. He felt her breath on his cheek, a familiar
warm zephyr carrying the scent of her mouth.

"Why are you hiding out here?" he asked, dreading an
answer which would name another man.

"This is Suzie Chamfer's house, I'm only borrowing it,"
she explained. His expression at once relaxed and she almost caught her breath as she understood his anxiety. They
passed each other awkwardly in the cluttered hallway as
she showed him into the miniature drawing room. He
reached out and caught her hand; she almost sprang into
his arms.

Relief and excitement overwhelmed them both. They
crushed together to kiss, grasping each other to breathless-
ness as they tried to repossess all the months of their separation. Her firm, cool flesh swelled against his lips, alive
with tiny pulses like a hillside running with hidden streams.

She felt his arm tighten around her waist and read his
mind. "The stairs are too narrow—you can't carry me," she
whispered.

"Who says?" Her feet left the ground and she luxuriated
in his strength. It was an awkward journey upstairs but he
achieved it and laid her in the centre of the bed. Once
naked, they strained against each other as if they could fly
into atoms and fuse into one being. They were fiercely hungry and satisfaction was all the sweeter for being so long
denied.

Afterwards Jo lay against him, her face on his chest,
wishing she could breathe his body into hers. Sadness stole
down on her unexpectedly, dripping from the alien antique
lace which Suzie had lavished all around the bedroom. The
thought of a home of her own sprang up, and with it the
vision of the defiled privacy of her apartment.

Before she knew it tears were pouring from her eyes and

she pulled away and sat up, angry with him, with herself and with the world for its cruelty.

"What is it?" he demanded, amazed to see that she was weeping.

She could not speak but pushed away his embracing arm.

"Don't push me away. I love you, you're unhappy, I want to know why. Tell me." He was angry himself now.

She shook her head. "It's no good, though, is it? We can go on forever like this. Every time we're together it's as if we've never been apart, but it doesn't mean anything, it can't. Loving you, you loving me. It's hopeless."

"Why should it be hopeless?" Slowly, he began to piece together her reasoning and see that he had misunderstood her. "Jo, I've felt as if I was half dead this last year. I thought it was just an after-effect of the war—a lot of the men who were in the Falklands were pretty screwed-up. The Everest thing showed me that it was something else. I'm not a person who was meant to be alone. I need people, and I need one pêrson in particular, and that's you. I *have* to be with you. I want to be with you, forever. What I mean is, I want to marry you."

Her face, already pale, turned white and blank with shock. "You can't marry me and anyway it would never work out," she half-whispered.

"I can do what the hell I want." He spoke very gently but his conviction was unmistakable. She looked at him in fear and wonder, searching for signs of weakness but seeing none. He had engaged the full power of his will and she could imagine nothing and no one withstanding it. "And as for it working out, that's up to us, isn't it?"

She smiled briefly. "My mother has a theory that it takes two to screw up a good relationship."

He reached out for her again and this time she did not resist. "I know what kind of life I want, I need you to live it. If you think you can bear it. But whatever it costs me, or anyone else . . ."

"What are you going to do?" She condemned herself for being preoccupied with her own fears and unaware of his struggle.

"I've been asked to work with the Nansen Trust . . ." She began to speak but he continued, "and the question is whether I can. It will mean being virtually a statesman, working abroad with governments . . . everyone's appalled, of course. Especially my father. If I'd wanted to spend the rest of my life playing at mountaineering or in the Marines, they'd all have been quite happy."

"I don't think your parents would have been happy if you weren't," she argued and he kissed her forehead. "Haven't you ever wondered how your father must feel, walking one pace behind your mother all the time? You have a kind of freedom which he doesn't, haven't you?"

"You see—I do need you to keep me straight about things. It's not them, it's everyone else, of course. Running around like headless chickens. So many people have got so much invested in our family. But I swear, if the men who say they speak for this country can't see a way to allow me to make some contribution to the world because of who I am, then I'll change it."

"You can't do that."

"I can. I'll resign. I'll give up my right of succession. I've thought it through and I will go that far. But however it works out, Jo, I'm not going to be an object in a palace, taken out and paraded through the streets every now and then. I'd go mad. And whatever happens, I will need you. You're the only person who can give me the strength to do it. And anyway, if I have to jack it all in, we won't get far on my salary alone."

"Not with your taste in clothes, that's for sure."

He was silent as long as he could bear to allow her to consider. "So—what do you think?"

"I can't think," her mind was spinning with fears and possibilities. "I know I love you. I don't know if I can do the rest of it. I wish I wasn't so weak—it's unbearable being hunted and spied on all the time . . ."

"I know, I know."

"I mean, I should be able to bear it, I was born into it just like you were, but . . ."

"It'll only be until we're married, things will quieten down then and we can live somewhere impossible to get at."

"Like the third moon of Neptune, maybe?"

"So you will marry me, Jo?" She felt a tremor run through both his arms and his chest heave as he snatched a deep breath. The palpable force of his emotion and the pleading catch in his voice were irresistible.

"Yes." The word seemed so large that her voice wavered as she spoke.

"Well, you could sound more cheerful about it."

Argument flew to her lips, but she decided to kiss him instead.

Outside on the street, Detective Henshaw wearily drove the Prince's Jaguar around the block again, hoping this time to find a place to park. He was hungry but not surprised. The staff were agreed that nothing ever went according to plan when the American woman was involved in it.

CHAPTER XXVI

THE TAXI TOOK Martha to an apartment block halfway between Buckingham Palace and New Scotland Yard, a pompous, red brick enclave of crisply decorated flats which were used to accommodate diplomatic guests. She opened the window of her small bedroom and sniffed the thin, humid air of London. It brought back memories, and she was surprised that so many of them were good.

There was scarcely time to do more than this, and dive into her single suitcase for a warmer blouse, before she had to leave again for the police headquarters. She walked through the twisting lanes of Westminster, choosing to pass in front of the mother of Parliaments like a mere tourist. In her modest clothes, no one turned to look at her. In Kingston she was accustomed to a certain measure of anonymity. Here she was used to being recognised wherever she appeared, to stepping out of taxis instead of walking the streets. For a short while she felt her old personality walking with her like a dazzling shadow.

At the police headquarters she was shown into an interview room where a thickset blond man rose to his feet as she entered. She felt her face split into the widest possible smile as she shook hands with Inspector Henshaw.

"The boss doesn't know about this yet," he confided, pulling up his chair to the utilitarian metal desk. "And I expect he won't like it when we break the news. He's always telling me I'm an old woman about security."

"How is he?" she asked, surprised how much she cared about the answer.

"Bloody terrible," was the uncompromising reply, and before he could say more the glass door opened and two other detectives joined them. "This is Inspector Lynch, he's head of the team who've been watching your man over here." A slim, clean-cut man with fair hair shook her hand. "And Inspector Carter of the Anti-Terrorist squad I believe you already know."

"Pleased to meet you again, ma'am." Carter was her adversary from Kingston. When she saw how the other two detectives treated him, Martha realised he was their senior.

Lynch cleared his throat. "I'll open the batting, shall I?" They nodded. "The man known as Ruben Santiago has been in and out of Britain for over a year now, travelling between London, Paris and Amsterdam. He has had several meetings with known officers of the IRA."

"Was he involved in the murder of Patrick Hamilton?" Martha leaned her head on her hand, suddenly feeling tired.

"We can't tie him in with that. He was in fact in London on that day, but it was, if you like, a routine car-bombing. The IRA wouldn't use him for something so simple. However, Santiago has been in contact with the man's widow—that's, er, your friend, I believe?" He sounded as if the idea of anyone being Martha's friend was hard to credit. She masked her feelings, annoyed with herself already for having made a powerful enemy.

"Santiago's been in touch with her since she has been back here. In fact, they're becoming quite friendly, meeting two or three times a week. Between us," he nodded at Henshaw, "we've also logged quite a few encounters between Mrs Hamilton and various members of the government and aristocracy, and of course with Prince Richard. That in itself represents a security risk, but the man's been exceptionally careful in his career, he's got no record of any kind anywhere in the world and simply deporting him would be difficult."

"In Jamaica he had diplomatic status—what about here?" Martha forced herself to smile. "If he's attached to the embassy, you could ask for him to be withdrawn."

"Santiago has a Bolivian diplomatic passport, and we considered asking the embassy to withdraw him, but it would only be a short-term measure. He's got so many aliases we'd probably have him back within a week under another name."

"It also wouldn't necessarily remove the threat he represents," Carter added. "For the past few years the IRA have favoured the kind of device known as a sleeping bomb, which can be put in place weeks before it is detonated. It was that kind of bomb which killed Lord Mountbatten, and which nearly wiped out the government in Brighton last year. It's actually detonated by a radio signal, so that can be done from quite some distance away. If Santiago has already planted such a device, he wouldn't need to set it off himself, anyone with the right information could do the job. From the terrorist's point of view, that's the beauty of it. In fact, if he's got away clean all these years that's probably the way he works."

"So—are we assuming Prince Richard is the target?" Martha turned inquisitorial eyes on Henshaw, but it was Carter who answered her.

"Our information is absolutely positive on that point." She felt as if someone had poured cold water down her spine and shivered involuntarily. "We took a lot of information from one of these so-called supergrasses in Belfast last year, and he was quite definite. Because the Prince served with the Marines over there, and because he's thought to be unpopular . . ." The man faltered, suddenly aware that his observation could be taken personally by the grave black woman listening to him. Public opinion was divided about Prince Richard; half the country felt he was the only young member of his family with any guts or glamour, the rest considered him to be the extravagant, arrogant womaniser the *Daily Post* painted him—if not worse.

"So you see," Henshaw broke in, "that's where you can help us."

"I don't *quite* understand . . ." Martha was not in a co-operative mood. She was hungry, and jet-lagged, and bitterly sure that her free legal clinic in Kingston needed her that afternoon much more than anyone in Britain, especially Richard.

"Everything points to the fact that Santiago will use Mrs Hamilton to get to Richard. Without her knowledge, of course. It's the only way. We go over the cars every day with dogs, check out everywhere he goes before he gets there. Short of posting a sniper outside the Palace, using someone who's in his company as a carrier for a bomb is the best method."

"So you thought that I . . ."

"With your connections with them both," Henshaw said firmly.

"Could perhaps find out what's going on."

"I find that a suggestion in poor taste, Inspector."

"I'm sorry." He obviously was not.

"Why not just ask her what's going on, take her house apart?"

"If he knows he's under suspicion, Santiago will disappear immediately and we'll lose him."

Martha turned the proposition over in her mind. Once her initial emotional reaction died down, she could see the detectives' logic. "Can we put Prince Richard himself in the picture?"

"I'd advise against it," Henshaw said at once. "He's got a very cavalier attitude to security and he's in a peculiar mood at the moment."

"Oh?" She gave him a cold look which quite wiped from Henshaw's mind the many evenings he had sat in the back of the Prince's Jaguar trying not to hear the conversation between the two of them in the front seats.

"Unpredictable," Henshaw explained uneasily, at the limit of his expressive range. "He's been unpredictable ever since the Falklands, if you ask me."

"I still think he needs to know if his life is in danger." She looked around the table and eventually saw agreement on three embarrassed faces. "And I suppose, with my *connections*, that will be my job?" She sighed and told herself to get energised. Distasteful as it might be, this was something she had to do. It was not just part of her job; it was a kind of peace-making, the vital resolution of her years in London.

Lynch coughed and adjusted the cuffs of his striped shirt. "I don't quite understand your status here . . ."

"Nor do I," she replied with rapid irony. "But if I can assist you gentlemen, I'm happy to do so." She rose to her feet and picked up her notes, addressing Henshaw. "When can we have a meeting with the Prince? The sooner the better, don't you think?"

"I slipped us into the diary tomorrow morning," Henshaw told her. "He's safe tonight, he's . . ." There was another sudden pause of embarrassment.

Martha raised her eyebrows. "Seeing another lady, perhaps? You can't shock me, Inspector Henshaw. I'd be more surprised if you told me he was staying at home."

She felt herself smiling again the next morning when the green baize door in his office opened and Richard appeared at last, radiating charm which she knew at once was pumped up for the occasion. Even through his deep tan she recognised the crumpled quality of his skin and hollows of exhaustion around his eyes which suggested that he had not slept well. His lips were a little bruised. They were, she remembered, particularly susceptible to damage. He used zinc cream to save them from sun and wind, but there was no protection against kissing. She felt much older than he was, careworn and responsible. It seemed unthinkable, now, that once she had been the one to send him back to the Palace with the same marks of love on his face.

"So you're only talking to me now because there's the prospect of a great case in it for you, is that it?" She marvelled at his gift for wiping away separation. Like a spotlight, he turned his full attention on her. Having been accustomed all his life to conducting his most important relationships in capsules of time, he had perfected the art of creating immediate intimacy. A footman brought them coffee, and he sat opposite her on a yellow brocade sofa.

"Not entirely. I just got so angry with the boys from Scotland Yard coming out to Kingston and treating me like a dumb nigger." A giggle, her first for many months, escaped her lips. "So this is your office," she looked around the room with interest.

"You never saw it before."

"We had better places to go."

"We certainly did."

In silence, they reached for the cups. The scrape of bone china echoed in the quiet room.

"So—how do I look?" he asked suddenly, drinking his coffee in one gulp.

"I'd say you look . . . rough," she replied. He laughed and ran his fingers through his hair.

"Oh, it's good to have you back in London, Harley. Rough! I don't feel it. I'll tell you why in a minute. Let's get Henshaw in and get the police business over with." He reached for the telephone on his desk and summoned the detective; Martha, assuming the finesse which the men seemed to think she should have, explained the situation.

"So it seems quite likely that this man has been hired to kill you, and that he's using Mrs Hamilton in some way."

"Poor, poor Tory." A weight of concern visibly bowed his shoulders, but Martha sensed that it was not a deep feeling. Now that he had given his heart elsewhere, Richard was thinking of himself, of the gossip the affair would provoke when it became known—as it inevitably would—and the embarrassment of an old lover who had gone to the bad, with the inevitable reflection on himself. "What a terrible time she's had, and now this. Are you sure?" he looked at Henshaw.

"There is no doubt," Martha told him firmly. "But we are quite sure that she's an innocent victim, she doesn't know she's being used."

"She's always an innocent victim, isn't she?" Martha dropped her eyes, noticing with surprise that the Persian rug on the floor was more than a little worn. "You don't agree?"

"It's not for me to discuss . . ." With time and distance between them, Martha had come to look upon Victoria as a moral coward. The Englishwoman always found a strategy to avoid every unpleasant reality, whether it was drugs, infidelity or simply the British veneer of politeness which reduced all other peoples to insignificance. She was weak but Martha did not despise her for it in the way she now judged Richard.

"No, tell me, Harley. She certainly isn't exactly her old self, you know. She's unpredictable, she says strange things sometimes—I can't tell you precisely, but something isn't right with her."

"It's just an instinct I have, nothing concrete," Martha refused to be drawn. "She's never mentioned this man Santiago to you?"

He shook his head. "I suppose you want to double up on security, Henshaw?"

"I'm afraid so, Sir."

"Well, for once I'm not complaining. I don't feel like being murdered by the IRA this morning."

"I'd like to give the orders right away, Sir."

Richard nodded his dismissal and the man left. There was another silence in the room while he walked up and down in front of the cold fireplace, deep in thought.

"Can I tell you something?" he asked her, looking almost wicked. "A secret. Nobody must know, not yet."

"You can tell me anything," she assured him, crossing her long legs. "But if it's truly classified stuff I'd as soon not know."

"It's not exactly classified. I was seeing Jo last year, you know that don't you?"

"The world knows it, Rich." Sometimes he was so out-of-touch she wanted to scream; she remembered that. She remembered it as one of the many proofs that he lived in a different world. When their own exploits had been on the front page of every newspaper in the world, he had hardly been conscious of it.

"Well, she's in London now and last night she agreed to marry me."

There had been a brief, inexplicable premonition of what he was going to say, and she quickly smoothed her expression. The smallest cloud of jealousy passed across her face, but she wiped it away with a smile. "Rich, that's wonderful. You two always did speak the same language. Can I be the first to congratulate you?" She rose gracefully, conscious of her utilitarian blue suit, and kissed him on the cheek. In the formal room, surrounded by reminders of his status, she felt that even this gesture was too intimate. He seemed like a different man in his own setting. "But I thought you and Jo were all finished."

"I thought we were too. She found it very difficult, being with me."

"So what changed?"

"I think she did. She isn't different, but she's somehow more herself since she made that film with her mother."

"And I hear they've both been nominated for Oscars."

"Yes, I'll have to say goodbye to her when she flies back for the ceremony next month. Until then . . ." his voice trailed into silence. He looked out across traffic in the street below to the greyish, exhausted grass of the park.

"You don't sound very happy, Rich."

"I'm anxious, anxious for her. It was different for us, we were trying to shock people and you could cope with all the attention."

"Come on, I enjoyed it. I felt really proud, standing beside you in front of the whole world. It was only when I understood that the picture wasn't telling the whole story that I changed my mind. I think Jo knew that all along. She's much more sophisticated about the world than I was."

"I'm afraid of losing her again, Harley. If a thousand paparazzi descend on us the way they did before . . ." His fists clenched involuntarily.

A delicious idea occurred to her. She turned towards him and took his arm in an old, familiar gesture. "Listen, I have to be in London for a while—why don't we spend some time together? I mean publicly, of course. As publicly as possible. I mean, all the papers think you're seeing Victoria again . . ."

A look of surprise flashed into his eyes. "I didn't know—nobody told me . . ."

"Well, they do. But listen, if we're seen together again, the press will go crazy. I know the way their tiny minds work. They'll be so busy playing off the English Rose against the Dusky Beauty they won't even know Jo's in town. If I've got the hounds of hell barking around my door, they won't even think of sniffing out a third girlfriend, now will they? Let's do it, Rich. I'd like to help Jo and I'd really enjoy putting on an act to get revenge on a few photographers. But I must get this meeting with Victoria over first, I don't want her to turn hostile on me." She spoke with some doubt. This was a meeting to which she was not looking forward.

"You're a very, very generous woman," he told her, taking both her hands. "OK—if Jo agrees, let's do it."

At one o'clock that morning he arrived at Suzie Chamfer's house from the annual dinner of the British Alpine Association, glorious in full evening dress and pale with exhaustion. He found Martha there with Jo, the two women curled into the bright chintz sofas with a charged atmosphere all around them.

"Why didn't you tell me?" Jo demanded at once with angry eyes. "Why didn't you tell me someone was trying to kill you?"

"I wasn't told until today," he looked across her head at Martha, who widened her eyes in a "Who knows what goes on in her mind?" expression.

"You should have told me at once," Jo insisted. She had a way of winding her arms around his waist that he loved, and she made a hesitant move towards him now, but then withdrew, disturbed.

"Harley came to tell you, I thought that was just as good. Better. She knows more about it than I do."

Jo sighed and said nothing, aware that he did not understand her distress and ashamed of herself for giving way to fear. She felt that destiny was playing cat-and-mouse with her, giving her an inch of joy on the one hand and taking a mile of misery on the other. It seemed such a familiar trick to snatch Richard away the instant she had found him again. The awful cruelty of it fascinated her, although she told herself she was being unreasonable.

"I'm sorry," she whispered later when they were alone. "Sometimes I feel as if it was some law of the universe that I have to be unhappy. I feel I've got too much and some catastrophe has to occur to restore the natural order. It's selfish of me. You're the one who's in danger. Aren't you worried, Rich?"

He shook his head. "If we only knew it, there's probably someone out there trying to kill every one of us most of the time. It's been like that all my life. I suppose I just accept it."

She sighed, wondering if she could accept it also. All her life she had been aware of people watching, hostile strangers whose interest had never been idle. This was the first time she saw the ultimate end of that evil curiosity.

"Did Harley talk to you about her idea to throw the press off the scent?" he ventured, holding her close.

"Uh-huh. She's a sweetheart, isn't she? I just would rather you dated a couple of SAS men. But I suppose even that wouldn't do any good if they were really out to get you."

"That's better." Her light-hearted fatalism pleased him; it was the way all his family thought about the particular dangers of their position.

"If we're going to get anywhere as a couple," she responded sharply, "you're going to have to stop patronising me."

Later, in the pale, sleepless hours of the early morning, she said, "Martha's terrified of this meeting with Victoria. I don't know why, I think she's afraid that Victoria will guess everything. I said I'd set it up for her, make it like a college reunion."

"Good idea." He was almost asleep.

"We're seeing her the day after tomorrow." He murmured another acknowledgement. Jo felt acutely alone. Victoria, she discovered as soon as she picked up the telephone to suggest the meeting, filled her with contempt.

The reunion with Victoria took place at her own house. In her suggestible condition, the idea of giving a little lunch for her girlfriends seemed attractive to her, particularly since Jo was suddenly so famous. She was able to ignore the fact that the three of them had Richard in common as well as Cambridge.

The three women sat on the hard *faux-bamboo* chairs in the breakfast room and conversed uncomfortably.

"I expect you've seen me in the newspapers—isn't it dreadful?" Victoria, who rarely had to open her own wine, was struggling with the bottle of white Mâcon. Jo helpfully took it from her.

"Very embarrassing," she said shortly. "They print such lies, don't they?"

"Not *all* lies," Victoria gave a small, crooked smile as she took the opened bottle and poured the wine. "I can't say anything, of course, but I am seeing quite a lot of Richard nowadays. We're going to be at Nicky Brompton's birthday party next week, for instance."

"Uh-huh." Jo and Martha were both aware of Richard's plans for that evening.

"I think he'll always be a little in love with you," Martha added gamely, inwardly shocked at Victoria's odd, whimsical manner and her unfocused stare.

"It is funny, the three of us, isn't it? Do you remember telling our fortunes that night at Girton, Jo?"

"Uh-huh. I can remember doing it, I can't remember what the thing told us." Jo was dismayed to find that she could not master her emotions. The knowledge that this cool, impeccable façade of Britishness concealed a woman whose lack of principle had led her to endanger the life of the man they all loved, filled her with fury. Acting the scene was a strain she was afraid she would be unable to bear; all she wanted to do was to lay hands on Victoria and shake her into recognition of her crime.

"I can't remember what it said either. Except it told you to go home, didn't it, Martha? That was right. We should have written it all down. It's funny how life turns full circle and comes round to the beginning again, isn't it? Do have some salad." Victoria handed the bowl of lettuce and tomato across the table and Jo helped herself in silence.

As the awkward conversation continued, Jo forced herself to observe Victoria's behaviour as an exercise to preserve her self-control. Soon the cause of the Englishwoman's decline became obvious to her. She had researched her role in *The Dawn of Dreams* partly by talking to tranquilliser addicts and now she cursed herself for not recognising the same signs in her former friend. The pockets of panicky confusion in Victoria's mood, the apathetic base note in her personality, the shallow expressions of off-key emotion—everything checked out; Jo announced that she was dying to see over Victoria's new house, and was airily invited to wander upstairs. In the bathroom cabinet she discovered an obsessively tidy stack of bottles which confirmed her diagnosis.

She returned to the breakfast room and tried to take part in the nostalgic discussion which Victoria herself had launched with Martha, but was lost for words. In silence she reviewed the Englishwoman's progress from a fresh, well-trained girl to a woman lost in self-delusion.

Jo found no pity for her former friend. To be weak was permissible; to pretend to be strong and superior, instead of acknowledging the frailty, was foolish. To let that pretence master you, so that your will was sapped and your conscience deadened, was wicked. Victoria, she found, had always displayed a kind of passive arrogance which was characteristic of English people of her class. She was a feeble, formless thing with no identity of her own. A hollow shell of received attributes, from her history and her peers, concealed her instability and she never questioned their viability in case the whole construction collapsed.

After an hour and a half, Jo pleaded a long-awaited call from her mother and left. Martha opened another bottle of wine and tried to get Victoria to open her mind.

"You were so unhappy with Patrick, I could see," she prompted.

"Yes, I was," Victoria agreed, combing her hair with her fingers.

"Did he have affairs?"

"Oh yes. But I made him stop, you know. I put my foot down. It's the only way, you'll find out when you're married." Martha strained her ears to hear Victoria's own admission, but none came. Santiago was still in town, and had visited the house the day before but the Englishwoman remained impenetrably superficial.

At last Martha stood up to leave and began the usual exchanges of parting.

"What a *very* smart handbag," she said, picking up the little gilt-trimmed object from the hall chair. "Chanel! This is *the* thing to have right now, isn't it? My, it's heavy." She examined it with fascination, thinking of it as the talisman of the mad world which still attracted her.

"That's the chain," Victoria explained. "Can you believe there's a six-month waiting list for these? A friend gave me this as a present."

"What a friend—hang on to him, baby!" Did something spark in the misty depths of Victoria's eyes at that remark? If it had, it was too brief for Martha to read.

She took a cab around to Jo's temporary home and found her fidgeting angrily in the narrow drawing room. "I'm sorry, I couldn't stay longer, it was really getting to me," she explained. "She's gone, isn't she?"

"She was like that when she lived in Kingston, but I thought it was just the strangeness of the place and the fact that Patrick was playing around and she hated Jamaica."

Jo shook her head, her rich brown hair stirring about her shoulders like agitated kelp. "It's drugs, Martha. She's on tranqs, trust me, I know. I've seen enough of them to be suspicious and I found a stash in the bathroom. That's how she can do this. Her mind's in pieces. You can see that she's doped, can't you?"

"No—but I remember in Cambridge . . ."

"Exactly. My guess is she's been popping Valium ever since."

Martha shook her head, reluctant to believe. "She's always so correct."

"And she looks strong, in control, above reproach even. No one would suspect, would they? She's had so much tragedy in her life, more than she could deal with. People just think she's grieving, I'm sure that's what Richard thinks."

There was a silence in the exuberantly cluttered little room.

"I think in a way it's a good thing," Jo forced herself to

be positive. "If you get your conviction and she's an accessory, they won't send her to jail, will they?"

"Maybe not, but you can never tell what a judge will do in court on the day." Martha spoke with weary irritation. "But it doesn't make it any more likely that I'll be able to get through to her."

"No. I'm sorry, Martha, I wasn't thinking straight. Her brains are totally scrambled, you won't get anything out of her except accidentally. She can't relate to anything. Who am I to talk? I can't relate to Richard being blown up, either. Right now being a Valium junkie seems like a good life plan."

"Let's just get through the next few days," Martha advised, seeing her friend's distress.

She was hard put to take her own advice the following morning, when a call came asking her to meet Inspector Carter at his office in Scotland Yard.

"As a matter of courtesy," he announced, self-importantly folding his hands on his spotless, cheap blotter. "I thought I should let you know that the West Germans have asked us to co-operate in a big anti-terrorist operation of theirs and arrest Santiago. I had him picked up last night and we're holding him until their team can get here to interrogate him. They suspect him of the killing of five British soldiers over there last year. I'm sorry, but their request would take priority over any similar request from Jamaica."

Martha concealed her anger. Santiago was her reason for being in London; what the man was effectively doing was cheating her of a victory and inviting her to leave town. She suspected a stirring of the monstrous British establishment, that sleeping crocodile which lay camouflaged and invisible to the naïve eye until it opened its jaws for a victim.

"Thank you so much for letting me know, Inspector." She purged her expression of irony.

"My pleasure." He was equally neutral. "Give my regards to Kingston."

"Since I'm here in London and the weather isn't too bad, I think I'll stay on a few days." The flash of displeasure in Carter's dull eyes was gratifying.

"Your friend Mrs Hamilton will still be under surveillance," he added, unmistakably warning her to keep her distance. "We can't rule out the possibility that Santiago has planted some kind of device around her to be detonated by someone else."

She quit the ugly concrete building in a fury and sought the familiar distraction of frivolity. After all, she was to go to the Royal Opera House with Richard that evening for the first of their public outings, and she needed something to wear. From her apartment she telephoned her favourite designers in search of clothes. No one in fashion ever bought dresses; they borrowed them from designers for their brief lifespan at the height of style, months before they were due in the shops. A hot dress would be wearable for six weeks or so, after which no woman with serious pretensions to elegance could be seen in it. Scented and soiled with cosmetics, it would be returned to the source, to be kept as a sample, sold on to a less demanding customer or put into the end-of-season discount sale.

Spectacular in pink off-the-shoulder silk satin from the Emanuels and a borrowed chip of the Cullinan diamond, she accompanied Richard to the ballet that evening with a murderous expression.

"Surely it's good news if Santiago's in custody," he argued as they withdrew in the first interval to the tiny room, like a red velvet cell, behind the royal box. "I can't say I'm not grateful to have one less terrorist hit-man after my blood."

She sighed and sipped her champagne, a little mellowed by the cool effervescence. "It's just a power play," she explained wearily. "Carter and his bosses want me off the scene before I cause a scandal."

"You can't blame them," he chided humorously. "It is one of your best tricks."

"There were only a couple of photographers out there when we came in," she said to shift the ground of the discussion to something less contentious.

"Wait until we come out," he advised. "They're like sharks. One gets the scent of blood and next thing there are hundreds of them."

"I almost miss Cowley," she said, finishing the wine as the bell sounded for the next act. "He'd been around so long. I keep looking for his ugly face."

Richard said nothing and took her arm to escort her back to her seat. As the performance continued he glanced at her proud profile, illuminated by the light from the stage and animated with pleasure.

"You like the ballet, don't you?" he asked as they began their progress down to the foyer after the final curtain call.

"I've always loved the idea, even when I'd never seen it. It's another part of the great unattainable white ideal, I suppose. My teacher at school told us black girls couldn't be ballerinas so I was fascinated by the whole thing immediately."

"Do you want to come again?" As they left the protection of the Opera House interior, a barrage of cameras began.

"I'd adore it," she told him with her old rich laugh. "Just when we thought it was safe to go back into the water . . ."

Henshaw drove them smoothly to the Palace, and she stopped for half an hour of tea and conversation. In Richard's sitting room a black leather jewel box, worn smooth by years of reverent handling, was open and she unclasped the diamond tear-drop and returned it to its home.

"How long do you think it will be before it's worn again?" The opulence of the jewel, and the knowledge that it was probably among the smallest of the vast hoard of priceless gems stored close by, suddenly overwhelmed her.

"Years. Decades. They're pretty contentious pieces now, Granny's chips. Because they were given by South Africa. Too hot to handle, like the fur coats. Mother almost never wears any of them, although she likes this because it's quite small."

Martha laughed, because the central diamond was bigger than her thumbnail and so brilliant that it had reflected flashes of light like shoals of fish across the full width of her bare shoulders.

"What shall I choose for Jo?" he asked her; the question had been heavy on his mind for days. "My mother will choose an heirloom piece but I think she should have something modern for a wedding present."

"Aquamarines? No, too pale. Not emeralds, they're too intense. Nothing heavy, because she hates heavy jewellery, says it gives her a headache to wear big things. I think a diamond necklace, pretty but not massive. She has such a lovely long neck." She laughed again. "I can't believe this conversation, it's just unreal, isn't it? You're a lucky man, you know that."

For a moment in the muted light it seemed as if he blushed.

Later, as Henshaw drove her home, Martha looked curiously at the back of his thick, muscular neck. Now that she had met the detective among fellow policemen, she appreciated how much of his robust personality was muted by the effort of patience which his role as a royal guard demanded. He even seemed more masculine when he was outside the confines of the court.

"Don't you get sick of watching and waiting and driving and being treated like part of the furniture?" she asked him suddenly.

"Sometimes," he confided. Even his Yorkshire accent was more distinct out of Richard's aura. "But it's my job."

"I'm glad it's not mine," she said, almost to herself. "You know Santiago's been arrested?"

"I was informed, yes."

"Well, what do you think about it? If you say that's not part of the job I'll hit you."

"Don't do that, miss. You've got a longer reach than me. I think it was inevitable. Carter didn't get where he is by letting situations get out of control. I expect you're disappointed."

"Yes," she agreed shortly, her mind moving on to other things. They passed a luggage shop and Victoria's Chanel handbag floated into her consciousness. Something about it had seemed worrying, but she could not decide what.

* * *

RICHARD FOUND THAT he could see the world with Jo's clear eyes now that he was sure of her. Within a few days a tornado of speculation roared through the press as he appeared to be courting both his old loves simultaneously.

Clive Fairbrother, in his first days at the Palace, reported the gossip of the court to him with amazement. "Are you sure you know what you're doing?" he asked, determined never to be schooled in the obsequious ways of his new colleagues. "The staff are chattering like a bunch of galahs and they're sure your mother's going to be mad if you don't sort things out."

"Don't worry, Clive. I know exactly what I'm doing. Six

months and we can leave all this behind us, I promise you. If you feel like feeding them a bit of information, you can just let slip that I'm going to Garrard to order a ring today. Don't worry, it's the truth." He and Jo had made a drawing of the ideal jewel the previous evening, and he unconsciously patted the breast pocket of his jacket where it lay.

"Just tell me one thing—am I going to like this woman, whoever she is?"

Richard paused, totally unaccustomed to considering the preferences of subordinates in this way. "I hope so," he rejoined. "I like her."

"You must do if you're going to all this trouble to make sure you get her."

Within twenty-four hours the news that a ring had been commissioned had leaked from the Palace to Sean Murray, who sounded his hunting horn louder and longer than ever before as he ordered the story to be splashed.

A few days later Richard requested a meeting with his mother and saw at once, from the crisp set of her lips and the cold light in her eyes, that his strategy had succeeded.

"I hope you're coming to tell me what all this is about," she said at once, before he had taken his usual seat on the small white brocade sofa in her drawing room. "Your father is absolutely appalled."

"It's quite simple really," he told her, leaning back with confidence. "I've been able to take your advice."

"What does that mean?"

"That I've persuaded Jocasta Forbes to marry me." In Richard's understanding, Jo's own initiative, so long considered and so painfully taken, was of no significance. He had already forgotten that she had taken the first step towards him.

A brilliant smile transformed his mother's expression, like the sun breaking out over a stormy sea. "But I don't understand, I thought . . ."

"So did everyone. It's a pretty complicated situation, but we needed a smoke-screen. Jo can't bear being harassed by photographers the whole time."

"I can't blame her, after everything she's been through." He could see that his mother was positively bubbling with delight. "Well, this is simply marvellous, I am so pleased." She rose and was expecting to kiss him, but he did not move.

"But that isn't the only thing, Mother. About the Nansen job . . ."

"You really had set your heart on that, I know."

"Don't you agree, though? It's what I ought to do. I'm not worth much if I run out on it, am I?"

"You've always been so worried about what you were worth." She sat on the edge of her desk and folded her arms. "Yes, you know I agree with you. Your father . . ."

"You'll get round him somehow," he announced with confidence, standing up to receive her embrace.

"I suppose I shall have to or heaven knows what you'll do next." She pointed at a copy of the *Daily Post* on a side table with an ironic expression. "I must say you've been extremely clever. After all this nonsense he'll probably agree to anything half-way sensible."

It was as she predicted, and a few days later Jo was invited to the Palace for tea to meet a family unanimously welcoming and approving of all Richard's decisions.

"There, you see," he said as he drove her home. "Everything's going to be just fine. I just wish you didn't have to leave."

She showed a flash of annoyance. "All the time I've been around you I've heard you saying your family needed you or your job demanded this or that—it's the same for me, can't you understand that? Jesus, Rich, I've worked so hard for this—and so has my mother."

"All right, relax, I didn't mean it." He had spoken carelessly, forgetting how sensitive she was. "I'm proud of you, you know that."

"Sometimes I think you're also jealous," she goaded him, hurt and wanting to inflict some pain in return.

"Well, I'll admit that. I am. I've always been jealous of anyone with real ambition. There—now I've owned up, can we stop quarrelling?"

Jo left the next day with a sense of foreboding which she could not dispel. Martha, trying to offer comfort, had passed on the news of Santiago's arrest, but Jo had not been consoled. "You said anyone could activate that kind of bomb," she explained. "I can't get it out of my mind, especially since I know that Victoria isn't in her right mind."

"I promise you, there is nothing to worry about now," Martha spoke with all the authority she could command.

"And if you fluff your speech to the Academy, I'll never forgive you."

The BBC were broadcasting the Academy Awards ceremony on the evening after the event in Los Angeles, the same date as Nicky Brompton's ostentatious celebration for his fortieth birthday. It was Martha's first free evening since her arrival in London, and she was planning the luxury of a solitary night with the television.

At six o'clock she lay in the bath, trying to relax and recapture her sense of who she was. A dozen days in London, resuming all the spurious glamour of her old personality, had disoriented her. It was as if there was a parallel universe of triviality which she had once inhabited, and into which she could occasionally pass, by changing dimension. Once there, all she cared about was the look of things.

The Chanel handbag stuck in her mind like a symbol of that superficial existence. "Why would anyone wait six months to buy a handbag?" she asked herself aloud. "Why it wasn't even well made . . ."

The observation reverberated around the steamy, high-ceilinged room. The Chanel handbag Victoria flaunted so proudly had not been well made. It was an obvious fake. It had been suspiciously heavy. It had been given to her—indeed, it was the kind of flashy status symbol she would have instinctively left to the nouveaux-riches to flaunt.

Almost slipping in her haste, Martha scrambled out of the claw-footed iron tub and lunged for the telephone, calling Henshaw's special number. "Where are you?" she demanded.

"Waiting for the boss and then off to pick up Mrs Hamilton before the Brompton do," his voice hissed over the radio connection.

"Where's Santiago?"

"Still in custody. Why?"

"I've just remembered something. He gave her a handbag. See if she comes out with a black handbag with a gold chain strap and a little emblem like two linked letter Cs on it. I think that if he has planted an explosive, it may be in that." It seemed an impossibly slight deduction when she explained it to a man, but Martha was certain and he heard that although he could not follow her reasoning.

"I'm going over to Mrs Hamilton's right now, I'll see you when you get there."

"I'll get a car sent over for you, that way we can stay in touch."

Unreasonable alarm galvanised her long limbs. You can't *know* that Richard is in danger, you're being foolish, she argued as she dragged clothes over her damp skin, jumping to the window ten times in ten minutes until she saw the police car enter the courtyard below. Snatching up her new pink wool coat at the last moment she dashed to the lift, slamming the door behind her. On their way across town to Kensington the radio crackled and Henshaw's voice was heard loudly inside the interior of the car. "There's been some IRA movement—two men and a woman were clocked at Heathrow this morning," he informed them. "But they've lost two of them. They're going to pick up the third, just in case." Martha thought even Henshaw's normally calm tones sounded tense.

"Does Rich—does His Royal Highness know what's happening?"

"Ah—I mentioned something."

"Henshaw, you must tell him!" She realised she was almost screaming.

"I'm sorry, miss."

"Chickie, please, you must!"

There was a silence and only static came from the radio. "Very well, miss. I think you're right. I've no *specific* orders."

The detective's flat voice was devoid of emotion, but Martha was seized by a ferocious terror for Richard's life. She stopped herself from urging the driver, who was diving through side streets with practised ease, to go faster.

The street on which Victoria lived was barred with white tape. Three more police cars were already waiting out of sight of the house, and Richard's Jaguar, with Henshaw at the wheel, was drawn up by the front steps. As Martha's car rolled forward to a halt, the front door opened and Victoria, in a wide-skirted pink taffeta gown, stepped out on to the porch with Richard.

"Is that the bag you mean?" one of the officers asked Martha.

In the pool of light from the still-open door she saw it clearly. "Yes, that's the one."

"Right. Best take cover, miss." Another officer firmly pulled her behind the pillars of a neighbouring porch. She saw Henshaw get out of the Jaguar and approach the couple with another policeman, and heard Victoria's voice raised in uncomprehending panic. Fear made the whole scene unreal to Martha, like a distant dream enacted by puppets.

"Just give us your handbag, Mrs Hamilton," Henshaw spoke in a reassuring tone.

Victoria looked at Richard. "Why do they want my bag?"

"I don't know, Tory, but I think you should do what they say." Very slowly, she pulled the bag off her shoulder and handed it to Henshaw, who handed it to the man beside him. Alone, he took it into the centre of the road and kneeled down to examine it. Lipstick, keys and a pen spilled out. Some tissues blew away in the light evening breeze.

In a few moments the man stood up and called to the others. "Looks like we hit the jackpot," the officer said to Martha. They beckoned her and she joined them, to be shown the lining cut open and a layer of greyish putty inside it.

"I don't understand, there must be some mistake." She heard Victoria's clear voice resound from the steps and saw a uniformed policewoman talking to her. Richard turned to her and was saying something in a low voice.

"Let me go with her," Martha ran up the steps. "Victoria, there's no mistake. You were taken in by that friend of yours, the one who gave you the bag?" The grey eyes were more clouded than ever. In all her exquisite evening clothes and jewellery, Victoria suddenly looked like a large expressionless doll.

"Are they arresting me?"

"Yes they are, they must, you do understand that, don't you? But I'll come with you."

"But Richard . . ." she looked around at him pleadingly.

"I can't interfere, Tory, you know that."

He stepped back, instantly assuming the carapace of majesty, and Harley heard her own breath hiss through her teeth with shock. Victoria herself suddenly drew away, her hands clutching each other at her breast, some realisation of what had taken place dawning. "Yes. Yes, I suppose I do. Very well then." With the dignity bred into her stock for centuries, she picked up her shimmering skirt and stepped down to the pavement.

Later she sat with Martha in a dirty interview room at the police station, still resplendent in her diamonds with her hair immaculately in place. She had given a statement and signed it, and accepted with subdued good grace the necessity to spend the night in a police cell.

"I'll get you some sensible clothes," Martha promised, noticing that grime had already attached itself to the hem of the dress. Victoria had endured the entire ordeal with composure, admitting her "friendship" with Santiago but nothing more, unruffled, polite, the image of British *sang froid* to the last, thanks to her habitual intake of chemicals.

"That would be kind of you." Victoria looked around the bare room with an air of alert interest. "This is quite an experience, isn't it? I can't imagine that man being a terrorist."

"Victoria, you know you're addicted to your pills, don't you?"

"Nonsense. I just take something to sleep when I need it."

"Oh, for God's sake! Do you mean you're too doped to know? Jo said you would be . . ."

"What's she got to do with it?"

"Never mind. Victoria, I shouldn't tell you this but somebody's got to make you face it. You've got a serious drug problem, you've lost touch with reality and you were manipulated by Santiago who intended to assassinate Richard. You saw the explosive yourself in the handbag he gave you. What do you think all this is about?"

A blurred dismay widened Victoria's grey eyes. "Is that . . . ?"

"Yes. You're in serious trouble, Victoria, you could be charged as an accessory."

"But that's dreadful . . ."

"Not as bad as it would have been if Santiago had succeeded."

"No. No. Of course not." Her voice was very small now as the realisation took root. "I could have killed him, couldn't I? And other people as well. And . . . and myself, I suppose."

"Yes."

Victoria's pale skin was as white and dry as paper and she suddenly seemed smaller. "What can I do?" she asked in a feeble voice, pulling at the sleeve of Martha's coat.

"Tell the truth," she advised wearily. "As much of it as you can remember. You may not go to prison. We'll get a doctor to see you and perhaps we can prove you didn't know what you were doing."

"I certainly didn't." Self-justification momentarily enlivened the Englishwoman and she sat upright on the hard chair, then slumped once more. "That's very good advice, Martha. I'll remember to tell my lawyer in the morning." Victoria's face had sagged suddenly, as if deflated. At that moment it was easy to guess how she would look when she was old.

"Oh dear," she said, drawing in her arms and legs, and tears began to fall on her skirt.

She wept quietly for an hour, with Martha standing helplessly offering her tissues, and then collected herself and sat silent for a while. "Why do you think he chose us?" she asked in something like the old, dreamy voice of her girlhood. "Richard, I mean. The three of us? It is strange, isn't it? You're in love with him too, I can tell. And Jo was, all along, I should think."

"Do you think he chose us? Maybe we chose him?"

An unaccustomed expression of irony spread over Victoria's empty face. "Wouldn't any woman choose Richard? I think he must be just about the most desirable man in the world."

"But loving him's a bitch, let's be honest about that."

Victoria sighed. "Yes. But you wouldn't want him to be like any other man, would you?"

"I think we just made him be what we wanted him to be." Martha stretched as she formed her thoughts into words and looked at her fingernails, naturally shell-pink but unpainted now for years. "We weren't in love with him. We were in love with love, at least I was. And we wanted our Prince to come, some day. A Prince is someone you make up, who comes along and puts right whatever you've missed in life. We were all missing something, and we thought Richard was the answer."

Jo, Martha reflected, had found her own answer. "And a

real Prince is someone who only comes along when he isn't needed any more," she continued.

"You do talk nonsense, Martha. But I'm glad you're here."

* * *

IN NICKY BROMPTON's blue chintz bedroom, Richard sat on the bed alone and watched the television. He was exhausted from the tension of the evening. The noise of the party was a distant roar from two floors below. He watched the tawdry procession of Oscar winners patiently for half an hour. Jo did not win the title of best actress; neither did Lorna Lewis and the camera lingered cruelly on her tight, small features as Meryl Streep made her short speech of acceptance.

He found he was biting the corner of his thumbnail, waiting to see Jo. The camera roamed tantalisingly among the crowd; he saw half-a-dozen women who looked like her from a distance but proved to be older, more painted or just someone else.

She was also nominated in the category of most promising newcomer, and at last he saw her. She glanced at the camera nervously as if looking at him, then her gaze moved onwards and he felt ridiculously rejected.

The clips unrolled slowly. The bloated, plain girl in *The Dawn of Dreams* seemed to be somebody else, which he acknowledged as proof of her artistry. Cher, in a mass of white beads and flesh-coloured net, was opening the envelope. He heard Jo's name and found himself standing up and applauding all alone in the middle of the Chinese carpet on Nicky's bedroom floor.

"I suppose it is traditional to thank your mother in these speeches," she began, "but in this case I really can't skip that formality." He lost track of what she was saying as she continued. He could see from her face that she was very tense and he wanted to hold her and tell her she was wonderful and tell her he loved her. "What do you want?" he asked himself aloud, "a personal message from the stage?"

"Every year," she was continuing in a different tone, "the Academy makes an award to somebody whose contribution to the motion picture industry is recognised as outstanding. The Special Award is a token of the love and esteem of the film community and indeed of the entire world, and it now gives me the greatest possible pride and pleasure . . ."

He clicked his tongue in irritation. "Typical American overkill," he muttered. "God, who wrote that speech?"

"Presented to Lorna Lewis, known to you in a dozen different roles but to me only as . . . my mother." There was a rapturous ovation from the crowded auditorium and the camera showed Lorna Lewis, visibly in tears, being helped to her feet by her husband and escorted to the stage. He saw Jo walk quickly over to the steps to meet her mother with a kiss.

"Your shoes hurt," he murmured tenderly as he recognised her discomfort in her high-heeled sandals.

"They certainly did," said her soft voice behind him.

"What!" He jumped from the bed as if someone had thrown him off it.

"I knew you'd be here." She was standing in the doorway wearing the jeans she had travelled in, her hair loose and her eyes shining.

"How . . . how long . . . ?" She walked towards him and he wrapped his arms around her, unused to his dreams coming true with so little effort.

"Long enough. I wrote that speech. It's the sort of thing one does at that sort of occasion. You can apologise now."

"I'm sorry." He kissed her as if to make sure she was real.

"That's OK. You know, I've worked out that we're going to be luckier than other couples."

"How's that?"

"Well, at least when we're apart we can watch each other on television."

"Yes," he agreed, "there is that."

"Look," she said, pointing over his shoulder at the screen. "Mother starts crying again here. She was so happy."

Twenty years ago, Christina Fortune disappeared. Now she's come home to claim what's rightfully hers. But is she an heiress...or an imposter?

_F_ortune's
_C_hild
by Pamela Simpson

Other women had claimed to be Christina Fortune, missing heiress to one of the world's largest shipping empires. Now this beautiful, self-assured woman has stepped forward, daring to take what she insists is hers. From Hawaii to exotic Hong Kong, she must fight to gain control of the family business, fight to convince them all that she is Christina.

❏ 29424-5 $5.99/$6.99 in Canada

◆

Uncovering the heart of corruption,
the price of power, and the danger of desire...

_M_ortal
_S_ins

by Dianne Edouard and Sandra Ware

Washington Post reporter Alexandra Venée's search for the truth behind the death of a prominent politician sets in motion a shocking series of events that will expose the dark secrets of her twisted family ties, the violent struggle within the Church, and the corruption and betrayal that reach from the Louisiana bayous of her childhood to the highest corridors of power.

❏ 28929-2 $4.99/$5.99 in Canada